# The Dalemark Quartet

BOOKS BY DIANA WYNNE JONES

*Archer's Goon*
*Black Maria*
*Dogsbody*
*Fire and Hemlock*
*Hexwood*
*The Homeward Bounders*
*The Power of Three*
*A Sudden Wild Magic*
*A Tale of Time City*
*The Time of the Ghost*
*The Tough Guide to Fantasyland*

THE CHRESTOMANCI QUARTET
*Charmed Life*
*Witch Week*
*The Magicians of Caprona*
*The Lives of Christopher Chant*

WIZARD'S CASTLE
*Howl's Moving Castle*
*Castle in the Air*

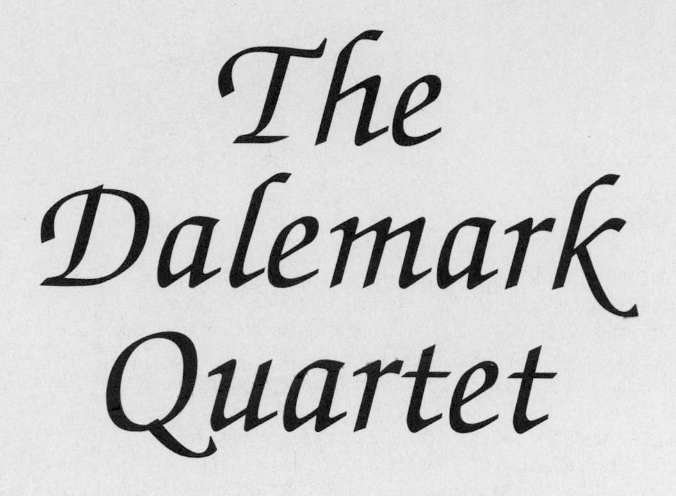

# The Dalemark Quartet

CART AND CWIDDER
DROWNED AMMET
THE SPELLCOATS
THE CROWN OF DALEMARK

*Diana Wynne Jones*

First UK publication 1975 by Macmillan London Ltd
Published 1993 by Mandarin, an imprint of Reed Consumer Books Ltd.
First US publication 1977 by Atheneum
Published 1995 by Greenwillow Books, an imprint of HarperCollins*Publishers*


First UK publication 1977 by Macmillan London Ltd
Published 1993 by Mandarin, an imprint of Reed Consumer Books Ltd.
First US publication 1978 by Atheneum
Published 1995 by Greenwillow Books, an imprint of HarperCollins*Publishers*


First UK publication 1979 by Macmillan London Ltd
Published 1993 by Mandarin, an imprint of Reed Consumer Books Ltd.
First US publication 1979 by Atheneum
Published 1995 by Greenwillow Books, an imprint of HarperCollins*Publishers*


First UK publication 1993 by Mandarin, an imprint of Reed Consumer Books Ltd.
First US publication 1995 by Greenwillow Books, an imprint of HarperCollins*Publishers*



Maps by David Cuzic

Published by arrangement with
Greenwillow Books
an imprint of HarperCollins*Publishers*
1350 Avenue of the Americas
New York, New York 10019

visit our website at www.sfbc.com
visit Greenwillow's website at www.harperchildrens.com
ISBN: 0-7394-3389-X

PRINTED IN THE UNITED STATES OF AMERICA

# The Dalemark Quartet

# CONTENTS

# *Cart and Cwidder*

*For Rachel*

# 1

"DO COME OUT OF that dream, Moril," Lenina said.

"Glad rags, Moril," said Brid. "We're nearly in Derent."

Moril sighed reproachfully. He had not been in a dream, and he felt it was unfair of his mother to call it that. He had merely been gazing at the white road as it wandered northward, thinking how glad he was to be going that way again, and how glad he would be to get out of the South. It was spring, and it was already far too hot. But that was not the worst of the South. The worst, to Moril's mind, was the need to be careful. You dared not put a foot, or a word, out of place for fear of being clapped in jail. People were watching all the time to report what you said. It gave Moril the creeps. And it irked him that there were songs his father dared not sing in the South for fear of sounding seditious. They were the best songs, too, to Moril's mind. They all came from the North. Moril himself had been born in the North, in the earldom of Hannart. And his favorite hero, the Adon, had once upon a time been Earl of Hannart.

"You're dreaming again!" Lenina said sharply.

"No, I'm not," said Moril. He left his perch behind the driving seat and climbed hastily into the covered back of the cart. His mother and his sister were already changed into their cheap tinsel-trimmed show dresses. Lenina, who was pale and blond and still very beautiful, was in silver and pale gold. Brid, who was darker and browner, had a glimmering peacock dress. Lenina hung Moril's suit above the rack of musical instruments, and Moril squeezed up to that end to change, very careful not to bang a cwidder or scrape the hand organ. Each instrument was shiny with use and gleaming with care. Each had its special place.

Everything in the cart did. Clennen insisted on it. He said that life in a small cart would otherwise become impossible.

Once Moril was changed, he emerged from the cart as a very flamboyant figure, for his suit was the same peacock as Brid's dress and his hair was red—a bright, wild red. He had inherited Lenina's paleness. His face was white, with a few red freckles.

"You know, Mother," Brid said, as she had said before every show since they left Holand, "I don't think I like that color on Moril."

"It makes people notice him," said Lenina, and went to take the reins while Clennen and Dagner changed in their turn.

Moril went to walk in the damp springing grass on the roadside, that was rough-soft under his toes, where he could have a good view of the cart that was his home. It was painted in a number of noticeable colors, principally pink and gold. Picked out in gold and sky blue along the sides were the words *Clennen the Singer*. Moril knew it was garish, but he loved this cart all the same. It moved softly, because it was well sprung and well oiled, and ran easily behind Olob, the glistening brown horse. Clennen always said he would not part with Olob for an earldom. Olob—his real name was Barangarolob, because Clennen loved long names—was harnessed in pink and scarlet, with a great deal of polished brass, and looked as magnificent as the rest of the turnout. Moril was just thinking that his mother and Brid on the driving seat looked like two queens—or perhaps a queen and a princess—when Clennen stuck his head out of the canvas at the back.

"Admiring us, are you?" he called cheerfully. Moril smiled and nodded. "It's like life," Clennen said. "You may wonder what goes on inside, but what matters is the look of it and the kind of performance we give. Remember that." His head popped back inside again.

Moril went on smiling. His father was always giving them odd thoughts to remember. He would probably want this one repeated to him in a day or so. Moril thought about it—in the dreamy way in which he usually gave his attention to anything—and he could not see that their turnout was like life. Life was not pink and gold. At least, some of theirs was, he supposed, but that was only saying the cart *was* life.

He was still pondering when they came under some big trees covered with pale buds, and the canvas cover went down with a bit of a clatter, revealing Clennen and Dagner dressed in scarlet and ready for the show. Moril scampered back and climbed up with them. Clennen smiled jovially. Dagner, whose face was tight and pinched, as it always was before a show, pushed Moril's cwidder into his hands and Moril into the right place without a word. He handed the big old cwidder to Clennen and the panhorn to Brid, and took up a pipe and a long, thin drum himself. By the time they were all settled, Olob was clopping smoothly into the main square of Derent.

"Ready," said Clennen. "Two, three." And they struck up.

Derent was not a big place. The number of people who came into the square in response to their opening song was not encouraging. There was a trickle of children and ten adults at the most. True, the people sitting outside the tavern turned their chairs round to get a better view, but Moril had a vague feeling, all the same, that they were wasting their talents on Derent. He said so to Brid, while Lenina was reaching past him to receive the hand organ from Dagner.

"All your feelings are vague!" Lenina said, overhearing. "Be quiet."

Undaunted by the sparse crowd, Clennen began his usual patter. "Ladies and gentlemen, come and listen! I am Clennen the Singer, on my way from Holand to the North. I bring you news, views, songs and tales, things old and things new. Roll up, draw up chairs, come near and listen!" Clennen had a fine rolling voice, speaking or singing. It rumbled round the square. Eyes were drawn to him, for his presence matched his voice. He was a big man, and not a thin one, though the scarlet suit made his paunch look bigger than it really was. He had a good sharp curl of ginger beard, which made up for the bald patch at the back of his head—now hidden by his scarlet hat. But the main thing about him was his enormous, jovial, total good humor. It seemed to fetch people by magic or multiply those there out of thin air. Before his speech was over, there were forty or fifty people listening to it.

"So there!" Brid said to Moril.

Before the performance could start, however, someone pushed up to the cart, calling, "Have you got any news from Holand, Clennen?" So they had to wait. They were used to this. Moril thought of it as part of the performance—and it certainly seemed to be one of their duties—to bring news from one part of Dalemark to the others. In the South particularly, there were few other ways in which people could get to know what was happening in the next lordship, let alone the next earldom.

"Now, let's see," said Clennen. "There's been a new earl invested for the South Dales—the old one's grandson. And they tell me Hadd has fallen out with Henda again." This surprised nobody. They were two very quarrelsome earls. "And I *hear*," said Clennen, stressing the *hear*, to show that he was not trying to stir up trouble, "I *hear* the cause of it had something to do with a shipload of Northmen that came into harbor at Holand last month." This caused confused and careful muttering. Nobody knew what to make of a ship from the North coming into Holand, or whether they were breaking the law to think of it at all.

Clennen passed on to other news. "The Earl of Waywold is making new money—copper and goodness knows what else in it—worth nothing. You get more than two thousand to one gold. Now the price on the Porter—you've all heard of the Porter, I suppose?" Everyone had. The Porter was a notorious spy, much wanted by the earls of the South for passing illegal information and stirring up discontent. Not one of the earls had been able to catch him. "The price on the Porter's head now being two thousand gold," said Clennen, "it's to be hoped that he's not taken in Waywold, or you'll have to collect your reward in a wagon." This caused some cautious laughter. "And the storm last month carried off the lord's roof in Bradbrook, not to speak of my tent," said Clennen.

Lenina, by this time, had sorted out the strips of paper on which she had written messages from people in other places to friends and relatives in Derent. She began calling them out. "Is there someone called Coran here? I've a message from his uncle at Pennet." A red-faced young man pushed forward. He confessed, as if he were ashamed of it, that he could read, and was handed the paper. "Is there a Granny Ben here?"

"She's sick, but I'll tell her," someone called.

So it went on. Lenina handed out messages to those who could read, and read them out to those who could not. More people hurried into the square, hearing there was news. Shortly there was a fair throng of people, all in great good humor, all telling one another the latest news from Holand.

Then Clennen called out: "Now I'm putting my hat on the ground here. If you want a song of us, too, do us the favor of filling it with silver." The scarlet hat spun neatly onto the cobblestones and waited, looking empty and expectant. Clennen waited, too, with rather the same look. And after a second the red-faced Coran, grateful for his message, tossed a silver coin into it. Another followed, and another. Lenina, watching expertly, muttered to Brid that it looked like good takings.

After that the performance began in earnest. Moril did not have much time even for vague thinking. Though he did not do much of the singing, his job was to play treble to the low sweet notes of his father's big cwidder, and he was kept fairly busy. His fingers grew hot and tingly, and he leaned over and blew on them to cool them as he played. Clennen, as he had promised the crowd, gave them old favorites and new favorites—ballads, love songs, and comic songs—and some songs that were entirely new. Several of these were his own. Clennen was a great maker of songs. Brid and Dagner joined him for some of them, or played panhorn, drum, and third cwidder, and Lenina played stolidly on the hand organ. She played well—since Clennen had taught her—

but always rather mechanically, as if her mind were elsewhere. And Moril fingered away busily, his left hand sliding up and down the long, inlaid arm of his cwidder, his right thrumming on the strings until his fingertips glowed.

Every so often Clennen would pause and send a cheerfully reproachful look toward his hat. This usually caused a hand to come out from the crowd and drop a small, shamed coin in with the others. Then Clennen would beam round at everyone and go on again. When the hat was more than half full, he said: "Now I think the time has come for some of the songs out of our past. As you may know, the history of Dalemark is full of fine singers, but, to my mind, there have never been two to compare with the Adon and Osfameron. Neither has ever been equaled. But Osfameron was an ancestor of mine. I happen to be descended from him in a direct line, father to son. And it was said of Osfameron that he could charm the rocks from the mountains, the dead from their sleep, and the gold from men's purses." Here a slight raising of Clennen's sandy eyebrows in the direction of the hat called forth an apologetic penny and a ripple of laughter from everyone. "So, ladies and gentlemen," said Clennen, "I shall now sing four songs by Osfameron."

Moril sighed and leaned his cwidder carefully against the side of the cart. The old songs only needed the big cwidder, so he could have a rest. In spite of this, he wished his father would not sing them. Moril much preferred the new, full-bodied music. The old required a fingering which made even the big mellow cwidder sound cracked and thin, and Clennen seemed to find it necessary to change his deep singing voice until it became thin, high, and peculiar. As for the words—Moril listened to the first song and wondered what Osfameron had been on about.

> "The Adon's hall was open. Through it
> Swallows darted. The soul flies through life.
> Osfameron in his mind's eye knew it.
> The bird's life is not the man's life."

But the crowd appreciated it. Moril heard someone say: "I do like to hear the old songs done in the right way." And when they were over, there was a round of applause and a few more coins.

Then Dagner, with his face more tight and pinched than ever, took up his cwidder. Clennen said, "I now introduce my eldest son, Dastgandlen Handagner." This was Dagner's full name. Clennen loved long names. "He will sing you some of his own songs," said Clennen, and waved Dagner forward into the center of the cart. Dagner, with a grimace of pure nervousness, bowed to the crowd and began to sing. Moril could never understand why this part was such a torment to Dagner. He knew his brother would have died rather than miss his part in the performance, yet he was never happy until it was over. Perhaps it was because Dagner had made the songs himself.

They were strange, moody little songs, with odd rhythms. Dagner made them even odder, by singing now loud, now soft, for no real reason, unless it was nerves. And they had a haunting something. The tunes stuck in your head and you hummed them when you thought you had long forgotten them. Moril listened and watched, and envied Dagner this gift of making songs. He would have given—well—his toes, anyway, to be able to compose anything.

> "The color in your head
> The color in your mind
> Is dead
> If you follow it blind,"

Dagner sang, and the crowd grew to like it. Dagner was not remarkable to look at—he was thin and sandy-haired, with a large Adam's apple—and people expected his songs to be unremarkable, too. But when he finished, there was applause and some more coins. Dagner flushed pale purple with pleasure and was almost at ease for the rest of the show.

There was not much more. The whole family sang a few more songs together and wound up with "Jolly Holanders." They always finished with that in the South, and the audience always joined in. Then it was a matter of putting away the instruments and replying to the things people came up to say.

This was always rather a confused time. There were the usual number of people who seemed to know Clennen well; the usual giggly girls who wanted Dagner to tell them how he composed songs, a thing Dagner could never explain and always tried to do; the usual kind people who told Moril he was quite a musician for a youngster; and the usual gentlemen who drifted up to Lenina and Brid and tried to murmur sweet nothings to them. Clennen was always very quick to notice these gentlemen, particularly those who approached Brid. Poor Brid looked older than she was in her show clothes—she was really only just thirteen—and she did not know how to deal with murmuring gentlemen at all.

"Well, you see, my father taught me," Moril explained.

"They come into my head like—er—ideas," Dagner explained.

"It is Lenina, isn't it?" murmured a gentleman at the head of the cart.

"It is," said Lenina.

"I didn't quite hear what you said," Brid said rather desperately to another gentleman.

"I don't go to Hannart. I had a little disagreement with the Earl," said Clennen. He swung round and, with one comprehensive look, disposed of the man Brid could not hear and also the one who thought Lenina was herself. "But I'm going through Dropwater and beyond," he continued, turning back to his friends.

Lenina had collected the money and was counting it. "Good," she said. "We can stay at the inn here. I fancy a roof over my head."

Moril and Brid fancied it, too. It was the height of luxury. There would be feather beds, a proper bath, and real food cooked indoors. Brid licked her lips and gave Moril a delighted grin. Moril smiled back in his milky, sleepy way.

"No. No time," said Clennen, when at last he was free to be asked. "We have to press on. We're picking up a passenger on the road."

Lenina said nothing. It was not her way. While Brid, Moril, and even Dagner protested, she simply picked up the reins and encouraged Olob to move.

# 2

"WHERE ARE WE picking up the passenger?" Brid inquired when they were three miles or so beyond Derent and her discontent had worn off somewhat. She was back in her everyday blue check and looked rather younger than she was.

"Couple of miles on. I'll tell you where," Clennen said to Dagner, who was driving.

"Going North, is he?" Dagner said.

"That's right," said Clennen.

Moril, in the ordinary rust-colored clothes he preferred, and in which, to Brid's mind, he looked a great deal nicer, trotted along beside the cart and hoped vaguely that the passenger would be agreeable. They had taken a woman last year who had driven him nearly crazy with boredom. She had known a hundred little boys, and they were all better than Moril in some way, and she had at least two long stories about each boy to prove it. They took someone most years, going North. Since North and South had begun their long disagreement, very little traffic went between. Those who had no horse—and to walk meant the risk of being taken up as a vagrant and clapped into jail—had to rely on such people as the licensed singers to take them as paying passengers.

The disagreement had begun so far in the past that not many people knew its cause: The North had one version, the South another. But it was certain that three kings of Dalemark had died, one after another, without leaving a proper heir to the throne. And almost every earl in the land had some kind of claim to be king. Even before the last king ruled from Hannart in the North, there had been quarrels and wars, and the country showed signs of breaking up into two. And when the Adon, who was the last king, died, his heirs were not to be found. Civil war began in earnest.

Since then the only rulers of Dalemark had been the earls, each in his own earldom, with the lords under them. No one now wanted a king. Keril, the present Earl of Hannart, said publicly that he had no claim to the throne. But the disagreement ran deeper than ever. The men of the North claimed that half the land was enslaved, and the earls of the South said the North was plotting against them. The year Brid was born, Keril, Earl of Hannart, had been proclaimed a public enemy by every earl and lord in the South. After that the only people who dared travel between were accredited traders and licensed singers, and they had to prove that their business was harmless or they might be arrested anywhere in the South.

Moril had met some of the traders and quite a few of the singers. Clennen did not speak highly of any of them, except perhaps the singer Hestefan, whom Moril had not met. But Moril had never heard any of them complain of having to take passengers. He thought they must all be very patient people.

"What about payment?" asked Lenina.

"You wait and see," said Clennen, with a laugh.

"That's all very well," said Brid, returning to her discontent. "But why do we always have to take someone? Why can't the stupid North make friends with the silly South?"

"You tell me," said Clennen. And after Brid had stammered for a minute, he laughed and said, "Would *you* make friends with someone you knew would stab you in the back if he got the chance? Remember that. Mind you, there was a time when the South was as free a place as the North. Remember that, too."

This was a bold thing to say in the South. The last rebellion had been stamped out very harshly indeed, and the strict laws were still in force. You did not say anything that suggested you were discontented with the ways of the South. The countryside was known to be full of spies and informers, watching and listening to give warning of rebellious thoughts.

That was why, when Clennen spoke of North, South, and freedom in the same breath, Moril saw Lenina look round the hedges to make sure no one was listening. He found himself doing the same.

But the hedges, though the leaves were already dusty, were still thin enough to see through. Nothing moved in them but birds. The only people they saw, for the next mile or so, were in the distance, planting vines on a hillside, until they came to where a road branched off to another vineyard. There, on the triangle made by the turning, a man was waiting. At his feet he had a huge round bottle half encased in a straw basket. He waved, and Dagner drew up. Olob turned his head and looked at the huge bottle with evident misgiving.

"Evening, Flind," said Clennen. "Is that our payment there, by your feet?" The man nodded. He seemed disinclined to smile, though Clennen smiled broadly at him. "I hoped it was," said Clennen. "Where's the passenger?"

Flind jerked a thumb. The passenger, probably in an attempt to keep out of the sun, was sitting behind the bottle in its shadow. He looked very hot, very untidy, rather discontented, and rather younger than Dagner.

"Help him into the cart," Clennen said to Moril.

Moril did his best, but the passenger shook off his helping hand. "I can get in by myself," he said, "I'm not a cripple." He climbed in very nimbly and sat on the floor. The canvas cover was half up, and he seemed glad of its shade. Moril looked vaguely after him and hoped it was the heat that made him feel so disagreeable. He knew from bitter experience that someone around Dagner's age could make life very unpleasant if he was steadily disagreeable for some hundreds of miles. This could be worse than the woman last year. He looked at Brid, who made her squeezed-lemon face back.

Clennen and Flind, meanwhile, were heaving the huge jar through the tailgate of the cart. It took a good deal of effort, and a lot of space once it was in. Olob almost laid his head backward over his shoulders in an attempt to show his strong disapproval of it.

"Are you really taking our payment in wine?" said Lenina.

"Can you think of a better one?" said Clennen. "My dear girl, there's only beer to drink in the North! Count your blessings. We'll broach it this evening, shall we? Or would you rather wait until we're going through Markind?"

"Oh—this evening," said Lenina, smiling a little.

Clennen latched the tailgate, waved to Flind, and they went on. Olob made a very expressive business of getting the cart under way again. Brid was quite sorry for him, straining in front of all that extra weight, but everyone else knew that the cart was so well sprung and greased that Olob could hardly feel the difference. Dagner made no bones about flicking him with the whip.

"What a lazy horse!" exclaimed the passenger.

"They're often the wisest ones," said Clennen.

The passenger, realizing he had been snubbed, put his chin on his knees and sighed gustily. Brid and Moril took turns at eyeing him through the gap in the tailgate. He was burlier than Dagner, though he was younger, and much the same height. But he was more remarkable-looking, because he was a queer combination of dark and fair. His hair was tawny-fair, and there was a lot of it, like a lion's mane, only rather more untidy, and his eyes were a pale blue-green. But his eyebrows were thick and black, and his skin very brown. His nose put them in mind of an eagle. He still had that fed-up look, which they decided must be due to more than the heat.

"Perhaps his grandfather's dying, and they sent for him, and he doesn't want to go," Brid speculated. Moril was content to leave it vague. He simply hoped the passenger would not vent his annoyance on them.

A mile or so farther on Clennen said: "We haven't got your name, lad. There's a lot in a name, I always think. What is it?"

"It's Kialan," said the passenger. "With a *K*."

"Even with a *K*, it's not half long enough for me," said Clennen.

"Well, what do you expect me to say? It's really my name!" the passenger protested.

"I like longer names," Clennen explained. "Clennen's too short for me, too. Lenina—my wife's name—is too short. But my children all have good spreading names, because I could choose them myself. The lad driving is Dastgandlen Handagner, my daughter is Cennoreth Manaliabrid, and the one with the red hair is Osfameron Tanamoril."

Moril ground his teeth and waited for the passenger to laugh. But, in fact, he looked rather awed. "Oh," he said. "Er, do you call them all that when you want to speak to them?"

"And the lazy-wise horse is Barangarolob," Clennen added, perfectly seriously, as if he were simply anxious for Kialan to know. Dagner gave a little whinny of laughter, which might have come from Olob. Kialan looked piteous.

"Take no notice," said Lenina. "They're Dagner, Brid, and Moril for short. And the horse is Olob."

Kialan looked relieved. He gave another gusty sigh or so and took off his coat. He must have been hot in it, because it was a thick coat, of good cloth. Brid whispered that it must be his best one, but Moril had lost interest in Kialan by then and did not care. Kialan folded the coat—not as carefully as such a good garment deserved—and used it as a pillow while he pretended to go to sleep. Brid knew he was only pretending, because he started up every time any travelers passed them and looked through the opening of the cover to see who they were.

There was not much traffic on the road. Mostly it was slow wagons, which Olob trotted past without any difficulty, sending spurts of white grit from beneath the cartwheels, until Moril, trotting in the rear, seemed to have hair the same color as Clennen's. But there were a few horsemen, and these overtook Olob as easily as Olob overtook the wagons. Once, quite a group of riders came past, raising a whirl of white dust, and were scanned by Kialan with great interest. One of the group seemed equally interested in them. He craned round in his saddle as he passed to get a good look at the cart.

"Who was that fellow?" Clennen said to Lenina.

"I couldn't say," she answered.

"Funny," said Clennen, "I seem to have seen him before." But since the man was a perfectly neutral-looking person, neither dark nor fair and neither young nor old, Clennen could not place him and gave up the attempt.

Shortly after that, as the sun was getting low, Olob left the road of his own accord and jolted the cart among gorse bushes into a heathy meadow. He stopped near a stream.

"Olob thinks this'll do," Dagner said to Clennen. "Will it?"

"You don't really let your horse choose where to stop!" Kialan exclaimed.

"He doesn't often let us down," said Clennen, surveying the meadow. "Yes, very nice. Horses have a gift for stopping, Kialan. Remember that."

The fed-up look settled on Kialan's face, and he watched, a little scornfully, while Dagner unharnessed Olob and led him off to drink. He watched Moril wiping the dust off the cart and Brid collecting firewood.

"Don't offer to help, will you?" Brid muttered in his direction.

While Lenina was cooking supper, Clennen fetched the big cwidder down, polished it, tuned it carefully, and beckoned Moril. Moril came reluctantly. He was rather in awe of the big cwidder. Its shining round belly was even more imposing than Clennen's. The inlaid patterns on the front and arm, made of pearl and ivory and various colored woods, puzzled him by their strangeness. And its voice when you played it was so surprisingly sweet and quite unlike that of the other cwidders. Clennen took such care of it that Moril still sometimes thought—as he had when he was little—that this cwidder was an extra, special part of Clennen, more important than his father's arm or leg—something on the lines of a wooden soul.

"Let's have that song of Osfameron's," said Clennen.

Moril liked the old songs so little that he was making very heavy weather of learning them. Clennen corrected him, made him go back to the beginning, and twice stopped him in the middle of the second verse. To make matters worse, Kialan came over and stood himself in front of Moril, listening. Moril, in self-defense, went into a dream between two notes, and stopped. He was with the Adon, on a green road in the North.

"Do you really need to teach him?" said Kialan.

"How else," asked Clennen, "do you think he'd learn?"

Kialan seemed a bit confused. "Well—I sort of supposed they picked it up—from giving shows," he said.

"Or it grew naturally, along with hair and fingernails?" Clennen suggested.

"No—I—Oh, that's silly!" said Kialan, and to Moril's relief, he drifted away. But he drifted back when Moril had finished and Brid took his place. Kialan caught Moril's sleeve. "I say, you all know all this music, but I suppose you can't even read and write, can you?"

Moril removed his sleeve. "Of course I can," he said. "My mother taught us." Before Kialan could ask any more impertinent questions, he scurried off among the gorse bushes to the stream. He stayed there, lost in vagueness, watching the bright water hurry over the different brightness of the stones beneath, until he heard Brid shouting.

"Supper! *Wash*, Moril!"

Supper was not very good, and what little bread they had was stale. "I say, this tastes peculiar!" Kialan said, pushing his share about on his plate.

Lenina's face, which never had much expression, went quite blank. "I meant to buy bread and onions in Derent," she said. "But there was no time."

There was a heavy pause. Then Clennen said, "Look, lad, we've got to travel more than a hundred and fifty miles together, you and us. It needs a little give-and-take, don't you think? I'd hate to have to break a good cwidder over your head."

The sun was setting then, and the light was red. But Moril thought that this did not entirely account for the color of Kialan's face. Kialan, however, said nothing. He silently accepted some of the wine and drank it, but he did not speak again until much later. By then Clennen had become very jolly with the wine. Beaming in the firelight, he leaned back against the wheel of the cart and said to Dagner, "Give us that new song of yours."

"It's not quite ready yet," said Dagner. But, since this was not a performance, he willingly fetched his cwidder and picked out a sketch of what Moril thought was a very promising tune. And without a trace of nervousness, he half sang, half spoke the words.

"Come with me, come with me.
The blackbird asks you, 'Follow me.'

No one will know, no one will know,
Wherever you go, I shall go.
Come with me. Morning spreads,
Clouds are high in milky threads,
The moon looks like a white thumbnail,
Larks are singing up the dale.
The sun is up, so follow me.
I'd like us to go secretly
Along the road, across the hill
Where water runs and woods are still."

"And then I think the first four lines again," Dagner said, looking up at Clennen.

"No," said Clennen. "Won't do."

"Well, I needn't have them again," Dagner said humbly.

"I mean the whole thing won't do," said Clennen.

Dagner looked very dashed. Kialan seemed unable to stop himself saying indignantly: "Why? I thought it was going to be a jolly good song."

"The tune's all right, as far as it's gone," said Clennen. "But why spoil a tune like that with those words?"

"They're jolly good words," Kialan insisted. "I liked them."

"It's the words I seem to want," Dagner said diffidently.

"I see," said Clennen. "Then in that case don't utter them again until we're in the North—unless you want us taken up for rebels."

Dagner tried to explain. "But I—it wasn't. I was just trying to say how much I liked traveling in the cart and—and so on."

"Were you?" said Clennen. "And haven't you heard the songs the freedom fighters used to sing here the year of the rebellion—oh, it'll be sixteen years ago now, the year you were born? They never dared say a thing straight out, so it was all put sideways—'Follow the lark' was one, 'Free as air and secret' another went, and the best known was 'Come up the dale with me.' The lords here still hang a man on the spot for singing words like that."

"And I do think that's ridiculous!" Kialan burst out. "Why can't people sing what they want here? What's the matter with everyone?"

Brid and Moril looked at his firelit face with interest. It began to seem as if Kialan might be a freedom fighter. They felt they could forgive him much if he was. Clennen, however, simply seemed amused.

"I hope there's not someone behind the gorse listening to you," he said. Kialan's head jerked round toward the nearest looming bush. "See?" said Clennen. "That's why, in one easy lesson, lad. No one can trust anyone anymore. It comes of uneasy rulers paying uneasy men to make the rest uneasy, too. It's not always been like that, you know. Dagner, what did I say outside Derent?"

Dagner's mind was woefully on his unsuitable song. "Oh—er—something about life being only a performance, I think."

"I knew I could trust you to get the wrong saying—and the wrong saying wrong," Clennen said tolerantly. "Anyone?"

"You said the South was once as free as the North," said Brid. "You said it to me, really."

"Then remember it," said Clennen.

# 3

AFTER ONE NIGHT attempting to share the smaller tent with Kialan and Dagner, Moril took to creeping into the cart along with Brid and the wine jar. As he told Brid, even the wine jar took up less space than Kialan, and it did not have knees and elbows. Moril had woken up three times to find himself out among the guy ropes in the dew. He resented it. He resented Kialan, and he wished Dagner joy of him. It was hard to tell if Dagner got on with Kialan or not, because he was such an untalkative person. Dagner was like Lenina in that way. It was quite impossible to tell what Lenina thought about Kialan—or, indeed, about anything else.

Kialan, in spite of Clennen's rebuke, seemed unable to stop making outspoken remarks. "You know, that cart is really horribly garish," he said, on the second morning. Perhaps he had some excuse. It was standing against the dawn sky, as he saw it, and Moril's red head was just emerging from it. The effect was undeniably colorful, but Brid was keenly offended.

"It isn't!" she said.

"I expect you're too young to have much taste," Kialan replied. Brid swore to Moril that she was Kialan's enemy for life after that one.

What Moril resented most—apart from Kialan's elbows and the fact that Kialan never made the slightest attempt to help with any of the chores—was the superior way Kialan stood by and listened in whenever Moril had a music lesson. Unfortunately he had them fairly frequently in the next few days. They were taking—perhaps for Kialan's benefit—a more direct route to Flennpass and the North than usual. It meant that they did not pass through any large towns and only two villages. Lenina bought supplies in the first, but they did not perform in either. Clennen took the opportunity to grind away at the old songs with Moril, to keep Brid hard at the panhorn, and to rehearse a number of songs with all of them.

Kialan stood by and put Moril off continually. Moril came so to resent it that he took refuge in more than usual vagueness. He would sit on his perch behind the driving seat staring up the white road unreeling ahead between the gray-green slopes of the South, basking in the hot sun—which never tanned him however long he sat in it—and dream of his birthplace in the North. It always saddened Moril that his father would never go to Hannart because of his disagreement with Earl Keril. He longed to see it, and he had built up in his mind a complete image of what it was like. There was an old gray castle in it, rowan trees, and blue hills of a certain spiky shape. Moril saw it clearly. He saw the whole North with it, spread over the gray-green southern landscape as if it were painted on a window: dark woods and emerald dales, the queer green roads from olden days which led to places that were not important any longer, hard gray rocks, and the great waterfall at Dropwater. In it lived all the stories of magic and adventure that seemed to go with the North. The South had nothing to compare with them.

Hearing Kialan talking behind him, Moril thought that the North had one new advantage. Kialan would leave them there.

"I've said that six times now," Kialan said. "Do you spend *all* your time a thousand miles away?"

Moril was annoyed. His family could accuse him of dreaminess if they wanted, but Kialan was a stranger. "You've no right to say that," he said.

It was possible Kialan did not realize how annoyed Moril was. "You see," Brid explained to him later, a good long way behind the cart, "even when you're angry, you always look so sleepy and—and *milky*, that he probably didn't even notice you were attending. Not," she added tartly, "that he'd have noticed anybody's feelings but his own, mind you."

What Kialan had replied was: "Oh, good grief! I know you're the fool of the family by now, but you don't have to be rude as well as stupid!"

"And the same to you!" Moril retorted, and took Kialan completely by surprise by butting him in the stomach. Kialan fell backward heavily—and painfully, Moril hoped—onto the wine jar. Whereupon Moril found the prudent thing to do was to hop out of the cart double quick and scud off down the road behind it. And for the rest of the day he was forced to walk well in the rear for fear of Kialan's vengeance.

But it was Clennen who took the vengeance. When they camped

for the night, he beckoned both Kialan and Moril up to him. "Are you two going to make up and apologize?" he inquired. Moril looked warily at Kialan, and Kialan looked most unlovingly back. Neither answered. "Very well then," said Clennen, and banged their heads together. Nothing seems harder than another person's head. Moril could only hope that Kialan had seen as many stars as he had. He was rather surprised that Kialan did not say anything to Clennen. "Next time, I'll do it harder," Clennen promised. Then, as if nothing had happened, he went on to give Moril a lesson. And to Moril's annoyance, Kialan stood by and listened just as usual.

The following day they reached a market town called Crady, and it came on to rain—big warm drops that seemed like part of the air and very little to do with the moist white sky. The raindrops made dark brown circles in the dust of the road and raised a delicious smell of wet earth. But it meant everyone crowding into the cart to change in great discomfort. Moril was not surprised that Kialan got out.

"I'm not really interested in your show," he said to Clennen. "I'll meet you on the other side of Crady, shall I?"

"If you like, lad," Clennen said cheerfully. Brid and Moril exchanged seething glances in the hot dim space under the cover and wondered why Clennen did not box Kialan's ears for him. But the only thing which seemed to perturb Clennen was the rain. "We shall have no audience in the open," he said. "I'll see what I can do. We'll go in with the cover up."

It was lucky that they did. By the time they came to the marketplace, the rain was coming in white rods and bouncing up off the flagstones. Olob was wearing his most long-suffering expression, and there was not a soul in sight. But Clennen had friends in Crady, just as he had everywhere else. Half an hour later they were installed under the great beams of a warehouse on the corner of the marketplace, and a crowd, damp but interested, was gathering into it.

They gave an indoor kind of show. After Clennen had told everyone about Hadd and Henda, the Waywold money, the price on the Porter's head, and the cost of corn in Derent, and the usual messages had been handed out, they sang songs with a chorus that the audience could join in. Dagner did his part early. Then, when good humor and attention were at their peak, Clennen told one of the old tales. This pleased Moril highly. He always felt rather too hot indoors, and playing the cwidder made him hotter still. But during a tale he was only needed once or twice. All the stories had places where there was a song. For the rest of the time Moril could sit on the dusty chaff of the floor with his arms wrapped round his knees and drink the story in.

Clennen chose to tell a branch of the story of the Adon. It had to be only a branch because, as Clennen was fond of saying, stories clustered round the Adon and Osfameron like bees swarming. The songs which came in where the story needed them were the Adon's own, or Osfameron's. Moril always thought the old songs sounded rather better set in their proper stories, though he still wished the silly fellows had tried to sing more naturally. But their doings made splendid tales. Moril listened avidly to how Lagan wounded the Adon and the wound would not heal until Manaliabrid came out of the East to him. Then came the story of the love of both Lagan and the Adon for Manaliabrid, and how the Adon fled with her to the South. Lagan followed, but Osfameron helped them by singing a certain song in the passes of the mountains, so that the mountains walked and blocked the way through. And Lagan was forced to turn back.

Here Clennen lowered his rich voice to say: "I shall not sing you the song Osfameron sang then, for fear of moving the mountains again. But it is true that since that day the only pass to the North is Flennpass."

The Adon for a time roamed the South with Manaliabrid, singing for a living, until Lagan found where they were. Then he stole away Kastri, the Adon's son by his first wife, and the Adon followed. But Lagan was something of a magician. He made Kastri invisible and took on the shape of Kastri himself. And when the Adon came up to him, unsuspecting, Lagan stabbed him through the heart.

Here came Manaliabrid's lament, which Moril was supposed to sing. He took up his cwidder for it, glancing as he did so into the warm blue-gray depths of the barn at the attentive audience. To his surprise, Kialan was there. He was standing at the back, very wet and draggled, listening with as much interest as anyone there. Moril supposed he had decided he preferred a performance to a soaking after all. And he was annoyed with Kialan for coming. His head was full of grand things, journeys, flights, fighting, and the magic North of once-upon-a-time. Kialan was the everyday world with a vengeance. Moril felt as if he had a foot on two different worlds, which were spinning apart from one another. It was not a pleasant feeling. He took his eyes off Kialan and concentrated on his cwidder.

Then Clennen went on to how Manaliabrid asked Osfameron for help. Osfameron sang, and made Kastri visible. Then he took up his cwidder and journeyed by a way that only he knew, to the borders of the Dark Land. There he played such music that all the dead crowded in multitudes to hear him. Once they were gathered, Osfameron sang and called the soul of the Adon to him. And—this part always gave Moril a delicious shiver—Clennen once more lowered his voice to say:

"I shall not sing you the song Osfameron sang then, for fear of calling the dead again."

Osfameron led the Adon's soul back and restored it to his body. The Adon arose, defeated Lagan, and reigned as the last King of Dalemark. He was the last king because Manaliabrid's son, who was to have been king after him, chose instead to go back to his mother's country. "And since that time," said Clennen, "there have been no kings in Dalemark. Nor will there be, until the sons of Manaliabrid return."

Moril gave an entranced sigh. He had hardly the heart, after such a story, to join in "Jolly Holanders," and he only managed to sing with an effort. After it he crept away to the other end of the barn to avoid the usual crowd, and sat under the cart, brooding, while Clennen greeted his friends and Dagner failed to explain how he made up songs. If only such things happened nowadays! Moril thought. It seemed such a waste to be descended from the singer Osfameron, who knew the Adon and could call up the dead, and to live such a dull life. The world had gone so ordinary. Compare the Adon, who lived such a splendid life, with the present-day Earl of Hannart, who could think of nothing better to do than to stir up a rebellion, so that he dared not show his face in the South. Or you only had to think of the difference between that Osfameron, Moril brooded, and this one, Osfameron Tanamoril, to see how very plain and ordinary people had become lately. If only—

Here the plain and ordinary life interrupted in the person of Lenina, carrying the chinking hat to the cart. She was followed by the usual kind of murmuring gentleman. "And it must be sixteen years now—" this gentleman was murmuring.

"Seventeen," Lenina said briskly. "Moril, come out of that dream and count this money."

Moril unwillingly scrambled out from under the cart. As he did so, Clennen turned his head, and his voice boomed across the barn. "No, I didn't care for him at all, last time I was in Neathdale." With his voice came a look that caused the murmuring gentleman to wither away into the crowd. Moril watched him wither, a little puzzled. He seemed to be the twin of the murmuring gentleman in Derent.

The takings were not bad, which pleased Lenina. And Clennen was in good humor because an old friend of his had made him a present of a beefsteak. It was beautifully red and tender and wrapped in leaves to keep it fresh. Clennen stowed it carefully in a locker. He talked jovially of supper as they drove through Crady in the slackening drizzle. Kialan, to Brid's contempt, was waiting for them under a tree just beyond the town.

"Huh!" said Brid. "Not interested in our shows, isn't Mr. High-and-Mighty! Did you see him, Moril? Drinking in every word!"

"Yes," said Moril.

While the red steak fizzled over the fire, Brid said mock-innocently to Kialan: "Father told one of the Adon stories at the show. Do you know them at all?"

"Yes. And a dead bore they are, too," said Kialan. "All that magic!"

"You *would* say that!" said Moril. "I saw—"

"Silence!" said Clennen. "You're interrupting the steak. Not another word until it's ready to eat."

The steak was certainly worthy of respect. Even Kialan had nothing to say against it. They went on again after supper. In his carefree way, Clennen seemed to be quite as anxious as Moril to see the North again. He refused to let Olob choose them a meadow until the sun was nearly down and the sky ahead and to the left was a mass of lilac clouds barred with red.

"Imagine *that* over the peaks of the North Dales," he said. "But even in the South, Mark Wood is fine at this time of year. There's nothing to beat a tall beech in spring. And do you know the Marsh at all, Kialan?"

"A little," said Kialan.

"If we'd time, I'd take you through it just for the flowers," said Clennen. "But it's too far east, more's the pity. The ducks there make your mouth water."

"There are rabbits in the South Dales," Dagner suggested.

"So there are," said Clennen. "Look the snares out tomorrow."

By the end of the following day the landscape had begun to change. The rolling gray-green slopes gave way to higher, greener hills, and there were more trees. It was like a foretaste of the North. Moril began to feel pleasantly excited, although he knew that they were only entering the South Dales. Tholian, Earl of the South Dales, was reputed to be a tyrant fiercer even than Henda. It was still a long way to the North. Beyond these green hills lay the Uplands and Mark Wood, before they came to Flennpass and the North at last.

Nevertheless, budding apple trees made a pleasant change from rows of vines. The nights were slightly cooler, and rabbits were plentiful. Every night Dagner went off to set snares round about the camp, and to Moril's surprise, Kialan made his first helpful gesture and went with Dagner.

"It's only because he likes killing things," Brid said. "He's that type."

Whatever the reason, Kialan was surprisingly good at catching and skinning rabbits, and Lenina was good at rabbit stew. Since they had wine as well, they fed very well for the next few days. Moril was almost grateful to Kialan. But Brid was not in the least grateful because every time they stopped in a town or village to give a show, Kialan would put on his act of not being interested and announce that he would meet them outside the town. And every time, unfailingly, they would see him among the audience, as interested as anyone there.

"Two-faced hypocrite!" Brid said indignantly. "He's just trying to make us feel small."

"That wouldn't do you any harm," Lenina said, in her dry way. Brid was more indignant than ever. It was becoming clear that Lenina rather approved of Kialan. Not that she said anything. It was more that she did not say any of the things she might have done. And when Kialan tore his good coat in the wood, Lenina mended it for him with careful neat stitches.

Kialan seemed far more surprised than grateful when Lenina handed him the mended coat. "Oh—thanks," he said. "You shouldn't have bothered." His face was red, and he seemed actually a little scornful of Lenina for doing it.

"Nothing to what I am!" said Brid. "He can go in rags for all I care."

The day after this they entered the part of the South Dales which was the lordship of Markind. They never gave shows in Markind. Brid's dislike of Kialan came to a head while Olob was patiently dragging the cart up and down the steep little hills of this lordship. The reason was that Clennen, who never disdained an audience, began to explain to Kialan exactly why he always hurried through Markind without giving a performance.

"I took Lenina from here, you see," he said. "From the very middle of Markind, out of the Lord's own hall. Didn't I, Lenina?"

"You did," said Lenina. She always looked very noncommittal whenever Clennen told this story.

"She was betrothed to the Lord's son. What was his name? Pennan—that was it. And a wet young idiot he was, too," Clennen said reminiscently. "I was asked in to sing at the betrothal—I had quite a name, even in those days, and I was a good deal in demand for occasions like that, let me tell you. Well, no sooner did I come into the hall and set eyes on Lenina than I knew she was the woman for me. Wasted on that idiot Fenner. That was his name, wasn't it, Lenina?"

"He was called Ganner," said Lenina.

"Oh, yes," said Clennen. "I remember he reminded me of a goose somehow. It must have been the name. I'd thought it was his scraggy neck or those button eyes of his. Anyway, I thought I'd rely on my looks being better than his and deal with Master Gosler later. For the first thing, I concentrated on Lenina. I sang—I've never sung better, before or since—and Lenina here couldn't take her eyes off me. Well, I don't blame her, because I don't mind admitting that I was a fine-looking man in those days, and gifted, too—which Flapper wasn't. So I asked Lenina in a song whether she'd marry me instead of this Honker fellow, and when I came up to get my reward for my singing, she said yes. So then I dealt with him. I turned to him. 'Lording,' I said, most respectful, 'Lording, what gift will you give me?' And he said 'Anything you want. You're a great singer'—which was the only sensible thing he said that evening. So I said, 'I'll take what you have in your right hand.' He was holding Lenina's hand, you see. I still laugh when I think of the look on his face."

While the story went on—and it made a long one, for Clennen went over it several times, embroidering the details—Brid and Moril walked by the roadside out of earshot, watching the fed-up look settle on Kialan's face. They had both heard the story more times than they could remember.

"I suppose the thing about being a singer is that you like telling the same story a hundred times," Brid said rather acidly. "But you'd think Father would remember Ganner's name by this time."

"That's all part of it," said Moril. "I always wonder," he added dreamily, "what would happen if we met Ganner while we were going through Markind. Would he arrest Father?"

"Of course he wouldn't," said Brid. "I don't suppose it's true, anyway. And even if it did happen, Ganner must have grown into a big fat lord by now and forgotten Mother ever existed."

Since this was Brid's true opinion of the matter, it was a little unreasonable of her to be so angry when she found Kialan shared it. But one is seldom reasonable when one dislikes someone. They stopped for lunch, and Clennen, thoroughly in his stride, went on embroidering the story.

"Lenina's a real lady," he said, leaning comfortably against the pink and scarlet wheel of the cart. "She's Tholian's niece, you know. But he cast her off for running away with me. And it was all my fault for playing that trick on Gander. 'Lording,' I said to him, 'give me what you have in your right hand.' Oh, I shall never forget his face! Never!" And he burst out laughing.

Kialan had heard this at least three times by then. Moril had rarely seen him look so fed up. While Clennen was laughing, Kialan got up quickly to avoid hearing any more, and stumped off without looking where he was going. He nearly fell over Moril and Brid and became more fed up than ever.

"Blinking bore your father is!" he said. "I'd be quite sorry for Ganner if I thought there was a word of truth in it!"

"How dare you!" said Brid. "How *dare* you say that! I've a good mind to punch your nose in!"

"I don't fight with girls," Kialan said loftily. "All I meant was I'm sick of hearing about Ganner. If your father remembers it that well, why on earth can't he get the poor fellow's name right?"

"It's part of the *story*!" screamed Brid, and threw herself at Kialan.

Kialan, for a second or so, tried to keep up his claim not to fight girls, with the result that Brid punched his nose twice and then boxed his ears in perfect freedom. "You spiteful cat!" said Kialan, and grabbed both her wrists. It was in self-defense. On the other hand, he squeezed her wrists so painfully that he hurt Brid rather more than if he had hit her. She lashed out at his legs with her bare feet, but finding that made no impression on Kialan, she sank her teeth into the hand round her wrists. At this, Kialan lost his temper completely and punched Brid with his free hand.

Dagner never let people hit Brid. He surged up from his seat in the hedgerow and fell on Kialan. Moril, since Dagner seemed to be doing his best to strangle Kialan, thought he had better get Brid out from between them and entered the fray, too. They made a grunting furious bundle. Brid would not unfasten her teeth and Kialan would not let go of Brid. Clennen heaved himself up, strolled over, and wrenched Dagner away from Kialan and Kialan away from Brid. Everyone, including Moril, fell with heavy thumps, this way and that. Clennen might have been fat, but he was also strong.

"Now stop!" said Clennen. "And if you've anything more to say about my story, Kialan, say it to me." He looked cheerfully down at Kialan, angrily sprawled on the roadside sucking his bleeding knuckles. "Well?"

"All right!" said Kialan. "All *right*!" Moril could see he was nearly crying. Brid was crying. "You can keep on saying you'll never forget Ganner—or whatever he's called—all you like," said Kialan. "I don't believe you've even met him! You wouldn't know him if he came walking down the road this minute! So there!"

The cheerfulness died out of Clennen's face. It was replaced by a very odd look. Kialan noticeably tensed at it. "Do you know Ganner then?" Clennen said.

"No, of course I don't!" said Kialan. "How could I? I don't suppose he exists."

"Oh, he exists all right," said Clennen. "And I'm sure you don't know him. Yet you're right. I've seen Ganner three times this month and not known him till this minute." He laughed again, and Kialan relaxed considerably. "Not a face that stands out in a crowd," he said. "Eh, Lenina?"

"I suppose not," agreed Lenina, and continued calmly slicing cold sausage.

"*You* knew him though, didn't you?" Clennen said. "In Derent, and on the road, and again in Crady?"

"Not till he said who he was," Lenina said, quite unperturbed.

There seemed suddenly to be a situation ten times worse. All through lunch Clennen looked at Lenina in a tense, troubled way. He seemed to be expecting her to say something and, at the same time, carefully not saying all sorts of things himself. And Lenina said nothing. She said nothing so positively and obviously that the air seemed sticky with her silence. It was hateful. The rest of them picked awkwardly at their food, and no one spoke much. Kialan did not say anything. It was obvious, even to Brid, that he was kicking himself for causing the situation—as well he might, Moril thought.

When the food was finished and the cart packed again, they went on, still in the same heavy silence. At last Clennen could bear it no longer.

"Lenina," he said, "you're not regretting all that, are you? If you want that kind of life—if you'd rather have Ganner—just say the word and I'll turn Olob toward Markind this moment."

Moril gasped. Brid's mouth came open in her tear-stained face. They looked at Clennen and found he seemed quite serious. Then they looked at Lenina, expecting her to laugh. It was so silly. Lenina was as much part of their life as Olob or the cart. But Lenina did not laugh, nor did she say anything. Not only Brid and Moril, but Dagner, Kialan, and Clennen, too, stared at her in increasing anxiety.

They came to a fork in the road. One branch led west, and the milestone said MARKIND 10. "Do I turn here?" asked Clennen.

Lenina gave herself an impatient shake. "Oh no," she said. "Clennen Mendakersson, you must be a very big fool indeed to think such a thing of me."

Clennen burst into a roll of relieved laughter. He shook the reins, and Olob trotted past the turning. "I must say," he said, laughing still, "I can't see how you could prefer Ganner to me. He couldn't have made the songs I've made to you, not if his life depended on it."

"Then why did you think I did?" Lenina asked coldly. The trouble was not over yet.

"Well," Clennen said awkwardly. "Money and all that. And it's what you were bred to, after all."

"I see," said Lenina. There was silence again for quite half an hour, except for the plopping of Olob's hooves and the light rumble of the cart. Kialan was unable to bear it. He got out and walked ahead, whistling the "Second March" rather defiantly. The others sat with their heads hanging, wishing Lenina would make peace. At last she said, "Oh, Clennen, do stop sitting there watching me like a dog! I'm not going to take wings and fly, am I? It's lucky Olob has more sense than you, or we'd be in the ditch by now!"

Then the trouble seemed to be over. Clennen was shortly laughing and talking again. And Lenina, if she was silent, was silent in her usual way, which everyone was used to. Brid and Moril got out of the cart, too, though they did not go near Kialan. Brid was still too angry with him.

# 4

THAT NIGHT THEY camped in one of the many little valleys Markind abounded in. There were woods up its steep sides and a meadow in the bottom, containing a small peaceful lake full of newly hatched tadpoles. Dagner and Kialan went off to set their snares. Lenina put herbs on the fire against the midges, and the fragrant smoke streamed sideways and settled across the lake in bands. Brid and Moril, quite unworried by insects, waded into the shallows of the lake and tried enthusiastically to collect tadpoles in an old pickle jar. Moril had just lost most of them by accident when he looked up to find his father watching them.

"You want a bigger jar," Clennen said. "And both of you want to remember what I said to Kialan about give-and-take."

"*He* doesn't remember it," Brid said sulkily.

"He's never had to learn it before," said Clennen. "That's his trouble. But it's not yours, Brid. A fight takes two."

"Did you hear what he said?" Moril demanded.

"I'm not deaf," said Clennen. "He's entitled to his opinion, like everyone else. And it wouldn't hurt you to find some opinions of your own instead of borrowing Brid's, Moril. Now get that slime off your fingers before you touch my cwidder."

While Moril was having his lesson, Kialan came out of the woods and into the lake, where he tried to teach Dagner to swim. The sight of them splashing about was a great distraction to Moril. It grew worse when Kialan tried to persuade Brid to learn to swim, too. Brid claimed to be afraid of leeches. Nothing would induce her to go above her knees in water, but she agreed to learn the arm movements. Moril could hear her laughing. It looked as if Kialan were trying to make friends.

Moril became more distracted than ever. Perhaps, after all, Kialan was not bad at heart—only tactless. Moril tried to decide what he thought. It really rankled with him that Clennen believed he borrowed Brid's opinions. Moril considered that he thought long and deeply—if rather vaguely—about most things. But he knew he had agreed with Brid, quite unquestioningly, both about Kialan and about the Ganner story. And it looked as if Brid had been wrong about both. Moril did not know what he thought.

"I suppose I ought to be used to you being up in the clouds by now," said Clennen. "Do you want to swim, too?"

"No," said Moril. "Yes. I mean, is that story about Ganner true then?"

"Word of honor," said Clennen. "Except it's the fellow's face I seem to have forgotten, not his name. I may embroider a detail here and there, but I never tell a story that isn't true, Moril. Remember that. Now go and swim if you want to."

Clennen was clearly very relieved that Lenina was not leaving for Markind. He drank a great deal of the wine that night to celebrate. The level in the huge bottle was almost down to the straw basket when he finally rolled into the larger tent and fell asleep. He was still asleep next morning when Dagner and Kialan went off to look at their snares. When Brid and Moril got up, they could hear him snoring, though Lenina was up and combing out her soft fair hair by the lake. Brid attended to the fire, and Moril tried to attend to Olob. Olob, for some reason, was tetchy. He kept flinging up his head and shying at shadows.

"What's the matter with him?" Moril asked his mother.

Lenina's comb had hit a tangle. She was lugging at it fiercely and not really attending. "No idea," she said. "Leave him be."

So Moril left off trying to groom Olob and turned to put the currycomb back in the cart. He found himself looking at a number of men, who were pushing their way through the last of the wood into the clear space by the lake. They were out almost as soon as Moril saw them, six of them. They stood in a group, looking at Moril, Brid kneeling by the fire, Lenina by the lake, the cart, and the tents.

"Clennen the Singer," one of them said. "Where is he?"

Olob tossed his head and trotted away round the lake.

"He's not here," said Brid.

Moril thought he would have said the same. The men alarmed him. It was odd to see six well-dressed men outside a wood in the middle of nowhere. They were very well dressed. They wore cloth as good as Kialan's coat, and all of them had that sleek look that comes from always living in style. Each of them wore a sword in a well-kept leather scabbard, belted over the good cloth of their coats, and Moril did not like the way the hilts of those swords looked smooth with frequent use. But the truly alarming thing about them was that they had an air of purpose, all of them, which hit Moril like a gust of cold wind and frightened him.

"My father won't be back for ages," he said, hoping they would go away.

"Then we'll wait for him," said the man who had asked. Moril liked him least of all. He was fair and light-eyed, and there was an odd look in those eyes which Moril did not trust.

Lenina evidently felt the same. "Suppose you give me your message for Clennen," she said, coming forward with her hair still loose.

"You wouldn't like it, lady," said the man. "We'll wait."

"Moril," said Lenina. "Go round the lake and fetch your father."

Moril thought that was clever of her. It would deceive the men, and Dagner and Kialan might be some help. He tossed the currycomb into the cart and set off at a trot. But Clennen chose that moment to crawl out of the tent like a badger. He stood up, with his eyes red and blinking inside a tousled frill of hair and beard.

"Somebody call me?" he said sleepily.

Moril stopped, helpless. Everything went so quickly that he could hardly believe it was happening. The six men pushed forward in a body, overwhelming Lenina for a moment, and then leaving her in the open, clutching Brid. Their swords caught the pink early sun. The group round Clennen trampled a bit. Clennen, sleepy as he was, must have put up something of a fight. A man stumbled sideways into the lake. Another fell in with a splash. Then the six men, swords sheathed again, went running away from the lake in a group. One glanced into Clennen's tent and then the smaller one. Another took a quick look into the cart as they passed.

"Nothing here," he called.

"Look in the woods then," said the fair one. And they were gone.

Clennen lay where he had fallen, half in the lake, with blood running out of him into the water.

Before Moril could move, there was a thumping of racing feet. Dagner shot past him round the lake and surged onto his knees in the water beside Clennen. "Have they killed him?"

"Not quite," said Lenina. "Help me move him."

Moril stood where he was, some distance away, and watched them heave his father out of the calm sunny water. Brid's face was grayish white, and her teeth were chattering. Dagner's mouth kept twisting about. Moril could see his hands shaking. But Lenina was quite calm and no paler than usual. As they turned Clennen over, Moril saw a cut in his chest. Bright red blood was gushing from it as fast as the river ran in Dropwater, steaming a little in the cold air over the surface of the lake.

At the sight, the bright trees, the lake, and the sunny sky dipped and swung in front of Moril. Everything turned sour and gray and distant. He could not move from the spot. Up in the woods behind him, he could dimly hear the six men crashing about and calling to one another, but they could have been on the moon for all the fear and interest Moril felt. His eyes stared, so widely that they hurt, at the group by the water.

Lenina, without abating her calm, tore a big strip from her petticoat, and another, to stop the bleeding. "Give me yours," she said to Brid, and while Brid, shaking and shivering, was getting out of her petticoat, Lenina said in the same calm way to Dagner, "Get the small flask from the cart."

Moril stared at his mother working and telling Brid what to do. The only sign of emotion Lenina showed was when her hair trailed in the way of the bandages. "Bother the stuff!" she said. "Brid, tie it back for me."

Brid was still trying to get a ribbon round Lenina's hair when Dagner scudded back with the flask. "Do you think you can save him?" he asked, as if he were pleading with Lenina.

She looked up at him calmly. "No, Dagner. The most I can do is keep him with you for a while. He'll want to have his say. He always did." She took the flask from Dagner and uncorked it.

Moril desolately watched her trying to get some of the liquid from the flask into Clennen's mouth. It was not fair. He felt it was not fair on his father at all, to die like this, first thing in the morning, miles from anywhere. He ought to have had warning. Dying was a thing someone like Clennen ought to do properly, in front of a crowd, with music playing if possible.

Music was possible, of course. Moril found himself beside the cart, without quite knowing how he had got there. He scrambled up and seized the nearest cwidder. It happened to be the big one. In the ordinary way, Moril would not have chosen it. But being inside the cart made him feel sick and queer, so he simply took what came first to hand and backed hastily down with it.

While he was getting its strap over his back, he realized that Clennen's eyes were open. And it was clear that Clennen shared Moril's opinion. Moril heard him say, rather thickly, but quite strongly, "This came out of the blue, didn't it? I'd have preferred to have notice."

Moril put his hands to the strings and began to play, very softly, the weird broken little tune of "Manaliabrid's Lament." The cwidder responded sweetly. The old song seemed more melodious than usual, and because of the water, it carried out across the lake until the valley seemed full of it. Moril heard its echo from the woods opposite.

His ears were so full of the sound that he did not hear much else of what Clennen said. Clennen's voice became weaker, anyway, after that first remark, and he spoke to Lenina in what was only a murmur. Then he spoke to Brid for a while, reaching out to hold her hand, which made Brid cry. After that, it was Dagner's turn. Clennen was very weak by then. Dagner had to put his head right down near his father's face in order to hear him. Moril played on, as softly as he could, watching Dagner listening and nodding, and wondered vaguely at the amount Clennen seemed to have to say. Then Dagner looked up and beckoned to Moril.

"He wants to talk to you. Quickly."

Moril did not dare take off the cwidder for fear of wasting time. He hurried over to Clennen with it bumping at his thighs and knees, and hoisted it away sideways as he knelt down. Clennen's face was paler than Moril had ever seen a face before. His eyes did not seem to reflect the sky, or Moril bending over him, though it was clear he could see Moril.

"Got the big cwidder, have you?" Clennen said. Moril nodded. He could not manage to speak. "Keep it carefully," said Clennen. "It's yours now. Always meant to give it to you, Moril, because I think you've got the ability. Or will have. But you have to come to terms with it, and with yourself. Understand?" Moril nodded again, though he did not understand in the least. "You're in two halves at present," Clennen went on. "Often thought so. Come together, Moril, and there's no knowing what you might do. There's power in that cwidder, if you can use it. Used to be Osfameron's. He could use it. Handed down to me. I couldn't use it. Only found the power once, when I—" Clennen paused for breath. Moril waited for him to go on, but nothing happened. Clennen stayed as he was, with his eyes open looking at Moril, and his lips parted. After a while, Moril realized that this was all there would be. He got up and carefully, very carefully, put the cwidder back in its place inside the cart.

Brid was crying loudly. Lenina was standing very upright beside the lake, as calm as ever. Dagner seemed to have frozen into the same sort of calmness, facing her. And Kialan was coming slowly toward them round the lake with a bundle of dead rabbits.

When he reached them, Kialan stopped. He looked at Clennen and, for once, seemed not to know what to say. "I'm—terribly sorry," he said at length.

"It was going to happen sometime," said Lenina. "Will you help us dig a grave, please?"

"Of course," said Kialan. "Here?"

"Why not?" said Lenina. "Clennen never had a home after he left Hannart, and we can't take him there."

"Very well," said Kialan, and he laid the rabbits down and unhooked the spade from its clips beneath the cart. Dagner went and fetched the pickax, and the two set to work. Lenina watched and seemed ready to take Kialan's advice, as if, in some odd way, Kialan were in charge just then. "I think we should mark the spot," Kialan said as he dug.

"How?" said Lenina.

"Is there a spare board in the cart?" Kialan asked.

"Find him one, Moril," said Lenina.

Moril managed to work free one of the spare boards Clennen always carried under the floor of the cart and, on Kialan's instructions, he sawed off a piece about three feet long. Then he relieved Kialan at the digging for a while. Kialan took out his sheath knife and carved away at the board, quickly and competently, as if this were another thing he was good at. When he had finished, the board had letters deeply and neatly cut into it. CLENNEN THE SINGER.

"That do?" said Kialan.

"Very well," said Lenina.

When the grave was ready, Kialan, Dagner, and Brid put Clennen into it. Moril did not like to see his father topple into the hole. Nor did he like to see the earth going in on top of Clennen's face and clothes. Rather than watch, he fetched his own cwidder and stood back a little, playing another lament, a newer one that had been made for an earl of Dropwater killed in battle. He went on playing while Brid put the turf back in place and Kialan trenched his board in until it was standing upright at the head of the grave, as it should. And now that there was nothing but a grave to be seen, Moril began to feel that something was missing. They should all be feeling and doing something else. They should be angry. Clennen had been murdered. They should be trying to bring the murderers to justice. But none of them thought of it. It was out of the question, here in the South. The six men had been far too well dressed.

"There," said Kialan, wiping his hands on his coat.

"Thank you," said Lenina. "Now I must change. This dress has blood on it. And you, too, Brid. Kialan, I think it would be a good idea if you changed your coat for Dagner's old one."

Kialan agreed to this, although Moril did not think Kialan's good coat was more than a little earthy. When everyone was changed and cleaned, Lenina told Dagner to catch Olob and harness him to the cart. Kialan picked up his bundle of rabbits.

"Leave those," said Lenina. "We don't need them."

"Well, I don't fancy them at the moment, either," said Kialan. "But—"

"Leave them," said Lenina. Kialan did as he was bid. Now Lenina seemed to be definitely in charge. It was she who took the reins when Olob was ready and drove out of the valley.

Brid and Moril looked back. It was a very beautiful valley. Probably, Moril thought, it was a good place to be buried, if one had to be. Brid cried. Dagner did not look back. He had sunk into a silence as profound as any of Lenina's. He did not look at anything, and no one liked to speak to him.

Lenina drove northward for a mile or so, until she came to a road that turned off to the left. Then, to Moril's surprise, she swung the cart into it.

"Hey! Where are we going?" said Moril.

"Markind," said Lenina.

"What? Not to Ganner!" demanded Brid, halting in the middle of a sob.

"Yes. To Ganner," said Lenina. "He said he would have me and mine if ever I was free, and I know he meant it."

"Oh, but no! You can't!" said Moril. "Not just like that!"

"Why not?" Lenina asked. "How do you think we shall live, without a singer to earn us money?"

"We can manage," said Moril. "I can sing. Dagner can—Dagner . . ." His voice tailed away as he thought of Dagner and himself trying to perform as Clennen did. He just could not see Dagner doing it. He did not know what to say, so he stopped, fearing he might be hurting Dagner's feelings. But it looked as if Dagner was not listening. "Father wouldn't like us to go to Markind," Moril asserted. He was sure of that, at least.

"I can't see that your father has much say in the matter now," Lenina answered dryly. "Get this clear, Moril. I know well enough that your father was a good man, and the best singer in Dalemark, and I've done my duty by him for seventeen years. That's half my lifetime, Moril. I've gone barefoot and learned to cook and make music. I've lived in a cart in all weathers, and never complained. I've mended and cleaned and looked after you all. There were things your father did that I didn't agree with at all, but I never argued with him or crossed him. I did my duty exactly in every way, and I've nothing to reproach myself with. But Clennen's dead now, so I'm free to do as I choose. What I'm choosing is my birthright and yours, too. Do you understand?"

"I suppose so," Moril mumbled. He had never heard Lenina say anything like this before. He was frightened and rather shocked to see that she must have been *not* saying it for longer than he had lived. He thought it was wrong of her, but he could not have said why. He thought she was altogether wrong, but he could not find any words to set against her. All he could do was to exchange a scared, helpless look with Brid. Brid said nothing either.

It was Kialan who spoke. He sounded rather embarrassed. "It's not my place to object," he said. "But I do have to get to Hannart, Lenina."

"I know," said Lenina. "I've thought of that. You can pose as my son for the moment, and I'll find someone to take you North as soon as I can, I promise. Hestefan's in the South, I know, and Fredlan may be, too."

Kialan looked exasperated as well as embarrassed. "But Ganner must know how many children you've got!"

"I shouldn't think so," Lenina said calmly. "People who haven't got children themselves never bother to count other people's. If he wonders, I'll say you've been ill and we'd left you at Fledden."

Kialan sighed. "Oh well. Thanks, anyway."

"Remember that," Lenina said to Moril, Brid, and Dagner, and Moril felt very queer, because "Remember that" was such a favorite saying of Clennen's. "Kialan's your brother. If anyone asks, he's been ill in Fledden."

Olob plodded toward Markind. He did not look happy either, Moril thought, looking at the droop of Olob's head. Moril was so miserable himself that he could almost hear it, like a droning in his ears, and he could not hide away in vagueness, much as he tried. He felt vividly and horribly attentive to everything, from the leaves in the hedge to the shape of Kialan's nose. Kialan's eagle nose was so different from Dagner's, Brid's, or Moril's that surely anyone could tell at a glance he was no relation? Why did he have to be a relation, anyway? And had Clennen known he wanted to go to Hannart? Clennen would not have gone there because he never went to Hannart. And why had the six men killed Clennen? Who were they, and what were they looking for in the wood? And why, why, why above all, had Clennen given Moril a cwidder he did not want in the least?

I shall never play it, Moril thought. I'll polish it and string it, and maybe tune it from time to time, but I don't want to play it. I know I should be grateful, because it must be very valuable—though it *can't* be old enough to have belonged to Osfameron; he's long ago in a story—but I don't like it and I don't want it.

Markind came into view at the other end of a valley. Without meaning to, Moril looked at it as he always looked at a new town. Sleepy and respectable, he thought. Bad takings. Then he remembered he was supposed to be going here to live, not to sing, and tried very hard to look at the pile of yellowish gray houses with interest. He found he was more interested in the villainously freckled cows which were grazing in the small green meadows outside the town.

Lenina looked at these cows with pleasure. "I remember I always liked those speckles," she said. She encouraged Olob to trot, and the gray and yellow houses approached swiftly. Moril's heart sank rather—and he had thought it was low enough before.

Soon they were winding up a gravelly street between quiet old houses. The houses were tall and cold and shuttered. There were very few people about. Even when they came to the main square and found a market going on under the high plane trees, there were still very few people, and these all sober citizens who looked at the gay cart with strong disapproval. Lenina drove past the stalls looking neither to right nor to left, and drew Olob up in front of a round-topped gateway in a massive yellow wall. Two men who seemed to be on guard at the gate peered round it at the cart in evident astonishment.

"Had you business here?" one of them asked Lenina.

"Certainly," Lenina answered haughtily. "Go and tell Ganner Sagersson that Lenina Thornsdaughter is here."

They looked at her in even more astonishment at that. But one of them went off into the spaces behind the thick yellow wall. The other stayed, frowning wonderingly at Lenina, the cart, and her family, until Moril scarcely knew where to look.

"What's the betting we get a message back to say, Not Today Thank You?" whispered Brid.

"Be quiet, Brid!" said Lenina. "Behave properly, can't you!"

Brid would have lost her bet. The man who had gone with the message came back at a run, and they could hear a number of people behind the gate, running too. The two halves of the gate were flung wide open.

"Please drive in," said the man.

Lenina smiled graciously and shook the reins. Olob plodded forward, disapproval in every line of his ears and back, into a small deep courtyard lined with interested faces. Ganner was standing in the middle of it, smiling delightedly.

"Welcome back, Lenina!" he said. "I never thought I'd see you so soon. What happened?"

"Some men killed Clennen this morning," said Lenina. "They looked like the pick of somebody's hearthmen to me."

"Not really!" exclaimed Ganner. Then he looked a little worried and asked, "Does that mean it happened in my lordship then?"

"Yes," said Lenina. "At Medmere."

"I'd better send some hearthmen over to investigate," said Ganner. "Anyway, come down and come in. Are these your children?"

"My three sons and my daughter," said Lenina.

"What a lot of them!" said Ganner, looking a little daunted. But he smiled gallantly at all four. "I'll do my best to look after you all," he said. Moril could not find it in his heart to dislike Ganner, much as he had intended to. It was so plain he meant well. If, to someone who had been used to Clennen, he seemed a very ordinary person, then that was hardly Ganner's fault, Moril supposed.

"He doesn't look much like a goose," Brid whispered, in some disappointment. Kialan had to bite his lip. Moril looked at Ganner gallantly helping Lenina down from the cart and smiling at her in a way that showed he adored her. Apart from that smile, he really seemed perfectly normal and ungooselike.

"Oh dear, oh dear!" Ganner exclaimed, as they all got down. "Shoes! Boots! Can you only afford one pair of boots?"

Lenina glanced along their line of bare feet, interrupted by Kialan's scuffed boots. "We don't usually bother with them," she explained. "But Collen has tender feet."

"I must make sure you all have shoes this instant!" Ganner exclaimed distractedly.

"You know, I think he may be a goose after all," Brid said, with considerable satisfaction.

# 5

BY THAT AFTERNOON Moril was wondering if it was only that morning they had left Clennen buried by the lake. It felt like last century. There had been so many changes. After a good breakfast, followed by the attentions of a tailor, a bootmaker, and Ganner's old nurse, followed in turn by an astonishingly good lunch, Moril scarcely knew himself. He looked in a mirror—it was a thing he seldom had the chance of doing, so he looked long and often—and he saw a smoothly combed red-haired boy in a suit of good blue cloth and a pair of soft rust-colored boots. The boots, to tell the truth, pleased him enormously. But he did not look in the least like his idea of himself. Dagner and Kialan had become spruce, gentlemanly figures in the same kind of blue clothes, and Brid a young lady in bright cherry color. They were all four behaving very soberly and politely, not because Ganner insisted on it—because he did not—but simply because Markind was the sort of place where you could behave in no other way.

The biggest change was to Lenina. She was splendidly dressed, too, and she had done her hair the way ladies did. Her cheeks were pinker than usual, and she laughed and chattered and hurried about with Ganner on a hundred errands. Moril had not often seen her laugh, and he had certainly never seen her so talkative. She was like a different person. That troubled him. It troubled him far more than learning she was going to marry Ganner that same evening.

Moril quite liked Ganner. Ganner told Moril he could do just what he liked and go anywhere he wanted, and obviously meant it. He was a very good-natured man. Moril quite liked the other people in the house, too. He liked Ganner's old nurse specially. She fussed rather, and she said rather too often that she had always known Lenina Thornsdaughter would come back to them, but she called Moril "My duck" and said he was a "blessing." And while she was dressing him, she told Moril a story about a lord of Markind who had been outlawed. Moril had not heard the story before, and he drank it up. But he felt strange. Everything felt strange.

Moril took Ganner at his word and explored the house. He found two gardens and the kitchens. He looked at the cellars and the small rooms under the roof, but in between each exploration he found himself drifting into the stableyard. The cart had been put away in a coach house there, just as it was, wine jar, cwidders, and all, down to the string of onions under the driving seat. It was just the same, yet somehow it already looked smaller and dustier and a little faded. Moril spent a lot of time talking to Olob, who was standing dejectedly in a stall nearby and seemed glad of his company. Moril stole sugar for him from the kitchen, which was easy to do because everyone there was in a great bustle, preparing for the wedding feast. Olob ate it politely, but he looked sad, and he was sweating rather.

"Poor fellow," Moril said sadly. "I'm hot, too. It's being in a house."

As the afternoon drew on, Moril became hotter still. Being between walls so oppressed him that he wondered whether to go out and walk in the town. But Markind had not inspired him with any wish to see more of it. He wandered to the stableyard and then into one of the gardens. Brid was there. She was feeling much the same, for she had taken off her cherry-colored boots and was sitting with her feet in one of the goldfish ponds.

They exchanged sad, polite smiles, and Moril went on into the second garden. Behind him he heard Ganner's voice.

"My dear little girl! You'll catch your death like that! Do please dry your feet and put your boots on. You'll worry your mother."

Moril felt sorry for Brid. Then he suddenly felt even more—desperately—sorry for himself. He needed to be somewhere else, out in the open. He looked round wildly, upward, everywhere. And a sturdy creeper growing up the thick yellow wall of the house gave him an idea. He slung himself onto it and started to climb.

It was extremely easy, except for the last bit, which needed a long stride and a heave across some crumbly stonework. Then he was on the wide, leaded roofs. It was splendid. Moril looked round, into the town, out across the valley, and over to valleys beyond. He turned north and looked at the misty blue peaks there, where he had so longed to go, and Kialan—lucky Kialan!—was going soon. But that made him sad. So, presently, Moril began to patter about across the leads and among the chimneys. He skirted courtyards and looked down into the gardens. Then he ran along a narrow part to another wing and looked down into another court.

And there was Ganner, horrified and gesturing below. "Come down! Come down at once!"

Moril looked. There was a lead pipe and an easy flight of windows. Obediently he swung his legs over the edge of the roof.

Ganner stopped him with a hoarse shriek. "No! Stop! Do you want to break your neck? Wait!" He ran away and presently ran back with a crowd of men carrying a ladder. With them ran a group of horrified maids, and the old nurse, wringing her hands.

"My duck! Oh my duck!"

Moril sat sadly on the edge of the roof, swinging his legs and watching them all pothering with the ladder. He knew what was wrong with Ganner now. He was a fusspot.

The ladder finally thumped against the wall beside him. "You can come down now," Ganner called. "Go very carefully."

Moril sighed and got onto the ladder. He came down rather slowly out of sheer perverseness. He decided when he got near enough he would say to Ganner, "But you told me I could go anywhere I wanted." When he judged he was low enough for it to be most effective, he turned round to say it.

A man was just coming in through the door to the courtyard—a fair man with light, untrustworthy eyes, who checked for a moment when he saw Moril twenty feet up a long ladder, staring at him. Shrugging slightly, the man strolled over to Ganner and said something to him. Ganner replied. The man shrugged again, said another word or so to Ganner, and strolled out of the courtyard.

Moril forgot what he intended to say. Instead, as soon as he was down on the ground, he said, "Who was that man here just now? The fair one, who spoke to you."

Ganner looked uneasy, so uneasy that Moril's chest went tight and he felt sick. "Oh—er—just someone who's my guest here," said Ganner. "Now you are absolutely *not* to get on the roof again! It's extremely high, and the leads are quite unsafe. You might have been killed!"

"Killed, my duck!" said his nurse.

Moril bore with a long scold from both Ganner and the nurse, without listening to a word. Both of them would have scolded anyway, but Moril was fairly sure that Ganner was scolding mostly as an excuse not to discuss the fair man. Moril did not want to discuss him. His one desire was to get away and find Lenina.

Lenina was in the great hall of the house. Presumably it was the same place where Clennen had sung and then played the trick on Ganner seventeen years before. Lenina was gaily organizing the tables for the wedding feast, and doing it as if she had done nothing else all her life. Moril had to pull her sleeve to get her to attend to him.

"Mother! One of the men who killed Father! He's staying here."

"Oh, Moril, don't interrupt me with stupid stories!" Lenina said impatiently.

"But I saw him," said Moril.

"You must have made a mistake," said Lenina. She pulled her sleeve away and went back to the tables.

Moril stood, shocked and troubled, in the middle of the hall. He saw quite clearly that his mother did not want to believe him. She had put Clennen and all that part of her life behind her and she did not want to be reminded of it. Yet if Ganner had had a hand in killing Clennen, this was the last place she ought to be—the last place any of them ought to be. Moril looked at gay, busy Lenina, shook his head desolately, and hurried away to find Brid.

Brid was hurrying through the garden in the opposite direction. "Moril—!"

"One of the men who killed Father," said Moril. "He's staying here."

"I know. I saw him," said Brid. "Did you try to tell Mother?"

"Yes. She wouldn't listen."

"She wouldn't listen to me either," said Brid. "She doesn't want to know, I think. Moril, what are we going to do? We can't stay here, can we? Do you think Ganner had Father killed?"

Moril thought about it. He remembered that though Ganner had obviously been very pleased to see Lenina, he had not perhaps been entirely surprised. And he did not like it at all. "I don't know. He *could* have done. Only he's a bit too feeble to think of it, isn't he?"

"And why not do it years ago if he felt that bad about Father stealing Mother off him?" said Brid. "But I don't care whether he did or not. I'm not staying here, and that's final!"

"Mother *is* staying," said Moril. "I'm afraid that's final, too."

"Then we'll have to do without her," said Brid. "I can cook, and we've got good clothes now. The only thing is, I'm not very good on the hand organ."

Moril did not feel as if they had come to a decision. It was as if he had known all along that they would leave. "But can we manage?" he said. "Give shows and all without even Dagner?"

"Dagner will have to come, too," stated Brid. "He'll have to. He's

Father's heir, and he ought to. Besides, he shouldn't stay here even more than us. If it was old days, he'd have to avenge Father."

Moril was dubious. Wherever Brid thought Dagner's duty lay, Moril knew Dagner would want to stay with Lenina. He knew, without knowing how he knew, that Dagner had always been closer to his mother than to Clennen. And how could Dagner take up the singer's trade when he was terrified and nervous at every show? "But would Dagner do it—on his own? I mean—"

"I know just what you mean," said Brid. "But I can manage Dagner. I can always manage him when there aren't any parents around to interfere."

"Let's go and find him then," said Moril.

Neither of them had seen Dagner for a considerable while. Since they had not the least idea where to start looking, they drifted quite naturally to the stableyard first, to have a look at Olob and the cart.

Dagner was in the stableyard, polishing Olob's harness, and Kialan was helping him. Both of them looked a little blank when Moril and Brid came in.

"Do you two haunt this yard, or something?" Kialan said irritably.

Moril decided to take the bull by the horns. "We're taking the cart and leaving," he said. "Are you two coming?" Kialan was clearly astonished and stared at Moril with all the annoyance of someone who cannot believe his ears.

"I've got to go anyway," said Dagner. "Father asked me to take Kialan to Hannart. But there's no need for you two to come."

"Oh, yes, there is!" said Brid. "One of the men who killed Father is in this house, and if that isn't a reason for going, give me a better one!"

Dagner and Kialan exchanged glances, and Kialan screwed his mouth up. "True?" Dagner said to Moril.

"I saw him," said Moril. "The fair one with queer eyes. But you didn't see them, did—"

"Yes, I did," said Dagner. "We were only in the woods. That one was the leader. Kialan, I think that settles it, don't you? We'd better leave at once, as soon as I've said good-bye to Mother."

"Don't be an idiot!" said Moril. "If you tell Mother we're going, she'll tell Ganner. And he's such a big fusspot that he's bound to say it's dangerous and stop us going."

Kialan and Dagner looked at one another again. "He's got a point there, Dagner," Kialan said. "Ganner is an awful old woman. He's bound to come after us, anyway. What do you say to waiting until the wedding feast has started and he's too busy to notice we're missing?"

Dagner pondered anxiously. He looked purple and bent with worry. "No," he said at length. "No, we daren't. Not if this other fellow's here." He jerked his head to the end of the yard. There was a big old gate in the wall there, bolted and peeling. "We've found out that leads to a back street. You two get those bolts back while I harness Olob, but don't open it till I'm ready."

Kialan helped Dagner pull out the cart and back Olob between its shafts, so they were ready almost as soon as Brid and Moril had done their part. The bolts were very stiff and rusty. Brid wanted to fetch the oil from the cart, but Moril would not let her. "No," he said. "I've an idea to fool Ganner." It took them quite a while, and cost Brid a pinched finger, to waggle the bolts back without.

"Ready," said Dagner. Olob came toward the gate, almost dancing with pleasure at being at the work he was used to. Brid and Moril swung the gate creaking open. Brid went up into the cart, with the easy spring of long practice, and sat down to get her boots off. The cart rumbled through and crunched on the gravel of the lane outside, which was so narrow that Olob for a moment seemed likely to run into the shuttered house opposite. Moril stayed inside the stableyard and carefully bolted the gate again. It looked, to his satisfaction, as if it had never been opened at all. He took a running jump at it and managed to hook his fingers in the top, where the gate did not quite meet the wall above. From there, he swarmed up onto the thick top of the wall itself. Kialan stood up in the cart to help him jump down.

"Good idea," he said. "Let's hope Ganner wastes a lot of time trying to find out which way we went."

# 6

IN THE LATE afternoon Markind seemed to be deserted. As they clattered northward through its shuttered, respectable streets, Moril was ready to swear that there was no one around to notice even such a noticeable cart as theirs. Nevertheless, Dagner was as tense as if he were giving a performance. He did not relax even when they were out of Markind. Instead of looking for a main road, he struck into the first small lane that went north and kept turning round uneasily as he drove to see if Ganner was following them.

Olob clattered along with a will, with his ears gaily pricked. The lane, and then the other lanes they took after it, led through apple orchards where the trees were bursting into bloom. The sun was mild and warm. Moril sat smiling sleepily and happily, listening to the familiar beat of Olob's hooves, the wine sloshing about in the great jar behind him, and the blackbirds singing in the apple trees. This was the life! He was sure they could manage, whatever Lenina thought. A cuckoo sang out, cutting across the songs of the blackbirds.

"O—oh!" said Brid. Tears began rolling down her cheeks. "Father said to me—by the lake—he hadn't heard a cuckoo yet this year. And he was sorry he was going to miss it." Her face screwed up, and her tears ran faster than ever. "He told me to listen for him, on the way North. And Mother goes and drives straight off to Markind! How could she!"

"Shut up, Brid," said Dagner uncomfortably.

"I shan't! I can't!" cried Brid. "How could she! How could she! Ganner's so stupid. How *could* she!"

"Will you be quiet!" said Dagner. "You don't understand."

"Yes, I *do*!" Brid cried. "Ganner and Mother arranged to have Father murdered—that's what happened!"

"Don't talk such blinking nonsense!" Kialan said sharply. "That had nothing to do with either of them."

"How do *you* know?" Brid wept. "Why did she go straight off to Ganner like that?"

"Because she's always wanted to, of course!" said Dagner. "Only she couldn't, because she thought it wasn't honorable. I *told* you you didn't understand," he went on, in an odd, agitated way. "You're too young to notice. But I've seen—oh, enough to know Mother hated living in a cart. She wasn't brought up to it like we are. It was all right while we were in the Earl of Hannart's household—we had a roof over our heads and that wasn't too bad for her—but—I suppose you don't remember."

"Not very well," Brid admitted, sniffing. "I was only three when we left."

"Well I do," said Dagner. "And Father *would* leave, though he knew Mother didn't want to go. And in the cart she had to bring us up and keep us clean and cook—and she'd never done anything like that in her life till then. And sometimes there was no money at all, and we were always on the move and always—well, there were other things she didn't like Father doing. But Father always got his own way over them. Mother never had a say in anything. She just did the work. Then she saw Ganner again in Derent, after all those years, and she told me it had brought her old life back to her and made her feel terrible. I just don't blame her for going back to what she was used to. You can see Ganner's not going to order her around like Father did."

"Father didn't order her around!" Brid protested. "He even offered to take her back to Ganner."

"Yes, and I thought Mother was really going to call his bluff for a moment then," said Dagner. "He knew darned well Mother wouldn't go, because it wasn't her duty, but he had an anxious moment all the same, didn't he? And then he took good care to point out how much cleverer he was than Ganner."

"That was just his way," said Brid.

"It was all just his way," said Dagner. "Look, Brid, I don't want to pull Father to pieces any more than you do, but in some ways he was—oh, maddening. And if you think about it, you'll see he and Mother weren't at all well matched."

Moril was blinking a little at all this. It was so unlike Dagner to talk so much or so clearly. He marveled at the way Dagner managed to put into words things Moril had known all his life but not truly noticed till this moment. "Don't you think Mother was fond of Father at all?" he asked dolefully.

"Not in the way we were," said Dagner.

"In that case, why did she run off with him like that?" Brid asked, triumphantly, as if that clinched the matter.

Dagner looked pensively at a new vista of apple trees coming into view beyond Olob's ears. "I'm not sure," he said, "but I *think* that cwidder had something to do with it."

Moril swiveled around and cast an apprehensive look at the gleaming belly of the old cwidder, resting in its place in the rack. "Why do you think that?" he asked nervously.

"Something Mother said once," said Dagner. "And Father told you there was power in it, didn't he?"

"There probably is, if it belonged to Osfameron," Kialan observed in a matter-of-fact way.

"Don't be silly! It can't be that old!" Moril protested.

"Osfameron lived not quite two hundred years ago," said Kialan, and he really seemed to know. "He was born the same year as King Labbard died, so it can't be more than that. A cwidder'd surely last as long as that if you took care of it. Why, we've—I've seen one that's four hundred years old—though, mind you, it looks ready to drop apart if you breathed on it."

Moril cast another look, even more apprehensive, at the quiet, prosperous shape of the old cwidder. "It can't be!" he said.

"Well," Dagner said diffidently, "you get used to thinking things like that were only around long ago, but—I'll tell you, Moril—didn't you get the impression you kept Father alive with it this morning?" Moril stared at Dagner with his mouth open. "I thought so," Dagner said, a trifle apologetically. "I've never heard it sound like it did then. And—and Father was dead awfully quickly after you left off, wasn't he?"

Moril was appalled. "Whatever am I going to do with a thing like that!" he almost wailed.

"I don't know. Learn to use it, perhaps," said Dagner. "I must say I was glad Father didn't give it to me."

Everyone subsided into thoughtfulness. Brid sniffed wretchedly. Olob clopped steadily on for a mile or so. Then he took a look at the sinking sun and decided to choose them a camping ground. Dagner dissuaded him. He refused to let Olob turn off the road three times, until Olob got the point and did not try again. They went on and on and on, downhill, uphill, through small valleys, pastures, and orchards.

The sky died from blue to pink and from pink to purple, and Brid could bear no more.

"Oh, do let's *stop*, Dagner! Today seems to have gone on for about a hundred years!"

"I know," said Dagner. "But I want to get a really good start."

"Do you think Ganner will really follow us?" said Moril. "He ought to be glad we've gone. Then he needn't fuss about roofs and things."

"He's bound to," said Kialan. "A man with a conscience—that's Ganner. He'll probably send some of his hearthmen out tonight and set out himself first thing tomorrow. That's what—I mean, if it had been just Dagner and me, he—"

"Go on. Say it. You think Moril and I shouldn't have come," Brid said bitterly.

"I didn't *say* that!" snapped Kialan.

"Just meant it," said Brid.

"No, he didn't," said Dagner. "Stop being stupid, Brid. The thing is, I left without explaining to Mother, and even if I had explained, she wouldn't have wanted you two to go. So I know she'll ask Ganner to come after us. If he does catch us up, you and Moril will have to go back, I'm afraid."

"Oh *no*!" said Brid, and Moril felt equally mutinous.

"That's why I hope he doesn't catch us," Dagner said. "Because I don't think I could give a show on my own, and I was wondering how on earth I'd manage."

This admission mollified Brid greatly. She refrained from grumbling, although they went on until the light was all but gone. Then Dagner at last permitted Olob to select them a spot on top of a hill. This meant their camp was windy, a fact which Brid bitterly pointed out while they were fumbling around trying to put up the tent in the breezy semidark.

"Yes, but we can see people coming," said Dagner.

"And there are thistles. I've just trodden on one," Brid complained.

"Then why on earth don't you put your boots on?" demanded Kialan.

"Oh, I couldn't! I'd spoil them," Brid said, quite shocked.

Kialan roared with laughter, which seemed to restore Brid's frayed temper. She took it quite cheerfully when Moril discovered the only food they had was bread and onions.

"I *knew* we'd need those rabbits," Kialan said dejectedly.

"We all had a good lunch," said Brid.

Moril had the notion of frying the bread and onions together. Unfortunately it was then so dark that he could not see to fry. The mixture he turned out of the frying pan was extremely singed, and it was only eaten because everyone was very hungry. Then they settled down to sleep. It seemed to Moril, waking and resettling himself round the wine jar during the night, that Kialan and Dagner kept watch, turn and turn about, until dawn broke. Certainly they both looked very jaded in the morning.

Nevertheless, as soon as the sun was up and Olob fed, Dagner had the cart on the move again. They ate the last of the bread as they went. Brid moaned a little, and Dagner promised they would buy more food in the next village they came to.

"What with?" said Brid.

That was a nasty moment. There was no money in the locker where Lenina usually kept it. She must have taken it out in Markind. And none of them had any money in the pockets of their fine new clothes. For a while, it looked as if they would have to give a show before they could eat. Then Brid thought of going through the clothes locker, turning out pockets. There were a few coins in the pockets of Clennen's scarlet suit, and a further few fell out of Kialan's old good coat when Brid picked it up.

"May we use these? We'll pay you back," she said.

"Of course," said Kialan. "I'd forgotten I'd got any."

When they came to a village, Dagner drew up on the outskirts and sent Brid and Moril shopping, shouting after them at the last minute that there were no more oats for Olob. The rule was that you bought oats first—for where would you be with Olob undernourished?—and they were dear in those parts at that season. Brid and Moril came glumly back with oats, a loaf, half a can of milk, a cold black sausage, and a cabbage. Knowing that Dagner would certainly put off giving a performance if he could, Brid prepared to do battle.

"That's all we could afford. If we don't give a show tomorrow, we'll starve," she announced, dumping the meager purchases in the cart.

"We're going to," Dagner said, to her surprise. "Father said we were to be sure to perform in Neathdale, and I think we'll be there by tomorrow. Have you found it?" he asked Kialan, who was frowning over the map. It was not a good map. Clennen knew Dalemark like the back of his hand and only kept a map for emergencies.

"If this place *is* Cindow, Neathdale's quite a way to the northwest," said Kialan. "Is it worth it? It would be almost as easy to go by the Marshes from here."

"Yes, I've got to go. And he said we'd be bound to get news there," said Dagner. "Let's get going. And," he added, "I suppose we'd better have a bit of a practice this evening."

As Olob went on, Moril, sighing rather, went and fetched the old cwidder. When he had vowed not to play it, he had been thinking of an idle life in Markind—if he had thought of the future at all—but now, whether Dagner played pipes or treble cwidder, and Brid pipes or panhorn, someone was going to have to play tenor to them. That meant Moril on the big cwidder. And he had always been in awe of it, and never more than now. By way of coming to terms with it, he laid it on his knees and polished it as Clennen had taught him. Brid gave him the note on the panhorn, and he tuned it. And tuned it again. And retuned it. As fast as he got a string to the right pitch, it went off again. All he could produce was the moaning twang of slack strings.

"I think the pegs are slipping," he said helplessly.

"Let me have a go," Brid said competently. But she could not get it tuned either.

"Let me look at the pegs," said Kialan. He looked, and seemed fairly knowledgeable, but he could not see anything wrong. He handed it on to Dagner. Dagner, who knew most of all, hitched the reins round his knees and spent half an hour trying to get the cwidder tuned. In the end he was forced to hand it back to Moril in the same state as before.

"Isn't that all we needed!" said Brid. "Perhaps it's in mourning. After all, we all should be, and look at us!"

"Try playing a lament," Kialan said thoughtfully.

"Why?" said Moril. "Anyway, I hate the old songs."

"Any lament," said Dagner. "You played your own treble over the grave, didn't you?"

Moril tried it. He began singing the "Lament for the Earl of Dropwater," and brought the cwidder in as softly as he could after the first line. The discord was horrible. Brid shuddered. But Dagner took up the song, too, and the cwidder seemed almost to follow his lead. The notes came right as Dagner sang them. To Moril's astonishment and secret terror, the cwidder was in tune by the end of the first verse. He sang the chorus, and first Brid, then Kialan, joined in.

"This was a man above all other,
Kanart the Earl, Kanart the Earl!
You'll never find his equal, brother.
He was a man above all other."

The cwidder sang on, as sweetly as it had for Clennen. Tears poured down Brid's face. Moril felt tearful, too. They sang lustily through the whole song, and sad though it made them, they felt heartened, too. The oddest effect was on Olob. His pace dropped to a slow, rhythmic walk, and he went for all the world as if the cart was a hearse.

"Put it away," said Dagner, "or we'll never get to Neathdale."

Moril put the alarming cwidder carefully back, and they made better progress. As before, Dagner would not let Olob stop at the usual time or in the usual kind of place. A little before sunset he took Olob right off the road into a high, lonely field full of big stones, where they could see a good way in most directions.

"There hasn't been a sign of Ganner!" Moril protested.

"Well, there won't be, until we see him arriving, will there?" said Kialan.

They demolished the sausage and held their practice. To Moril's relief, the big cwidder now behaved perfectly. But there were other difficulties. Without Clennen or Lenina, they found they could not do half the songs in the way they were used to. They had to work everything out afresh. And Dagner did not in any way take Clennen's place. He refused to do more than a third of the singing, and that was the only thing he was firm about. Otherwise, he simply made suggestions, and he was quite ready to be overruled by Brid or Moril. The younger two felt lost. They were used to Clennen's kind but entirely firm way of telling them exactly what to do. Sometimes they were annoyed, and several times they were tempted to get very silly. It was only the grim thought that their next meal depended on this practice that kept them from breaking into loud arguments or louder laughter. Moril felt he had never truly missed Clennen till then.

Yet, in the middle of thinking that, he remembered what Dagner had said about Clennen's always having his own way. It occurred to him to wonder if Clennen had not, in fact, kept them all a little too dependent on him. Maybe this was why it seemed so hard to manage without him.

While they practiced, Kialan lay full length on a rock above them, listening and also, Moril suspected, acting as lookout. This elaborate caution began to irritate Moril. After all, it was Moril and Brid who stood to lose if Ganner found them, not Dagner and Kialan. In the morning he was exasperated to see that they had been on watch again. Both of them looked tired out.

Brid was furious. "How on earth do you think you're going to give a performance, Dagner, if you can hardly keep your eyes open? I've never known you so silly! We *depend* on you!"

"All right," Dagner said wearily. "You drive and I'll have a sleep in the cart. But wake me if—if—"

"If *what*?" snapped Brid.

"If anything happens," said Dagner, and lay down beside the wine jar with a groan. Kialan flopped down on the other side of the jar, and both of them fell asleep before Olob had the cart in motion.

It was left to Brid and Moril to find the way to Neathdale. They did it, too, half cross and half proud of themselves. The map did not help much. They were forced to follow their noses across country, turning into any road that seemed to go northwest and hoping for the best. Once they arrived in a farmyard and had to back out of it, pursued by the barking of dogs and the squalling of hens and roosters. Kialan and Dagner did not even stir. "Stupid fools," said Brid. They were still asleep when the cart came out on a rise above Neathdale.

"We did it!" said Moril.

"Unless Olob knew the way," Brid said, trying to be fair. "But I don't think even he can have come to it this way before."

Neathdale was a big cheerful-looking town lying across the main road north to Flennpass, in the last level ground before the Uplands. They could look across even its tallest buildings from where they were to where the South Dales mounted like stairs to the Mark Wood plateau.

"Say four days, and we'll be in the North," Moril said yearningly.

"Four days," said Brid promptly.

The scuffle that followed on the driving seat woke Dagner and Kialan at last. "What's the matter? What's going on?"

"Nothing. Only Neathdale," said Brid. Dagner's sleepy face at once became pinched and tense and mauvish. Brid set herself to soothe him. "We always used to get good takings here," she said. "There must be hundreds of people who remember us and know Father. I'm going to do the talking, mind, and I shall talk about Father and say who we are—though they can read that on the cart anyway."

"The cart ought to be repainted with Dagner's name," Moril observed. He did not think Brid was soothing Dagner in the slightest, but he did not mind helping.

"You'd hardly get the name on," Brid said brightly. "Dastgandlen down one side and Handagner up the other, I suppose."

"Isn't Neathdale the seat of Earl Tholian?" Kialan asked, tactlessly cutting through the soothing.

"Not really. His place is outside a bit, over to the east," Dagner said. He pointed with a hand that shook noticeably. A great white house was just visible, among trees, on the other side of Neathdale.

"Blast you, Kialan!" said Brid. Kialan looked at her in surprise. "Oh, it doesn't matter," said Brid. "Just if this show goes wrong, I'll blame you. Dagner, I think we'd better put on our glad rags now."

"No," said Dagner.

"What do you mean?" said Brid.

"Just no," said Dagner. "We'll give the show as we are. We're quite respectable."

"Yes, but we always change," Brid protested. "It gives you a feel."

"That was Father's idea," said Dagner. "And he was right in a way. It went with his style to come rolling in, singing and glittering. He could live up to it. But if I go in dressed in tinsel and singing my head off, people are just going to laugh."

"You think that because you're nervous," Brid said persuasively. "You'll feel better once you're changed."

"No, I won't," said Dagner. "I'll feel ten times worse. Brid, I just haven't got Father's personality, and I can't do the same things. I'll have to do them my way, or not at all. See?"

Brid, by this time, was near tears. "Do you mean you're not going to give a show at all then?"

"Not Father's kind," said Dagner, "because I can't. We'll give a show all right, because we'll starve if we don't, and you can introduce us and explain what's happened, and maybe it'll be all right. But if I find you boasting and ranting about us—that goes for you, too, Moril—I'll stop. We'll just have to be plain, because we're not Father."

Brid sighed heavily. "All right. But I'm going to put my boots on, anyway. I need a feel." She brightened a little. "I've always hated the color of your suit, Moril. You look nicer like that."

"Thank you," Moril said politely. Dagner had suddenly brought it home to him that, for the first time in their lives, they were about to give a show entirely on their own. He had never, as far as he knew, been nervous before. Now he was. As Brid drove downhill toward Neathdale, Moril sat clutching the big cwidder with hands that were icy cold and sweating at once, and it would have been hard to say whether he or Dagner was the more nervous. The houses came nearer. Quite desperate, Moril laid his cheek against the smooth wood of the cwidder. "Oh, please help me!" he whispered to it. "I'll never manage. I can't!"

"Can you stop a moment?" said Kialan.

Brid drew up. Kialan immediately swung down from the cart to the road. Brid looked at him somberly. "Now you're going to give us that about not being interested in our shows, aren't you? Well don't. I won't believe you. I've seen you listening to every show we've given."

Kialan looked up at Brid's stormy face and seemed nonplussed. Then he laughed. "All right. I won't give you that. But I'm going to meet you on the other side of Neathdale all the same. See you." He set off at a good swinging pace toward the town, with his hands in his pockets, whistling "Jolly Holanders."

"I give up!" said Brid. But both her brothers were too nervous to reply.

# 7

THE MAIN SQUARE at Neathdale was always busy. It was not very large, but it had a handsome fountain in the middle and four inns on three of its sides. There was also a corn exchange and two guildhalls, which added to the coming and going. The fourth side was occupied by the gray frowning block of the jail. When Brid drove the cart into the square, it seemed busier even than they had remembered. It was packed with people. The reason, they saw, as Olob patiently shouldered his way toward the fountain, was that there had been a public hanging that morning. The gallows was still there, outside the jail, and so was the hanged man. A number of people outside the inns were raising tankards jeeringly in his direction.

The dangling figure made them all feel sick, although it meant a good crowd. Dagner turned green. Moril clutched his cwidder hard and swallowed. Brid could not resist leaning down and asking the nearest person who it was who had been hanged.

"Friend of the Porter's," was the cheerful reply. It was a cheerful whiskery man Brid had chosen to ask, and he looked as if he had enjoyed every second of the hanging. "Some say he *was* the Porter," he added, "but you can't tell. He wouldn't admit to anything. Taken up last week, he was, on the new Earl's orders."

"Oh, is there a new Earl?" Brid said blankly, trying to keep her eyes from the swinging criminal.

"Sure," said the man. "Old Tholian died more than a month back. The new Earl's the grandson. Got a real nose for the Porter and his like, he has. Good luck to him, too!"

"Oh yes. Very good luck," Brid said hurriedly, terrified of being arrested for disloyalty to the new Earl.

"Leave off, Brid, and let's get started," Dagner said irritably.

Brid smiled rather falsely at the whiskery man and hitched up the reins so that Olob knew to stand still. Then she blew a blast on the panhorn for attention. When sufficient people had turned their way, she stood up and spoke. Moril marveled at how cool she was. But Brid was like Clennen that way. An audience was meat and drink to her.

"Ladies and gentlemen," she called, "please come and listen. You see the cart I'm standing in? Many of you will know it quite well. If you do, you'll know it belongs to Clennen the Singer. You'll have seen it coming through Neathdale, year after year, on its way North. Most of you will know Clennen the Singer—"

She had aroused people's interest by then. Moril heard someone say, "It's Clennen the Singer."

"No, it isn't," said someone else. "Who's the pretty little lass?"

"Where's Clennen, then? It isn't Clennen," said other people. Finally, someone was puzzled enough to call out, "Where is Clennen, lass? Isn't he with you?"

"I'll tell you," said Brid. "I'll tell you all." Then she stopped and simply stood there, upright and conspicuous in her cherry dress. Moril could see she was trying not to cry. But he could also see she was making it plain to the crowd that she was trying not to cry. He marveled at the way she could use real feelings for what was in fact a show. He knew he could not have done it.

Brid stood there silent long enough for murmurs of interest to gather and grow but not long enough for them to die away. Then she said: "I'll tell you. Clennen—my father—was killed two days ago." And she stood silent again, struggling with tears, listening attentively to murmurs of sympathy. "He was killed before our eyes," she said. At the height of a loud murmur, she came in again, loudly, but in such a calm way that Moril and most of the people present thought she was speaking quietly. They hushed to hear her. "We are the children of Clennen the Singer—Brid, Moril, and Dastgandlen Handagner—and we're doing our best to carry on without him. I hope you'll spare time to listen to us. We know our show will not be the same without Clennen, but—but we'll try to please you. We hope you'll forgive any faults in—in memory of my father."

She got a round of applause for that. "Put your hat out, then, and let's hear you!" someone shouted. Brid, with tears running down her cheeks, picked up the hat she had ready and tossed it on the ground. Several people put money into it at once, out of pure sympathy for them. Brid could not help feeling pleased with herself. She had made a considerable effect without boasting once—in fact, she had done the opposite, which, she thought, ought to please Dagner.

Though Dagner was far too nervous to show any pleasure at all, Brid knew he was not displeased because he left her to do all the announcing. That meant that Brid could more or less choose what they sang. She did her best to put together the things they had practiced in the order she thought would be most impressive. She began them with general favorites. Moril felt terrible. Without the deep rolling voice of Clennen, they sounded to him thin and strange, and they lacked the body Lenina usually gave them on the hand organ. Moril began to feel they had nothing to offer the crowd, except perhaps some well-trained playing on cwidder and panhorn.

Brid felt much the same. To encourage them, she announced that they would now play, in trio, the "Seven Marches." That was one thing she was sure they could do well. And they did. The most successful part was when Dagner, on the spur of the moment, signaled to Brid to play soft during the "Fourth March," and played his treble cwidder in double time against Moril's slow and mellow tenor. They looked at one another while they were doing it. Moril knew they were neither of them exactly enjoying it, but they were both by then desperate for some applause from the silent crowd, and they had the dour kind of satisfaction of knowing they were giving an exhibition of real skill. They were rewarded by a burst of clapping and a little shower of coins falling into the hat.

Then they did Clennen's "Cuckoo Song," which always made people laugh. After that Brid, feeling that the sooner Dagner got his part over, the better he would be for the rest of the show, announced that Dagner would now sing some of his own songs.

Brid was glad she had said "some." Dagner was so nervous that he only managed three. If she had not said "some," it was probable that he would only have sung one. Moril was disappointed and Brid exasperated, and it was altogether a pity, because the crowd liked Dagner's songs. "The Color in Your Head" went down particularly well. Brid could tell he had the crowd's sympathy. They thought of him as bravely following in Clennen's footsteps and wanted to encourage him. But Dagner was mauve and shaking, and he stopped.

Crossly Brid took the center of the cart and sang herself. Moril, without being told, came to her aid on the cwidder, while Dagner gasped to himself in the background. Brid did well. An audience always helped her. She sang a number of ballads, though she was forced to avoid "The Hanging of Filli Ray," which she did best, because of the corpse dangling on the gallows behind the crowd. Her success was undoubtedly the patter song, "Cow-Calling," which she did instead of "Filli Ray." Brid always enjoyed it. You started with a sort of yodeling cry, to the whole herd, then you called the cows one by one, and each verse you added a new one.

> "Red cow, red cow, my lord's thoroughbred cow,
> Brown cow, brown cow, the woman in the
> town's cow,"

Brid sang, and no one looking at her could have realized that she was frantically wondering what else she could put into their unusually short show before her voice gave out. At "Old cow, old cow," inspiration came. Brid bowed at the end of the song. Coins clattered into the hat.

"Now, ladies and gentlemen, my brother Moril will sing four songs of Osfameron."

Moril gulped and glared at Brid. He had never performed any of the old songs in public before. But Brid had gone and announced him, so he was forced to take the center of the cart, with his wet hands shaking on the cwidder. To make matters worse, he suddenly met Kialan's eye. Kialan was standing near the fountain, looking cool, attentive, and slightly critical. From where Moril stood, the hanged man on the gallows appeared to be dangling over Kialan's head. Moril took his eyes off both of them and began to play. He knew he was going to make wretched work of it.

For a short while he could attend to nothing but the queer fingering and the odd, old-fashioned rhythms. Then his tension abated a little, and he was surprised to discover that his performance was pleasing him. As Moril's voice was naturally high, he did not need to sound cracked and strained, the way Clennen did. And not being yet expert and not anyway liking the noise the old fingering made, he found he had been unconsciously modifying it, into a style which was not old, nor new, but different. Osfameron's jerky rhythms became smoother, and Moril felt that if he could have spared time to attend to them, he might almost have understood the words:

> "The Adon's hall was open. Through it
> Swallows darted. The soul flies through life.
> Osfameron in his mind's eye knew it.
> The bird's life is not the man's life.
>
> "Osfameron walked in the eye
> Of his mind. The blackbird flew there.

He would not let the blackbird's song go by.
His mind's life can keep the bird there."

It sounded good to Moril. And it was his own doing, he was positive, and not the cwidder's. When he had finished, however, there was silence in the square. The crowd had never heard the old songs done that way and did not know what to think. Kialan made up their minds for them by clapping loudly. Other people clapped. Then came a burst of applause which made Moril feel ashamed of himself—he was only a learner, after all—and more coins went into the hat.

The applause seemed to worry Olob. From then on he became restive. He tossed his head, he stamped, he tried to go forward, and he threatened to back. Brid pulled him up, and he backed in earnest, throwing Moril into Dagner. Brid had to take the reins up again, which put her half out of action. Seeing this, Dagner pulled himself together and led into some songs with rousing choruses, hoping the crowd would join in. He had little luck. People were in the mood for listening. But they had come to the end of all they had practiced, so Dagner was forced to go on to "Jolly Holanders" and finish.

Olob was still behaving like a colt, so Moril got down and went to his head. The crowd shifted away from the cart. Moril heard Brid say to Dagner, "Shall I go shopping? I know what to get," and the hat chinking.

"No, I'll go," said Dagner. He still seemed nervous, although the show was over. He took the hat and climbed down from the cart. Almost at once, several men that Moril recognized as friends of Clennen's came up and crowded round Dagner.

"What's this, Dagner? What's this about Clennen?"

The upshot was that Dagner went off to have a drink with them, taking the hat. Moril did not see which inn they went to because he found himself being talked to by a kindly man just then. This man first gave Moril a pie, then told him—in a fatherly way—that he had sung the old songs all wrong, and things were going to the dogs if people could take those kind of liberties.

Moril took a leaf out of Dagner's book. "Yes, but I can't do it like my father did," he said with his mouth full. He was extremely grateful for the pie, or he would have told the man his real opinion of the old songs.

When the man had gone, muttering that he didn't know what the young were coming to, Moril remembered that Brid would be a prey to murmuring gentlemen. He looked up at the cart, wondering what he would do if she was. There was—or had been—a murmuring gentleman. Brid was glaring at him like a tiger, and the gentleman was retreating, very red in the face. "I do hope Dagner remembers the shopping," Brid said to Moril, pretending the gentleman had never existed.

So did Moril. They waited, and waited, Moril at Olob's restive head and Brid in the cart, for well over an hour. Moril saw Kialan at intervals, hanging about in the square, evidently waiting, too. But Kialan made no attempt to come near them. Moril rather irritably wondered why not.

Olob tossed his head furiously. Brid said, "There's Dagner!" Moril saw Dagner hurrying back across the square with the empty hat rolled up in one hand. "Where's the shopping?" Brid wondered. Dagner waved cheerfully and came hurrying on. He had almost reached the cart when two large men advanced, quietly and purposefully, on either side of Dagner. One took Dagner's shoulder in a large hand.

"What—?" said Dagner, trying to shake free.

"You're under arrest, in the Earl's name," said the man. "Come on quietly and don't make any trouble now."

For a moment Moril had another glimpse of Kialan, looking absolutely horrified, in the crowd beyond the fountain. The people near, seeing someone being arrested, drifted quickly away from around the cart. Kialan seemed to get lost in a moving group and was gone the next second. Moril stood by Olob's head in an empty space, quite irrationally angry with Kialan. Not that anyone could do anything if the Earl took it into his head to have Dagner arrested, but even Kialan would have been better than no one. He looked despairingly at Dagner. Dagner had only time for one hopeless look back before the two men led him away across the square toward the jail. The crowd hurried away from all three—as if Dagner had a disease, Moril thought angrily. He wished Dagner would walk upright, instead of going bent and guilty-looking.

"I've never been so furious in my life!" said Brid. "Never! Of all the unjust—" She stopped, and looked uneasily round the empty space by the fountain, realizing she was on the way to getting herself arrested, too.

The two men vanished with Dagner inside the frowning jail. Moril had never felt more lonely. "I've just realized," he said. "We didn't have a license to sing, did we?"

"We're entitled to operate on Father's for six months," said Brid. "Father told me, and I *know* that's the law. I hope Dagner remembers. They can't *do* this! They're just trying—"

A man approached across the empty space, rather grudgingly, carrying what looked like a sack of oats. He stopped some way off the cart. "Your brother ordered this," he said. "Do I take it away again?"

"You'll do no such thing!" Brid said haughtily. "It's paid for—that I do know. Put it in the cart."

"Please yourself," said the man unpleasantly. He dumped the sack on the flagstones and went away.

That was nasty, somehow. Moril saw that everyone was going to avoid them now. Angrily he supposed that Kialan had deserted them in the same way. He left Olob, who seemed to be quietening down, and dragged the sack over to the cart. "What shall we *do*, Brid?"

"Do?" said Brid, more furious than ever. "I'll tell you what to do. I'll have to stay here, in case Dagner ordered anything else, but you're to go over to the jail at *once* and ask to see Dagner. Go on. Tell them he's related to the Earl. Say Mother's Tholian's niece. Make a fuss. Ask them to send for Ganner. Make it quite clear that we're well connected. And when you see Dagner, tell him to do the same. Go on. They're just trying to frighten us into paying for another license, I know they are!"

Obediently Moril scurried off across the square. He was so shaken that he could think of nothing else to do, even though he knew in his heart that it was no good. In the South, when they arrested people, even for small offenses, it took more than a boy talking about noble relatives to get them out of prison. At the least it took a lot of money. And as they had not got a lot of money, the doors of the jail could well have closed on Dagner for good. Moril wished Ganner had found them, after all. By the time he reached the cold archway into the jail, he was heartily wishing they had never left Markind.

"Please," he said to the man on duty there, "I want to see my brother."

The man looked down at him, not unkindly. "Clennen the Singer's son?" Moril nodded. "And how old are you, lad?" asked the man.

"Eleven," said Moril.

"Eleven, are you?" said the man. "They don't hang your kind till they're fifteen, you know, so you're lucky." Moril thought this was meant to be a joke and smiled politely. "Look, lad," said the man. "Take some good advice. Get in that cart of yours and drive off. You won't do any good here."

Moril looked up at him in helpless irritation. "But—"

"Be off!" said the man, urgently. Footsteps were coming through the dark passage behind him. Moril could see the man meant kindly, but he did not move. He waited to see if the person coming would let him see Dagner.

The man who came was one of the two who had arrested Dagner. He glanced at Moril, without seeming very interested. Then he looked again—sharply. "That's another of them, isn't it?"

"Yes, sir," said the man at the gate, and he gave Moril a reproachful look, as much as to say, "Now see what you've done."

"Come with me, lad," said the other man. Moril, with his stomach hopping as it had never done before, even before this last show, followed him into the dark passageway, through a dismal courtyard and up some stone stairs. They went into a blank room with yellow walls and a bench by one of the walls, where the man told him to sit and wait. Then he went out and locked the door.

Moril sat on the bench for some time, feeling terrible. He wondered if he was arrested, too. It looked like it. He tried to see out of the window, but it was high up and barred. He dragged the bench over to it, but he still could not see much except gray walls. There was no hope of wriggling out between the bars. He dragged the bench back to its original position and sat on it again.

Then the most dreadful part began. He could not bear being shut between walls. He was hot. He was trapped. The room seemed to get smaller every second and the ceiling seemed to be moving down on him. He thought he would have to scream. He nearly did scream, when a fortunate stain on the wall opposite caught his attention. It was almost the shape of the mountains between Dropwater and Hannart.

Moril thankfully escaped into a dream. He imagined snow-capped mountains and forgot he was too hot. He imagined wide valleys and the sky overhead, and the small room became easier to bear. He thought of the old green roads of the North and of Osfameron and the Adon walking along them. He became Osfameron himself. He and his friend the Adon made their way to imaginary Hannart. On the mountain, they were ambushed by enemies and fought their way clear. Then they went down into Hannart and strolled under the rowan trees outside the old gray castle, composing a song of victory together.

The door opened, and another man told Moril to come along now, quickly.

Moril came back to the present with a jump. He was scared and vibrating and small. He was aware of every stone and stain in that oppressive room, of the grain in the wood of the door, and the dirt in the fingernails of the man's hand holding it open. He even knew there were six hairs in the mole on the man's nose. As he got up, he suddenly remembered Clennen by the lake, saying, "You're in two halves at present." And he wondered if this was what Clennen had meant.

The man ushered him into a large, imposing room, with a heavy old table at one end. An elderly man sat behind the table, with a younger one who was taking notes. Moril could see by the gold chain round the elderly one's neck that he was a justice.

"Stand in front of the table and answer clearly," said the younger man, pausing in his writing and pointing his pen at Moril.

Moril did as he was told, still vibrating. He knew every bulge in the rather pointless carving on the wall above the justice. He could tell how many wrinkles there were in the forehead of the justice—fifteen yellowish folds.

The justice wrinkled these folds up and looked at Moril. "Full name?"

"Osfameron Tanamoril Clennensson," said Moril. "I'd like to see my brother, please."

"Quite a mouthful," remarked the Justice, while the other man wrote it down. "Osfameron?"

"He's my ancestor," said Moril. Seeing that the yellow folds of the justice were lifted toward him with slight interest, he explained, "I was called after him. And could I see Dagner, please?" The yellow folds drew closer together. "My brother," Moril said patiently.

"Your brother?" said the justice. The other man passed him a sheaf of papers, and he drew the folds of his forehead together over them until it looked like smocking. "Some other mouthful down here," he said.

Moril, with a little wobble to his stomach, realized the papers must be Dagner's answers to the questions they had asked him. He wondered what Dagner had said and wished he knew. For if he gave different answers from Dagner's, the justice might well convict Dagner of all sorts of things he had never done. "We call him Dagner for short," he explained carefully. "And I'd like to see him, please."

"You can see him presently, if you answer my questions truthfully," said the justice. "You come of a family of singers, is that true?"

"Yes," said Moril.

"And you traveled with your father, giving shows?"

"Yes," said Moril.

"How long have you been doing that?"

"All my life," said Moril.

"Which is how long?"

"Eleven years," said Moril.

The younger man leaned over. "The elder boy said ten years."

The justice smocked his forehead at Moril, calculating how old he was. He looked weary and shrewd, and Moril was just a doubtful fact to him. Moril saw that to follow Brid's advice and talk of being related to the Earl and to Ganner would do no good, simply no good at all. He knew Brid would have done it. But he was not going to try.

"I was a baby when we started," he explained.

"From Hannart?" said the justice sharply.

"Yes, but I don't remember," Moril said, knowing well enough that if he admitted to his true feelings about Hannart here, he could convict both himself and Dagner. "My father said he had a quarrel with Earl Keril."

They checked that off against Dagner's answers, and it seemed to be right, to Moril's relief. But they seemed dissatisfied, and they became more dissatisfied as the questions went on.

"Where did you last perform before Neathdale?"

Moril thought. It seemed very long ago. Fledden? Yes, because that was the last place before they were in the Markind lordship and stopped performing. That was where Lenina had mended Kialan's coat. "Fledden," he said.

"Who did your brother talk to in Fledden?"

"Nobody," said Moril. He remembered particularly, because no girls had come up to Dagner for once, and he had talked to Dagner himself.

"But you weren't with him every moment you were in Fledden, were you?" said the younger man.

"Yes, I was," said Moril. "We were all in the cart, you see. Father always made us stay in the cart together in towns."

"Always?" said the justice, smocking his folds severely. "You don't mean to tell me your brother never went off on his own."

Moril realized he could convict Dagner of poaching rabbits unless he was careful. "No, never," he said. "Dagner's not interested in anything much except making up songs." And to divert attention from the idea of poaching, he added, "Dagner hasn't done anything you could arrest him for—and our license is in order, honestly."

The justice sighed irritably. "I'm not concerned with your license, boy. Your brother has been arrested for passing illegal information—"

"*What!*" said Moril.

"—and I want to know where he got it," said the justice. "That surprises you?"

"I should just say it does!" said Moril. "He couldn't have done! You must have made a mistake."

"Our agents are very reliable," said the justice. "What makes you think it's a mistake?"

"Because Dagner wouldn't. He's just not interested. He's only interested in making songs. Besides, there's nowhere he *could* have got information," Moril said frantically.

"That sort of assertion is not at all helpful," said the justice. "I fancy both you brothers are concealing something. You say you last performed in Fledden. That must have been a week ago. Where have you been since?"

"Markind," said Moril, wondering why on earth Dagner had not mentioned it. "Then we came here by Cindow."

The justice and the younger man looked at one another, and seemed incredulous. It was clear that they thought Markind the last place where anyone could obtain illegal information. Moril took heart a little. "Why Markind?" snapped the younger man.

"My father was killed," Moril explained, his voice wobbling a little.

"We know. At Medmere. Why did you go to Markind?" said the younger man.

"My mother went to marry Ganner," said Moril.

"*Ganner!*" they both exclaimed, and both looked at Moril in flat disbelief. "Ganner is Lord of Markind," the justice said, as if he thought Moril did not know.

"I know," said Moril. "Mother was betrothed to him before she married Father, and she went back there."

"Very likely," the justice said cynically. "In that case, why did you and your brother leave?"

Angry tears came into Moril's eyes. "Because I saw one of the men who killed Father there, if you must know! And if you don't believe me, ask Ganner!"

"I most certainly shall," said the justice. The other man murmured something to him and they looked at one another, the wrinkles of the justice smocked into a tight yellow bunch. Moril saw Brid had been right after all to tell him to mention Ganner. But like Brid, the justice had jumped to the conclusion that Ganner had had Clennen killed, and the younger man was wagging his eyebrows at him to warn him that Ganner was far too important to be accused. The justice showed himself neither very nice nor very just by giving a cynical little laugh, smiling and shrugging. Moril supposed he should be glad, if, as Kialan had said, Ganner really had nothing to do with Clennen's death. Then the justice turned to Moril again and Moril saw, sadly and rather bitterly, that there was one law for Ganner and quite another for himself and Dagner. "Did your brother talk to any strangers in Markind?"

"No," said Moril. "Only Ganner's household."

"Then who did he talk to between Markind and here?"

"Only us," said Moril.

"Listen, my boy," said the justice, "you're not being very helpful, are you? Perhaps it will jog your memory if I remind you that your brother's crime is one for which he will be hanged in due course. Therefore, I can put you in prison for withholding information."

Moril felt sick. "I *am* being helpful," he said. "I've *told* you it's a mistake. But if you're only going to believe me if I tell you Dagner's guilty, then it's no use asking me questions. Because he didn't do it!"

The younger man half stood up, looking savage. Moril blinked and waited for them to hit him, or clap him in a cell, or both. But they did neither. The younger man, after a dreadful pause, told Moril coldly to go and sit down at the other end of the long room. Moril did so. He sat on a hard shiny stool near the door and watched the two conferring together in low voices. There were footsteps beyond the door, so that he was unable to hear anything that was said, though he thought he caught Ganner's name more than once. Then they called him back to the table.

"We're going to let you go, boy," said the younger one. "We've come to the conclusion you know nothing about this matter."

"Thank you," said Moril. "Can I see my brother now?"

The younger man glared at him and was obviously going to refuse. But the justice said irritably, "Oh, very well, very well. I said you should if you answered my questions. I wouldn't like you to go away thinking we're unjust here."

Moril thought Brid would have made the obvious answer to this. He held his tongue, with a bit of an effort.

# 8

THE MAN WHO HAD fetched Moril before came back. He took Moril downstairs to a great gloomy room with guards at the door. In the middle of this room were two rows of benches about three feet apart. People were sitting facing one another at intervals along these benches. Those on the farther bench were all prisoners. Moril could see they were, because they all had a dingy, sullen, dejected look and held their heads hunched forward. He had once seen a dancing bear with the same look. And the people on the nearer bench were plainly visitors, from not having that look, and being brisker and more nervous. There seemed to be guards everywhere, standing about in a bored way, and the nervous looks of the visitors were mostly directed at the guards. The room rang and whispered with shuffling feet and sad conversations.

The man told Moril to sit on the nearest bench. After a while two guards led Dagner through a door at the other end. Dagner had the same dingy, dejected look already. He looked unexpectedly small between the guards. Moril was sure he remembered him bigger.

They sat Dagner down on the bench opposite Moril. "You can have ten minutes," they told Moril. Then they left them to talk. Moril swallowed and could not think what to say.

"Just a moment," said Dagner. "Look at the room behind me, will you, and tell me if there's anyone you think can hear what we say."

Moril looked. The nearest guard was a good way off, talking to another. "No. They're two cart lengths away at least." He was about to turn round and see if there was anyone behind him.

"Don't move, you fool!" said Dagner. "I can see it's all right behind you."

"Then that's all right," said Moril. "I saw the justice and I told them it's all a mistake. They can't really think you were passing information, can they? It's just not true."

"Yes, it is," said Dagner. "I did."

Moril stared at him.

"Father asked me to," Dagner explained. "I had to give a message and some money to one of our men here. I didn't manage very well," he said sadly. "I wasn't sure—anyway, I think the one I gave it to must have been the spy. And when I think how relieved I was once I'd got rid of them, I—well, it's no use thinking of that, I suppose."

"But, Dagner!" Moril said, quite horrified. "They'll hang you for that!"

"You don't think I don't know that, do you?" Dagner said irritably. "Is there still no one near?"

"No," said Moril. "Dagner, it isn't true, is it? You're joking."

"I'm not joking," said Dagner. "If you don't believe me, take a look at that wine jar—unless they've searched the cart by now. But that's not important. What *is* important is that you've got to get Kialan into the North. You and Brid just have to go on and get him to Hannart if you can. Can you do that, Moril?"

"I suppose so," said Moril. "But I think he sloped off when they arrested you."

"No, he didn't," said Dagner. "He'll be waiting outside Neathdale, like he said."

"If you think so—Dagner, *why* is it so important?"

"Ask Kialan," said Dagner, with his eyes on someone behind Moril. "I ordered some flour and some more oats," he went on, rather artificially. "And there was a friend of Father's letting me have a side of bacon cheap. And onions. You can get bread on the way."

"And eggs," agreed Moril. "And I'll polish your cwidder for you, I promise."

"You needn't bother," said Dagner. "Right, he's gone. Now, listen. There are two things I want you to tell Kialan. One is that Henda *has* asked a ransom for him—"

"Ransom for Kialan?" said Moril. "But he's—"

"Never mind. Just tell him," said Dagner. "And the other thing is far more important. Earl Tholian is gathering an army and—"

"Tholian? He's dead," Moril objected, and he had a muddled and upsetting notion of an army of ghosts.

"This is the new Earl. He's called Tholian, too. Don't keep interrupting. There's someone on his way over behind you," said Dagner. "The point is that nobody in the North knows, and there's nobody going through but you and Kialan. Have you got those two things?"

"Ransom and Tholian," said Moril. "There's somebody coming behind *you* now."

The guards behind Dagner came right up to him. "Come on. Time's up."

"We haven't had anything like ten minutes," Moril pointed out.

"Too bad. The justice wants to see him. On your feet, fellow," said the guard.

Dagner got up and climbed back over the bench. He made Moril a face as he was marched off, which Moril thought was intended for a smile. Moril himself, feeling utterly crushed, wandered to the door and was shown briskly through to the entrance again.

"You're out again, are you?" said the man on duty. "You've been lucky."

Moril had not the heart to reply. He did not think he was lucky, particularly as the first thing that met his eyes outside was the two dangling feet of the hanged man.

Beyond the dangling feet, Brid was sitting in the cart looking haughty and impatient. The cart was still in a clear space, and the sack of oats had been joined by a number of other sacks and bundles, all of them too heavy for Brid to lift by herself.

"Where have you *been*?" she demanded, as soon as Moril was near enough. "I thought you were never coming back! What's the matter? You look like a jug of spilled milk."

Moril was feeling so lost and peculiar that all he could do was to go to Olob. He put his arms round Olob's neck and rubbed his forehead on Olob's nose.

"Well, tell me!" said Brid. "Have you seen Dagner?"

"Yes," said Moril.

"Did you tell him to say what I told you?"

"No," said Moril.

"Why *not*? Moril, I shall hit you in a moment if you don't tell me sensibly what happened!"

"I can't," said Moril. "Not here."

"Why *not*?" Brid almost shouted.

Moril realized that he must stop her attracting attention to them. "Please, Brid. Shut up," he said, looking at her as meaningly as he could from beside Olob's nose. "Let's get these sacks loaded and get on."

Brid began to see that something terrible might have happened. "Without Dagner?" she said, in a more subdued voice. Moril nodded, tore himself away from warm, soft, friendly Olob, and began to heave at the nearest sack. Brid came down and joined him. "Moril, for goodness' sake!" she whispered angrily. "It can't be that bad! You're behaving as if they're going to *hang* Dagner."

"They are," said Moril.

Brid went white, but she did not really believe him. "Oh no!" she said. "Not on top of everything! Why?"

"Get these things in, and I'll tell you when we're moving," Moril said.

They loaded the cart, and Brid drove out of the square. When they came into the cobbled streets, where the cart made sufficient clatter to cover up whispers, Moril told Brid what had happened. It turned Brid so sick and weak that had Olob been that kind of horse, he could easily have got out of control.

"I can't believe it!" she kept saying.

She was still saying it when half a mile out of Neathdale, Kialan pushed his way out of a hedge and came to join them. When he first looked at them, he was smiling, as if he were relieved. Then he saw there were only two of them, and his smile vanished. He looked along the cart to make sure Dagner was not there, and then at their faces. When he climbed up to join them, his brown face was tired and yellowish. "What happened?" he said. "Better drive on."

"Moril says they're going to hang Dagner for passing information," said Brid. "He says Father told Dagner to do it. And I can't believe it! I just can't believe it!"

"Oh," said Kialan. "They got him for that, did they? I thought that was too much of a risk on top of everything else."

"You're mighty cool, aren't you?" said Brid. "But I suppose Dagner's not your brother!"

There was a pause, in which Kialan tried to control his feelings. But his natural outspokenness won. "All right," he said. "So he's not my brother. So you think I don't know how you feel. You just thank your stars, my girl, that you don't have to stand there and watch them hang Dagner, like I had to with *my* brother!" Brid and Moril turned round in the driving seat to stare at Kialan. But they turned back, because there were large, angry tears running past Kialan's high-bridged nose, and more tears filling and reddening his light blue eyes. "I always thought the world of Dagner, anyway," he said. "I remember him quite well from when we were small."

There was silence, except for horse and cart noises. Brid encouraged Olob to make the best speed he could up the first steep hill to the Uplands. It was horrible to be urging Olob away from Dagner. There were tears in Brid's eyes, too.

"Why did they hang your brother?" Moril asked at length.

"No reason," Kialan said angrily. "It was Tholian's idea—that pale-eyed murdering swine who killed your father—but I didn't hear Hadd or Henda or any of the others making much objection. They just had us put on trial first, to make it seem respectable. And then it came out that I was only fourteen—"

"Oh! I thought you were older!" said Brid.

"People do," said Kialan. "But I was fourteen in March. Tholian was furious, because the rest of the earls said it was against the law to hang me for another year. But they hanged poor Konian, and the ship's captain, and all the crew they could catch, and they made me watch. It was just like our luck to land when all the earls had got together to invest that brute Tholian! His grandfather died the week before."

They were now high enough above Neathdale to have, at that moment, an excellent view of the same Tholian's mansion. Moril looked down at its long white front, peaceful and pompous and bowered among trees, and felt like a mouse running over the paws of a cat. He wished the cart was not so very pink and noticeable.

"I'm beginning to think," Kialan said miserably, "that I bring bad luck on people. First Konian, then your father, now Dagner—and goodness knows what happened to the people who helped me escape from Hadd!"

"If you don't mind my asking," Brid said cautiously, "who are you exactly?"

"My father's the Earl of Hannart," said Kialan. "And if you want to dump me out and drive off, I won't blame you."

Moril looked round for Tholian's mansion again. To his relief, it was now hidden by a bend in the road. He was glad. He felt as if this piece of news had put them suddenly in great danger. He was limp with terror, although he knew that they must have been in exactly the same danger from the moment Kialan joined them. Any earl of the South—not only Tholian—would have been overjoyed to get his hands on Kialan. His father was their chief enemy. Anyone found helping Kialan was bound to be savagely punished. Moril thought back, terrified, to Kialan walking through towns so as not to seem to belong to them, sharing the cart in full view of travelers on the road, and even being introduced to Ganner as one of them. And if that was Tholian he had seen in Markind, Moril could hardly bear to think what a risk it had been. Clennen could not have known who Kialan was. He would never have done it for the son of someone he had quarreled with. But it looked as if Lenina had known.

"I should have known you were from the North," Brid said ruefully, "when you said your name was spelled with a *K*. They don't use *K*'s in the South, do they? I wondered why Mother told Ganner your name was Collen."

Kialan chuckled slightly. "Your mother's a cool one, isn't she?"

"I suppose she is. But look here—" said Brid. "What were you and your brother doing in the South? Didn't you know what would happen?"

"It was an accident," said Kialan. "Do you remember that storm at the end of April?"

"Yes. We nearly lost the big tent. Remember, Moril?" asked Brid. Moril nodded.

"Well, we nearly got drowned," said Kialan. "We'd been to our aunt on Tulfer Island, and the storm hit us on the way home. We were blown all over the place, and the boat was sitting half under water with sea pouring in, and I don't think the captain knew where we were any more than I did. He said we'd have to get to the nearest haven before we sank. And we did. And it turned out to be Holand. And there were all the earls of the South, smacking their lips at us. To tell you the truth," Kialan said, "I didn't even feel frightened at first. I was so glad to be on land again."

"We were near Holand then," said Brid. "But we never heard—oh, yes, Father gave it out as news, didn't he? Is that how Father came into it?"

"Don't you think he was bound to be in on it?" asked Kialan. "He didn't tell me much, but I'm sure he arranged it all. I know the people who helped me escape seemed to spend all the time waiting for messages from the Porter to know what to do next."

"What? Father?" Moril said, puzzled.

"Yes. Your father," said Kialan. "You don't mean to tell me you didn't know he was the Porter?"

"He was *not*!" Brid said angrily. "The Porter's a spy with a price on his head."

"Yes, of course, in the South," said Kialan. "They were mad to catch him here, because he was the main agent for the North. You must have known! He brought all the important messages and most of the refugees. They must have come in this cart. And he organized people here against the earls—I know that, because Konian told me. Konian sent a message to your father for help, during the trial, but it didn't get to him quick enough."

There was a somber pause. Olob clopped patiently upward, zigzagging with the road across the steep hillside, while Brid and Moril tried to take in what Kialan had said. "I thought," Moril said, "that your father had quarreled with ours?"

"So did I," said Kialan. "But I think that was a pretense. I found out last year—I wish people told me things!—because my father vanished and I needed him for something. And Konian told me to shut up, because he'd gone to meet Clennen the Singer like he always did, but no one was supposed to know. I think they arranged what to do next then."

"I refuse to believe that my father was a common spy!" said Brid. "Why didn't he *tell* me? He ought to have told me! It's so sneaky, somehow!"

"Don't *shout*!" Moril said, with an anxious look round at Tholian's mansion, which had come into view again, lower down and farther off.

Kialan laughed outright. "But he wasn't sneaky! That was the splendid thing about him! I couldn't believe he really was the Porter at first. I saw this fat man with a great big voice, who spent all his time trying to impress people, and I thought there'd been an awful mistake. Then I saw him go into towns, in this shocking bright cart, in a scarlet suit just to make sure people didn't miss him, and sing his head off, and call out at the top of his voice that the price on the Porter's head was two thousand in gold. It was incredible! Then he and your mother would call out messages and hand out notes, right in front of everyone, and I knew half of them were illegal. But no one would believe it, because it was all done so openly. Nobody thought he was anything more than a very good singer. And I really think Clennen thought that was the best joke about it."

Moril blinked a little at this view of his father. But Kialan had hit Clennen off in a way. Clennen *had* treated their shows as a rather serious joke. If he was really the Porter all along, then that would be why. "I suppose that's where Dagner went wrong," he said sadly. "Trying to be secret."

"Dagner was awfully stupid to think he could carry on where Father left off, anyway," said Brid.

"He didn't," said Kialan. "Dagner wasn't trying to do that for a moment. But Clennen asked him to finish off the important things if he could. Then he was to go North and stay there. And the message to Neathdale was important because it was about a spy who'd got in among them there."

Moril sighed. He did not say that Dagner thought he had given the message to that very spy. There seemed no point. He said, "Dagner said I was to tell you Henda has asked for a ransom for you. And Tholian is gathering an army."

"Oh damn!" Kialan said wearily. "Then I'll *have* to get through somehow, won't I? You saw Dagner? Tell me."

Moril told Kialan all that happened to him in the jail. He could not help speaking low and looking nervously at Tholian's mansion each time it came into view. He was relieved when they crossed the brow of the first hill and could not see it anymore.

"You were lucky, Moril," said Brid. "If you'd known all the things Kialan's just told us, we might be in jail at this moment." Moril nodded soberly. He certainly could not have acted the surprise he felt when they told him what Dagner had been arrested for. But he knew it had been the merest good luck that he had not happened to mention Kialan.

"I couldn't think," said Kialan, "why Clennen made such a point of not telling you two anything. He wouldn't let me say who I was, and neither would Dagner. But I think it saved our skins. I wish it could have saved Dagner's."

"You don't think Dagner was really arrested because of you?" Moril asked.

"I did at first," said Kialan. "I thought we'd all had it, all the time I was sitting in the hedge. I could hardly believe it when I saw the cart coming. No. I think Dagner's trouble is separate, and thanks to you, Moril, they think he just did a bit of freedom fighting on the side. But I hope it doesn't get round to the Earl. Tholian will put two and two together all right."

"Why did Tholian kill Father?" said Moril.

"He was looking for me," said Kialan, "and he didn't want anyone to know, because I'm supposed to be Hadd's prisoner—or Henda's, only they were still arguing about that when I escaped. Dagner thought that maybe the Neathdale spy—or perhaps it was the fellow they hanged—might have given Tholian a hint about your father. But he couldn't have known much, or we'd all have been arrested. Tholian's the sort who says dead men tell no tales, so he kills Clennen and then beats the woods for me."

"If only we'd known!" said Brid. "Where were you all that time?"

"Up a tree," said Kialan, "rabbits and all. They were crashing about searching all the time you were playing that cwidder, Moril, and it worried them like anything. They kept saying that blessed boy and his music made their heads go round. Tholian suggested going back and killing you, too, but none of them could quite be bothered to. And when you left off, they'd had enough and they went."

"Could you pass it me?" said Moril. Kialan obligingly crawled back to the instrument rack and reached the big cwidder over to the driving seat. Moril took it and clutched it to him. It felt fat and hard and comforting. Apart from the fact that it seemed to have saved both his life and Kialan's, it was in its rather more awesome way as good as Olob's nose. He felt he needed it, somehow, after the events of today.

"Play something," suggested Kialan.

"No, don't," said Brid. "Not until we've decided what to do. We're slap bang in the middle of Tholian's earldom, and we've obviously got to get North, and everyone knows this cart. And we've no money. I daresay Father meant to go this way because it would have looked suspicious if he didn't, but I vote we turn east and try to get North through the Marshes."

Kialan fetched the map out and scowled at its sketchiness. "I suppose we could try the sea," said Moril. "We might find a boat that wants a singer."

Kialan glared at the map. "We'd take ages, either way. And we can't be more than four days off Flennpass here. Don't either of you understand? Tholian's getting an army together to invade the North, and Henda's sent to my father to say he'll ransom me, so my father thinks I'm a prisoner and daren't do a thing! And I suppose," he added, "Henda's message is the first news my father gets that we're not both drowned. If you don't mind, I'd like to get North as quickly as I can—but it's your cart, of course."

Moril glanced at Kialan and decided that his hectoring tone had much to do with the tears in his eyes. Brid did not notice. "Oh, *is* it our cart?" she said. The result was that Kialan managed to laugh, rather sheepishly.

"We'll go straight on," Moril said, suddenly deciding. "We'll do it Father's way and be quite open about it. It worked for him, and it worked for me in the jail."

Brid and Kialan seemed to be relieved that Moril had taken the lead. But as Olob dragged the cart into the level ground of the first Upland, they began to make nervous objections.

"Innocent little children is all very well," said Brid. "What about when the Earl hears of Dagner doing the Porter's business?"

Moril looked round on fields with green corn showing and sheep grazing. The hills of the North towered against the sky, so high and blue-gray with distance that, on first glance, Moril took them for a bank of cloud.

"A certain pink cart will be looked for," said Kialan. "Could you paint it?"

"Dark green would be best," said Brid. "But we've no money."

A village came in sight, looking very small against the hills of the North. Moril roused himself before Kialan and Brid could have any wilder ideas. "Tholian knows me," he said. "He recognized me up a ladder in Markind. That's the trouble with having red hair."

"Wear a hat," said Kialan.

Moril turned round to quell Kialan. "What about this village?" As he said it, he realized that Kialan was tired out. His face was as white as such a brown complexion could be, and there were dark rings under his eyes. All the watching at night and the suspense in Neathdale had been rather too much for him. "Get down in the cart," Moril said, taking pity on him. "I'll put the cover half-up."

Kialan lay thankfully down beside the wine jar, and Moril pulled the canvas forward until it hid him. They drove straight through the village, Brid holding the reins and Moril sitting beside her, gently strumming the cwidder. On the heights above the village there was an odd little gray tower, belonging to the Lord of the Uplands. Brid looked at it and quivered with terror, knowing as she did that the Earl of Hannart's son was hidden in the cart. But Moril knew it was no different from any other risk they had run without knowing. The tower and the mountains made him think of his imaginary Hannart. He felt soothed and peaceful.

Several people looked up, or out at doors, hearing the cart and the cwidder. When they saw what it was, they smiled and waved. Brid did her best to smile and nod back. Then a woman came out of a house and walked beside them.

"Have you been through Neathdale today?"

"Yes," said Moril.

"They tell me there was to have been a man hanged."

"Yes," said Moril. "He was. We saw him."

"I knew it!" the woman said, smiling. "He was bound to come to it!" She seemed so gleeful that Moril thought she must have hated the hanged man, until he noticed the tears in her eyes. Then he saw she was just trying to hide her feelings. He wanted to say something kind to her, but she left the cart and went back into her house. Moril wondered whether Clennen had known her, and what her connection was with the hanged man.

# 9

A MILE OR so beyond the village, Olob looked at the sun moving into the blue mountains and turned toward a cart track which led away to the left. Brid tried to stop him. "No, Olob. We must get on."

"Let him find a place," said Moril. "I told you. It's no good looking guilty. Besides, we haven't eaten a thing since this morning."

"You had a pie, you lucky pig!" snapped Brid, but she gave in and let Olob pull the cart into a secluded grassy space under a cliff. A stream ran in a trickle of green mosses down the rock face. Moril came down from the cart, feeling shaky at the knees.

"If we're going to camp this near the village," said Kialan, emerging from hiding, "then we'd better set a watch tonight."

"What for?" said Moril. "Nobody's going to bother to come at night, not after three children. And if they come while we're awake, we'll hear them."

"I'm going to watch, all the same," said Kialan.

"No you're not," said Moril. "There's no point."

"Bossy, aren't you, all of a sudden!" Brid snapped. Then she rounded on Kialan. "And if you make yourself ill staying awake every night, what are we supposed to do with you?"

Moril realized that Brid was angry because she was tired and miserable. So he said nothing and simply began to get Olob out of the shafts. Kialan must have realized it, too, because he said wearily, "Oh, all right. I give in," and started collecting firewood.

Brid investigated the provisions Dagner had bought. "What am I supposed to do with all this flour?" she demanded. "And no eggs!"

It looked as if Dagner's idea had been to stock the cart with enough food to last them until they reached the North. But as Brid said mournfully, his mind must have been on that message, for the only useful things he had bought were the bacon and a large cheese. Among the less useful things were lentils, candles, and a big bunch of rhubarb.

"Look at this!" said Brid, wagging the rhubarb about. "What was he *thinking* of?"

"Waste of money," agreed Kialan. "Did he use all you earned?"

"Yes," said Brid. "Every penny. And there's not even any bread."

They had a rather strange supper of fried bacon, cheese, and experimental pancakes made out of flour and water. Brid, after nibbling one, promptly put them in the frying pan that held the bacon, and Kialan thought of melting cheese over them to improve the taste. This left them still so empty that they finished the meal with about a quart each of stewed rhubarb; luckily, Lenina had left some sugar in the cart.

Moril felt better after that. He got up, fetched the bucket, and carefully cleaned the cart. It was looking very dusty and uncared for, and to his mind, it had a furtive, illegal look. He thought about Dagner as he worked. He wondered what he had to eat in prison and how soon he would be tried and hanged. Or did the questioning by the justice count as a trial? Moril feared that it did. He wondered again what Dagner had said when they questioned him. Then he thought of Dagner trying to carry on Clennen's work in Dagner's way. It had not seemed wise. Dagner had been nervous and secretive, and he had made a fatal mistake. But on the other hand, Dagner was so unlike Clennen that it was probably the only thing he could do. Moril thought about himself going back to Clennen's way and wondered if that was wise. He was not like Clennen either. But he did not know what he was like. He supposed that sooner or later he would have to find out, and then do things in the way best suited to what he found.

Brid and Kialan were washing the pans. Kialan was looking exhausted. Tears kept coming into Brid's eyes, and she angrily wiped them away with the back of her greasy hand. And they were both pretending they were cheerful.

"Do you think if we mixed the cheese in with the flour, they'd taste better?" Brid said.

"What about rhubarb? Sort of fritters?" said Kialan.

"Ugh!" said Brid. "When I see Dagner, I'll—" She wiped off another set of tears and said brightly, "He must have had his reasons, I suppose."

Moril tipped away the dirty water, wondering if there could be three more unhappy people in Dalemark. Kialan must know he was a danger to himself and his companions. His landfall in Holand must have been horrible. And since then, Moril realized, Kialan's life had been one long, tense escape, which was not over yet. As for himself and Brid, they had seen their family simply dwindle away, until it was down to their two selves. And Kialan had been fond of Dagner, too—fonder than he had realized.

Moril stopped himself in the midst of a snuffle of self-pity. No. Last year, as soon as they were safely in the North, Clennen had told them some of the other things that happened in the South. Whole families had been arrested. The older ones had been hanged, and children younger than Moril had been left with nothing in the world, and nobody dared help them for fear of being arrested, too. Clennen had told them how Henda had calmly doubled his taxes last year and turned those who could not pay out to starve, and how old Tholian had hunted an old man with dogs for not raising his hat to him fast enough. Moril knew there must be hundreds of people in the South even worse off than he was. They had a horse and cart, and Clennen had left them with a means of earning a living and a license to do it. If it came to the worst, they could go back to Markind. Moril did not like the idea. He tried to tell himself that they could not go back, because of Kialan. But he knew that was not it. Lenina would help Kialan. The reason for his not liking it, he was forced to admit, was that he was not at all clear whether they had deserted Lenina, or she them. And it made him uncomfortable.

"We'll give more shows," he said, putting Lenina out of his mind. He went to the cart to polish the instruments and stopped at the sight of the wine jar taking up so much room inside. "Do you know anything about this wine jar?" he called to Kialan.

"No—oh, you mean the papers?" Kialan said, coming over to the cart. "Dagner had a look in Markind, because he had to find the message for Neathdale. They're down inside its basket."

Moril scrambled up to look. Kialan took down the tailgate and told him where to put his hand down between bottle and basket. Brid hurried over and watched Moril fish about, feel paper, and pull it out. "What are these?"

"Messages that weren't so important," said Kialan. "Lucky they didn't search the cart, wasn't it?"

Brid and Moril held the papers into the sinking sun and spelled out, in Clennen's writing: "For Mattrick. Someone in Neathdale—I think Halain—smells of lavender. Dirty washing through Pali and Fander in future."

"Lavender!" said Brid. "Really, Father!"

The other notes said the same, and were marked to be delivered to places between Markind and Neathdale.

"Go and put those all on the fire," Moril said, handing them to Kialan. "Now do you believe we can read?"

Kialan grinned and took the papers. While he was stuffing them under the embers and the air was filling with the strong smell of burning paper, Moril busily worked his hand on round the wine jar. Halfway round, he felt more papers. He pulled them out and unfolded them.

These were all in different people's writing. Some of them seemed to have come from parts of the South they had not visited in years. Others concerned the places they had passed through, and these were mostly in Lenina's writing. Moril felt oddly glad to see his mother's small, bold writing. He could see that whatever Lenina had thought, privately, of Clennen's freedom fighting, she had most scrupulously done what Clennen wanted while he was alive—even at the risk of being hanged for spying. It was queer to find her so honorable, but Moril liked it. Among other things, she had written: "Crady—169 taken north to Neathdale" and "Fledden—24 pressed yesterday, with horses." The other notes said much the same.

"What do you think this means?" said Brid.

Kialan came over to look. "Do you think," he said, after some puzzling, "those might be for my father or someone in the North? It could be about the army Tholian's gathering."

"You know, I do believe that's it!" said Brid. "They mean how many men went for soldiers from each place. Don't you agree, Moril?"

"Probably," said Moril. It seemed a bit boring to him. "We'd better take them North, then." He put them back and, just to be on the safe side, went on working his hand round the other side of the jar. There were cold, hard things. He gripped one and pulled it out. "I say!" It was a gold piece. "Whose is this?"

They were all mystified. Brid suggested that it was payment for taking Kialan North, but, as Moril and Kialan rather scornfully pointed out, if Clennen had organized that, he would have been paying himself. No other explanation seemed likely, either.

"Anyway, that means we can buy food tomorrow," Brid said. "Father couldn't mind that."

"Don't be a big idiot!" said Moril. "When did we ever have a gold piece before? Someone's going to think we stole it, and if *we* get arrested, the whole thing's going to come out." Carefully he slipped the coin back behind the basket again.

Brid sighed. "A whole bottleful of gold! Oh, all right. I suppose you're right and it would look odd. I'm going to bed. Get out of the cart."

Moril helped Kialan put up the tent. By then Kialan was so tired that he dragged a blanket into it and fell asleep before the sun set. Moril felt too agitated to go to sleep straightaway. He sat against the cliff, with Olob companionably cropping grass nearby, and strummed on the cwidder for comfort. He did not play any particular song, just snatches of this and a bar or so of that. It seemed to express the state of his feelings. He still found it hard to believe that his father had been a notorious agent. Of all the discoveries of the last few days, that one was hardest to take. He had thought he knew Clennen. Now he saw he had not. He wondered when Dagner had found out and how he had felt. And he made an effort to think of Clennen in this new light.

But somehow, he did not want to think of his father. He wanted to forget the blood gushing into the lake, and he did not want to consider how Clennen could be so public and so private at one and the same time. Instead, by degrees, Moril took refuge in hazy memories from much earlier. He thought of the cart rolling down a green road in the North. Clennen was singing in the driving seat, Lenina doing some mending beside him, and the three children were playing happily on the lockers. The sun shone—and, somewhat to his surprise, the cwidder began to produce a muzzy sound. It was a very queer noise. Moril did not like it, and Olob looked round at it disapprovingly.

"Time for bed," Moril said to Olob. He got up and went to put the cwidder back in the cart.

Inside, the cart was hot, and Brid and the wine jar seemed to fill it. Moril hesitated, thinking of the active elbows and knees of Kialan. But he could not bear the heat, so he took a blanket and wriggled into the tent with Kialan.

Luckily Kialan was so exhausted that he did not move in his sleep. Both he and Moril woke feeling fresher and happier. Brid was the somber one, but she improved after a breakfast of bacon steaks fried by Kialan. Then Moril fetched Olob's harness to clean. He was determined that their turnout should be as spruce and innocent as he could get it. Kialan, without being asked, went to groom Olob. And Moril realized that not only had Kialan done his full share of the chores ever since they left Markind, but nobody had either noticed or thanked him.

"You don't have to do Olob," he said. "I'll do him."

"Am I supposed to stand around and watch you wear yourself out, or something?" said Kialan. "Move, Olob, you lazy lump."

"Well, you used to," said Brid, scrubbing the frying pan. "And you're an earl's son."

"I thought I'd get that sooner or later!" Kialan said with his most fed-up look. "I didn't know what needed doing at first, and there always seemed loads of you to do it, anyway. But if you two are having to earn money now, it's only fair you don't do everything else."

"Moril," said Brid, going very somber again, "do you think we really *can* earn money? I mean, even with Dagner, we sounded so—so thin and pale, didn't we?"

"No, you didn't," said Kialan, at work on the farther side of Olob. "You just gave a different kind of show. Only I think you made a mistake in not building it round Dagner more. You should have got him to sing again, Brid. He'd have done it in short bursts, and his songs are really good."

"They are, aren't they?" Brid said sadly. "And now—"

"Moril," said Kialan, appearing under Olob's nose, "you can't happen to remember Dagner's songs, can you? Enough to play them yourself?"

"I never thought of that!" said Moril. As soon as he had finished the harness, he fetched out the instruments. While Brid set to work polishing them, Moril took up the big cwidder and tried out the first song of Dagner's that came into his head. For some reason, it was the song Dagner had never finished, the one Clennen had forbidden him to sing until they were in the North. Moril stopped after the first few notes, to make sure nobody was about. There seemed to be no one, so he went on. He found he wanted to finish it for Dagner. It seemed the only thing he could do for him.

Dagner had only sketched out part of the tune. Since Moril had no idea what Dagner intended, he let the words take him, this way and that, through a melting blackbird phrase:

"Come to me, come with me.
The blackbird asks you, 'Follow me.' "

—and then to a kind of birdsong triumph in

"Wherever you go, I will go."

Kialan seemed almost awestruck. But Brid, as soon as she realized what song it was, looked up the cliff and down the slope to make sure they were not overheard. Moril knew he was breaking the law. But he wanted to finish the song, so he went, rather defiantly, on to

"The sun is up."

The cwidder produced a shrill and defiant sound. Moril, cross with himself for being scared, tried to recapture the first melting tone and only succeeded in making a scratchy, bad-tempered tinkle. Dagner would have hated it. Moril thought of Dagner and put in the first four lines again at the end, as Dagner had suggested he might. But he was not thinking very clearly of Dagner himself—more of Dagner as part of that happy family on a green road in the North that he had pictured the night before. And just as he had last night, he heard the cwidder making that odd, muzzy noise.

Moril sprang up and sprang back. He could not help it. The cwidder fell on the turf with a melodious thump.

"Moril!" said Brid. "You'll break it!"

"It was splendid!" said Kialan. "Don't stop."

"I don't care!" Moril said hysterically. "I've a good mind to jump on it! The blessed thing was playing my *thoughts*! It played the way I was thinking!"

Brid and Kialan looked at one another, then at Moril. "Don't you think," Kialan said, "that that's the way it works? It's your thoughts that bring out the power."

"But it never did that for Father!" said Moril. "He told me! He said it only did it once."

"Well," Kialan said, rather awkwardly, "he couldn't really use it, could he? It wasn't his kind of thing."

"Except just that one time," said Brid. "Which proves it, Moril. Because it must have been when Father saw Mother in Ganner's hall. And he wanted her to love him instead of Ganner so much that he managed to make the cwidder work, and she did love him enough to come away with him."

After that Moril went and put the cwidder away. Brid got it out again and polished it for him, but he pretended not to notice. When Olob, the cart, and all the instruments were gleaming with care, they set off again through the first Upland, toward the steep hill to the second. Brid drove. Moril sat beside her, trying out another of Dagner's songs on his small treble cwidder. But it was no good. The treble cwidder just felt foolish and flimsy and shrill, and it sounded terribly ordinary. As Olob settled into a slow, heaving walk up the steep hill into the next Upland, Moril was forced to turn and ask Kialan to put the little cwidder away and pass him the big one.

The matter-of-fact way Kialan handed it to him made Moril feel much better about it. Moril took the cwidder thankfully. It felt right. He was not sure now whether it was a comfort or a burden, but if Kialan could accept so easily that it was a powerful and mysterious thing, so could he. But he knew he was going to have to learn to control the thing. You could not earn your living with a cwidder that whined if you were miserable and croaked if you were cross. "How should I start?" he asked Kialan over his shoulder.

Kialan hesitated, not because he did not understand Moril, but because he was not sure how Moril should start. "Understanding yourself, perhaps?" he asked. "I mean, I've no idea either, but try that. Er—why didn't you stay in Markind, for instance? Was it just seeing Tholian there?"

Moril, by this time, was sure that it was not. "Why didn't *you* want to stay?" he asked Brid, as a start. "Duty to Father?"

"Like Mother, you mean?" said Brid. "N-no. A bit of that. I do prefer Father's outlook to Mother's, but it was really almost more like the way Mother went back to Ganner. It's what I'm used to—this—and nothing else felt right."

Moril felt that went for him, too. But there was more to it than that. He could have persuaded Brid to go back to Markind after Dagner was arrested, but he had not thought of it, even. He had not wanted to go back when he had found out how dangerous their journey North really was. And he was still going North, as if it was a matter of course. Why?

"Why, Moril?" asked Brid.

"I was born in the North," Moril answered, rather slowly. "When I—er—dream of things, it's always the North. And the North is right and the South is wrong."

"Bravo!" said Kialan.

Moril turned to smile at him. He found himself turning from the towering unseeable hills of the North to a low, blue vision of the South, beyond Kialan's head. "But I still don't understand," he said.

At the top of the hill there was a village, a very small place, simply ten houses and an alehouse, clinging to the steep brow of the hill.

"Don't let's perform here," said Brid. "There's a bigger place farther on, I know."

They went past the village into a wider Upland, full of grazing sheep. By the middle of the morning Moril's cwidder was sounding melancholy. "I can't see us getting much," he said. "Not just the two of us."

"Would it help at all," said Kialan, "if I were to pretend to be Dagner?"

Both their heads whipped round his way. It was almost a marvelous idea.

"Would they remember Dagner from last year?" said Kialan.

"We didn't perform in the Uplands at all last year," said Brid. "But—"

"I've been thinking," said Kialan. "No one but the earls knows I'm in the South. And it's so out of the way here that no one's going to know Dagner was arrested unless we tell them. I think it would be safe enough—and a bit in your father's style, too."

Moril made the obvious objection. "You can't sing." They looked at one another for a moment. Moril remembered Kialan listening in to his lessons with Clennen, appearing in the crowd whenever they gave a show, and seeming so knowledgeable the time the big cwidder went out of tune. "Or can you?" said Moril.

"Not as well as you," said Kialan, "but—may I borrow one of these cwidders for a moment?"

"Go ahead," said Brid.

Kialan took up Dagner's cwidder and tuned it without needing to be given a note. Moril and Brid looked at one another. Neither of them could do that. And from the moment Kialan started to play, they knew they were listening to a gifted person very much out of practice. If he did not sing as well as he played, it was merely because he was the age when his voice still moved troublesomely from low to high. Moril vividly remembered the trouble Dagner had had at the same age.

What Kialan sang was a song of the Adon's, one that Clennen never sang in the South.

> "Unbounded truth is not a thing
> Cramped to time and bound in place—"

"Ooh!" said Brid, looking nervously round.

"No one about. Shut up!" said Moril.

Kialan did that part meticulously in the right old style. But then he gave Moril a bit of a wink and dropped into the same kind of different fingering Moril had used in Neathdale. The song seemed to come alive.

> "Truth strangely changes space,
> By right of its reality.
> It moves the hills containing me
> Wider than the world, or small
> As in a nut. Truth is free
> And laws are stones, or not at all,
> And men without it nothing."

"Oh, I liked that!" said Moril.

"I took a leaf out of your book," Kialan said, rather apologetically. "I don't like the old style either, and I don't see why old things should be sacred. Wow! I'm out of practice, though! Do you think I'll be any use to you?"

"You know you will," said Brid. "You big fraud. If you're that good, why on earth didn't you say so before? Father would have put you in the show, instead of making you walk through all the towns."

"I know he would!" Kialan said feelingly. "He'd have dressed me in scarlet and flaunted me. I didn't quite like to say anything at first—you were all so excellent—and as soon as I realized what your father was like, I'd have died rather than tell him. It was frightening enough walking."

The upshot of this was that Olob quietly pulled the gleaming cart onto the green of the village a mile or so on, and three people stood up to sing and play. Moril and Kialan were nervous, Brid, as usual, as confident as a queen. Moril did one or two of Dagner's songs, but mostly they sang ballads, since those were Brid's specialty and Kialan's voice was not equal to anything more difficult. A scattering of people listened and clapped. Someone asked for an encore, and Brid gave them "Cow-Calling." They got a little money, enough to buy eggs, milk, and butter, and a woman gave Brid a basket of somewhat withered apples. It was not a raving success, but it was no failure either.

"We can do it!" said Brid.

Moril smiled, and strummed his cwidder as they took to the road again. Every so often he played a tune in earnest, and Kialan would come in, too, on Dagner's cwidder. Kialan was getting more in practice every moment. They experimented, and tried for effects and new settings. Moril had seldom enjoyed making music so much. He almost wished the distance to Hannart were twice as long.

# 10

THEY HAD A SORT of cheese omelet for lunch, sitting on a point of green land between two brisk streams. Kialan would have it that what they were eating was scrambled eggs. Brid disagreed. Moril did not join in the argument because he was listening to the sound of the water. It made him think of the North. The sound of water running was never far away in the North. He was dreamily considering whether one could make a tune that captured the noise when Brid shook him sharply and told him they were moving.

"You didn't have to do that!" said Kialan.

"Why not? You know how maddening he is when he goes into a dream," Brid retorted.

"Yes, but it's just his way," said Kialan. "He's about six times as awake as most people, really. I bet he heard every word we said—didn't you, Moril?"

"I suppose I did," Moril said, in some surprise.

"Can I drive this next stretch?" Kialan asked.

Neither Brid nor Moril objected. Letting Kialan drive Olob seemed the best way to show he was a full member of the company now and not a passenger any longer. So Kialan held the reins, and Olob clopped onward through the lonely Upland. Moril sat beside him, still strumming the cwidder, looking dreamily round at the hills, the flocks of sheep, and the occasional shepherd in the distance.

They came to a steep rise to the third and last Upland. It was the highest and also the most beautiful of the three climbs, because it was clothed in trees the whole way up. The road, though it was the main road, dwindled to a rutty lane, damp and stony, boring its way upward through the woods. The sunlight fell in gay splashes through the bright leaves of springtime. All three of them looked upward and grinned at the way their faces became speckled and greenish.

But Olob, whether he objected to Kialan's holding the reins or to having to climb two steep hills in one day, became steadily more restive. At first it was simply tossing his head and stopping. Kialan persuaded him to move again, each time with more difficulty. But, as they went on upward, Olob took to trampling this way and that, so that the cart wheels caught in the hawthorns at the side of the road. Kialan grew exasperated. The fourth time Olob did it, Kialan lost his temper and swore at Olob. Olob promptly turned right across the road and seemed to be trying to climb the sheer bank into the woods. Moril thought the cart would overturn. The wine jar fell over and knocked Brid sideways, with a dreadful twanging of cwidders.

"Let me take him," said Moril.

Kialan crossly handed him the reins. Moril propped the cwidder across his knees and worked with both hands and some shouting to persuade Olob back onto the road again. Olob refused to come out of the bushes.

"What's got into him?" said Kialan.

"No idea," said Moril. As he said it, two memories came to him. One was of almost exactly the same conversation, between himself and Lenina, just before Tholian came out of the wood and killed Clennen. The other was of Olob behaving like a colt in Neathdale, just before Dagner was arrested. "Quick!" he said to Kialan. "There are enemies near, and Olob knows. Get out and go through the woods until we've passed them."

"How *can* he know?" said Kialan, with his most fed-up look.

"I don't know, but he does. Father always said he wouldn't part with Olob for an earldom, and I think that's why. Get *out*, I said!" Moril said urgently.

"Do as you're told, Kialan!" said Brid from the tilted bottom of the cart.

Kialan, entirely unconvinced, swung himself grudgingly down from the cart. As Olob was halfway through a bush, up the right bank of the road, Kialan went up beside him by the space he had cleared, and vanished among the trees higher up. Moril could hear his cross footsteps swishing along the steep hillside.

"Go quietly!" he said, but he could tell Kialan took no notice. Moril dumped the cwidder in the canted cart and went to Olob's head. Olob was most unwilling to leave the bush. "I know, old fellow, but we've got to go on and look innocent," Moril said. "*Come* on, now!"

It took some time to get Olob back on the road. When he did

consent to come, Brid had to lean on the cart to keep it upright. Then she climbed in and tried to set the wine jar and the instruments to rights. Olob reluctantly climbed onward. Above them in the woods, Kialan's feet kept pace with the cart, swishing loudly and cracking twigs. Moril wished he would not make so much noise.

Olob toiled round three corners and Brid still seemed to be busy in the cart. "What are you doing?" Moril asked.

"Putting my boots on," said Brid. "If there *are* enemies near, I'm going to look respectable. And I'm putting the sharp knife down the right boot." She joined him shortly, looking flushed and determined, firmly booted. "I'll drive," she said.

Moril gave her the reins and hung the cwidder round his neck by its strap, which, he supposed, was his way of looking respectable. His boots, by this time, were nothing like as new and smart as Brid's. Brid was better at managing Olob. Olob put on a great act of this being the most difficult climb of his life and did everything in his power to suggest that they turn back, but Brid kept him going. Beyond the protesting clatter of his hooves, Moril listened for Kialan, but he could not hear him any longer. By this time they were near the top of the climb. They rounded what must have been the last corner, and Olob shied.

"Clever Olob," Brid remarked.

There was a stout wooden trestle in the road. It did not fill the road, but it was placed so that there was no room for a cart to pass on either side. There were a number of men with it, one of them sitting on the trestle. To Moril's dismay, they were all in full war gear. Each of them wore a steel cap and a steel breast-plate with a pointed front—which gave them all chests like pigeons—over jackets and trousers of tough leather. They wore great black boots and long swords in black leather scabbards.

Brid drew the alarmed Olob up. "Would you mind moving the trestle? We need to get by," she said haughtily. She was frightened and daunted, but there were enough soldiers to make her feel as if she had an audience.

Three of the men strolled forward. None of them made any effort to move the trestle. "What's your business?" said one. The other two strolled on and looked over the sides of the cart to see what was in it.

"Drunkards, by the look of this wine," one said, and both of them sniggered a little.

"We're singers," said Brid. "Can't you see?"

"In that case, let's see your license," said the first man, and held out his hand for it. Brid, after a moment's hesitation, fetched the license out of the locker under the seat and handed it to him. He looked at it casually. "Which of you is Clennen?"

"That's my father," said Brid. "He was killed four days ago."

"Then you haven't got a license," said the man. "Have you?"

"Yes, we have," said Brid. "We're entitled to sing under that license for six months. That's the law, and you can't tell me it isn't."

"That may be the law in the other earldoms, but not in the South Dales," the man said, grinning. "You haven't read the small print." He unrolled the parchment and pointed vaguely to the bottom of it. When Brid leaned over to look, he took it out of reach and let it roll up again. "Too bad," he said. "You'd better come and explain yourselves."

"It doesn't say that at all!" Brid said furiously. "You're just using it as an excuse. That license is perfectly in order, and you know it!"

The man stopped grinning. "You'll do as you're told," he said. He nodded to one of the other men, who took hold of Olob's bridle. The rest moved the trestle aside. The one holding Olob hauled on him and Olob, passively resisting for all he was worth, was forced to move reluctantly on. Brid and Moril were towed after him, feeling quite helpless. It was clear that someone—Tholian, probably—had given orders that all travelers were to be stopped. Moril looked back to see the soldiers putting the trestle across the road again and sitting on it to wait for any other comers. He wondered about jumping off the cart and running. But there was a soldier walking on either side of it and it did not seem worth trying. Their only hope seemed to be to use Clennen's method and appear as open and innocent as they knew how.

They went fifty yards or so—a difficult jerky fifty yards, because Olob was extremely frightened and did not want to move, in spite of the names the soldier called him—and came to a steep road branching to the right. The soldier dragged Olob into it. Moril had forgotten this road. It worried him that Kialan would have to cross it on his way to the last Upland.

"Where does this road go?" he asked Brid.

"To a sort of extra valley at one side," Brid said. "We camped here the year before last. Don't you remember? Moril, they will let us go, won't they?"

Moril glanced down at the soldiers. "We haven't done anything wrong," he said carefully. But the wine jar came into his mind as he said it, and he wondered why on earth he had not left it behind somewhere.

A twig snapped in the wood up to the right. Moril looked up. And looked away quickly, in case the soldiers noticed. He had a very clear sight of Kialan staring down at the cart, alarmed and rather puzzled, as if he had not gathered what was going on. Moril stared at the steep road ahead and tried to will Kialan to cross the road while he had the chance and go on North. But he was very much afraid Kialan intended to follow the cart.

The trees opened like the end of a tunnel, and they came out into the valley. Brid gave a little moan. Beyond two groups of soldiers, evidently on guard, were tents, weapons, horses, and many more soldiers, as far as they could see. It was a long, thin valley, and winding, so that half of it was out of sight. But they had no doubt that the part of it they could not see was also full of soldiers and weapons and tents.

The nearest tent was a very large one. There was a chair outside it, and in that chair sat Tholian. His head turned as the cart came out from among the trees. As far as he could tell from this distance, Moril thought Tholian smiled. And he saw that Clennen's method was not going to help them here. In fact, he doubted if any method was going to be much use.

"Get down," one of the soldiers said to Brid and Moril.

They climbed down, Brid a little awkward in her boots, Moril clutching the cwidder, and stood where they had a lower and even busier view of the teeming valley ahead. Moril dimly remembered that the year before last there had been fields and crops growing here. There was no sign of them now. As they were taken toward Tholian, he saw nothing but men drilling and training, all down the valley. It was filled with orders and curses, and the thick warm smell of many people and horses. The grass, and any crops there might have been, were trampled to earth, except for a green stretch round the large tent where Tholian sat.

Tholian signaled to the soldiers to make Brid and Moril stand to one side of the patch of grass, and turned his pale eyes from them to the soldiers. "Just these two in the cart?" he asked.

Moril seized the opportunity to look over his shoulder to see what had become of Olob and the cart. He was glad to find one of the soldiers struggling to tie the unwilling Olob to a tree beside the road.

"Could I have your attention, cousin?" he heard Tholian say, and he turned back hurriedly. Tholian sounded irritated. But when Moril looked at him, he was smiling. He could have been friendly in spite of his queer, shallow eyes. "We are related, aren't we?" he said.

Moril thought about it. "I suppose so. But it's Mother who's your cousin."

"Once removed," said Tholian. "Which makes us twice removed, I believe."

"I'm surprised you acknowledge it at all," said Brid. "Considering—"

"Why not?" said Tholian. "It doesn't hurt you. But don't deceive yourselves into thinking your mother's going to get a penny of dowry out of me. I'm content to do as my grandfather wanted. Ganner's a fool if he thinks I'm going to make him rich on Lenina's account."

This seemed a very odd thing for Tholian to start talking about. Moril wondered if he was a trifle mad. "I shouldn't think Ganner does think that," he said.

"He's fond of Mother, you see," explained Brid.

Tholian laughed. "Fool, isn't he?" He was so contemptuous that Brid all but sprang to Ganner's defense. "But I stayed for the wedding," Tholian said, before Brid could speak, "which was more than you did. You threw Ganner into a fine old fuss by leaving like that, you know. Your mother took it much more calmly. So I promised them I'd look out for you on the road and send you back to Markind when I found you."

"That was kind of you," Brid said coldly. Nevertheless, both she and Moril were beginning to feel distinctly easier. If Tholian were regarding them simply as silly young relations and himself as doing Ganner a favor, then the position was nothing like as bad as they had feared. It would be exasperating to be sent back to Markind, but at least Kialan, with luck, could get North on foot from here.

"Didn't Mother recognize you?" Moril said slowly, rather puzzled at the way Tholian was now being a friend of the family.

"Of course," Tholian said, not at all disconcerted. "But as I'm Ganner's overlord, there wasn't much she could say. Not that she would. She has a way of saying things in silence, your mother. By the way, what became of your brothers?"

They saw he had just been showing them how much he knew. It gave them both a jolt. Moril reacted best, because he was able to rely on his habitual sleepy look. He went on staring at Tholian in a vague, friendly way, though he had never felt less vague or less friendly in his life. But Brid was so shaken that she had to put on an act.

"Funny you should ask," she said, with artificial brightness. "We don't quite know—"

"Yes, we do, Brid," Moril said, fearing she was going to babble herself into trouble. "Dagner went back to Mankind." It was a risky thing to say, but Moril knew that if Tholian already knew that Dagner had been arrested and why, it did not matter what he said anyway.

"Did he, indeed?" said Tholian, and there was no telling whether he had heard about Dagner or not. "And what about the other brother—er—Collen, was it?"

Moril knew Tholian had not seen Kialan in Markind. If he had, none of them would have been allowed to leave. He must have heard Ganner talk about him later. And no one would be surprised to find Ganner had got something wrong. Moril opened his mouth to say they had not got another brother, but Brid, to his annoyance, came in first, with tremendous verve: "Oh, Collen! He's so stupid you never know *what* he'll do! But we think he went with Dagner."

"Curious," said Tholian. His untrustworthy eyes slid over Brid, and over her again. "Now I thought I was reliably informed that there were three of you giving a show in Updale this morning."

That had obviously been a fatal mistake. But how could they have known Tholian was so near? The only thing to do was to say that the third one had been Dagner. Moril drew a breath to say it, but once more, Brid rushed in. "Yes, of course. But that's what I was telling you. Collen went back after that. He said he was going to Neathdale and he—er—he got a lift in a farm wagon."

Moril sadly wished that Brid would let him do the talking. Brid was not as clever as she thought she was. No doubt she had thought she was doing very well, but she had first admitted Kialan's existence and now that he was quite near, and Moril knew there was no need to have done either. Tholian had never seen Kialan in their company. He was only going by guess. But now he was almost certain. He was looking at Brid, worrying her by just looking, and obviously enjoying the way he was worrying her.

"I don't think you quite understand the position," Tholian said when Brid, flushed and alarmed, had dropped her eyes from his pale ones to her boots. "I'm ready to send you both back to Markind safely, in exchange for Kialan Kerilsson. Not otherwise. Is that understood now?"

"I don't understand you at all," Brid said valiantly.

Tholian looked at Moril. "Do you?"

Moril tried to repair some of the damage Brid had done by saying, "Not really. Who's this person you're talking about?"

The only result of this was that Tholian turned his eyes back to Brid. "Keril," he said, "as I'm sure you know, is Earl of Hannart." Without bothering to turn round, he snapped his fingers to some of the men near. They came hurrying up. "Listen," said Tholian. "Kialan Kerilsson is about five feet seven, solidly built, with a dark complexion and fair hair. His nose is aquiline and his eyes are much the same color as mine. Start searching the woods for a boy of that description."

The men at once turned and went hurrying farther into the thronged valley. Brid, as Moril knew she would, showed her consternation by saying, with horrible brightness, "What a queer kind of person that sounds!"

"No, no," said Tholian. "Just a typical Northerner." Beyond him, captains waved their arms and shouted orders. In a matter of seconds, quite a surprising number of soldiers left off drilling and moved at a run toward the woods behind Moril and Brid. Moril could only hope that Kialan had had the sense to cross the road and go North as fast as he could. Tholian's eyes moved sideways to make sure his orders were being carried out and then turned back to Brid. "You seem worried," he said, and laughed at her.

"Not in the least," Brid lied haughtily.

"But you don't," said Tholian, looking at Moril. "Why not?"

Moril did not see why Tholian should make a game of him. "Why did you kill my father?" he said.

Tholian was not in the least discomposed. The cool way he took the question upset Moril more than a little. It reminded him of Lenina. "Now, why was it?" Tholian said, pretending to remember. Moril thought of Lenina coolly stopping Clennen's bleeding and saw an actual family likeness to Lenina in Tholian's calm face. He wished he had not seen it. "I was having a little trouble finding Kialan," said Tholian, "as I recall. But I think the main reason I killed him was that it was probable he was the Porter."

Brid gasped, which amused Tholian. Moril felt hopeless, though he managed not to show it. "If you thought that, why didn't you have him arrested?" he said.

"Legally, instead of murdering him," said Brid, who was in such despair that she no longer cared what she said.

"But that would have been a silly thing to do," Tholian said laughingly. "A man arrested and tried for crimes like the Porter's very easily becomes a hero. You hang him, and people take his side or even rebel in his memory. Besides, I've seen Clennen give his shows in Neathdale. And I really didn't see why he should be given the chance to put on the biggest performance of his life. He'd have enjoyed it too much."

"You—" Brid hunted for the nastiest word she knew. "Fiend!" she said. Tholian, of course, laughed.

Moril said nothing. Up till then he had disliked Tholian, and he was afraid of him, because he was powerful and had such queer eyes. But after that he hated him, violently and personally. He should have hated him before, he supposed, but the fact was that in an odd way, he had thought of Clennen's death almost as if it were an accident, unfair in the way accidents were. Now he knew Tholian had intended it to be unfair, he hated Tholian for it.

"And how did you find Father?" Brid said. "Did Ganner tell you, you murdering beast!"

Tholian, luckily for Brid, still seemed to find her funny. "Ganner? Oh no," he said. "I don't have to rely on Ganner for information. Though I must say, Ganner didn't seem to be breaking his heart over Clennen when I told him he was dead." He laughed. "I suppose we put Ganner in a bit of a spot," he said, "all turning up in Markind almost together that day." He looked at Brid, to see how she took that. Brid realized Tholian was trying to torment her. She stared haughtily away at the busy soldiers in the valley. Tholian's eyes looked past her, at something behind them. "One last thing," he said. "Never try to carry on like your father. It's stupid, and it never pays. If I'd copied my father, I wouldn't be here with an army."

There was a nasty reasonableness about this that annoyed Moril. "Yes, but you see," he said, "it was something that needed doing."

Tholian was not interested any longer. He stood up. "Bring him here," he said. "Move, can't you!"

A group of soldiers hurried up, dragging Kialan. Kialan was disheveled and red in the face. Twigs were clinging to his clothes. He was resisting, rather, but he also had his head bowed in the sullen way Moril had seen among the prisoners in Neathdale. It was the way you looked, Moril realized, when you were caught. You had it whether you were guilty or innocent. It did not surprise him that Kialan was caught. He had made the mistake of staying near the cart. No doubt he had hoped to help Brid and Moril. Perhaps, since he was now the eldest, he had felt responsible for them. But Moril did not feel one twinge of gratitude. He just felt sad. Kialan had hung about, and Brid had made sure Tholian guessed he was near. That was the trouble with people who thought too well of themselves.

# 11

"AH! KIALAN!" SAID Tholian. "Nice to see you where there aren't any other earls to interfere."

Kialan looked up at Tholian from among the soldiers, with his head still a little bowed, but did not answer. Moril noticed that it was indeed true as Tholian had said, that Kialan's eyes were almost the same color as Tholian's. It made him see the difference between them. For Kialan, scared and sullen though he was, had a direct and living look, and Tholian's eyes were blank and strange. It was clear that while Tholian thought of Brid and Moril as rather funny and not at all important, he thought of Kialan as quite another matter.

"I thought you'd appear on this road sooner or later," Tholian said. "But we were watching the Marshes, too, in case. I'm hoping to let your father know you really are our prisoner. You'll have to write him a letter."

"I'm blowed if I shall!" said Kialan. "Write it yourself."

"Very well. I will," agreed Tholian. "I suppose he'll recognize one of your ears if I send it with the letter. Hold him tightly," he said to the soldiers. He took a knife from a sheath at his belt and walked toward Kialan.

Kialan tried to back away and was held in place by two soldiers. "All right," he said hurriedly. "I'll write you a letter if you want." Moril did not blame him.

But Tholian took no notice. The blank look in his eyes did not alter. The soldiers screwed up their faces. Moril, sickened and terrified, realized that Tholian just wanted an excuse to hurt Kialan. He clutched the cwidder and wondered what he could do. Kialan, even more frightened, tried to duck his head away from the knife. "Hold him, I said!" said Tholian.

One of the soldiers took a handful of Kialan's hair. Brid, without really thinking what she was doing, plunged forward and tried to catch hold of Tholian's arm. She got no farther than the nearest soldier, who pushed her sharply away. Brid staggered back and bumped into Moril, jolting his right hand on the cwidder, so that he accidentally struck a long humming note from the deepest string.

An extraordinary buzzing numbness filled the air and seemed to be eating up Moril's brain. He could do nothing, and barely think. The noise pressed into his head and forced him down on his knees. Everything outside his head was gray and pulsating, burring and blurred, and the feeling went on and on and on. He thought he saw Tholian, looking a little bewildered, stand still and slowly sheathe his knife, while Kialan and the soldiers all shook their heads like people who have been hit. Brid pressed both hands to her eyes. Their movements made Moril feel sick. He knelt with his head bent, looking at the pulsing earth, and wondered if he was going to die.

Brid knelt down beside him. "Moril, are you all right? It was the cwidder, wasn't it?" Moril shook his humming head at her, wanting her to be quiet.

Everyone except Moril seemed to have quite recovered, except that Tholian looked puzzled, as if he had forgotten a word that was on the tip of his tongue. "Tie him up for now," he said to the soldiers, in a rather irritated way. "Get some rope, one of you."

"You made Tholian forget!" Brid whispered. "Do attend, Moril. You might be able to do it again." But Moril could not attend. His face was so white that Brid became worried, which meant that she was very cross with him in a harsh, snapping whisper which hurt Moril's numbed head. Then Brid suddenly jumped to her feet and dashed away from him. "You can't do that!" she shouted. "It's cruel!"

That jerked Moril to his senses. He looked up and saw Kialan had been tied with his hands behind him to one of the stakes that carried the tent ropes. The reason for Brid's outcry was that Tholian, not satisfied with merely tying him, had put a noose round Kialan's tied hands and was hoisting them up his back. The effect must have been like having both arms twisted at once. Moril could see Kialan was in agony.

Tholian turned to Brid as soon as he had made the rope fast. "Can't?" he said. "Go back to your brother." When Brid did not move at once, Tholian advanced on her, with his strange eyes blank. "Are you going to do as I said?"

Brid was frightened enough to turn and run back to Moril. As she came, she mouthed, *"Do something!"*

Tholian started off toward where several captains were hovering, wanting to speak to him. "Those two are not to move from there," he said over his shoulder to the soldiers round Kialan.

"Moril," whispered Brid. "The cwidder. Make it undo the rope."

Moril wished he could. He was sure the cwidder was quite capable of releasing Kialan, if only he knew how to work it. Osfameron had made it move mountains. But Moril had not the slightest idea how to begin and was very much afraid of making a mistake and bringing that awful humming into his own brain again. Kialan tried to give him a brave look although he was grinning with pain. Moril could see him struggling to get into a more comfortable position when there was no way of doing so. And Tholian might leave him like that for hours. It was worth a try.

Remembering the way the cwidder seemed to play his thoughts, Moril set himself to imagine Tholian's noose pulling and twisting Kialan into that unnatural position. It was horrible. His arms ached and sweat dropped out from under his hair. He thought fiercely, This must *stop*! and gently touched the slack bottom string.

It chimed like a soft, deep bell. Moril braced himself against the humming, but it did not come. Its effect, though it was not at all what he expected, was on Kialan alone. He saw Kialan's head suddenly drop and his knees give. He did not move, and it was clear that only the ropes were holding him up. Terrified, Moril clapped his hand across the string and stopped it vibrating.

Brid rounded on Moril with tears whisking down her cheeks. "You stupid idiot! You've killed him!"

"Shut up!" Moril whispered, anxiously watching both Kialan and the soldiers just beyond him. "They'll realize. Look. He's breathing. He's only passed out."

"But what about the ropes?" Brid whispered.

Moril shook his head. "I can't. I was trying to. I think I can only make it work on people."

One of the soldiers turned and saw Kialan sagging. When Tholian came back from talking to the captains, they pointed Kialan out to him. Tholian simply shrugged and passed by on his way somewhere else.

"I *hate* Tholian!" said Brid.

Moril said nothing. He knelt on the ground, nursing his cwidder, thinking as he had never thought in his life before. The soldiers, meanwhile, looked at one another, looked around to see how far away Tholian was, and undid the noose from Kialan's hands, so that Kialan slid to his knees with his head hanging almost upside down.

"Look, Moril," Brid whispered. "You did undo the ropes, sort of."

Moril had seen perfectly well, though he gave no sign of it. He was as alert as he had been in the jail in Neathdale. He could have told Brid exactly how many captains, troops, and horsemen there were in the part of the valley they could see. He was aware of every time a group of new recruits came marching in, and how many came in each group. Four groups arrived while he knelt and thought and while Kialan hung in a heap, head downward. Moril saw that they did not come by the road, but down through the woods, to keep their mustering secret. He also saw that almost every new arrival was miserable. They trailed their feet and held their heads at that sullen angle Kialan and Dagner had both held theirs when they knew they were caught. He could see that few of them had joined Tholian's army willingly. But he was thinking, thinking. For he was sure that the cwidder he was hugging on his knees was capable of saving all three of them and getting them North with news of Tholian's army. He knew how it could be done. The only thing he did not know was how to call up the power in the cwidder to do it.

Since it was his thoughts the cwidder responded to, Moril tried to understand how he might feed his entire self through it into the enormous power he knew was needed. His father had said Moril was in two halves. "Come together," Clennen had said, "and there's no knowing what you might do." Moril supposed Clennen had meant the way Moril was incorrigibly dreamy and also unbelievably alert at times, just as he was now. But as Kialan had noticed, he was often both at the same time, unless he went vague in self-defense. Moril thought that could not quite be it.

But there was another way he was in two halves. His mother was a Southern aristocrat, and his father a freedom-fighting singer from the North. As Dagner had said, there was no doubt it was a weird mixture. It was cold and hot, strict and free, restrained and outspoken, all at once. The trouble was, this did not quite add up to Moril. He did not think he had inherited much from his Southern ancestry—certainly none of the unfeeling tyranny that made his distant cousin Tholian so detestable.

But Tholian's calm cruelty had, in a horrible way, reminded him of Lenina. Moril remembered Kialan saying, "Your mother's a cool one." And that was it, of course. Lenina never lost her head, and neither did Moril. He knew that, if Brid had only let him, he could coolly have led Tholian to believe that none of them had ever set eyes on Kialan, just as Lenina might have done. Keeping your head was part of the strict standard of the South. It was the same strict standard that had kept

Lenina so loyal to Clennen, even though she hated life in the cart and disagreed with the freedom fighting. And Moril saw that it was the same kind of strict loyalty that had brought him North—only, with him, it was loyalty to the North.

After this followed something very uncomfortable, which Moril would not have faced if he had not had such a pressing need to use the cwidder. He had to admit he had deserted Lenina. He had gone off and left her when she had been trying to make them happy. He hoped he had not made her too unhappy, because he knew that seeing Tholian in Markind had only given him the excuse he had been looking for to go North. And going off like that, he had been trying to deny the Southern part of him—all the strict, honorable things which were the good aspect of the South. It did not do to deny them, even though he thought he had been doing it out of loyalty to Clennen.

Then he tried to find out what he had got from Clennen. Goodness knew what strange blood the singers came from. They could all sing and play. They saw a little more than most people, and some of them dreamed dreams. But Moril knew that all he had got from Clennen himself were ideas of freedom and his love of the North. The rest was the common stock of the singers.

The puzzling part was that these two halves added up to three quite different people: Brid, Dagner, and Moril. Brid had Lenina's sharpness and some of Lenina's efficiency, and she had Clennen's love of an audience, without Clennen's gifts—though she thought she had them. Dagner had far more of the gifts, but he had all Lenina's reserve, and more. In fact, it had been very much in Lenina's manner that Dagner had set off North to finish Clennen's work for him, knowing he had not the personality to do it. None of them had inherited the largeness that made Clennen what he was. And why had Clennen not told Brid or Dagner they were in two halves?

Moril found himself suddenly at a dead end. He saw he would have to get at the cwidder's power some other way. He had to. The third batch of recruits had just arrived. The valley was filling with soldiers, and the North did not know. And the Earl of Hannart would not dare move because of Kialan. And Moril knew Kialan was actively in danger from Tholian. Tholian passed several times, and each time he looked at Kialan's hanging body as if he wanted it awake and writhing.

Moril thought of the cwidder itself. Though Osfameron could use it on things, it seemed that Moril was only going to make it have an effect on people. That was right for music, in a way. You performed, and people listened and were affected by it. So what did you put into a performance to bring out the power?

Moril did not know. He had only the vaguest idea what he had done to make Kialan unconscious. All right, he thought. What *didn't* my father do, that he could never use the power more than once? And he thought of Clennen, from day to day, as he had known him, huge, genial, and sociable—and boring Kialan stiff by telling the same story three times over. He thought of the way Clennen had been the Porter, quite openly, enjoying deceiving people by the simple fact that he did it all in public, as obviously as possible. Kialan had been positive that this was what Clennen enjoyed particularly. Then Moril thought of Clennen saying "Remember that" so often—almost as if he hoped one of them might write all his sayings down one day. Perhaps Brid would, Moril thought, smiling a little. Then he remembered a particular saying of Clennen's, the day they picked Kialan up. Clennen had said the cart was like life. "You may wonder what goes on inside, but what matters is the look of it and the kind of performance we give." Later on Clennen had asked Dagner about another saying, and Dagner had got this one wrong. "Something about life being only a performance," Dagner had said.

And that was it, Moril thought. Clennen was all performance. Layers of performance. He was the best singer in Dalemark and he used it to play the Porter, and he was the Porter because he was using his sincere feelings about freedom to play the singer—to and fro, over and under, Clennen had performed, even to his own family. His whole life had said, "Look at me!" He had known he was a performer, and he had used that knowledge, just as Brid had used her real sorrow to perform with in Neathdale. But he could not use the cwidder. It was not going to say, "Look at me!" It did not work like that.

If you did not say, "Look at me!" what was the right way? With a joyous feeling of being on the right track, Moril thought of Dagner next. Kialan had called what was really Dagner's performance "a different kind of show." Moril felt warmly grateful to Kialan. Kialan pointed things out. If only because of this, Kialan deserved to be rescued and taken back to the warmhearted, cocksure, outspoken North where he belonged.

But Dagner—Dagner had been diffident. He had never said, "Look at me!" because he was shy when people did. What he did was to show people his thoughts—a little—in his songs. "Look here," he seemed to say. "Excuse me. This is what I think. I hope you like it." And people did like it—not in the way they appreciated Clennen but as if they had been told something new.

Moril knew he was unable—at least for the present—to make something new, just as he was unable to use his real feelings for show, like

Brid. That left the old songs, Moril's own specialty. Did they help? Yes, they did—thanks to Kialan again. Kialan, just this morning, had sung that song of the Adon's, and it might have been made about this very cwidder! Unbounded truth! Moril thought, in rising excitement. Not a thing cramped to time and bound in place! Neither was the cwidder when its power was used.

He had it, then. You performed. But you did not say "Look at me!" Nor could you say, like Dagner, "This is what I think." If Dagner's diffident way had been right, Clennen would have given the cwidder to Dagner. No. You had to stand up and come straight out with it. "This is *true*," you had to say. "*This is the truth.* And, though I may not get it over very well, it just *is*." And it was horribly difficult to do.

Moril blinked a little, nerving himself up. The fourth group of new recruits was shuffling its way through the valley, and Tholian was coming back again. With him were the same hearthmen who had been with him by the lake. They all had the same unpleasant look of purpose, too. When they reached Kialan, Tholian jabbed at him with the toe of his boot. Kialan flopped.

"Bring him round," he said. "He's going to write me a letter presently." Then he looked across at Brid and Moril, and his eyes were like an owl's caught in a strong light at night. They knew he had no intention of sending them back to Markind.

"Moril," Brid said humbly, "do you think you can do anything?"

Moril scrambled stiffly to his feet, carefully not bumping the cwidder. "I'm going to try," he said, and began to play.

He started with a little sequence of chords, repeated over and over, in a rocking rhythm. He had to start slowly, while he found the thought the cwidder would respond to. He was terrified that Tholian would realize what he was trying to do and stop him, but, though all the men round Kialan glanced irritably at Moril, they obviously had no idea that he was doing anything important. Moril's fear faded. "Not all of you are bad," he told them through the cwidder. "Some are just afraid, others are not good, and you are doing wrong." Over and over, he told it.

And to his relief, the cwidder began to hum under his hands. He had got it right. Moril could feel the power gather in it and then, slowly, go humming out over Tholian and his men, right off down the valley, and turn the corner to the part out of sight. The movements of everyone he could see grew slack and a little aimless, and Tholian yawned. Moril thrummed on. He would have rejoiced, except that he knew he was going to have to bring the lowest string in soon, and he was afraid of it. If its power ate into his own head this time, that was the end of his plan. Cautiously he struck it. *Sleep*, it sang, heavily sweet, off down the valley, following the humming path of the power he had already built up. *Sleep*. Tholian's head turned slowly, and he looked at Moril, mistily puzzled. Moril himself was wide awake. He knew it was all right. He had been caught in the power before because he had simply been thinking *No, no, no!* without meaning anything else. Now he meant *Sleep, all you out there*.

Tholian seemed to understand what Moril was doing. He came slowly toward Moril, lurching as if he was very tired. "Break that blessed thing!" he said. His voice was slurred, but he was fighting the cwidder's power for all he was worth.

Quickly Moril passed into a proper tune, a lullaby.

"Go back to the time
When your feelings were blind
When they rocked you and sang
Go to sleep."

If Moril had thought about it, he would have realized he was in fact making up something new. But he did not notice, because all he wanted to do was to put Tholian to sleep. The lullaby was like a gust of power. It held Tholian to the spot. Tholian knew what was happening, but he was helpless. Moril played the tune again, louder, and took pleasure in holding Tholian in place while the tune swept beyond him, out into the valley.

Tholian rubbed his eyes and tried to take a grip on himself. Beyond him, the men round Kialan yawned and the marching and cursing in the valley faded away. The air was clear for the full force of the song, and Moril gave it to them. *Go to sleep*. It went down the valley in slow waves, washing first over Tholian, then on and out. Tholian's eyelids drooped, his knees bent, and he dropped forward onto the trampled ground with his head in his arms. There he made one final movement of resistance and fell asleep. After him, the other people dropped down, too, back and back into the valley. Horses stood still and men keeled over beside them and lay sleeping. Beside Moril, Brid fell sideways and slept curled up as if she was still kneeling. That was a pity, but Moril did not see how he could have excluded her. He played on, sending out wave after wave of sleep-song, until the valley seemed thick with it, and he could almost see it hanging in the air and pulsing gently. Under it every soul was dead to the world.

At last, a little apprehensively, Moril left the cwidder still humming, hoping like that to make the power last, and went through the heavy, silent air to Kialan. He was still tied up. Tholian's friends had not untied him, though they had been about to. Moril went back through the humming silence and fetched the knife out of Brid's boot. "Thanks," he whispered, and he thought Brid stirred a little. With the knife he hacked through rope after tough rope, until Kialan rolled loose on the grass. He was still unconscious.

Moril bent down and shook him. "Kialan!" he said.

Kialan came round as he heard his name. Moril was almost sorry, because Kialan's face was suddenly full of pain and misery.

"It's all right," Moril whispered. "Everyone's asleep. Quick. I don't know how long it'll last."

Kialan climbed to his feet. He was very stiff and winced with every movement. He stared at Tholian, lying on the earth with his head in his arms, at Brid, and out at the silent, humming valley, full of a sleeping army. "Ye gods!" he said. "Was that the cwidder?"

"Yes," said Moril. "Quick." He ran back to Brid and shook her. Brid rolled about, but she did not wake.

Kialan came limping after him. "Suppose you leave her asleep?" he suggested. "Then when she wakes up, you'll know it's worn off."

Moril saw that was an excellent idea. The thing about Kialan, he thought as he raced for the cart, was that he had brains. Olob was dozing, too, which was more serious. Moril snapped his fingers under his nose. "*Olob!* Barangarolob!" And Olob shook his head and looked at Moril wonderingly. Moril untied Olob and brought him toward Brid at a run, much though Olob objected to going near even sleeping enemies. As he hauled on the bridle, he thought how queer the valley looked with everyone in it lying asleep except for the lonely upright figure of Kialan. He dragged Olob up to Brid and opened the tailgate of the cart to make it easier to get her in. Then he gently put the cwidder back in its rack. It was still vibrating faintly.

"Throw the wine jar out," said Kialan. "Let's make the cart as light as we can."

Moril heaved out the great jar. It landed with a sploshy thump that ought to have woken the dead, but Brid, who was nearest, did not stir.

Kialan laughed. "Present for Tholian. Information he knows and money he doesn't want. He can drink our health."

Moril gave a muffled giggle at the idea, but he did not speak. He had a feeling that the one thing most likely to wake the sleepers was his voice. He climbed into the cart and threw out most of Dagner's purchases: candles, flour, lentils, and the remains of the rhubarb.

"Oh, he'll love those!" panted Kialan. Though he was still very stiff, he managed to lift the head and shoulders of Brid and heave the upper half of her into the cart. Moril took her shoulders and dragged her right in, where she settled with a little sigh. Kialan climbed in beside her. Moril latched the tailgate and got onto the driving seat.

"Now, Olob," he whispered. "Run. Run for your life."

Olob tossed his head and set off. He did not exactly run, but he took the cart briskly across the trampled earth to the road by which they had entered the valley. Moril looked over his shoulder as they went under the trees. Tholian was lying beside their heap of provisions. Beyond him, Moril thought he could see a faint haze vibrating quietly over the whole valley. The cwidder's power still held.

"What about those soldiers by the trestle?" Kialan said, as Olob clattered down the steep road.

"I don't know," Moril said anxiously. He had no idea how far the cwidder's power spread, and the trestle had been behind him as he played. When they came to the main road, Moril held his breath and Kialan craned sideways to get a sight of the trestle.

Those soldiers were asleep, too. Most of them were sprawled in the road, pigeon breastplates upward, snoring. One was asleep with his arms on the trestle, in a most uncomfortable position. Kialan gave a wild little laugh. "He'll be stiff when he wakes up!"

# 12

IT WAS A SHORT, steep climb up the last of the hill. Then they came out onto the green spread of the last Upland. They could see Mark Wood in the distance, gay green and bronzed by the afternoon sun, and beyond it, looking deceptively near, the gray bulk of the Northern mountains.

"Now you *must* run, Olob," said Moril.

Olob ran. It could not be called a gallop—Moril had never known Olob to gallop in his life—but he ran, and ran as fast as Moril had ever seen him go. Behind him the lightened cart wove from side to side and bounded in the ruts of the road. Kialan wedged his feet against the side of the cart and tried to hold Brid in one place, but they nevertheless pitched and rolled and bounced until it was a marvel Brid did not wake up. But Brid slept on, stirring once or twice when she hit the side of the cart, but never coming out of her deep sleep. Moril began to hope that it would last until they reached Mark Wood. Once they were there, they could hide the cart among the trees, with a good chance of escaping Tholian.

"How did you work it?" Kialan called jerkily above the rilling of wheels and banging of hooves. "The sleep."

Moril could not explain, any more than Dagner could explain how he made songs. "By thinking," he said. "You said a lot of things that helped me."

They jounced and battered another half mile. "I had a weird dream," Kialan called, "while I was tied up. I dreamed—wow, what a bump!—I dreamed you took me along to your father's grave, by the lake, and opened that board I carved, just as if it was a door. Then you said, 'Do you mind getting in here for a while? I'll call you when it's safe to come out.' And—I say, what happens if we lose a wheel?—and I went in and went to sleep. What do you think of that?"

"I don't know," said Moril. "I might have done. There's no one behind, is there?"

There was no one, though they could hardly believe it. The wide Upland seemed empty. They rattled, wagging this way and that, through a village, and that seemed asleep, too. Olob pounded on, blowing now, and Brid still slept. The sun sank, and Mark Wood was nearer. Twilight seemed to come from the trees and soak into the green landscape around them. Big clouds were building up beyond the mountains. The sunset shot them with fierce pink and lakes of moist yellow.

"You know," jerked Kialan, "when I thought—in the valley—that we weren't going to get away this time, I wanted to apologize. I was pretty awful when I first came into the cart, wasn't I?"

"We were, too," Moril called over his shoulder. "We didn't know what had been happening to you. Was it horrible in Holand?"

There was a bouncing, battering pause. "Ghastly," said Kialan. "But it wasn't only that. I didn't understand. I thought you were all—beggars or something, and I thought—oh, of fleas and ignorance and so on for the whole way North. And I was fed up."

Moril laughed. "You looked it."

They reached the verge of Mark Wood almost as the sun set. Olob had not run so far for years. Moril could see steam rising off him in the thickening twilight. His sides were heaving under the scarlet harness, and there were flecks of foam along him. The road went upward into the trees, under a sloping cliff, and, though it was not a steep rise, Olob slowed down.

"I'll have to let him walk," Moril said, acutely sorry for him. "He's had enough."

So Olob fell to a weary plod, and everything suddenly seemed ten times more peaceful. They could hear birds cawing and calling in the great beech trees above.

"Good gracious!" said Brid, sitting up. "Where are we? Why do I feel so bruised?"

Moril knew it was bound to happen, but he wished it had been farther into the wood and not just when Olob was tired out. They explained to Brid. She was rather indignant.

"Using me as a kind of sleep measure! I like that!"

"It was a jolly good idea," said Kialan, "though I says it as shouldn't."

But Brid had realized that Tholian was probably after them by now and changed to being as nervous as a cat. She turned her head back over her shoulder and implored Moril to get in among the trees quickly. Moril looked over his shoulder, too. Between the tree trunks, he could see the darkening green of the Upland and a long stretch of the road. It was empty.

"I will when we get to the top of this hill. Olob's tired."

The dark gathered quickly under the trees, but it was still light enough to see. Brid squawked faintly. There were people among the trees on horses, coming slowly down the hill on the cliff side. But Olob gave no sign of alarm. Moril trusted Olob and kept on the road, in spite of Brid's imploring whispers. All the same, it was rather frightening the way that the horsemen, as soon as they saw the cart, turned toward it and increased their pace. They came fairly thudding down on them.

There were three of them. They drew up beside the cart, and Olob stopped walking. Kialan stood up and stared at the foremost rider, and the rider stared back.

"You blinking idiot! What did you have to come South for?" Kialan said, and burst into tears.

Somehow, though they would never have dreamed of addressing Clennen as a blinking idiot, Brid and Moril had no doubt that the rider was Keril. They watched Kialan jump awkwardly down, and the man dismount and hug him, and they were sure of it.

"Konian—they *hanged* him!" Kialan said.

"I know. We heard from a fisherman," said Keril. "It was you I came for. I was hoping Clennen might know—where *is* Clennen?" he asked.

"He's dead," said Brid, and began to cry, too.

Moril sat on the driving seat and felt tears trickling down his face. As far as he knew, he was crying for the whole situation, because he was on his own now, and always would be.

"There's an army," said Kialan. "Tholian's gathered an army to attack the North. In a valley over there. They're probably after us now."

Keril exchanged glances with the two other riders. "We've a small force in the wood. How big is this army?"

"Pretty big," Moril said, sniffing. "There were five hundred men, divided into three troops, and a hundred horsemen in the part of the valley we saw. But that was probably only a quarter of it."

"How do you know?" said Kialan. "Did you count?"

"No. I just know," said Moril. "And recruits came in four batches, while we were there, twenty-three in the first, and thirty-two in—"

"Too many for us, in fact," said Keril. "Thanks, lad. Let's get back to our camp and get fortified."

The Northerners' camp was along the cliff, chosen with an eye to defense. When tired Olob dragged the cart up to it, there was already a bustle of preparation. The campfires were being put out and the two provision wagons dragged across the only place where it could be reached from the wood. These preparations should have made Moril feel alarmed, but in fact, he felt safer and happier than he had been for days. He could see by the light of the few lanterns that the mere fifty or so men bustling about had, many of them, the same dark-fair coloring as Kialan. Moril remembered now that it was something you only saw in the North. Keril was the odd man out, because he was dark, though his nose was the same shape as Kialan's.

They were taken into a tent, where they had the best meal they had had since Markind. While they were eating, Moril gathered that the Earl had been camping here for two days. The night before, he had ridden South almost to Neathdale in hopes of meeting Clennen and hearing news of Kialan, and he had been meaning to do the same that night, too. It was Henda's message offering to ransom Kialan that had brought him South. Up till then, everyone in Hannart had supposed that Kialan had been hanged, too.

In a tired and muddled way, they told their part, as far as Dagner's arrest. Keril, who had been sad rather than astonished at Clennen's death and not at all surprised to hear of Lenina returning to Markind, broke in angrily when he heard of Dagner. They felt sure he was thinking of Konian, too, when he said, "Fancy hanging a boy that age! I wish I could *do* something—er, Moril—is that your name?"

"Not really," said Kialan. "His name's Osfameron. And Brid's Manaliabrid."

Keril forgot his anger and threw back his head and laughed.

"What's so funny?" said Brid. She was sensitive about their names.

"Well, history repeating itself, I suppose," said Keril. "Kialan's the Adon, you see."

"No, he isn't," said Moril. "The Adon lived two hundred years ago. Kialan told me."

"But the heir of Hannart is always called the Adon," Keril explained, and was sad, thinking of Konian.

Moril and Kialan looked at one another by the light of the carefully shaded lantern. Moril was thoroughly put out. If Kialan was the Adon, then he had been living the life of his dearest imaginings for nearly a month without realizing it. It had not seemed like that at all. Yet, thinking of the weird dream Kialan had told him of, he suspected that it might have been history repeating itself indeed. "Why didn't you tell me?" he said.

"I didn't sort of think," said Kialan. "I was just me, trying to get home." He was thinking about his dream, too. He nodded toward his father. "Tell him about the cwidder."

Moril told Keril how he put Tholian and his army to sleep. Keril marveled a little, and he asked Kialan to confirm it, but he took it, on the whole, in the same matter-of-course way that Kialan did. "May I see the cwidder?" he said.

Moril felt his way out of the tent to the cart and came back with the cwidder. Keril took it and held it under the light of the lantern. He ran his fingers down the inlay, over the strange patterns. "Yes, this *is* the one," he said. "I used to think Clennen was boasting when he said it was Osfameron's, but I wasn't much of a hand at the old writing in those days." His square, practical-looking finger pointed to a line of swirls and dots made of slivers of mother-of-pearl. "Here it says, 'I sing for Osfameron' and there"—his finger moved to another line of signs—"it says, 'I move in more than one world.' " He smiled at Moril and handed the cwidder back. "Be careful of it."

Moril fell asleep that night hugging the cwidder, and as far removed as he could from Kialan's knees and elbows. They were a little crowded because Keril had given up his own tent to Brid. Moril had meant to do some more thinking, but he was far too tired. He awoke at dawn, because somebody came to talk to Keril, very annoyed with himself. For he was sure that, by reading the strange writing, Keril had really told him how to use the cwidder as Osfameron had used it.

There was no time for thinking for a while. The man had come to tell Keril that a troop of riders had gone by on the road during the night and that the same troop had just come galloping back, probably on their way to report to Tholian. Both times they had been going too fast to notice the camp.

It was clear the riders had been looking for the cart. Tholian must have assumed that Moril, Brid, and Kialan were driving North as fast as they could. Since the riders had not found them, Keril knew Tholian would think Kialan had already reached the North, and his news with him. "And if I were Tholian," he said, "I'd be on the march now, before the North can be ready for war. We'd better hurry."

They broke camp and went. The cart went, too, with a strange youthful horse between the shafts, for more speed. Olob looked so disconsolate that Brid said she would ride him. "He'll let me," she said, "if no one puts a saddle on him. I hate him to feel neglected." So she rode Olob bareback with her boots on—for, after all, she was in company with an earl—and Olob did not seem to object. He was just rather slow. Brid had some difficulty keeping up with the cart, where Moril sat with his cwidder, thinking. The cart was being driven by a large slow-spoken Northerner called Egil, and Kialan had borrowed Egil's horse.

"You know," Brid said to Moril, "I do wish Kialan hadn't turned out to be the Adon. I feel embarrassed about liking him."

Moril was very busy thinking, but he chuckled at this. "You'll get used to it."

"You're *hopeless*!" said Brid, not as angry as she meant to be.

Kialan's turning out to be the Adon was important to Moril's thoughts, too. It was one of three things he kept trying to put together in his mind. The other two were what the writing said on the cwidder and his own discovery about the way you had to tell the truth with it. He thought it was odd how easily one got used to new ideas. What had seemed an entirely new thing yesterday was an old idea today, which he could use to take him on somewhere else. He went on trying to put ideas together while the band of Northerners hurried through Mark Wood.

They were not taking the road because Keril dared not risk being seen. There were clearings and villages all along the road and probably enough people in them to hold the small number of Northerners up until Tholian came to wipe them out. So they worked their way North through the trees. It was easy enough for the riders, but heavy going for the cart and the wagons. And everybody was worried about the final stretch, where they would have to come out of the trees in order to get to Flennpass. Once they were in the pass, they would be safe. It was guarded by Fort Flenn, which was the southernmost fort of the North.

Night came before they were out of the wood. Keril was anxious at their slow progress, but they had been traveling all day and they were tired. They had to risk camping for the night. After supper, round a carefully shaded campfire, they told Keril their doings in more detail. Kialan said things which confirmed Moril's feeling that his time in Holand had been more horrible than they had realized. Keril became so angry and sad that Kialan changed the subject and talked about the wine jar.

"I regret leaving Tholian all that gold," he said. "He can have the rhubarb with pleasure, and the papers, but we should have taken the money out."

"Set your mind at rest," said Brid. "I did. I put it in the money locker."

Everyone laughed. Brid wanted indignantly to know what they took her for, leaving a sum like that in a wine jar.

"But I wish I knew whose it was, and where Father got it from," she said.

"I think," said Keril, "that it was probably the remains of what I gave him for expenses. I gave him a hundred gold every year in Dropwater. No," he said when Brid offered to give it back. "Keep it. You deserve it. You can use it as pocket money when you're living in Hannart."

In this way they gathered that Keril intended them to live with him in Hannart.

"That's frightfully nice of you," Brid said awkwardly. "Because I don't know what else we'd do, do you, Moril?"

"It's the least I can do," said Keril. "I owe Clennen a great deal. If it hadn't been for him, we'd have had no news from the South worth having." Then he told them things about Clennen they had not known before. Keril had met Clennen in the South in the days when he was still only the Adon, and they had both helped in the uprising there. But Keril's father died, and he had to go North. Clennen stayed in the South, until soon after he met Lenina. Then, what with old Tholian's fury and the failure of the uprising, Clennen found the South too hot to hold him. He went to Hannart and became singer to the court. Dagner, Brid, and Moril had all been born in Hannart. It had been Clennen's idea to go South again when they heard reports of what was going on. The Porter had been his idea, too. But Keril had thought of staging the quarrel so that no one would suspect Clennen was Hannart's agent.

Moril sat staring into the fire, dreaming of Hannart.

"What is it, Moril?" Kialan said jokingly. "Dreams coming true?"

Moril looked up and grinned. He did not say anything, but he went to sleep sure that Kialan had just told him the way the cwidder really worked.

He thought it out as he rode in the cart next day. It came to him first as a memory. It had rained in Crady, so Clennen had told one of the stories of the Adon indoors, and Moril had looked up to see Kialan in the audience. He had been annoyed, because he thought of Kialan as part of dreary, everyday life, and he had felt as if he had a foot in two worlds which were spinning apart from one another. Yet Kialan was the Adon—or *an* Adon—all the time. And the cwidder itself said, "I move in more than one world."

It came on to rain just then, though not as heavily as it had rained in Crady. Moril smiled and lifted his face into the wet. They were nearly in the North, and it rained a lot there. His smile became rather rueful as he realized that in none of his dreams of Hannart or hazy imaginings of the cart on green roads had he ever thought of its raining. The cwidder had made a muzzy sound. And that was the point. That kind of dream was not true. There were true dreams, but they had to be part of life as well, just as life, to be good, had to embody dreams, or a good song had to have an idea to it. The Adon's song Kialan had sung had been saying that. But Osfameron's song had gone one farther and talked of the other worlds the cwidder moved in.

Moril thought of the way life and dreams had met for him, willy-nilly, on this journey. But he knew they met in him naturally, too, when he could be miles away, thinking, and yet count all the soldiers in that valley, or every beech tree they were passing at the moment. He saw that Clennen had not got it quite right. He had been too practical to see. The important thing was that Moril *was* in two halves. Provided he knew what was true in both, he could use the cwidder as it should be used. He could send ideas through it, into reality.

About midmorning, they came to the end of Mark Wood. Moril looked past Egil's broad back at the mountains at last, vividly close, and the deep V in them that was Flennpass. The rain had stopped, but the clouds over the mountains were heavy with more. It was a gray, threatening scene. Fort Flenn was out of sight, behind a sharp peak, since it was at the North end of the pass, but Moril could see the South's answer to it. The wood had been cleared for a mile or so in front of the pass, so that no one could go in or out of it unseen. He looked at the mountains across a desolation of tree stumps, charred from frequent burning, with new bright green bushes and saplings springing up between, because it had not yet been cleared this year.

The Northerners stopped at the edge of the trees. Moril did not at first know why.

"The Lord of Mark, I think," Keril said to his captain. "Tholian must have set him to watch for the cart."

Moril leaned round Egil, and his stomach fluttered at the number of the horsemen drawn up across the pass in the distance. They were clearly Southerners, and in war gear, and there were at least twice as many of them as there were Northerners in Keril's band.

"He can't be expecting us," said the captain. "I'll take an oath no one saw us come through. It'll give him a fair old shock when we ride out at him."

"I know," said Keril, "but I'd be more comfortable if we were twice the number."

"Oh come!" said someone else, laughing. "One Northerner's worth ten Southerners. Any day."

Moril thought for a moment. Yes. Everyone believed that. None of the band was particularly worried, and even Brid was looking confidently at Keril, sure they would get past the Lord of Mark without trouble. Northerners were famous fighters. But Keril was evidently thinking it was more important to get through to the North than to get courageously killed on the way.

"Would you like there to seem more of us?" Moril called over to him. "I think I can do it."

Keril made a bit of a face. "I only wish you could."

"I bet he can," said Kialan.

Moril slung the cwidder round his neck and began to play the "Eighth March." It was never played in the South, for obvious reasons. But, as Clennen often said, it went to such a brisk time that only the North thought of it as a march.

"We are the men of the North, the North,
And I'll tell you how much we're worth,
we're worth—
One man is as good as ten Southern men
And each of us marches as ten."

For a moment, until the cwidder began to hum, Moril was afraid he had got it wrong after all. But the hum increased and became almost like a lighthearted whistling, and the wood was suddenly full of men, horses, and wagons. Some of the Northerners cried out in alarm.

Kialan burst out laughing. "Oh, well done, Moril! Only nine more pink carts are a bit much!"

Moril glanced from side to side and could not help laughing. There were indeed nine more pink carts. One of them had a tree apparently growing through it. And a false Moril sat in each playing an illusory cwidder. What he had done was to reflect their own band nine times over, just as the song said. After all, it was an illusion that one Northman was worth ten Southerners. And the riders and wagons were exactly that, like reflections in a mirror. The Northmen realized. People began to laugh and wave at their own reflections. Consequently, the false nine-tenths waved and laughed also.

Keril laughed with the rest. "Keep playing, Moril. Off we go."

Moril played on gaily, and they moved out from among the trees, the real and the false men together. They rode among the bushes and stumps under a stormy sky, toward the road, and the real men had to go round saplings and the larger stumps, but Moril's illusions went straight through everything in their path. When they reached the road, there was a good deal of confusion and much laughter. The Northmen tried to get out of the way of their own shadows, until they grasped that there were four reflections on the left and five to the right, and that the fifth band from the left was the real one, entitled to use the road. Once they had sorted that out, they trotted on in fine style, many of them singing the "Eighth March" as Moril played. And on either side the nine repetitions went straight through the landscape, pink carts through bushes and horses through saplings.

Moril sat in the midmost pink cart beaming with elation. It was the most splendid proof that he had done his thinking right. The whistling hum of the cwidder in his hands, calling the strange army into being, took on an extra note, like a sort of purring, as it reflected Moril's pleasure and amusement. Behind him, Brid and Kialan thought it one of the funniest things they had seen. They thought it even funnier when Olob sensed enemies near and began prancing about, setting the nine other Olobs prancing, too, and the nine other Kialans grabbing at his bridle to help Brid control him.

By the pass the Lord of Mark's force drew uneasily together, seeing five hundred apparent Northmen riding merrily toward them. As Keril's band drew nearer, they could see the enemies' uneasiness mounting. Ordinary Northerners maybe they could face. But what was to be done with enemies who went straight through small trees and seemed none the worse for it? When they were near enough to distinguish faces, and only a hundred yards from the camp the Lord of Mark had set up to the right of the road, a group of the Southerners panicked and had to be brought back by some others. Moril could see a man who must be the Lord of Mark riding up and down imploring his men to keep calm. He laughed. Then two shadow wagons and a pink cart went right through the camp without disturbing so much as a guy rope. A number of the Southerners wailed with terror. Moril thought, Why not? and threw in the lowest string. *Run*! it boomed beneath the gay tune.

The Lord of Mark broke and ran, and his men with him. They galloped frantically away to right and left along the mountains and vanished in the bushes, leaving Flennpass open. A roar of laughter went up from Keril's band.

Brid's voice cut through it. "Moril! *Look*!"

Moril glanced back. Huge numbers of horsemen were on the dark edge of Mark Wood, and more were among the trees. The horses' legs were all moving steadily, but they were too far away for sound to carry, and the riders seemed to glimmer along as if they were an illusion, too. Only they were no such thing. They were the forefront of Tholian's army.

# :‖ 13 ‖:

MORIL GAVE THE alarm with a sweep of his hand on the cwidder. Though Keril also looked over his shoulder, it was only to confirm what the cwidder said. In that same moment they were all going hell for leather for Flennpass and Fort Flenn at the other end of it. The ghostly nine-tenths had gone as if they had never been. Moril knew there was no time for illusions. As the cart bucked and wove along, he hung on to the side and looked back.

Tholian's army was coming at a steady speed across the cleared stretch. If anyone saw the cart, or the sudden decrease in the size of their band, there was no sign of it. The host of horsemen simply came onward. It might be pursuing Keril, but it looked more as if their band would be merely the first incident in the invasion. Tholian had no need to hurry, since the North was unprepared. Olob knew the army was behind and Brid could not control him. Kialan had taken the reins and was dragging him along with Egil's horse. Moril thought this might well make Olob worse. Olob had never really accepted Kialan. But there was nothing Moril could do.

They swept into the pass with a gathering thunder of hooves. It held a good road between clifflike walls, which narrowed at the Northern end. They had to string out as they went, with the cart and the wagons bouncing in the rear. Egil and the other drivers were using their whips. Brid was smacking Olob. Moril thought they would just make it to the fort, though it would be a close thing—and it seemed closer every second. The army behind had no wagons with the vanguard to slow them down. They were catching up steadily. As Keril's troop came to the narrowest part of the pass, where the fort stood chunkily above on the skyline, Moril looked round to see the first line of Tholian's cavalry coming into the wide end of the pass, and multitudes of others milling behind.

Keril had reached the fort, when Moril looked back, and was shouting to the people inside. There was a moment's delay. But the defenders must have seen all that happened. A sudden black space appeared where the great gate had been, and some of the Northmen rode into it. The space between the cliffs was filled with noise, the huge drumming of a mass of hooves, and some sharper sounds. Moril thought the fort was firing on the enemy.

Things began to fall around the cart and bounce off the wagons. They were not from the fort, but from the advancing army. Moril could do nothing but hope. It was long-range, and he thought it must be difficult to fire from a cantering horse. But to Olob, struggling against Kialan's impatient hand on his bridle, it was the last straw. In his terror, he turned clean round, dragging Kialan and Egil's horse with him. Brid lurched and hung on to his mane. A number of the Northmen saw what was happening and turned back to help. And the narrow end of the pass at once became a dangerous bottleneck, full of riders trying to go two ways at once. Egil roared out a curse and pulled the cart up. Moril jumped down, with the cwidder slung across his shoulders, and ran toward Olob.

"Let him go!" he shouted to Kialan. "Olob, stop it!"

Luckily, Kialan had the sense to let go. For, as Moril ran up, Olob reared, frightened out of his wits. There were just too many enemies for him. Moril had to dodge his lashing front hooves, and Brid slid helplessly down his back, over his tail, and onto the ground. And as Olob stood high above them, screaming and slashing, an unlucky bullet took him clean through the head. His great brown body came down between Moril and Brid with the force of a falling oak. He was dead before he hit the ground.

They stared at one another over the huge corpse.

"Olob now," said Brid.

"Right!" said Moril. "That does it!"

Keril's captain had been sorting out the bottleneck. Now he galloped up and held down his hand to Brid. "Catch hold, lass! Up you come!" Brid caught hold and scrambled up behind him.

Kialan shouted to Moril and held down a hand to him, but Moril did not attend. He raced to the cliff at the side of the pass and climbed it like a maniac with the cwidder bumping and booming on his back. He was at the top in seconds—how, he never knew. Heaving deep breaths, he went scrambling along the cliff edge until he had a view down into the pass. He saw Kialan, not very far below him, at the gate of the fort, waving and shouting something. He seemed to mean there was a door in the fort at the top of the cliff. Then he went into the fort, and the gate shut.

But Moril, now he knew the Northmen were in the fort, was not interested in the door. He looked Southward along the pass. It was packed with Tholian's horsemen more than halfway along. They were going more slowly now, because of the narrower space, and beyond the wide end of the pass, as far as he could see, there were more riders coming. It was truly an invasion.

Moril stood up and slung the cwidder in front of him. He felt a spatter of rain. There looked to be a storm coming, which was all to the good. For a second he gazed up at the heavy bruiselike clouds, feeling a little awed. He thought anyone would who was about to use the cwidder as Osfameron had used it.

Then he looked down into the pass where Olob's body lay in the middle of the road. The nearest riders were not so far from it now. He struck one sharp, rolling chord, and the power in the cwidder swelled with it. There was no humming, but he could feel the power. "You're not coming North," he said to the jostling riders. "And this is why." He struck two more chords. The power almost choked him. The answer was a great dagger of lightning, green and perilous, lancing down over the cliffs. A peal of thunder followed, and Moril led it on, pealing the lowest note of the cwidder, so that the power in it could grow. When it stopped, he spoke, in the way the singers spoke an incantation. He said:

> "Kialan and Konian were caught in a storm.
> The one you hanged in Holand had not
>   harmed anyone,
> Nor had Kialan when you caught him.
> This is for Konian first."

He struck another chord, followed by a swinging, hanging, frantic phrase, and felt the power in the cwidder grow again. Then he said:

> "Unlucky Clennen lies by a lake in
>   Markind,
> The singer you stabbed on suspicion only
> And prevented him performing. This is for
>   the Porter Clennen."

He struck a sharp chord and a rolling one. The first horsemen were now right beneath him. They did not pause when they came to Olob but trampled over him and on. Moril saw, but he looked beyond them, to the center of the pass. Tholian was there, jostled on either side by his favorite friends. Moril waited, quite confident and implacable, and let them come on while the power in the cwidder grew yet again. Then he spoke his last stave:

> "There was no mercy shown by the magistrate
>   in Neathdale
> To Dastgandlen Handagner. There was death
>   in the South
> And weeping in the Uplands. Now war comes
>   North,
> And all through Tholian. This is for Tholian."

He struck the cwidder again, and again, and yet a third time, vengefully. The power grew enormous, until it possessed Moril, the sky, the clouds, and the entire pass. Then, as Moril had known they would, the hills began to walk.

They started mildly and slowly, as if the mountains on either side of the pass were shrugging their shoulders. But in a second or so, the shrugging was a deep rhythmic jigging. The tops of the cliffs bent and marched, regularly inward and downward, walking, piling, inescapably trudging together to fill the pass. The thunder pealed and was drowned in the grinding of ton after ton of rock, moving and jogging inward. Almost lost in the greater din was the lesser screaming of men and horses. At the far end of the pass Moril could see riders swirling and struggling to get back or get out. But leisurely, sleepily, rhythmically, the mountains were filling the center. The cliff Moril was on marched with the rest, downward and forward. Moril leaned backward to keep his balance and let it take him, until he was standing at the head of a heap of jumbled rocks, almost over the place where Olob had been shot. The rocks were piled into the rift, choking it so that it was no longer a pass.

Moril did not spend long looking, because the rain came down, and the torn surfaces of the rocks were black with it. But he knew, as he turned round to keep the cwidder from the worst of the wet and stripped off his coat to cover it, that Tholian was underneath somewhere and Barangarolob had plenty of company. He looked across to see that the fort was safe, as he had intended. It was there, standing on a steep-sided block of steady rock, and Keril was picking his way over the ruin of the cliff toward him.

"I've just done something really horrible," Moril said to him. "Haven't I?"

Keril jumped from one rock to another and then onto the one where Moril stood. "I don't think we had much chance of holding the pass otherwise," he said.

"You don't understand," said Moril. "I did it because of Olob." He leaned against Keril and burst into tears. Keril took off his own coat, wrapped it round Moril, and led him quietly back over the rocks to the fort.

They left the fort the following day, after a big force of men from the North Dales arrived there to make sure the Southerners did not attempt to attack over the fallen rocks. Moril did not see as much of the journey to Hannart as he would have liked. He was exhausted and spent most of the time asleep in one of the wagons. Every so often he woke to find they were on a green road, or in a wood where the trees were still only budding in the later spring of the North, and went to sleep happy. He was awake to see the Falls at Dropwater, which he would not have missed for worlds. And by the time they reached Hannart he had come to himself again.

He was disappointed but not really surprised, to find Hannart a city far larger than Neathdale, in the center of a big valley. Flags were flying in honor of their arrival. There were crowds of people carrying flags or flowers. Hannart was full of flowers in fields, in gardens, on trees, and growing wild, thick as the grass, on the steep sides of the mountains. Moril could smell them as soon as they entered the valley. At the end of the valley was a great tall thing, like a castle four times life-size, picked out in gold and blue and green.

Moril stared at it. "Whatever is that?"

"That's the steam organ," said Kialan. "Haven't you heard about it? They'll probably play it tonight. It makes the most splendid noise."

"I wish someone had told me," said Moril.

There was a feast that night, in their honor, and as Kialan had thought, the steam organ played. In a strong steamy smell of coal and oil, it thundered out well-known tunes, like a mountain singing, or the grandfather of all music, and made Brid and Moril laugh. It seemed most fitting that Hannart should own such a thing, because the place was full of music, not only then, but at all times. Cowbells clinked in the steep meadows. Women called the cows home in a kind of song, not unlike Brid's "Cow-Calling" song. In the city there were tunes for crying everything that was on sale and for telling the hours of the watch. There was singing and dancing somewhere almost every night. The saying was that you could tell someone came from Hannart because whatever they did, they sang, and if they did not sing, they whistled.

Keril lived right in the center of the city, in a house twice the size of Ganner's. Unlike Ganner's house, it was always open. The cheerful people of Hannart seemed to use its front courtyard as another part of the main square. There was always someone there, gossiping or selling something, and, if anything unusual happened, they came on into the rest of the house to tell Keril about it. Since there were also large numbers of people who actually lived in the house, Moril found it almost impossible to sort out who came from where.

Brid loved it. She had never been happier in her life. "I often remembered it, but I didn't think it was real!" she was fond of saying.

Moril enjoyed it, too. He liked the liveliness, the carelessness, and the way people rushed up to Keril and said what they pleased. He could not imagine anyone doing that in the South. Moril liked Keril. He liked Halida, Kialan's mother. He enjoyed being with Kialan, and he loved the perpetual music. But he was too hot in the city and far too hot in the house. He kept having to go out on the hillsides. At night it was worse, and he slept in one of the gardens when he could. When Halida realized this, she gave him a room on the ground floor, opening on one of the gardens. Moril was grateful, but he hardly went into the room, and he only slept there if it was raining.

Brid and Kialan consulted about it and went to see what Keril thought.

"Yes," said Keril. "I'm afraid he'll be off again, one of these days. I hope not yet, though. I owe it to Clennen to see he has an education."

After that Brid watched Moril like a hawk. Moril showed no sign of wanting to leave. He seemed perfectly happy getting the education Keril thought he should have. He spent long hours playing his cwidder with Kialan, arranging songs and trying to make new ones. He rode with Kialan and Brid and walked on the hills with them. It was just that he was too hot indoors, and there was something at the back of his mind he did not want to think about yet.

Now Flennpass was blocked, there was very little news from the South. It was nearly a month before some fishermen brought news that Tholian had indeed been killed by the fall of rocks, and his army, most of it having been unwilling, anyway, had packed up and gone home. Some time after that, a trader arrived to say that things had gone very quiet in the South. Yes, he said, when Keril questioned him, the lords and earls were very shaken. But the cause of the quiet was the ordinary people. They did nothing, but they seemed powerful. The earls were afraid of them. They dared not even try for peace with the North, in case that stirred up a revolution.

A month later still a cart drove into Hannart. By the black mud on its axles, it had clearly come north through the Marshes. Apart from the mud, it was gaily painted in green and gold, and trim enough. It was driven by a very pretty girl. Beside her on the driving seat sat a dreamy-looking man with a thin face and a thin, graying beard, who smiled round at the gaiety of Hannart with a look of mild pleasure. The small gold lettering on the side of the cart said he was HESTEFAN THE SINGER.

The people of Hannart realized that here would be both music and more news of the South. Numbers followed the cart as it jogged through the streets and drove into the front court of the Earl's house.

"Oh look! A singer!" Brid said to Kialan.

"Do you know him?" Kialan asked Moril.

"I've heard of him," said Moril. He looked at Hestefan's mild face and dreamy eyes, and it came to him that he would probably look like that when he was older.

The cart stopped. The mottled gray horse blew, as much as to say, "Good—that's enough for today, thank you." The canvas cover came back a little, and a third traveler rather hesitantly stood up in the cart.

"*Dagner!*" shrieked Brid, Moril, and Kialan.

They rushed up and hurled themselves on him. Dagner, grinning and blushing mauve with pleasure, climbed out of the cart and was thrown against it by their onrush.

"What happened?" said Brid.

"How did you get out of prison?" said Moril.

"Ganner got me out," Dagner said when he had got his breath back. "Ganner's a good fellow. I got to like him a lot. He did follow us, you know, but he went back to Markind when he didn't find us. Then—I don't know what you said to that old snob of a justice, Moril, but when they had me up in front of them again, they didn't seem at all sure I was guilty and kept asking me about Ganner. So I told them he was marrying Mother, and they sent all the way to Markind to ask if it was true. It was marvelous. As soon as Ganner heard I was in prison, he came to Neathdale and raised a real stink. And while he was doing it, news came that Tholian was dead. Ganner upped and sacked the justice, and said he was in charge now. It was marvelous! He let half the other prisoners go, too. But seeing that I really had been passing information, Mother thought I'd better go North for a while and got Hestefan to take me."

"How is Mother?" asked Moril.

"Terribly happy," said Dagner. "Runs about all the time laughing.

I don't know why—she laughed when she heard Flennpass was blocked and said you and Brid must have made it to the North. She sent me with a letter for you both."

Brid and Moril snatched the letter and bent over it eagerly. It was a good long letter, all about Lenina's doings in Markind. Lenina wrote of everything from the speckled cows to the roof where Moril had walked, and reminded Brid of this and Moril of that, and sent Ganner's love—and to Moril, it was like a letter from a distant acquaintance. He felt it might just as well have been written to the baker's boy round the corner. He was sad that he should feel like that, but he could not help it.

"What a lovely letter!" said Brid. "I shall keep it."

While they were reading it, Hestefan's pretty daughter had driven the cart away to the stables. Moril was annoyed, because he had wanted to talk to Hestefan. He dashed away to the stables, but the green cart was already standing empty in the coach house beside their battered and faded pink one. Moril went back to the courtyard, where Dagner, delighted to see them all again, was being uncharacteristically chatty.

"Shall I tell you something really silly?" he said to Kialan as Moril came up. "You won't believe this!"

"Try me," said Kialan.

"Well," said Dagner, "I'm the Earl of the South Dales. They won't have me," he said hastily, as Kialan burst out laughing. "Nothing will possess them to invest me. But it's true. Tholian wasn't married, and all his cousins were killed, too, when Flennpass collapsed—you *must* tell me about that, by the way—and the only living heir left was me. And Moril after that. Honestly."

Moril stood silent in the crowded courtyard and left Brid and Kialan to do the exclaiming. Now he knew what it was that he had not wanted to think about. He had done that. He had worked a huge destruction and killed so many people that Dagner was now an earl. Everyone no doubt thought he had done right. He had saved the North, prevented a war, and avenged Clennen and Konian. But Moril knew he had not done right. He had done it all because Olob was killed. With the cwidder in his hands, he had behaved as if it was for Konian, for Clennen, for Dagner, and for the North, but it had all been for Olob, really. He was ashamed. What he had done was to cheat the cwidder. That was the worst thing. If you stood up and told the truth in the wrong way, it was not true any longer, though it might be as powerful as ever. Moril saw that he was neither old enough nor wise enough to have charge of such a potent thing as that cwidder.

That night, there was a feast in honor of Dagner, Hestefan, and

Fenna, Hestefan's daughter. Keril asked Hestefan to sing. Hestefan sang, old songs, new songs, and many that Moril had never heard. When he sang, you forgot it was Hestefan singing and thought only of the song. Moril was impressed. Then Hestefan told a story. It was one Moril did not know. And while Hestefan was telling it, he found he forgot who was telling it and simply lived in the story. Moril realized he still had a lot to learn.

After that they wanted Dagner to sing. Dagner was nervous, but surprisingly ready to perform.

"Huh!" said Brid. "He just wants to impress Fenna, that's what."

Whatever the reason, Dagner took his own cwidder, fetched for him by Kialan, tuned it, and sang the song Moril had tried to finish for him. He did it nothing like the way Moril had made it go. The new parts of the tune were quite different from Moril's, and he had changed the beginning. It now went:

"Follow me, follow me.
The blackbird sings to follow me.
No one will know where we go—
All that matters is we go."

Kialan looked at Moril and made a face to show that he liked Moril's version better. Moril smiled. Everyone had to do things their own way. While Dagner went on to sing his "Color" song, Moril slipped quietly away, fetched the old cwidder, slung it on his shoulders, and went to where Hestefan was refreshing himself with beer beside an open window. Hestefan looked as if he was too hot, just like Moril.

"Please," Moril said to him, "will you take me with you when you go?"

"Well," Hestefan said dubiously, "I was thinking of slipping off now, while nobody's noticing."

"I know you were," said Moril. "Take me, too. Please."

Hestefan looked at him, a vague, dreamy look, which Moril was positive saw twice as much as most people's. "You're Clennen's other son, aren't you?" he said. "What's your name?"

"Tanamoril," said Moril. "I'm called Osfameron, too," he added, as an inducement.

Hestefan smiled. "Very well then," he said. "Come along."

# Drowned Ammet

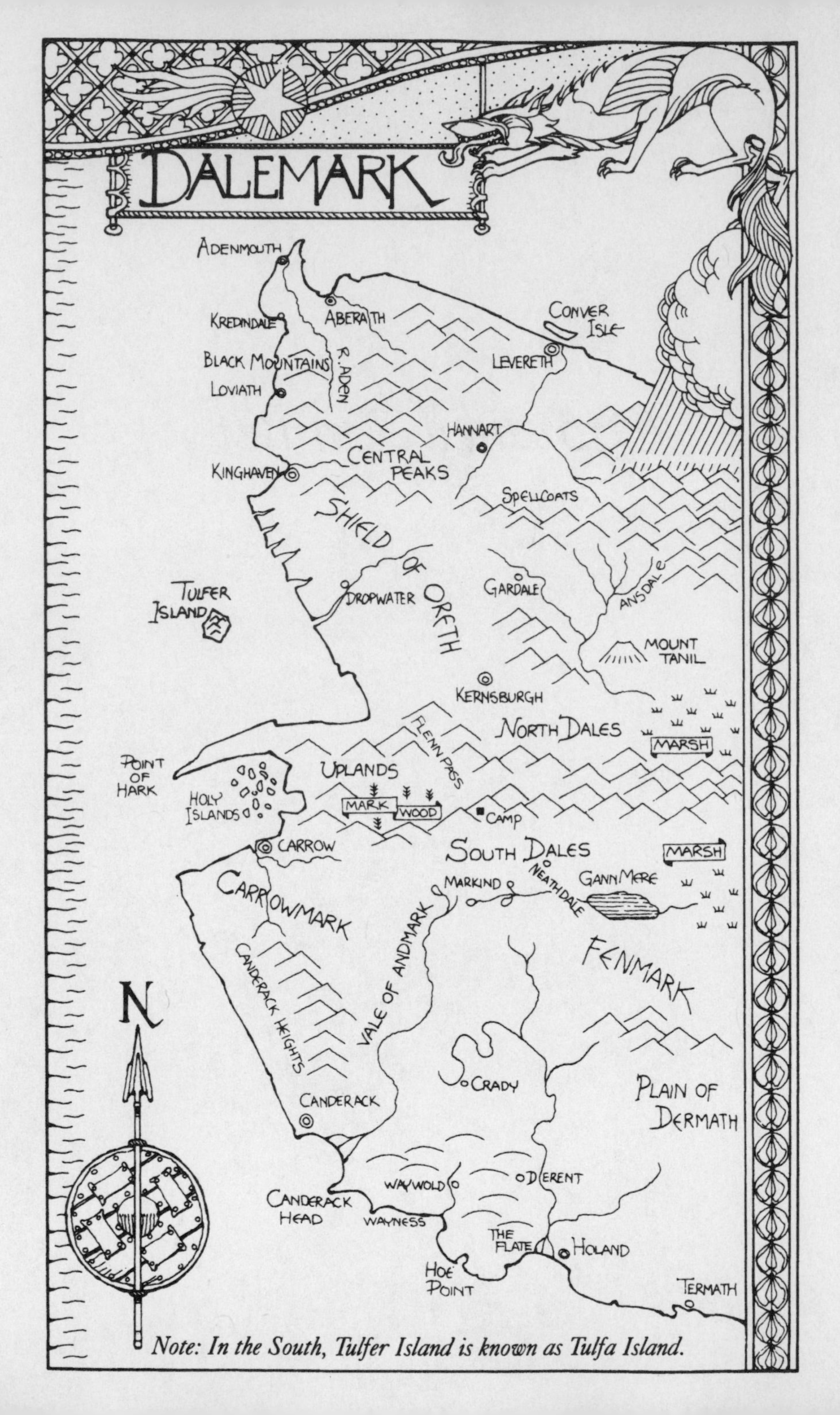


*Note: In the South, Tulfer Island is known as Tulfa Island.*

*For My Mother*

# CONTENTS

# PART ONE

# *Free Holanders*

# 1

PEOPLE MAY WONDER how Mitt came to join in the Holand Sea Festival, carrying a bomb, and what he thought he was doing. Mitt wondered himself by the end.

Mitt was born the day of the Holand Sea Festival, and he was called Alhammitt after his father. Perhaps the first sound Mitt heard as he burst bawling into the world was his parents laughing about both these things.

"Well, he took his time," said Mitt's father, "and chose his day all right. What does this make him? A man of straw, born to be drowned?"

Milda, Mitt's mother, laughed heartily at this, because the Sea Festival was something of a joke. On that day, every autumn, Hadd, the Earl of Holand, was required by tradition to dress up in outlandish clothes and walk in a procession down to the harbor carrying a life-size dummy made of plaited wheat. The dummy was known as Poor Old Ammet. One of Hadd's sons walked after him carrying Poor Old Ammet's wife, who was made entirely of fruit, and her name was Libby Beer. The procession that went with them was both noisy and peculiar. When they reached the harbor, they said traditional words and then threw both dummies into the sea. Nobody knew why this was done. To most people in Holand the ceremony was just an excuse to have a holiday, eat sweets, and get drunk. On the other hand, everyone would have thought it horribly unlucky not to have held the Sea Festival.

So Milda, even though she was laughing until her dimple was creased out of existence, bent over the new baby and said, "Well, I think it's a lucky birthday to have had. He'll grow up a real free soul, just like you—you wait! That's why I'm calling him after you."

"Then he'll be common as dirt," said Mitt's father. "Just like me. You go into town and shout 'Alhammitt' in the street, and half Holand will come to you." And they both laughed at the thought of the common name they were giving their baby.

Mitt's early memories were full of his parents' laughter. They were very happy. They had the good luck to rent a smallholding on the Earl's land in what was known as the New Flate, only ten miles from the port of Holand. It had been reclaimed from sea marsh by Earl Hadd's grandfather and grew lush emerald grass, big vegetables, and corn in narrow yellow stripes between the dikes. Dike End holding was so fertile and the market of Holand so near that Mitt's parents had plenty to live on. Though Earl Hadd was said to be the hardest man in Dalemark, and other farmers in the Flate were always being turned out of doors for not paying their rent, Mitt's parents always had just enough money to go round. They laughed. Mitt grew up running carelessly along the paths between the crops and the dikes. It never occurred to anyone that he could drown. When he was two, he taught himself to swim by falling into a dike when his parents were busy. Since no one was there to help him, he had to help himself. He struggled to the bank and got out, and his clothes dried in the stiff breeze as he ran on.

The sound of that breeze was as much part of his early memories as his parents' laughter. Apart from the hill where Holand stood, the Flate was flat as a floor. The wind blew straight across from the sea. Sometimes it came storming in, laying the grass over, chopping the sky reflected in the dikes into gray Vs, and hurling the trees sideways so that their leaves showed white. But most days it simply blew, steadily and constantly, so that the dikes never stopped rippling and the leaves of the poplars and alders went *rattle-rattle* up and down the banks. If the wheat was ripe, it rustled in the wind, stiffly, like straw in a mattress. The constant wind sighed in the grass and hummed in the chimney, and kept the sails of the big windmills always turning, *creak-thump, creak-thump*, to pump the water to the dikes or grind the flour. Mitt used to laugh at those windmills. It was the way their arms pawed the air.

Then one day, shortly after Mitt had taught himself how to swim, the wind suddenly dropped. It did that sometimes in early summer, but it was the first time in Mitt's life that he had known the Flate without wind. The sails of the windmills creaked and stood. The trees stopped moving. There was blue sky in the dikes, and trees upside down. Everything went quiet and unexpectedly warm. Above all, there was suddenly an extraordinary smell. Mitt could not think what was happening. He stood on the bank of the dike nearest the house with his ears tipped to the silence and his nose lifted to the smell. The smell was cow dung and peat and trampled grass, mixed with smoke from the chimney. But that was only in the foreground. Beyond that was the smell of fresh things growing—cow parsley, buttercups, a hint of may, and strongest of all, the heavenlike scent of willows budding. While, at the back of it, there and not there, so that Mitt almost missed it, was the faint boisterous bite of the distant sea.

Mitt was too young to think of it as smells, or to realize that the wind had simply stopped. He thought it was a place. It seemed to him that he had got an inkling of somewhere unspeakably beautiful, warm, and peaceful, and he wanted to go there. Yes, it was a land. It was not far off, just beyond somewhere, and it was Mitt's very own. He set off at once to find it while he still remembered the way.

He trotted to the end of the dike, crossed the footbridge, and continued trotting, northward and inland. He passed all the places he knew, impatiently—they were obviously not his land—and trotted on until his legs ached. Even then he was still in the New Flate, lush and green, with its dikes, poplars, and windmills. Mitt knew his land was different from the Flate, so he was forced to toil on. And after a mile or so, he came out into the Old Flate. Here it was different, all right. The ground was wide and treeless and covered with pinkish marsh plants. In some places, long lines of rushes and green scum showed where there had once been dikes and farms, but now it was all flat and blank. Nothing seemed to be alive there but mosquitoes and plaintive marsh birds. In the wide distance, it was true, there were one or two islands of higher ground with trees and houses on them. The roads to them crossed the pink waste on causeways, raised up like the veins on an old man's hand. Otherwise there was nothing until, away on the edge of the distance, there was what Mitt took for a line of clouds but was in fact the beginning of the land above sea level, where Holand joined Waywold.

Mitt was a trifle daunted. This was not the kind of land he had in mind. His vision of his perfect place faded a little, and he was no longer sure this was quite the way to it. Nevertheless, he set forward bravely into the dismal landscape. He felt he had come too far to turn back now. After a while he thought he saw something moving, out in the marsh. He set his eyes on the movement and waded toward it. It was extremely dangerous. There were snakes in the Old Flate. And if Mitt had walked into one of the scummy pools, he could have been sucked down into it and drowned. Fortunately he had no idea. And even more fortunately the moving things he could see were a troop of the Earl's soldiers combing the Flate for a runaway revolutionary.

Mitt could see they were soldiers before long. He stood on a clump of rubbery plants, with the marsh sucking and gobbling around him, and wondered whether he ought to go near them. When people in the New Flate talked about soldiers, they talked as if soldiers were something to be afraid of. There was a causeway quite near Mitt. He wondered if he ought to climb up on it, out of the soldiers' way. While he was wondering, a muddy horse heaved itself onto the causeway from the marsh behind it. The young officer on its back reined in and stared at the sight of such a very small boy standing all alone in the middle of the Flate.

"What on earth do you think you're doing?" he called to Mitt.

Mitt was rather pleased to have company. "I'm looking for my home," he told the officer chattily. "I come a long way, too."

"I can see you have," said the officer. "Where is your home?"

"There." Mitt pointed vaguely northward. He was busy examining his new acquaintance. The gold on the officer's coat took his fancy. So did the officer's face, which was very smooth and pale and narrow, with a nose that went out much more sharply than any noses Mitt had known before and a mouth which Mitt somehow thought of as clean. Altogether Mitt felt he was a person worthy of knowing about the perfect place. "It's all quiet, with water," he explained, "and it's my place where I'm going to, but I can't find it yet."

The officer frowned. His own small daughter had been found marching out into the Flate only yesterday, saying she had a house on a hill that was hers and she had to find it. He thought he knew the signs. "Yes, but where do you live?" he said.

"Dike End," Mitt said impatiently. It was unworthy of the officer to ask such things. "Of course. That's where I come from, and I'm going to my home."

"I see," said the officer. He waved at the distant soldiers. "Come here, one of you!"

The several troopers who came running at his shout were somewhat astonished to find not a full-grown revolutionary but an extremely small boy. "He shrunk with the wet," one suggested.

"He says he lives in Dike End," said the officer. "One of you take him home and tell his parents to take more care of him in future."

"Dike End's not my home. It's where I *live*!" Mitt protested.

Nevertheless, he was taken back to the New Flate almost dangling from the hand of a huge trooper in the Earl's green uniform. Mitt was sullen at first, disappointed and vaguely humiliated. And he was deeply disillusioned about the officer. Mitt had told him a valuable secret, and the officer had barely even listened. But the trooper was a cheerful man. He had children of his own, and it had been hot, wet work, hunting the revolutionary in the windless Flate. The trooper was pleased to have a rest. He was very jolly to Mitt, and before long Mitt cheered up and chatted happily about how far he had walked and how he thought he would like to be a soldier, too, when he grew up, and a sea captain as well and sail the Earl's ships for him.

When they came to the New Flate, people came to doors and gates to stare at Mitt trotting along with his hand stretched above his head in order to reach the great warm hand of the trooper. The stares were unloving. Earl Hadd was a hard man and a vindictive one. The soldiers were the ones who carried out the Earl's harsh orders. And lately the Earl's second son, Harchad, had taken command of the soldiers, and he was even harder than his father, and a good deal more cruel. But since, all over Dalemark, an earl in his earldom had more power than a king, in the times when there were kings, Harchad and his soldiers did exactly as they pleased. Therefore, soldiers were hated heartily.

Mitt understood none of this, but he saw the looks. "Don't you look like that!" he kept crying out. "This is my *friend*, this is!"

The trooper became steadily more uncomfortable. "Take it easy, sonny," he said every time Mitt cried out. And after a while he seemed to feel the need to justify himself. "A man's got to live," he told Mitt. "It's not work I enjoy, but what can a poor boy off the harbor edge do? When I get my bounty, I aim to take up farming, like your dad does."

"Did you fall in the harbor?" Mitt asked, fixing on the only part of this he understood.

They came to Dike End. Mitt's parents had missed Mitt about half an hour before, and they were by then in a panic. Mitt's father received him with a great thump, and his mother hugged him frantically. Mitt did not understand the reason for either. The vision of his perfect land had faded by then. He was not sure what he had gone away to do.

The trooper stood by, very stiff and correct. "Boy was found out in the Old Flate," he said. "Said he was looking for his home, or some such story."

"Oh, Mitt!" Milda cried joyously. "What a free soul you are!" And she hugged him again.

"And," said the trooper, "Navis Haddsson's compliments and would you keep more of an eye on him in future."

"Navis Haddsson!" exclaimed both Mitt's parents, Milda in considerable awe, and Mitt's father with surprise and resentment. Navis was Earl Hadd's third and youngest son.

"Big of Navis Haddsson," Mitt's father said sarcastically. "Knows all about bringing up boys, I suppose?"

"Can't say, I'm sure," said the trooper, and he made off, having no wish to get into an argument with such a thickset and aggressive person as the elder Alhammitt.

"Well, I think it was very kind of Navis to send us our Mitt back like that!" Milda said when he had gone.

Mitt's father spit in the dike.

All the same, Milda remained extremely impressed by the kindness of Navis. She told people about it whenever her husband was not by to resent it, and most people she told were impressed, too. Earl Hadd and his family were not, as a rule, kind to anyone. After that Milda took a great interest in Navis for a while and found out everything about him that she could. There was not very much known. The Earl's eldest son, Harl, and his second son, Harchad, were the Earl's favorites and the ones people heard most about. But about the time Navis sent Mitt home, Navis was enjoying a little more of the Earl's favor. The reason was that three years or so before, the Earl had chosen Navis a wife, as he had chosen wives for his other two sons. Milda heard that Navis and his wife adored each other and went everywhere together. Then Navis's wife gave birth to a daughter. That was the reason the Earl was pleased with Navis.

The Earl valued granddaughters. He did not like girls in the least, but he needed granddaughters because he was an extremely quarrelsome man. Granddaughters could be married off to other earls and lords, who would then become Hadd's allies in his quarrels. But so far only Harl's wife had had a daughter. So when Navis's wife, too, had a daughter, Hadd was delighted with them. Milda learned that Navis's wife was expecting a second child shortly, and Hadd was gleefully expecting another marriageable granddaughter.

The baby was born the following month. He was a boy, and Navis's wife died having him. It was said that Navis was so stricken with grief that he could not be bothered to find a name for his son. The nurses were forced to ask Earl Hadd to think of a name, and Hadd was so annoyed at not having a granddaughter that he called the boy Ynen, which was the name of a lord he particularly disliked. Hadd was consoled later on that year when Harl's wife and Harchad's both had girl babies. As for Navis, he gave up his commission in the Earl's army and fell into total obscurity. It was soon quite impossible to learn anything about him or about his children, Hildrida and Ynen.

Mitt did not quite forget his perfect land. He remembered it, though a little fuzzily, next time the wind dropped, but he did not set off to look for it again. It was plain to him that soldiers only brought you back again if you went. It made him sad. When an inkling of it came to him in silence, or in scents, or, later, if the wind hummed a certain note, or a storm came shouting in from the sea and he caught the same note in the midst of its noise, he thought of his lost perfect place and felt for a moment as if his heart would break. But then he would shake off the feeling and laugh with his parents.

It seemed to Mitt that the three of them could laugh at anything. He remembered laughing with Milda one evening during a rainstorm. Mitt was trying to learn his letters. He found them so difficult that he had to laugh. Then the door came clapping open in a gust of rain, blowing everything in the house to the end of the room, and there stood Mitt's father, soaking wet and laughing, shouting above the gale that the cow had calved. At that the door came off its hinges and fell on Mitt's father. And they all laughed till they ached.

The very funniest thing happened when the calf had grown into a young and gamesome bull. Mitt and his parents were all in the pasture, trying to mend a place where the dike bank was giving. The bull stood watching them, rather interested. Life was a little dull in the pasture. Then Hadd's rent collector climbed over the fence and stalked irritably over to the dike.

"I've been all the way to the house," he said. "Why couldn't you—?"

The bull, with a look of pure mischief in his merry red eye, lowered his horns and charged. He would not have dreamed of harming any of the family, but the rent collector was another matter. And in a misty, bullish way, he may have noticed that the family was not altogether pleased to see the rent collector. Anyway, up went the rent collector in a graceful arc, moneybag and all, and down he went again, moneybag and all, into the dike, where he gave out a truly tremendous splash. He came up. He swore horribly. He floundered to the bank and tried to get out. The bull was there to meet him and simply prodded him back in again. It was the funniest thing Mitt had ever seen. It never occurred to the rent collector to cross the dike and get out on the opposite bank where the bull could not reach him. He kept floundering up, clutching his moneybag. And prod, prod went the bull, and the rent collector was sitting in the dike again. Over and over again, with the rent collector, floundering, reeling, sitting down *splash*, and squawking "Can't one of you control this beast!" and Mitt's parents leaning head to head, too helpless with laughter to do a thing about it. It was Mitt, laughing as hard as anyone, who at last hooked his finger in the ring on the bull's nose and let the raging rent collector scramble out. And the rent collector was not pleased.

"I'll teach you to laugh, boy!" he snarled.

He did. Next time he came for the rent, he asked double. When Mitt's father protested, he said, "Nothing to do with me. Earl Hadd needs the money."

Probably Hadd was short of money. The rents were put up all over the Flate. Rumor said that there were riots in the town of Holand, and the Earl needed to pay more soldiers to deal with the rioting. But only at Dike End was the rent doubled. That was the rent collector's private revenge. And there was nothing Mitt's parents could do about it. Theoretically they could have gone to law and accused the rent collector of extortion. But the rent collector was the Earl's official, and judges always upheld the Earl's employees against ordinary people—unless, of course, you gave the judge a big enough bribe. Mitt's parents had no money for bribes. They needed more than they had to pay the rent collector. They had to sell the bull.

Next quarter they sold the mule. Then some furniture. And by that time they were in a vicious circle: The more things they sold from the farm to pay the rent, the less they had to make money with to pay the next quarter's rent, and the more things they had to sell. Mitt's parents stopped laughing. That winter Mitt's father took to spending most of the week away in the port of Holand, earning what money he could there, while Milda tried to run the farm with what help Mitt could give. It was desperately hard work. Milda's pretty face acquired a seam of worry down one side—a sort of pucker where her dimple had been. Mitt hated that pucker. He did not remember how his father looked at that time. He remembered a curt, bitter voice and his father's square back plodding away from them down the causeway to Holand to find work.

He could not have found much work. He spent longer and longer away in Holand, and brought very little money back, but what he did bring enabled them to drag on at Dike End for the following summer. But Milda on her own was a poor, forgetful manager. Mitt did all he could to help, but they lost money steadily. There were still a few times when Mitt was able to lie on his back by the dike, looking up at the rattling leaves, and think yearningly about his perfect land. As times grew harder, he seemed to want it more and more. He longed to set off again to find it, but of course he was older now and he knew he had to stay and help his mother.

Then quarter day came round again, and there was no money at all. It did no good for Milda to beg the rent collector to wait a day or so. He came back the next day with the bailiff and three of the Earl's soldiers, and Mitt and Milda were turned out of Dike End. A short while before Mitt's sixth birthday, he helped his mother pack their few belongings into a handcart and push it into Holand to join his father.

# 2

MITT ALWAYS HATED to remember that first winter in Holand. His father was living in one room in a big tenement block down by the harbor. Mitt and Milda joined him there. The tenement had perhaps once been the house of a wealthy man. Outside, on its greenish, peeling walls, there were the remains of pictures—once fine paintings of garlands of flowers and people out of stories, sheaves of wheat, and bunches of fruit. But they were so old that Mitt could not quite tell what they were, and anyway, the inside of the building was what he saw most. The large rooms had been chopped into as many small ones as possible, so the house was crowded as full as it would hold of people. It was filthy. The buckets on the dark stairs stank. Bedbugs lived in all the walls. They came out at night and bit, viciously. What with that, and the strangeness, and the noise of all the people, Mitt could not sleep very well. He lay awake and listened to his parents quarreling as they had never quarreled before.

Mitt could not understand what the quarrels were about. It seemed as if his father was not pleased to have them with him in Holand. "Hanging round my neck!" he put it. He wanted them to go back to Dike End. When Milda shrieked at him that there was no rent, he cursed her for laziness.

"Why should I work my fingers to the bone to keep you in idleness?" Milda screamed at him. But after a week of quarreling, she found a job in a workroom which made fine embroidered hangings, and she was there, sewing, from early morning until light failed in the evening.

After this the quarrels Mitt's parents had became even harder for Mitt to understand. His mother kept saying to his father, "You and your

Free Holanders! *Free* Holanders! There's no such *thing* as freedom in this place!" Mitt had no idea what that meant.

Mitt was shocked and shattered by the town of Holand itself. He hated the dirt and the noise and all the people. His job for the day was to carry their bucket to the waterfront and tip it in the harbor. As Milda said, the one advantage of living in that tenement was that you did not have to go far to get rid of your rubbish. Mitt hated the smell on the greasy waterfront, where fish scales glimmered on the flagstones like sequins on a dirty dress. The crowded harbor appalled him. There were tall ships with many masts and pennants flying, merchant ships, ships of the Earl's fleet, loading and unloading going on most of the time. In between were small boats, packed and bustling, rowing boats, cutters, jollyboats, and a good hundred fishing boats. Mitt was always glad when the fishing fleet sailed out, because the crowded water seemed a little emptier then.

After Mitt had brought the bucket back to the door of their room, he was all on his own once Milda had found work. He had nothing to do but keep out of the way of the other children. He hated them most of all. They were town children, shrewd, nimble, and knowing. They made rings around Mitt. They jeered at him for not understanding town ways. They made him look a fool, then ran away laughing.

Mitt hid from them, usually, in the dark holes and corners of the house or the waterfront. But one day he felt he had had enough of that and ran away instead, up the hill from the harbor, into the better part of the town. Here, to his surprise, the streets were cleaner, and became wider and cleaner still as he went upward. The air smelled almost fresh. There was a tang in it of the sea, and an autumn smell from the Flate. Better still, most of the houses were painted, and unlike the tenement, the paint was fresh and bright, and Mitt could see what the pictures were about. He walked slowly, looking at trees and fruit, red swirls and blue flowers, until he came to a particularly fine tall house, where the painting was in gold as well as other colors. On one gable, a stiff sort of lady in a green dress held out a very purple bunch of grapes to a stiff man on the other gable, whose hair seemed to be solid gold. Mitt much admired them. They reminded him a little of the figureheads on the fronts of the big ships. And perhaps because of the fresh air smell, they made him think of his perfect land.

He was standing lost in admiration and daydream when a servant of the merchant who owned the house came out with a stick and told him to be off. He called Mitt a guttersnipe and said he had no business to be there. Mitt ran away, terrified. As he went, he looked back and upward. And there, on the very top of the hill, was the Earl's palace, larger, whiter, brighter, and with more gold paint than any other house in Holand. Mitt felt it was squashing him. He felt like a pip in a cider press.

That was the last time for many years that Mitt remembered his perfect land. Holand quashed it out of his mind entirely and left him simply bewildered.

When Mitt's birthday came, a few days later, and with it the Sea Festival, that was bewildering, too. Everyone had a holiday, so there were more people about than ever. Mitt watched the Festival procession, hoisted onto the shoulders of a kindly man called Canden, who seemed to be a friend of his father's. Down the street came a boiling and a bubbling of brightly clothed people. There was terrific shouting and yelling, and ribbons, fruit, and flowers on everyone. Some had silly hats. Images went by on sticks—heads of cows and horses, with hats and ribbons on, too. Big boys went tearing in and out of the procession, shouting and swirling wooden rattles. It was noise, noise, noise. Every so often came a group of people playing the traditional tune on traditional instruments. There were pipes called scarnels, which sounded just like their name, and triangular stringed things you played with a horsehair bow. They were cruddles, and they sounded just like their name, too. And the groups of musicians were so far apart from one another that it was only by accident that they played the same part of the tune as the rest. Then, *drub, drub, drub*, came people banging at horsehair drums and drowning out even the scarnels. In the midst of it, Mitt glimpsed a straw dummy, fantastically looped with cherry-colored ribbons, riding along in somebody's arms.

"Look," said the kindly Canden. "There's Poor Old Ammet. That's Earl Hadd carrying him."

"What's he going to do with him?" Mitt asked anxiously. He had never heard of Earl Hadd doing anything good with anything.

"Throw him in the harbor, of course. For luck," explained Canden.

Mitt was horrified. Earl Hadd must be quite heartless. He thought of Poor Old Ammet being tipped into the harbor just like the bucket of muck Mitt tipped in daily, and Poor Old Ammet sinking, soaking, drowning, his ribbons getting spoiled. "Doesn't he float?" he asked tensely.

"Not too often," Canden said, quite unaware of Mitt's state of mind. "Mostly he falls to pieces and sinks in the harbor or just outside it."

"He doesn't!" Mitt said frantically.

There was another friend of Mitt's father's standing beside Canden. He was called Dideo, and his face was a mass of tiny lines. Mitt thought Dideo's eyes looked like two shiny fish caught in the net of his skin.

Dideo said, "He doesn't always fall to bits—Old Ammet. If the tide's right, he goes out on the tide in one piece. Or they say he does. Floats for miles. And those in a boat that can find him and pick him out have a lucky boat ever after, they say."

If anything, Mitt found it even more distressing to think of Poor Old Ammet floating, floating, all on his own out to sea. He tried to change the subject. "Who are those boys with rattles?"

Canden glanced at the procession, where boys in red and yellow trousers were having great fun whirling their rattles under the noses of cruddle players. "Boys from the Palace. All them in the procession come from the Palace," he told Mitt, and turned to Dideo again. "I've never seen Old Ammet float. He goes down almost as quick as Libby Beer."

"Would they let me run about with a rattle?" Mitt interrupted desperately.

"No. You're born a nobody," said Dideo. "He does float," he said to Canden. "You've not been in Holand long enough to know, but he was picked up once, a good ten miles out, by the old *Sevenfold*, and I heard every man on that ship made a fortune afterward. That was the only time I ever knew it happen, though," he added regretfully. "I was about Mitt's age at the time." Here he looked up at Mitt and, finding him inexplicably white and tearful, nudged Canden.

Canden took Mitt down and peered at his face. "What's the matter? Would you like an Ammet of your own?"

"*No!*" said Mitt.

Nevertheless, he arrived in front of a stall where dozens of tiny straw Ammets were for sale. With them came another friend of Mitt's father's, a man with a dour, blank face, called Siriol, who stood by without saying anything while Canden and Dideo bent over Mitt, doing their best to please him. Would Mitt have this Ammet here? Or how about this one with blue ribbons? And when Mitt firmly refused to have anything to do with Poor Old Ammet in any color ribbons, Canden and Dideo tried to buy him a wax model of Libby Beer instead. But real and enticing though the wax fruit looked, Mitt did not want Libby either. She was thrown into the sea just like Poor Old Ammet. He burst into tears and pushed her away.

"But they're lucky!" Canden said, quite mystified.

Dour-faced Siriol picked up one of the toffee apples from the other end of the stall and stuffed it into Mitt's damp fist. "There," he said. "That'll please you best, you see." He was quite right. Mitt forgot his distress, somewhat, in the difficulty of getting his teeth through the toffee into the apple underneath.

There was some mystery about these friends of Mitt's father's. Mitt knew his mother did not care for them. He heard her objecting to them every night when his parents quarreled. Her objections seemed to mount steadily through that winter, until around the new year, when Mitt heard her say, "Oh, I give in! Only don't blame me when the soldiers come for you!"

It must have been about a week after Milda said this, in the very heart of winter, when Mitt woke up suddenly in the middle of the night. A red light was flickering on the ceiling. He could hear crackling and distant shouting, and smell smoke. One of the big warehouses on the waterfront was clearly on fire. Mitt could see it, when he raised himself on one elbow, blazing into the sky and down into the dark water of the harbor. But what had woken Mitt was not that. It was the slow shuffling outside the door of the room. The sound made Mitt's back prickle. He could hear Milda trying to light the lamp, whimpering with haste and annoyance because she could not get the wick to burn. Then the light came at last, and Mitt saw his father was not in the room. Milda ran through the room with the lamp, making lurching shadows as she ran, and tore open the door.

Canden was on the other side of it. He was clinging to the door frame to hold himself up. Mitt could not see him well because Milda was holding the lamp all wrong, but he knew that Canden was either hurt or very ill, or both. He could see it in Canden's face. He had a feeling that the part of Canden which was behind Milda and the doorpost was the wrong shape. It did not surprise him that Milda gave a dreadful strangled scream.

"Eeeeh! What—? I knew it would go wrong!"

"Harchad's men," said Canden. He sounded disgusted. "They were there waiting for us. Informers—that's what they were. Dideo, Siriol, and Ham. They informed on us."

After that Canden gave a quiver of indignation and slid down the doorpost to the floor. Milda knelt down to him, hugging the lamp and whimpering. "O ye gods! What do I *do*? What can I do? Why doesn't somebody help?"

After that doors began cautiously opening and shutting up and down the stairway. Ladies came in nightgowns and old coats, with more lamps or candles. There were troubled whispers and soothing words, while Milda rocked about on her knees, moaning. Mitt was too appalled to move. He did not want to look at Canden or his mother, so he lay and looked at the ceiling instead. The bustling ladies thought he was asleep, and after a while he must really have gone to sleep. Canden was not there in the morning. But he had been there. He had left a stain on the floor. And Mitt's father was still not there either.

Mitt knew both of them were dead. Nobody told him, but he knew. What he did not know and wanted to be told was what had happened. He wanted to know why ladies in the tenement came and told Milda, "I should lie low, if I was you. You don't want to get yourself arrested, too." Milda stayed away from work for a while, sitting very still by the window. Her face was so drawn in by worry that the seam where her dimple used to be looked more like a puckered scar than a line. Mitt hated her face like that. He crouched beside her feet and asked to be told what had caused it.

"You're too young to understand," said Milda.

"But I want to know," said Mitt. "What's happened to Dad?" He asked at least forty times before he got an answer.

"Dead," said Milda. "At least, I hope that's what he is, because they all say it's better to be dead than have Harchad after you. And I shall never forgive them that did it to him—never, never, never!"

"What did Siriol and Dideo and Ham do?" Mitt prompted her.

"Leave me be, if you know so much!" Milda said irritably. But Mitt went on asking, and in the end Milda told him as much as she knew.

It seemed that when Mitt's father had found it so hard to get work in Holand, he had felt so bitter against the Earl that he had joined a secret revolutionary society. There were a lot of them in Holand. The Earl's son Harchad had spies and soldiers hunting out these societies night and day, at all times. But when he found one and marched the members off to be hanged, there was always another to take its place.

The one Mitt's father joined was called the Free Holanders. It was composed mostly of fishermen who felt there should be more justice and better living for the ordinary people of Holand. Their ambition was to have the whole city rise against the Earl, and, as far as Milda knew, they had never done much except talk about it. But when Milda and Mitt had been turned out of Dike End, Mitt's father was so angry that he had tried to stir the Free Holanders to action of some kind. Why not set fire to one of the Earl's warehouses, he said, to show the Earl they meant business?

Canden and the other younger Free Holanders were delighted by the idea. It would hit Hadd where it hurt, they said—right in the moneybags. But the older members, particularly Siriol, Dideo, and Ham, were clean against it. If they fired a warehouse, they said, the Free Holanders would be hunted down by Harchad's men, and how would that help the city to rise and overthrow the Earl? The society split in half over it. The younger members went with Mitt's father to fire the warehouse. The older members stayed at home. And when the younger ones reached the warehouse, Harchad's men were waiting for them. All that Milda knew beyond that was that someone had managed to start a fire even so and that no one had come back from it except Canden to say that Siriol, Dideo, and Ham had informed on them. And Canden was dead, too.

Mitt considered all this. "Why did Siriol and them inform, though?"

The crease of worry down Milda's face drew into a tighter seam. "Because they were frightened, Mitt, like I am now."

"Frightened what of?" Mitt asked.

"Harchad's soldiers," Milda said, shivering. "They might come banging at this door any moment now."

Mitt considered what he knew of soldiers. They were not so frightening. They brought you home when you were found wandering in the Flate. "How many soldiers are there? More than everyone else in Holand?"

In spite of her misery, Milda smiled. To Mitt's relief, the crease on her face turned into a dimple again for a moment. "Oh no. The Earl couldn't afford that number. And I don't suppose he'd bother to send more than six or so to come and take *us* away."

"Then," said Mitt, "if all the people in this house, or all the people in Holand, all got together, they ought to be able to stop the soldiers, oughtn't they?"

Milda was forced to laugh. It was quite beyond her to explain why everyone in Holand lived in dread of soldiers, and even greater dread of Harchad's spies, so she said, "Oh, Mitt, you're a real free soul, you are! You don't know what fear means. It seems such a waste when Hadd and the Free Holanders have done for us between them, it does really!"

Mitt realized that by talking in this sturdy way, he had managed to comfort his mother. He had sent the hateful crease of worry out of her face twice. Better still, he had made Milda comfort him by calling him a free soul. Mitt was not sure he knew what a free soul was—it never occurred to him that his mother had no idea either—but he thought it was a splendid thing to be. By way of earning it, he said stoutly, "Well, you're not to worry anymore. I'll make it all right for you."

Milda laughed and hugged him. "There's my Mitt!"

# 3

MIRACULOUSLY, NO soldiers came for Milda and Mitt. It seemed as if Dideo, Siriol, and Ham had contented themselves with getting rid of the younger half of the Free Holanders and had not bothered to include wives and families. All the same, Milda and Mitt had a hard time of it for a while. When, after a week or so, Milda dared to go back to work, she found her place had been taken. Mitt was furious.

"It's the way things are in this town," Milda explained. "There's hundreds of poor women willing to work their fingers into blisters. And the rich people have to have their curtains ready on time."

"Why?" said Mitt. "Can't the poor people get together and tell the rich ones where they get off?"

That was the kind of question which made Milda call him a free soul. Mitt knew it was, so he made a point of asking such things. It was a great comfort to know he was a free soul who did not know what fear was, while Milda was out trudging from workshop to workshop. Mitt himself, hungry and miserable, spent the days hanging round the back doors of counting houses, or on the edges of boatbuilders' yards, hoping to be sent on an errand. Few errands came Mitt's way. He was too small, and there was always the crowd of bigger, quick-spoken city boys to jostle Mitt aside and run the errand instead. And of course they jeered at Mitt, too. But Mitt would tell himself that *he* was a free soul, he was, and wait patiently on. It helped him greatly.

At night Mitt had horrible dreams. He dreamed repeatedly that Canden was coming shuffling to the door again. Then the door would open, and there would be Canden, hanging on to the doorpost and slowly falling to pieces like Poor Old Ammet in the harbor. "All dead," Canden would say, as pieces dropped off him, and Mitt would wake up trying to scream. Then Mitt would lie and tell himself sternly that he did not know what fear was. In the middle of the night that was not always so easy to believe. But sometimes Milda woke up when Mitt yelled. She would tell Mitt stories she had learned as a girl until he went back to sleep again.

Milda's stories made good listening. There was magic and adventure and fighting in them, and they all seemed to happen in North Dalemark in the time when there were kings—though there were earls in the stories, too, and ordinary people. Mitt puzzled about the stories. He knew Holand was in South Dalemark, but this North Milda talked about seemed so different that he wondered for a while if it was real.

"Do they have kings still in the North?" he asked, to see what Milda would say.

But Milda knew disappointingly little about the North. "No, there's no kings anymore," she said. "I've heard they have earls in the North just like we do, only the earls there are all freedom fighters like your dad was."

Mitt could not understand how an earl could be anything of the sort. Nor could Milda explain.

"All I can say is I wish there *were* kings again," she told Mitt. "Earls are no good. Look at Hadd—us poor people are just rent on two legs to him, and if we do anything he doesn't care for, he claps us in prison, or worse."

"But he can't put everyone in prison," Mitt objected. "There wouldn't be anyone to catch his fish for him or sew his clothes."

"Oh, you are a free soul, Mitt!" Milda exclaimed.

Mitt was not sure when or how it happened, but in the course of these talks he had with Milda in the night, it began to be understood between them that Mitt was one day going to avenge his father and put right all the wrongs in Holand. It was an accepted thing, even before Milda found work. She found work fairly soon, in another sewing house, because the one thing she could really do well was fine embroidery. They managed to pay the rent on their room in time to prevent the landlord turning them out. But they were still short of food. Milda spent the rest of her week's earnings on a new pair of shoes.

"To celebrate," she said. "I just happened to see them. Aren't they pretty?"

Mitt would have been very hungry indeed had not Siriol, the dour-faced informer, sent round his daughter, Lydda, with a basket of sea fry. Lydda was a fat, meek girl of twelve. She showed Milda how to cook the fry, and she much admired Milda's pretty new shoes. Perhaps she described them to her father. At any rate, Mitt and Milda had a square meal, and there were still enough fish for breakfast. Milda put them out on the windowsill of their room to keep fresh. The ants came out of the wall in the night and ate them up. When Mitt opened the window to fetch in breakfast, all he found was some tiny scraps of bone. He was looking miserably at them when Siriol came clumping up the dark stairs in his clogs and came into the room without being invited.

"Lost your breakfast, I see," he said. "You'd better come round to mine and have some. And best thing I can see, Milda, is for him to sail with me in future. I was thinking of taking an apprentice."

"Well—" said Milda.

"Free Holanders look after their own," said Siriol.

Knowing what he knew about Siriol, Mitt was speechless. He had to stand there and let Milda do the refusing for him. But to his astonishment, Milda smiled gratefully at Siriol, thanked him over and over again, and agreed that Mitt should sail with Siriol.

"I don't need breakfast," was all Mitt could think of saying.

"Be round at my place in half an hour," Siriol said, and clumped away again.

Mitt rounded on Milda. "But he informed!" he said passionately. "What did you want to go and agree for?"

Milda shrugged, with the crease in her face very deep and bitter. "I know. But we have to live. And maybe you'll see your way to getting even with him if you keep close to him."

Mitt was mollified by that. And it made a great deal of difference that he had a job, too. Siriol was very scrupulous. Mitt had an apprentice's share of the takings, so that when the catch was good, he earned nearly as much as Milda. That almost made up to him for the kind of job it was. He did not like fishing. He did not like Siriol. He hardly knew which he disliked most.

Fishing was a mixture of boredom, hardship, and frantic bursts of work. Siriol was sour and surly and insisted that everything should be done exactly right. Mitt very soon learned that he was not allowed to make a mistake. The first day he forgot to coil a rope as Ham had shown him. Siriol picked up the end of the offending rope—which had a knot in it—and hit Mitt across the back with it. Mitt glared at him.

"Do it," said Siriol. "Do it right. Or else. You'll be glad to know how one of these days."

Small as Mitt was, he shared watches with big, slow Ham, who was Siriol's partner. He learned to patch the much-patched sail, to mend nets, and to gut fish. Siriol and Ham taught him to steer, at first by day, which was simple, then to find his way by night, by the stars, or in pitch dark, by the feel of the wind and the water, and the pull of the sails. They taught him to smell bad weather before it was near enough to hurt. Mitt also learned what chilblains were and how it felt to be too wet and too cold for too long. And he learned all these things, loathing them, until they were second nature, and learned them so young that they were with him all his life.

One thing that surprised Mitt was that he was never in the least afraid at sea. He expected to be. When he first climbed gingerly down into the *Flower of Holand*, and she rocked, and he knew there were only salt-swollen old boards between him and sinking into the sea like Old Ammet, he had to tell himself very hard that he was a free soul who did not know what fear was. Then *Flower of Holand* went dipping out to sea with all the rest of the fishing fleet, and he forgot all about it. Sailing was just a job, like Milda's sewing. And it was good to have a job and earn money when the host of bigger boys hanging round the waterfront had no such thing.

Sometimes, on a fine day, when Siriol's boat went bluntly out of the harbor on the tide, rich people's pleasure boats would be putting out, too, from the West Pool. The West Pool was a shallower mooring just beyond Holand, where the dues were so high that only wealthy people could keep boats there. Mitt enjoyed watching them. But Siriol and Ham had nothing but contempt for them. They spit in the water when they saw them.

"Rich men's toys," said Siriol. "Half out of the water in this little breeze! Put one of those in a gale, and she's under in five minutes." Siriol's respect was reserved for the stately merchant ships. Let the *Proud Ammet* or the graceful *Lovely Libby* come nodding out of Holand, crowding up sail as she came, then Siriol's face would light up, and Ham's also. "Ah!" Siriol would say. "That's a ship for you!" And he would look round his thick and fishy *Flower of Holand* as if she disappointed him.

After a year of fishing, Mitt felt himself the equal of any boy in Holand. He did not grow much—probably because he had to work so hard—but he was as tough and quick-witted as any lad on the waterfront, and much quicker-tongued. He knew every bad word there was. He had a retort for everyone. Boys and girls alike treated him with respect now. Indeed, many of them would have liked to make friends with Mitt. But Mitt kept himself to himself. These children, or children like them, had made his life a misery when he first came to Holand, and he found he could not forget it. He preferred grown-ups. He cracked jokes onshore and on board that made big slow Ham guffaw and even Siriol smile.

That pleased Mitt. It made him feel grown-up and independent—a proper free soul.

It was just as well Mitt was independent. Milda had simply no sense of economy. It became a habit with her to "just happen to see" something whenever she came home with her wages. One week it would be a huge iced cake, the next, a pair of pretty earrings.

"You have to keep up your self-respect," she told Mitt when he protested. "I'm being ground underfoot, I am, and if I don't keep my spirits up somehow, I shall just go under, I know I will!"

This was all very well, but if Mitt was out and the thing Milda "just happened to see" cost more money than Milda had, she did not scruple to take Mitt's hard-earned money, too. Mitt had to hide his money, or they would have starved. He felt terribly put upon and responsible. One evening, when he crawled home, tired out, to find Milda had bought a whole tub of oysters, it seemed like the last straw. She had opened the tub, too, and left it in the sun under the window. It was already smelling rather queer, and the ants were swarming up the sides of the tub to investigate.

"What did you want to buy that for!" Mitt yelled.

Milda was injured. "Oh, Mitt! I thought they'd be such a treat for you."

"But there's thousands of them!" Mitt bawled. "How are we going to eat all that lot? If you wanted oysters, I could have *got* you oysters—for nothing, from Dideo. Honest, you need more looking after than a kid! How am I going to pay Siriol out for informing, or do anything else, if you're going to carry on like this?"

"You sound just like your dad," Milda said coldly. "Let me tell you, those oysters were a bargain at two silver, and you ought to be grateful."

"Two *silver*!" Mitt raised both his chilblained hands to the blotchy ceiling. "That's no bargain. That's daylight robbery, that is!"

Mitt and Milda—and the ants—had oysters for supper and for breakfast, and after that they both felt unwell, although the ants seemed as lively as ever. Ham kindly helped Mitt throw the rest of the tub into the harbor.

"And she went and paid two silver for them!" Mitt groaned.

"Don't be too hard on her. She's used to better things," Ham said. "She's a lovely good woman, she is."

Mitt stared at him. "If I didn't feel sick as a dog already," he said, "I would after I heard you say that!" And he went back upstairs, muttering, "Lovely good woman!" to himself in the greatest disgust. Of course he knew his mother was still young and pretty, in spite of that hateful crease on her face where her dimple should have been, and he knew she was not like those other ladies in the tenement who were always down on the waterfront, making up to the sailors whenever a ship came in, but for Ham to say *that*! Mitt had never noticed that Ham deeply admired Milda. Ham was too slow and shy to let Milda know it. And Mitt's feeling was that all women were born stupid and grew worse.

Alda, Siriol's wife, was the worst of the lot. Mitt supposed he should be thankful that his mother did not spend all her money on arris, the way Alda did. Alda was usually too drunk to sell the fish Siriol, Ham, and Mitt had caught. She sat on a barrel at the corner of the stall, while Lydda stood dumbly behind the heaps of fish, letting people have them too cheap. It pained Mitt to his soul. After all their trouble, out half the night pulling in fish in the drizzling rain, a rich merchant's housekeeper or a mincing man from the Palace had only to appear and point to a pile of sweet whitebait, and Lydda would humbly halve the price. It was not fair. The ones who could afford to pay the full price always got it cheap. But that was Holand all over.

At length, Lydda's spineless meekness was more than Mitt could bear. If the fish was to go cheap, he felt it should go cheap to the right people. He elbowed Lydda aside and tried selling the fish himself.

"Hadd, Hadd, haddock!" he shouted. "Fit for an earl, and dirt cheap, too!" When people stopped and stared, Mitt took up a haddock and waved it about. "Hadd," he said, "ock. Come on. He won't eat you. You eat *him*." He picked up an eel in the other hand. "And here's an earl—I mean a Harl—I mean an eel—for sale. Who wants a nice fresh Harl for supper?" It was great fun, and it sold a lot of fish.

After that Mitt always sold the fish. Lydda weighed and wrapped it, while her mother sat on her tub chuckling at Mitt and breathing arris fumes over the customers. Mitt was often very tired. His hands were chapped and covered with little cuts from the fish scales, winter and summer, but it was worth it, just to be able to shout rude things about Hadd.

"You want to watch it, Mitt," Siriol said whenever he heard Mitt's sales talk. But he let Mitt go on. After all, there was always a laughing crowd round the stall, buying fish. Even the Palace lackeys sniggered as they bought.

Then one day, as soon as *Flower of Holand* was out of the harbor and no one could overhear, Siriol amazed Mitt by asking him if he wanted to join the Free Holanders.

"I'll have to think," Mitt said. And he missed selling the fish that next morning, in order to hurry home and ask Milda what he ought to do, before she went to work. "I can't join, can I?" he said. "Not after what they did to Dad?"

But Milda went dancing round the room, her skirts held out and her earrings swinging, and her dimple deep and clear. "This is your chance!" she said. "Don't you see, Mitt? This is your chance to get back at them at last!"

"Oh yes," said Mitt. "I suppose it is and all."

So Mitt became a Free Holander, and great fun it was, too. At first it was simply the great fun of being in the secret, with, behind that, the further secret that he was only in it to get revenge for his father. Mitt grinned to himself at both secrets all through long, boring watches when he was alone at *Flower of Holand*'s tiller, and the stars wheeling overhead seemed to glimmer with sheer glee.

"Ah, shut up, he's useful!" Siriol said to Ham when Ham protested. "Who's going to bother with a lad who looks just like all the other kids? People think boys don't count. Look at the way he gets away with selling fish. He's safer than what we are."

Taking messages for the Free Holanders was pure bliss to Mitt. He reveled in going unnoticed through the crowded streets. It was good to be small and ordinary-looking, so that he could get the better of Harchad's soldiers and spies. He would memorize the message carefully and slip off after selling the fish, mingle with the crowd in this street, watch a fight in that alley, loiter round the barracks, joking with the soldiers, and still go unsuspected. He was Mitt of the free soul, who did not know the meaning of fear. And the greatest fun of all was when he chanced to be in a street while soldiers stopped off both ends of it and questioned everyone in it about their business.

Harchad ordered this done quite often, as much to keep people properly subdued as to catch revolutionaries. In a tense silence, broken only by the clopping of soldiers' boots, his men would go from person to person, searching bags and pockets and asking each one what he was doing in this street. Mitt delighted in inventing business. He loved giving his name. It was marvelous to have the commonest name in Holand. Mitt, with perfect truth, could call himself Alham Alhamsson, Ham Hamsson, Hammitt Hammittsson, and Mitt Mittsson, or any combination of those that he fancied. He enlivened boring hours of fishing by thinking up new ways to fool Harchad's men.

The only trouble about being a Free Holander was that Mitt did not understand what the meetings were about. Once the novelty wore off, they bored him to tears. They would sit in someone's shed or attic, often without a candle even, and Siriol would start by talking of tyranny and oppression. Then Dideo would say that the leaders of the future were coming from below. Below what? Mitt wondered. Someone would tell a long tale of Hadd's injustice, and someone else would whisper things about Harchad. And sooner or later Ham would be thumping the table and saying, "We look to the North, we do. Let the North show its hand!"

The first time Ham said this, Mitt felt a shiver of excitement. He knew Ham could be arrested for saying it. But Ham said it so often that Mitt lost interest. He found he was using the meetings to make up sleep in. He never got enough sleep in those days.

Mitt felt this would not do. If he was to get his revenge on the Free Holanders, he needed to know what they were up to. "What do they think they're doing?" he asked Milda. "It's all looking to the North, or whisper, whisper, about Harchad, or tyranny and that. What's it *about*?"

Milda looked nervously round the room. "Hush. They're getting at rebellion and uprising—I hope."

"They don't get at it very fast," Mitt said discontentedly. "There's no plans at all. I wish you could come to meetings and see if you could make some sense of them."

Milda laughed. "I might—I bet they wouldn't have me, though."

When Milda laughed, the crease on her face gave way to a dimple again. It was a thing Mitt always tried to encourage if he could. So he said, "I bet they would have you. You could stir them up a bit and get them to come out with something. I'm sick of old tyranny and the rest!" And since this made Milda smile broadly, Mitt did his best to keep her smiling. "Tell you what," he said. "While I'm getting back at them for informing, I'd like to get back at old Hadd, too. I'd like to give him what for, because of him trampling you underfoot all these years."

"What a boy you are!" said Milda. "You don't know what fear is, do you?"

After that, it was understood between Mitt and Milda that the mission of Mitt's life was a double one. He was to break the Free Holanders and rid the world of Earl Hadd. Mitt was sure he could do it. So was Milda.

Milda joined the Free Holanders, too. Mitt was delighted. He had high hopes of it. Milda came to meetings, and she talked as eloquently as anyone there. She loved to talk. She loved leaning forward over the secretive night-light and seeing everyone's listening face shadowy and attentive. But the sole result was that Milda became as ardent a freedom fighter as anyone there. She talked revolution to Mitt whenever he was at home.

"Flaming Ammet!" Mitt said disgustedly. "It's like being at a meeting all the time now!"

All the same, Milda's talk did make things clearer to Mitt. He was soon able to talk of oppression and uprising, tyranny and leadership from below, and feel he knew what it meant. And when he had leisure to think—which he sometimes did while *Flower of Holand* ploshed her sturdy way to the fishing grounds—he decided that what it amounted to was that there were two parts to Dalemark: the North, where people were mysteriously free and happy, and the South, where the earls and the rich people were free and happy enough, but where they made darned sure that ordinary people like Mitt and Milda were as unhappy as possible.

Right, Mitt said to himself. I reckon that sums it up. Now let's get busy and *do* something about it.

But the Free Holanders seemed simply content to talk, and Mitt became increasingly annoyed by them. He was very pleased when another secret society actually killed four of Harchad's spies. Siriol was not. He told Mitt, with a glum sort of gladness, that things would be very much worse now. And they were.

Harchad imposed a curfew. Anyone found in the streets after dark was marched away and never seen again. Siriol forbade Mitt to carry messages during that time. Mitt did not quite understand why he should not.

Then a thief on the waterfront tried to rob a man. He knocked the man down and was taking his money when he found a gold button with the wheatsheaf crest of Holand on it, hidden in the man's coat. The thief knew it was the badge Harchad gave all his spies, and he was so frightened that he jumped into the harbor and was drowned. Mitt did not understand this story at all.

"Well, if you don't, I'm not telling you," was all Siriol would say.

Then Earl Hadd quarreled with four other earls at once. Everyone in Holand groaned. Much as they detested Hadd, they almost admired him for being so very quarrelsome. "Fallen out with Earl Henda again, has he?" the women in Milda's sewing shop would say. "Honestly, I never knew anyone like him!" This time, however, Hadd fell out not only with Henda, but with the earls of Canderack, Waywold, and Dermath, too. And so powerful were these earls, and owned so much of South Dalemark between them, that there was some doubt in Holand whether Hadd could hold his own against them all.

"Bitten off more than he can chew this time for sure, the old sinner," Dideo said to Mitt. "Maybe this is where the Free Holanders get their chance."

Mitt hoped so. But Harl, Hadd's eldest son, managed to put himself into Hadd's good books by suggesting a way to deal with the four earls. Harl, fat and indolent though he was, could sometimes be seen with his brother Navis and a crowd of beaters, servants, and dogs, walking over the Flate and shooting birds with a long silver-inlaid fowling piece. Harl was allowed to use a gun, being an earl's son. No one else was, apart from lords and hearthmen, because there had been so many uprisings in the South. Big ships carried cannon, as a protection against the ships of the North, but guns were otherwise banned. But, said Harl, why not give all the soldiers guns as well? That would make the four earls think twice before attacking Holand.

Hadd agreed that it would. And that put paid to the hopes of Mitt and the Free Holanders. Up went rents and taxes and harbor dues. The people of Holand admitted grudgingly that Hadd was up to everything, even while they groaned.

"It's not right," said Ham. "Give Harchad's men guns and they'll be ten times worse than they are now. But you have to admire Hadd. Fair play."

But Hadd took other precautions, too. The Earl of Canderack, since most of the coast north of Holand was his, owned a fair-size fleet he could send against Holand if necessary. Holand also had its fleet. But to be on the safe side, Hadd betrothed his granddaughter Hildrida to the Lord of the Holy Islands, north of Canderack. The ships of the Holy Islands were famous. As Siriol remarked to Ham, the Holy Islands fleet was probably the main reason why the North had not long since conquered the South and brought freedom to everyone. Milda, as she sewed with three other women at a great bedspread to be covered with blue and gold roses, thought of it from another point of view. One of the women said that Lithar, Lord of the Holy Islands, was twenty years old. And, another added, Hildrida Navisdaughter could only be about nine.

Milda remembered she had once been interested in Navis and his family. "Then in that case I don't think it's fair at all!" she said warmly.

# 4

IT DID NOT SEEM fair to Hildrida Navisdaughter either. She thought at first she was in trouble. She and her brother, Ynen, had gone sailing. They had been tired of being told they were too young to go out in a boat alone and of being taken tamely up and down the coast by the sailors the Earl employed to sail his family. Ynen had wanted to sail a boat himself. So they slipped away and borrowed their cousins' yacht. It had been splendid fun, and very frightening, too. Ynen had nearly laid the boat on her side, just outside the West Pool, before he got used to the wind. And they had twice found themselves nearly aground in the shoals beyond. But they had managed. They had brought the yacht back and not even bumped the jetty.

Then, as soon as she reached the Palace, Hildy was told her father wanted to see her. Naturally she thought he had found out about the sailing.

Too bad for him! Hildrida thought, while she was having a good dress put on and her windblown black hair brushed. I shall be very angry. I shall say we're never allowed to do *anything*. I shall say it's *my* fault, and I shan't let him send for Ynen. And I'll tell him that it doesn't matter whether we drown or not. It's not as if we were important.

The lady-in-waiting who led Hildrida by her hand through the lofty corridors to Navis's rooms rather thought Hildrida must have found out what was in store for her. She had never seen her so white and stormy. The lady-in-waiting was glad she was not in Navis's shoes.

Navis was well aware that his daughter had an awkward personality. He had taken refuge in a book. When Hildy was shown in, she found him sitting on the window seat, with his calm profile outlined against the Flate beyond the window, and his eyes on a song by the Adon. She was exasperated. The ladies-in-waiting told her that Navis was still grieving for her dead mother, but Hildy found that hard to believe. To her mind, Navis was the coldest and laziest person she knew.

"I'm here," she said piercingly, to stir him up a bit. "And I'm not sorry."

Navis winced a little and kept his eyes studiously on his book. But like the lady-in-waiting, he assumed that Hildrida had already heard about her betrothal, and he was heartily relieved. "Then, if you're not sorry, I suppose you're glad," he said. "Whoever told you has saved me a great deal of trouble. You may run away and boast now if you wish."

Hildy was taken aback at not being scolded. But it seemed to her that her father was washing his hands of her, just as he always did, and she wanted to do battle with him instead. "I never boast," she said. "But I could. We didn't sink her."

Navis was puzzled enough to take his eyes off his book and look at Hildy. "What are you talking about?"

"What did you send for me for?" Hildrida countered.

"Why, to tell you that you've just been betrothed to the Lord of the Holy Islands," said her father. "What did you think it was for?"

"Betrothed?" said Hildy. "Without asking *me*!" It was such a bombshell that, for the moment, she clean forgot she had been sailing. "Why wasn't I *told*?"

Navis found himself facing a blazing white daughter, out in the open, as it were, without a book to hide behind. "I am telling you," he said, and hastily picked up his book again.

"When it's too late!" Hildrida said, before he could find his place again. "When it's done. You might have asked me if I minded, even if I'm not important. I'm a person, too."

"Most people are," Navis said, rather desperately scanning his page. He wished he had not chosen to read the Adon. The Adon said things like "Truth is the fire that fetches thunder," which sounded unpleasantly like a description of Hildrida. "And you are very important now," he added. "You're forming an alliance with Lithar for us."

"What's Lithar like? How old is he?" Hildrida demanded.

Navis found his place and put his finger on it. "I've only met him once." It was hard to know what else to say. "He's only a young man—twenty or so."

"Only—!" Words nearly failed Hildy. "I'm not going to be betrothed to an old man like that! I'm too young. *And* I've never met him!"

Navis hastily got his book in front of his face again. "Time will cure both those objections."

"No, it won't!" stormed Hildrida. "And if you go on reading, I'll—I'll hit you and then tear that book up!"

Realizing that strong measures were necessary, Navis laid his book down. "Now listen, Hildy. This is something that happens to all our family. Your cousin Harilla is being betrothed to the Lord of Mark, and what's her name—Harchad's daughter—to one of the—"

Hildy interrupted with a screech. Her father could call her Hildy all he liked—usually only Ynen did—but the thought of being lumped in with the dreadful girl cousins was too much for her. "Just you unbetroth me!" she said. "And do it at once, or you'll be sorry!"

"You know I can't," said her father. "It's your grandfather's doing, not mine."

"Then he'll be sorry, too!" Hildy proclaimed, and swept to the door.

Navis called after her. It was easier talking to her back. "Hildrida! Don't make an undignified scene, there's a good girl. It won't do any good. I advise you to go to the library instead and read about the Holy Islands. You'll find they're rather interesting."

Hildy paused, with her hand on the doorknob. Islands were places surrounded by water, weren't they? Perhaps she could turn this bombshell to some advantage at least. "I ought to learn to sail, oughtn't I, if I'm going to the Holy Islands?" she said.

"Yes, I suppose so," Navis said. Rather relieved to find her no longer raging, he added consolingly, "But you won't be going for some years yet."

"Then I've got time to learn," said Hildy. "If I promise not to make a fuss, will you get me a boat of my own?"

"Er—if you like," said Navis.

"I do like. But you must give the boat to Ynen, too, because he never gets anything," said Hildy. "Or I shall make a fuss to Grandfather and all over the Palace."

By this time Navis's one desire was to be left in peace with his book again. "Yes, yes," he said. "If you run away like a good girl and don't make a scene, you and Ynen shall have the best boat money can buy. Will that do for you?"

"Yes, thank you, Father," Hildy said, primly and bitterly, and swept out.

The Palace people kept out of her way. Even her cousins, when they saw Hildrida marching, white, upright, and staring like a mask out of the Sea Festival, knew better than to cross her path. They all knew Hildrida had inherited her temper from Grandfather Hadd himself. Only

Ynen dared go near her, and he dared not say a word. Hildy swept to her own room. There she collected all the ornaments, from the gilded clock to the gold-painted chamber pot, put them in a heap on the floor, and broke them with the poker. Ynen crouched on the window seat, wincing at the carnage. He still dared not say a word when Hildy flung aside the poker, somewhat bent, and went to sit by her dressing table, where she stared long and earnestly at the thin white face in the mirror. She had left the mirror unsmashed on purpose.

"I am a person," she said at last. "Aren't I?"

"Yes," said Ynen. "What happened, Hildy?"

"And not a Thing," said Hildy. "What's happened is I'm betrothed. And nobody told me, just like a Thing. Do you think I should sit quiet and not mind and *be* a Thing? The girl cousins are betrothed, too."

"They'll make a fuss," Ynen predicted. "Have you been forbidden to go sailing?"

"No," said Hildy. "We're getting a boat out of it. You have to get between the islands somehow. I think I shall go to the library now." And she got up and went. Ynen went with her. He was still mystified, but he was used to that. He knew he would have to be very patient and tactful if he was to hear more about this promised boat.

The library was very tall and built of speckled marble, with a domed window in its high ceiling. Hildrida, looking very small, followed by the even smaller Ynen, marched across to the librarian. "Give me all the books you have on the Holy Islands," she said.

Rather astonished, the librarian went away obediently. He returned shortly with one big old volume and one small newish one. "Here we are. Not too much, I'm afraid. I advise you to take the little book. It's easy, and it has pictures."

Hildrida gave him a scathing look and took the big book. She marched to the nearest table and opened it. Rather helplessly, the librarian gave Ynen the small book and left them to it.

"This book is all pictures," Ynen said dolefully. "Read me yours."

"Quiet," Hildy said severely. "I'm concentrating." But she did not like to think of Ynen sitting humbly there with nothing to do, and, besides, the book was the difficult, old kind that is easier to read aloud. So she read, " 'Indeed men say that the Holy Isles been of all places in the South marks the sole place where enchantment abides.' "

"I like that," said Ynen. "What are marks?"

"The old name for earldoms. Quiet. 'Of legends that do there pertain, there is said by some to be a certain enchanted Bull which appears, no man can say how, now on one isle, now upon another. By some it is said that this Beast may grant wishes, and certainly to see it is deemed by all a great good fortune. Further, there may be heard in clear weather a strange piping among the islands, most piercing and pleasant to hear, though no piper can be seen, and which goeth like the Bull from island to island. This has been heard by many, and many good ships been foundered following the sound. Withal come the horses of the sea, and, it is said, at times the Sea himself in the likeness of an old fellow of the Islands, who will oft speak fair with those that meet him, but oftentimes be rough and violent. For this reason, the men of the Islands count themselves holy and favored above others. And certainly the Holy Islands are a fair place, mild, fruitful, and full of fair havens.' "

"They sound wonderful," said Ynen. "I'd like to go there."

Hildy shut the book. "You shall," she said. "You can come with me when I go. I think I shan't make an undignified scene after all. I'm important. There's no magic Bulls in Mark, are there?"

"I didn't know there were any anywhere," said Ynen. "When are we getting our boat?"

"I don't know. But Father promised," said Hildy.

Later that day their cousin Harilla learned that she was betrothed to the Lord of Mark and lay on the stairs, drumming her heels and screaming, while everyone near ran for smelling salts and made a great to-do. Hildy managed to smile a little. It was a dry, stretched smile, but very dignified. And as, one by one, her four other girl cousins learned of their betrothals and promptly followed Harilla's example, Hildy's smile grew more and more dignified. She was still not exactly glad to be betrothed, but she did almost feel it was worth it when the yacht *Wind's Road* was towed into the West Pool.

Navis kept his promise lavishly. He had heard of the smashed ornaments, of course, but knowing Hildrida's temper, he felt she had shown great self-control. *Wind's Road* was twice the size of the cousins' boat—Navis did not think his children were old enough to sail alone, so he provided space for a crew, as befitted the grandchildren of an earl—and she was sheer beauty, from the golden ears of wheat carved on her prow to the rosy apples decorating her stern. Her hull was blue, her cabin white and gold, and her canvas snowy. She carried two foresails, too, to Ynen's joy. In fact, Hildy felt that the look of pure bliss on Ynen's face almost made up for any number of betrothals.

# 5

THAT AUTUMN, when the Festival procession poured, scraping and banging and colorful, down to the harbor to drown Poor Old Ammet, it was guarded by soldiers with the new guns. Mitt did not like watching it. Each Festival brought back his nightmares about Canden falling to pieces in the doorway. But the tenement was so near the harbor that it was hard to avoid watching. This year Dideo came to lean out of the window between Mitt and Milda, with his netted eyes wistfully on those new guns.

"The stuff they use in those," he explained, "can blow a man up, used right. Years back I used to sail with a man who could get the stuff, and we went after fish with it. You might call it unfair to the fish, but I know to this day how to make a bomb. And I was thinking that a bomb in the midst of Old Ammet could rid the world of Hadd and give us uprising all over Holand in one moment."

Mitt and his mother exchanged a long, startled look over Dideo's gnarled hat. That was it! What an idea! They discussed it excitedly as soon as the procession was over and Dideo gone.

"If you were to get a bomb and throw it at old Haddock—you *do* throw bombs, do you?" said Milda. "You could shout out that Dideo and Siriol set you on."

"But I might not be heard," said Mitt. "No—I'd have to get myself taken. Then when Harchad comes to ask questions, I tell him the Free Holanders set me on to do it. But how can we get hold of some of that gun stuff?"

"We'll get some," said Milda. "We'll think of a way. But you'll have to do it before you're old enough to hang. I couldn't bear to think of you taken and hanged!" She was so excited that she went out and spent the rest of her wages on fruit and sweets to celebrate.

Mitt looked at the bundles of toffee apples as dourly as Siriol. He sighed. He saw he would have to put off throwing any kind of bomb until he had earned enough money to rent another farm for Milda. She would certainly starve if he was arrested and she left to manage all by herself. He thought he might have to wait until he was at least as old as Dideo.

It did not happen that way. A week later Mitt came home from selling fish, smelly, slimy, and pinched with cold. He wanted only to go to bed. But to his annoyance, his mother was entertaining a visitor. The visitor was a square, sober-looking man, with an air that reminded Mitt vaguely of something—or someone—else. He was wearing much more respectable clothes than most people wore on the waterfront, and to Mitt's further annoyance, Milda had squandered her money this week on a bottle of Canderack wine for this visitor. Mitt stood in the doorway glowering at him.

"Oh, Mitt!" Milda said happily. She was looking very pretty, and the dimple was back in her face. "You remember Canden?" Mitt did remember Canden—too well. He was still having nightmares about him after the Festival. He had to hold hard to the doorpost when he heard the name. Milda, quite unaware how Mitt was feeling, said, "Well, this is Canden's brother, Hobin, all the way from Waywold. My son, Mitt, Hobin."

The visitor smiled and came forward, holding out a square, useful-looking hand. Mitt shuddered, clenched his teeth, and put out his own fishy hand. "I'm all covered with fish," he said, hoping the visitor would not like to touch him.

But the warm, square hand seized his and shook it. "Oh, I know what it's like to come in dirty from work," Hobin said. "I'm a gunsmith myself, and sometimes I think I'll never get the black off. You go and wash and don't mind me."

Mitt smiled shakenly. He realized Canden's brother was a very nice man. But that did not alter the fact that he had a nightmare for a brother. Mitt went over to the bucket in the corner to wash, hoping that Hobin would go back to Waywold at once and never be seen in Holand again.

That hope went almost immediately. "Yes, I've got a tidy little house, up in Flate Street," he heard Hobin telling Milda. "Workshop below, plenty of room to live upstairs. Earl Hadd's done me proud."

Mitt realized that Hobin had come to live in Holand. He was so dismayed that he called out, "And who did Earl Hadd turn out of there, in order to do you proud?"

"Oh, Mitt!" said Milda. "You mustn't mind him," she told Hobin. "He's a real free soul, Mitt is."

Mitt was furious. She had no right to tell a stranger private things like that. "Yes," he said. "Bit poor and common for you here, aren't we?" And, to make sure that Hobin would not want to visit them again, he wandered round the room swearing as hard as he could. He could tell that worried Hobin. He kept giving Mitt sober, concerned looks. It worried Milda, too. She apologized for Mitt repeatedly, which made Mitt angrier than ever. When Hobin at last put out his hand to say good-bye, Mitt turned his back and pretended not to see it.

"You didn't have to be like that, Mitt!" Milda said reproachfully when Hobin had gone. "Didn't you understand? He's a gunsmith! And you can see he was fond of Canden. If I can only get him to join the Free Holanders, then we can have that bomb—or a gun would be better. You could shoot Hadd from this very window, then!"

Mitt only grunted. He knew he would rather take a gun off a soldier in the open street than get one from Canden's brother.

To Mitt's acute misery, Hobin called again, repeatedly. It took months of visits before Mitt could forget Hobin had a brother who fell to pieces in his nightmares. When he did, he found he quite liked Hobin. Meanwhile, Hobin was firmly but kindly resisting all Milda's persuasions to become a freedom fighter. He agreed that the earls made life needlessly hard. He agreed that things were bad in Holand. He grumbled at taxes like everyone else. But he did not hold with freedom fighting, he said. He called Canden—sadly and a little severely—a boy who played with fire, and when Milda talked eagerly of injustices, he smiled and said it depended on her circumstances. After a while he took to scolding her kindly for buying him wine she could not afford.

Ham grew increasingly gloomy over that winter. Mitt could not understand why, until the spring, when *Flower of Holand* was gliding out on the tide one morning.

Siriol said, "Your ma going to marry that Hobin?"

"*No!*" Mitt said indignantly.

"Good for the cause when she does," Siriol said.

Ham sighed. "Good for her, too," he said nobly. "Hobin's a good man."

Mitt was furious. And when Siriol and Ham proved right, it made another grudge he bore them. Milda did marry Hobin. And all through the wedding Mitt was muttering to himself that he would get Siriol and Ham for this if it was the last thing he did. Probably will be, too, he thought. Since last Festival, he had been living as if there was nothing to look forward to, beyond the moment he somehow planted a bomb under Earl Hadd. The only good thing he could see in this wedding was that he would be living in reach of a store of gunpowder.

Milda and Mitt moved into the upper part of the house in Flate Street, some way west of the waterfront. It was a good house, though small and peeling. It even had a yard with a mangle in it, and a target on its dingy brick wall where, to Mitt's interest, Hobin tested the guns he made. Mitt had his own room for the first time for years, and though he was far too proud to admit it, very lonely he was in it, too. Milda gave up her sewing and bustled round their four upstairs rooms, singing and laughing, and the crease of worry seemed to have left her face for good. It saddened Mitt. He had only been able to send that crease away from time to time, yet Hobin had banished it forever. Hobin offered to send Mitt to school, but Mitt preferred to go on working. The Free Holanders would not find much use for a boy who was tied up at lessons all day. And besides, Mitt felt that freedom fighting was almost the only tie left between himself and Milda.

It was then that Hobin showed a surprising strictness. "You're a fool, Mitt," he said. "You've got a brain and you ought to learn to use it, not waste your time talking freedom with a bunch of boatmen who don't know what the word means. You'll wish you'd done otherwise when you grow to be a man."

This kind of argument is always irritating. Mitt twisted about and did not answer. He wanted to say he was not going to grow up—he was going to kill Hadd instead—but with Hobin's sober blue eyes fixed on him, he did not like to.

"Well, if you *must* work," said Hobin, "you can do one job and one only. You can learn my trade from me, or Siriol's from him, or you can sell fish if you want. But you do no more than one."

Mitt passionately wanted to go on selling fish. He enjoyed shouting out rude things about Hadd even more than he loved fooling Harchad's soldiers. Fishing—well, he was glad of any excuse to stop doing that. On the other hand, he knew that he would have far more chance of getting his hands on some gunpowder if he was Hobin's apprentice. He shifted about, kept his eyes on the floor, and finally swallowed his annoyance enough to say grudgingly, "I'll learn your trade, then."

"You did quite right, Mitt," Milda said, and hugged him delightedly. That consoled Mitt somewhat.

But it was unexpectedly awkward when Hobin went with Mitt to Siriol's house to explain to Siriol and buy out the remainder of Mitt's apprenticeship. Alda threw both arms round Mitt and gave him an arris-scented kiss on both cheeks. Slow tears trickled down Lydda's face. "I shall miss you on the stall, Mitt," she said. Mitt was prepared for this.

But what he had not been prepared for was the look of disappointment and resignation on Siriol's face.

"I should have thought of this," Siriol said, and he got out the arris bottle and poured everyone a glass, by which Mitt knew that this was a special occasion. "Yes, I should have thought," Siriol said when they were all sitting stiffly round the table. "You got right on your side, Hobin, and Mitt's worth a better trade than fishing. But it's not easy for me—having no son of my own."

Hobin looked uncomfortable. Lydda and Alda cried. Mitt sat squirming on his stool. "It made me feel all slimy, sort of," he told Milda afterward. "As if I was covered in fish juice. *And* I can't abide the taste of arris."

Siriol fetched the crumpled paper that Milda had signed on Mitt's behalf nearly two years back. At first he refused to take any money for it. Hobin insisted. Everything got more and more awkward, until Ham was called in to witness the bargain. Ham clapped Hobin on the shoulder, and wrung Mitt's hand until Mitt wondered if he would have the use of it again, and was generally so cheerful and so pleased for Mitt that all the awkwardness vanished. Everyone had another glass of arris—Mitt poured his secretly into Alda's glass—and then he and Hobin came away.

"But I feel bad, I do, really," Mitt told Milda. "As if I owe it them to tell them we need the gunpowder."

"Well, why don't you tell them?" Milda said. "Dideo knows how to make a bomb. It wouldn't do any harm to get them to help."

"You mean, bring the Free Holanders into it, really?" Mitt said. It seemed a very good idea.

Unfortunately Hobin came in at that moment and caught the words *Free Holanders*. Again he showed surprising strictness. "I'm not having freedom fighting talk in this house," he said. "Silly cloak-and-dagger stuff! And don't get the idea I'm scared of Harchad either. He knows I can go back to Waywold if I want. What gets me is the way those boatmen don't grow up. It's like a game to them, just like it was to Canden. Nobody's playing that silly game in my house!"

Mitt and Milda could only continue their talk in utmost secrecy, either in snatched moments or when Hobin was out at the Gunsmiths' Guild. The upshot of their planning was that Mitt lied himself blue in the face to Hobin and managed to attend the next meeting of the Free Holanders. There he laid before them his suggestion: that he steal enough gunpowder for a bomb and plant it under Hadd when he next carried Old Ammet down to the harbor to drown.

The suggestion made a startled hush. Ham broke it by saying reproachfully, "It wasn't because of the gunpowder I was glad for you, Mitt. I hope you don't think that."

"Funny. I made sure you was expecting it," said Mitt, who could seldom resist teasing Ham.

"Now, Mitt—" Ham began.

"Hush," said Siriol. "Learn to take a joke, Ham. Mitt, that's a risk. Horrible risk. You'd get taken."

This was fighting talk from Siriol. He was really considering the idea. Highly delighted, Mitt made haste to assure Siriol that he had no intention of being taken. "Suppose I was dressed up in red and yellow, like the Palace boys. They'd not know who I was until it was too late. I can run."

"I know you can run," said Siriol. "Your ma never agrees, does she?"

"Ask her," said Mitt. "Only not when Hobin's there. She can sew the clothes if we can get her the stuff."

Siriol pondered, long and deep.

"Mitt looks just like any other lad I ever saw," Dideo said persuasively. "Half the time I don't recognize him myself. And I would love to get making a bomb." Indeed, all the other Free Holanders were loving the thought, too. They leaned forward, murmuring eagerly across the night-light.

"Boom!" said someone. "Up goes Hadd. Lovely!"

"And all Holand rises to us!" said someone else. "He can do it, Siriol."

"Quiet!" said Siriol. "I know he can do it. But he has to get away after. This is going to take careful planning."

Mitt scampered home to Flate Street, wholly delighted. "We did it!" he whispered to Milda when she met him anxiously on the stairs. "We're on!"

"And you're not afraid at all?" Milda whispered, wonderingly.

"Not a bit," said Mitt. And it was true. He was looking forward to it. He felt dedicated.

The Free Holanders began to lay their plans, carefully and thoroughly as Siriol did everything. Mitt and Milda laid theirs. And all of them very soon realized that it would not be next Festival that Mitt planted his bomb. As Siriol said, they would need to study the road the procession took, and the way the soldiers were placed, to find out where and when would be the safest time for Mitt. And he had to look into escape routes and possible hiding places for Mitt afterward.

As Mitt had no intention of escaping, he never attended when Siriol talked of things like this. But after the first week he spent as Hobin's apprentice, he knew that it would take him years, literally, to steal enough gunpowder to make Dideo a bomb. Hobin was only allowed enough gunpowder to test the guns he made. Harchad's arms inspectors called once a week to make sure there was no more. Sometimes they made surprise visits, to make doubly sure. They would weigh the powders and count the guns, and, unless their seal was on everything, Hobin was not allowed to work. They were a great annoyance to Mitt, though Hobin did not seem bothered by them. He would joke with them, almost as if they were friends.

Gunpowder, Mitt discovered, was made of three things, which Hobin mixed, very carefully, himself. One was charcoal, which Mitt never bothered with. Dideo could get that easily. But the sulfur and the saltpeter were, as far as Mitt knew, impossible to get any other way than by stealing them. Mitt supposed they must be made somehow, but he never found out how. They were delivered in sealed bags by the inspectors and locked away by Hobin. It was months before Mitt was allowed even to touch any. He had to spend his time instead melting lead and casting boring little bullets in a string of small sausage-shaped molds. And watching, watching.

Hobin himself was the other great drawback to Mitt's plans. He was such a careful man, and so patient. Mitt suspected that even without inspectors, Hobin would have kept all his things under lock and key anyway. And he was much in demand. There was scarcely an hour when there was not someone else in the workshop besides Mitt and Hobin. Troopers and captains came, bringing guns which had problems. Other gunsmiths came, to consult Hobin on difficult technical matters. Mitt discovered that Hobin had invented a way of making a gun shoot true, by putting a spiral groove up the inside of the barrel. That was why the bullets Mitt so boringly cast were pointed, and not round like the shot Harl used when he shot birds on the Flate. Twice Hobin was actually summoned to Harchad to be consulted. By the time Mitt had graduated to carving butts and even weighing a little powder, he had grasped that Hobin was the best gunsmith in South Dalemark. Mitt was quite proud, and glad on his mother's behalf. But it did mean he had chosen the very worst man to filch from. Hobin had a name for honesty. He was respected in the Guild. And for a long time Mitt dared not do anything but pretend he was honest, too.

Hobin was truly anxious for Mitt to learn, and to become what he called "a decent citizen." Mitt had to wear better clothes—which were certainly warmer in winter, but which he despised on principle. He had to wash when they came up from work. Once a week he was forced to wash all over in front of the fire, in spite of his conviction that washing took the strength out of you. And every evening Hobin produced a book. It was called *A Reader for the Poor*, and it bored Mitt to tears. "If you won't go to school, you must learn at home," Hobin said, and he made Mitt read a page aloud every night after supper.

Mitt's only wonder was that he did not die of boredom in the first year. It seemed to him that he only came alive when he began to be able, at last, to take Dideo tiny packets of sulfur and saltpeter. Then it was even better than running errands for the Free Holanders. Mitt would lie to Hobin, as he told Milda, like a fishmonger's scales, and slip off into the streets with his packet, knowing that if he was caught with it on him, there would be trouble indeed. It was a marvelous feeling of danger, and marvelous to know he was getting somewhere at last.

He did not get on very fast, either as a gunsmith or a thief. Hobin was a patient man, but he sometimes grew irritated with Mitt. Mitt's mind was wholly on filching powders. He did not intend to be a gunsmith, so he attended to Hobin as little as he attended to the plans Siriol insisted on making about a hiding place for him after his bomb was thrown. Meanwhile, Milda had a baby, and another the year after. Mitt was rather astonished to find himself with two sisters long before he had a bomb. They were rather a nuisance. They would cry, and they would cut teeth, and they would take up Milda's time when Mitt needed her. But they would not believe they were nuisances. Whenever Milda dumped a sister in Mitt's arms, the baby would start to laugh and gurgle, as if Mitt liked her.

Mitt started to grow then. That astonished him, too. He was used to being the smallest boy in the street. Now he was one of the bigger ones, with long, long, thin legs. The woman who had stolen the red and yellow cloth to make Mitt's bomb-throwing clothes from had to steal more, and Milda put off making them until she was sure Mitt would not grow out of them.

"All to the good," Siriol remarked. "If you keep on this way, you'll have changed so after a year's hiding that even Harchad's spies won't know you."

The trouble was that Mitt needed a lot to eat, and Hobin became increasingly hard up. Hadd put the rents up again all over Holand. His guns had done very little good. Every other earl in South Dalemark had hastened to get guns, too. Hadd was forced to bargain for peace, and bargains cost money. Hobin, Mitt was glad to see, grumbled just like everyone else. He led a petition from the Guild of Gunsmiths, asking to be allowed to raise the price of guns. Hadd refused.

"Now don't you think there's some use to freedom fighting?" Mitt asked him.

"It only makes things worse," said Hobin.

"No, see," Mitt said persuasively, "you could set all the earls fighting one another, then have an uprising, and the North would come and help us. They'd have to!"

"If the North did any such thing," said Hobin, "you'd find the earls would stop fighting one another and start on the North. And you'd find yourself on their side, Mitt. You couldn't help yourself. You're born a Southerner. The North knows that better than you do. It's history. It'll take more than an uprising to make things better in Holand."

"The trouble with you is you're so patient!" Mitt said.

In spite of his patience, Hobin began to look a little worn by springtime. There were the babies and Mitt to feed. And Milda was still rushing out and "just happening to see" expensive things, though these days it was mostly furniture. Hobin began to talk seriously of moving back to Waywold.

"We can't do that!" Mitt told Milda in a panic.

"I know. Not after I've trained you all these years," said Milda. "But he'd stay if only Hadd was gone. Run and catch Siriol." And she broke a whole bowl of eggs to give Mitt an excuse to go out.

Mitt was lucky enough to catch Siriol just as he was boarding *Flower of Holand*. Siriol stood on the quayside and thought so long that Mitt wondered whether to suggest he would miss the tide. "Ah," said Siriol. "Well. You better do it this autumn then."

"This autumn it is!" Mitt agreed, and the muscles at the back of his legs jumped with excitement. "And thank goodness! After three flaming years, I can't wait much longer!"

# PART TWO

# The Sea Festival

# 6

THERE WERE GREAT GALES that spring. The sea broke the dikes in two places, and even in the harbor, boats blew this way and that and masts snapped. Siriol could not put to sea for a fortnight, and few people in Holand went out much because the wind in the street filled your face with sand and salt until you could barely see. Mitt was kept very busy. The old Earl of the South Dales died, and all the earls of the South began to gather in Holand to invest the new Earl, as the custom was. People asked one another whether Hadd would manage to quarrel with them all or only half of them. Mitt thought Hadd must be determined to. Hobin was busy making and mending guns day and night. The Palace must have bristled with them. Mitt got little chance to look at any earls. He saw one windswept fine person, who looked as if he would very much rather have been indoors, but no one could tell Mitt if he was an earl or not.

"Down with him, anyway!" Mitt muttered, and hurried back indoors.

Then a strange boat was sighted, beyond the shoals, beating her way to the harbor. There was intense excitement. The boat was said to be a Northerner. Mitt could think of nothing else.

"We'd best settle this for you before you ruin any more bullets," Hobin said. He and Mitt put on pea jackets against the gale and went out to look, along with most of the rest of Holand.

The ship was wallowing in the great waves outside the harbor wall, black in the yellow stormy light. Though all her canvas was in and she was riding only on the rags of a storm sail, Mitt saw at once that she was indeed a Northerner. She had the square rigging which few ships in the South used these days. People round Mitt shook their heads and said it was daft to go out in this gale with a little square-rigger like that, but then Northmen were all daft. And it was clear the ship was in bad trouble. For some minutes Mitt doubted that she would make the harbor at all. Then she rounded the wall, and it was clear she would be safe.

The harbor was lined with soldiers to meet her. Behind them, a lot of ordinary people had come out with knives and stones. And Mitt watched with the most extraordinary mixed feelings. He was glad the ship was safe. But how *dared* they! How dared they put into Holand harbor like this! The ship wallowed her waterlogged way to the quayside. When some of the sailors on board saw the soldiers waiting, they dived into the harbor rather than be caught.

"What cowards!" he said to Hobin.

"They haven't a chance, anyway," said Hobin. "Poor devils."

The Northmen who stayed on board were taken prisoner as soon as soldiers could jump onto the ship. The crowd hid most of it from Mitt. But he had a glimpse of them being taken uphill to the Palace, a bunch of soaking, draggled fellows with fair hair and brown faces, who all had a thicker, healthier look than anyone in Holand, even though they were plainly almost too exhausted to realize what had happened to them. Mitt's shaken thought was that they looked like people. He had expected them to look mysteriously free. But they held their heads low and shuffled along, just like anyone else taken by Harchad's men.

Their arrival caused quite as much excitement up at the Palace. Everyone had been in a ferment there, anyway, because of the investment of the new Earl. Feasts and fuss and arrangements had gone on for a week now. All the children were bundled out of the way and ordered to be seen and not heard—and not seen unless asked for. There was much excited peeping and giggling. To Hildy's scorn, all the girl cousins decided that the new Earl of the South Dales was *terribly handsome* and spied on him whenever they could. They all wished they had been betrothed to him and not to whomever they *were* betrothed to. Hildy herself thought Tholian looked rather unkind. She made the mistake of telling Harilla so.

"All right, Lady Be Different!" said Harilla. "I'm not telling you my spyhole for that. Go and find your own."

Hildy did not mind. Ynen and she were better than any of them at finding places where they could see what was going on. They watched a great deal of the feasting and music, until it was obvious that the Lord of the Holy Islands was not going to arrive.

"Why not?" Hildy wondered.

"I don't think he's anyone's hearthman," said Ynen. "His job is to keep the North's fleet out."

Then it was learned that one Northern ship at least had slipped through. Half the earls were convinced that it was the first of an invasion. The messages, the orders, and the bustling about made Hildy think of an ants' nest stirred with a stick, and there were more still when the soaking prisoners were marched in. The prisoners were questioned. It came out that two of them were nobly born—and not only that, they were the sons of the Earl of Hannart himself. The excitement was feverish. The Earl of Hannart was a wanted man in the South. Ynen reported to Hildy that when he was a young man, the Earl of Hannart had come South and taken part in the great rebellion, just as if he were a common revolutionary.

The fate of the Northmen was no longer in doubt. They were all put on trial for their lives.

Now it is a fact that if you are brought up to expect something, you expect it. Hildy and Ynen were used to people being tried and hanged almost daily. It did not worry them particularly that the Northmen were going to be hanged. Most of the Palace people said they had asked for it by putting into Holand anyway. But Hildy and Ynen were very anxious to catch a glimpse of the Earl of Hannart's sons while they were still alive to be seen. It was not easy to do. Hadd was afraid that some of the freedom fighters in Holand might attempt to set the Northerners free, and nobody was allowed near them who had no business to be. But on the last day of the trial Hildy and Ynen managed to stand in an archway near where the younger son was being kept prisoner.

They saw soldiers come out. They saw their uncle Harchad in the midst of them, and with him the Earl's son. When they came level with the archway, Hildy was astonished to see that the Earl's son was quite young—no older than Harchad's own son—just a big boy, really. And when they were beside the archway, Harchad suddenly turned and kicked the Earl's son. Instead of glaring or swearing at Harchad, as Hildy herself or any of the cousins would have done, the boy cringed away and put one arm over his head. "Don't!" he said. "Not anymore!"

Hildy stared after the soldiers as they marched the prisoner away to the courtroom. She had sometimes seen revolutionaries cringe like that. She had thought that was the way common people behaved. But that an Earl's son should be brought to behave like that shook her to the core.

"I wonder," she said. "Is Uncle Harchad very cruel, do you think?"

"Of course he is," said Ynen. "Didn't you know?" And he began telling her some of the things he had heard from the boy cousins.

Hildy stared at him. Even though she realized Ynen was quite as shaken as she was, some of the things he said made her feel so sick and cold that she had to run at him with both arms stretched out and bang him against the side of the archway to shut him up. "Oh be quiet! Don't you *mind*!"

"Of course I mind," said Ynen. "But what can I do?"

The prisoners were hanged the following day. Hadd gave permission for the Palace children to watch if they wanted. Ynen said he did not want to. Hildy was trying to decide whether, after what she had seen, she wanted to or not when a message came from Navis. He forbade Hildy and Ynen to watch. Hildy found she was relieved.

But in some ways a dreadful thing you do not see is more dreadful. Hildy tried not to watch the clock, but she knew the exact moment when the executions started. When a groaning sort of cheer came up out of the courtyard, Ynen covered his ears. What made it seem all the more dreadful was that their cousin Irana was carried out screaming, their cousin Harilla actually fainted, and all the rest, boys and girls alike, were sick as dogs.

"It *must* have been horrible!" Hildy said, quite awed.

After that neither she nor Ynen went near their uncle Harchad if they could help it.

The gales dropped, and the earls all went home. Hildy's cousin Irana Harchadsdaughter ran feverishly from window to window trying to get a last glimpse of the Earl of the South Dales.

This sentimental behavior so disgusted Hildy that she said, "I don't know why you carry on like that. He hasn't even looked at you. And I bet he's twice as cruel as your father is. His eyes are even meaner."

Irana burst into tears. Hildy laughed and went out for the first sail of the year in the yacht *Wind's Road*. But Irana went weeping to her cousin Harilla and told her how beastly Hildy had been.

"She said that, did she?" said Harilla. "Right. It's time someone taught Lady Superior a lesson. Come with me to Grandfather. I bet he doesn't know she's gone out sailing."

Hadd did not. He was in a very bad temper, anyhow, having quarreled furiously with Earl Henda. And the coming of the ship from the North had brought home to him just how important it was to have an alliance with the Lord of the Holy Islands. The thought that this alliance was at that very moment in danger of drowning in a squall was almost too much for him. He was so angry that Harilla was almost sorry she had gone to him. She got her face slapped, as if it was her fault. Then Navis was summoned. Hadd raged at him for half an hour. And when Hildy came in, she found herself in the worst trouble of her life. She was utterly forbidden ever to go sailing again, in any kind of boat whatsoever.

For three days after that, even Ynen hardly dared go near Hildy. She stole a fur rug from her aunt and sat wrapped in it, up on the leads of the roof, looking out over the lovely whelming sea, streaked gray, green-blue, and yellow where the sandbanks were, too angry even to cry. It's just the alliance. He doesn't care about *me*, she thought. Then, after two days, she remembered she would be able to sail once she got to the Holy Islands. I wish I could go now, she thought. Away from this horrible cruel place. She spent the rest of the day making a loving drawing of *Wind's Road*. When it was finished, she cut it carefully in half and labeled one half "Ynen" and the other "Hildrida." Then she crossed out "Hildrida" and wrote "Ynen" on that half, too. After that, she came down from the leads and handed both halves to Ynen.

"There you are. She's all yours now."

Ynen sat holding both halves of the drawing. He was glad, but it seemed a shame. It was the high price Hildy had to pay for being important. Ynen reflected that this autumn he would at last be old enough to take part in the Sea Festival. He swore to himself that if he died in the attempt, he would catch his grandfather one on the nose with a rattle. Hadd deserved it if ever anyone did. Then he thought about the Earl of Hannart's sons and hoped Uncle Harchad would be in the procession, too. He would catch a whopper.

Down in Holand, they were still talking about the Northmen. As Milda said, it seemed hard to hang them when they had only come in for shelter. Hobin said it was only to be expected. Mitt gradually forgot his mixed feelings. As time went on, he remembered more and more his glimpse of the Northerners shuffling like all prisoners. It came to something, he thought, when the tyranny of Holand could make free men of the North look so abject. In fact, as a free soul himself, he despised the Northmen a little for it. Come autumn, and I'll show them! he thought.

Most people were sorry for the Northmen. Feeling ran high against Hadd all that summer. Then rumors were heard that the North had defeated the South in a great battle and blocked the last of the passes in the mountains between them. After that even people who were in favor of Hadd began saying it was Hadd's fault. He had let them in for a shameful defeat by hanging twenty innocent men.

"Good," said Siriol. "Things are going our way nicely."

The Free Holanders were planning long and carefully all through that summer. Among other things it suddenly dawned on Mitt and Milda that no one must connect Hobin with Mitt when Mitt threw his bomb. Give Harchad's spies half a clue, as Mitt said, and Hobin would be hanged. Mitt was confident that he could lie well enough to keep Hobin out of it. "I've had years of practice," he said. "The wonder is that I know how to tell the truth these days. But will Hobin keep himself out of it?" That was the trouble. Hobin seldom bothered to watch the Festival. But he might take it into his head to do so, and if he saw Mitt being arrested, he was quite capable of going with Mitt and spoiling everything. "That's the worst of him being so honest," Mitt said.

Mitt took this problem to the Free Holanders. They put their heads together. The result was that Ham, who had always liked Hobin, struck up a proper friendship with him. The two of them went for walks together, out in the Flate, all that summer. Ham managed surprisingly cunningly. He got Hobin used to longer and longer walks. By the end of the summer they were spending all day in the Flate, having supper at an inn, and not getting back to Holand until after nightfall.

"See?" Ham said, with his big, slow grin. "Then on the day of the Festival, we go out to High Mill, twenty-odd mile, and we'll be seen. I'll make sure the innkeeper swears to us."

Then, to Mitt's exasperation, another society of freedom fighters put its oar in. It was called Hands to the North. It tacked notices to the gates of the Palace and the barracks which promised, in crude writing and even cruder language, to kill Hadd during the Sea Festival. "AND AS MANY ER THE REST ER YU AS WE CAN GIT."

"That's torn it!" Mitt said as soon as he heard the news. Milda broke the eggs again, and a jug of milk for good measure, and she and Mitt both seized a baby apiece and hurried round to see Siriol. "What shall we do?" said Mitt. "There'll be spies and soldiers all over now. Who are these Hands to the North anyway?"

"Not any lot I know," said Siriol. "This is bad. It could have the Earl stopping the Festival."

"He'd better not!" said Milda. "I've trained Mitt for this for years. And the clothes won't fit him if we have to wait another year."

Siriol thought, in his customary unhurried way. "If the Palace thinks of staying at home," he said, "we'll hear it soon enough on the grapevine. Meanwhile, it wouldn't do no harm to see if we couldn't start a bit of a panic. Go round letting on that it'll be terrible bad luck for Holand to stop the Festival, and that kind of thing."

So the Free Holanders dropped a word here and another there. Most of them were content simply to hint at dire bad luck. But Mitt felt he could not leave things so much to chance. Whenever Hobin was not by to listen, Mitt would whisper passionately to anyone who happened to be in the workshop, of floods, fires, famines, and plagues. "And that's just the least of what'll happen if old Hadd's too scared to hold the Festival," he would conclude, and pull a dreadful face to suggest all the other unspeakable kinds of bad luck. When Milda was out shopping, she said things even more highly colored.

Four days later the rumor came back to Mitt when the arms inspectors called on their weekly visit. "Hear what they're saying?" said one. "They say if Hadd stops the Festival, the sea rises up and spews out monsters over Holand, and all manner of ignorant nonsense."

"Yes," said the other. "Monsters with heads like horses and horns like bulls. I mean, I know it makes you laugh, Hobin, but you must admit it shows how much happier everyone would be to know there *is* going to be a Festival this year."

Hobin was still laughing after they had gone. "Monsters!" he said. "Don't let me catch you listening to that sort of nonsense, Mitt."

"No fear!" said Mitt. Secretly he was awed by the way the rumor had grown.

Next day Hadd announced that the Festival would be held as usual. Hadd was no coward, and no fool either. The news Harchad's spies brought him showed him well enough how much he was hated in Holand. He knew that to cancel the Festival might be the thing that could spark off a real revolution. So he did not cancel it. But he forbade any of his grandsons to take part in the procession. The procession, this year, was to consist of servants and merchants and their sons—all people who did not count.

The news was a great blow to Ynen. He had looked forward to the Festival for months. He had *counted* on hitting Hadd with a rattle. He had dreamed of himself whirling the rattle round and round under Hadd's great pointed beak, closer and closer, and at last, *bash*. But now . . . It did not console Ynen in the least that he was allowed to come to the feast afterward. And it was the last straw to learn that his father was to be in the procession. Harl was quite content to stay in the safety of the Palace. Harchad, of course, would be busy supervising the soldiers and spies posted to keep Hadd safe. But someone in Hadd's family had to carry Libby Beer, and Hadd chose Navis. Navis was his most expendable son. Besides, Hadd did not like Navis much.

"It's not fair!" Ynen said to Hildy out of his disappointment. "Why is Father allowed in the procession, and not me?"

"Now you know how I feel," Hildy said unsympathetically. Girls were never allowed in the procession at all.

When this news filtered down through devious ways to the Free Holanders, Siriol was rather pleased than otherwise. "Less chance of our Mitt being recognized," he said.

The other safety measures were much more disturbing. In the week before the Festival, all boats were ordered to the far side of the harbor.

Siriol had to move *Flower of Holand* to a distant mooring, where she was bumped and rubbed by six other boats crammed in round her. He grumbled furiously. He grumbled even more when, for two days before the Festival, no boats were allowed in or out of the harbor, and all were searched by soldiers every few hours. At the same time Harchad had all the tenements on the waterfront knocked down, and a large rubbly space cleared in front of the harbor. This was more serious. The street where Mitt was supposed to join the procession vanished. They had hastily to choose the next inland. Milda and Mitt were furious. They had lived in one of those tenements.

"The whole lot down, just to keep his nasty old pa safe!" said Mitt. "Talk about callous tyranny!"

"They should have come down years back," said Hobin. "They were nothing but rats and bedbugs. And 'callous tyranny' is the kind of talk I'm not having."

"But those poor people are turned out in the street!" Milda protested.

"Well, it's cleaner there," said Hobin. He was combing his hair and getting ready for a Guild meeting. "Anyway, to my certain knowledge, three trades have offered them room in their guildhalls, Gunsmiths included. But there's new houses being built for them, back in the Flate."

"The Earl's building them houses?" Mitt asked incredulously.

"No," said Hobin. "Would the Earl do a thing like that? No. It's one of the sons—Navis, I think." He put on his good jacket and went away downstairs, as far as Mitt could see, rather annoyed with Navis for stealing the Gunsmiths' thunder.

"He'll come back talking of Waywold," Mitt said as the door slammed. "You see. Still, it won't matter you going back there after tomorrow."

"Mitt, I'm nervous!" said Milda. "All our planning!"

Mitt felt pleasantly excited, no more. "Don't you trust me or something?" he said. "Come on. Let's have a look at those clothes."

Milda laughed excitedly as she fetched the red and yellow costume from its hiding place under her newest carpet. "I don't think you know the meaning of fear, Mitt! Honest, I don't! Here, now. See if they fit."

It was a strange and rather ridiculous costume. The breeches, which came halfway down Mitt's thin calves, had one yellow leg and the other red. The jacket was red and yellow in the opposite halves. Mitt was a bit thin for the jacket. But he buttoned it up and added the jaunty cap, which had a double crown like a cock's crest. "How do I look?"

Milda was delighted. "Oh, you do look handsome! You look just like a merchant's son!"

Mitt looked in the little mirror, all prepared to agree. He felt very fine. And he had rather a shock. He looked good, it was true. But there were things in his face one never saw in the smooth faces of wealthy boys—lines which made it look old and shrewd. It was the knowing face of the poor city boys who ran about in the streets, fending for themselves. And yet—this was the thing which shocked Mitt most—it was a babyish face, too. Under the lines there were empty curves, emptier than in any boy's face he had ever seen, and his eyes stared as round and wide as his baby sisters'. Mitt made haste to alter it by putting on his most joky smile. The empty cheeks puckered, and the eyes leered long and sly. Mitt flipped the crest of his cap. "Cock-a-doodle-do!" he said. "Roll on, Festival!" Then he turned away from the mirror and did not look in it again.

# 7

ON THE DAY OF THE Festival, Ham called for Hobin soon after dawn. That's got rid of him! Mitt thought, hearing them clattering away downstairs. To tell the truth, he had not slept as well as usual. But since this was a holiday, he stayed in bed another good hour. I reckon they'll be questioning me all tonight, he thought. I better get all the rest I can. But when Milda called him, he was very glad to jump up and put his own holiday clothes on, on top of the Festival costume. They were supposed to be spending the day at Siriol's house. So they went there first, Milda, the two babies, and Mitt, very bulky and warm in his double set of clothes. They were not to go to the side street until word came that the procession had already left the Palace.

The procession left the Palace a little before midday. Ynen watched it from the upstairs window of a merchant's painted house. He was crowded round with hearthmen and hearthmen's sons, all of whom had strict instructions to keep Ynen safe. Ynen could hardly see for them. His was the first and worst position anyway. The other boy cousins were all in houses from which they could see the cleared space by the harbor. Ynen could see it only if he craned, and if he craned, someone was sure to take hold of the back of his jacket and pull him respectfully back inside.

Ynen could hardly bear it, even before the first of the procession came past. When at last he heard the *thump, thump, thump* of the horsehair drums, followed by the squealing of scarnels and joined finally by the groaning of cruddles, his frustration was almost boundless. Perhaps he was not very musical. It struck him as the most exciting sound in the world. Then he heard shouting. Then the lovely, lovely din of the rattles. And at last came the first of the procession, ribbons fluttering from silly hats, banging and blowing and scraping as they marched, with a beribboned bull's head bobbing among them, and the lucky boys with rattles tearing in and out between their legs. Lucky red and yellow boys.

"Oh, why can't all the revolutionaries drop dead!" wailed one of the hearthmen's sons.

Ynen wished they would, too. But for Hands to the North, he would be down there in the stirring din and the bright colors. And here came Grandfather, looking strange and rather silly. Ynen had an excellent view of Hadd's cantankerous old face under a hat loaded with fruit and flowers. On Hadd's shoulders, and trailing behind him, was a magnificent creamy mantle, embroidered with scarlet and cherry red and gold. Over that was draped a garland of wheat-ears and grapes. Not much of the rest of Hadd was visible, because Old Ammet was in the way. Ynen had very little attention to spare for Old Ammet. All he saw was ears of wheat bristling at head, hands and feet, cherry ribbons, and a girdle of apples. Ynen was chiefly impressed with Hadd's skinny legs, cased in scarlet stockings, strutting underneath Old Ammet. Ynen giggled at the important way those legs walked. He had not realized before how vain his grandfather was and how much he enjoyed being an earl. At the sight of those red, strutting legs, Ynen longed to seize a rattle and whirl it in his grandfather's face. To his annoyance, the red and yellow boys were on their best behavior. None of them dared wave a rattle at Hadd. If only they would! Ynen thought, craning, and being pulled back.

Navis came next. Ynen giggled again. His father's feet were in buckled boots, so his legs did not look as ridiculous as Hadd's. But he had ribbons at his knees and fruit in his hat. And juice was coming out of Libby Beer and running into Navis's ribboned sleeves. Flies were following her. Navis was looking hot and bothered—most unusual for him—and obviously wondering if he could get Libby Beer to the harbor still in one piece.

Behind Navis were two merchants who had been pressed into the procession. One wore a hat with ears, the other a hat with horns. They looked right idiots, and they knew they did. All the boys at the window shrieked with laughter. Ynen leaned out again and yelled insults, which were drowned by the next batch of cruddle players. After that the procession was all music, things on sticks, boys with rattles, until it got smaller and smaller and wound downhill out of sight. Ynen sat back with a sigh. He desperately envied Hildy. She and the girl cousins, as the most important of Hadd's grandchildren, had seats at the window of a house on the very edge of the cleared space.

Mitt was by now in the side street, with Milda, Siriol, and Dideo, hastily climbing out of his own clothes. In front of them were the backs of the crowd lining the main street. They were solidly Free Holanders and their families. Most of them had been there since dawn to make sure of the position. Mitt could already hear the thumping and skrawking of the procession, very near. As he passed his jacket to Siriol and put the crested cap on his head, a bull's head on a stick went by above people's heads. The noise was deafening.

"Be careful, Mitt," said Siriol. "And remember you say, 'I've come to meet Flind's niece,' to the one that meets the cart at Hoe. If he says, 'She's expecting another little one,' then it's all right to go with him. Got that?"

"Yes, all in my head," Mitt said, attending to this no more than he usually did when Siriol talked of such arrangements. The din of the scarnels was making the back of his legs jump.

"Old Ammet's coming!" said someone in the crowd. "Pass it back."

"Old Ammet in sight."

Siriol handed Dideo the lighted taper. Dideo bent over the bundle he was carrying.

"Oh, Mitt, be careful!" Milda said. She was smiling and looking sad, both at once. Mitt looked from her to the sister in her arms, and then down at the other sister, unsteadily standing and holding Milda's hand. They upset him. He could not think of anything to say to them.

He was glad when Dideo passed him a bundle on a strap. It was scarlet to match Mitt's left side, and it had a stiff twist of paper coming out of it, which sent off little puffs of smoke. "There," said Dideo, and his face was netted in smiles. "That's long enough to last to the cleared space." He patted Mitt's shoulder as he hung the bag on it.

Siriol passed Mitt a rattle and banged his other shoulder. "Off you go. Good luck."

Mitt slipped in among the crowd, and they parted to let him through. He was on, after years of waiting, and he could hardly believe it. He came to the soldiers, who stood in a line in front of the crowd. They ought to stop him.

A soldier glanced down and saw the red and yellow suit. "Sorry, sonny," he said, and moved to let Mitt by.

Mitt was in the roaring, skirling, streaming procession. For just one second, he was small and sort of blunt and did not believe he was really there. But he was. And there was Hadd. Mitt had not seen Hadd close to before, but he knew him by Old Ammet in his arms. The bad-tempered old face was exactly what he expected. That face, Mitt told himself, is asking to have a rattle under its nose before it gets blown up. And he was off to do it, whirling from one side of the procession to the other, rattle spinning, crested cap flopping, and keeping a wary eye on the puffing bundle under his arm as he went.

He caught up with Hadd just on the edge of the cleared space. Hildy saw him clearly, from where she sat at the window jammed in among her five cousins. They had soldiers in the room with them, soldiers downstairs, and soldiers lining the new open space by the harbor. They were safe. Nevertheless, the cousins were very nervous and disposed to scream at things. They screamed when the first musicians came between the soldiers and straggled across the open. They screamed at the bull's head.

"Oh, look!" screamed Irana, as Mitt ran in front of Hadd, whirling his rattle neatly under Hadd's irascible nose as he went.

Mitt checked after he had done that. Holand looked so strange with no waterfront buildings and all the shipping cleared to one side of the harbor, that he had another moment when he could hardly believe it was real. But the bundle under his arm fizzed. Sparks puffed out with the smoke. Mitt knew the time had come to get rid of it. He turned and plumped it down at Hadd's scarlet feet. Then he did not know quite what to do next.

Hadd's legs stopped walking. His bad-tempered look did not alter. He simply stopped and stood like a statue, with Old Ammet beneath his chin. Both of them stared at Mitt, and Mitt stared back. And the cousins round Hildy screamed in earnest at the sight of the smoking bundle on the ground. Behind Navis, everyone in the procession began to run into the backs of the people in front, and still Hadd stood, and so did Mitt. Hildy could not think what the boy thought he was doing. It seemed stupid behavior, even for a revolutionary. Old Ammet seemed to be staring at him, unblinking as a cow over a gate, from under raised wheat-ear eyebrows, as if he shared Hildy's wonder.

Sparks poured out of the bundle. Navis saw that nobody else was going to do anything. He hoisted Libby Beer to his shoulder and dashed forward. This was more what Mitt had expected. He got ready to pretend to run. But to his astonishment, Navis took no notice of Mitt. Instead he aimed a great kick at the fizzing bundle. Mitt saw the ribboned leg go out, the buckled boot connect, and the bundle, in an arch of smoke, sail away behind into the open space.

And the fellow hasn't a hair out of place! Mitt thought, rather astonished. He wanted to shout to Navis, "Hey! I dedicated a lifetime to this lot! And you just wasted it!"

By this time the merchant with ears on his hat had pulled himself together, too. He made a rather dubious grab for Mitt. Mitt dodged him easily.

This made Mitt think: Might as well give them a run for their money.

He turned to run. As he did so, the explosion came and sent him reeling. The force of it rattled all the windows and sent a gust into Hildy's face. The cousins screamed again. The rest of the procession came jostling out from behind Navis, some of them demanding to know what had happened, some of them after Mitt. Hadd turned and made a sign to one of the captains that Mitt should be taken alive. Since Hildy now knew that this was the worst way to be taken, she shivered a little as she watched the boy running. He ran like a deer, ribbons fluttering, dropping his rattle as he ran, straight toward the soldiers coming out from the edge of the crowd to meet him. Hildy thought that if it had been her, she would have run to the edge of the harbor and jumped in.

So would Mitt have done if he had meant to escape. But he was supposed to be caught. His ears hurt from the explosion. They seemed to be plugged with wool. He saw the soldiers mouthing as they came but could not hear a word. Mitt dodged and swerved as only someone brought up in the poorer parts of Holand could. Looks more natural, he thought. A huge hand snatched at his face. Mitt ducked under it and twisted sideways. A blurry face mouthed curses. A bevy of big boots clodhoppered at him from all directions. This way and that went Mitt, that way and this. He leaped a boot, dodged another, missed an enormous stretching arm, and tripped over another great boot. A jerk and a sudden coldness on his back told him—where his furred-up ears could not—that his jacket had been grabbed and torn. He was flat on his face and up again in one moment. But he was still not caught. He felt his jacket leave him, jerk, jerk, and he was still sprinting forward. Too good to last, Mitt thought, and he dived, pushing and shoving, among the big bodies of the ordinary people crowded behind the soldiers.

Come on, some of you! Stop me! he thought. But no one succeeded, though Mitt thought some of them tried. Just barely, he could hear their voices now: "Stop him! Don't let him get away!"

Ah. Ears come to their senses again, Mitt thought. Good. Couldn't see myself lip-reading all the questions I'm going to be asked.

He pushed on, very glad he was not deaf. And shortly, the voices round him were saying, quite loudly, "What's happened then?" and, "Who are you shoving?"

Mitt, to his extreme astonishment, plunged out from the back of the crowd into a narrow street. Hey! he thought. This won't do. He stopped. He turned round and saw the backs of the people filling the street heaving and bumping about as the soldiers tried to force their way through after him. He cast a longing look up the narrow street. He could really almost get away. They would not run fast in those boots.

Better make it easier for them, Mitt thought, sighing. And he went back into the crowd.

Out in the open space, the procession had re-formed and was straggling toward the water's edge. Hadd behaved as if nothing had happened at all. As soon as Mitt vanished among the soldiers, he went on walking as if the whole thing were not worth thinking about. Hildy could not help admiring him. That was how an earl should behave! Hadd's behavior was so dominating that Hildy and everybody else were soon watching the procession going up and down the quays, drumming and droning and skirling, as if Mitt had never existed.

Mitt was in the crowd just beneath Hildy's window. He found he was still wearing one red and one yellow sleeve. They were a nuisance, so he took them off and threw them on the ground. He seemed to have lost his cap. He stood there in his threadbare undershirt, hoping the soldiers would recognize him by his two-colored breeches. But he was surrounded by tall citizens and nobody saw him. Above the noise of the procession he could hear the boots of the soldiers hammering away up the narrow street.

Right fools, some people are! Mitt thought. Better make myself obvious.

He squirmed his way along the painted wall of the house until he came to its front door. It had six steps up to it, for fear of flooding, as did most houses in Holand. People were crowded on the steps, staring out toward the harbor. Mitt climbed up and squeezed in among them. He was easy enough to see, had anybody been looking his way. But everyone was watching the Festival.

The procession had formed into a line along the jetty, with Hadd and Navis in the center. The heads on poles were lowered. Garlands were taken off. Everyone waved these downward, pretending to beat the water. In fact, the water was too far below to reach, but the Festival went back to the days when Holand harbor was just a low ring of rocks and none of it had been altered since. The same old words were said:

> "To tide swimming and water welling, go now and come back sevenfold. Over the sea they went, on the wind's road. Go now and come back sevenfold. For harbor's hold and land's growing, go now and come back sevenfold."

This was repeated three times by everyone in the procession. It was a growling, ragged chorus. Yet, by the third repetition, Hildy's arms were up in goose pimples from sheer awe—she did not know why. Mitt's eyes pricked, as they always did, and he was annoyed at himself for being so impressed by a load of out-of-date nonsense. Then the musicians gave vent to a long groaning chord. Hadd raised Poor Old Ammet above his head, ready to throw him in the harbor.

A little star sparkle of flame blossomed for a second on one of the ships tied up at the side of the harbor. Hadd jerked, half turned, and slid quietly to the ground. It looked at first as if he had suddenly decided to lay Poor Old Ammet carefully at Navis's feet. Then came a tiny, distant *crack*.

Nobody understood for a moment. One of Hildy's cousins laughed.

After that there was a long, groaning uproar. Mitt's voice was in it. "Flaming Ammet! I been *diddled*!" The fat woman beside him was saying, over and over again, "Oh, what bad luck! What terrible bad luck!" Mitt had no idea whether she meant bad luck to Hadd or to Holand. The ladylike girls overhead somewhere were screaming. Mitt leaned his head against their painted front door and cursed. All he could think of was that the unknown marksman had cheated him. "Half my life, and now it's wasted!" he said. "Wasted. Gone!"

Overhead the cousins hung on to Hildy and to one another, whimpering and crying. Hildy found herself saying, "Ye gods, ye gods, ye gods!"

A soldier in the room behind shouted, "He's in that boat—*Proud Ammet*! Run, you, and we'll get him!"

"They mustn't leave! We're not safe!" screamed Harilla.

They had already left. The door behind Mitt burst open, and soldiers pelted out of it. Mitt leaped clear. But he had no chance to make himself obvious. Everyone on the steps was pushed off and toppled in all directions. The fat woman landed almost on top of Mitt and knocked him sprawling. By the time he had picked himself up, and then her, the soldiers had pelted off.

"Shut *up*!" Hildy snapped at Harilla. She was trying to see what was happening on the waterfront. Navis was bending over Hadd, and the rest of the procession was crowding round. Soldiers were running. People from the crowd were surging forward to see. Uncle Harchad, keeping prudently among a crowd, was running, too. Hildy saw her father stand up and point to the boat where the shot had been fired, wave to the soldiers, and wave the crowd back. Then he stooped again, and stood up holding Poor Old Ammet. He turned this way and that with him, showing people what he was doing, and then threw him into the harbor with the traditional shout. Then he picked up Libby Beer and slung her after.

Hildy felt a mixture of pride and horrible embarrassment. She could see her father was trying to assure the citizens of Holand that this did not mean unmitigated bad luck. But it was doubtful if anybody noticed. People were surging about. Numbers were leaving. Soldiers were running out to *Proud Ammet* along the curving harbor wall. There were screams and shouts which drowned Navis's voice. Nevertheless, the rest of the procession followed his lead. In a ragged, unconvinced way, garlands began to loop out from the quay and fall on the water. By this time Uncle Harchad had reached the waterfront. Hildy watched him and Navis kneel down beside her grandfather, with red and yellow garlands sailing around them, until the harbor seemed full of bobbing fruit and wet flowers, and wondered what they were feeling. She could see Hadd was dead, but she seemed to have no feelings about that at all.

# 8

THE FAT WOMAN was very grateful to Mitt. She clung to him, and he had to help her to the street beyond the house. "You're a sweet boy," she kept saying. "Come on up to the stalls, and I'll buy you something."

Mitt refused. He had to be where the soldiers were. It was the only thing left for him to do. Half his life's work had fallen to someone else's bullet. Hands to the North, curse them! he thought. He knew he would never get a chance to be revenged on Hadd now. But the other half remained. He had to get caught and get questioned and, with the utmost reluctance, let out that it was Siriol, Ham, and Dideo who set him on to plant the bomb. So, as soon as he had shaken off the fat woman, he went back to the waterfront.

By the time he got there, the other murderer had very thoroughly stolen his thunder. Soldiers were shouting to people to get back and get home, while other soldiers tried to open a path for what was left of the procession, carrying Hadd's body. More soldiers were in and out of the house where the screaming girls were. The place was full of groups of people hurrying purposefully this way and that, in uniform, in Festival dress, or in holiday best. The result was utter confusion. The only thing which did not seem to be happening, Mitt thought bitterly, was the revolution the Free Holanders had confidently expected once Hadd was dead.

Mitt shrugged. For lack of any better plan, he did as he used to do three years back and joined a hurrying group of total strangers. With them, he was swept right across the waterfront to the other side of the harbor. And when we're there, I bet we hurry all the way back again, he thought.

He was right. An officer stopped them near the harbor wall. "Only authorized persons past this spot."

Mitt's group obediently turned away. "Alham must have gone up Fishmarket then," someone said, in a worried, busy voice, and they all set off again in the opposite direction.

Mitt lagged and let them hurry away. He could see the masts of the smaller boats from here, sawing the sky as heavy soldiers jumped from one to another, hunting the murderer. Even the masts of the big ships were swaying sedately, so many were the soldiers searching them. A group of seamen who had been on the ships were being herded and prodded roughly along the harbor wall. They'll catch *him* all right, Mitt thought resentfully.

A new group of people surged up beside him. These were clearly important. They were officers in braid, well-nourished men in good cloth, with, in their midst, a tall, thin man with a pale jagged profile. The man's clothes had a wonderful sober richness. Mitt saw the sleek glint of velvet, and fur, and the flicker of jewels, worn where they did not show, because the man was too used to having them to bother with their value. Mitt knew that pale, jutting face, though he had never, to his knowledge, seen the fellow before. It had the same bad-tempered lines as Hadd's. The nose was the one he had whirled his rattle under. The rest of the features were like the ones he had seen advancing on him behind Libby Beer to kick the bomb away. This could only be Harchad.

Proper flinty flake off the old block, he is, Mitt thought, looking up at him with interest. Wearing six farms and ten years' fishing on his back, and *he* don't care!

"Oh, stop bleating, man!" Harchad snapped at the man with the most braid. "Those seamen are to be questioned till we get something. I don't care if you kill them all. And I want the brat who threw the bomb, too. He was obviously an accomplice. I want him brought to *me* when you find him."

Mitt's stomach, for the first time in his life, gave a cold little jolt. He lowered his eyes from Harchad's face and gently backed away. Wonder how he'd look if he knew I was right beside him, he thought. Accomplice, was I? O flaming Ammet! I think everything's gone wrong. He tiptoed hurriedly sideways to join the nearest group of hurrying citizens.

The man in braid shouted. "There he is now! That's him!"

"Who?"

"The brat who threw that bomb."

Mitt had the merest glimpse of them all staring at him. Harchad's face jutted out of the rest in a way that dried Mitt's mouth, tongue and all, and almost wrung a scream out of him. It was as horrible as his nightmares about Canden. He turned and ran, mindlessly. His only idea was to make his legs go faster than their fastest. He had to get away from the gathering shouts behind him. He had to escape from that face. He shot across the waterfront, not knowing whether he hit people or avoided them as he ran. He dived into the nearest road and ran there for all he was worth. It filled with banging feet behind him. Mitt ran harder still, turned a corner and ran, and ran again, and went on running. The only thing in his mind was the shouting and ringing feet behind him, and he did not stop running until they had grown faint and died away.

When his breath came back, he wandered wearily round a corner into the next street. He was deeply ashamed of himself. What had got into him? What had made him, the free soul, fearless Mitt, who had never turned a hair during all the errands he had run for the Free Holanders—what had possessed him—to panic at the mere sight of Harchad and run away? Mitt could not understand it. What had made everything go so wrong?

"Here, love. Have hold of this and cheer up."

Mitt looked up to find himself in an airy, respectable street, quite some way above the waterfront. It was full of handsomely painted houses. Mitt dimly remembered the one just up the hill from him, with the double gable and the two stiff figures painted on it. The street was full of quiet, cheerful people in respectable holiday clothes, who were buying things at the stalls which lined the street. It did not seem as if a whisper of the events at the harbor had reached this far. All was peace and sober enjoyment.

The person who had spoken to Mitt was a woman behind one of the stalls. She was leaning forward across rows of little Ammets and Libbys, holding a toffee apple out toward Mitt. She smiled when he looked, and waggled the apple invitingly on its stick. "Here. Take this for luck. Your face is as long as Flate Dike, my love."

Mitt did his best to grin. Running had filled his mouth with thick, bitter juice. He did not want a toffee apple. But he could see the woman meant to be kind. "Oh, no, thanks, lady. I just lost a lifetime's work, see, and I'm off my food a bit."

"Well, then, you need an appetizer," said the woman, and she tried to push the toffee apple into Mitt's hand.

Mitt found he really could not bear the thought of sticky toffee and sour apple, and he backed away. "No, thanks, lady. Honest. Much obliged."

"Please yourself," she said. "But I've got to give you *something* now I've started, or it's bad luck for both of us. Here." She picked up one of the little images of Libby Beer from the line on the front of the stall and held her out to Mitt. "You can have her then. I'm just clearing up to go, anyway." Mitt did not know if the woman really wanted luck or if she was simply trying to cheer him up, but he took the little image and tried to grin again. "And don't try eating her. She's made of wax," said the woman. "The year's luck to you."

"Luck to you, ship and shore," Mitt said politely, just as he should. He wandered on down the street, clutching the knobby little figure and wondering what to do with it. Perhaps I could make Harchad a present of her, he thought.

He was three stalls lower down when boots hammered on the flagway behind him. Six soldiers with an officer at their head swung round the corner the way Mitt had come and halted by the woman's stall. "Hey, you. Anyone. Seen a boy in Festival breeches, no jacket, very skinny?"

The sober respectable hum in the street died away completely. Nobody moved. Mitt froze, bending over the stall beside him, pretending to look at little Ammets. He tried to will himself to make a dash down the street and bring the soldiers after him. But there was no question of that, somehow. He could only wait for the woman who had given him Libby Beer to give him away.

"Yes, indeed, I have seen him, sir," she said. "Just this minute. I offered him a toffee apple, and he went away down the street."

The soldiers nodded and came on down the street.

Mitt stood with a bright imitation Libby Beer in one hand and the other stretched out to touch the plaited corn of an Ammet and still could not move. He did not blame the woman. Other people had seen her talking to Mitt, and she dared not deny it. In the old days it used to make him amused and rather scornful, the way even respectable people like these went in dread of Harchad's soldiers. It made him think he must be the only free soul in Holand. But now he did not seem to be a free soul any longer. He dared not move. He had to stand there till the soldiers saw him.

The boots clomped by. Mitt could see and feel everyone's eyes moving between him and the green uniforms. But nobody said a word. The boots clomped on to the end of the street and faded out of hearing. There was sighing and shifting all round. Someone behind Mitt, who must have blocked the soldiers' view of him, said, "Go on, lad. Run while the going's good." Mitt did not see who said it, but he ran.

Isn't that Holand people all over! he thought as he ran back round the corner and plunged downhill toward the harbor again. Where they could be, they were kind. But you could never count on it. Yesterday this kindness had amused him. Now there did not seem to be anything left to laugh at. Tears trickled across Mitt's cheeks as he ran, as he thought of all those years of planning gone to waste.

I wonder if there's something wrong deep inside of me, he thought. It don't surprise me. He tried to wipe the tears off his face and found he was brushing it with something knobbly. He looked, and there was the little Libby Beer, made of wax cherries and rose hips and miniature apples, glistening with his tears. "Goh!" said Mitt, and stuffed her angrily in his scarlet pocket. Crying did no good. Next time he met any soldiers, there would be no mistake. He was going to get caught.

He came down into the old town, through a street of peeling houses breathing the smell of the poor quarters out through their open front doors—the smell of too many people, dirt, damp plaster, and cheap food. All the children from the houses were playing in the road. There was hopscotch nearest, marbles a little way on, and then two of the running, shouting kind of games. And through the shrill yells, Mitt sensed more soldiers coming. The rhythm of their boots was in the very air.

Mitt did not decide what to do. He moved without thinking, round the hopscotch to the game of marbles, and dropped down to squat in the ring of smaller boys. It was a trick he had often played three years back. Unless the boys were doing something very secret, they usually did not mind. But as he hurriedly wiped the tears off his face with his wrist, Mitt was amazed at himself. Here, he thought. What am I doing?

The rhythm of boots beat in the dirty pavement under him and a green block of soldiers swept round the corner. When they saw the children, the *clump-clump* of their boots slackened and became a slow puttering. They had broken step and were coming slowly down the street, looking very carefully indeed.

The yelling and the games stopped. The children stood in awkward rows, staring. The small boys round Mitt were not really playing marbles anymore. They were waiting for the soldiers to pass. And Mitt crouched with them, in such terror that he could hardly see or feel. He had not known it was possible to be so frightened. He knew he stuck out like a sore thumb among these children. He was half as big again as any of them. His red leg blazed and his yellow leg shone. And he could not trust little kids like these not to give him away, either by accident or on purpose, for spoiling their games. At any moment a shrill voice might say, "That's the one you want, mister."

As the soldiers puttered toward him, Mitt no longer had any doubt what he was doing. He was trying not to be caught. And as wave after wave of pure fear swept over him, he knew he was going to go on trying. By the time the soldiers were level with him, his terror was worse than the worst pain he had ever known. Mitt crouched down over his blazing legs, squeezing himself into himself to look as small as possible, and forced himself to put out a hand, take a marble, and roll it casually into the middle of the ring. He had to fight his terror every inch in order to move at all. He thought he could have rolled Siriol's boat across the pavement more easily. The effort made him weak.

As soon as the marble left his hand, he was sure he had done the wrong thing. The boy next to him shot him a nasty look. The puttering boots went slower, as if the movement had attracted their attention. Mitt almost lost his senses, he was so terrified. Time swam forward, sickeningly slow and blurred.

The boots puttered down past the hopscotch, stopped, and started again, in step this time. *Clump-clump-clump*, they went, away into faintness.

"Buzz off," said the boy. "You spoiled my go."

Mitt stumbled to his feet. He felt dizzy, and as cramped as if he had spent a winter night fishing. He had to limp down the street. None of the games started again. The children watched Mitt as they had watched the soldiers. Bad, that was bad. They would tell of him to someone. Mitt hoped they would not tell too soon because he felt far too tired to run. He felt like curling up in the nearest doorway and crying himself to sleep.

Get a hold of yourself! he thought angrily. You're on the run, that's all. People go on the run all the time in this place. I don't know how it keeps happening, but it's like I can't help myself from running. What's gone wrong with me? This was a question Mitt simply could not answer. He only knew that he had got up this morning, intending, as he had intended for the last four years, to finish Hadd and the Free Holanders at one stroke. And now he had failed to finish Hadd, his one idea seemed not to be caught.

Oh, now, wait a minute! Mitt stopped and pretended to loiter in a yard doorway. There were still the Free Holanders. If he was too scared to get himself caught, he could easily just go to Siriol's house, or Dideo's. Where Mitt went now, Harchad's spies would swiftly follow. It was just as good a way of getting the Free Holanders caught. But the reason Mitt stopped, leaning on the doorpost and gaping at nothing, was that he was not even tempted. "Not even tempted!" he repeated to himself. And it was true. It was nothing dramatic. Mitt could not tell himself he would rather die than go to Siriol's house—he knew he would do anything rather than die—but he was still not going there. Or to Dideo. "What do you think they are then? Friends?" Mitt asked himself derisively.

It seemed as if they were. He remembered the smile on Dideo's netted face when Mitt brought him the first little packet of saltpeter, and Siriol glowering at him over a rope's end but never hitting him more than just that once. And I reckon he ought to have done, Mitt thought. He ought to have knocked me through a Mitt-shaped hole in the side of *Flower of Holand*, over and over. He found himself smiling a little. Siriol always understood his jokes, and Ham scarcely ever did. Then there was Alda, puffing arris at everyone, and Lydda going to marry that sailor off *Lovely Libby*. I got to know them too well, Mitt thought.

It did no good to stand there, smiling and staring. Mitt walked on. He supposed his best plan was to use the escape arrangements Siriol had so carefully made for him.

"No!" Mitt exclaimed. It was not that he did not want to use them. He did. He would have given his ears to. But he could not remember a thing about them. Thinking he would not need to escape, he had attended to Siriol's plans probably even less than he had listened to Hobin telling him about guns. He had a vague idea there was a cart somewhere and a password. But that was absolutely all he knew. Of all the fools!

But what was he to *do*? He could not spend the rest of his life sneaking round the streets of Holand. If he looked for all the carts he could find, he would certainly be caught. The soldiers would think of that. He dared not go home. That would get Hobin and Milda arrested, too. The only thing he dared do was take to the Flate, like so many freedom fighters before him. But he knew a bit about that. You got hunted down there. And it was a miserable life unless you were lucky enough to have a gun and could shoot marsh birds for food. Mitt had no gun. He knew where guns were, though: locked up in Hobin's workshop. And he dared not go near there. Oh, it went round in circles. *Why* hadn't he attended to Siriol? Mitt knew why, really. He had simply not thought of anything beyond the moment when he was to plant that bomb. I must be flaming insane! Mitt said to himself. *Do* something, can't you!

He wanted to go home, that was what he wanted to do. And he dared not.

Or dared he? Hobin was out for the day. Milda was at Siriol's with the babies. If Mitt went there, spies would follow. But spies would probably go there, anyway, because Hobin had gunpowder. Suppose Mitt were to go there, take gun and ammunition, and make it look like a burglary? It would have to look like a burglary, anyway, because he would have to break locks and the seals of the inspectors to get anything. Hobin could not be blamed for being burgled. It would be a way of keeping suspicion from him. In fact, the more Mitt thought about it, the more it seemed his duty to go and burgle Hobin. Then do what? Go out in the Flate and try to get North, Mitt supposed.

It made a considerable difference to have a purpose again. Mitt felt far less tired. Flate Street was quite near. Mitt purposely doubled the distance to it. He wanted to be seen in as many places as possible, to confuse the spies. When he finally arrived behind the high greasy wall which cut the light off the back of the workshop, Mitt was fairly confident that any spy trying to trace him would not arrive until tomorrow. He thought two days was more likely. But he said tomorrow, because it never paid to underestimate Harchad's spies.

The wall made one side of an alley, with another sightless wall opposite. Mitt stood facing it, breathing deeply. He had to reckon on being seen going over the top of the wall. If he allowed time for whoever saw him to fetch help and break down the front door of the workshop—or fetch soldiers to do it—there should just be time to take what he wanted and then break the place up a bit. But it was only a very short time. Mitt knew it might be a close thing. He wished his knees would not tremble and his heart knock so. He was not *used* to being frightened like this.

# 9

"AND I MISSED *everything*!" was Ynen's disgusted comment when at last Hildy arrived back at the Palace and he managed to find her.

The Palace was all doubts and hushed voices and indecision. Only one thing was certain: Hadd was dead, and Harl was now Earl of Holand. But when you had said that, you had said everything. Nobody knew if there was an uprising, or whether to take off the Festival clothes, or what would happen about the feast which had been prepared. Harl did nothing but sit in his room. He had not given one order. Harchad came and went and gave orders perpetually, but nothing seemed to come of them.

"Well, in that case there can't be an uprising," Hildy said rather snappishly when Ynen told her what it had been like. "We didn't see anyone but soldiers all the way back." She felt as if she wanted to be alone, but Ynen looked so lost that she stayed with him. They wandered stairs and corridors together, among people who had as little idea as they had what to do.

Ynen told Hildy some of the rumors about the murderer. He had been caught; he had not been found. He was a discontented seaman; he was a dangerous revolutionary and an agent for the North. He was a superb marksman; he was a fool who had fired a lucky shot; he had used a new secret weapon from the North. He had poisoned himself; he had jumped into the harbor and escaped. No one knew what the truth was. "Now tell me what it was *like*, by the harbor," Ynen said.

"I don't know," Hildy said, quite honestly. "Anyway, you know what it's like when Harilla has hysterics." But she did try to describe what had happened. It was not Ynen's fault he had missed it.

"Did Father really do all that?" Ynen asked. "I didn't know he could move fast enough." He added wistfully, "I *wish* I could have seen that boy twirl a rattle under Grandfather's nose."

"It wasn't as funny as you think," said Hildy. "It—it was queer. He didn't run away. I suppose he's caught by now." Then she found she really did need to be alone and went to her room. But Ynen came with her, and she had not the heart to tell him to go away. He sat curled up on the window seat, while Hildy sat cross-legged in the middle of her big square bed.

Here Hildy tried for the hundredth time to sort out how she felt. It was a very shocking thing that her grandfather had been murdered. That she knew. And it was a shocking time to kill him. Everybody said it meant terrible bad luck. Hildy found she was still far more embarrassed than proud at the way her father had tried to save the day. It was the way nobody had noticed that made her so uncomfortable. But about the actual murder, she simply felt awed and respectful—and subdued all over, so that she moved gently and quietly and wanted to be alone. She could not manage to feel strongly about it. And this was odd, because she knew that somewhere, about something, she felt very strongly indeed. She was raging with feelings, but she did not know what *about.* It reminded her of the way she had felt when her father had told her she was engaged to Lithar.

Here Hildy sprang up. "Wait," she said to Ynen when he sprang up, too. Ynen sat down with a sigh, and Hildy sped to her father's rooms.

She knocked at the heavy door. There was no answer. Hildy, a little hesitantly, turned the handle and went in. There was no one in the first room. She went on to the second.

Navis was sitting by the window, still in his Festival clothes. Perhaps he was trying to sort out how he felt, too. At any rate he was not reading the book he had in his hand. He was staring out into the Flate.

Hildy saw at a glance that he had gone back to being cold, idle, and proud. There was little chance of anybody making him do anything which was not absolutely necessary. Hildy ground her teeth with fury. How could he rise to the occasion at the waterfront and then sink from it like this? And if he was still mourning about her mother, Hildy had no sympathy for him whatsoever. He had been like this far too *long*!

"Father," she said.

Navis jumped slightly. "Did I forget to lock my door?"

"I'll go away in a minute," said Hildy. "Are you sorry Grandfather's dead?"

"Er," said her father. "He was an old man."

Hildy thought angrily that *that* was no way to speak. She wondered whether to flatter him by saying she thought he had behaved extremely well by the harbor. But it was beside the subject, it was not true, and she did not think it would rouse Navis, anyway. "I came to ask you," she said, champing at the words because she was so angry, "if I need to marry Lithar now."

"What's that got to do with the situation?" Navis asked.

"Grandfather arranged it," Hildy said, trying to be patient. "But I don't want to marry him. So will you cancel it, please?"

Navis looked at his book as if he would rather attend to that than Hildy. "I think you'll find the alliance is prized quite as much now."

"What does that mean? *Can't* you cancel it?" Hildy demanded.

"I doubt it," said her father.

"Don't you *care*?" said Hildy.

"I fancy I do," Navis admitted. "But with things in this state of upheaval—"

Hildy lost her grip on her temper. "Ye gods! Nobody cares in this place! You're the worst of the lot! You just sit there, after all that happens, and you don't even care that nobody even knows if there's going to be a feast or not!"

"Don't they?" Navis asked, rather surprised. "Really, Hildy, there *is* nothing to do at the moment but sit. I'm very sorry—"

"You're *not* sorry!" raved Hildy. "But I'll make you sorry! You just wait!" She turned to storm out of the rooms.

Navis called after her. "Hildy!" She turned round to find him looking oddly anxious. "Hildy, will you make sure you and Ynen stay where I can find you?"

"Why?" Hildy said haughtily.

"I may need you in a hurry."

This was such an unlikely thing that Hildy simply made a scornful noise and crashed out of her father's rooms, slamming each door behind her as hard as she could. She was so angry, and so determined to make Navis sorry, that she reached the gallery outside her uncle Harl's rooms on a surge of blind fury and had almost no idea how she got there. She was fetched back to her senses by running into her cousins Harilla and Irana. They were hurrying the other way. Harilla's face was still streaked with red from her recent hysterics. Irana's was red all over.

"It's no good," Irana said. "If you're going where I think you're going. They're both pigs."

Harilla gasped, "I wish I was dead!" and burst into tears. Irana led her away.

Hildy wondered what was the matter with them this time. When she saw that there were guards outside her uncle's rooms, she supposed that meant Harl had refused to see them. She marched up to the guards, prepared for battle. But they stood aside, most respectfully, and one opened the door for her. Hildy marched on into the antechamber, rather puzzled. The servants there bowed. She heard her uncle Harl's voice from the room beyond.

"I tell you I owe the fellow a favor! He killed old Haddock, didn't he? Let him get away."

"Don't be an ass, Harl!" snapped Uncle Harchad's voice.

"With my blessing," added Harl.

"Look, Harl, if we don't catch him—" Harchad broke off irritably as Hildy came in.

Harl looked at her and let out a great guffaw. He was sitting in great comfort, with his shoes off and his feet on a chair. A table under his beefy elbow was crowded with wine bottles. He seemed very happy. He was grinning and sweating with happiness all over his big, bluff face. Harchad, on the other hand, was sitting tensely on the edge of his chair, nervily twiddling a full glass of wine. His face was paler than usual.

"Ha! Ha!" bellowed Harl. "Now it's Hildrida. That makes the full set of them. We haven't any more, have we, Harchad? Daughters and nieces and things?"

"No," said Harchad. He did not seem to find it funny. "If you please, Hildrida. We are trying to talk business. Say what you have to say quickly, and then go."

Hildy stared at them. She had never paid much attention to her uncle Harl before. He had always been a lazy, sober, silent man—and so ordinary. Nothing he said or did was ever remarkable. But now Uncle Harl was drunk, drunker even than the soldiers got on their nights off. And he was not drowning his sorrow either. He was celebrating. And Uncle Harchad was no more sorry about Grandfather than Harl was. But he was frightened: scared stiff in case he got shot next.

Harl pointed a drunken finger at Hildy. "Don't say it. We know. All the rest said it." He put on a high, squeaky voice. " 'Please, Uncle, will you break off my betrothal, please?' Who's she betrothed to?" he asked Harchad.

"Lithar," said Harchad. "Holy Islands. And the answer's no, Hildrida. We need all the allies we can get."

"So it's no good asking," said Harl. He wriggled his stockinged toes at Hildy and produced strange cracking sounds.

At this Hildy's anger blazed up again. "You're quite wrong," she said haughtily. "I wasn't going to ask. I was going to tell you. I am *not* marrying Lithar or anyone else you try to choose for me. I'm quite determined about it, and you can't make me."

Her two uncles looked at one another. "She's quite determined, and we can't make her," said Harl. "This one had to be different. Her father's Navis."

"I'm afraid you'll find you're mistaken, Hildrida," said Harchad. "We *can* make you. And we will."

"I shall refuse," said Hildy. "Utterly. There's nothing you can do."

"She'll refuse utterly," said Harl.

"She will not," said Harchad.

"She can if she wants," said Harl. "She'll be married by proxy, anyway. Can't expect Lithar to come all this way. You refuse, my dear girl," he said to Hildy. "Refuse all you want if it makes you happy. It won't bother us." He wriggled his toes at Hildy again, and once more they cracked. Harl was impressed. "Hear that, Harchad? That noise was my toes. Wonder why they do that."

Hildy clenched her teeth in order not to scream at him. "Lithar might bother if I refuse."

Harl bawled with laughter. A small smile flitted on Harchad's face. "Well, it'll be you he takes it out on, won't it?" said Harl. "That doesn't worry me!" He lay back in his chair and grinned at the idea.

"All right," said Hildy. "Don't say I didn't warn you." She swung round and swept out, with her back very straight and her chin up, willing herself not to let the tears in her eyes fall until she was past the attendants, and then the soldiers. Then she ran. She ran to find Ynen. He was the only person in the Palace who was kind.

She could not find him. She dried her tears on her sleeve and searched grimly, high and low, right down to the kitchens. The cooks there were cursing. Hildy discovered that Navis had bestirred himself sufficiently to cancel the feast. She was angrier than ever. To think that out of what she had said to him, this was the one thing he had attended to! She wanted to bite something and tear things up. She stormed to her own room, wondering if a sheet or a curtain would be best to tear.

Ynen was there, still curled up on her window seat. By this time he was feeling very doleful. Hildy was a little ashamed to think she had clean forgotten telling him to wait.

"Hildy," he said plaintively before he noticed her state of mind. "Why is it all so miserable?"

"Can't you *think* why?" Hildy snapped. She seized the coverlet on her bed, a good handful in each hand, and wrenched. It gave way with the most satisfactory ripping noise.

Ynen's eyes widened. He wished he had not spoken. Now he knew he would have to say something else, or Hildy would turn on him for sitting there like a dumb idiot. "Yes," he said. "It's because nobody's even pretending to be sorry Grandfather's dead."

"How right you are!" Hildy snarled. Carefully, almost with enjoyment, she tore a long strip off the coverlet.

Ynen watched her anxiously and kept talking. "People are more sorry about the Festival being messed up. They go on about bad luck. And the awful thing," he said hurriedly as Hildy began on another strip, "is that I don't care about Grandfather either. I just feel sort of shocked. It makes me think I'm wicked."

Hildy finished the second strip. Then, fists up and elbows out, she began on a third. "Wicked! What a stupid way to talk! Grandfather was a horrible old man, and you *know* he was! If people didn't do exactly what he wanted, he had them killed, or tried them for treason if they were lords." She dragged the third strip down to the selvage and wrenched to tear that. She began on a fourth. "The only people who dared argue with him were other earls, and he quarreled with them all the time. Why should you be sorry? Even so," she said, rending the fourth strip loose, "I felt sick when I heard Uncle Harl calling him old Haddock."

Ynen judged that Hildy's temper was cooling. He risked laughing. "Everyone called him that!"

"I wish I'd known," said Hildy. "I'd have said it, too."

This encouraged Ynen to believe she was almost calm again. "Hildy," he said, "that was rather a good coverlet."

It had been a good one. It was blue and gold, and worked in a pattern of roses. The sewing women down in Holand had taken a good month to embroider it. Hildy's four furious strips had left it a square of ragged, puckered cloth about four feet long. "I don't care," said Hildy. Her rage flared up again. She seized the puckered square and tore it and tore it. "I hate good things!" she raged. "They give us good coverlets, and golden clocks, and beautiful boats, and they don't do it because they like us or care about us. All they think of is whether we'll come in useful for their plans!"

"Nobody thinks I'm useful at all," Ynen said. That was the reason for his misery, but he had been ashamed to say it before.

Hildy glared round at him, and he shrank. "I could murder them for thinking that!" she raved. "Why do you *have* to be useful? You're nice. You're the only nice person in this whole horrible Palace!" Ynen went pink. He was very flattered, but he would like to have been told he was useful, too. And he wished Hildy would realize that she was quite as alarming raging *for* him as she was raging *at* him. "I intend to teach them a lesson," Hildy proclaimed.

"They probably won't notice," Ynen said. "I wish we could go and live somewhere else. Somebody told me Father preferred living in the country. Do you think if I asked him—?"

Hildy interrupted him with a squawk of angry laughter. "Go and ask one of the statues in the throne room! They'll pay more attention."

Ynen knew she was right. But now he had talked about going away from the Palace, he knew it was the one thing he really wanted to do. "Hildy, couldn't we go out for the rest of the day? I hate the Palace like this. Couldn't we go sailing—oh, I forgot. You're not allowed to anymore, are you?"

"Don't be a fool! The place is full of revolutionaries. They won't let us go out," said Hildy. But she could see from the window behind Ynen that it was perfect weather for sailing. "Won't all the sailors have a holiday today?"

Ynen sighed. "Yes. I wouldn't have a crew." Still, it had been a good idea. "Suppose we rode out to High Mill then?"

But Hildy stood looking from the window to the ruins of her coverlet. There was going to be trouble about that. It was a silly thing to get into trouble about on its own. She ought to do something worse. She was aching to do something really terrible and show everybody. She remembered Navis had asked them to stay where he could find them. That decided her. "Let's go sailing, Ynen," she said. "And let's give them a fright. Let's knot the coverlet and hang it out of the window, and make them think we've run away." Ynen looked at her dubiously. "I can crew," said Hildy. "You can be captain because it's your boat."

"You don't mind getting into awful trouble?" said Ynen.

"I do not," said Hildy.

Ynen jumped up, so full of pleasure and mischief that he looked like a different boy. "Come on then! We'll need warm clothes, and we'd better pinch some food, too. We'll have to sneak out past the kitchens, anyway."

Hildy laughed at the change in him as she snatched up two strips of coverlet and knotted them together. She pulled the knot tight. There was an ominous ripping noise. "It wouldn't bear a sparrow, this stuff," she said.

"It's only got to look used," Ynen pointed out. "Pull it as tight as you can without tearing it." He helped her make the knots and then to tie the fraying strip to the window frame and let it down outside. It did not reach very far. "It'll do," Ynen said hopefully. "We could have jumped down onto the library roof."

Hildy leaned out beside him. Their rope dangled a pitiful sixteen feet. The library dome was twenty feet or more below that. "They'll wonder how we didn't break our necks," she said. "Go and get warm clothes. I'll come to your room when I've changed."

Ynen raced off, hardly the same boy who had sat miserably on Hildy's window seat half the afternoon. Hildy, as she changed into a short woolen dress, sea boots, socks, and a pea jacket, told herself she was doing right. Ynen was so happy. She still felt wonderfully rebellious, but she was also just a little scared. There were people in Holand with bombs and guns. She had seen them.

"They won't know who we are," she told her reflection in the mirror. "And I'm sick of being important." She took her hair down and did it in pigtails, to look as ordinary as possible, and collected dust from all the corners where she could find it and rubbed it on her face. Then she threw her good clothes to the back of a closet and set off for Ynen's room.

Her cousins Harilla and Irana were coming along the passage. Hildy dodged behind a grand china vase. She heard them go into her room. Harilla was saying: "Well, Hildy, did they let you break off your betrothal? You needn't think—Oh!"

Hildy dodged out from the vase and ran, as quietly as she could in sea boots. "Quick!" she told Ynen. "Harilla found the coverlet."

"It would be her, wouldn't it?" said Ynen.

They could tell the alarm was up as they crept down toward the kitchens. There was a great deal of noise and running about. But everyone seemed to believe that Hildy and Ynen would be found in the direction of the library. It was easy to avoid the people running there from the kitchens, and once they reached the kitchens, there were very few people left there. They heard someone whistling and dishes clattering, but the sounds echoed with emptiness. Ynen risked opening the door of a pantry.

"Look at that!" he said. The pantry was full, from floor to ceiling, with pies—glazed pies, golden pies, puffy pies, tarts, flans, pasties, and pies with flowers and birds on them. "Pass us a couple of those sacks," said Ynen. "Let's make it look as if we took enough for a week."

They pulled the pantry door to behind them and, in the half-dark, seized what pies came first to hand and stuffed the sacks with them. While they were doing it, footsteps hurried outside, backward and forward. They waited for whoever it was to go away, and took the opportunity to eat a pasty each.

"Seems quiet now," Hildy whispered.

They wiped gravy and crumbs off their mouths and tiptoed out. The kitchen gate was just beyond. The footsteps had been Uncle Harchad's. He had done them a favor. The soldiers who should have been on guard at the gate were standing stiffly just inside the kitchen door up the passage, listening to Harchad, along with the scullions left in the kitchen.

"And you're absolutely sure neither of them has gone past?" they heard Harchad saying.

"Quite sure, sir."

"If you see them, I want them brought to me, understand? Not to Earl Harl," said Uncle Harchad.

Nobody saw or heard Ynen and Hildy tiptoe to the gate, open the small postern carved in the big door, and slip out of it with their sacks.

# 10

MITT TOOK A LAST deep breath, hurled himself across the alley, and ran up the wall. If you are light and strong and determined, you can get a long way up a wall like this. Mitt's feet scrambled, his breath sawed, and his fingers caught and slipped in the greasy bricks overhead. His right hand managed to clench in a crumbly crack. He threw the other arm over the top of the wall. Then, with a rasping slide and a slither, he was over and down, in his own backyard, terrified at the noise he had made.

It was queer. It looked like a strange backyard already. Mitt had not remembered it so small and grimy, or the target on the wall so pitted, or the mangle so rusty. As he stole over the slippery earth, he could hardly believe that just as usual, he would be able to slide up the workshop window and unlatch the back door. Yet just as usual, he put his arm in and the cold latch clicked upward under his fingers. He pulled open the door, *creeeak*, and slipped round it into the grimy, gloomy workshop.

Remember to break that window, Mitt thought. Noisy. Pity. Do it last. He crept across the room and picked up a crowbar. He looked at the rack of finished guns—locked, with the seal of Holand dangling from the lock—and the chests of powder—each kind separate, and locked, with the seal of Holand dangling there, too. He wished Hobin was not so careful. He was going to have to break everything, mix his own powder, make his own cartridges.

There was a soft, purposeful movement behind him. Mitt's heart hammered, and his tongue suddenly grew too fat for his mouth. He whirled round, with his hand wet on the crowbar. Hobin was just latching the door which led upstairs to the house.

"That you, Hobin?" Mitt said weakly. Cold despair set in. Everything was going wrong. Hobin should have been out at High Mill, but he was here instead, and wearing his good clothes, as if he had never been out for a walk at all.

Hobin nodded. "I was hoping you'd be along. You've got some sense left, I see." He walked deliberately across the workshop, even more solid and grave than usual. Mitt could not help backing away, even though he knew he would be cut off from the back door. And he was. Hobin stationed himself by the back window, and Mitt knew he was doing it on purpose.

"But you went out," said Mitt. "With Ham."

"And I came back," said Hobin. "Without him."

"And—" Mitt pointed jerkily upward with the crowbar. "My mother. She in?"

Hobin shook his head. "At Siriol's, isn't she? We'd best keep her out of this. Mitt, what kind of fool do you think I am to get taken in by someone like Ham? And what did you think you were aiming to do?"

Mitt swallowed. "I—I came for a gun. I was going to make it like robbers broke in. Honest, Hobin, I wasn't meaning to get you into trouble."

"No, I mean out there on the waterfront," said Hobin.

"Oh," said Mitt.

"You do take me for a fool, don't you?" said Hobin. "I can tell my gunpowder to a grain. I knew it was you taking it, but I never thought it was you who was going to use it. Who was the one that shot the Earl? Another of your precious fishermen?"

"I don't know. Hands to the North, I suppose. Hobin," said Mitt, "let me have a gun. Then I'll go away and never bother you again. Please. Everything went wrong."

"I saw it go wrong," said Hobin. "I was right by you when you chucked your fizz-bang. And it was lucky for them, after that Navis kicked it away, that none of them caught you. Then there was nothing I could do but hope you'd have the sense not to trust those fishermen to get you away. Because you're in really bad trouble, Mitt. And it's not funny. Not this time."

"I know!" said Mitt. "I know! There'll be spies here by tomorrow asking for me."

"Tomorrow!" said Hobin. "You must be joking! They'll be here by sundown. I give them till then to notice it was one of my guns shot the Earl."

"One of yours? How can you tell?" Mitt wished Hobin would come away from the back door. He felt trapped.

"It had to be one of mine to throw straight over that distance," said Hobin. "And it fired first time. Now do you see why I keep well in with the arms inspectors? Or was that what you were counting on?"

"No, I was not," Mitt said wretchedly. "Why do you think I set Ham on you? What did you do with Ham, anyway?"

"Nothing, only gave him the slip," said Hobin. "Being the fool he is, he's still walking round in the Flate looking for me. No, I didn't see you thinking that way, but I couldn't help being riled over Ham. I could see through Ham easier than through that window." Hobin pointed to the grimy glass and came away from the back door at last. Mitt eyed the distance and was wondering whether to dash for it when Hobin said, "What did you aim to do when you'd pinched a gun?"

Mitt heard keys jingle. He looked round to see Hobin unlocking the rack of guns. He could hardly believe it. He knew the risk Hobin was running. "Go out on the Flate," he said. "See here, I don't want you in trouble. Make it look as if I stole it."

Hobin looked at him over his shoulder, almost as if he was amused. "You keep taking me for a fool, Mitt. I'm not giving you one of these. If a man can make one gun, he can make two, can't he?" The whole rack of guns swung out from the wall. Hobin took two loose bricks out of the wall where it had been and reached into the space they left. While he was fumbling inside it, he said, "I wish you'd tell me what made you start on this freedom fighting nonsense, Mitt. Was it your father, or what?"

"I suppose it was," Mitt admitted. It seemed like confessing to one spot when you had measles, but it was the best he could do. Like an admission of failure, he laid the crowbar gently down.

"I thought that was it." Hobin wriggled the bricks back into place and swung the rack back to its usual position. He turned round carefully, carrying a strange, fat little gun. "And I hoped you'd grow up, Mitt," he said. "You've got your own life to live." Gently he spun the strange fat barrel of the gun round. Mitt had never seen a gun like it before. "Have you ever thought," Hobin asked, "what kind of man leaves you and Milda on your own like that?"

This was such an untoward question that Mitt was quite unable to answer it. "What kind of gun is that?" he said.

"The one I had in my pocket while you were planting your banger," said Hobin. "In case of trouble. I kept it loaded for you. But I can only let you have the six shots in it, so go easy on them. I can't cheat the inspectors much more than you can."

"*Six* shots?" said Mitt. "How do you do for priming?"

"You don't. Ever thought what I did with those percussion caps I set you making?" Hobin said. "They're in here, see, on the end of the cartridges, and the hammer fires them off. There's a barrel for each shot. You spin the next one up after you've fired. It doesn't throw far, or I wouldn't let you have it. This is to get you out of trouble, not get you in it, see. If it wasn't for Milda and the girls, I'd have kept you with me and sworn myself blue in the face you were with me all along, like I used to for Canden. But there's them to consider, too. There you are."

He put the gun in Mitt's hands. Like all Hobin's guns, it was beautifully balanced. Mitt hardly felt the weight of the chubby six-holed barrel at all. "What did you make this for?"

"Experiment," said Hobin. "And because one of these days there's going to be a real uprising here in the South. The earls can't hold people down forever. So I've made ready. I hoped you'd be patient and be ready, too. But there. You'll find your pea jacket on the stairs, and my belt to carry the gun in."

Mitt went to the stair door. There, sure enough, were his old pea jacket and the belt. "You—you had this all ready," he said awkwardly.

"What did you expect?" said Hobin. "Sometimes I think I'd make a better freedom fighter than any of you. I put a bit of thought into it. And I'll give you some advice, too. Don't go out in the Flate."

Mitt stopped in the middle of fastening Hobin's belt round himself. "Eh?"

"Eh?" said Hobin. "You're all the same. Do what the other man did. You've got a brain, Mitt. Use it. They'll expect you out in the Flate. You'll be caught by tomorrow lunchtime if you go that way. What you want to do is go up along the coast and see if you can't get a boat at Hoe or Little Flate. Or it's worth looking at the West Pool."

"Over those mucky dikes?" said Mitt.

"That won't kill you, and it's nearest. But I don't know what guard they set over their boats there. See how you go. And if you get anywhere in Canderack or Waywold where there's a gunsmith, go to him and tell him I sent you. They'll all know me. Come on," said Hobin. "I'll give you a lift up over the wall."

Mitt pushed the gun into the belt and put on his jacket. "But what are you going to tell them when they come—these spies?"

"Nail up this window for a start," said Hobin. "Then you may have tried to break in, but you didn't manage it. I'll be very grieved and disappointed in you, Mitt. You'll never darken my door again."

Though Hobin smiled slightly as he said that, Mitt knew that he was not likely to see Hobin again. As he went across the yard with him, Mitt felt unexpectedly wretched about it. He had never treated Hobin right, never even thought of him in the right way. He wanted to apologize to Hobin. But there seemed no time to say anything. Hobin had his hands joined ready for Mitt to tread in. Mitt sighed and put his foot on them.

"Happy birthday," Hobin whispered. "Luck ship and shore."

There had been so much else on Mitt's mind that he had clean forgotten it was his birthday. He wanted to thank Hobin for remembering. But Hobin heaved. Mitt went upward. He had only time for a hasty grin down at Hobin, before he was on top of the wall and slithering over the other side.

No one seemed to have seen him. Mitt set out into the depressed corner of Holand between the causeway to the West Pool and the dunes. It was not far. Flate Street was some way west to start with. And Mitt saw Hobin had been right to tell him to go this way. He only saw one party of soldiers, and these he hid from in a doorway, fingering the fat little gun as they passed and thinking: Better not come too near. Hobin gave me a birthday present you won't like.

The soldiers passed without seeing him. Mitt went on. The town petered out into marsh and shacks made of pieces of boat. There was no one about at all. Mitt, the seagulls, and the rubbish thrown into the pink marsh plants had it all to themselves. Mitt was glad of his coat. There was a fresh wind ripping over the dunes on his left, from the sea, which brimmed to the horizon above the dunes and looked higher than the land. Ahead was a bright green stretch where a network of brackish dikes broke through the dunes. Mitt would have to cross those in order to get to the seawall of the West Pool. He was still not too keen on the idea. But beyond that black line of wall there were masts—several hundred pleasure boats, large and small, awaiting Mitt's pleasure.

Good old Hobin! Mitt thought, making squelching strides through the pink marsh.

Then he came to the dikes. They were gray-green muddy ditches, just too wide to jump, threading the squashy green turf in front of the wall as intricately as the patterns Milda used to embroider on hangings for the Palace. Once they had been simply sea marsh. Now they were where the Palace sewers came out. As the tide was going out, they were running sluggishly, with scummy bubblings and a foot of gray mud above the waterline.

"Yuk!" said Mitt, and looked rather desperately toward the causeway, wondering whether he dared go that way instead. There were people on it. He could see them moving between the trees. Once again that awful, unusual fear seized him. He was afraid to move at all. I better wait for dark, he thought.

But the people, whoever they were, continued flickering slowly to and fro between the trees. Mitt, with his hands shaking, tore up an old stake and prodded the nearest ditch with it. The nasty water was only knee-deep.

I'll have a go, thought Mitt. He slithered down into the sour, salty mud. "Oh yuk! Shershplottle-shloosh! What filthy filth!" said Mitt. He waded through and climbed out. "Careful of that gun, now," he warned himself. A couple of yards on was another ditch. "Second sewer," said Mitt, sliding in with a shudder. "And now"—as he climbed out—"here comes another."

He was struggling out of that ditch when there were shouts from the causeway. Figures ran between the trees and leaped gingerly down on the green morass—green figures, darker than the marsh. Harchad had thought of the West Pool, too. Mitt went down, through and up out of that next dike quicker than the rats through the garbage on the waterfront. He was through the next two before the running soldiers reached their first. As he plunged down yet another slimy bank, he saw them stop there, about a hundred yards away.

Take them a while to bring themselves to go in, he thought. The wall of the Pool was about a hundred yards away, too. Mitt knew he would never get there. It was hopeless. He doubled over and ran along the ditch, splashing and squelching, keeping one hand over his coat and the gun. "Keep it dry. You might get one or two with it," he said to himself. The ditch bent and joined another one. When Mitt looked up, the wall of the Pool was quite a bit nearer. There was a buttress he might climb up. But he would have to come out of this ditch to get to it. Mitt rolled out and dived across the moist green turf.

Something went *pheeew* past his head and thudded *smick* into the bank of the dike beyond.

Mitt found himself up and running. He was so frightened that he felt as if he had got some dreadful disease. His legs hurt, his breathing hurt, and he felt giddy. Bullets were going *pheeew-smick* all round him now. He thought he was like a chicken, running about with its neck wrung. He was sure he was dead.

Hey! thought Mitt. He was on the edge of another dike. *Pheeew-smick.* He threw up both arms, spun round, and fell. While he was falling, he had time to hoik Hobin's belt round him, so the gun was at his back, out of harm's way. He fell on his face on the cold, salty turf and let himself slide over sideways into the bubbling slime in the dike. He hardly noticed the smell.

There was one more shout from the distance, then businesslike silence.

Good, thought Mitt, and began to claw his way along below the bank on hands and knees.

"There are a lot of people," Ynen said uneasily when he and Hildy were halfway along the causeway. "Soldiers, I think. By the Pool gate."

They stopped, confounded, and humped their sacks of pies to the side of the road, where the trees hid them.

"It must be the uprising," said Hildy. "Do you think they'd let us past if I offered them a gold piece? I've got one."

"I don't know. There are an awful lot of them."

They loitered forward, under the trees. It was hard to know what to do. The soldiers might not stop them. On the other hand, Uncle Harchad had told the guards by the kitchen to bring them to him. He could have sent the same message to these soldiers.

"And it would be the most terrible waste if they sent us back *now*," said Hildy.

Before they were near enough to see or be seen clearly, they saw the figures at the end of the road flicker to the side of it, one after another, and disappear through the trees. It looked as if they had jumped off the causeway.

"Don't they want us to see them?" Hildy said, and stopped, thinking of bombs and revolutionaries.

"Oh come on!" said Ynen, and began to run. "Quick! While they're away."

Hildy caught him up, and they ran hard, with the pies butting at their shoulders and the trees flicking past on either side. There was a salvo of little blunt bangs down below the road. Between the flicking trees they saw puffs of smoke and a flash or so. It sent both Hildy and Ynen over to the other side of the road, where they ran still, but more slowly. Neither of them wanted to run straight into a battle.

But the firing stopped after a round or so. Ynen panted to Hildy to hurry, to get to the gate before the soldiers came back. But no soldiers appeared. They reached the big pitch-painted gates before they saw them. There were about twenty soldiers, all down in the marsh to the left, jumping and slithering among the smelly dikes there. They were peering into each one they came to, and shouting to one another to cover the next one. Some had poles and were prodding the mud.

"They're looking for someone," Ynen said, greatly relieved. "I bet it's the murderer."

"I suppose they shot him," Hildy agreed. "Ynen, how lucky!

They've left the gates open. They must have been searching the Pool." It did not really occur to them that someone's misfortune had caused their good luck.

Mitt slithered up that buttress. Like a horrible great slug, I am, he thought. He rolled onto the top of the wall. Left a slimy trail like one, too, he thought, looking at the wide smear of gray-green mud behind him. Below, the soldiers were prodding at ditches, convinced he was dead. Mitt rolled off the wall and thumped onto the jetty beyond before any of them chanced to look up and find reason to revise their opinion. He lay propped on his elbows, panting, clammy and almost tired out, and wondered which of these many little boats he had better get into. He knew it would have to be one he could manage easily alone. For that reason he rejected the beauty moored about ten yards down. "Too big, my lovely," he told her. "One of them Siriol used to spit at, too."

He looked round the rest. Some were big, some tubby, some the merest cockleshells. They all gleamed with splendid paint. Mitt thought he was weighing each one up as he looked at it, but in fact, all he was doing was comparing them with that blue beauty ten yards away and finding them trash in comparison. He did not have time to make himself decide reasonably. A soldier down in the marsh yelled. Mitt bolted on hands and knees like a monkey. He was rolling across the blue beauty's cabin roof before he had time to think. She had a steering well—purest pleasure boat stuff, Mitt thought, dropping down into it. At least it hid him from the soldiers.

But not for long. Before Mitt had believed it possible, footsteps were pattering on the jetty outside. He tore open the double cabin doors and dived inside. If he had not been in such a hurry, he would have stopped then and stared. He never could have imagined a ship's inside could be so beautiful—blue blankets and blue plush, a charcoal cooking stove, white paint and gold, and everything carved and ornamented and cleaned until it was more like a floating palace than a boat.

Ah, I always said the best wasn't good enough for me! Mitt thought, tiptoeing in a trail of green slime to the far end of the cabin. The boat's name was embroidered on all the blankets. Mitt could not resist pausing to spell out the name all this luxury went under. *Wind's Road*, he read. Very suitable. Suits me fine.

The next second *Wind's Road* dipped and swung under people's feet. "Isn't she beautiful!" Ynen said, dumping his sack on a locker. Mitt fumbled open a gilded cupboard, sweating with panic, and found himself confronting a bucket with a gilded seat. The bucket seemed to have roses painted all over it.

Flaming Ammet! thought Mitt. There really *is* nothing but the best on this ship! He shot the polished brass bolt to the cupboard with slimy, shaking fingers, and leaned against the gilded wall, listening to feet scampering and shrill, haughty voices calling overhead.

# PART THREE

# *Wind's Road*

# 11

"HELP ME GET the mainsail up, and then stand by to untie her," Ynen said. "Oh, look at this! She's all over mud! I knew those blessed sailors used her for lobsters when my back was turned!"

"I'll wash it down when we're sailing," Hildy said. "But do let's get going before those soldiers come. Most of the mud's only on the sail cover." She jumped on the cabin roof and helped Ynen unlace the cover.

Ynen unlaced busily beside her. He was not often angry, but he was now. Someone had been on *Wind's Road*, the apple of his eye, the one lovely thing that was truly his own, and made a mess of her in his absence. He could not forgive them. "Honestly!" he said. "Green, smelly mud! You trust people, and they go and take advantage of you."

"Father said you can't blame people for that," said Hildy. "I'll fold from my end, and be *quick*! He said the poor see the rich as their natural prey."

"Just the kind of thing he would say!" Ynen said irritably. "Fold it, don't just scrunch it! Mind you, he was probably right. I'll ask for a guard in future."

"Some soldiers have just come through the gates," said Hildy, causing Mitt to stand stiffly in his cupboard with his hands clenched. He had no idea who these arrogant fugitives could be or why they were in such a hurry, but he knew they could not be in too much of a hurry for him.

"Cast off the moorings and push her off, then," Ynen called, "while I get the sail up. Make sure you don't push us out of the deep channel, though."

Yes, and hurry up about it, for Old Ammet's sake! Mitt thought.

In a flurry of thumping, Hildy untied the mooring ropes and threw them on the planking, ready to be coiled later. Then she heaved on the jetty with all her might. Mitt gathered from the shifting and dipping what was happening. He heard the rhythmic *rattle, rattle* as Ynen sent the mainsail up, hand over hand, and then a further pounding of feet combined with a stiff tilting, as Ynen bounded to the bows to get the foresails up, and Hildy plunged to the tiller and turned *Wind's Road* to catch the wind. After that came a slow *ripple, ripple. Wind's Road* got gently under way and slid along the channel toward the open sea.

They won't find us so easy to stop now, Mitt thought. Whoever these rich youngsters were, they could handle a boat all right. He supposed it was lucky they could. But he was still scared stiff. He could not see them getting away with it.

Hildy and Ynen anxiously watched the harbor wall glide by and wished it would glide faster. Four or five soldiers were now running along the jetty behind, stumbling among ropes and shouting.

"What are they saying?" Ynen wondered.

Hildy gave a nervous giggle. "*Stop*, I think."

"What am I supposed to do? Pull on the reins?" Ynen said, and laughed, too.

Soldiers appeared on the harbor wall, struggling up from the marsh behind, most of them muddy and all in a great hurry. No sooner did they see *Wind's Road* sliding proudly past and beginning to lean a little in the sea wind than they became quite frantic. They shouted to one another and yelled at Hildy and Ynen to come back. One or two raised their guns.

"They're awfully close," Hildy said.

"I know, but I daren't leave the channel," said Ynen. The soldiers seemed so angry that he thought he had better pacify them. He jumped up onto the seat of the steering well, with his foot on the tiller, and waved. "It's all right," he shouted cheerfully. "We're only going out for a sail."

A soldier sighted along a gun at him. Ynen overbalanced out of sheer astonishment and pitched down into the well, kicking the tiller as he went. As *Wind's Road* veered, the shot fizzed slantwise across where Ynen's head had been, only just missing the lovely whiteness of her mainsail.

"Ye gods!" said Hildy, and plunged for the tiller. Wind was hard in the sail, and she could feel the deep keel dragging in the mud of the Pool. Another shot zinged across behind Hildy's head.

Ynen rolled over as if he had been stung and stared anxiously up at the sail. "Filthy swine! If he's holed my canvas, I'll have his guts for garters!"

Hildy dragged the tiller across. *Wind's Road*, her sail now properly filled, gathered majestic speed and foamed past the end of the wall. If the soldiers fired any more shots, they were lost in the sudden buffet of waves and the singing of the fresh wind. "They can't possibly stop us now," said Hildy. "But, Ynen, they fired at us! What *did* they think they were doing?"

"They must all be filthy revolutionaries," Ynen said. He was still very shaken. "I'll make sure they're all hanged when we get back."

"I think it must have been a mistake," Hildy said, almost equally shaken.

Mistake all right, Mitt thought, shaking all over. They thought one of you was me. Now you had a taste of the way the rest of us feel. Don't like it, do you? What did I have to go and choose this boat for? I can't do a thing right today, can I? If only I'd got on any of the other ones, I could have sat tight and let the soldiers think these two was me.

"It must have been a mistake," Ynen agreed, recovering. "I was just furious in case they'd spoiled the boat. We can sort it out when we get back."

"We might not be able to," said Hildy. "Don't forget we'll be in awful trouble when we get back."

"Oh, don't let's think of that now," said Ynen. "Hand over the tiller. I want to stand well out to miss the shoals."

It was beyond Mitt to imagine what these two thought they were doing. First they ran from the soldiers as fast as he had. Now they talked about going back. The one thing Mitt was certain of, was that he was going to change that idea for them. He wriggled the bolt quietly back and came out of his gilded cupboard. There he suddenly felt tired out. He stood listening to the sea frilling briskly past the hull and the creak and rattle of ropes. Feet batted the roof as Hildy began coiling ropes and resetting the foresails. Then came the clank and slosh of a bucket being dipped overboard. Rubbing and trickling sounds told Mitt that someone was washing off the mud he had brought aboard.

That's right, he thought. Bustle about. Siriol taught me to keep my boats particular. Ah, I feel like a wet wash leather! And since it was obvious that neither of his companions was intending to come into the cabin, Mitt flopped onto the port bunk for a rest. He could wait a bit to change their plans. The cabin, as small places do, quickly got up a fug. The mud on Mitt, the blankets and the floor dried in big green flakes. Mitt drowsed.

When Hildy had washed the deck, she joined Ynen in the well. "I love the way the wind blows in your face and makes your eyes all cool," she said.

"It's my favorite feeling," Ynen said.

Mitt hoped they would not go on like this. He did not want to hear their silly private thoughts. He was glad when Hildy said, "The land's a long way off already."

"The tide's running out," Ynen explained. "We'll be past the shoals in a minute. Then we'll turn north."

"I like the south best," Hildy objected.

"So do I. But the wind's wrong. We'd be close-hauled, and I wouldn't dare tie the mainsheet when we had supper."

"But there's a current to the north, isn't there? If we get into that, we'll never get back before dark, not close-hauled," Hildy pointed out.

"I wasn't going that far," said Ynen. "I want to be back in daylight because of the shoals. I thought we'd go north till slack water, and then have supper, and then come back when the tide turned."

"Supper at slack water sounds a nice idea," Hildy admitted. "And you are captain."

Mitt thought supper at any time was a nice idea. And you'll share it three ways, he thought. Two for me and one for you. Then we'll see about who's captain, and carry on up North. He bestirred himself enough to fetch out Hobin's gun and see how it had fared in the dikes. To his relief, it was dry. He laid it by his head, within easy reach, and dozed again. *Wind's Road* rose and fell. The wind creaked in her sails. The water splatted past. Ynen and Hildy did not talk much. They were too happy. Time and the land slid away.

The next thing Mitt knew, *Wind's Road*'s motion was a more sluggish one. Hildy was saying angrily, "Why did you tell me you knew if you didn't?"

Ynen answered patiently, in the overfirm way people use when they are trying to convince themselves as much as the other person, "I do know. That must be Hoe Point over there, and I'm sure Little Flate is in the dip beyond it. All I said was that we'd come a bit farther than I expected."

Mitt blinked at the gilt and white portholes and was surprised to see it was still daylight, if they had come that far. *Wind's Road*, even allowing for the tide which helped her, was a fine, fast boat. Unless it was tomorrow, of course. So much had happened to Mitt today that he felt as if it had gone on for a fortnight, even before he boarded this boat.

"Are you saying you think we've got into that current?" Hildy asked sharply. "Because, if so, we'd better turn straight round now."

"No, no. It's only slack water," Ynen assured her anxiously. "I can tell it's slack water by the way she's sailing."

Mitt thought about the new motion of *Wind's Road*. It felt much more as if she were in a current to him, which suited him perfectly. In which case they were not where that flaming amateur at the tiller thought they were.

"Where does the current begin?" Hildy demanded.

"That's the trouble," Ynen admitted. "It may be Hoe Point, or it may not be till Little Flate. I'm not sure."

Mitt cast his eyes to the elegant ceiling. The current began off Hoe Point, and Hoe Point came after Little Flate. I thought everyone knew that, he thought. Anyway, what's the fuss about? You can go right out to sea and get out of it again.

But *Wind's Road* was simply a pleasure boat. Ynen had never been out of sight of land in her. And he had always had sailors with him before who knew the coast. "I think perhaps you'd better fetch me the chart," he said to Hildy. "It's in the rack over the port bunk."

"I think I'd better, too," said Hildy, and she set off.

Whoops! thought Mitt, as he heard her coming. The time had come for him to act. He snatched up Hobin's gun and cocked it as he scrambled off the bunk. Then he grabbed open the door and whirled through it, just as Hildy was trying to come in.

They collided heavily. Hildy was slightly taller than Mitt and weighed a great deal more. But Mitt was moving twice as fast. Hildy crashed over backward with a shriek. Mitt was thrown against the cabin. The gun went off with a bark and a jerk and all but kicked itself out of Mitt's hand. It was like being hit over the wrist with a hammer. The shot, in a spatter of splinters, plowed across the deck and into the sea. The well filled with sharp-smelling smoke.

"Ye gods!" wailed Hildy. She thought her back was broken.

Mitt choked for breath against the cabin door and peered resentfully through the smoke at the gun. He thought Hobin might have warned him that it kicked like that. Then, as the smoke cleared, he saw Ynen in front of him, hanging on to the tiller and the rope from the mainsail, very white in the face, and staring at the long splintered groove in *Wind's Road*'s beautiful planking. A right ninny, Mitt thought. Cares more about his boat being damaged than he does about his brother—sister, I mean. Hildy was painfully up on one elbow, glaring at Mitt. Mitt looked at both of them with the utmost contempt. They both had such a smooth look, with their skin well filled and their hair thick and dark and healthy. He could see neither had gone hungry in their lives. What aroused his dislike most—though he did not realize it—was that

Hildy and Ynen both inherited their looks from their father. Mitt looked at Ynen and saw a gentle version of Hadd's nose and at Hildy and saw the narrow, pale face of both Navis and Harchad, and though he did not recognize either, he detested them both on sight. And since his opinion of females was low, anyway, he encountered Hildy's glare and thought: She makes me sick—worse than her brother!

It was not surprising that they felt much the same about Mitt. They stared at Mitt's young-old face and his lank, dull-colored hair. They saw his bony hand was gripping a gun that looked like a collector's piece, that his pea jacket was ragged, and that green mud was peeling from his long, skinny legs. They knew he must be riffraff from the waterfront. They suspected he was a thief, too. They thought he was disgusting.

"Well, we know what the soldiers were after. And where all the mud came from," said Hildy.

"Are you badly hurt?" Ynen asked her. He felt very helpless. He dared not let go of the tiller to help Hildy, nor did he dare turn straight round and head back to Holand, much as he wanted to, for fear this disgusting stowaway loosed off with his gun again.

"No. I'm all right," said Hildy, and struggled to her feet. "He missed me, of course."

"I was not aiming to hit you," Mitt said with great scorn. "You ran into me like a whole herd of cows. You want to look out. This is a hasty kind of gun."

"I like that!" said Hildy.

"If it's that hasty, why don't you put it away?" Ynen suggested.

Mitt ignored him. He looked up at the sail and the streaming flag at the masthead. It was a fair wind for the North, all right. The land was low blue hummocks to his right. It took Mitt only one glance to spot Hoe Point nearly a mile astern. The hump Ynen had taken for Hoe Point was Canderack Head. Mitt was impressed. It was still an hour off sundown, too. He could not help grinning.

"Well, well," he said. "A good fast boat you got here. All set for the North, aren't we?"

Ynen's face went rather whiter as he grasped what the stowaway might be planning. "We're not going to take you North," he said. "If that's what's in your mind."

"Not got much choice, have you?" said Mitt. He pretended to rub the gun on his sleeve. He did not really rub it, because he was very much afraid it would go off again. "I've got this gun, haven't I?"

"You can shoot me if you want," said Ynen. "But I'm not taking you North." He wondered if it would hurt very much and thought that it probably would. He could only hope he would die quickly.

"Ynen, don't be an idiot!" said Hildy.

"He thinks I wouldn't dare," said Mitt. "Well, I would. Because I happen to be a desperate man." That sounded good. And it had the advantage of being true. Mitt began to enjoy himself. "If you won't take me North," he said, "I wouldn't kill you. I'd just put a bullet in your leg. Maybe both legs." He was pleased to see Hildy glaring at him. "Then in her," he said. "And then it would be rather a pleasure to knock this boat about a bit—scrape off the pretty paint, carve silly pictures in the decking, and so on."

As Mitt had hoped it would, this threat truly upset Ynen. "You dare touch my boat, you guttersnipe!"

"He doesn't know any better," said Hildy.

"I thought that would worry you," Mitt said in high glee. "All you've got to do to stop me is carry on as you are. Just keep sailing North."

Ynen and Hildy exchanged a miserable look. They seemed to have gone from perfect happiness to a nightmare in a matter of seconds. Hildy wondered what had possessed her to lead Ynen into this. She had known there were revolutionaries at large. They should have stayed in the Palace. Ynen was thinking mostly of that current and how he could persuade the boy that *Wind's Road* simply could not take him all the way North.

"Look here," Ynen said, trying to sound fair and reasonable. "We can't go North. We have to be back in Holand tonight or people will worry. What do you say to our landing you somewhere on the way back? How about—" Ynen looked over at the land and could not help feeling extremely uneasy about the shape of it. "Hoe Point?" he said doubtfully.

Mitt gave what he hoped was an evil laugh. "Go on! You couldn't get back to Holand tonight even if you went this second! You're in a nice fast northerly current, and in this wind you'll be lucky if you make it back by morning. Hoe Point is where that current starts, and that's Hoe Point back there, you flaming amateur! Look at your chart if you don't believe me." He saw he had demoralized them. Ynen's face was warm pink, and he was staring at Hildy as if the end of the world had come. Mitt was so pleased that he added, "I was sailing out of Holand before you were born." That was a mistake. Hildy gave him a jeering look. Mitt scowled at her. "Just sail North and don't give me any trouble," he said. "And you won't have any trouble from me. I can't say fairer than that, can I?"

Hildy sighed to cover up her thoughts. Unpleasant as this boy was, he did bluster rather. To judge by Ynen's face, he was right about the current, but that did not mean he had thought of everything. "I suppose we'd better humor him, Ynen," she said. She stared hard at Ynen, slowly shutting her eyes and opening them, to show him that the boy would have to sleep sometime.

Mitt knew that, too. Even a sweet boat like *Wind's Road* would take three or four days to reach North Dalemark waters. No one could stay awake that long. Mitt was tired to death already. He felt his only course was to keep these children thoroughly intimidated by being as rough and dangerous and brutal as he could. He seemed to have made a fairly good start. So, while Ynen was nodding gravely at Hildy to show her he understood, Mitt roared out, "Right, then. Now that's settled, go and get out your eatables. I'm starving. Hurry up!"

Hildy gave him a poisonous look. But it was fully suppertime, and she was hungry herself. She got up and dragged one of the sacks of pies out of the locker. Ynen took a careful breath, hoping it was not his last, and said, "I'd rather you didn't speak to my sister like that."

"What's she done to deserve any better?" Mitt said nastily. "You watch it." He was annoyed to see the two of them exchanging a look which was anything but intimidated. "Come on. What's in that sack?"

He was relieved to see it was pies. He had been wondering how he could eat and still keep hold of Hobin's gun. He was afraid that if he let go of it for a moment, he would find himself being pushed overboard. But he could eat a pie with one hand.

The pies were scarcely as tempting as they had been. Gravy had run and juice had leaked, and then mingled and soaked back into other pastry. But Mitt was not in a state to care. He had not properly eaten anything since breakfast. He intended to go on with the intimidation by eating with great gobbling noises and huge slurpings, but as soon as he had a pie in his hand, he forgot everything but how hungry he was. He only thought of eating. He was hardly able to attend to the splendid, unusual tastes, he was so frantic for food. He ate five steak pies, a pheasant patty, six oyster puffs, a chicken flan, four cheesecakes, and nine fruit tarts. He thought, as he drew at last to a gentle halt, that his gluttony had served to intimidate the children almost as well as making noises. They were staring, looking thoroughly chastened. Mitt managed, with no effort at all, to produce a monstrous belch, to make sure they knew exactly how rough and foul he was.

In fact, Ynen and Hildy were simply awed. They had not known it was possible to be so hungry.

That explains those thin legs, Hildy thought, looking at them. The sun was melting down into the sea, in a buttery haze. By its strong yellow light, Hildy saw that most of the mud had flaked off the boy's legs, showing him to be wearing odd old-fashioned breeches, with one leg red and the other yellow. The sight gave Hildy such a jolt that she burst out, "I know who you are! You threw that bomb Father kicked away!"

# 12

MITT LOOKED FROM Hildy to Ynen. He saw the likeness now. His huge meal had left him slow and almost unbearably sleepy. His first thought was that it was funny. Hadd ruined him. Navis spoiled all his plans. And now these were Navis's children who were willy-nilly rescuing him. He chuckled. "Now that's what I call justice," he said. "Navis is your pa then?"

Hildy stuck her chin up and did her best to overawe Mitt. "Yes," she said haughtily. "And I'll have you know that I am betrothed to Lithar, Lord of the Holy Islands."

"Oh, shut up," Ynen said uncomfortably. "You sound just like the cousins."

Hildy had been imitating her cousin Irana boasting of her betrothal. She was annoyed with Ynen for noticing. She turned her back on him and looked hopefully at Mitt, hoping she had upset him by it at least.

Mitt laughed. "Betrothed!" People got betrothed at Lydda's age, when they were eighteen and grown-up. Hildy was only a little girl in pigtails. "Bit young for that, aren't you?" Then the implications struck him. He was quite as alarmed as Hildy could have hoped, but he kept on laughing. He dared not let them see he was upset. This girl was important, all right. He remembered Milda telling him about Lithar. That made certain that ships would pursue them from Holand, and more ships would be out to meet them from the Holy Islands. Mitt knew he was going to have to make them take this boat right out into the ocean. It was going to take days, and even then he might be caught. Just to think of it made him feel tired. "Well, it's your business," he said. "Doesn't worry me." He stood up. "I'm off for a visit to that silly bucket in the cupboard. The one with roses on. No tricks while I'm gone now."

Ynen's face was pink in the yellow light. "They aren't roses. They're poppies," he said.

"Roses," said Mitt. "And with a golden rim, too. Amazing the way your kind has to have things pretty!" He went into the cabin.

Ynen shouted after him, "Your kind built this boat!" Then, as soon as Mitt was at the end of the cabin, he whispered to Hildy, "What are we going to *do*?"

Now that Mitt had laughed at Hildy for being betrothed, she was determined to get the better of him. "I've got an idea," she whispered, "to make him go to sleep."

"Then we'll turn round," Ynen agreed. "What idea?"

"What are you whispering about?" Mitt yelled.

They dared not whisper anymore. Ynen looked at the long splintered groove in *Wind's Road*'s planking and shivered. It was getting hard to see now. The sun had swum down below the horizon, leaving a yellow sky spread with straight black clouds. The sea was a melting, lighter yellow, as if the light had soaked into it. Hildy's face was dark. "We're saying we ought to have a light at the masthead," he called. "It's the law."

"Haven't you noticed?" Mitt bawled. "I got nothing to do with the law."

"Unlike you, we were brought up to be lawful," Hildy called. "Can I light the lamp in the cabin at least?"

Mitt came out of the cupboard and fumbled his way through the cabin. It was certainly getting dark. He felt sour and grim, and he ached all over. The red and yellow breeches would not do up properly after his great meal. He came out of the cabin and flopped down on the lockers. "Please yourself," he said. He was horribly weary.

Hildy smiled slightly and went into the cabin, where she was some time fiddling about before the lamp came on, as yellow as the sky outside. Then she moved on to the fat little water barrel, which was clamped to a special shelf above the stove. She undid the clamps and shook it. The barrel was completely full, so full that it did not even slosh. It took all Hildy's strength to shake it convincingly, but she had been prepared for that, because it was always kept full. No one dared let Hadd's family go thirsty.

"Oh dear!" Hildy said. She was surprised how convincing she sounded. "There's no water in this at all! I'm horribly thirsty, too." This was true, but she thought she could bear it in a good cause.

As soon as she said this, Mitt realized that one of the many things wrong with him was an appalling thirst. It was all those highly spiced pies he had eaten. The thought of going without water for all the time it took to get North nearly made him burst into tears. Ynen was almost equally dismayed. His mouth suddenly seemed quite dry, and he had a moment when he would have liked to report those negligent sailors to Uncle Harchad. He licked his sandpapery lips and said, "They sometimes keep wine in the lockers over the starboard bunk. Have a look, Hildy, for Old Ammet's sake!"

Hildy turned round to hide a triumphant smile and fetched the two bottles she had already found there. One was a half-full bottle of wine. The other was a square bottle of arris. It had been full before Hildy had poured a generous dollop of it into the wine. One way or another, she thought she had done for this wretched boy.

"Which will you have?" she said, showing Mitt the bottles in the twilight.

Mitt knew the rough, foul drink was arris. But he hated it too much. "I'll have the wine," he said, and he snatched the bottle from Hildy, feeling he could make up on roughness and foulness that way, and took a long, guggling swig from it before Hildy could get him a cup from the cabin. He intended to drink the lot. But it tasted rather unpleasant. He passed Hildy back the bottle, a good deal less than a quarter full.

Hildy distastefully wiped the neck of the bottle and shared the rest into two cups for herself and Ynen. They sipped it and settled down to wait, while twilight grew into night.

Shortly, Ynen began to feel cheerful and Hildy slightly dizzy. As for Mitt, the wine, on top of his weariness, on top of his huge meal, had the inevitable effect. The low black humps of land kept spreading under his eyes like inkblots. The stars came out and looked fuzzy. His head kept dropping forward. At length he stood up unsteadily.

"Going to have a lie-down," he said. "No stunny fuff, now. Got ears in the back of my head." He staggered off into the cabin, while Hildy and Ynen each stuffed a fist into their mouths in order not to scream with laughter, and flopped heavily down on the port bunk.

Hildy nudged Ynen meaningly and sat down with her back against the lockers, where she could see into the cabin. They waited for Mitt to fall asleep. But, with the best will in the world to do so, Mitt could not go to sleep. The movements of *Wind's Road* and the movements the wine had set up in his head seemed to be in direct conflict. Sometimes he was convinced the boat had got into a whirlpool. Sometimes he was sure his legs were high above his head. He sat up several times to see what was going on. And each time the elegant gilded cabin was exactly as it should be, gently rising and falling, and the lamp swinging. At length he realized the queer things only happened when he had his eyes shut. So he kept them open.

The result was a set of horrible, half-waking dreams. Mitt stared at Harchad's face in a gilded porthole, paralyzed with terror. He ran endlessly from soldiers. He struggled through innumerable dikes. Several times he was shot in the stomach. Once he threw his bomb in front of Hadd, and Poor Old Ammet bent down, put out his straw arms, and threw the bomb in Mitt's face. "You're in really bad trouble," he said, and he sounded just like Hobin. Then he fell to pieces like Canden. Mitt sat up with a yell of horror. After this, when he lay down again, things got a little quieter, until it was Libby Beer's turn. She ran at Mitt, with her fruity eyes wobbling on stalks, and kicked the bomb at him. "I brought you up to do this, Mitt," she said reproachfully. Then the bomb exploded, and Mitt started up with a scream.

Hildy and Ynen wished he would stop yelling and go to sleep. They wanted to turn round and sail home. The yells perturbed them. The boy must be disgustingly sinful. And the sounds made them think of the things they had heard about Uncle Harchad, and that terrible day the Northmen had been hanged. Meanwhile, true night came on, and Ynen became frankly terrified. By this time he had been at the tiller longer than he had ever been in his life. He had never sailed at night before. He was cold and cramped and tired, and scared of shoals he could not see. What he could see scared him even more. It was not dark the way it was in a closed room. The sea was there, faintly, all round, heaving and swelling limitlessly. The sky was a huge empty bowl, dark blue, covered with a littering of stars, and the land was only a feeling, far away to the right. The sail noises, and the swish and fizz of waves passing, only seemed to show how small and lonely *Wind's Road* was. Ynen suddenly became aware of fathoms and fathoms of empty water underneath them, too. He was hanging all alone in the middle of nowhere. Ynen clenched his teeth and kept the Northern Cross grimly over *Wind's Road*'s bowsprit, and it was all he could do not to yell out the way the boy in the cabin kept doing.

It was midnight before Hildy dared signal that Mitt was asleep. In fact, he had been asleep all along, but so restlessly that Hildy had not realized. She pulled the cabin door quietly shut and shot the elegant little bolt home.

"Thank goodness! You go to the foresails," Ynen whispered.

Hildy crept forward, round the starboard side, to avoid any noise near Mitt. Ynen could see her clearly against the pallor of the sails. As soon as she was ready, he put the tiller over hard. *Wind's Road* surged round. Her sails ran out to the end of their ropes and swung back. The wind seemed suddenly twice as strong. Ynen kept his foot against the tiller and hauled in the mainsail frantically. Hildy collected the clapping foresails and dragged them the other way. *Wind's Road* stood still, head on to the wind, and seemed to flap and tremble in every part. Then she was round, tipped over much farther, and apparently rushing through the water, but actually making very little way against the current. Ynen hauled in the mainsail as close as he could, in order not to waste time tacking, and they were now headed back to Holand. Hildy came back to the well, and they both sagged with relief.

Holand meant safety and bed and warm rooms. They had got the better of that dreadful boy. That was their first thought. Then they both remembered the trouble they would be in once they were back. That could not be helped, but they did wish the thought of the trouble did not go along with an empty, forsaken feeling. It was no good pretending Navis would defend them from the uncles. On the other hand, Uncle Harchad might forgive them a great deal if they brought him the boy who had thrown the bomb.

Hildy and Ynen peered at one another's faces, trying to see what the other thought about that. The boy was a criminal. He had tried to murder their grandfather. Perhaps he was a friend of the man who had actually done so. But all the same, he was a human being, much the same age as they were, and having bad dreams in the cabin. They both thought of Uncle Harchad kicking the Earl of Hannart's son, and the Earl's son cringing. It was easy enough to replace the Earl's son with a picture of that skinny, cocksure boy, and quite as unpleasant.

"We could put him off at Hoe Point, couldn't we?" Ynen whispered, and relieved Hildy's mind considerably.

Mitt, as he slept, was encountering Poor Old Ammet and Libby Beer at once. They rushed at him, one from either side. The world spun about and went wrong somehow. When Mitt opened his eyes, he knew the world was still wrong. It was going with a blunt, blundering, bucking motion, and tipping the wrong way. Those early years with Siriol had put some things deep in Mitt's brain. Funny, he thought. Close-hauled against a current. *Flaming Ammet!* He snatched up Hobin's gun and burst out of the cabin. He did not even notice the door had been bolted.

Outside, he had only to feel the wind on his face to know he was right. The children's smitten faces in the lamplight confirmed it. So did the Northern Cross low down behind them.

"Turn her back round!" he yelled. "You sneaking idle rich, you! You think you can do just as you like, don't you! Go on, turn her back round!"

At this, despite the waving gun, Hildy lost her temper. He spoiled her entire scheme, and then he shouted insults. "Don't you talk to me about doing just as we want!" She was so angry that she stood up and yelled in Mitt's face. "You sneak aboard our ship, and order us about like dirt, and eat our food, and make us go where *you* want to go, and then you have the nerve to say *we* always do what we want! You're worse than—than Grandfather! He was honest about it at least!"

*"Honest!"* bawled Mitt. "Haddock honest! Don't make me laugh. He was robbing all Holand for years!"

"So you try to murder him, and order us about like dirt on top of that!" Hildy screamed.

"You *are* dirt, that's why!" Mitt thundered, waving the gun. "Turn this boat back round!" Ynen clutched the tiller and feared for Hildy's life. In fact, neither he nor Mitt noticed that Mitt had not even remembered to cock the gun. He had not spun the empty barrel on either.

Hildy did not know and did not care. "If we're dirt, I shudder to think what your family is!" she roared.

"Oh shut up!" Mitt pointed the gun at Ynen. "Turn this boat round, I said!"

For the second time that night Ynen thought he was about to be shot. It gave him a cool kind of resignation. "You did try to murder our grandfather," he said. "Give me one good reason why we should do anything to help you."

Mitt noticed he was pointing the gun at Ynen and realized that Ynen did not regard the gun as a good reason. It sobered him rather. He felt considerable respect for this smooth-faced, hawk-nosed little boy, though, as for his sister—! "Well then," he said, "your precious grandfather bust up my family. Is that a reason?"

"How did he do that?" Ynen asked, shivering with cold and weariness.

Hildy added angrily, "Whatever he did, *we* didn't do anything to you!"

"I'll tell you," said Mitt. He rested his arm on the cabin roof and began to talk, jerkily and angrily at first, and then more reasonably, as he realized neither of them was trying to interrupt. He told them how he had been born at Dike End, and how the rent had been doubled, and how this had forced his father to work in Holand and then forced them out of the farm. He told them how his father had never found proper work and so joined the Free Holanders, and how he had been betrayed over the warehouse—though he did not mention names—and disappeared, leaving Milda and himself to manage alone. He described how they had lived after that, and he could not help thinking, as he talked, that this was a funny kind of way to tell your life story, with *Wind's Road* bucking through the water in the dark, and the half-lit faces of Hadd's grandchildren staring up at him as he talked. He told them about

Hobin. "And if it hadn't been for him," he said, "we'd have been turned out into the street when they knocked the houses down to make the Festival safe."

"They didn't just turn them out, did they?" Hildy said. "I thought—"

"Father had houses built for them," said Ynen. "But I don't think anyone else was going to bother. All the same," he said to Mitt, "you and your mother weren't there then. You were all right. You still haven't given me a reason."

"Isn't that a reason?" Mitt demanded. "There was Hobin never daring to put a foot wrong for fear of the arms inspectors, and us near on as hard up as ever because Hadd would put the rents up all the time. But never the price of guns—not he! We had to pay through the nose to support those soldiers, so that they could make us scared to stir hand or foot. You don't understand—can't you think how it feels when everyone you know is scared sick all the time? You couldn't trust people. They'd turn round and tell on you, anytime, even if it weren't you done it, because they didn't want to get marched off in the night themselves. That's not how people should be."

"It isn't," Hildy agreed.

"I grant you that," said Ynen. "But you're talking about everything. You haven't told me one thing Grandfather did to *you*. I still don't see why we should help you. But I've heard things about Uncle Harchad. I don't mind landing you at Hoe Point, so you'll have a chance to get away."

Yes, Mitt thought, in full view of all the ships coming out to look for them. Very safe. Talking to this boy was like bashing down a weak little plant that kept springing up again in your face. "You might as well take me back to Holand and be done," he said. "If I'm not caught landing, I'll be caught in the Flate straight after."

"Well, you did throw a bomb," said Ynen. "And I can't see why you did. There must have been lots of people in Holand far worse off than you. Why did *you* do it?"

That was a home question. Twenty-four hours earlier Mitt could have given all sorts of answers. He could have told them at least that it was to be revenged on Siriol, Dideo, and Ham. But he had gone out of his way *not* to be revenged. And he had run and run and run. He did not know what he thought he had been doing. He was reduced to answering with another question. "Could *you* have seen things so wrong and not think you ought to do something about it?"

This in its turn was a home question to Ynen and Hildy. They had indeed seen things wrong. All Ynen had done was wish he could whirl a rattle in Hadd's face. All Hildy had done was tear a bedspread and make empty threats. Then they had gone out sailing—a piece of defiance which had thrown them in the way of this boy. And he had not only told them more things that were wrong but had demanded that they help him. With the result that they were now sailing back to Holand to deliver him to Uncle Harchad.

"Ynen—" said Hildy.

"I know," said Ynen. "All right. We'd better take you North. Hildy, could you go to the foresails again?"

Mitt was rather taken aback. He knew he had not given Ynen a reason. He felt dishonest, and shamed. What would happen to these two in the North? He thought of the Northmen shuffling through Holand to be tried and hanged. "See here," he said. "All you got to do is land me near Kinghaven or whatsits—Aberath—and I'll do nicely. Or you might try Tulfa. Then you go back to the Holy Islands. You'd be all right there if she's betrothed to Lithar—What's your name, by the way?"

"Hildrida," said Hildy. "Hildy for short. And this is Ynen. What's yours?"

"Mitt," said Mitt.

"Oh, not another Alhammitt!" said Hildy. "That must make at least twenty I know!"

"Common as dirt," agreed Mitt.

Ynen had been thinking over what Mitt had suggested. Tired as he was, he began smiling. "Let's go to the Holy Islands, Hildy. I'd love to see them."

Hildy just could not see herself sailing up to the Holy Islands and announcing she was Lithar's future wife. The idea made her stomach squirm. But she looked at Ynen and decided he was too tired to be argued with.

Mitt could see how tired Ynen was, too. He remembered how he used to feel on a long stint aboard *Flower of Holand*. "How about you getting some rest, now we seem to know where we're going?" he said. "I can sail her for you. Can she?"

"Naturally I can," Hildy said haughtily.

So it was settled that they divide the rest of the night into three watches. Ynen reluctantly took his numb hand off the tiller and watched Mitt settle into his place. He felt very dubious as he stumbled off to the cabin. But he supposed that if Mitt could tell in his sleep when they turned the other way, he must be able to handle *Wind's Road*. As Ynen lay down, he heard Hildy walking uncertainly forward over the roof, half blind from the light of the cabin. He saw Mitt's bony hand pushing the tiller firmly over. Once more *Wind's Road* surged round. Her sails ran out, clapped, and filled. Ropes rattled as Mitt and Hildy reset them. And shortly Ynen felt the tug and surge of *Wind's Road* riding properly northward, and he knew Mitt could indeed manage her. He fell asleep, to the creak of ropes and the hurrying of dark water.

# 13

THE NIGHT SEEMED extraordinarily long. Mitt stayed at the tiller for as much of it as he could. He wanted to get a good start Northward. It felt good to be handling a boat again, particularly a responsive racing boat like *Wind's Road*. But with the good feeling went long, mindless boredom. There was nothing to do but watch the slowly wheeling stars and listen to the whelming of the huge sea. Mitt did make several honest efforts to decide just what he thought he had been doing back in Holand. But every time he started to think, he came to, some time later, to find he had been thinking of nothing at all. At length the stars began taking little jumps through the sky. Mitt did not know if he had been asleep while they moved or not, but he saw he had had enough. He hitched up the tiller and woke Hildy.

Hildy was so sleepy that she took her watch almost unconscious. It seemed a very long time. Then Hildy found herself doubled painfully over the tiller in a paler world. The sea was dark and glossy. A white wave fizzing past had woken her. Hildy hobbled off like an old woman and woke Ynen.

Ynen, much more refreshed by six hours' sleep than Hildy felt he had any right to be, went gaily out into whitening dawn. The bank of mist where the land was seemed too near. Ynen corrected their course and tightened ropes, and sang while the sun came melting red and yellow out of the mist. Now it was settled, and they were going North, it felt like the best holiday Ynen had ever had. When Mitt came out a while after, *Wind's Road* was sailing briskly in a brisk wind, under a streaky gray sky. The land was a chalky smudge, and the vigorous gray waves were galloping North, too, dividing into two lines of white round

*Wind's Road*'s eager bows. Hildy crawled out later still, groaning. It was so early.

They got the pies out. They were staler, soggier, and much less appetizing. "I reckon," Mitt said, "that they'll be old enemies by the time we make Kinghaven—if they last till then."

"They ought to. We've got two sacksful," said Ynen, and could not help laughing at the look on Mitt's face.

"Then it's only water that's the worry," said Mitt.

"Well, actually, the water barrel's full up," Hildy confessed.

For a moment Mitt could hardly credit that he had been so taken in. Then, to Hildy's relief, he shouted with laughter. "I bet you were mad when I didn't have the arris!" he said. "Us rough fellows are supposed to love that, aren't we?"

Hildy bent her head, embarrassed. She was even more embarrassed when Mitt tasted the water and remarked that it was some of the sweetest-tasting water he had ever drunk. She and Ynen were both shuddering at its musty wooden taste.

Ye gods! What must the water be like down in Holand! Hildy thought. She was so uncomfortable that she jumped up and fled across the cabin roof, babbling that she thought the foresails needed looking at.

"Want a hand?" Mitt called.

Hildy did not know what to say and did not answer. Mitt was just getting up to help her when Ynen said, in great surprise, "I say! What on earth are those doing here?"

Mitt looked. To his astonishment, a number of half-submerged apples were bobbing in the waves beside the boat. He watched them apparently climb a wave, then get left behind by it, the way floating things do. There were dozens of them—bright red and yellow water-sodden apples, all round *Wind's Road*. And there were what looked like wisps of grass as well, and some almost waterlogged flowers.

"Oh, I know!" said Ynen. "Those must be the garlands from the Festival. I suppose the tide brought them out into the current."

"No good to eat, are they?" Mitt wondered.

There was a scream of excitement from Hildy. She was pointing, jabbing her finger seaward, at something floating ahead. For a nasty second Mitt and Ynen both thought it was a drowned person. There was sodden flaxen hair and an outflung hand. Then it rolled and seemed simply a mat of white reeds.

"Can't you see!" screamed Hildy. "It's Poor Old Ammet!"

*Wind's Road* veered and shivered in the excitement of that moment. Ynen almost let go of the tiller. Mitt ran from side to side. Whatever the differences between them, they were all three Holanders, and they knew this was the lucky chance of a lifetime.

"We'll miss him, we'll miss him! Hurry up, Mitt!" Hildy screamed. "Bring me the boathook!"

Mitt plunged round on Ynen and seized the tiller from him. "You go. I'll bring her round for you."

Ynen knew the maneuver was probably beyond him. He let go of the tiller almost before Mitt had it and shot up along the deck, snatching up the mop and the boathook as he went. He thrust the mop at Hildy, and the two of them, waving their implements, balanced jubilantly on the pointed prow. As Mitt took *Wind's Road* racing past Old Ammet and then round again toward the wind, he was very much afraid either or both of them would join Old Ammet in the water. But they clung on. Mitt let the mainsail out with a long rattle, to take the speed off *Wind's Road*, and she plowed on, *bash-bash-bash*, with waves smacking at her bows and spraying Hildy and Ynen thoroughly. When they were a few yards off the floating straw figure, Mitt turned *Wind's Road* right into the wind, and she stood almost still, shaking and flapping. Hildy and Ynen both threw themselves on their faces and lunged at Poor Old Ammet.

Their efforts were agony to Mitt. They knew nothing about how to get things out of the sea, those two. Hildy prodded. Ynen was hanging right under the bowsprit like a monkey, wasting Mitt's accurate work by pushing Old Ammet farther and farther away. It was so clear that they were going to lose him that Mitt hitched the tiller up and set off to help. *Wind's Road* promptly jigged round sideways to the waves, where the strong wind threatened to fill her sails again. Mitt saw that she could capsize that way and hurried back to the tiller.

"Flaming mind of your own, you have!" he told *Wind's Road*. "Sail me or I'll drown the lot of you—that's you!"

That jigging gave Ynen the extra foot he needed. He managed to get a grip on Old Ammet with the boathook. Hildy planted the mop on him to steady him, and together they tossed Poor Old Ammet aboard like the stook of corn he was.

Mitt marveled that he could have taken that intricate mass of plaited corn for a drowned man. Old Ammet still had arms, legs, and a tufted head, but he was now more the shape of a starfish than a person. Most of his fine red ribbons were gone, and his face was cockeyed and blurred. He was a Poor Old Ammet indeed. All the same, they were delighted to see him. They all shouted, "Welcome aboard, Old Ammet, sir!" which they all knew was what you said. Mitt turned *Wind's Road* joyfully back on her way again, while Hildy and Ynen first did an unsteady dance of triumph on the cabin roof and then set about fixing Old Ammet to the prow like a figurehead—which was the other thing you were supposed to do.

Poor Old Ammet was limp and waterlogged. It was no easy matter to make him into a figurehead. Ynen fetched rolls of twine and rope. Mitt called advice. Hildy ransacked the cabin for things which might support that weight of wet wheat. Mitt called so much advice that Hildy snapped, "Oh shut up! We all know you get Old Ammet out of the sea every year!"

There was really no answer to that. Mitt shut up, bitterly annoyed, and soothed himself by muttering, "Flaming females! They're all the same. It goes right through." He watched, haughtily, Old Ammet being threaded on a besom, a gilded picture rail, and two wooden spoons and then being lashed to half the door of the gilded cupboard that concealed the rose-covered bucket. Then he was tied very firmly across the bowsprit, where he lifted and fell proudly to the movements of the boat. Mitt knew he could not have done it better himself. So he said knowledgeably, "He'll stiffen up. He's full of salt. Mind you, he may niff a bit." Then he gave way to honest pride. "Looks good, doesn't he?"

Ynen and Hildy thoroughly agreed. "But," Hildy said, "why doesn't anyone ever find Libby Beer?" She lay down to peer under the mainsail, as if she expected to find Libby Beer just in the offing, in the other half of the gray, leaping sea.

"She's all grapes and squashy berries," said Ynen. "She must get waterlogged in no time. It would be a miracle if we had her, too."

Mitt laughed and slapped the knobby pocket of his red and yellow breeches. "I clean forgot to this moment! Miracle it is. Here. Look." He dragged the little wax model of Libby Beer out of his pocket. Like Poor Old Ammet, she was rather the worse for wear. The wax berries were flattened, with cloth marks imprinted on them, and the ribbons were muddy strings. But she could hardly have delighted Ynen and Hildy more had she been new and gay and gleaming.

"Oh, beautiful!" said Ynen. "We must be the luckiest boat in the world. May I lash her to the stern?"

"Carry on," said Mitt.

"She's lovely!" said Hildy, fingering Libby Beer while Ynen unrolled more twine. "I've always wanted one of these, but they won't let us buy things at the stalls. Those little tiny rose hips. How did you get her?"

"While I was on the run," said Mitt. "Lady at a stall gave her me for luck."

"You mean she knew you were running away?" Hildy asked, reluctantly giving Libby Beer to Ynen to be tied behind the tiller.

"No," said Mitt. He fixed his eyes on the gently heaving horizon and wished this silly female would understand what Holand was like for the likes of him. "She found out I was on the run just after, when the soldiers came asking. She gave me Libby Beer to cheer me up—I had a face as long as Flate Dike, see, not knowing where to go or what I dared do. Then, when the soldiers asked, she had to say she seen me. She didn't dare not tell. That's how people are. It's different for you."

Ynen considered this while he tied careful knots round the wax figure. "We're on the run, too, now—in a way. Why is it different? If a fisherman sees *Wind's Road*, he'll tell. And I don't feel miserable about it."

Mitt knew Ynen had missed the point. He thought of Milda, Hobin, and the babies, of all the waterfront people who used to laugh at him selling fish, all the dozens of people he would never see again, and he was almost exasperated enough with Ynen to push him from the stern where he was crouching, into the sea. "But you've not put yourself outside the law, have you?"

"Yes, we have, in another way," Hildy said. She thought Ynen had missed the point, too, and the only way to cover it up seemed to be to let Mitt know that they had their difficulties as well. She told him about their pretended escape with the bedspread and their real escape with the pies. Mitt tried not to grin. It was all a game to them.

It did not seem to Ynen that he had missed any point. He looked admiringly at the little Libby Beer, already shiny with spray, and proudly over at Old Ammet, lifting and falling at the bowsprit, while he thought over all he now knew about Mitt. It did not add up properly. He wanted to know why. "Look here," he said. "You must have known you'd be on the run, and what it would be like, once you'd thrown the bomb. Didn't you make *any* plans to get away?"

"Were you standing there waiting to be blown up?" Hildy asked, thinking this would explain Mitt's odd behavior on the waterfront.

Mitt eyed the heaving horizon. He supposed he might as well tell them, if they could tell him about their silly escape with their pies. There was something odd about Hildy's story, though—something not quite right. Mitt felt that as strongly as Ynen evidently felt it about his. "They made plans—the Free Holanders," he explained, "but it wasn't in me to listen, because I was planning to get myself taken. I was aiming to kill Hadd, and when they caught me, I was going to tell them the Free Holanders set me on, to pay them out for informing on my father. It was them that informed on him. I've been planning that half my life.

You might say my mother brought me up to do it. And your pa goes and spoils it in half a second. That's what had me standing there—the waste!"

There was silence from Ynen and Hildy. Mitt did not wonder he had shocked them. He took his eyes off the horizon and caught them exchanging a look that was not shocked but deeply puzzled.

"And so it *was* a waste!" he told them aggressively. "Three years I saved gunpowder. Five years me and my mother planned it. And your pa kicks the bomb instead of grabbing me. Then I run straight at those fool soldiers, and they lose me. What was I supposed to do after that? Walk in the Palace gates and say, 'Here I am'?"

"It's not that," said Ynen. "You keep saying everyone informs because they're frightened—and I believe you—but why do you blame the Free Holanders for informing and not the woman who gave you Libby Beer?"

"She wasn't a friend of mine, was she?" Mitt said gruffly.

There was a further silence, puzzled and uncomfortable, filled only with the sound of *Wind's Road*'s ropes pulling in a wind that seemed to be slackening. Hildy and Ynen looked at one another. They were both thinking of the Earl of Hannart's son and wondering how to say what they thought.

"I don't understand about mothers," Hildy said cautiously. "Not having one myself. But—" She stopped and looked helplessly at Ynen.

"You do know," Ynen blurted out, "your mother does know, does she, the kind of things that happen when people get arrested for your kind of thing? Do you know about my uncle Harchad?"

Harchad's face, and the terrible fear that had gripped Mitt when he saw it, seemed to have mixed in Mitt's mind now with his nightmare of Canden shuffling to the door. Under his thick jacket, his skin rose in gooseflesh. But he was not going to let Hildy and Ynen know how he felt. "I've heard things about Harchad," he conceded.

Hildy shivered openly. "I saw. One thing."

"That's why we said we'd take you North," said Ynen.

"Thanks," said Mitt, and he stared woodenly at the horizon. He was not sure quite what was the matter with him. He felt sick and cold. He shook Canden and Harchad out of his mind, but he still felt as if a load of worry had fallen on him, making his head ache and drawing his face into a strange shape. Ynen and Hildy stared, because Mitt's face seemed all old, with scarcely any young left in it. "See here," Mitt said, after a minute, "I feel wore out again. Mind if I go for a lie-down?"

Hildy took the tiller without a word. Mitt plunged into the cabin, onto his favorite port bunk, and fell heavily asleep.

"Ynen, what did you have to go and say all that for?" Hildy whispered, wholly unfairly.

"Because I didn't understand," said Ynen. "I still don't. Why has he gone to sleep like that?"

"I think it's because you—we—upset him more than he wanted to think about," Hildy answered. "He's in an awful muddle. It must be lack of education."

"He's muddled me, too," Ynen said crossly. "I don't know whether to be sorry for him or not."

The slackening wind brought a drizzle of rain. Ynen and Hildy found a tarpaulin and wrapped it round their heads and shoulders. The rain increased, and the wind strengthened slowly, until the sea was so choppy that Hildy found it hard to steer and hold the sail rope, too. The sail was yellow-gray and heavy with rain.

"Miserable!" she said. Water dripped off the end of her nose and chin.

"I wonder if we ought to take in a reef," Ynen said.

Just before midday, the choppiness woke Mitt. Wind's changed, he thought. Coming more off the land.

He stumbled muzzily out into the well to find a real downpour. Rain was battering down into the well and swirling along the planking, going *putter, putter* on the tarpaulin over Hildy and Ynen's heads, and making myriad pockmarks in the yellow-gray waves alongside. Mitt was not sure he liked the angry tooth shape of all those pockmarked waves.

"I've been wondering if I ought to reef—just in case," Ynen said to him.

Mitt looked at him, frowning sleepily against the cold water in his face. Beyond Ynen, the little figure of Libby Beer was shiny as new with rainwater. Beyond her, dim behind veil upon veil of silver rain, was what looked like a mountain walking up the sky from the land, monstrous, black and impending.

"What do you think about reefing?" Ynen asked.

Mitt stared at that mountain of black weather, aghast. Last time he had seen anything like it, Siriol had made for Little Flate as fast as *Flower of Holand* could move, and they had hardly got there in time. This was twice as near. There was no chance of making land. Those two had been sitting with their backs to it, but all the same! "Flaming Ammet!" said Mitt.

"Well, I thought I'd reef," Ynen said uncertainly.

"What am I doing standing here letting you ask?" Mitt said frantically. "You should have woke me an hour ago. Three reefs we'll need, and let's be quick, for Old Ammet's sake! I bet this boat handles real rough."

Ynen was astounded. *"Three?"* Hildy was so surprised that she lost her hold on the wet tiller. *Wind's Road* tipped about, and the boom swung over their heads. Mitt caught it, braced himself against the weight of wind and sopping sail, and tied it down with such haste that Ynen began to see he was in earnest. He slipped out from under the tarpaulin and scrambled onto the cabin roof in the hammering rain, to the ropes that lowered the mainsail. When he saw the weather the tarpaulin had been hiding from him, he did not feel quite so surprised at Mitt's command. Ynen had never been out in any weather so black himself, but he knew when the sky looked like that, you saw all the shipping making for Holand as fast as it could sail. He let the huge triangle of the sail down a foot or so. Mitt began tying the resulting fold down against the boom by the little strings that dangled from the canvas, and tying as if for dear life. "We have got a storm sail," Ynen called.

Mitt shook his head, knowing how long it would take two boys to get in this mass of great wet sail and bend on another. "We'd be caught with our pants down. Maybe we are, anyway. She rides awful high. Get tying. Quick!"

They tied cold, wet reef knots until their fingers ached. Hildy stood on the seat, with her foot on the tiller, and laced away at the sail over her head. Mitt and Ynen crawled up and down the cabin roof, tying knots there. They did it again with a second fold, and then all over again with a third. By this time, *Wind's Road*'s sail was an absurd little triangle, with the long bare mast towering above it. The rain was coming in gusting clouds now. They could see nothing much beyond a gray circle about thirty feet across. But, inside that circle, the waves were yellow-green, heaving high and pointed. The bare mast swept back and forth. The deck was up and down, sickeningly steep both ways.

"Don't untie that boom till we got the foresails in," Mitt shouted at Hildy. Somehow the weather was much louder, though it was hard to tell what was making the noise. Mitt and Ynen hauled and grappled at the clapping sails in the bows, slithering on the wet planks round Old Ammet. One moment they were skyward, soaring into lashing rain. The next Old Ammet was plunging, like a man on a toboggan, down and down a freckled tawny gray wave side.

Ynen swallowed giddily. "Is it going to be bad?" he yelled.

Mitt did not try to deceive him. "Real shocker!" he bawled back. But he thought it was just as well that he did not have breath to spare to explain to Ynen that these autumn storms sometimes went on for days. Mitt knew they would be drowned long before the day was out.

Now he was fully awake, he knew, with nasty vividness, that *Wind's Road* would capsize. He could feel it in the movement of her. She was only a rich man's pleasure boat, after all. And as Old Ammet launched himself furiously down another freckled hill of water, Mitt was as terrified as he had been when he crouched among the marble-playing boys in Holand. He was blind with panic. It was as if he had run away from himself and left the inside of his head empty. Mitt knew this would not do. It was no use thinking Ynen could manage by himself. He had to run after himself, inside his head, and bring himself back with one arm twisted up his back before he was able to pick up an armful of soaking sail and stagger with it to the hatch. He thought, as he pushed and kicked it down and clapped the cover on and banged the bolt home, that there really was nothing left of the old fearless Mitt anymore. He had never been in charge of a boat before. He wanted to whimper because Siriol was not there.

He and Ynen crawled back across the seesawing cabin roof. Hildy, seeing them coming, obeyed instructions and started to untie the lashings round the boom. She knew they had been idiots, she and Ynen, sitting under that tarpaulin and letting the storm creep up on them. She had been trying to behave with smart efficiency ever since. She did not want people like Mitt thinking her a fool. But she had no notion how fierce the wind was now. She loosened the main knot.

The wind tore it all out of her hands. The sail slammed round sideways, jerking *Wind's Road* broadside on to the next huge wave. The boom mowed across the cabin roof and caught the side of Ynen's head with a *thuck*. It knocked him clean out. He was carried helplessly with it toward the side.

# 14

HILDY SCREAMED. Mitt flung himself after Ynen and just managed to catch him round the ankle with both hands. Water thundered down over them, hard and heavy, and fell away, sucking and rilling, pulling Ynen against Mitt's straining arms and dragging both of them down the tilted cabin roof. Mitt had no idea how they survived, any more than Hildy. Hildy knew *Wind's Road* had gone like a bullet, slantwise through the top of that wave. But how she came to have the fighting tiller in one hand and the sail rope in the other she did not know.

"Ye gods! I'm sorry!" she screamed at Mitt when she saw him, drenched and horrified, sliding down from the cabin roof and heaving Ynen after him.

"Don't dare do that again!" Mitt screamed back. *Wind's Road* was plunging downhill now, and he made use of it to slide Ynen into the cabin. Ynen was alive, to his great relief, stirring and muttering miserably. Mitt did not dare linger with him. He wedged him hurriedly in place with blankets. "Don't move!" he bawled, though the cabin was almost quiet. "You took a knock there." *Wind's Road*, trembling sickeningly, mounted upward again. Mitt threw himself downhill into the well and wrestled the tiller out of Hildy's weak hand. The storm was too loud even for screaming now.

Mitt found he had arrived just in time. The huge autumn storm roared and howled and bashed around them. *Wind's Road* was half sideways in the trough between two heaving walls of water, caught in the backwash of the last wave. Worse still, while she wallowed there, half the thundering gale was blocked by the water. The sail was coming smashing across and threatening to capsize her. Mitt, as he worked at the sluggish tiller, shrieked and made gestures at Hildy to pull the rope in and hold the sail. It seemed a lifetime before she understood and the rope came yelling over its blocks into her hands. She still had a silly, puzzled look on her face, but Mitt had no time to attend. He could only thank Old Ammet he was stronger since he was last in a boat. *Wind's Road* was the hardest thing he had ever had to handle. She would *not* come about. They were creeping crabwise up a great slope of water, up and up, until they were hanging, almost over on one side, just beneath the raving crest of the wave. *Wind's Road* had suicidal urges. Mitt felt her going over, and heaved on the flaccid tiller.

The full force of the storm hit them as he did so. Mitt and Hildy both screamed. Their voices burst out of their throats without their being able to help it. The wind hit with a roar and a crash. The sail rope yelled out from between Hildy's fingers, nearly dislocating both her shoulders. Great lumps of water loomed and fell, smashing across the bows, banging down on the cabin, thundering over Hildy and Mitt, until they were as bruised as they were wet, and went fizzing and boiling away behind.

The man in the bows with the flying fair hair understood their danger and leaned into the wave, dragging at *Wind's Road*'s forward rigging. *Wind's Road* did not want to come, but Mitt thought the man dragged her round by main force. He saw him clearly for a moment, with his hair as white as the snarling spray, gesturing aside the horses that were trying to overwhelm *Wind's Road*. Then *Wind's Road* lashed herself over the edge and down another watery hillside, and Mitt had all his work cut out to hold her straight. Beside him, Hildy, to his relief, was trying to help the sail rope as it came rattling in again when *Wind's Road* plunged.

Mitt could not hold her straight. *Wind's Road* went down into that valley of water and wallowed sideways, with every intention of never coming up. But the man was there against the foam-laced surface of sliding black water, wrenching *Wind's Road* straight for him. Mitt wanted to thank him, but by that time *Wind's Road* was on her sickening way upward again to lay herself sideways to the next wave top.

And so it went on. Mitt thought they went from sudden death to sudden death so often that they lost count of how long. The world was a lathering uproar, and *Wind's Road* hit and buffeted until she jerked all over. Mitt and Hildy were bashed by water until they hardly felt it. Water fizzed into the cabin and swirled round Ynen. The tarpaulin floated round the well, mashed up and neglected, and got in the way, but neither Hildy nor Mitt had time to get rid of it. Hildy's attention was all for the rope, either yelling out or rattling in, and Mitt's for battle with the tiller, *Wind's Road*'s yawing death urges, and the gestures of the fair-haired man when the wind hit with a clap and a shout.

He and Hildy got quite used to seeing him, up there in the bows, either gray with storming rain or whiter against the black side of a wave. They were glad to see him there. But the horses bothered them both. They were beautiful gray horses galloping, arching their necks under flying manes, dashing up the slopes of waves, frolicking and rearing on the crests. Mitt and Hildy never had time to look at them properly, but they saw them all the time out of the corners of their eyes. They knew they were imagining things. Sailors told stories of horses playing round doomed ships, frolicking at the death of mortals. Mitt and Hildy would much rather not have seen them. They kept their eyes ahead on the next danger coming. But there were still horses galloping on both sides of the boat, though ahead there was nothing but fizzing foam and shuddering waves and occasionally the man with the flying light hair.

*He's* doing us no harm, that's for sure! Mitt thought.

In the cabin Ynen got to his elbows and put a hand to the big tender lump on the side of his face. He could have sworn somebody had shaken him and told him to get up. But he was all alone, lying among sopping blankets. "Ugh!" he said. He could feel *Wind's Road* yawing and staggering, and he wondered what was causing this awful sluggish movement.

The cabin door slammed open against the stove, and a wave of dirty water rushed down on Ynen, soaking him to the bone. He stared uphill at two pairs of slithering feet and more water bashing across them. Ye gods! he thought. The water we must be shipping! He scrambled up while he was thinking it and climbed uphill into the well.

The first thing that met his eyes was the lovely head of a thoroughbred gray horse, flying past among the rain and spray. It was gone at once, as if it was galloping faster than *Wind's Road* could sail. Ynen was hit by the rain and gasped. It was lashing down. He could hardly see the withered and wind-whipped figures of Mitt and Hildy, let alone the woman kneeling on the stern behind them. It was as much as Ynen could do to make out that this woman had long red-gold hair, flapping and swirling in the wind. He saw she was giving Hildy a hand with the rope—or he thought she was, until he realized she was pushing at the tiller as Mitt braced his feet and shoved it. The rain made Ynen very confused. But he realized the woman was pointing at the locker where the pump was.

"Yes, of course," Ynen said to her. He was still dazed, but he clipped the lid of the locker up, moved the tarpaulin off the scuppers and began to pump.

The storm raved on for another hour or more. Ynen pumped away, without a hope of emptying the boat, but perhaps doing just enough to prevent *Wind's Road*'s swamping. Sometimes he wished, in the fretful way one does in dreams, that the lady in the stern would help him, too, though he knew she had enough to do with Mitt and Hildy. Sometimes he thought the man up in front might come back and give him a hand. He knew this was an ungrateful thought. The man had stopped *Wind's Road* from turning over several times, and he was keeping off the horses, too. But Ynen's arms ached so.

At length the roaring and thundering grew less. *Wind's Road*, from sliding up and down, went to heaving and lurching, and from that to a staggering *slap-slap-slap*, with only the odd spout of water coming aboard. They sailed through a brown light. The rain hissed down and seemed to flatten the tossing sea further. Then the rain stopped. Ynen, pumping and pumping, felt far too hot.

"We did it!" Hildy said. "It's over." As she said it, Ynen heard the squelching that meant the bilge was nearly dry. He straightened his back thankfully.

There was a blinding sun right in front of the bows, low on the edge of the sea. The storm clouds were above the sun in a heavy black line, getting smaller and smaller. It was hot. *Wind's Road* had steam rising from her decking and salt crystals forming like frost on her. The small triangle of sail sagged. There was a mess of tangled ropes everywhere, and *Wind's Road* was riding with a surge and swing unlike any Ynen or Hildy had ever experienced. Mitt knew it for the surge and swing of deep ocean. He looked back, across the little salt-coated figure of Libby Beer, away and away over empty sea. There was no land.

Weak and trembly though they all were, they burst out talking and laughing, in overloud hoarse voices, telling one another what each had thought the worst bit was. Ynen said it was when he saw the boom on its way to hit him. Hildy said it was the horses.

"No," said Mitt. "It was that first time she tried to capsize, just before we saw the man."

"I thought that, until the horses kept being there," said Hildy. "And I tried to tell myself I was just imagining them because I was so scared and tired. But I knew they were there."

"I saw one quite close to, just before Libby Beer told me to pump," Ynen said. "Didn't they go fast!"

"Hey, look," said Mitt. "We haven't all run mad, have we?"

"Of course not," said Ynen. "Libby Beer was sitting behind you, helping you sail her, and Old Ammet was standing in the bows stopping her sinking and keeping the horses off. I saw both of them."

Hildy looked anxiously at the big purple bruise on the side of Ynen's face and then at the tiny, salt-coated figure of Libby Beer on the stern. "I didn't get a chance to turn round, but isn't she rather small?"

"Old Ammet got carried away in that first big wave, for sure," Mitt said, and hoisted himself weakly on the cabin roof to see.

He could see a bundle of whitish straw, gently rising and falling in the bows. He crawled forward, hardly able to believe it. Old Ammet was still there, contrary to all reason, every plaited wheat stalk of him, miraculously in one piece. There were strips of seaweed wrapped about him and tangled in his wheaten hair, as if he had got his lost ribbons back, changed by the sea to green and brown. But round his neck, broken and sodden, was draped a garland made of wheat, burst grapes, and drooping flowers.

"Come and look at this!" Mitt yelled.

They left *Wind's Road* to sail herself and stood in a row with their clothes steaming, looking down at Old Ammet and his garland from the Festival. "I think we ought to thank him, and Libby Beer," said Hildy.

Mitt was very self-conscious at the idea, but he made himself growl, "Thank you, sir," with Hildy and Ynen, and then turn round and say, "Thank you, lady," to Libby Beer. After all, he had seen Old Ammet with his own eyes.

Then Hildy started to shiver violently. Mitt knew what was needed. He waded through the soaked blankets on the cabin floor and fetched the bottle of arris. He made Hildy and Ynen have a good swig and then took one himself. They stood about in the well going *"Um-pwaugh!"* and making awful faces.

"Shocking taste, isn't it?" said Mitt. "Wait a moment, though. There comes a sort of *boing* inside, and then it warms the insides of your ears."

The *boing* came. It made them feel so much better that they got out the pies and fell on them ravenously. Their hands shook as they ate, and their fingers were white, wrinkly, and blistered, even Mitt's, which had got a little soft-skinned in Hobin's workshop.

"I can't sail all through the night," Hildy said wearily.

"We've got a sea anchor," said Ynen, and looked at Mitt to see what he thought.

Mitt was dog-tired, too. But he knew autumn storms could come one on top of the other. He did not know what to do.

"I know," said Hildy, and she crawled forward to the mast. Mitt, with Ynen nodding and yawning beside him, stared at the soles of her feet and heard her say, "Please, Old Ammet, can you look after the boat tonight? But if there's another storm, could you wake Mitt up and tell him, please?"

"That's right! Pick on me!" Mitt called. "Tireless Mitt they call me. Think I don't wear out or something?" He turned to the figure of Libby Beer. "Excuse me, lady. She wants you to wake me if there's trouble. She thinks I'm made of the same stuff as what you are. So, if I'm needed, and you have to give me a nudge, do you mind waking her up, too? She can sit and feed me nips of arris."

The cabin was crowded and close that night. Nobody needed blankets, so they hung them in the well to dry. They all slept like logs, even Hildy, who had the small forward bunk which had been designed for her when she was nine. If Old Ammet or Libby Beer had tried to call Mitt in the night, he did not hear them. But all seemed well in the morning. The sea was flat, and the sun made a liquid yellow path to the gently drifting *Wind's Road*.

"I think I hate pies," said Hildy.

"You want to try mixing about a bit," Mitt told her. "You know—cherry flan and steak. Makes a change."

"You're cheating," said Ynen. "Those were squashed together, anyway. Try oyster and apple, Hildy. It's—well, it's different."

After this decidedly strange breakfast, they cleaned up *Wind's Road* and got very hot doing it. The heat told them all that they could not yet be very far North. None of them had the slightest idea where they were. As there was no land in sight, no chart Ynen could produce was any use to them. The only thing they were sure of was that they had been blown out into deep ocean, probably more west than north.

"I'll steer north and east," Ynen said. "When we sight land, I'll keep it just on the horizon, until we see somewhere we can recognize. Tulfa Island should be easy to find. And we know that belongs to the North. Let's get the sails up."

Shortly, with sails set again, in a light wind, *Wind's Road* was sailing on. Mitt sat lazily just above Old Ammet, listening to the water running past her sides and admiring the way her bows cut the sea sweetly asunder. In fair conditions *Wind's Road* was a beauty, he thought. He could hardly believe she had been doing her damnedest to drown them all yesterday.

"There's something to port over there," Ynen called. "Can you see what it is?"

Mitt looked too far, then too near, and finally saw a small dark thing lolloping on the swell, about a quarter of a mile away. "Could be a boat," he called.

"That's what I thought," Ynen called back, and pushed the tiller over, with a fine *ruckle-ruckle* of water from *Wind's Road*'s elegant bows.

"Hey! What are you doing?" Mitt called, jumping up.

"Going to look. If it's a boat, it will have been in the storm," Ynen said and, for the first time for over a day, he gave Mitt a frankly unfriendly look. Hildy, beside him, gave Mitt the same look.

Mitt felt hurt, and irritated. "You don't have to look at me like that! I don't want to get seen and caught, do I?"

"If there's anybody in it, they can't possibly hurt you," said Ynen. "But I have to make sure. It's the law of the sea."

"Or weren't you brought up to keep to any law?" said Hildy.

Mitt felt Hildy need not have said that. He knew the rule as well as she did. "Don't talk so stupid!" he said. "Can't neither of you get it in your heads this isn't a pleasure trip?" Then, as Hildy went white and drew in her breath to make a powerful answer, Mitt added, "But please yourself—please yourselves. Don't mind me. I'm only the passenger." He could see the thing was a boat now, but only a small one. It looked to be just a ship's cockboat, torn loose in the storm. No danger there, Mitt thought.

But when *Wind's Road* had leaned nearer, in a pleasant riffling of water, they saw the boat was larger than that, about a third the size of *Wind's Road* herself. There was a mast in it, still flying tag ends of rope and some fluttering pieces of sail. There was no sign of life in it.

"It *was* in the storm," Hildy said, rather hushed.

"I'll go alongside," said Ynen.

Mitt stood up to offer to do that for him. Ynen pretended not to see. *Wind's Road* was his. Mitt sat down dourly by the mast. So Ynen did not trust him not to sail straight past then? Very well. Mitt grinned as Ynen went about too soon and hit the smaller boat a fair old wallop. Ynen winced at the damage to *Wind's Road*'s paint. The smaller boat simply bobbed about. It was salty, battered, and draped with seaweed. It had to be hard to sink, Mitt thought, to have survived the storm. It was empty, except for a tangle of tarpaulin in the bottom. Ynen had scraped *Wind's Road* for nothing, by the look of it.

Hildy read the name painted on the stern of the derelict. *"Sevenfold II."*

"Funny!" said Mitt, coming to look. "That's a big merchant ship out of Holand. She was tied up in harbor there the day of the Festival. What's her boat doing here with a sail in it?"

"She must have sailed out later and got caught in the storm," Ynen suggested. "I suppose her crew took to the— Oh, dear!"

The tangle of tarpaulin heaved and humped. A wet and unkempt head was thrust out, as if its owner was shakily on his hands and knees. A hoarse and wretched voice said, "Take us aboard, for pity's sake!"

No one had expected this. Hildy and Ynen were quite as dismayed as Mitt. In fact, it was Mitt who first pulled himself together and said, "Up you come, then. How many are you?"

"Just me, guvnor," said the man, and seemed to fall flat on his face again.

Mitt exchanged a resigned and dubious look with Ynen and swung himself down into the bobbing derelict. The worst of it was it could be someone who knew him. He heaved back the tarry canvas. Underneath were several inches of water and, lying sprawled in it, a soaking, unshaven man in sailor's clothes. He was a square, powerful sort of fellow—the kind of man you could trust to survive a storm, Mitt thought, taking the man under the arms and trying to heave him upward. He was no one Mitt knew. But when Mitt had wrestled the fellow to his knees, he thought the man had a faintly familiar look. He must have seen him around on the waterfront. One thing was certain about him. The man was a good deal better nourished than most people in Holand. Mitt simply could not lift him.

They only got him aboard *Wind's Road* because the man seemed to come to his senses enough to help a little. Mitt boosted. Hildy leaned over and dragged. The man, groaning and feebly scrambling, pulled himself over the side into the well and collapsed again. It took them some time to pull and push him into the cabin and get him onto a bunk. Meanwhile, Ynen left *Sevenfold II*'s boat to bob by itself and sailed on.

"Would you like a drink of water?" Hildy asked, thinking the man must be parched with thirst.

The answer was a growl, in which the only words they caught were "little lady" and "arris."

"Give him a nip of it," Mitt said. "Bring him around."

Hildy fetched the bottle and put it to the man's pale, waterlogged lips. He took such a long drink that she was alarmed. When at length she managed to drag the bottle away, the man made a feeble pounce after it. "Arragh!" Hildy backed away quickly. He seemed like an angry wild beast. But he became calmer almost at once and mumbled something else with "little lady" in it. "S'some sleep," they heard him say.

"That's right. You drop off. Do you good," Mitt said heartily. He took Hobin's gun off the rack above the bunk, where he had left it, and put it in his belt, just to be on the safe side.

Hildy, in much the same spirit, put the arris bottle in a locker and shot the bolt. She looked back as they left the cabin and saw that the man's eyes were wide open. He could have been watching. But he could also have been half unconscious. "Do you think he's all right?" she whispered.

"You do get rough types," Ynen said, very much wishing he had left *Sevenfold II* to drift.

"He'll survive," said Mitt, "if that's what you were asking. Must be made of iron to be still alive. Let's hope he'll be more agreeable when he's had some sleep."

"So do I," said Hildy. The man's eyes were still wide open, staring from a broad pale face covered with long black stubble.

# 15

FOR THE REST OF that day, the new passenger slept, with his face turned to the wall. Everyone felt this was the best thing he could do. They left him alone and almost forgot he was there.

Ynen stayed at the tiller. It was his way of claiming *Wind's Road* back after the storm. He did not exactly resent Mitt's taking charge then, but *Wind's Road* was *his*. She was the loveliest and the luckiest boat out of Holand, and Ynen loved her passionately. This left Hildy and Mitt nothing much to do but lounge on the cabin roof. Hildy understood Ynen perfectly. Mitt was amused, though he had to admit that if he had had the luck to own *Wind's Road*, he might well have been just the same. And a bit more careful of my paint, he thought.

*Wind's Road* clipped her way elegantly northeast. No land came in sight. While they watched for land, they fell to talking, mostly about Holand. Mitt irritated Hildy because he would seem to think that life in the Palace was one of perfect bliss. So she told him what it was really like. It was beyond her to describe properly the emptiness and the lonely, neglected feeling she and Ynen had lived with, but she could tell Mitt how Hadd was as much of a tyrant in his own home as he was in his earldom.

"Everybody was so—so obedient that they'd no characters," she said. "The aunts were just fine ladies. And those cousins! All 'Yes, Grandfather,' and 'No, Grandfather,' and pretty dresses and despising people who didn't feel like being obedient."

"The boys were worse," Ynen said feelingly. "They had such a good opinion of themselves under the obedience."

"Like the uncles," said Hildy. "I don't think Uncle Harl ever did anything but crawl to Grandfather while he was alive and go around looking smug and being boring. But when Grandfather got shot, Uncle Harl got drunk to celebrate. It made me feel awful. And I will say this for Father—he wasn't like that."

"Then what was—*is* he like?" Ynen asked resentfully. "You got more sense out of a fish on a slab!"

"Except fish don't make jokes at your expense," Hildy added.

"Ah, now I've had quite a bit of dealings with fish, on slabs and off," Mitt said. "Sad look, they often have. And speaking as an authority, as you might say, I get to feel quite sorry for your pa, hearing you talk. Happy family, weren't you?"

"*Sorry* for him!" said Hildy.

"I know. That's a fine thing, coming from me, isn't it?" said Mitt. "But as far as I can see, he's not let do anything, except maybe play soldiers or go out for a shoot now and again. All he's let do is sit about in the happy family and take orders, and since he's not booked to be Earl or anything, he'll be doing that till he dies. Not much of a life, is it? On a slab, you might say, until he's under one."

Hildy and Ynen sat digesting this unusual view of their father for some time. Even then, all Ynen could think of to say was, "Well, I don't know," which he said very dubiously indeed. They seemed so perplexed that Mitt tried to cheer them up by telling them stories from the time he used to fish with Siriol and how he used to sell the fish. He amused Hildy and Ynen mightily. Hildy nearly rolled overboard laughing, and Ynen doubled up over the tiller. But this led to another difficult moment.

Ynen straightened up, tenderly shifted *Wind's Road* a point or so, and asked: "Is Siriol a Free Holander? He seems to have been very kind to you."

"Yes." Mitt went to pick at a blister the storm had raised on the cabin paint. He caught Ynen's eye and stopped, trying to grin. The puzzled, serious look he was growing to dread was settling on Ynen's face. "All right. He was one of them that informed," Mitt said. "Only don't start asking things again! I tell you straight I don't know *how* I feel about him. So he was good to me. So I didn't want to go near him after the bomb, for fear I brought the soldiers on him. That's all I know."

Ynen's mouth opened to ask another question. Hildy saw Mitt's face had gone elderly. She nudged Ynen and hastily got out the pies. The survivor from *Sevenfold II* was still asleep, so Hildy left a rather withered steak pie between his face and the cabin wall. When she came out into the well again, Mitt was still elderly, and she could tell from Ynen's face that he was going to ask more questions any minute.

Hildy began to talk brightly about the Holy Islands. She was not sure why she did, except that it was clear to her that Mitt's feelings were in a most painful muddle, and she knew a little how that felt. Perhaps the Holy Islands was not a good choice of subject. Hildy's feelings about them and about Lithar were in as bad a muddle as Mitt's about the Free Holanders. Because of this, and because she was so anxious to keep off Mitt's feelings, Hildy began to boast. All through the long afternoon, while *Wind's Road* ruckled her way gently through small blue waves, Hildy sat on the cabin roof and boasted about Lithar's famous fleet and the beauty and the strangeness of the Holy Islands. She told Mitt about the magic Bull, the mysterious piping, and the old man of the sea and his horses. She told him the Holy Islands were the most favored place in Dalemark. Before long, she began to feel that she was indeed extremely lucky to be going there, and she told Mitt all over again about the fame and beauty of the Holy Islands, in even more glowing terms.

On the third repetition Mitt felt he had had enough. "All right," he said. "You were so lucky to be betrothed, you ran away the first opportunity. So stop swanking."

"Yes, do stop, Hildy," said Ynen, who was as bored as Mitt.

Hildy was furious. "Why should I?"

Ynen looked at her whitening face and did not answer. Mitt could see Hildy was angry, too, but he did not see that was any reason for holding his tongue. "Because you said three times," he said, "that you're going to be Holy Hildrida. You're going to ride about on a bull, blowing a little whistle and hopping from island to island, granting everyone wishes. Now tell us how poor old Lithar feels about it. Pretty sick, I shouldn't wonder."

Hildy stood up on the cabin, so blazing white that Ynen winced. How dared Mitt make fun of her! She had only been trying to help him, too! And he repaid her like the street boy he was. She was so angry that she wondered whether to jump down on him where he sat in the well and hurt him as much as she could. Mitt grinned up at her, not in the least dismayed. Hildy realized he was probably stronger than she was. "You," she said, "are just a horrible little murderer, and don't you forget it!" She turned on her seaboot and stalked to the bows of the boat.

Mitt saw he had gone too far. He was sorry at first. Then, as Hildy continued to sit, white and blazing, looking out over Old Ammet, he became resentful. "Give me the tiller," he said to Ynen. "You need a rest, anyway. And go and tell that sister of yours to jump in."

Ynen took Hildy a pie instead. She refused to speak to him. He took a pie to the man from *Sevenfold II*. The man had not eaten the first pie. Ynen was just going away when the man roused a little. When

Ynen asked if he wanted a pie, he growled. The only word Ynen heard was "guvnor." He leaned over, rather nervously, and asked the man his name. The man growled to call him Al, guvnor. Then he reached out and snatched the pie Ynen was just taking away again. Ynen retreated to the well, feeling he was the only good-tempered person aboard.

"He's horribly hard to get on with," he said to Mitt.

"He's a right brute," Mitt agreed. "Mind you, he may be better tomorrow."

They settled the watches for the night, with Ynen having to run back and forward between Mitt and Hildy because Hildy would not speak to Mitt. Mitt took the dawn watch. He wanted to be on hand in case they reached land then.

But by morning there was still no sign of land. The wind was brisker, and the day promised to be clear. Mitt leaned against the side of the well, with his foot up on the seat, humming a tune and feeling fresher and calmer than he had felt for years. He wondered what he would do when he reached the North. Go back to fishing, he supposed, or get work on a farm. But he was sure there were a hundred other things, as yet unthought of, which he could do quite as well.

He was so cheerful and confident that he was really hurt when Hildy came out of the cabin and pushed past him without a word. "What am I supposed to have done—bar teased you a bit?" he demanded.

"And why should I put up with that?" asked Hildy. "It's not your place to criticize me."

"Oh, go and get a nice long drink of arris!" Mitt said disgustedly.

Hildy was looking at him, uncertain whether to laugh or fly at his throat, when *Wind's Road* vibrated to a string of swearwords. Hildy had never heard the like. Even Mitt had seldom heard so many at once. Al stuck his head out of the cabin and gave Mitt a bloodshot look.

"Isn't there a razor in this godforsaken tub?"

"There may be," said Hildy. "The sailors often leave things. I'll look."

"I didn't mean you, little lady. I meant him," said Al. "Let him look."

"I'm steering," said Mitt. "And I don't know where to look."

Al gave him another bloodshot look. "Then she'd better do it," he said, and went inside again. Hildy followed him, and found a razor. Mitt stood outside, scowling, hearing things like, "It'll be none the worse for a bit of sharpening, little lady," and the sound of Hildy stropping the razor. "This is all the soap you have, is it? Thank you, little lady, much obliged, but a man needs a bit of hot water to shave with." That meant

Hildy had to get the charcoal stove alight, draw water, set it to boil, and work away at the stove bellows. Mitt watched her working away with a set, cross look on her face, while Al sat at his ease on the bunk, and wished they had left that boat to rot.

When Ynen came out, he was wishing the same, though all he said was "No land yet?"

All Mitt said was "No. I reckon that storm blew us a good long way out." But he could see Ynen knew how he felt.

Al emerged from the cabin at last, rubbing his smooth chin and looking satisfied. He climbed on the cabin roof and stretched. He was square and stocky. His face, now they could see it properly, was square, too, and unremarkable except for some bitter creases round the mouth and a general look of being well pleased with itself. His clothes, in spite of being faded and creased by the sea, were better than Mitt had realized, and he had a well-nourished look that made Mitt think he must have been mate or perhaps bosun on *Sevenfold II*.

"What are you staring at?" Al demanded. Hildy was looking at him resentfully. Ynen was puzzled because he had a feeling he had seen Al before somewhere. Al laughed and looked round *Wind's Road*. "Lucky ship, eh?" he said, nodding from Old Ammet to the little Libby Beer. Then he nodded at Mitt. "Hand that tiller over, and let's have something to eat."

"I'll do it," Ynen said, opening the locker where the second sack of pies still lay untouched.

"Don't you, guvnor," said Al. "Let him."

"It's still Mitt's watch," said Ynen.

"Yes, but it's his station," said Al. "It's not your place to cook."

"Nobody's cooking," said Mitt. "And what do you take me for?"

Al shrugged his wide shoulders. "Servant. Bodyguard, by the look of that gun you got there."

Mitt looked down in annoyance, wishing he had buttoned his coat over Hobin's gun. "I'm no servant," he said.

"Don't tell me!" Al said, laughing loudly. "I suppose you come aboard and held the guvnor and the little lady up at gunpoint!"

Mitt could not look at anyone. Hildy seized the sack out of Ynen's hands and dumped it on the cabin roof. "Help yourself," she said. "That's what everybody else is doing on this boat."

"Thank you kindly, little lady," said Al. "After you. After the guvnor." He would not touch a pie until Hildy and Ynen had each taken one. Then he took one himself, remarking that Mitt could eat when he came off duty. Ynen promptly passed Mitt his own pie and took another. But Al was clearly not a man to pick up hints. He waved a piece of oyster patty at Ynen and asked with his mouth full, "And where, may one ask, is this boat bound, guvnor?"

They munched in uneasy silence. They all realized that they had forgotten to invent a story to tell him. "Kinghaven," Ynen said at last, in a haughty way he hoped would shut Al up.

Al ducked his head respectfully. "Sorry I spoke. Sorry I spoke, guvnor. Never wish to offend the gently born. Friends in the North, have you? Not many Holanders could say the same. I mean, I know you'll pardon me for mentioning it, but I can see this boat's from Holand by the images back and front. Not a deep-water boat, either, is she? Pleasure vessel, more like."

Hildy drew herself up, as her aunts did when they were displeased. "Yours was hardly even that, was it?"

Al shut his eyes and muttered things. "Oh, it was horrible! Filthy little tub. Never been so seasick in my life!" That surprised them, in a sailor, but Al's other remarks had so alarmed them that they all tried to look sympathetic. Al grinned. "I lay down in the bottom and let it all happen. Only thing I knew how to do. That was after I lost my gun. Damned wave took it off me. I regret that gun. It was as good as the one you got there." Mitt found Al's eyes open again, staring at Hobin's gun in his belt. "Mind if I have a look?" said Al.

"Sorry," said Mitt. "It's got sentimental value. I never let anyone else touch it."

"Fair enough," said Al, to Mitt's considerable relief.

Mitt finished his pie, handed the tiller to Hildy, and retired to the cabin, sick of Al already and hoping heartily that it would not prove far now to Kinghaven. They must all make sure to give Al the slip there. Mitt did not trust Al. He disliked his elaborate deference to Hildy and Ynen, his plain intention of not doing a hand's turn, and, above all, his smug and prying manner.

Above him, Mitt could hear Al asking if they had anything to eat but pies. He added discontentedly that it seemed rather a rich diet. Yes, let's have you seasick again, Mitt thought, and went up the cabin to the rosy bucket.

When he came out, Al's voice was in the well, saying, "Oh, no offense, little lady. It's not my place to question the provisions. I just thought you could get that lazy boy to catch a few fish now and then. His kind get above themselves if they're let stay idle."

"You can fish if you want," Ynen said. "We don't want you idle either."

"That's right, guvnor," Al agreed heartily. "I'll go and set him to it, shall I?"

There was a frustrated silence in the well. Al bent down and entered the cabin. Mitt braced himself against the remaining half of the cupboard door, ready to whisk past Al and out on deck. Al would soon find Mitt was nobody's servant. Al advanced. Mitt waited his moment and shot forward. But instead of sliding by under Al's elbow, Mitt found himself hurtling into Al's solid body and grunting with the impact. He was seized in a punishingly strong grip. Al laughed in his ear. "No, you don't!"

Nothing like this had happened to Mitt for years. He was as humiliated as he was angry. He struggled hard. They bashed against the cupboard, a bunk, and the cupboard again. "Let go of me!" panted Mitt as they bounced against the gilded door.

Al, by this time, had both Mitt's hands helpless under one brawny arm. "Right you are," he said. He plucked the gun out of Mitt's belt and let go of Mitt the same instant. Mitt was flung against the bunk again.

"How dare you!" said Hildy.

"Give that back, please," said Ynen.

Both of them had come into the cabin, too, which explained why *Wind's Road* was tipping about so, Mitt realized, as he was rolled onto the floor.

Al raised the gun. "You see to the boat, guvnor," he said, and walked toward the cabin door. Ynen, Hildy, and Mitt, too, backed out in front of him in a dismayed cluster, treading on one another along the tipping floor. Ynen seized the tiller and set *Wind's Road* to rights again, while the other two crammed themselves beside him, as far as they could get from Al in the cabin doorway.

"That's right," said Al. "Now this is much more comfortable. I didn't feel safe with this gun where it was. Went off once already, didn't it?" he said, pointing to the splintered groove beside the well. He turned the gun over admiringly. "Where did you pinch this?" he asked Mitt. "This is one of Hobin's—one of his specials."

Mitt set his face sullenly. He was not going to discuss Hobin with Al.

"Well, it's in good hands now," Al remarked. "Five shots in it. Got any more?"

"No," said Mitt.

In rippling, rope-creaking silence, Al swung himself up to sit facing them on the cabin roof, with his legs dangling and the gun laid across one knee. Mitt watched his square, smug face and was almost shamed enough to cry. He knew he was having a very vivid experience of exactly how Ynen and Hildy felt when he first came out of the cabin himself, and it made him feel sick. It seemed hard on Ynen and Hildy to be having it again.

"Now let's make sure we understand one another," Al said comfortably. "I've been having a good deal of trouble lately, and it's made me nervous. I don't want any more, understand—guvnor? Little lady? You?"

"The name's Mitt," said Mitt. "What trouble?"

"I'll tell you," said Al, "so you won't get any wrong ideas about me. I'm a marksman. Best shot in the South—so do remember I don't want more trouble, won't you? That's why I'd rather be on the right end of this gun—nothing personal. As for the trouble, I had the good fortune to be employed by a noble gentleman in Holand—well, let's call him Harl, shall we?—to take one of my best shots at a certain Earl—let's call him Hadd, not to beat around the bush—"

Hildy's eyes and Ynen's slid sideways to each other. *Wind's Road* veered. Mitt had to nudge Ynen before he realized. Mitt felt nearly as bad himself, and the nature of the badness dragged his face elderly again.

"And I did," Al said earnestly. "It was as sweet a shot as you ever saw and dropped Hadd like a stone. But then the trouble started because I had to get away, hadn't I? Naturally, Harl had promised me I'd be safe, but I knew better than to trust that kind of promise. Noble gentlemen who make these arrangements always prefer you to be dead, too. You can't blame Harl. I'd have done the same myself. So I made a little outlay of my own, on some soldiers, not to search a certain ship's boat where I was. But there were so many soldiers, and they got so eager, that I had to knock a couple into the water and then cast that filthy tub loose. And I got shot at, and rowed after, and if I hadn't happened to catch the tide, I wouldn't be here now. So I don't want more trouble this time. You don't blame me, do you, little lady?"

"I can't honestly say," said Hildy, "that I don't."

Al blinked a little at this, and scratched his tousled head. He smiled incredulously at Ynen. "She's a sharp one, your sister. She is your sister, isn't she? Lucky I never mind what people say." He moved Hobin's gun round on his knee until it pointed to Mitt. "You. Find some tackle and catch us a fish for lunch."

"If you don't mind what people say—no," said Mitt.

Al snapped back the trigger so that Hobin's gun was ready to fire. "You can say what you like as long as you do it," he said, and the look he gave Mitt made it quite clear he intended to shoot him.

"There may be some tackle in one of those lockers," Ynen told Mitt, in the slow, serious way people only use when they are truly frightened.

# 16

FOR THE REST OF the day Mitt sat fishing. Not venison, oyster, or pheasant tempted any fish to bite. Mitt sullenly watched the line trailing a little pucker in the sea and hated Al more every hour. It was no comfort to see Ynen and Hildy hated him, too, for Al had divided them from Mitt in every possible way.

Al liked talking. He lounged on the cabin roof, between Mitt and the well where Ynen and Hildy were, laying down the law about this, telling them the truth about that, and always treating Hildy and Ynen with great deference and Mitt with none at all. He told them the North was nothing like as free as it was cracked up to be, that a diet of pies would give them scurvy, and that Waywold was a better place to live than Holand. Then he came round to Poor Old Ammet and Libby Beer.

"Funny superstition, having a couple of dummies in your boat," he said, waving from the straw figure to the wax one. "It's not as if you Holanders believed in them. When I was in Waywold, they had a saying there that Holanders kept gods they didn't own to. And that's true. I bet you didn't know they were gods one time."

"They're all right now," Mitt said.

"And we know they're something special," said Ynen.

"Surely you do, guvnor. No offense. But I've been in the Holy Islands all this year past, and I know a bit more than you do. They call those two things gods there. That's how the islands got their name, see. But—this is a funny thing—they don't call them anything there. You ask what are the names of these two dummies, and people just look at you. Oh, they're funny people—half crazed with god fearing, if you ask me—and all the gods are is two dummies."

"I think you might let Mitt stop fishing now," said Hildy.

"Little lady," said Al, "you've a kind heart, and he can stop when he's caught a fish. You hear that?" he said to Mitt. "She's a nice girl—considerate. All her kind are like that. They can afford to be nice, and frank, open, and generous, too. They've got the means behind them, see, where your kind and mine can't afford it. It's a high-priced luxury, being nice is."

Mitt humped his shoulders bitterly. He was sure Al was right. Al could not have chosen any better way of describing the way Ynen and Hildy had treated him all along. It hit the nail on the head.

Ynen said to Hildy as Al talked on, "Who *is* he? I've seen him before somewhere."

Hildy knew Ynen had a far better memory for faces than she had. "I don't care who he is," she said. "I'm going to push him in the sea." She meant it.

But Al was too old a hand to let any of them have a chance to harm him. Having divided them from one another, he talked until he had bored them into numbness. Then he demanded food. Then he talked until nightfall, and still no land was in sight. By now they all thought of land as the thing which would rescue them from Al.

"Well," said Al, as soon as supper was over, "I think I'll be turning in."

They made an effort to suggest he took a watch during the night.

"Who, me?" said Al. "I don't know the first thing about this game. I'm a landsman."

"You had a sail up in that boat," Ynen said. "And you're a Holander. I've seen you. Holanders aren't landsmen."

"I never denied it, guvnor. But that was all years back, before your time. Good night, then." And, since none of them could stop him, Al went into the cabin and fell asleep with the gun hidden under his body where nobody could get it.

While Mitt was dourly stowing the fishing tackle back in the locker, Hildy looked vengefully into the cabin. "He's just like the cousins, Ynen, only I hate him more."

"I hate him harder every time he calls me guvnor," said Ynen.

"He's bound to," Mitt said, kicking the locker to vent some of his feelings. "He's respectful of you." It was on the tip of his tongue to ask them if he had been as bad as Al, but he had not the heart to. He knew he had been. Instead he found himself arranging the night's watches, in a constrained and businesslike way, and taking the dawn watch himself again. Mitt felt in his bones it would be dawn when they sighted land.

In fact, the numb hatred they all felt for Al was very different from the way Ynen and Hildy had felt about Mitt. Ynen pondered about this while he steered *Wind's Road* into darkness. Mitt had scared them horribly at first. But Ynen had never felt unequal to him, the way he felt with Al. As soon as Mitt had started to argue, Ynen had stopped being scared. There were things they had in common with Mitt, but with Al there was nothing. You could not trust him or argue with him. Ynen hoped the wind would be fresh tomorrow, because if it was and if Al stayed on the cabin roof, he was fairly sure he could bring himself to give the tiller a quick shove and sweep Al off the roof with *Wind's Road*'s boom.

Hildy spent her watch thinking wretchedly of Uncle Harl. Ye gods! It was as if she, or Ynen, had paid Al to shoot Navis. Hildy felt so sickened that she was truly thankful Mitt had forced them to sail North, out of that horrible situation. Only now they had Al on board. Hildy knew they were going to need all their cunning, and Mitt's, too, to escape from Al once they did reach land. And she had quarreled with Mitt. Of all the stupid things to lose her temper over! After what Al had said, Mitt was not going to believe in anything friendly Hildy said. Hildy hated Al for the way he had treated Mitt. It was like Uncle Harchad and the Earl of Hannart's son, except that Al had used words instead of kicks.

She tried to show Mitt she was friendly by being very pleasant when she woke him up for his watch. Mitt hardly spoke to her. He pretended to be very sleepy and stumbled past her into the well, mumbling. When he took the tiller and set *Wind's Road* heeling away into the faintly silvering sea, he was too perplexed and miserable to notice what he was doing. The awful similarity between himself and Al was all he could think of. "He did it for money, and I did it for a cause—that's all the difference I can see," he said to himself. "But what cause?"

He felt a sharp nudge on his back. He looked up to find *Wind's Road* yawing about in a white sea, against a white sky. The wind had dropped and changed. It was quite a bit colder. Mitt set *Wind's Road* to rights, buttoned his coat, and turned to have a good look at Libby Beer. She was a tiny, dark figure, too far away to have nudged him. Yet she had.

"See here, lady," Mitt said to her, in his misery, "can I talk to you? Will you answer?" The little dark knobby shape did not move or make any sign. "What I want to know," said Mitt, "is: Am I going to end up worse than Al if I started so young?" Libby Beer gave no sign of having heard. "All right," said Mitt. "I promise to leave murdering alone in future. Will you help me now?" There was silence, except for the fitful rilling of water. "I can't seem to think things in my head without talking them," Mitt explained. "I went through life thinking I was on the right side—one of the good ones, you know—and now I can see I'm as bad as Al. So I got it all to think about again. I want to know what I thought I was doing there in Holand." There was still no sign from Libby Beer. She sat at the end of the tiller among her twine lashing, and the faded colors began to come back to her because the sun was rising. Mitt did not dare talk anymore, in case someone in the cabin heard him. He stared round the welling yellow waves. There was still no land in sight.

No land came in sight all that day. The wind sank to a light, fitful breeze, in which they all buttoned their coats and shivered. It was so much colder that they were sure they must be in Northern waters. That was their one comfort. The pies were smelling strange, the water was low, and got lower still when Al refused to shave in seawater—and there was Al.

Al announced he was bored. "You must have brought a pack of cards or some dice with you," he told Mitt, evidently thinking he was the most likely one.

Since Libby Beer had nudged him in the dawn, Mitt felt just a little more equal to Al. "Me?" he said. "People in my station can't afford games."

Al roamed about grumbling for a while. Then he suddenly went below and came up with the bottle of arris. "This'll have to do then," he said. "Should just be enough. Mind you, little lady, I'm not grumbling, but you should be sure your bottles are full before you sail."

He settled himself on the cabin roof and got drunk. They could all see Hobin's gun stuck in his belt, but Al's hand was never far off it, and he patted it lovingly from time to time. Al sang a little. Ynen looked yearningly at the sail. But the wind was so light that he knew the boom would only give Al a gentle bump if he did swing it over. He sighed and handed the tiller over to Hildy, hoping she would have better luck.

When Al had drunk half the arris, he began to talk again. They all closed their ears. It was easy to do. They were all half asleep after their night watches. For an hour not one of them heard a word Al said. Then he began to laugh uproariously and shout at them.

"I tell you, I've been around all right! And my advice to you is *two games at once!* Rich against rich—they pay better—but rich against poor, if you can't have that. I'll tell you—I'll tell you—*Come here and look, the lot of you*!"

Hildy was steering, but Ynen and Mitt did not dare disobey. Reluctantly they went toward the cabin roof, where Al was fumbling and pawing at his jacket and staring at them with angry, unfocused eyes. As they reached him, he managed to turn the top of his jacket inside out, to show the drab strip of tape in the lining. Fixed to the tape was a tiny round piece of gold with a wheatsheaf crest on it.

"There. Know what that is?"

"Yes," said Ynen. "You're one of Harchad's spies."

Al slapped himself with triumph. "Right!" he said. "Right, right, right! Been Harchad's man for seven years now. So you see what I done?" he asked shrewdly, and became earnest and confiding before either of them could answer. "Rich against rich is the best way. Harl pays me to shoot old Haddock. Harchad gives me a bounty to shoot old Haddock. Offers of safety from both. Al's all right whatever happens, see."

"Just what we'd have expected of you, Al," said Mitt.

Ynen was quite unable to stay near Al any longer. He backed away beside Hildy and was glad when she took a chilly hand off the tiller and squeezed his arm so hard that it hurt.

Al seemed quite content to concentrate on Mitt. He laughed and waved one finger under Mitt's nose. "You take my advice and go in for the double game. Do what I done. You can't beat the earls, so you join them. Find freedom fighters, join them with the Earl's blessing. Then bust them up. I done that all over South Dalemark. Harchad pays—wants information. Earls pay. Lovely life."

Mitt felt his face being pulled elderly as he listened. There seemed no end to the similarities between Al and himself. He turned away from Al's wagging finger and saw that Hildy and Ynen were as hard hit as he was. Their heads were hanging at wretched doll-like angles, and their faces were blurry. Mitt would have liked to say something—something rude to Al, at least—to cheer them up. But he was in such a blazing misery himself that he thought: Being nice is a high-price luxury. Why should *I* bother? He jumped up onto the decking and scrambled toward *Wind*'s *Road*'s bows.

"Hardest bunch of freedom fighters are in Waywold," said Al. "Where are you going?"

"To talk to Poor Old Ammet," said Mitt. "He's better listening. He keeps quiet."

"But the cushiest job," said Al, as if Mitt had not spoken, "was in the Holy Islands. They don't know the meaning of freedom fighting there—only I'm not telling Harchad that. I'm on to a real good thing there." He laughed. "They think the world of me. And all because of my name. Did you know my name was Alhammitt? But I'm not telling that in Holand. I'd have half Holand coming and trying to set themselves up in style there."

"Oh shut up!" Hildy whispered.

But Al talked on, until there was very little arris left in the bottle. Then he sang the "Ballad of Fili Ray." It was about a man who was hanged.

"At least he knows what he deserves!" Ynen said. "Hildy, I know where I saw him before. He was in the Palace last week. The first time I saw him, he was with Uncle Harchad. The other time was out at the back, where Father was having those new houses built. Al came out and talked to Father there, I'm afraid."

Hildy knew, by the dead, sick feeling inside her, that she had feared this all along. "You—you think Father paid him to shoot Grandfather, too?" If Navis had been expecting someone to shoot Hadd, it would explain his unusual presence of mind.

"I don't know," Ynen whispered wretchedly. "He kicked Mitt's bomb away."

"But that could have been because it wasn't part of the plan," said Hildy, and they both looked over to Mitt's hunched shape beyond the mast. They were both quite sure Mitt would want nothing more to do with them now.

The song stopped. Al drank the last of the arris. Then he stood up and staggered toward the well. Hildy and Ynen, both thoroughly frightened, pressed back against the stern and stared up at his swaying, grinning face. There was simply no knowing what Al would choose to do next.

"Funny thing, guvnor and little lady," Al said slurrily. "You look as though you seen a ghost. Another funny thing—I don't feel quite myself. Think I'll go and lie down." He came off the edge of the roof and collapsed on his knees in the well. Neither Hildy nor Ynen could bear to touch him. They turned their feet sideways out of his way, as he floundered round and crawled into the cabin. After two attempts he got onto a bunk and was shortly snoring.

"The gun's underneath him again," Hildy said hopelessly.

They waited for Mitt to come back to the well. It seemed the most important thing in the world that Mitt should come and be friendly with them. It had nothing to do with the fact that they were both sure Mitt was the only one who might get the better of Al. It was that if Mitt disowned them, then they were disowned indeed. But Al snored for two hours before Mitt moved. Old Ammet was as little help to Mitt's misery as Libby Beer had been, although Mitt reached out several times and pleadingly touched the stiff, salty straw of him. Mitt knew he would have to talk to someone. The only way he could think was aloud.

*Wind's Road*'s movement altered. The dip and swing of her became shorter and stronger, though the wind was still the merest chilly breeze.

Mitt knew they must be in coastal waters again. He jumped up, but there was still no sign of land. He hurried across the cabin roof to tell Hildy and Ynen what he thought, but when he looked at them, below him in the well, he wondered if he was going to be able to speak to them at all. Their searching expressions, and their very faces, put him off. Ynen's nose had blistered in the weather, but it was still Hadd's nose. Hildy's two pigtails were loose and puffy, and wisps of black hair blew across her narrow cheeks, but the sharp, tanned face was like Harchad's even so.

Hildy made an effort to talk about Navis. "I know what you're thinking—" she said to Mitt.

"I'm no good at thinking," Mitt said sadly. "Not like you." It sounded much nastier than he intended. Hildy took it for a snub and did not go on.

After that none of them tried to talk about anything important, much as they all wanted to. The things Al had said were like a sore place none of them wanted to touch. This had a very odd effect. They found themselves chattering, and even laughing, about things that were not important, so that someone who did not know might have thought they were three great friends. They got the pies out again and picked out the parts that were still good. The rest—more than half—they had to throw in the sea.

They had just finished eating when Hildy exclaimed, "Seagulls!" White birds were bobbing on the water behind, riding high and light like *Wind's Road* herself. Others wheeled above the well on big bent wings, each with a bead of an eye watching for more pie. Ynen looked at Mitt.

"Land," said Mitt. "Can't be too far off."

They exchanged excited looks. Not only was the long voyage nearly over, but if they could reach land while Al was still asleep, they had a real chance of getting away from him. Ynen tiptoed into the cabin and rustled all the charts there were off the rack above Al's bunk. Al did not move. He tiptoed back to the well with them. Most of the charts, naturally enough, were detailed maps of the water round Holand, but there was one which showed the whole curved coastline from Aberath in the far North to the sands round Termath in the South. Just above the middle of the curve, there was the large diamond-shaped block of Tulfa Island, about thirty miles out from Kinghaven. Below Kinghaven was the wicked spike of the Point of Hark, dividing North from South Dalemark waters. Below that again, much closer inshore, was a scatter of small and large blobs that were the Holy Islands.

"We should recognize that," Ynen whispered, pointing to Tulfa Island, "and I think we'd know the Point of Hark, too. It looks like sheer cliff. I wish we knew how far North we'd come."

"There'll be light on Tulfa, if—" Mitt began.

Al surged out of the cabin like a bloodshot bear. "What's all this whisper, whisper, guvnor? Can't a man sleep?"

The three of them exchanged baffled looks. "Seagulls wake you?" asked Mitt.

"You don't get charts out for seagulls," said Al. He gave the horizon the benefit of his bloodshot look, and seemed as annoyed as they were at finding no land there. "Fuss about nothing. Where's the food?"

They took pleasure in assuring him that all the pies were gone. There was, in fact, a hunk of cheesecake left, but none of them saw any reason to waste it on Al. Al annoyed them by taking the news philosophically. He said his stomach was not too good, anyway, and turned to go back to his bunk.

It occurred to Ynen that if Al was this alert, the thing to do was to make use of him. "How well do you know the coast?" he asked him.

"Like the back of my hand," Al said over his shoulder. "Told you I'd been around, guvnor."

"Then could you stay on deck?" said Ynen.

Al said nothing. He simply went into the cabin and back to sleep again.

But as things turned out, they had no need of Al, nor of the charts, that day. The wind continued light. No land appeared. It was clear that they were in for another night of standing watches.

"We'd best turn due North," Mitt said. "We could run aground in the night on this course." And again he settled to take the dawn watch.

Ynen called Mitt earlier than usual. The sky was hardly beginning to pale. But Ynen was horribly sleepy. He kept nodding off and kept feeling that gentle nudge in his back from Libby Beer. The last nudge was not quite so gentle. Ynen jumped awake, into air that was chilly and muggy at once, and knew something was different. *Wind's Road* was riding in a high, jerky way. Ynen had not felt the like since the day they picked up Poor Old Ammet, and, for a moment, he was as terrified as he had been that first night, when there was space all round him and Mitt crying out in the cabin. He put his hand on Libby Beer to steady himself and realized that the only thing to do was to wake Mitt.

"I think we must be in coastal waters," he said to Mitt as he fell onto the warm bunk Mitt had just left.

Mitt knew they had been in coastal waters since yesterday. He got to the tiller before he was really awake. While he was furiously jerking the rope from the mainsail, which Ynen had tied in a manner Siriol would have given him the rope's end for, Mitt could tell *Wind's Road* was in alarmingly shallow water. He searched that paler side of the sky, but there was only misty darkness. Yet while he searched, he could hear the roar and rumble of waves breaking.

"Flaming Ammet! That's a reef somewhere," Mitt said. He wiped a sudden sweat out of his eyes and stared forward into the paling dark. He thought his eyes were going to burst out of his head with the strain. He could hear the waves clearly, but he could not see a thing.

The figure with flying light hair, half hidden by the foresail, was pointing right and slightly forward. Yes, but which? Rocks there, or go there? Mitt wondered frantically. The tiller swung firmly left under his hand. *Wind's Road* leaned right, in the crisp wash and guggle of a current. Waves crashed over to Mitt's left, and he saw the dim white lather above the rocks she had only just missed.

"Phew!" said Mitt. "Thanks, Old Ammet. Thanks, Libby. Though I don't know what call you have to keep on helping, with me and Al on board. I suppose you got Ynen and Hildy to consider. Thanks all the same."

He heard the waves round more rocks ahead as he said it. This time he did not hesitate to turn *Wind's Road* as soon as he saw the light-haired figure pointing. He was pointing the other way almost at once. Waves crashed on both sides of *Wind's Road*, and the white spray showed whitish yellow in the growing light. Mitt found he was following Old Ammet's pointing arm through a maze of rocks it made him sweat just to think about. Once or twice, in spite of Old Ammet's care, *Wind's Road*'s deep keel grated, and she was snatched sideways in an undertow. Then Mitt would feel Libby Beer's strength on the tiller, pulling them to rights. Frightened as he was, Mitt smiled. The light was growing all the time. If this kept on, he was going to see them as they really were. Old Ammet looked more of a man every second. If Mitt pushed his eyes sideways, he had glimpses of a long white hand behind his on the tiller. It was worth the danger.

The last reef he saw clearly for himself. It was a welling and a milling of yellow water. It was nearly light. Then it was full day. The sun was up, making the sea look as if it was scattered with broken glass. The mainsail was cloth of gold; the island ahead was half golden, and the birds circling it were stabs of dazzling white; and the mist over to the right was a molten bank. The only sign of Old Ammet was a tuft of sunlit straw beyond the mast. Libby Beer was back to a colored knobby thing, tied with string. And Mitt was so disappointed that he could think of nothing else.

Then he came to his senses. He bent down and whispered into the cabin, "Island ahead! Come and look!"

# PART FOUR

# *The Holy Islands*

# 17

THERE WERE SOUNDS of heaving and stumbling inside. To Mitt's disgust, it was Al who appeared, blinking and rubbing his bristly chin. Al glanced at the island. Then he calmly opened the locker and helped himself to the last hunk of cheesecake. Munching it, he surveyed the island again. Ynen and Hildy came out into the well. They looked first at the vanishing cheesecake, then at the island.

"That's Tulfa Island," Al said, with his mouth full.

"Are you sure?" asked Ynen. "I thought it was bigger than this." The island was no more than a great rock, surrounded by drifting seabirds that kept up a long, melancholy crying.

"Positive," said Al. "You want to turn into that mist there."

"I'll try," Mitt said doubtfully. There was little wind now, and that fitful. He put the tiller over and hauled in the mainsail. *Wind's Road* went dipping and swinging gently toward the mist that hid the land.

"Watch out!" said Ynen. "The land's awfully close!"

It was, too, Mitt realized. It was a low green hump in the mist, only about a hundred yards off. He put the tiller hard over again. *Wind's Road* turned elegantly and leaned along outside the mist. "This must be wrong!" Mitt said angrily to Al. "There's no land this close to Tulfa. Do you know where we are or not?"

"I've a fair idea," said Al. "Turn round again."

To do that would mean tacking. Besides, Mitt did not trust Al in the least. He hesitated, and looked over his shoulder, beyond Libby Beer. And he saw a tall ship gliding out of the mist. The sun was just catching her topsails and the gold on her many pennants. Mitt turned back again. "What the—?"

The silence of Ynen and Hildy almost warned him. Al had Hobin's gun in his hand again. Mitt found himself looking into its six deadly black little muzzles. "You do what I say," said Al. He came a step closer. Mitt resigned himself to being shot. He felt, very fiercely, that it was a pity. He would never be able to sort himself out now. On the other hand, he supposed he deserved it. He was afraid it would hurt.

Then, most unexpectedly, Al hit him instead. A great blow caught Mitt hard in the stomach, and he sat down, hawking and gasping, hard on the lockers, feeling very angry, rather foolish, and quite helpless. *Wind's Road* yawed about in the douce breeze. Ynen put his hand out for the tiller and took it back again when the fat little gun pointed his way. There was no danger. *Wind's Road* simply swung and creaked and drooped, rather as Mitt was doing.

The tall ship came gliding closer. They could hear the ropes of her many sails creaking, see the dew from the mist shining in drops on her canvas, and pick out every grain in the wheatsheaf carved on her prow. She stood over *Wind's Road* like a house and took the last of the wind from her sails. Al grinned up at her tall side, highly pleased with himself.

"This has worked out wonderful," he said. He jumped up on the cabin and ran along, shouting, "Hey, *Wheatsheaf*! Hey, there! Bence! Is Bence aboard that thing?"

The tall ship turned. Her creaking sails flapped gently against the wind, until she and *Wind's Road* floated a yard or so apart. Mitt, holding his aching stomach, looked up to see a row of heads watching them, and a man on the highest part leaning over the rail to shout to Al.

"Al! Where did you take off to? There's been no end of askings and botherings and wanting to know where you were. Want to come aboard?"

Al laughed heartily. "What do you think, Bence? I'm sick of this tub. See it gets stowed in harbor, will you, and throw us a rope."

"What about them?" Bence asked, moving his head toward Hildy, Ynen, and Mitt.

"They can come with their tub," said Al.

Orders were shouted high above *Wind's Road*. Two small, agile men came over the side of the tall ship and descended on ropes like two rapid white-headed spiders, until they landed lightly on *Wind's Road*. While she was still dipping and swinging, they handed their ropes to Al. He took hold of them and was hauled up, with a heavy scramble or so, until he reached the ship's rail, where a mass of hands reached out to pull him aboard. The tall ship turned at the same moment. Her sails creaked and filled. The air was loud with rippling for the few seconds it took her to vanish into the mist as quickly as she had come.

Hildy, Ynen, and Mitt were left bobbing in *Wind's Road* with the two small brown sailors. But they seemed to be rid of Al. They gave long breaths of relief about that, even while they were looking dubiously at the sailors. Ynen hurriedly took hold of the tiller. *Wind's Road* was his.

The sailors seemed in no hurry. They stood together by the mast, looking over *Wind's Road*, down at Old Ammet, up at the poor tattered pennant, over beyond Ynen to Libby Beer, and exchanging small singing murmurs. Quite suddenly, they came briskly to the well and swung themselves down into it.

"Will you move out and give us some room, little ones?" one of them asked cheerfully. He had a soft singsong accent, the like of which none of them had heard before.

Ynen clenched his fingers round the tiller. "This is my boat."

"Then you must continue to steer her," said the sailor.

"But you must be guided by us. The road has hazards," said the second sailor. "And will the other little ones go up before the mast to give us room?"

Mitt was so fascinated by the singing talk that he did not gather straightaway that the men were asking him to move. He got up, holding his stomach, and saw that Hildy still had not understood. Mitt nudged her, and she jumped, feeling as if she had been dreaming. They scrambled stiffly onto the roof of the cabin. The sailors settled on either side of Ynen as naturally as if they sailed *Wind's Road* every day, and gave him gentle instructions what to do. Mitt and Hildy knelt on the cabin roof and stared, while *Wind's Road* turned and heeled softly into the now-thinning mist.

They were little brown men with dark eyes and oddly light hair, as fair as light new rope. They felt safe, somehow. They were as warm and brown as the earth itself. Even Ynen felt lulled and peaceful with them. Mitt and Hildy could not shake off a feeling that they were dreaming—a good dream that they had dreamed several times before.

"This is a fine sweet boat," one sailor remarked. "Will you take in the foresails a fragment—Jenro will do it, little one. You steer left now."

Jenro, the second sailor, put his brown hand to the ropes that led to the foresails. Ynen was a little shamed to see how much better *Wind's Road* sailed. "Very sweet," Jenro agreed. "What is the name she goes under?"

"*Wind's Road,*" said Ynen.

The dark eyes of the two sailors met across him. "Is it so?" said Jenro. "Who comes sailing on the *Wind's Road*? What are the names of them?"

Ynen looked up uncertainly at the dreamy faces of Hildy and Mitt. There seemed no harm in saying. "My name's Ynen. My sister's called Hildrida, and our friend's name is Alhammitt."

Mitt blinked. Both sailors were looking at him, smiling warmly. He smiled back. They both made a little gesture, almost as if they bowed. Rather surprised, Mitt ducked his head back at them.

"This is Jenro, and I am Riss," said the first sailor. "Remember us in times to come."

"Yes. Yes, of course," Mitt said uncertainly.

*Wind's Road* had come gently past the green hump in the mist. The mist cleared steadily as she sailed. When Mitt looked away from the sailors' faces, he was astonished to find they were sailing among islands—more islands than he could count at a glance. Some were green and steep, with gray rocks standing above the green and trees clinging to the rocks. Some were green and low. Some were quite small. Others, in the distance, were clearly several miles long. Mitt could see houses on nearly all of them, usually near the shore, as if the sea were their road and the island their farm or garden. Sheep and cows grazed in pastures that mounted above the houses. Smoke rose from the chimneys. The sea space round them was so sheltered that it was warm and calm as a lake. Mitt could smell the salt of the sea mingling with the smell of earth, smoke, and cattle, in a close, queer mixture. He looked round, sniffing, warm and delighted, wondering why he felt so happy and so much at home, and everywhere he looked he saw the astonishing emerald green of more islands.

"Where *is* this?" Ynen said suspiciously.

Jenro smiled at him. "The Holy Islands, little one."

Hildy's head went up. The dreamy feeling left her and left her feeling strained and rather sick. She retreated to the mast and knelt there by herself, nervously clasping her hands and gripping them with her knees. She seemed to feel better like that. Ynen looked dubiously at Mitt. This was not the North. Mitt still had to get away, and Ynen wanted to apologize. He was surprised that Mitt did not seem either annoyed or frightened. Mitt supposed he ought to be. But he was entranced, smiling and sniffing. Seabirds and land birds flew over, uttering their different cries. Jenro, with a mixture of pride and politeness, began to tell Ynen the names of the islands as they passed them, while Riss softly put in a word here and there about the steering. Their voices made Mitt feel as if this was a song he had heard a long time ago, which he had never managed to learn the words to.

"That was Chindersay, and there Little Shool. Big Shool is after. Then Hollisay and Yeddersay and Farn—"

"—to the right here, then left immediately—"

"—and Prest and Prestsay. High Tross there beyond. The large one is Ommern."

"—your mainsheet out here, but with care. The wind gusts after Tross. And a sweet way to the right as you go—"

So *Wind's Road* threaded gently between tall emerald slopes and past low green humps, and Mitt listened and listened, trying to remember that song.

"Then you have Ommersay and Wittess, and we come out past lovely Holy Isle, the holiest of all. After, you will see Diddersay and Doen and the three Ganter Islands—"

Mitt thought it was not quite a song he had in mind. It was the astonishing turfy smell of the islands, or a mixture of the two. Anyway, had he not once, years ago, thought he knew this place and set out to find it? Navis came into it somehow. Mitt was so pleased to remember this much that he scrambled over to Hildy and beamed at her. "Hey, I take it all back about this place! You're going to love it here!"

He was rather hurt at the pale, haughty way Hildy looked. "This," she said, squeezing at her fingers, "isn't the North."

"Who cares?" Mitt said. "I think I'll have a go at staying here myself. I wouldn't mind—I really wouldn't mind!"

"—left now—"

"—and there is Trossaver, with Lathsay beside—"

*Wind's Road* slipped between long, high Trossaver and lump-shaped Lathsay and came into a wide space ringed with islands, where there was ship upon tall ship at anchor. One was just hoisting sail. Another was gliding in through a wide gap opposite, as if it were coming off patrol, but most were anchored, with bare masts. Among the anchored ships Mitt recognized the *Wheatsheaf*. She had no doubt sailed fast on wind above the islands that *Wind's Road* was too small to catch, but she was evidently so far ahead of them that Mitt suspected Riss and Jenro had sailed them on a tour of the Holy Islands. That suited Mitt, but he wondered why.

They sailed toward a long horseshoe-shaped jetty, with a host of little ships tied to it. Behind it was a small town of gray and white houses, with what looked to be the Lord's mansion rising above them at the back. The mainland was beyond again, as green and rocky as the islands, as if the town was also on an island.

"That is the Isle of Gard. The hardway to the land is behind," Jenro explained.

"And a fine fleet in harbor," Riss added proudly.

Hildy tried to unbend. "There are more ships here than in Holand," she said. She thought she sounded as condescending as her aunts. She saw Ynen wince a little. So she became angry with everyone and did not say any more.

As *Wind's Road* approached the jetty, Riss and Jenro sprang into sudden activity. Mitt had hardly had time to climb to his feet and offer to help before the sails were down, ropes out, and *Wind's Road* was quietly nudging the jetty stonework, tied up and her long journey over. Mitt and Ynen stared at one another, tired, sad, and a little aimless. Riss, meanwhile, was out on the jetty, talking to a number of large blank-faced men who were standing there.

"Will you go with these?" he said, coming back to Mitt and pointing to the men. "They are not of the islands."

They were clearly not of the islands. They were dark and heavy, like a lot of men in Holand. But since they were standing in a line along the jetty, Mitt did not see he had any choice in the matter. "I suppose so. All of us?"

"If you will," said Riss. "We shall see you." He and Jenro both shook hands with Mitt, smiled warmly, and trotted away along the jetty. Feeling rather deserted, Mitt, Ynen, and Hildy scrambled out on the jetty, too. The men closed round them to lead them away. It was alarming. But it was also very silly because for a minute or so none of the three of them could walk. When they stepped forward, the ground was either unaccountably missing, or it came up and hit them before they were ready for it.

"Too long at sea!" gasped Mitt. "You have to wait."

The large men waited, silent and impatient, while Ynen fell into Mitt, and Hildy into both of them, and Ynen and Mitt shrieked with laughter, and even Hildy was forced to smile. None of the men smiled, even when they were able to set out through the town, rolling like old sailors and giggling as they went. They were not able to notice the town much, though Mitt did see that there were fields in it, confusingly, among the houses, with cows or wheat stubble in them, and that, every so often, there was a short square-topped pillar about as high as his waist, where people had carefully laid flowers, fruit, and ears of corn. But they saw few people because it was still early morning.

They came to the mansion and were taken inside through a small door. Hildy relaxed a little. The small door meant they were probably prisoners, which must mean that nobody knew who she was. She was glad of that because she could soon put that right. Mitt was not so sure. He had simply no idea what was happening. The only thing seemed to be to wait and see.

They staggered their way up a flat flight of stone stairs to a sunny stone landing. They waited, while one of the men went to knock on a door. Then—*bang*! There was an explosion somewhere. All the windows rattled. All three of them jumped violently, and Mitt, at least, burst out in cold, trickling sweat all over. He was nearly as scared as he had been in the storm. But the large man did not turn a hair and did not pause in knocking on the door. There was a voicelike noise from beyond it. The large man opened the door.

"They're here. Shall I show them in?"

"If you like," said someone inside.

The man jerked his head. Hildy, Ynen, and Mitt trooped through the door into a long, sunlit room smelling of food and gunsmoke—as queer a mixture, though less pleasant, as the mixed smell of the islands and the sea. The food smell came from the table near the door. Al was sitting beside it, with his back to the table and Hobin's gun supported over the back of his chair. Another table was against the wall at the other end of the room. There was a row of bottles on it and cups balanced on the bottles. One bottle was smashed. Al fired again as soon as the door was shut. It was deafening. A cup jumped and shattered, and there was a great deal of laughter.

"Got the hang of this flaming gun now, Lithar," said Al.

"About time," said Bence, the captain of the *Wheatsheaf*. He was sitting on a chair by the window, eating an apple.

The third man said, "Oh, Al! I *have* missed seeing you do that!"

Lithar's clothes were nearly as rich as Harchad's, but he looked nothing like so well in them. He had a mop of fairish hair over the brown face of a Holy Islander and a long, long chin. He seemed quite well built, but he sat in a strange, hunched way which creased his clothes in all directions. When he looked toward them, Ynen, Hildy, and Mitt were uncertain how old he was, because his face was oddly lined, old and young at once. Like Mitt's face, Hildy thought, and she looked at Mitt to compare the two. But Mitt was young and undernourished, whereas—

With a horrible jolt, Hildy realized Lithar was a near imbecile. It was as if her whole future, and her whole past, too, fell away and left just herself—a small girl with untidy hair—alone in a sunny smoke-filled room. Hildy had not realized how much she had built on Lithar and the Holy Islands. She seemed to have founded on them everything which made her into Hildrida and not one of her cousins. It was not exactly her fault, but she had done the building. And it was all unreal. It had not even gone; it had just never been.

It was the same with Mitt. He took one look at Lithar, and one look at Hildy, and he knew that what was happening to Hildy now had happened to him in Holand. But he had not admitted it. Everything he had thought of as being Mitt—the fearless boy with the free soul, the right-thinking freedom fighter—had fallen to pieces there, as thoroughly as Canden in his dream, or Old Ammet in the harbor, and he had been left with what was real. And it had frightened him to death. Mitt thought his face must be as yellow pale as Hildy's. I hope neither of them are fools enough to say who they are, he thought. We better all make off North, quick.

"Who are you?" Lithar asked, with a surprised wag of his long chin.

Mitt and Ynen opened their mouths to begin on two separate false stories, but Al got in first. "Little present I brought you," he said, without turning round. "Don't you like it?"

Lithar giggled. "Well—not terribly, Al. Unless they do tricks. Are you acrobats or something?" he asked them. "Untidy children, aren't they?" he said to Bence.

Al hitched his chair round and leaned close to Lithar, in a way that could only be described as possessive. "They're untidy because they've been at sea. Forgot to take their hairbrushes with them. But you know who they are? Who she is? She's your little betrothed. Harl's niece, from Holand. The brat with the long nose is her brother."

Hildy said, "How did you—?"

Al grinned at her. "You sit on top of the cabin, little lady, boasting for half a day how you was betrothed to Lithar, and then you ask me how I know! Be reasonable!"

"I thought you were asleep," said Hildy.

"Not me," said Al. "Too seasick. Well, Lithar? Aren't you going to thank me?"

Lithar, to help himself absorb what Al said, had put a forkful of food in his mouth. It looked like some of the tastiest sea fry Mitt had ever seen. He and Ynen looked at it longingly. They were ravenous. Lithar chewed, wagging his brown boot toe of a chin. "I suppose she'll grow," he said discontentedly, with his mouth full. "But I don't want her brother."

"Yes, you do," said Al. He went back to eating sea fry, too, but paused to wave his loaded fork to Bence. Mitt thought it was cruel. "Here, Bence," Al said. "Tell us that news from Holand you gave me on the boat." Bence raised his eyebrows and looked at Hildy and Ynen as if he did not want to say anything in front of them. Al angrily waved another forkful at him. "Get on with it!"

Bence was the ruddy, hairy kind of man who looks strong-minded but is really rather weak. He was obviously well under Al's thumb. "I just wondered—" he said. "Well, the news from Holand is that the old

Earl was shot some days back, and his sons had a set-to over the earldom. Harl, the eldest son, killed Harchad, the second son, and family. And Navis, the third son, and family took fright and ran away. That's all I heard, Al."

Hildy and Ynen stared desolately at one another, while Al laughed loudly and pointed his fork at Lithar. "Understand?" Lithar nodded intelligently and plainly did not understand. "Harl," Al explained, "has come out on top. But Navis isn't dead, or not yet. You've got Navis's family here. You want the girl, anyway. She's worth alliance, and bargains and a lot of money. But you want the boy, too. He's a nuisance to Harl. Harl's got boys of his own, and he'll pay high to be rid of this one. And if the unexpected happens, and Navis comes out on top, then you've done him a favor instead, see? Don't worry about the girl. She'll grow."

"Sure to. They all do," Bence said heartily.

Lithar's lined face was riven with bewilderment, but he gave Hildy a formal smile, still with his mouth full, and Ynen a doubtful nod. Then he pointed his fork at Mitt. "But who are you? Al keeps not talking about you."

"I'm just a nobody," Mitt said quickly.

Al tipped his chair back and looked at him. "Don't be too sure of that. Murderer, aren't you?"

Lithar was delighted. "Oh? Like you, Al?"

"No—though he flaming near got in my way," said Al. "I bear you a grudge for that," he told Mitt. "Harl's going to want him, too, Lithar. He had a go at killing Hadd. It didn't come to much, but he'll make someone to blame—satisfy a crying need nicely, you might say. You offer to send him back for a price."

Lithar cocked his long face intently. "How much should I ask?"

Mitt wanted to say something, but he was in such terror that his mind was blank. How had Al known? He must have given himself away just as Hildy had, thinking Al was asleep, and his red and yellow breeches were on him to prove it.

Ynen looked at Mitt's face and knew exactly how he felt. Ynen felt bad. They had promised Mitt to take him North. Something Al had said came into Ynen's mind and combined with the way those sailors had behaved. "I don't think you should," he said to Lithar. "His name's Alhammitt."

"Half Holand's called that," Al said swiftly and loudly.

But Lithar looked at him reproachfully. "Now, Al. That isn't a name we take chances with in the Holy Islands. *You* should know that. I can't send him to Holand. I'm a god-fearing man."

"You're a superstitious ass," said Al. "You send him."

"I can't," said Lithar, and he smiled pleadingly, as if he wanted Al to forgive him.

Al's square face lost all its expression. He laid down his fork and picked up Hobin's gun again. It was empty. Al must have used all the remaining shots demonstrating it to Lithar. He grunted. Then he looked up in annoyance, because the door of the room opened. A little brown woman with white hair came in. She was a slim, upright person in a green-embroidered island dress.

"Clothing and food is prepared for the little ones," she said to Lithar.

Lithar giggled. "Little ones! A bit more respect, please, Lalla. You wouldn't believe how important they are! Shall I send them with her?" he asked Al. Al shrugged.

# 18

TO MITT'S HEARTFELT relief, Lalla took them out of that dangerous room. A crowd of small brown island women were waiting for them outside, with beautiful dark faces and hair either snowy white or light-fair. No one could have been kinder or more concerned than these women. They hurried all three of them upstairs again to rooms where baths were waiting.

Hildy and Ynen, in spite of the situation, were very glad to have a bath. Mitt was hugely embarrassed. He was not used to baths. He was not used to being undressed in front of strangers. Two of the kindly women helped him, soaping and scrubbing and then drying him. Mitt was afraid he seemed unpleasantly dirty. And they kept shaking their heads distressfully over him and talking about him in soft voices almost as beautiful as their faces.

"He is too thin, this one. Look at those legs on him, Lalla. But see the shoulders, and the span on them. There is the makings of a thick man, and the flesh of a sparrow to cover him." Mitt writhed.

At length, feeling rather as if he had been put through the mangle in Hobin's backyard, Mitt tottered out into a long, cheerful room with barred windows, where Hildy and Ynen were waiting to begin breakfast. Mitt hardly knew them. Hildy had been given a faded blue island woman's dress with white embroidery down the front, which made her look grown-up and haughty. Ynen's black hair was wet and shiny and smooth. He had been given a secondhand suit so faded that it was the color of blue-green distance. Mitt became very conscious of the good suit of new bottle green they had given him to wear. He had never worn anything half so good. It gave him a feeling there had been a mistake somewhere, because it was certainly better than Ynen's.

They were left alone to eat breakfast. There were piles of smoking sea fry, new bread, crusty outside and moist within, salty butter, and bunches of green grapes, smaller and sweeter than those of Holand. As Ynen said, it made a wonderful change from pies. But Hildy simply sat looking haughtier and haughtier and not eating.

Mitt found her very annoying. "Do eat," he said irritably. "Keep your strength up."

"I can't," Hildy said, tight and toneless. "Uncle Harchad's dead. And half the cousins."

"So what? Good riddance, if you ask me," said Mitt.

"Uncle Harl's a murderer," said Hildy. "He's no better than Al."

"Well, you knew that before," Mitt pointed out, "and you didn't let it put you off your food then."

"Yes, do eat, Hildy," said Ynen.

"Don't you see?" said Hildy. "Uncle Harl has probably killed Father, too." Two tears ran slowly down her narrow cheeks. "Because we got away, people think he was with us."

Ynen looked at Mitt, appalled. Mitt sighed, rather. He felt he had enough troubles of his own, without sharing theirs. "I always thought it was wrong somewhere," he said, trying to think it out, "what you told me about when you were coming away. Looks as if your Uncle Harchad may have been out to kill you."

"You mean," Ynen asked, "that when those soldiers fired at us in the West Pool, it wasn't because they thought we were you, it was because Uncle Harchad had given them orders to stop us?"

Mitt nodded. "Could be. Harchad or Harl. If you ask me, you were luckier than you knew there."

"Lucky!" exclaimed Hildy. "You call us lucky when Father's probably dead and Al's going to sell us to Uncle Harl!" Tears came down her cheeks in pulses. "Lithar's an imbecile!" she said. "And I boasted so! There's no such thing as luck. Life's horrible. I hate everything about it. I think I always have done."

"You like sailing in *Wind's Road*," Ynen said, rather hurt.

"With two murderers," said Hildy, "into captivity." She bent her head over the pale oak table and sobbed miserably.

Mitt was offended. "Stop that!" he said. "If I hadn't had to get away, you'd be lying dead in Holand at this moment, and you know it! Ynen's worse off than you, and he's not crying. All this means is that we've got to get out of here and go North. So will you stop crying and eat something!"

Tears whisked over the table as Hildy raised her head and glared at Mitt. "I don't think I've ever disliked anyone so much as I dislike you!" she said. "Not even Al!" She snatched up a bunch of grapes and began to eat without noticing the taste.

"How can we get away?" Ynen asked anxiously.

Mitt got up and tried the door. It was locked. Rather dashed, he looked over at the bars on the windows. Somehow he had not expected the island women to lock them in.

"Iron bars," said Ynen.

"Of course, stupid!" said Hildy. "This is a nursery. The bars are to stop babies falling out." Eating the grapes made her suddenly realize how very hungry she was. She began wolfing lukewarm sea fry. "Ye gods!" she said as she wolfed. "I haven't been shut in a nursery for—for some time."

Ynen and Mitt left her eating and went to look at the windows. They looked out on the mainland, rolling into green distance, and the shingly causeway which led to it from the back of Lithar's mansion. Little boats were drawn up to the causeway, nudging the shingle on either side. Immediately below them was a courtyard, with a gateway opening on the causeway. It was full of people, and people were walking backward and forward along the causeway, too.

"We could get down," Ynen said. "Next window along. There's a drain that goes right down to the yard wall. We'd better wait till there are fewer people and then try."

Mitt cautiously forced open the window over the drain and tried if he could get his head through between the bars. He found he just could. And, he knew from experience, where his head would go, the rest of him could follow, sideways on. Since he was bigger than Ynen, that meant that Ynen could certainly get through, and probably Hildy, too. So they settled down to wait until there were fewer people about.

The time came about an hour later. Mitt put his head through, turned his shoulders sideways, and shoved. He could hardly do it. He thought he must have grown. His stomach stuck. By the time he finally forced himself through onto the high sill outside, his stomach felt as if it had been pulled down near his knees. He turned round, hanging on to the bars, to help Ynen and Hildy through.

But Ynen could not get through. He was too well nourished. His shoulders were just too thick. He pushed and squirmed and squeezed, and Mitt pulled him perilously from outside, but it was simply no good. Ynen had to give up, bruised and miserable. Hildy was even worse. She was bigger than Mitt all over and could barely even get her head through. They stood unhappily against the window, while Mitt crouched outside with his knees aching from the strain, feeling both unsafe and obvious, wondering what they were going to do now.

"Do I come in or what?" Mitt said angrily.

"Could you come back up and unlock the door for—" Ynen began to say.

"Oh, ye gods!" said Hildy. "There's Father! Look!" Her face was suddenly bright red, and she looked as if she was going to cry again.

Mitt swiveled himself round on the sill to look. The man trudging along the shingle of the causeway was wearing farmer's clothes and big boots, but he was certainly Navis. Mitt knew him by the way he walked and, even at that distance, by the face that was so like Harchad's and Hildy's. "It is, too!" Mitt said. "You lot have the luck of Old Ammet!"

"It's not lucky at all," said Ynen.

"Mitt, go down and warn him, quick!" said Hildy. "Tell him we're prisoners and it's not safe for him here. Quickly, before Al sees him!"

"But he'll know me," Mitt objected.

Hildy shook the bars in her anxiety. "He can't possibly—not in those clothes. If you won't go, I'll have to shout, and someone will hear!"

"All right, all right!" said Mitt. "I'll tell him. I'll tell him to keep back on the mainland, and then I'll have a go at letting you out. Tireless Mitt does all the work again."

"Oh shut up!" said Ynen.

"And hurry up!" said Hildy.

Mitt made a face at both of them and slid down the drainpipe. Mitt to the rescue! he thought. He reached the yard wall without anyone noticing him at all. Nobody seemed particularly interested when he shot down from the wall and raced to the gate.

Navis was just about to come through it. Close to, Mitt saw that he looked tired and not very well shaved. The big boots were caked with mud. But Navis took no notice of Mitt as Mitt darted out of the gate to meet him. That encouraged Mitt. Navis did not remember him. He could only have seen Mitt for half a minute on the day of the Festival, after all.

"Hey!" Mitt said to him. "Don't come in here. It's not safe."

Mitt had reckoned without two things. Navis had been a fugitive, living on his wits, for days now. And he had Ynen's memory for faces. Or perhaps not only for faces, for he recognized Mitt mainly by his build and the way he ran. And since Navis had no reason to think Mitt would do him a good turn, he simply looked at Mitt as people do when they are surprised to find themselves addressed by a total stranger and walked past him into the courtyard.

Mitt was so annoyed by this haughtiness that he would have let Navis alone had it not been for Ynen and Hildy watching from above.

He ran after Navis and took hold of his sleeve. Navis shook Mitt's hand off and walked on. Mitt was forced to trot beside him, trying to explain.

"See here, it's not safe for you here. Lithar's wrong in the head, and the fellow who shot Hadd got hold of him and made him take Hildy and Ynen prisoner. They're up there, in that room with bars. Take a look."

Since there were so few people about, Mitt risked pointing. But Navis would not demean himself to look. He trudged on, trying to decide why this murdering brat should spin him a yarn like this and taking no notice of Mitt at all.

"Father's not listening!" Hildy said, with her head pushed against the bars. "Isn't that just like him!"

"He may only be pretending not to listen because it's safest," Ynen suggested hopefully.

Mitt hoped Navis was pretending, too. "Hildy and Ynen sent me," he explained, feeling sure this would convince Navis. But Navis tramped through the main doorway of the mansion into a large stone room without appearing to have heard. The room was full of people. Mitt hung back in the doorway, wondering whether he dared follow Navis in. They were mostly island people. The singsong of their talk rang round the room. Mitt decided that it was safe enough and ran after Navis to make one more attempt.

"Do come out of here," he said, dodging about near Navis's shoulder. "They'll sell you to Harl to kill. Honest."

Navis looked at someone beyond Mitt's head and called out loudly, "Will one of you take this offensive child away, please!"

Mitt sensed a movement in the crowd and got ready to run. "Can't you *listen* to me, you pigheaded idiot!" he said.

"Will you shut your unpleasing mouth?" said Navis. "Guard! Remove this, will you!"

Mitt turned and ran. But the guard was nearer than he thought. Two big men seized him as he turned. Mitt lost his temper then. He kicked and struggled and called Navis a number of names he had learned on the waterfront.

"Oh him again," Al said from behind Mitt. "Not to worry, sir. I'll take care of him, sir."

Upstairs in the barred nursery, Hildy and Ynen waited and waited. For a long time they were sure that whatever had happened between Mitt and their father, Mitt would come and unlock the nursery door any moment. They had great faith in Mitt's resourcefulness. But when the island women came and brought them lunch for two, even Ynen gave up hope.

"I don't think Mitt was even trying to make Father understand," Hildy said angrily. "And now he's just forgotten us. His kind are all the same!"

"I don't think he would forget," Ynen said.

"Yes, he would. He had a perfect chance to escape on his own, and he took it," said Hildy.

"I thought he felt he owed us—" Ynen began uncomfortably.

"He didn't feel anything of the kind," said Hildy. "His whole idea was that we owed him everything, because of his rotten life in Holand!"

This was so exactly the kind of thing Mitt had said himself that Ynen could not argue any longer.

Long hours later they were trying to play I spy. Hildy was far too dejected to concentrate. "I give up," she said. "There's nothing beginning with *T* in this room."

"Table," Ynen said drearily.

The door opened just then, and Lithar shambled in. Hildy did not realize. "How was I to know it was something as stupid as that!" she snapped, thoroughly bad-tempered.

Lithar stared at her, shocked. "I don't think I want to marry you," he said.

"That goes for me, too!" Hildy retorted. "I hate the sight of you!"

Lithar turned plaintively to Al, who had followed him in. Behind Al came two of the large men, with Navis between them. "Al," said Lithar, "I don't have to marry her, do I? She's not womanly." Al laughed and patted him on the back.

"There, Hildrida. You have just received your first compliment," said Navis. "Possibly your last, too."

"Where's Mitt?" Ynen said to Al. Al laughed and shrugged. "You do know, don't you?" said Ynen. "Have you killed him?"

Al chuckled. "Say hallo to your pa like a good boy."

"Not until I've told you what a foul brute you are," said Ynen.

"He's not very nice either," Lithar complained. "Let's go away."

"After you," said Al, and everyone went out of the room again, leaving Navis standing by the locked door.

Hildy and Ynen stared at Navis. He looked tired, dirty, and depressed. Hildy felt sorry for him. She was almost certain she was glad to see him. She went toward Navis to tell him so. But she did not quite dare and stopped. Then she somehow ran at him without thinking and threw her arms around him. For just a second Navis looked surprised. Then Hildy found herself being hugged, picked up, and swung round, and her father looking more pleased and more upset than she had ever seen him. When Ynen came shyly up, Navis spared an arm for him, too, so that they all hung together in a bundle.

"Who warned you to get away?" said Navis. "How did you manage in that fearsome storm?"

"Nobody. It was an accident. Mitt and Libby Beer and Old Ammet helped," they said, and they tried to tell him about their adventures in *Wind's Road*. After a little Navis let go of them and sat down to listen, pressing two fingers to the corners of his eyes as if he had a headache. They could not help noticing that he frowned and seemed to press harder every time they mentioned Al or Mitt.

"Why did you come here?" Ynen asked him at last. "Was—is Al in your pay? I saw you talking to him in Holand."

Navis looked up at Ynen in surprise. "Of course not. You must have seen him the time he came to offer—for a large sum of money, naturally—to tell me of a plot against the Earl. You can't imagine how often people did that," Navis said. He sounded very depressed. "I found Al very uncongenial. But I mentioned the matter to Harchad, and, ironically, I remember Harchad telling me in return that he had put an agent in the Holy Islands to keep Lithar in line, in case the North attacked. If I had known it was this same Al, I would have stayed well away. I came because there are boats here—prepared to pay high for being taken North—and trying not to hope there might be news of you two. But it seems that Al has decided that Harl would pay more for us than I would pay for a boat—which I'm sure is true—so we are being sold back to Holand."

There was a wretched silence.

"Wouldn't Uncle Harl let us go," Hildy asked, "if we all signed something to say we didn't want to be earls?"

Navis shook his head, with his two fingers lodged hard above his nose. "He doesn't trust me. He never has. Besides, I kicked him in the stomach when he came to arrest me. He was so annoyed that he came out in the Flate after me himself, in spite of the storm. He nearly trod on me while I was lying in a ditch. By which I knew he wouldn't easily forgive me."

Ynen laughed, though he was sure it was no joke. "But didn't Mitt try to warn you?"

He saw his father's forehead crease. "If Mitt is the boy who tried to blow up the Sea Festival—yes, he did. I thought he was lying and asked the guards to take him away. Al took charge of him after that. Is this one more mistake I've made?"

"Yes," said Ynen.

"You didn't know," said Hildy. "I never trust Mitt either. His ideas are all in a muddle. But if Al's killed him, I'm going to call on Old Ammet and Libby Beer for vengeance."

"I sincerely hope they answer you quickly," said Navis.

But when, about an hour before sunset, Al came into the nursery with a number of the largest guards, he was as sturdy and carefree as ever and rather more pleased with himself than usual.

"Up you get, sir," he said, "and you, guvnor. Bence is back from a little job I sent him on. The old *Wheatsheaf* is all ready, the tide's right, and we're going sailing again. It's not what I'd have chosen, being a landsman and inclined to queasiness, but we reckoned you'd not be able to give us the slip so easy at sea."

Navis stood up slowly. "You mean you're taking us back to Holand."

"Quick on the uptake, your pa," Al remarked to Hildy. "That's right, sir. We're taking you and the boy, and leaving the girl here."

"Why are you leaving my daughter?" said Navis.

Al looked at Hildy. Hildy wanted to hit him, to scream, to make a fuss in every way she could think of, but she felt she could not when her father was behaving so calmly. "Be reasonable, sir," said Al. "She's betrothed to Lithar. We've got to have a bargaining point. The money Harl offers has got to go up, and up again, and she'll be the reason. And if he won't offer enough, you may find we come sailing back here with you in a day or so. Look on the bright side, sir."

"Oh, is there a bright side?" said Navis.

"For some of us," Al answered genially. "I'll trouble you to step along now."

They said good-bye stiffly. None of them wanted to say anything important with Al there. Navis and Ynen were marched out by the guards. Hildy stood by herself in the middle of the room, with her hands clenched into useless fists, watching the door close behind them. She was determined not to cry till it shut.

The door opened again. Al put his head round it. "By the by, little lady," he said, "something tells me that Lithar may suffer a little accident on the voyage. He would come with us, you know. Then there'll be a new Lord of the Holy Islands for you to marry."

Hildy looked at that grinning face stuck round the edge of the door and was so angry that she shook all over. "If you mean it'll be you," she said, "I bet you have at least two wives already."

Every scrap of expression went out of Al's face. "Someone tell you their life story, did they?"

"No," said Hildy. "I just know. You're just that kind of man."

"Then you better keep that idea to yourself," said Al. The door snapped shut, and the key grated.

Hildy went on standing where she was, too miserable and frightened even to cry now. She knew she had been very, very foolish to say that to Al. But after all that had happened, it hardly seemed to matter. She thought she might as well sit down anyway.

She was just turning toward a chair, when she noticed that the door was swinging open again. Beyond, in the dark corridor, Hildy could see one of the little island women. She thought it looked like Lalla.

"Will you come out now?" asked the gentle island voice. "It is time to be leaving, if you wish to go."

"Oh, I do wish to go!" Hildy said, and hastened out to her.

Lalla turned and walked down the passage, and Hildy walked beside her. It was so strange to be free suddenly that Hildy did not quite believe it. It felt like a dream. Dreamily she went with Lalla down some stairs and along another passage.

"Where are we going?" she asked as they came to more stairs and went down again.

"Out to the hardway. Riss is waiting there for you."

Despite her troubles, Hildy was dreamily glad. Of the two little sailors, Riss was the one she had liked best. "Where will Riss take me?"

"To the North, if you wish to go there." They came to the end of the stairs and out into the big stone room where Mitt had made his last attempt to convince Navis. It was empty now, rather cold, and seemed dim because there was such a blaze of evening light from the arched doorway to the courtyard. Their footsteps echoed softly from the stone. Among the echoes Hildy heard Lalla ask, "Will you be wishing to come back to the Islands again?"

Hildy thought about it, as they crossed the ringing stone floor. She would not have been surprised to find she never wanted to come here again. But she found she did. The Holy Islands had somehow taken her heart while she was sailing through them in *Wind's Road* into danger. "I'd love to," she said. "But not if Al's here."

"We can rid you of your enemies," Lalla said, "if you are prepared to trust Alhammitt."

"Mitt?" said Hildy. "Is Mitt all right?" Then she became embarrassed that Lalla knew how little she trusted Mitt and wanted to explain herself. "It isn't what he did. It's what he thinks and the way he's been brought up. I mean, I know I'd probably be just the same if I'd been brought up on the waterfront, but I haven't. And I can't help the way I was brought up, either. I think mostly he annoys me. I suppose I annoy him. That's it, really."

As Hildy said this, she came to the doorway and a blaze of orange sunlight. There was a bull in the courtyard beyond. It was a huge animal, almost red in the low sun. There was power in every line of it, in each stocky leg and from its tufted tail and slim rear to its great shoulders and blunt triangular head. It seemed to be loose in the courtyard, with no one to control it. Hildy stopped short and stared at it. And the bull raised two wicked horns growing out of a mat of chestnut curls, and looked at Hildy. Hildy did not care for the look in its large red eye. She turned uncertainly to Lalla.

The blazing low sun had dazzled her, but Lalla seemed taller than she had thought. In the dimness, her hair seemed not white but red, or brown. But it was the same singing island voice which said, "It was only two things I asked you. Would you come again to the Islands, and would you trust Alhammitt?"

Hildy felt the ground shake under the weight of the bull as it trod nearer. It was unfair of Libby Beer to try and frighten her. "What happens if I say no to those questions?" Hildy asked defiantly.

The lady standing in the dimness might have been a little surprised. "Nothing will happen. You will go in peace and live quietly."

Then Hildy found that it was important to her to answer both questions truthfully. She stood thinking, while the bull twitched its tail and paced heavily in the sunlight. "Yes, I want to come here again," she said. That was the easy part. "And—and I suppose I do trust Mitt really. I did in the storm. It's just when I'm angry I notice the difference between us, but I don't think that's quite the same. Is it?"

She looked up to Libby Beer for an answer, but there was no one there. The stone room was empty. Shaken, Hildy looked out into the courtyard. That was empty, too.

"Didn't I answer right, then?" Hildy said. Her lonely voice rang round the room. Since there was no good to be done there, Hildy went out into the warm dazzle of the courtyard and walked over to the open gate. The damp scent of the Islands met her there. The sea hurried to the shingle of the causeway in a myriad small ripples, setting the waiting rowing boat nuzzling at the stones.

As Hildy's feet crunched on the pebbles, Riss stood up in the rowing boat and smiled warmly. "Will you thrust on the boat and climb in, little one? We will be stirring to your ship."

Beyond Riss, *Wind's Road* was moored in the deeper water between the mainland and the causeway. Hildy could see her swinging gently in the tide. She smiled at Riss delightedly.

"I think," she said, as she kicked off her shoes on the shingle and tied a knot in one side of her Island dress to keep it out of the way, "I think I've just been talking to Libby Beer."

"That is not the name we use here," Riss said. "She is called She Who Raised the Islands."

# 19

AL SLUNG MITT into a room which was probably a storeroom and left him there while he went to attend to Navis. It was a very small stone room with a skylight too small even for Mitt to squeeze out through. Mitt sat with his hands behind his head, glaring up at it and hating Navis with all his heart. All his troubles went back to Navis. He felt as if instead of kicking a bomb this time, Navis had actually kicked him in the teeth. And Mitt had only been trying to help!

"That's the last time I ever do anything for that lot!" Mitt said to himself, and fell into a prolonged and fierce daydream about what he would like to do to Navis. He imagined himself as a powerful outlawed revolutionary with several hundred seasoned followers at his back. He imagined himself conquering a town full of terrified lords and ordering them all to surrender. Out they came, with Navis among them, cringing Harchads, quaking Hadds, dozens of Hildys, and several frightened Ynens, all hanging their heads and shuffling, as the men from the North had shuffled through Holand. Mitt had them all killed, but Navis he saved till last for a truly frightful death.

It was most interesting. For years now Mitt had been too busy with other things to do any daydreaming. He found he had been missing something. He did the story over again, with a larger town, and made himself more powerful and even more merciless. He began to see that he really had it in him to become such a revolutionary. He felt considerable respect for himself. He did the story a third time and conquered all South Dalemark, pursuing Navis ruthlessly until at last he caught him.

He was halfway through killing Navis very slowly, with great attention to detail, when Al came back again. Mitt jumped up and backed into the far corner of the small space. Al's face had its most blank and unpleasant look. Because of what he had been thinking of doing to Navis, Mitt knew rather well how much Al could hurt him if he wanted to.

But Al simply leaned against the door and surveyed Mitt. "You're a real nuisance to me," he said, "and I'm going to have to get rid of you quick. How many people know where you are?"

Mitt stared at Al uncertainly. He did not know what Al thought he had done.

"Out with it," said Al. "Or do I have to knock your head in? Navis knows you were the one with the bomb. Does Hobin know about that? Hobin must've given you that gun. I don't see you pinching one of Hobin's specials. He's too careful of them. Does Milda know where you are, too?"

Mitt shook his head and went on staring at Al. Out of the distant past came memories of Al's voice shouting that the cow had calved, and Al's square back marching away toward Holand to find work, but he could not bring himself to believe it.

"If you was anyone else," Al went on bad-temperedly, "I could send you back to Holand with the other two and good riddance! But I'm not having you tell Hobin about me. He'd have it round every gunsmith in the country, and without Harchad to back me I'd never get near a gun again. He's made it hard enough for me as it is. And all because I happened to drink a bit too much one day and let out to him how I bust up the Free Holanders. He said he was going to Holand to look after you and Milda, but I know he did it just to spite me." Here Al noticed the way Mitt was staring at him, and laughed at him. "Say hallo to your pa, then, why don't you?"

"Aren't you proud of me at all?" Mitt asked him. Al stared at him. "Chip off the old block, and so on?" said Mitt.

At this Al spit on the floor as Mitt remembered him often spitting in the dike. "Proud of *you*! I've got three kids in Neathdale, and the lot of them put together never got in my way like you do. First thing you ever did was get lost and put me under an obligation to Navis. Then you let the bull get at the rent collector. Then you hang round my neck in Holand. Then, when I thought I'd seen the last of you years before, you bob up dressed like a side of bacon and dump a bomb in front of Hadd just when I'd got my sights lined up on him! I don't know what good you thought that would do. Mind you," said Al, "I didn't know who you were then, but if I had known, I'd have said it was Milda's fault. It looked just like one of her daft ideas."

Mitt was not much given to blushing, but he felt his face going warm and red at this. "It was my idea. So!" he said. He felt he had to defend Milda to Al. "She's all right, Milda is. It's just she's not too clear about what's real. You know, always throwing her money about—" Mitt stopped. That was exactly the truth about Milda, and he had always known she was like that. Milda never looked to the future, whether she was buying too many oysters or sending Mitt to be taken by Harchad. The fact was, neither of them had dreamed what it would be like. It was very painful to Mitt, the way Al was laughing about it.

"You don't have to tell me she's got no flaming sense!" Al said. "She'd have ruined me if I'd let her. And you're just the same. Fancy making friends of Hadd's grandchildren!"

"They're not my friends!" Mitt said angrily.

"You could have fooled me," said Al. "Swap jokes on the cabin roof with your enemies, do you? Told them half your life story, didn't you? And that Hildrida's no fool. If you say one word more to her, she's going to add it up with what I said and spoil all the plans I got for her. You finished yourself when you opened your big mouth, you did. You don't make friends with people like that. You batten on them."

There were hurrying footsteps outside the storeroom door. Someone shouted, "Al! Al, are you there? Lithar wants you."

"Coming!" Al shouted back. "I'll have to leave you to Bence to deal with," he said to Mitt. "Can't that gibbering fool manage for five minutes without me?" He banged out of the storeroom, muttering.

The bolts shot home. Mitt slid down into a heap in the corner. After a moment he wrapped his arms round his head, as if that could keep some of his misery off him. But nothing could. The horrible similarity between himself and Al was clearly no accident. Like father, like son. And as Mitt hated Al so vehemently, he hated himself, if possible, even more. He had set out to be a brute like Al, and it had not been his fault if he had failed. Worse still, everything he had thought he was doing it for turned out to be a complete sham. Al had betrayed the Free Holanders, not the other way round. Mitt felt as if his whole mind was falling to pieces, like Canden in his dream. There seemed nothing left of him at all.

"One thing you might have done, Al," he said from his corner. "You might have put me out of my misery quick, instead of running away to flaming Lithar!"

It was some hours before anyone came to put an end to Mitt's misery. By that time he was rolling groaning in the middle of the room. He barely had time to scramble up and barely time to glimpse the little brown sailor, Jenro, and another he did not know, and Bence standing in the doorway, before a large sack was pushed over his head and he was bundled head-down over Jenro's shoulder.

"Hey!" Mitt said, struggling miserably.

"Be silent, little one, and no harm will come," Jenro said softly.

"Hurry up," said Bence from the distance.

Mitt trusted Jenro and stopped struggling. The world began to bounce about as Jenro hurried somewhere with him. Mitt was uncomfortable with his head hanging down, but not badly so. After a short while he was swung up, swung down, and lowered surprisingly gently onto boards that dipped a little. Mitt heard water slapping quietly under the boards and guessed he was in a boat. He felt the boat sway, bumping as the two sailors hitched on the oars. Mitt tried to see through the sack where they were. It was a hairy, porous sack, which tickled his nose rather. He could see very little light coming through, which made him suspect that the boat was undercover somewhere and whatever was being done with him was a secret. He would have yelled, but for what Jenro had said.

The movements of the two sailors stopped. Jenro's soft voice said, "Then, Captain, you are settled that we must be stirring out to sea to throw this little one in?"

"Yes," Mitt heard Bence say from above somewhere. "And I'm coming with you to see it done."

"Captain, there is no need to do that," said the other sailor.

"Oh, isn't there?" The boat surged heavily as Bence landed in it. "I know you lot. When you say no need, I start to get suspicious. Cast off there."

The sailors said nothing. Mitt felt the boat move. The oars began a slow, sleepy *dip-creak-splash, dip-creak-splash*. Shortly, bright sunlight fell across the holes in the sack. Mitt thought they must be out in the harbor. They went on steadily in the sun, *dip-creak-splash, dip-creak-splash*. It was so soporific that Mitt nearly fell asleep, in spite of his misery.

Then he heard the gentle voices begin again. "Captain, throwing this little one in the sea is a thing we cannot do."

"But you wait to tell me till we're past Trossaver," Bence said from the distance. "You'll do it."

"Captain, there are two of us and one of you."

"All right. You can watch me do it, then," said Bence.

"But that is a thing we cannot do."

"You'll have to put up with it," said Bence. "Al wants it done. You always do what Al wants, don't you?"

"We would not do this for Al either."

Bence seemed really astonished. "Not for Al!"

"No," said Jenro. "For this one came on the wind's road, with a great one to guide him behind and before."

"What's that got to do with it?" Bence demanded. "You saw Al come on the same flaming boat."

"That matters not at all. The great ones contain multitudes."

"Don't you throw your religion at me!" said Bence.

The voices stopped. The oars dipped slowly and peacefully. Mitt grinned to himself inside the hairy sacking and rubbed his itching nose. He suspected that Bence was more likely to be thrown into the sea than he was. He thought Bence knew it, too. Mitt dozed off, soothed by the sound of oars and glad to forget himself. Every so often he woke up to find the argument going on again.

"What am I supposed to do when two of my best men don't do what I say?" he heard Bence demanding.

"We will do what you say," answered a gentle voice.

"Then I want this brat dumped in the sea."

"But that is a thing we cannot do."

Another time Mitt heard Bence say, "What do you think you're rowing all this way for, then? Are we just going to turn round and come back again, or what?"

"If you wish for us to turn round, Captain."

"I do not! I want this brat dumped in the sea."

"But that is a thing we cannot do, Captain."

The next time Mitt woke, Bence's nerve had broken. "I see," he was saying. "And if I lay a finger on him, it'll be me in the sea instead."

"You would not force us to that, Captain."

"Then what *can* I force you to?"

"If it is a thing that meets your mind, Captain, we can be stirring to an island and putting the little one on it. There are those where no mortal men live."

"Bother meeting *my* mind," said Bence. "It won't meet Al's."

"If you are not telling Al, we shall not be saying either."

"Hmm," said Bence. After a pause he said, "Well, it's not so different from dumping him in the sea, I suppose, provided it's uninhabited. Which island is it to be?"

"Lovely Holy Island is nearby. There is none on her but She Who Raised the Islands and the Earth Shaker."

"What's that supposed to mean?"

"No mortal soul lives there."

"I thought there was supposed to be a mad old priest living there."

"He does not live there. No mortal soul lives there."

"Oh, very well!" said Bence.

There was a noticeable increase in the creak and jerk of the oars. Mitt could feel the boat shoving through the water. After barely a minute the swing of the oars stopped. Shingle grated underneath and grated again. Mitt could hear waves rattling the pebbles of a beach.

"Hurry up!" said Bence.

Mitt was lifted and carried by two people. Their feet crunched on sand, and then his own feet were placed tenderly on what felt like turf. Jenro pulled the sack off him and smiled at him.

Mitt had a feeling Jenro was going to say something, perhaps tell him something important, but while Mitt was blinking and rubbing hairs from the sack out of his eyes, Bence was climbing angrily along the rowing boat at the sand's edge.

"Get back here," said Bence. "Or else."

The two sailors smiled at Mitt, and Jenro certainly winked, though Mitt could not see why, before they trotted back to the boat. Mitt stood, blinking still, while they pushed the boat off, twirled it with a deft shove of an oar, and rowed smartly away, getting smaller and smaller against the green of the nearest island. He thought they were going at least twice as fast as they had come.

Mitt felt desolate. The nearest island was far too far for him to swim. Holy Island towered above him in a tumble of rocks and green grass. Little trees and heather hung far above his head. It was wild, uncultivated, and deserted. To judge from the fresh, peaty smell, there was water somewhere, but there was no food except berries. Mitt could not see why Jenro had winked. He was going to starve to death.

He tried to remember what Holy Island had looked like from the other side, as they sailed past in *Wind's Road*. He thought it had seemed lower and greener, and—though he might be mistaken—he thought he remembered that the islands were nearer on that side. It was worth going to look, anyway.

Mitt set off round the island. There was no clear path. He was forced to wander up and down, between rocks and over slippery turf, sometimes almost down to the water's edge, sometimes quite far up the high hill, and, as he went, his miseries caught up with him again. He hated himself and Al and Navis—everything—so much that he wished someone really had drowned him. He no longer wondered why Hildy had exclaimed she hated life. It was not worth living.

The sun was low. Mitt was hot and under a cloud of midges. And he found his way round the island barred by a huge block of granite. Grumbling dismally under his breath, he scrambled his way to the top of it. A green meadow spread beneath him on the seaward side, bright in the golden evening. Beyond it the sea rolled and swashed in little waves. Mitt looked out over their golden ribbing and saw that the nearest two islands were only two hundred yards or so away. He could swim that easily. No wonder Jenro winked. Then he looked down at the meadow.

There was a bull in it. It was a huge animal, almost red in the low sun. Its great shadow stretched halfway across the meadow. As Mitt looked at it, the bull raised its triangular head, armed with wicked horns growing out of a mat of chestnut curls, and looked at Mitt. Its tufted tail swung. Keeping its red eyes on Mitt, it advanced toward the rock. Mitt could feel the granite tremble under the weight of it as it walked.

Now what am I supposed to do? Mitt wondered, crouching on top of the rock.

A woman came round the rock and looked up at Mitt. "You'd better not go that way," she said to Mitt, nodding toward the bull. She was wearing a green island dress with red embroidery, but Mitt thought she could not be an island woman. She was tall, and she had long red hair which blew round her in the sea breeze. Her face was very beautiful and rather serious. "Go up that way," she said, pointing to the island above the rock.

Mitt looked where she pointed and saw a path of trodden earth climbing steeply this way and that among the rocks. He looked back at the bull, which met his eye unpleasantly. "I suppose I'd better," he said, and he stood up. Then it occurred to him that the woman was standing in the meadow, only a few yards from the bull. "Are you safe there?" he said.

The woman smiled. It reminded Mitt of the way Milda smiled, when the crease went out of her face and the dimple took its place. "Thank you. I can manage him," she said.

As Mitt set off up the steep path, he saw the woman go toward the bull with her hand held out. The bull stretched its massive neck to nuzzle her fingers. Well, rather her than me! Mitt thought.

The path went backward and forward across the hill, diving between twisted trees and making hairpin bends over rocks. Mitt climbed with the rich smell of the earth and the sharp smell of turf in his nose. In his ears the plangent plash and roll of the waves became larger, but more distant. Mitt wondered where he was going and what good it would do when he got there. Then the path went round a rock with a tree growing out of it and entered a very small hanging dell, open one side to the sea, and greener than any of the islands. Mitt stood there to get his breath. There was a great view over the islands in the golden light, islands on one side floating green-gold in blue-gray sea, and islands on the other side blue-black against the sun, floating in silver-gold, like clouds in the sunset.

Mitt, hot and breathless and miserable as he was, felt very bitter at the sight. Times out of mind, as a small boy, he had dreamed of such a place. Now he had found it, and what good had it done?

He turned away and went on into the dell. It was moist and cool. To Mitt's pleasure, there was a trickle of water running down a rock. The sack had made him very thirsty. He put his hands and then his face into it and came out dripping. He noticed that beside him there was one of those stone pillars he had seen on the Isle of Gard. It was about as tall as a sundial, but wider. On it were two small figures, one made of green grapes and rowan berries, and the other of plaited stalks of wheat.

"Hey!" said Mitt. "Here's Libby Beer and Old Ammet!"

He was stretching out a hand to give Old Ammet a touch of greeting when he felt the dell tremble under the feet of a heavy creature. He whirled round, expecting to see the bull again.

A gray-white horse had stopped further down the dell and a tall man with flying light hair was dismounting from it. Mitt hastily brushed his wet face with his arm and backed against the short stone pillar. The man was Old Ammet. He came toward Mitt, smiling a little, with his long light hair blowing and swirling about his head and shoulders as if the wind were blowing half a gale in the dell. But there was no wind at all. He had a straight, grave way of looking, which reminded Mitt a little of Hobin, though his face was nothing like Hobin's. It was like no face Mitt had ever seen. One moment Mitt thought Old Ammet was a grand old man, and the next he seemed a handsome young one. And as Mitt saw these strange changes in Old Ammet, he was more frightened than he had ever been of any nightmare. With every step Old Ammet advanced, Mitt felt another wave of fear, until he was as terrified as he had been that time in Holand when he pretended to play marbles—right up to the moment when Old Ammet spoke to him. Then it all seemed perfectly natural.

"I was needing to speak with you, Alhammitt," Old Ammet said. His voice reminded Mitt of Siriol's, though it was also quite, quite different. "I have to ask you a question."

"You could have talked to me anytime," Mitt said, feeling a little resentful. "Why does it have to be now, when I'm all to pieces?"

Old Ammet's young face laughed, and his old face answered. "Because there was no doubt till now what you would do."

"What I want to do is get out of this place and go North," Mitt said. "What's so doubtful about that?"

"Nothing," agreed Old Ammet, out of his grave old face. "The men of the Islands will help you go North." Then his face blazed young and glad and eager, and he said, "It is also quite certain that you will come back."

"How did you know that?" Mitt asked. He knew it was true. He would have to come back to the Holy Islands. "When do I come?"

"That is for you to say," said Old Ammet, young and old at once. "And when you do, it is laid down that we shall deliver these Islands into your keeping. My question to you is: Will you take them as a friend or as an enemy?"

"As an enemy to *you*, you mean?" Mitt asked, highly perplexed by this question.

Again Old Ammet's young face laughed. "We are not the stuff of enemies or friends, Alhammitt. Shall I ask this way: Will you come as a conqueror or in peace?"

"How should *I* know?" Mitt said. "What do you mean coming and asking me questions like that? What do you mean coming and pushing me around? It's my belief you've been pushing me around all the time, you and Libby Beer, and I don't like people pushing me around!"

"Nobody has pushed you around," said Old Ammet. He looked as old as the Islands. "You chose your own course, and we helped you, as we were bound to do. We shall help you again. All I needed to know was what manner of help we must give you in times to come." And as if Mitt had already told him the answer to that, Old Ammet turned away and went to his horse. The corn color of his clothes and hair caught the sun and seemed to melt into it.

"Hey, wait!" said Mitt. He felt very resentful and very disappointed in Old Ammet. He had expected more from him somehow. "Well, what am I supposed to say? You might give me a bit of help over that, at least!" he said, hurrying after the melting, hazy figure. Old Ammet turned round, melting back to a young man, and Mitt found he had to stop. "Can't you give the Holy Islands to someone else? I don't deserve to get them," he said.

Old Ammet shook his blowing hair and smiled regretfully. "I'm not anyone's judge."

"But you could be," said Mitt.

"What good would that do?" said Old Ammet. "What is your answer?"

Mitt was glad to find that he had not, after all, yet answered Old Ammet's question. He thought about it. The first thing he wanted to do was to ask Old Ammet to come back in an hour or so, to give him time to think. But Old Ammet stood there, old and patient beside the tall gray horse, and the horse cropped the cool green turf with drops of bright water falling gently from its mane, as if, for both of them, there was all the time in the world.

"I'm bad at thinking without talking," said Mitt. "I'm like Al that way. We both love to talk."

"Then why not talk?" suggested Old Ammet.

But Mitt did not talk because it suddenly came to him that he had it in him to be far worse than Al. Mitt, if he wanted, really could become the person out of his recent daydream and go round the country putting people like Navis to death. Al did what he did for himself alone. Mitt would be doing it against people. Mitt looked up at Old Ammet and caught his face as it changed to young. He looked as splendid as Mitt's daydream. Yet beyond Old Ammet was the opening of the dell, and there lay the Holy Islands spread out between the evening sea and the sky. And Mitt knew he did not want to come back to them hunting people from island to island and putting them to death. It just did not fit. But if he came back as an enemy, he would. He had Old Ammet's word for it that he would come back. And it would be like destroying his own early daydreams.

He looked up at Old Ammet's face and caught it between young and old. "It'll have to be friends," he said.

Old Ammet, turned to old now, simply nodded gravely. It was no more than Mitt expected, but he was disappointed all the same. He had hoped Old Ammet would praise him, or at least reward him, for his decision. He was a very puzzling being, and, Mitt suspected, a very powerful one, too.

"What's your name?" he said. "It isn't really Old Ammet, is it?"

"Once," said Old Ammet, "it used to be the same as yours. But people have forgotten."

Mitt thought he had known that. Old Ammet and Alhammitt did not sound so very different. "And Libby Beer," he asked. "That's a silly sort of name."

Young Ammet smiled at Mitt, dazzling him by the heave and billow of his bright hair and the brightness on his clothes. "You can learn how to call both of us now you've decided. Go on up to our house and take what help you can from there. Remember to ask for our names." He pointed to the end of the dell. Mitt saw the path went on there, up into the rocks. While he was looking, Mitt had a feeling Old Ammet walked dazzling out of the dell, leading the horse, into the sky. But he was not sure. He was only sure he was gone.

"Well, I've met him at last," Mitt said, and he was wonderfully pleased now as he went on up the path.

It was not far, a short, steep climb through the rocks. Then Mitt came to the very top of Holy Island, into a strong breeze, and found a little gray building which looked as old as the island. Standing in front of it was an old, old island man with long white hair and a wrinkled brown face.

"Hey!" said Mitt, remembering that Jenro had said there was no mortal soul on the island.

"You've had a hard climb," the old man said in a gentle island voice. "Come and seat yourself on the bench here and be breathing."

"Thanks," said Mitt. "But I got to ask for their names first. That's what I come for."

"Sit down first. That will be needing a quiet mind," said the old man, pointing to a stone bench outside the house. Mitt went over and, a little impatiently, sat down. The old man sat creakingly beside him. "Will you eat?" he said.

"Well, I—Yes—Thanks!" said Mitt. The old man was suddenly passing him a large bunch of grapes and a flat loaf plaited like an ear of wheat, and Mitt had no idea where he got them from. "How about you?" he said politely.

"I am well, thank you," said the old man.

Mitt supposed that meant he was not hungry. He was very hungry himself. The loaf was better even than the bread they had that morning, and the grapes were sour-sweet, cold and juicy. He ate every scrap. "How about those names?" he said, munching.

"The names of the Earth Shaker and She Who Raised the Islands are strong things," said the old man, "even the least of them. Spoken aloud by the voice, they are too strong, unless the speaker has right in the heart of him. And I must tell you that the names of the Earth Shaker are cruel even then, as they are strongest. He who learns these names must never say them aloud, even sleeping, unless he wishes something perilous to follow. Will you still learn those names?"

Mitt was not sure. He did not like the idea that he might say something perilous in his sleep. He was about to tell the old man to forget he asked when he realized that Old Ammet had indeed rewarded him for his decision, and this was to be the reward. Frightening though it was, Mitt saw he would have to take it, or he would be going back on his decision. And when he thought of himself conquering and killing among the people of the Holy Islands, he knew his decision was right. "Yes, please," he said.

"And who was it sent you?" asked the old man.

Mitt answered without hesitation. "The Earth Shaker."

"Then I will be showing you," said the priest, "if you have taken enough of their gifts." He stood up as creakingly as he had sat down.

Mitt brushed the crumbs off his suit and got up, too. "Can you read?" asked the old priest.

"Just about," Mitt conceded.

The old man walked to the door of the house, but he did not go in. He signed to Mitt to go inside. "Look under them in the sun," he said. "And do not speak what you read until you have true need."

Mitt had to duck his head to get into the house. When he was inside, he was surprised to find it was not dark, as he had expected, but light and warm and quiet. The late sun was streaming in through windows placed curiously low down, nearly at the floor. The red-gold light fell on the end wall, on two hollows in the stonework. In one hollow stood Libby Beer, and in the other Old Ammet. They were not as grapes and corn, but as queer old statues of themselves as Mitt had just seen them. Mitt knew that whoever had made those statues had seen them, too. Libby Beer was carved smiling as she had smiled at Mitt, and Old Ammet was miraculously both old and young at once. Mitt wished he knew how to carve like that.

Look under them in the sun, the old man had said. Mitt took his eyes reluctantly off the statues and looked at the wall under the hollows. There was a mass of cracks there, as if something had hit the wall and all but smashed it. But as Mitt looked, he found that the sun was lighting some of the cracks and not others and that the lighted parts were forming letters. The letters fell together to form words, two words under each figure, and the words were names.

Mitt had always thought he could not read without saying what he read aloud. But he dared not do that now. It was one of the hardest things he had done, spelling out those words in his head. Three of them were such strange names, too, that he was not sure how to say them. Only one—the one immediately under the hollow where Old Ammet stood—was not so strange. It was almost Ynen, or like Ynen with an extra *Yn* to it. From this, Mitt gathered, though he could not say how, that the top name in each pair was the lesser name and went with the usual figures of Old Ammet and Libby Beer, made of corn and berries, and that the names below were the strong ones and went with Old Ammet and Libby Beer as they really were. After that he found them a little easier to remember. Even so, he walked to the door with his eyes up and his mouth moving, remembering hard.

"Will you let them stay easy? They will stay in you," the old priest said kindly, seeing his trouble.

Mitt blinked at him. "They will? They seem to get away every time I stop thinking about them."

"You will be saying them when you should not if you will not leave them lie," said the old man. "Now what you must be doing is going down that way." He pointed to the rocks on the landward side of the low gray house.

"But how can I get off the island that way?" Mitt said.

"The Earth Shaker will show you," said the priest.

Mitt shrugged and looked over at the green hump of the nearest island, a good half mile away. Still, where the old man pointed, there looked to be an easy way down. Mitt turned back to thank him, and he was gone. Mitt knew he had not had time to hobble off anywhere. He was simply not there anymore. Mitt could feel that the space by the house was empty somehow.

"And he felt like a real one, too," Mitt said. "I wonder who he was."

# 20

*WIND'S ROAD* HEELED gently westward in a peaceful evening breeze, threading her way among the Islands. When the sun went red and gold behind High Tross and the misty green hump of Holy Island beyond that, Hildy began to feel chilly. Riss told her there were coats below. Hildy went into the cabin. There she found that not only had the cupboard been repaired and the water keg refilled, but the forward bunk held a pile of coats and seaboots to fit both men and boys. Puzzled by this, Hildy put on one of the coats and came out, intending to ask Riss about it.

A sweet, haunting sound came to her. It seemed to be coming from Ommern. Hildy listened, enchanted, to a tune at once melancholy and filled with joy—at once a tune and at the same time only the broken pieces of a tune. Instead of coming from Ommern, as she had thought, it came from the green hump of Wittess. But when she turned that way, the sound came from Prestsay to one side. "Piping?" she said to Riss.

He nodded. "The greeting of the great ones."

Hildy leaned over the side of *Wind's Road* listening until she thought her heart would break, but whether with joy or sorrow she could not tell.

They heard the piping aboard the tall ship *Wheatsheaf*, too, as she tilted among the islands, carrying Navis and Ynen to Holand. They were in Bence's stateroom, with Al, Lithar, and two guards. Bence was stamping about above in a considerable rage. It seemed that the *Wheatsheaf*'s sails unaccountably kept losing the wind, and they were making very poor progress.

"Can't any of you trim a sail right!" Bence roared.

"It is the wind toward evening, and the islands taking the force from it," explained a gentle voice.

"Teach your flaming grandmother!" roared Bence. "You there! Stop sleeping along that yard and trim your sail!"

The piping came to Ynen's ears very sweet and fitful, sometimes like a melting song, sometimes as a wild skirling. He could not hear it properly for the roaring of Bence. "I wish he'd be quiet," he said to Navis.

From time to time Bence fell into an exasperated silence. Each time the piping came from a different quarter. Al wriggled his shoulders at it as if it made him itch.

"I wish they'd stop that flaming piping! What do they do it for?"

"Nobody does it," Lithar said in surprise. "It happens sometimes. Always near sunset, around suppertime. Shall we have supper?"

"If it makes you happy," Al growled.

Bence's steward brought in cold meat and fruit and wine. Al did not eat much, though he drank the wine. The rest had supper and listened to the shouts of Bence and the piping in between. The steward cleared the meat away, and they were still among the islands and the piping still sounded.

Mitt heard the piping, too, as he swung down the side of Holy Island, galloping the occasional steep stretch. The sound seemed to come from the heart of the island beneath his feet. It was the wildest, most joyful music he had ever heard. Mitt felt so glad and confident that he would have sung, except that he was afraid of spoiling the music.

But when he came down with a steep rush to the shingly shore and saw the well-known elegant shape of *Wind's Road* leaning past High Tross in the haze of evening, he nearly despaired again.

"They've got away! They've gone and left me!" he said. "*Wind's Road!* Hey, there! *Wind's Road!*" He jumped and waved and shouted, knowing they were too far away to see or hear him.

A sudden wave rose between Holy Island and green Ommern and traveled swiftly to the shore where Mitt was. It was so queer, all on its own, that Mitt stopped shouting and watched it. It rushed on, one lonely peak of water, and thundered down on the shingle beside Mitt in a mass of white water and the rubbly squeaking of pebbles. Mitt scrambled hastily out of range. Then he realized that the white foam of the wave was still standing high above his head. He found he was staring at one of the lovely white horses of the storm.

"Thanks, Ammet," Mitt said, laughing a bit nervously. He had ridden a horse only when he was a very small boy, and that was a cart horse. He edged toward the horse. It put its nose down and blew salty breath at him. Nervously Mitt grasped it by its rough wet mane, which it did not seem to like, and struggled onto its slippery back. The horse shook its head and rippled the skin under Mitt, but it did not throw him off.

"Can you catch that boat for us?" Mitt said to it.

The horse surged forward, joggled him, bounced him, and then seemed to be pure movement under him. Mitt found they were galloping across the sea itself, tossing spray, tossing the horse's mane, tossing Mitt. He fell forward and put his arms round the horse's neck. There were hard muscles in it, and it felt warm and cold together, like a hot day high on a mountain. Spray dashed into Mitt's face and the dark sea raced beneath. He could only bear to watch it out of one eye. He tried peering forward for *Wind's Road*, but she had sailed behind Wittess.

Wittess was straight ahead. Almost there. Underneath him. The horse galloped straight across the island without checking. The only difference was that its hooves thudded deep and drumlike, and turf flew into Mitt's face instead of spray. Out of the corner of his eye, he saw several people, who all shaded their eyes to see Mitt against the sun. They did not seem particularly astonished.

"Must have odd things happen all the time," Mitt said breathlessly to the horse as it thudded down to the sea again. Among the sound of its hooves, he could hear the piping again, strong and wild. The sound changed to whipping water, and the horse seemed to splash wet sunset out of the sea. In the dazzle Mitt saw the deck of *Wind's Road* just in time, almost underneath him, as the horse dissolved to a wave of gray, foamy water.

Hildy turned round almost too late. She saw Riss smiling, a welter of disappearing water, and Mitt's feet landing on the cabin roof. "You're not alive!" she said.

It was not very welcoming. "I'm not a ghost yet," Mitt said gruffly. "Where's Ynen then?"

"With Father and Al on the *Wheatsheaf*," Hildy said miserably. "He's taking them back to Holand. They went hours ago."

"Oh, well," said Mitt. He was going to say it was a pity, and then forget about it, when he saw Riss was smiling at him knowingly.

"The *Wheatsheaf* will be between Yeddersay and the outer island," Riss said. "Jenro is seeing to that. They will wait until the sun goes down and the piping stops, when they will know you are not coming."

"Oh," said Mitt. This was too bad! It was not enough to decide to come back as a friend. It seemed to mean he was expected to act as a friend, and to Navis, of all people, here and now. Ynen, Mitt did not mind. But he did not want to see Al again either. He shot a surly look at the bows of *Wind's Road*, where Old Ammet still lay, stiff and blond and bristly. It was all his fault.

But while he was looking, Mitt suddenly remembered, for no reason he clearly knew, the time when he had first seen Old Ammet in his other, better shape, standing by the bowsprit as *Wind's Road* hung on the slope of that monster wave, trying to turn over and drown them all. For a moment he felt like *Wind's Road* himself. But at that point he had already saved Ynen's life by grabbing his ankle just in time. Mitt sighed. It seemed as if it was his way to make friends without knowing he had—just as he had with Siriol, or Hobin, for that matter. Perhaps even Hildy and Navis were friends, too, deep down where it did not show.

"We better make haste to Yeddersay then," he said.

Riss looked dubiously up at the sail. He meant they were doing as much as the wind would let them.

"I'll see to it," said Mitt. He clambered sideways along to Old Ammet and gently, politely, touched the image on its shoulder. "Could you give us just a bit more wind, please?"

Hildy glowered after him. The pure annoyance on Mitt's face when he first realized what his decision meant made her feel anything but trustful of him. She saw the water ahead ruffle and darken. *Wind's Road* creaked. The sails tightened, and she heeled over with a much brisker rippling round her bows.

"Never fear," Riss said, thinking Hildy was staring at Mitt because she was afraid of him. "He has been on Holy Island."

"I wish he'd stayed there," Hildy muttered.

*Wind's Road* threaded among the Islands quickly now, accompanied by her own ruffle of wind. The sun was just touching the rim of the sea when she rounded Yeddersay, and there was Chindersay, and the piping came from Hollisay, loud and joyful behind them. And there, sure enough, was the *Wheatsheaf*, towering against the crimson sky, hardly moving at all, with her sails drooping and swinging about. They could have heard Bence bellowing easily on Hollisay.

"What are we going to do?" Hildy asked.

Mitt was not at all sure. "There are four things I can do, I suppose," he said. Then he had a bad moment, thinking he had forgotten those names. But, when he examined the inside of his head, they were there all right, safely stuck.

"Nothing, nothing, nothing, and nothing, I'll bet!" Hildy said scornfully. *Wind's Road* glided nearer the *Wheatsheaf*, and she saw that there happened to be two ropes dangling over her side, just where they would be within easy reach. Somebody trusted Mitt. "I'm sorry," she said. "I've been having a horrible time, you see."

"You're not the only one!" said Mitt, looking up at those ropes dangling over the steep side. Al was up there. Mitt was afraid the sight of him was going to drive those four strange names clean out of his head. It seemed to him that it would be as well to take precautions. As Riss was bringing *Wind's Road* up alongside the *Wheatsheaf*, Mitt hurriedly leaned right over the side and came up again with his hand dripping wet. "See here," he said to Hildy, "if I get in a fix, or you do, and if I don't seem to know what to say, shout this out." And he scrawled with his wet finger on the cabin roof, big crooked letters: *YNYNEN*.

Hildy looked at them. "But that's—"

"Don't say it!" Mitt said furiously. "Just keep it in your head, will you!"

Hildy saw that if she did not trust Mitt in this, she would have lied to Libby Beer, after all. "All right. I'll remember."

"Thanks," said Mitt, and he swept his wet hand over the name, as *Wind's Road* gently scraped against the side of the *Wheatsheaf*. The ropes hung head-high. Hildy and Mitt each seized one. There was no need to climb. The ropes went up with them, hauled by a dozen men above.

"What's going on there?" bawled Bence.

One of the ship's boats went down past Hildy as she went up. Another splashed into the water beyond Mitt, as he reached the rail. As they both set their feet on the decking, helped by any number of smiling island sailors, a third boat was going down. Mitt saw Bence stare, and then make for the ladder down to the deck where he and Hildy were.

"This is your way," Bence's steward said politely. Mitt and Hildy trotted beside him past masts and coils of rope, and past scores of sailors all busy getting down to the lowered boats, and arrived at the stateroom door just before Bence reached the bottom of his ladder. The steward opened the door for them, and they went in. Bence suddenly saw what his crew were doing and ran about shouting to them, instead.

Inside the stateroom the lamplight was not yet as bright as the sky. No one quite saw who they were until they were fully inside. Then Ynen was unable to stop himself calling out, "Mitt! Hildy, he's not dead!" Al jumped to his feet. Lithar recognized them both and said amiably, "I wondered where you two had got to."

"Bence!" bellowed Al.

"Mitt, I owe you an apology," Navis said.

Mitt nodded at him as cordially as he could. He hoped that by keeping a friendly expression on his face, he might make himself like

Navis. But the one Mitt was watching was Al. Hobin's gun was in Al's hand, and Mitt kept one eye on it, with a name waiting on his tongue.

"Bence!" yelled Al.

Bence arrived in the doorway, angry and sweating. "The flaming crew have got the boats out now!" he said. "They're all rowing away."

"Bence," said Al, "how did they get here? Him particularly."

"I don't know!" Bence said, blustering a little. "They were on that boat again—*Wind's Road*."

"Then you can go by this road," said Al. He brought Hobin's gun up, over his forearm, and fired at Mitt.

Mitt shouted out Libby Beer's lesser name as he saw Al's finger move.

With unbelievable speed, an apple from the table was in the air between Mitt and the gun. The bullet hit it. The apple burst all over the room, showering everyone with pulp, pips, and skin. The deflected bullet clanged into one of the lamps and broke its glass cover. Navis and his two guards put their arms up against a cascade of broken glass. After a stunned moment, everyone shook themselves and dusted off apple and glass.

Al looked from the gun to the broken lamp. "What did that?"

"I did," said Mitt. "And I can do it as often as you've got bullets. We came here to fetch Ynen and his father away North, and you might as well let them come. You ready?" he said to Ynen and Navis.

Ynen and Navis were already standing up. They might have left then, in that shaken moment, had not Lithar cried out. "Oh lovely! How pretty! You *do* do tricks then! Look at this, Al. Isn't it pretty?"

Everybody looked. It was irresistible. Lithar had a little apple tree growing on his knee. Its roots spread visibly over Lithar's trouser leg, sucking up the moisture from the apple pulp on it. Its leaves turned from spring green to summer dark as they looked. There was another growing on the table, and several more coming up on the floor. Lithar was delighted.

"Do another trick," he said. "These are beautiful."

Mitt almost agreed with him. Hildy agreed entirely. She leaned over the tree on the table and watched it grow in astonishment.

"Very pretty," said Al, giving Lithar's knee a cursory look as he passed. He took Hildy by her arm so suddenly and hard that she yelled. "Now get out," he said to Mitt. "You and your tricks. I give you a count of five before I break her arm, and a count of ten before I strangle her. One—two—"

Mitt could see Al meant it. He could see Hildy was too frightened to say the name he had told her. He could see Bence standing aside from the door to let him go. He could see Ynen staring at him helplessly.

"Four," said Al.

"A larger apple tree?" Navis suggested. "Heavy apples?" Mitt looked at him and saw that he was as tense and helpless as Ynen.

If he's that fond of Hildy, why does he try to hide it? Mitt thought irritably. He said Libby Beer's great name, before Al could come to five. It was a name that rang and reverberated, and became more awesome after it was said. It swelled inside the stateroom.

The result was nothing like Mitt expected. The *Wheatsheaf* shook from stem to stern as if she had hit a rock. They all staggered. There was a creaking and a hard rending. Bence, as soon as he heard it, turned and dived out of the door. The two guards hastily followed him, dragging Ynen and Navis with them. Lithar said, "What's happening?" and ambled out past Mitt with his tree flapping on his leg. But Mitt had to stay where he was because Al, though he was hanging on to the table with one hand, still had hold of Hildy's arm.

There was a huge creaking, followed by the sound of planks snapping and splintering. The end of the ship with the stateroom in it tipped, so that Mitt had to hang on to the door.

"This ship's breaking up!" he shouted at Al, through the din. "Let go of her!"

Al seemed to forget that he intended to strangle Hildy. He dragged her to the door and stared out. He, Mitt, and Hildy all ducked back as a mast as big as a tree, shrouds, sails, and all, crashed down on their end of the ship. The ceiling above them began to cave in under it. Mitt took hold of Hildy's other arm and Hildy pulled. Al was so bemused that he let go of her. Mitt and Hildy struggled over broken decking to an amazing sight.

There was an island growing through the middle of the ship. It was a wet shiny hump covered with shells and weeds and smelling like the waterfront on a hot day, and it was growing steadily. Navis, Lithar, Bence, and the guards were all on top of it, being carried upward as the island grew. Ynen was slithering anxiously down to them. Mitt stared round, weak with awe. The poor *Wheatsheaf* was in two shattered halves, on either side of the new island, and the surge and disturbance of its growth was rocking the ring of boats where the crew sat watching. Farther off, *Wind's Road*'s mast beat to and fro.

"What's happening?" said Ynen. "Hildy, what did he do?"

Grass was already springing on the wet hump. It grew faint and far apart at first, but it thickened as quickly as the apple trees had grown.

The muddy mound grew greener as well as larger. Some grass seemed to be rooting on the timbers of the *Wheatsheaf* as well.

Navis shouted and pointed. Mitt and Hildy both turned round to find Al close behind them, in the act of grabbing for them. Hildy threw herself to one side and Mitt to the other, where Mitt sat down with a wet *smick* which reminded him nastily of the dikes by the West Pool. As he landed, he saw Al grab Ynen instead and drag him by the leg down the muddy slope. The gun was still in Al's hand. Ynen put up a useless arm against it.

"Hildy! Help!"

"Mitt!" shouted Hildy. She pointed. She meant simply to shout that Ynen was in danger, but it came out with a stammer of terror. "Yn—ynen!"

The rough water round the new island spouted up into a point. A wing shape of water whipped across Al and Ynen, knocking them sprawling. Hobin's gun was flung against Mitt. Mitt had barely time to pick it up, before the new island was a hurricane of wind and water. Huge yellow waves crashed over what was left of the *Wheatsheaf* and broke halfway up the newly green hump. One wave, sluicing down, left Ynen clinging to the grassy mud between Mitt and Hildy. Though none of them could hear, or even think, Mitt hung on to Ynen, and Hildy leaned over him screaming, "It's all *right*!" until her throat was sore.

Then it was over. The sea was rippling and calm. The island had gone on greening in spite of the waves, and it was now as green a hump as the Ganter Islands. There was little of the *Wheatsheaf* left—just a few spars floating nearby. Nor was there any sign of Al. But where he had been there was a curiously shaped patch of green corn, growing and ripening, and crackling like fire with the speed of its growing.

The crew of the *Wheatsheaf* called remarks to one another and began rowing in to look at the new island. Navis stood shakily up at the top of the mound and shouted through the twilight to know if Hildy and Ynen were there.

Mitt shook the water out of his eyes. Ye gods! he thought. What happens if you say his big name?

A desperate thrashing in the water just below him caught his eye. He slid carefully down to look. Lithar's young-old face looked up at him imploringly. Mitt knelt on the salty turf, holding out a hand, and Lithar struggled toward it.

"You should learn to swim," Mitt said, catching hold and heaving him to land.

"Never could," said Lithar. "No more tricks, please."

The nearest boat arrived then, and Jenro leaned out of it. "I will stir you over to *Wind's Road*, you and the two other little ones and their father."

"Thanks," said Mitt. "And then you take Lithar home and look after him for me." He looked at Lithar, but Lithar was not attending. He was looking woefully at his knee. His apple tree had gone. "He's a bit in the head," Mitt explained.

"We know that he is," Jenro said, without expression.

"Do what I tell you," said Mitt. "You look after him. You. And don't let anyone else get at him." Jenro still looked expressionless. Mitt was exasperated. "You've got to have someone until I come back," he said. "And he needs looking after."

"Until you come back," said Jenro. He smiled. "Very well. Will you all five climb in and I will stir to the *Wind's Road*?"

Riss leaned down to help Navis, Ynen, Hildy, and Mitt aboard *Wind's Road*. As soon as they were up, he slid down into his own rowing boat and untied it.

"I think I'd better take first watch," said Navis, rather wearily, looking at the three tired children.

"You do that," Mitt said. He felt exhausted. He had barely strength to wave to Jenro and Riss.

They waved back. "Go now on the *Wind's Road* and return sevenfold," said Jenro. The island men sat in their boats and watched *Wind's Road* lean away North in the brown tag end of sunset, carrying Libby Beer behind and Old Ammet in her bows.

# The Spellcoats

PREHISTORIC
DALEMARK
AT THE TIME OF
THE SPELLCOATS
KANKREDIN
SOULNET
KARS
ADON
ROYAL
CAMP
FLOODS
SUBMERGED
PALACE
FLOODS
WATERSMEET
BLACK
MOUNTAINS
BROKEN
BRIDGE
RAPIDS
LAKE
RED RIVER
KARS
ADON'S
FIGHT
SHELLING
MILL
MARSH
N
WREN'S
VILLAGE
KING
HERE
KARS
ADON'S
CAMP

*For my sister Ursula*

# CONTENTS

# PART ONE

# The First Coat

# 1

I WANT TO TELL of our journey down the River. We are five. The eldest is my sister Robin. Next is my brother Gull, and then my brother Hern. I come fourth, and I am called Tanaqui, which is a name from the scented rushes that line the River. This makes me the odd one out in names, because my youngest brother is Mallard—only we always call him Duck. We are the children of Closti the Clam, and we lived all our lives in the village of Shelling, where a stream comes down to join the River, giving plentiful fishing and rich pasture.

This makes Shelling sound a good place, but it is not. It is small and lonely, and the people here are dark and unpleasant, not excepting my aunt Zara. They worship the River as a god. We know that is wrong. The only gods are the Undying.

Last year, just before the autumn floods, strangers came to Shelling from over the hills, carrying bundles and saying that our land had been invaded by strange and savage Heathens, who were driving all our people out. Hern, Duck, and I went and stared at them. We had not known that we had any land except the country round Shelling. But Gull says the land is very large, and the River only the center part of it; there have been times when Gull has said quite reasonable things.

The strangers were not very interesting. They were just like Shelling people, only rather more worried. They hired my father to ferry them over the River, which is wide here, and then went on their way beyond this old mill on the far side. But, a week after them, people arrived on horseback: very stern smart men wrapped in scarlet rugcoats, with steel clothes under that. And these men said they were messengers from the King. They carried a golden stork wearing a crown on a stick to prove it. When my father saw the stork, he said they were indeed from the King.

We stared at these men far longer than at the others. Even Robin, who was very shy then, left the baking and came and stood beside us with her arms all floury. The smart men riding past all smiled at her, and one winked and said, "Hallo, sweetheart." Robin went very pink, but she did not go away as she used to when the Shelling boys called such things.

It seemed these messengers had come collecting men to fight the Heathens. They stayed one night, during which time they had all the men and boys walk before them and told the ones who were fit that they must prepare to come to the wars. It seems they had the right. It seems the King has this right. I was very surprised because I had not known we had a King over us before. Everyone laughed. Hern pretended to laugh at me with Robin and Gull and my father, but he confessed afterward that he had thought Kings were of the Undying, and not really of this world at all. We agreed that a King was a better thing to have over us than Zwitt, the Shelling headman. Zwitt is an old misery, and his mouth is all rounded from saying no.

The messengers told Zwitt he must go to war, and for once he could not say no. But they also told Aunt Zara's husband, Kestrel, that he must go. Kestrel is an old man. My father said this must mean that the King's case was desperate indeed. It made Hern feverishly hopeful. He said if they took Kestrel, they would surely take boys of Hern's age, too. Gull said nothing. He just smiled. Altogether Gull was odious that evening.

Hern crept secretly away and prayed to our Undying, in their three niches by the hearth. He prayed to them to make him fit to go to war and swore that he would free the land from the Heathen if they did. I know this because I heard him. I was coming to pray, too. I must say I was surprised at Hern. He usually scoffs at our Undying, because they are not real and reasonable like the rest of life. It shows how much he wanted to go to war.

When Hern had gone, I knelt and implored our Undying to turn me into a boy so that I could fight the Heathen. I am as tall as Hern, and wiry, although Hern beats me when we fight. Robin sighs and calls me boyish, mostly because my hair is a bush. I prayed very deeply to the Undying. I swore, like Hern, that I would free the land from the Heathen if they made me a boy. They did not answer me. I am still a girl.

Then it was time for my father, Gull, and Hern to walk before the King's men. They chose my father at once. And they dismissed Hern at once, saying he was too skinny and young. But Gull has always been tall and sturdy for his age. They told Gull he could go to war if he wished and if my father agreed, but they would not press him. They were fair men. Of course Gull wished to go to war. My father, now he knew he had a choice, was not altogether willing to let Gull go, but he thought of poor old Uncle Kestrel, and he told Gull he could go, provided he stayed close to Uncle Kestrel. Gull came home delighted and boasted all evening. I told you he was odious then. Hern came home trying not to cry.

In the morning the messengers went to the next village to choose men there, giving the men of Shelling a week to prepare themselves. For that week we were weaving, baking, hammering, and mending for dear life, getting Gull and my father ready. Hern was like a broody hen the whole time. He made Duck miserable, too. Robin says I was as bad, but I deny it. I had found a way to comfort myself by pretending I was a very fierce and warlike person called Tanaqui the Terror of the Heathen. When the messengers came back to Shelling, I pretended they would hear of this person and send Zwitt to fetch her to lead our land to war. I told it to our Undying, to make it seem more true. I wish now that I had not done that. Sometimes I think this is what brought such troubles on us. You should not speak falsehoods to the Undying.

Robin says we all got worse, Hern, Duck, and I, every time Aunt Zara came in. She kept coming and thanking my father for taking Gull to look after Kestrel, and she kept promising she would look after us all when they were away. It was all words. She never came near us. But I think my father believed her, and it took a weight off his mind.

After a week the messengers came back, bringing some hundreds of men with them. That night, before they were to leave, my father and Gull naturally prayed to the Undying for safety.

Robin said anxiously, "I'd be happier if you took one of them with you."

"They belong by this hearth," said my father. He would not say any more about it. "Hern," he said. "Come here."

Hern would not come at first, but my father dragged him by one arm over to the Undying. "Now put your hand on the One," he said, "and swear that you will stay with Duck and the girls and not try to follow us to war."

Hern was red in the face, and I could see he was very angry, but he swore. That is my father all over. He never said much—they called him the Clam with good reason—but he saw what was in people's minds. After Hern had sworn, Father looked at Duck and me. "Do I need to make you two swear as well?"

We said no. Duck meant it. He had grown scared that week while he was sharpening my father's weapons. I was still fancying to myself that the messengers would send Zwitt in the morning to fetch Tanaqui the Terror.

So much for my fancies! Next morning all the men from Shelling marched away except Zwitt. Zwitt—would you believe this!—fell ill and could not go. What kind of illness is it that has a man in a fever in the morning and out fishing in the afternoon? Hern says it is a very rare and uncommon disease called cowardice.

We went with the rest of Shelling to wave the army off. I do not think I like armies. They are about five hundred men, which is quite a large crowd of people, dressed in all sorts of old tough rugcoats, and some in fur or leather, so that they look as brown and scaly as River mud. Each of these people carries bags and weapons and scythes and pitchforks, all in different ways, so that the army looks like an untidy pincushion or a patch of dead grass. There is a King's man riding at the side, shouting, "All in line there! *Left*, right, left, right!" The crowd of people do as he says, not willingly, not fast, so that the army flows off like the River, brown, sluggish, and all one piece. As if people could become like water, all one thing! We could hardly distinguish Father or Gull, though we looked hard. They had become all one with the rest. And as the army flows off, it leaves a dull noise, dust in the air, and a smell of too many men, which is not pleasing. It made me feel sick. Robin was white. Duck said, "Let's go home." As for Hern, I truly think he lost all desire to go to war that morning, just as I did.

Zwitt called everyone together and said the war would not last long. He said confidently that the King would soon beat the Heathens. I should not have believed a bad man like Zwitt. It was many months before we had news.

Life in Shelling went on, but it was small, quiet, and empty. The autumn floods came late. They were less than usual and smelled bad. Everyone agreed that the River was angry because of the Heathens—and they began saying other things, too, that we did not hear until later. The floods did not bring as much driftwood as usual, but they washed up strange fish, which nobody liked to eat.

Though Aunt Zara did nothing to help the four of us, we did not go short. We had vegetables from the garden, and the flour was milled from our field. Duck and Hern always catch fish. Duck can find clams by instinct, too, I think. The hens were laying well, even in the winter, and we had the cow for milk. Money for other things was scarce, because we had just laid in a great deal of wool when Zwitt's flock was sheared, before the Heathens came. This I combed and spun and dyed in the ways that my mother had taught Robin and my father, and they have taught me. My mother taught Robin to weave. I was too young to learn when she died, but Robin taught me, and now I do it better than she does. It is that same wool I am using now to weave our story. We did not find much market for my weaving in Shelling that winter. A number of children needed winter rugcoats. But my main—and my best—work is always for weddings. The girls' families buy my finest rugcoats, with stories and poems in them, to give to the boy they are going to marry. But there were no weddings, with the men all gone. And after we went across the River, no one wanted any of my weaving.

The floods had left us no driftwood to speak of, so we rowed across the River when the leaves started falling to cut wood from the forest on the other side. No one else in Shelling crosses the River. I asked Aunt Zara why once, and she said that the old mill was cursed by the River, and the forest round it, and that they were haunted by a cursed spirit in the shape of a woman. That was why the new mill was built, up along the stream. When I told my father what Aunt Zara said, he laughed and told me not to listen to nonsense. It is quite a pleasure to me to sit weaving in this same old mill, with this same cursed forest round me, at this very moment, and take no harm. There's for you, Aunt Zara!

The day we cut wood, the light was rich with the end of autumn. It was like a holiday. We broke the stillness of the trees by running about shouting, catching falling leaves, and playing Tig. I do not think there were any spirits who minded, in spite of what Robin said. And she ran about and shouted with us, anyway. She was far more as I remember her, that day, before she grew up and got all shy and responsible. We had lunch sitting on the grass by the old millpool, and after that we cut wood. When the River was pale in the dusk, we rowed back over, with wood heaped in such a stack that the boat was right down in the water and we had to sit still for fear of being swamped. My hair was like a real bush, full of twigs and leaves. I was really happy.

Next day Zwitt and some of the old people came to us with sour faces. They said we were not to pasture our cow with the others in future. "We do not give grazing rights to godless people," Zwitt said.

"Who's godless?" Duck said.

"The River has forbidden people to cross to the mill," Zwitt said. "And you were all there all yesterday. The River would punish you worse than this if you were older."

"It's not the River punishing us. It's you," said Duck.

Hern said, "You didn't punish my father for ferrying the strangers over there."

"Who told you we were there?" I said.

"Zara told me," said Zwitt. "And you watch how you speak to me, now your father's away. I won't stand for rudeness."

Robin wrung her hands when they had gone. It was her latest ladylike habit, but it meant she was really upset. "Oh dear! Perhaps the spirits over there are angry. Do you think we did offend the River?"

We were not having that. We respect the River, of course, but it is not one of the Undying, and we do not believe in spirits flocking around being angry at everything, the way Zwitt does. I told Robin she was growing up as joyless as Zwitt. Hern said it did not make sense to talk of a river's being offended.

"And if it is, *it* ought to punish us, not Zwitt," said Duck.

"I only meant that it *could* be offended," Robin said.

When we had finished arguing, Hern said, "It sounds as if Zwitt was afraid of my father."

"I wish he'd come back!" I said.

But the months passed and no one came back. Meanwhile, we were forced to move our cow to the edge of the River, just beside our house. We think that was why she never caught the cattle plague all the other cows got. Hern is sure it was. A great deal of mist came off the River that winter and hung about the pasture. Of course our cow was grazing peacefully in the mist most of the time, on the Riverbank, but the other people said it was the mist that brought the disease. When some cows died, and ours had never coughed once, they began giving us very black looks.

Hern was furious. He called them narrow-minded fools. Hern believes there are reasons for everything, and that curses and bad luck and spirits and gods do not make real reasons. "And why is it *our* fault their wretched cows die?" he demanded. "Because *we* offended the River, if you please! In that case, why is our cow all right?"

Robin tried to pacify him. "Hern, dear, don't you think it could be our Undying looking after us?"

"Oh—running river-stinks!" said Hern, and flounced out to the woodshed with such a look of scorn that Robin went into the scullery to cry—she cries a lot—and I stood on the hearth wondering whether to cry, too. I do not cry much, so I talked to Duck instead. It is no good talking to Robin, and Hern is so *reasonable*. Duck is young, but he has a lot of sense.

"Hern doesn't believe in the Undying," Duck said. "It's because they're not reasonable."

"Then why didn't he run away after the army?" I said. "He didn't, because he'd sworn on the Undying."

"He didn't because he saw the army," said Duck. "Anyway, the Undying *aren't* reasonable."

"Don't you believe in them either?" I said. I was truly shocked. Hern is one thing, but Duck is younger than me. Besides, we were standing right beside the Undying in their niches, and they must have heard Duck.

Duck turned to look at them. "You don't have to believe in things because they're reasonable," he said. "Anyway, I like them."

We both looked quite lovingly at our three Undying. Two of them are old. They have been in my father's family for generations. I can remember lying in my cradle by the fire, looking up at them. Hern says I could not possibly remember, but that is Hern all over. I do remember. The Young One has a face that seems to smile in the firelight, though by daylight you can hardly see his face at all. He is carved of a rosy kind of stone that has worn very badly. You can just see that he is playing a flute, but not much else. The One is even older. It is hard to see what he is really like at all, except that he is a head taller than the Young One. The stone he is made of generally looks rather dark, with glistening flecks in it, but he changes every year when he has been in his fire. The Lady is made of hard, grainy wood. When my father first carved her, just after Duck was born, I remember she was light-colored like the tops of mushrooms, but she has darkened over the years, and now she is brown as a chestnut. She has a beautiful, kind face.

Duck chuckled. "They're a lot nicer than Uncle Kestrel's lump of wood."

I laughed, too. Everyone in Shelling has such awful Undying. Most of them are supposed to be the River. Uncle Kestrel has a piece of driftwood that his father caught in his net one day. It looks like a man with one leg and unequal arms—you know how driftwood does—and he never lets it out of his sight. He took it to the war with him.

I remember this particularly. It was in the first part of the year after the shortest day, and there was a hard frost that night. It was the only frost that winter. I was cold. Right in the middle of the night I woke up out of a dream, freezing. In my dream my father was somewhere in the distance, trying to tell me something. "Wake up, Tanaqui," he said, "and listen carefully." But that was all he said, because I did wake up. It took hours to get back to sleep. I had to get in beside Robin in the end, I was so cold.

From what Uncle Kestrel said, I think that was the night my father died. It is hard to be sure, but I think so. I do not want to weave of this.

Before that came the terrible illness. Almost everyone in Shelling got it, and some of the smaller children died. The River smelled very bad. Even Hern admitted that this disease might have come from the River. It was much warmer than it should be for the time of year, and the River was very low and stagnant—a queer light greenish color—and we could not get the smell out of our house. Robin burned cloves on the edge of the hearth to hide it. We all had the disease, but not badly. When we were better, Robin and I went round to see if Aunt Zara was ill, too. We had not seen her in her garden for days.

She was ill, but she would not let us into her house. "Keep away from me!" she screamed through the door. "I'm not having either of you near me!"

Robin was very patient, because Aunt Zara was ill. "Now, Aunt, don't be so silly," she said. "Why won't you let us in?"

"Just look at yourselves!" screamed my aunt.

Robin and I stared at one another in great surprise. Robin had been very particular about our appearance, partly because she has grown fussy now she is old and partly to please Aunt Zara, who is even fussier. We both had our new winter rugcoats on, with bands of scarlet saying "Fight for the King," which I had woven to remind us of the King's messengers. The rest was a pattern of good browns and blue, which suit us both. My head was still sore from Robin's combing, so I knew my hair was neat and not the usual white bush. Robin's hair is silkier than mine, though just as curly. She had striven with it and put it into neat plaits, like a yellow rope on each shoulder. We could not see what was wrong with us.

While we looked, my aunt kept screaming. "I'm not going to have anything to do with you! I disown you! You're none of my flesh and blood!"

"Aunt Zara," Robin said, reasonably, "our father is your brother."

"I hate him, too!" screamed my aunt. "He brought you down on us! I'm not having the rest of Shelling saying it's my fault. Get away from my house!"

I saw Robin's face go red, then white. Her chin was a hard shape. "Come along, Tanaqui," she said. "We'll go back home." And she went, with me trotting to keep up. I looked at her as I trotted, expecting her to be crying, but she was not. She did not speak about Aunt Zara again. I spoke, but only a little, when Hern asked me what had happened.

"She's a selfish old hag, anyway," Hern said.

Aunt Zara recovered from the sickness, but she never came near us, and we did not go near her.

It was a long winter. The Spring floods were late in coming. We were longing for them, to wash away the smell from the River. I was longing for them in a special way. After my dream I was very anxious for my father, but I hid my worry in a new fancy: that he would come home in floodtime, before the One had to go in his fire, and everything would be all right. Instead no floods came, but at last men began to come back to Shelling from the wars. That was a time I do not want to tell about. Only half came back who had set out, weary and thin. My father and Gull were not among them, and no one would speak to us. Everyone looked at us grimly.

"What are we supposed to have done *now*?" Hern demanded.

# 2

Uncle Kestrel came home among the last. He came to our house first, leading Gull. We were frightened when we looked at them. None of us could behave as if we were glad, though Robin tried. Uncle Kestrel had turned into a real old man. His head nodded, and his hands shook, and his face was covered with scraggly white bristle. Gull was inches taller. I knew it must be Gull because of his fair hair and the rugcoat I had woven for him last autumn, though that was shiny with grease and almost in rags, but I would not have known him otherwise.

"Be easy on him," Uncle Kestrel said when Robin threw her arms round Gull. Gull hardly moved. "He's had a bad time. It was the Heathens in the Black Mountains did it. We were all in the siege there, and the slaughter."

Gull did not show he had heard. His face was empty. Robin led him to a seat, where he sat and stared. Duck, Hern, and I stood in a row looking at him. Only Robin remembered to ask Uncle Kestrel to come in. She bustled about for cake and drinks, and dug the three of us in our backs to make us help her. Duck fetched the cups. I pulled myself together and got out our best plum preserves, but my face kept turning to Gull, sitting staring, and then to Uncle Kestrel, so old. Hern just stood there staring at Gull as hard as Gull stared into space.

Uncle Kestrel is a very direct person. "Well," he said as soon as he was sitting down, "your father's dead, I'm afraid. Out on the plains, a long way from here."

We were all expecting that. None of us, not even Robin, cried. We just went pale and slow, and sat down without wanting to eat to hear what Uncle Kestrel had to tell.

Uncle Kestrel was glad of the good food. He beamed at Robin and ate a great deal. Whatever war had done to Gull, Uncle Kestrel came out of it completely natural. In the most natural way he broke off a big lump of cake, put it in Gull's hand, and closed Gull's fingers round it. "Here you are. Eat it, boy." Gull obediently ate the cake without looking at it—without looking at anything. "You'll find you have to do that," Uncle Kestrel explained to us. "He'll drink the same way. Now, to the sad news."

He told us how Father had died of wounds in the middle of winter, a long way off. I think, from the way he said it, that my father had dragged himself along pretending to be well for Gull's sake, because Gull had needed looking after even then. The fighting had been terrible. Our people were not used to it, and few of them had real weapons. The Heathen had good weapons, spears, and bows that could send an iron bolt through two men at once. "Besides being trained from their cradles to fight like devils," Uncle Kestrel said. "And they have enchanters in their midst, who conquer us with spells. They can draw the strength from you like sucking an egg."

Hern stared. "Piffle."

"You haven't seen them, lad," said Uncle Kestrel. "I have. You know them by their long coats. They've set their spells on the very River himself, knowing him to be our strength and our lifeblood. Take a look outside, if you don't believe me. Have you ever known him that color and smelling like he does?"

"No," Hern admitted.

"So, by fair means and foul," Uncle Kestrel said, "the Heathen have beaten us. They've brought their women and their children, and they mean to stay. The land is full of them. Our King is in hiding, bless him."

"What will we all do?" Duck asked in an awed whisper.

"Run away to the mountains, I suppose," said Uncle Kestrel. He looked worn out at the idea. "I've run from them for months now. But you five might stay if you wished, I think. This is a funny thing—" He glanced at Gull and began to whisper. I do not think Gull was listening, but it was so hard to tell. "The Heathen look almost like you do—the fair hair. He's had a deal to bear—Gull—from our side saying he was a Heathen changeling and bringing bad luck, and from the time the Heathen took him, thinking he was one of them." We all stared at Gull. "Be easy on him," said Uncle Kestrel. "As you see, they gave him back—this was in the Black Mountains—but he was not himself after that. Our men said he carried the Heathen's spells, and they might have killed him but for your father."

"How awful!" Robin said in a very high voice, like a sneeze or an explosion.

"True," said Uncle Kestrel. "But we had our good times." Then for quite a while he sat and told us jokes about people we did not know and things we did not understand, to do with the fighting. I am sure he meant to cheer us up. "That's what kept me sane, seeing the jokes," he said. "Now I suppose I'd better be off to see Zara." He got up and limped away. He did not behave much as if he was looking forward to seeing my aunt. Nor would I, in his shoes.

Robin cleared the cups away. She kept looking at Gull, and Gull just sat. "I don't know what to do with him," she whispered to me.

I went away outside, in spite of the smell from the River. I was hoping to be able to cry. But Hern was sitting in the boat, on the mud below the Riverbank, and he was crying.

"Just think of Gull like that!" he said to me. "He'd be better dead. I wish I'd gone after the army."

"What good would it have done?" I said.

"Don't you see!" Hern jumped up, so that the boat squelched about. "Gull had nobody to talk to. That's why he got like that. Why was I such a coward?"

"You swore to the Undying," I reminded him.

"Oh that!" said Hern. He was very fierce and contemptuous. The boat kept squelching. "*And* I swore to fight the Heathen. I could swear to a million things, and it wouldn't do any good. I just wish—"

"Stand still," I said. It suddenly seemed to me that it was not only Hern's angry movements that were making the squelching round the boat. Hern knew, too. He stood bolt upright with his face all tear-stained, staring at me. We felt the small shiver run along the banks of the River. The mud clucked, quietly, and a little soft lapping ran through the low green water. There were yards of bare mud on both sides of the River, but in a way that I do not know how to describe, it looked different to us. The trees on the other bank were stirring and lifting and expecting something.

"The floods are coming down," said Hern.

If you are born by the River, you know its ways. "Yes," I said, "and they're going to be huge this time."

Before we could say more, the back door crashed open, and Gull came out. He came out stumbling, feeling both sides of the door and not seeming to know quite where he was.

"The River," he said. "I felt the River." He stumbled over to the bank. I put out both hands to catch him because it looked as if he were going to walk right over the edge. But he stopped on the bank and swayed about a little. "I can hear it," he said. "I've dreamed about it. The floods are coming." He began to cry, like Robin sometimes does, without making a sound. Tears rolled down his face.

I looked at Hern, and Hern looked at me, and we did not know what to do. Robin settled it by racing out of the back door and grabbing Gull in both arms. She hauled him away inside, saying, "I'm going to put him to bed. It's frightening."

"The floods are coming down," I said.

"I know," Robin called over her shoulder. "I can feel them. I'll send Duck out." She pushed Gull through the door and slammed it.

Hern and I pulled the boat up. It was horribly hard work because it was stuck a long way down in the mud. Luckily Hern is far stronger than he looks. We got it up over the edge of the bank in the end. By that time the sick green water was racing in swelling snatches, some of them so high that they slopped into the grooves the boat had left.

"I think this is going to be the highest ever," Hern said. "I don't think we should leave it here, do you?"

"No," I said. "We'd better get it into the woodshed." The woodshed is a room that joins the house, and the house is on the rising ground beyond the bank. Hern groaned, but he agreed with me. We got three of our last remaining logs to make rollers, and we rolled that heavy boat uphill, just the two of us. We had it at the woodshed when the woodshed door opened and Duck came out.

"You did arrive quickly!" I said.

"Sorry," said Duck. "We've been putting Gull to bed. He went straight to sleep. It's awful having him like this. I think there's nothing inside him!" Then Duck began to cry. Hern's arm tangled with mine as we both tried to get them round Duck.

"He'll get better," I said.

"Sleep will do him good," Hern said. I think we were talking to ourselves as much as to Duck.

"Gull's head of the family now," Duck said, and he howled. I envy both boys for being able to howl.

Hern said, "Stop it, Duck. There's the biggest ever flood coming down. We've got to get things inside." The River was hissing by then, *swish* and *swish*, as it began to spread and fill. The bad smell of winter was mixed with a new damp smell, which was better. I could feel the ground shaking under us, because of the weight of water in the distance.

"I can smell it," said Duck. "But I knew there was time to be miserable. I'll stop now." And he did stop, though he sniffed for the next hour.

We jammed the boat into the woodshed. I said we ought to bring the hens in there, too. Hens are funny things. They seem so stupid, yet I swear our hens knew about the floods. When we looked for them, they had all gone through the hedge to the higher ground above Aunt Zara's house and we could not get them back. They would not even come for corn. Nor would the cow go into the garden at first. Usually her one thought was to get in there and eat our cabbages. We pushed and pulled and prodded her, because we were sure she was not safe on the Riverbank, and tethered her where she could eat the weeds in the vegetable patch.

"She'll eat those cabbages somehow," said Duck. "Look at her looking at them."

We were pulling up all the cabbages near her when Robin came out. "Oh good," she said. "Pull enough for at least a week. I think the floods will be right up here by tomorrow. They feel enormous."

We ran around picking cabbages and onions and the last of the carrots and dumped them on the floor of the scullery.

"No," said Robin. "Up on the shelves. The water's coming in here."

She is the eldest, and she knows the River best. We did as she said. By this time it was getting dark. The River was making a long, rumbling sound. I watched it while Robin milked the cow. There was brown water as strong as the muscles in your leg piling through between the banks. The mud was covered already. I could see the line of yellow froth bubbles rising under the bank as I watched. The color of the water was yellower and yellower, as it always is in the floods, but it was a dark yellow, which is not usual. The air was full of the clean, earthy smell the floods bring. I thought it was stronger than usual, and sharper.

"There's been different weather up in the mountains where the River comes from, that's all," Hern said crossly. "Shall I wake Gull up and give him some milk?"

Gull was so fast asleep that we could not wake him. We left him and had supper ourselves. We felt strange—half excited because of the rumble of the water outside, half heavy with misery. We wanted sweet things to eat, but when we had them, we found we wanted salt. We were trying to make Robin cook some of the pickled trout when we heard an odd noise. We stopped talking and listened. At first there was only the River, booming and rushing. Then we heard someone scratching on the back door—scratching, not knocking.

"I'll go," said Hern, and he seized the carving knife on his way to the back door.

He opened it and there was Uncle Kestrel again, half in the dark, with his finger to his mouth for quiet. We twisted round in our seats and looked at him as he limped in. He had neatened himself up since he was last here, but he was still shaking.

"I thought you were the Heathen," Hern said.

"They'd be better company for you," said Uncle Kestrel. He smiled. He took a jam tart from Robin and said, "Thanks, my love," but that did not seem natural any longer. He was frightening. "Zwitt's been at my house," he said, "calling your family Heathen enchanters."

"We're not," said Duck. "Everyone knows we're not!"

"Do they?" asked Uncle Kestrel. He leaned forward over the table, so that the lamp caught a huge bent shadow of him and threw it trembling on the wall, across shelves and cups and plates. It looked so threatening with its long, wavering nose and chin that I think I watched it most of the time. It still scares me. "Do they?" said Uncle Kestrel. "There are men in Shelling who have seen Heathens with their own eyes, and who remember your mother—lovely girl she was, my Robin—looked just like the Heathen. Then Zwitt says you dealt ungodly with the River—"

"That's nonsense!" Hern said. He got angrier with everything Uncle Kestrel said. It was good of Uncle Kestrel not to take offense.

"You should have gone over to the old mill by night, lad," he said, "like I do when I go for mussels. And it's a pity neither you nor your cow got the sickness the River sent."

"But we all got it!" Robin protested. "Duck was sick all one night."

"But he lived when others his age died," said Uncle Kestrel. "There's no arguing with Zwitt, Robin, apple of my eye. He has the whole of Shelling behind him. If Duck died, they'd have thought up a reason for that. Don't you see? Do none of you see?"

The huge shadow shifted on the wall as he looked round the four of us. I saw that we seemed to be strangers in our own village, but I had known that before. So had Robin from the look of her. Duck looked quite blank. Hern almost shrieked, "Oh, yes, I see all right! Now my father's dead, Zwitt's not afraid of us anymore!"

The shadow shook its head and bent across two shelves. "But he is, lad. That's the trouble. They're frightened. The Heathen beat them. They want to blame someone. And spells have been cast by the Heathen. Hear the River now!"

We could all hear. I had never heard such rushing. The house shook with it.

Uncle Kestrel said softly, "He's coming down like that to fight the Heathen at the Rivermouth. That's where they set their spells, I heard."

"Oh!" said Hern. He was going to be rude.

"I understand," Duck said just then. "Zwitt wants to kill us, doesn't he?"

"Now, Duck!" Robin protested. "What a silly idea! As if—" She looked at Uncle Kestrel. "It's not true!"

The shadow on the wall shook. I thought it was laughing. I looked at Uncle Kestrel. He was serious—just shaking in that new old-man way of his. "It is true, my Robin," he said. "Zwitt was at my house to blame me cruelly for not killing young Gull while I had him. Gull carries the Heathen spells for you, it seems."

Nobody said anything except the River for a moment, and that rushed like thunder. In the midst of it Robin whispered, "Thank you, Uncle Kestrel."

"How are they going to kill us?" Hern said. "When?"

"They're meeting to decide that now," said Uncle Kestrel. "Some want to throw you to the River, I hear, but Zwitt favors cold steel. They often do who haven't seen it used." He stood up to go, and to my relief the huge shadow rose until it was too big for the wall to hold it. "I'll be off," he said, "now you understand. If Zara knew I was here, she'd turn me out."

"Where is Aunt Zara?" I asked.

"At the meeting," said Uncle Kestrel. He may have seen me look. As he limped to the door, he made me come with him while he explained. "Zara's not in an easy position. You must understand. She's afraid for her life of being called one of you. She had to go. It's different for me, you know." I still do not see why it should be different for Uncle Kestrel. Even Robin does not see.

I opened the door for him on such a blast of noise from the River that I put my hands to my ears. It was louder than the worst storm I have known. Yet there was barely any wind and only a few warm drops of rain. The noise was all the River. The lamplight showed black silk water and staring bubbles halfway to the back door.

Uncle Kestrel bawled something to me that I did not hear as he limped away. I slammed the door shut, and then Hern and I barricaded the doors and windows. We did not need to discuss it. We just ran about feverishly wedging the heaviest chairs against the doors and jamming benches and shelves across the shutters. We wedged the woodshed door by pushing the boat against it. We made rather a noise blocking the window just over Gull's bed, but Gull did not move.

All this while Duck was standing leaning his head against the niches of the Undying, and Robin was still sitting over supper. "I can't believe this!" she said. Another time we went by, she said, "We've only dear old Uncle Kestrel's word for it. He's not what he was. He may have misunderstood Zwitt. We've lived in Shelling all our lives. They wouldn't—"

"Yes, they would," Duck said from the niches. "We've got to leave here."

Robin wrung her hands. She will be ladylike. "But how can we leave, with the River in flood and Gull like this? Where should we go?"

I could see she had gone helpless. It annoys me when she does. "We can go away down the River and find somewhere better to live," I said. It was the most exciting thing I have ever said. I had always wanted to see the rest of the River.

"Yes. You can't pretend you've enjoyed living here this winter," Hern said. "Let's do that."

"But the Heathen!" Robin said, wringing away. I could have hit her.

"We look like the Heathen," I said. "Remember? We might as well make some use of it. We've suffered for it enough. I suppose Aunt Zara thought we were Heathen when she told us to go away."

"No," said Robin, being fair as well as helpless. It makes a maddening combination. "No, she couldn't have. She just meant we look different. We have yellow, wriggly hair, and everyone else in Shelling has straight black hair."

"Different is dead tonight," Hern said. Clever, clever.

"We've only Uncle Kestrel's word," said Robin again. "Besides, Gull's asleep."

So we sat about, with nothing decided. None of us went to bed. We could not have slept for the thousand noises of the flood, anyway. It made rillings and swirlings, rushings, gurglings, and babblings. Shortly there was rain going *blatter, blatter* on the roof and *spaah* when it came down the chimney and fell on the fire. Behind that the River bayed and roared and beat like a drum, until my ears were so bemused that I thought I heard shrill voices screaming out across the floods.

Then, around the middle of the night, I heard the real, desperate bellowing when our cow was swept away. Robin jumped up from the table, shouting for help.

Hern sat up sleepily. Duck rolled on the hearthrug. I was the most awake, so I scrambled up and helped Robin unblock the back door. It came open as soon as we lifted the latch, and a wave of yellow water piled in on us.

"Oh help!" said Robin. We heaved the door shut somehow. It left a pool on the floor, and I could see water dripping in underneath it. "Try the woodshed!" said Robin.

We ran there, although I could tell that the cow's bellows were going away slantwise down the River now. Water was coming in steadily under the woodshed door. We pulled the boat back easily, because it was floating, but when we opened the door, the wave of water that came in was not quite so steep. Robin insisted that we could wade through the garden to the cow. We hauled up our clothes and splashed outside, trying to see and to balance and to hold skirts all at once. The rain was pouring down. That hissed, the River hissed and *gluck-glucked*, and the water swirled so that I half fell down against the woodshed. I knew it was hopeless. The cow was faint in the distance. But Robin managed to stagger a few yards on, calling to the cow, until even she was convinced there was nothing we could do.

"What shall we do for milk?" she said. "Poor cow!"

We could not shut the woodshed door. I tied the boat to one of the beams, and we waded back to the main room and shut that door. The woodshed is a step down. Soon water began to trickle under that door, like dark crawling fingers.

Robin sat by the hearth and I sat with her. "We shall drown if it comes much higher," she said.

"And Zwitt will say good riddance and the River punished us," I said. I sat leaning against Robin, watching water drip off my hair. Each drop had to turn twenty corners because my hair hangs in springs when it is wet. And I saw we would really have to leave now. We had no cow. We had no father to plow our field. Poor Gull could not do it, and Hern is not strong enough for that yet. We had no money to buy food instead, because no one would take my weaving, and even if we had, the people in Shelling probably would not sell us any. Then I remembered they were going to kill us, anyway. I thought I would cry. But no. I watched the firelight squeeze a smile out of the Young One's face, and Duck's mouth open and shut on the hearthrug, and the water from the woodshed trickle into a pool. Robin was soft and warm. She is maddening, but she does try.

"Robin," I said. "Did Mother look like us? Was she a Heathen?"

"I don't know," said Robin. "It's all vague. I think she had hair like ours, but I may be making it up. I don't remember. I don't even remember her teaching me to weave."

That surprises me still, Robin not remembering. She was nearly eight when our mother died. I was much younger when Robin taught me to weave, and I remember that perfectly. I can recall how Robin did not know the patterns for all the words, so that she and I together had to make quite a number up. I am not sure that anyone except my family will be able to read much of this, even of those who know how to read weaving. To everyone else, my story will look like a particularly fine and curious rugcoat. But it is for myself that I am weaving it. I shall understand our journey better when I have set it out. The difficulty is that I have to keep stopping because the clicking of my loom disturbs poor Robin.

# 3

NOW THE THING that finally decided us to leave was this. It was around dawn, though there was no light coming in round the shutters as yet. My neck ached down one side, and my mouth tasted bad. The fire was very low, but I could see Duck rolling and stirring in front of it. Hern was sitting on the table.

"The floor's all wet," he said.

I put my hand on the hearthrug to move, and it was like a marsh. "Ugh!" I said. It is a noise there is no word for.

At that the door to the bedroom swung open, and there was Gull in his nightshirt, feeling at the frame of the door as he had done before. I heard his feet splash in the water on the floor. "Is it time?" Gull asked.

"Time for what?" said Hern.

"Time to leave," said Gull. "We have to go away down the River."

Robin, I swear, had been asleep up to then, but she was on her feet, splashing about, trying to soothe Gull back to bed before he had finished speaking. "Yes, yes. We're leaving," she said. "It's not quite time yet. Go back to bed till we're ready."

"You won't go without me?" Gull said as she shoved him back through the door.

"Of course not," said Robin. "But we haven't packed the boat yet. You rest while we do that, and I'll call you as soon as breakfast's ready."

While she put Gull back to bed, Hern and I splashed about in an angry sort of way, filling the lamp and lighting it again and putting the last logs on the fire. Duck woke up.

"Are we really leaving?" he said when Robin came back.

Hern and I thought Robin had just been soothing Gull, but she said, "I think we must. I think Gull knows best what the Undying want."

"You mean, the Undying told him we must go?" I said. Early though it was, my back pricked all the way down with awe. Usually I only get that in the evenings.

"Gull must have heard us talking," said Hern. "That explains it just as well. But I'm glad *something* made up your stupid minds for you. Let's get the boat loaded."

Then I did not want to go at all. Shelling was the place I knew. Everywhere beyond was an emptiness. People came out of the emptiness and said things about Heathens with spells, the King, and war, but I did not believe in anywhere but Shelling really. I did not want to go into the nowhere beyond it. I think Hern felt the same at heart. We went slowly into the woodshed with the lamp, to push the boat out ready to load.

Water rolled in from the woodshed as soon as we opened the door. It came round our ankles like yellow silk, lazy and strong and smooth, and made ripples in the living room. Inside the shed the boat was floating level with the step. The lamp shone up from our startled reflections underneath it.

"You know," said Hern, "we can load it in here and just row out through the door."

I looked toward the door, dazzled by the lamp. I looked too low, where the land usually slopes toward the River, and I had one of those times when you do not know what you see. There was a long, bright streak, and in that streak, a smooth sliding. I thought I had been taken out of my head and put somewhere in a racing emptiness. There I was, upside down under my own feet—a bush of hair and staring eyes, wild and peculiar. I wonder if this is how Gull feels, I thought.

Duck did not like it either. "There's water high up, where the air usually is!" he said, and he waded over and tried to shut the door.

Hern was the only one of us who could shut the door against the force of the water. I always forget how strong Hern is. You would not think he was, to look at him. He is long and thin, with a stoop to his shoulders, very like the heron he was named for.

We argued a great deal over loading the boat and trailed up and down the ladder to the loft a great deal too often at first. Robin said we should take the apples. Hern said he hated last year's fruit. It was because none of us wanted to leave. Gradually, though, we grew excited, and the loading went quicker and quicker. Hern packed things in the lockers, shouting orders, and the rest of us ran to and fro remembering things. We packed so many pots and pans that there was nothing to cook breakfast in and almost nothing left to eat. We had to have bread and cheese.

Robin got Gull up and dressed him in warm clothes. The rest of us were in our thick old waterproof rugcoats, which I only make when they are truly needed, because it is double weave and takes weeks. My everyday skirt was soaked, and I did not want to spoil my good one. Besides, I had had enough of splashing about in a skirt in the night. I wore Hern's old clothes. I tried to persuade Robin to wear some of Gull's. A year ago she would have agreed. But now she insisted on being ladylike and wearing her awful old blue skirt—the one I made a mistake in, so that the pattern does not match.

The only warm rugcoat we could find which fitted Gull was my father's that my mother had woven him before they were married. My mother was mistress of weaving. The coat tells the story of Halian Tan Haleth, Lord of Mountain Rivers, and it is so beautiful that I had to look away when Robin led Gull to the table. The contrast between Mother's weaving and Robin's blue skirt was too painful.

It occurred to me while we were dressing Gull that there was not so much wrong with him as I had thought. He smiled once or twice and asked, quite reasonably, whether we had remembered fishing tackle and spare pegs for the mast. It was just that he stared so at nothing and did not seem to be able to dress himself. I wonder if he's blind, I thought. It did seem so.

I tested it at breakfast by pushing a slice of bread at Gull's face. Gull blinked and moved his head back from it. He did not tell me not to or ask what I thought I was doing, as Hern or Duck would have done, but he must have seen the bread. I put it in his hand, and he ate it, still staring.

"I tried that last night," Duck whispered. "He can see all right. It's not that."

We were sitting round the table with our feet hooked on the chair rungs because water was coming in from all the doors, even the front door, and most of the floor was a pool. There was a hill in the corner where my loom and spinning wheel stood, so that was dry, and so was the scullery, except for a dip in the middle. We laughed about it, but I did wish I could have taken my loom. The boat was so loaded by then that there was no point even suggesting it.

As I put the last slice of bread in Gull's hand, there was an explosion of sizzling steam from the hearth.

"Oh good gracious!" Robin shouted. She soaked us all by racing to the hearth. Water was spilling gently across the hearthstones and running in among the embers. Amid cloud upon cloud of steam, Robin snatched up the shovel and scooped up what was still alight. She turned round, coughing, waving one hand and holding up the red-hot shovelful. "The pot, the firepot, quickly! Oh, why do none of you ever help me?"

That fire has never been out in my lifetime. I could not think how we were to light it again if it did go out. At Robin's shriek, even Gull made a small bewildered movement. Hern splashed away for the big firepot we use in the boat, and I fetched the small one we take to the field. Duck took a breakfast cup and tried to scoop up more embers in that. He had only rescued half a cupful before the water swilled to the back of the fireplace and made it simply a black, steaming puddle.

"I think we've got just enough," Robin said hopefully, putting the lids on the pots.

Everything was telling us to leave, I thought as I waded with Hern to the woodshed to put the pots in the boat. The River had swung the outer door open again. It was light out there. Outside was nothing but yellow-brown River, streaming past so full and quiet that it seemed stealthy. There was no bank on the other side. The brown water ran between the tree trunks as strongly as it ran past the woodshed door. It was all so smooth and quiet that I did not realize at first how fast the River was flowing. Then a torn branch came past the door. And was gone. Just like that. I have never been so near thinking the River a god as then.

"I wonder if there's water all round the house," said Hern. We put the pots in the boat and waded back to see.

This was very foolish. It was as if, among all the other things, we had forgotten what Uncle Kestrel had told us. We climbed the slope beside my loom and took the plank off the shutters there. Luckily we only opened the shutter a crack. Outside was a tract of yellow, rushing water as wide as our garden, and not deep. On the farther edge of it, in a grim line, stood most of the men of Shelling. Zwitt was there, leaning on his sword, which looked new and clean because he had not been to the war. The swords of the others were notched and brown, and more frightening for that. I remember noticing, all the same, that behind them the yellow water had almost reached Aunt Zara's house. Where they were standing was a point of higher ground between the two houses.

"Look!" we called out, and Duck and Robin crowded to the open crack.

"Thank the Undying!" said Robin. "The River's saved our lives!"

"They're making up their minds to cross over," said Duck.

They were calling to one another up and down the line. Zwitt kept pointing to our house. We did not realize why until Korib, the miller's son, came past the line with his longbow and knelt to take aim. Korib is a good shot. Hern banged the shutter to just in time. The arrow met it *thock* a fraction after, and burst it open. Hern banged it shut again and heaved the plank across. "Phew!" he said. "Let's go."

"But they'll see us. They'll shoot!" I said. I hardly knew what to do. I nearly wrung my hands like Robin.

"Come along," Hern said. He and Robin took hold of Gull and guided him to the woodshed.

"Just a minute," Duck said. He splashed over to the black pool of the hearth and gathered the Undying down out of their niches. It shocks me even now when I think of Duck picking them up by their heads and bundling them into his arms as if they were dolls.

"No, Duck," said Robin. "Their place is by this hearth. You heard your father say so."

"That," said Duck, "is quite ridiculous nonsense, Robin. The hearth's in the firepots, and the firepots are in the boat. Here." He pushed the Young One into Hern's hands. I noticed Hern did not object. Because Robin was busy with Gull, Duck pushed the One at me. He kept the Lady himself. She has always been his favorite. The One felt heavy in my hands, cold and grainy. I was afraid of him and even more afraid of slipping in the water and losing him. I took him so carefully to the boat that they were all calling out to me to hurry and trying not to call too loud. I could hear Zwitt talking outside. He sounded near. They had a heavy blanket over the boat, hanging over the mast. Robin was holding it down on one side, Duck on the other. Hern had the boat untied and was standing ready to push it out of the shed.

"Get *in*, Tanaqui. You can be religious in the boat," he said. I climbed in carefully and found Gull lying in the bottom where Robin had put him. As soon as I was in, Hern started to push the boat. It was so loaded that he could hardly move it. I pushed up the blanket and offered to help. "Get down!" he snapped, red in the face, with his teeth showing.

As he said it, the boat was through the door, and the current took her sideways along the end of the house, all in seconds. I am not sure whether Hern meant to get in straightaway and did not have time or whether he meant to stay out and push us into deep water. At all events he was still surging through the edge of the floods with his hands on the stern when the boat came out beyond our house, in front of Aunt Zara's, and the Shelling people saw us.

They shouted. I had not seen how they hated us till I heard them shout. It was terrible. Some of them were wading in the water toward our house, and they ran through it toward us. Zwitt slipped over. I hoped he drowned. The others on dry land yelled and pointed at us and cursed. And Korib, on one knee, bent his bow to an arrow again.

"Hern! He's shooting!" I screamed.

Hern was trying to push us sideways into the deep River. He tried to get round to hide behind the boat at the same time. That pushed us the other way. We wove about. Korib shot. It was as good a shot as the first. Hern would be dead, but at that instant we reached the real Riverbank at last, and the ground went from under Hern. He disappeared up to his neck, and the arrow hit the rudder instead. Korib took another and bent his bow again.

Hern had the sense to hang on to the boat. If he had let go then, he would have drowned, for he lost his head completely. "My clothes are heavy!" he screamed. "The River's pulling me down!"

Duck and I climbed about over poor Gull, trying to heave Hern up, and Hern went hand over hand along the boat to keep out of Korib's aim. The boat tipped frighteningly, and Hern's caution was undone, because it spun round and let Korib see him again. The boat was spinning all the time after that. Every time I saw the bank, it was in a different place. Korib kept shooting, at Duck and me as well as at Hern, but we were too busy trying to get Hern aboard to be frightened. Afterward we counted six arrows stuck in the blanket, besides the one in the rudder.

We got Hern up in the end. Robin, by that time, had hooked the tiller in place and was trying to steer, but the boat still went round and round. Hern sat streaming beside Gull, very much ashamed and trying to laugh it off. "When your clothes are full of water, you can't swim, you know," he said. "They weigh a ton." We made him get into dry things.

By this time we were almost at the end of the part of the River we knew, right down to the thick forest. We had gone that fast. I took the steering from Robin and tried to stop us spinning so. It was not easy. The current ran so strong that if you pushed the boat at all sideways, you were spinning again before you could count five. It took all my skill, but in spite of what my brothers say, I am as good a waterman as they.

"This is dangerous," said Duck, watching me. "We can only go where the River wants. How can we get to the bank?"

Before I could say to Duck what I felt like saying, Gull said suddenly, "We can go where the River wants." He sat up with his back against a thwart. He seemed happy and dreamy, as he used to be when we went fishing on a summer day, and we were sure he was better.

This made us realize—as if we had not known till then—that we had left Shelling far behind, and we were glad. I do not think one of us has ever regretted it. We laughed. We talked over all the lucky things that led to our escape, which is a time none of us will forget, I think, and all the while we were going, fast as a swallow skims, straight down the center of the River, and the trees on the bank seemed to spin about with our speed.

We must have gone leagues that day, and in all those leagues there was nothing on either bank but flooded forest. All there was to see was tall bare trees, with the green just coming to the upper boughs and water winding among their trunks. They had a chilly, slaty look. I confess I was disappointed. It is often the way when you dream of doing something new; it is not so new after all.

When night came on, I tried to work the boat across the current to the eastern bank. Shelling is on the west bank. We did not think Zwitt had sent anyone after us, but we kept to the other side of the River for a number of nights all the same. This caution nearly drowned us that night. The River whirled; the boat whirled and went on whirling, despite all Hern, Robin, and I could do, pulling together at the tiller. Only Gull sat calmly. Duck picked up the Lady and hugged her to his chest. Then the River rushed beneath one side of the boat, and we tipped. I put out my hand and took hold of the One. But he felt so cold and hard that I put him down and picked up the Young One instead. It surprises me still that we came among the trees without sinking. I am sure it was because of our Undying.

We poled and pushed on the trees until we came to higher ground, where we landed and let some of the fire out of our firepots. We cooked pickled trout for supper, and very good it was. Gull seemed so far recovered that he was able to eat for himself.

"I think being back with the River is curing him," Hern said.

That night, after a long quarrel, we decided to sleep in the boat. Hern and Duck were for sleeping on land. Robin, with sound sense, said that if the Shelling men found us, we need only untie the boat to escape. Duck said we could just as easily run away into the forest. In the end Robin said, "Gull's head of the family. Let's ask him. Gull, shall we sleep on the land or in the boat?"

"In the boat," Gull said.

In the middle of the night Gull woke us up shouting and talking. Robin says he talked of disaster and Heathens at first, but when I woke up, he was saying, "All those people! So many people, all rushing. I don't want to go with them. Help!" Then he shouted for my father, and I could hear he was crying.

We all sat up, and Hern got the little lamp lit. Gull seemed to be lying asleep in the boat, but he was talking, and tears were running down his face. Robin bent over him and said, "It's all right, Gull. You're with us. You're safe."

"Where's Uncle Kestrel?" Gull said.

"He brought you to us because that was safest," Robin said.

"I'm not safe from the rushing people," said Gull. "Don't tell me to pull myself together and be a man. They want to take me with them."

We wondered who had told Gull to pull himself together. Probably my father. He was not called the Clam for nothing. He did not like people to talk about their troubles.

"Of course we won't tell you that," said Robin. "We'll keep you safe from everything."

"I want Uncle Kestrel," said Gull. "The people are rushing."

It went on like this for a long time. Each time it seemed that Gull was listening to Robin and she was getting him calmer, he would ask for Uncle Kestrel and talk about these rushing people of his. Robin began to look desperate. Hern and I suggested all sorts of things for her to say to Gull, and she said them, but after another hour it did not seem as if Gull was listening at all.

"What shall we do?" said Robin.

Duck had sat all this while cross-legged and half asleep, hugging the Lady. "Try giving him this," he said, and held out the Lady—by her head, of course.

It worked. Gull put both hands to the Lady and held her to his face. "Thank you," he said. Then he rolled over and went to sleep, with his cheek pressed against the hard wood. I could see Duck looking woeful at losing the Lady, but he did not say anything.

# 4

FROM THAT TIME ON, Gull was worse and worse.

When we woke next morning, we found the floods had risen to cover the place where our fire had been. The tree we had tied the boat to was twenty yards from dry land; after that we always slept in the boat. Gull was awake, too, lying with the print of the Lady on his cheek, but he did not move until Hern started poling us to the higher ground. Then he sat up and called out, "Where are you going? We must get on."

"Why must we get on?" Hern said. He was angry with lack of sleep.

"We must get down to the sea. Quickly," said Gull, and tears ran down his cheeks across the mark of the Lady.

"Of course we will," said Robin. "Be quiet, Hern."

"Why should I? This is the first I've heard about having to get to the sea," Hern said. "What's got into him *now*?"

"I don't know," Robin said helplessly.

This new idea of Gull's gave him no peace, nor us either. Whenever we stopped to eat, he wept and urged us to hurry on to the sea. When we stopped for the night, he was worse still. He kept us all awake talking of Heathens and people rushing and, above all, calling out that we must get on, down to the sea. I grew almost too tired to look at the River-banks, which was a pity because the land grew new and interesting after that day. On the day following, the sides of the River were steep hills, covered with a forest, budding all colors from powdery green to bright red, so full of circling birds that they strewed the sky like chaff. Among the trees and birds we saw once a great stone house with a tower like a windmill and a few small windows.

Hern was very interested. He said it looked easy to defend, and if it was empty, it would make a good place for us to live.

"We can't stop here!" Gull cried out.

"It was only an idea, you fool!" Hern said.

Altogether Hern became more and more impatient with Gull. It was hard to blame him, for Gull was very tedious. As the hills held the River in, we floated at a furious pace on a narrow, rushing stream, but we still did not go fast enough for Gull.

"I'd get to the sea tomorrow, if I could, just to shut you up!" Hern said to him.

Duck became as bad as Hern that day. He sighed sarcastically whenever Gull said we must hurry. He and Hern laughed and fooled about instead of helping us look after Gull. I smacked Duck several times, and I would have smacked Hern, too, if I could. I smacked Duck again that night, in spite of Robin shouting at me, when Duck would not let Gull have the Lady.

Duck jumped out on land, hugging the Lady. He was lucky not to fall in the water. We were tied among little brown bushes, with a slope of slimy earth above, where the bank was no bank at all and the River kept slopping our boat into the bushes and away. "She's mine!" Duck shouted, sliding and scrambling above me. "I need her! Give Gull the One. He's strongest."

I was so angry that I tried to climb out after him. But the boat slopped away from the bushes, and Robin caught the back of my rugcoat and hauled me back. "Leave him be, Tanaqui," she said. "Don't you be as bad as he is. Let's try Gull with the One."

We put the dark glistering One in Gull's hand, but he cried out and shuddered. "He's cold. He pulls. Can't we get on now?"

"Some of us have to sleep, Gull," I said. I was nearly as cross as Hern. I gave him the Young One instead, but Gull would not have him either. We had a dreadful night.

In the morning, Duck gave Gull the Lady, looking a little ashamed. But by that time Gull was not having the Lady either. Robin could hardly get him to eat. All he wanted was for us to untie the boat and go on.

"Fun and games all the way to the sea," said Hern. "Then what will he want?"

"I don't think he should go to the sea," said Duck.

"Oh, not you now!" said Hern. "Why not?"

"The Lady doesn't want him to go," said Duck.

"When did she tell you that?" Hern asked jeeringly.

"She didn't," said Duck. "I just had a feeling and knew."

Most of that morning Hern was jeering at Duck for his feeling. Robin snapped at Hern, and I yelled at Duck. We were very tired.

That was the day we came to the lake. The hills on either side of the River seemed to retire away backward, and before we were aware, we were out at one end of a long, winding lake. They tell me it is usually a smaller lake than we saw, but because of the floods, it filled a whole valley. We could see it ahead, white with distance, stretching from mountain to mountain. I think they were real mountains. Their tops went so high that gray clouds sat on them, and they were blue and gray and purple as Uncle Kestrel described mountains. We had never seen such a great stretch of water in our lives as that lake. In the ordinary way we would have been interested. Water in such quantity is restless. It is gray and goes in waves, *chop, chop, chop*, and lines of foam stretch like ribbons back from the way the waves are going. There was a keen wind blowing.

"What a horrible wind!" Duck said. He crouched down in the boat, hugging his precious Lady.

Hern said disgustedly, "There's *miles* of it! I hate seeing how far I have to go."

Maybe I said that, when I think. Hern and I both found the place too large. As for Gull, he struggled up and stared about. "Why have we stopped?" he said.

We had not stopped, but the current ran weaker in such a mass of water, and I think our boat had turned sideways from it as we came out into the lake. I could see beyond us a wrinkling and a lumping in the lake, more yellow than gray, where the River flood rushed through the larger waters.

"Get the sail up," I said.

"Don't order me about," said Hern. "Get up, Duck, and help."

"Shan't," said Duck. You see how angry we all were.

Hern was stepping the mast when Gull said, "What are you doing? Why can't we get on?"

"I *am* getting on, you mindless idiot!" said Hern. "I'm putting the sail up. Now shut up!"

I do not think Gull listened, but Robin said, "Hern, can't you show poor Gull a bit more sympathy?"

"I *am* sympathetic!" snarled Hern. "But I wouldn't be honest if I pretended I liked him this way. Tell him to keep his mouth shut, if I worry you."

Robin did not answer. We got the mast and the sail up, and Duck condescended to let the keel down. The keel is a thought of my father's, to make a flat riverboat sail well, and it is the best thought he ever had.

We raced through the gray waters, leaning. Gull lay quiet in the bottom. Duck sang. When he sings, you know why we call him Duck. Hern told him so. And through their new argument, I noticed Robin still said never a word. She was white and wringing her hands.

"Are you all right?" I said. She annoys me.

"I think we're going to drown," said Robin. "It's so big and so deep! Look at the huge waves!" I would have laughed at her if I had seen the sea then. But the boat did lean, and the water did churn. The shore on both sides was some miles off—too far for swimming—and I thought the lake was deep. I began to be as frightened as Robin. Hern did not say how he felt, but he did not steer near the middle of the lake where the current ran. He kept to one side, and drew nearer to the land there. Shortly we came to a point of land reaching into the lake, with trees on it. The trees grew down to the water's edge and marched on in. We sailed over the tops of trees right under water. Robin's eyes went sideways to them, and she gave a squeak at how deep the lake was. Her hand went out to the One, but she was too much in awe of him to pick him up. She fumbled round till she found the Young One. Her hands went white with clinging to him.

We passed more points of land and more submerged trees and came to a wide bay, where the lake had flooded up a side valley. In the distance we could see a green pasture at the edge of the water. It looked a good place to land. Hern steered that way.

Immediately Gull rose up and screamed at him to keep straight on. Hern looked at me expressively, and we sailed on.

There was an island on the far side of the bay, a miserable thing where a tuft of willow trees bent over a marsh. Gull let us land there because it was straight ahead. I think it had always been a marshy place, that island, perhaps a saddle of marsh low on the hillside, because around it in a wide ring we saw the heads of rushes—just their heads—pushing above the water. They were tall tanaqui mostly, bravely trying to flower in the Spring. The air was full of their scent as the boat came pushing in among them, disturbing marsh birds every moment.

Hern laughed. "Look! A line of baby brothers!" He pointed to a row of ducklings plodding after their mother among the willows. Duck flounced round with his back to Hern and fell into a deep sulk. Which Hern must have known he would do. My brothers are maddening.

We got out, lit a smoky fire, and ate. Gull would not eat. He just sat with food in his hand. Robin tried thrusting bread in his mouth, but he just sat with it there.

"Oh, I don't know what to do with you, Gull!" Robin cried out. Soon after that she fell asleep, leaning on a willow with the Young One in her lap and Gull sitting sightlessly beside her. Duck was still sulking. Hern and I got up and wandered over the island, but not together. He was at one end, and I was at the other, and I felt I did not care whether I ever saw him again.

I hated that island. The boughs of the willows rattled in the wind, like teeth chattering. They had bright yellow buds on, and the color looked thoroughly dreary against the gray water. The gray water went *crush, crush, crush*, among the tops of the rushes, bringing their scent in ripples. I looked down at the oily sort of peat under my feet, and I looked out across the gray miles of water to the purple line of land beyond, and I felt truly miserable.

Then I thought I heard my mother's voice behind me. "Tanaqui, for goodness' sake pull yourself together, child!" she said. "Are you too cross to think?"

Naturally I turned round. There was only the empty grove of willows, with Hern's back beyond them, and the other purple shore much nearer but quite as melancholy.

And my mother's voice spoke behind me again, by which I knew I was imagining it, because she would have had to be standing in the water, among the tips of the rushes. "You mustn't let Gull go to the sea, Tanaqui," she said. "Can't you see that? Promise me to stop him."

I turned round again, and of course there was nothing. "Might as well try to stop the River, the way he carries on," I said, just in case she could hear me. Then I thought what a fool I was. I did almost cry, but not quite. I went back to the fire instead.

Gull was not there. I was quite horrified for a moment. Then I found he had got back into the boat and was lying there, staring up at the gray sky. "You'd better stay there," I said to him. I went and looked at Robin, still asleep. I had a feeling, from what Uncle Kestrel said, that my mother had looked a little like Robin. If you look at Robin that way, not just as a person you know very well, she is very pretty. Her face is longish, but round and even, and her eyebrows are quite dark. She always calls her hair yellow and wriggly, but I think that is what people mean when they talk about golden curls. Her eyes are large and blue. Even with her eyes shut, and mauve shadows under them, she was pretty.

She woke up as I looked. "Why are you staring? What's the matter?"

"Gull's gone back to the boat," I said.

"By himself?" said Robin. "Oh, dear, what *is* the matter with him, Tanaqui?"

"He had a bad time in the wars," I said.

Duck came marching across from somewhere, carrying the Lady by her head as usual. "No, it isn't," he said. "Uncle Kestrel told you. The Heathens put spells on him, and now they want him to go to the sea."

"I don't think it's quite like that, Duck, love," Robin said, looking worried. "Tanaqui, I had a dream—"

But I have not heard to this day what Robin's dream was because Hern came rushing back just then, full of brisk talk about getting to the end of the lake by nightfall, and Robin must have forgotten her dream. Whatever it was, it made her happier. She was nothing like so scared of the lake after that.

That lake is huge. We sailed in it all that day and half the next. Beyond the island it became wider yet, until we could barely see the other shore. There were more islands scattered on it, and we learned not to sail too near them, because our keel got tangled with any trees or bushes that grew at their edges before the floods came. We had one lucky escape from a bush and another from a great torn bough, moving on the flood, which I did not see behind the sail.

I think the banks of the lake must have been quite crowded with people before the Heathen came. We saw planks floating and logs cut for winter, hen coops, barrels, and chairs. Duck saw two drowned cats, and I saw a dog. We all saw the corpse except Gull. That was horrible. We came quite near, because Robin insisted the person was alive, until we saw it was only the waves moving her. We thought it was a girl, but she was so small and the clothes so strange that it was hard to be sure. The long hair was browned with the water, but we could see it had been fair and curly.

"It's a Heathen," Duck said. He took the pole and turned her. Her throat was cut. Duck pushed her away with the pole quickly, and then he was sick. We all felt terrible. We none of us said anything, but we knew we did not dare to go near any of our own people. That corpse looked just like us.

We met no one living all the length of that lake. Once or twice we thought we saw other corpses, but we did not go near them. Nobody was sailing except us. Later in the day it rained. A big purple cloud hung over us, lower than the rest of the sky, and rain soused down on us out of it. Behind us the lake was silver with sun, and in front of us a mighty rainbow came down across some dark green pine trees growing on a point of land and buried itself in the lake at their roots. We saw the trees sunlit through the colors of the rainbow. But the rain cloud hung above us. "Just like our bad luck does," Duck said gloomily.

That point of land was a long way off. By the time we reached it, night was coming on and we decided to tie up there. Gull protested, but we were getting used to that.

"I'm sorry, Gull," Robin said. "We have to stop for the night." From Robin, that is steely firmness.

Gull would not get out of the boat. We all pulled and pushed at him, but he would not move. In the end we had to pole the boat round the point, where it was sheltered from the wind, and pull it up out of the water with Gull still in it. We did that because we did not trust him not to sail away while we were getting supper. In that place the land fell back and a marshy stream came down to meet the lake. The lake had come up to meet the stream a long way. Nowhere was dry. Rushes of all sorts grew there, and the flag irises were green already, with brown water round their roots. The evening filled with the scent of tall tanaqui and the smell of damp smoke. Robin could not get the fire to go.

"Look," said Duck, pointing down to where the reeds grew away under the water. A heron was standing there, with its head bent, looking for fish. "Look, a big brother, with long legs like sticks." Trust Duck to remember Hern's insult.

Hern roared with rage and dived at Duck.

Duck fled down among the tall rushes, hugging the Lady. "And a long nose!" he screamed back. Hern went galloping and squelching and roaring after him.

"Oh, go and stop them, Tanaqui!" Robin said. She was crouching over the fire, blowing it.

I went down among the rushes after my brothers, grumbling. I think it was too bad of them still. I could see where Hern had gone, from the path of trodden rushes and deep footprints filling with oily water, but even though it was getting dark, I was fairly sure that Duck had doubled back and was lying low uphill somewhere. When I came to the lake, all the light was in the water, and Hern was an angry shadow against it, with his head bent, glaring for Duck along the sopping shore. We were facing the pine trees on the point there, looking across the bay of muddy water from the stream and the lake.

Hern looked so like a heron, standing there, that I nearly laughed as I said, "Duck didn't come this way."

Hern turned round, saw I was laughing, and raised his hand to hit me. I turned to run away.

Then we neither of us moved because our mother's voice said, "Hern! Tanaqui!"

We both turned the same way, to look out across the gloomy inlet. From that I know Hern heard it as well as I did. And I know I saw a shape standing there, in the mist above the water, whatever Hern says.

I saw the dark body with a blur of whiter hair and a smudge of white face. The same voice said, "Stop fighting and look after Gull. You mustn't let him go to the sea, whatever you do. Take him down to the watersmeet."

"Take him where?" I said. "Mother, what's wrong with Gull?" I heard Hern laughing while I said it. "What's so funny?" I said.

"You standing there talking to trees and stones and half the boat," Hern said. "Take a look."

As he spoke, I saw it was true. The stern of the boat came out of the reeds a short way, with water showing beneath, and that was the lower half of the dark shape. The upper half was the trunk of a pine tree that seemed exactly above it. And above that I saw dimly that a bush was budding around a light-colored rock, high up on the point, making the hair and the face. "But there was a voice," I said. "You heard the voice."

"The heron," said Hern. There was indeed a bird crying out. The cries grew fainter as I listened, and I heard wingbeats. "We're all tired out," said Hern. "That's what did it. I just hope Gull lets us get a proper night's sleep tonight, or we'll be as bad as he is."

"It didn't seem like being tired," I said. I felt very foolish.

"Well, it wasn't Mother," said Hern. "She's dead. I admit I made the same mistake for a second, but don't say a word to Robin, will you? You'll only upset her."

I agreed to that. So many things upset Robin. We went back among the rushes and helped Robin get supper. Duck appeared when it was ready. Hern gave him a look in the firelight, but he did not say anything, and Duck sat down hugging the Lady and said nothing either.

Gull would not eat. He lay in the boat, growing colder and colder, and would only say, "Why can't we go on?" Robin heaped all our blankets around him, but he never grew warm. Nor would he eat in the morning. But at least he was quiet that night. Duck gave him the Lady without being asked, and we had hours of good sleep.

We went on down the lake next day. By the middle of the morning we could see the high purple land standing right across our way, and we thought it was the end of the lake. But we could see no way for the River to flow out. Hern said that it must flow out, since the current in the middle of the lake was still strong. We agreed that we would eat lunch somewhere on the high purple shore and then look for the rest of the River. So as the land approached, Hern took down the sail, intending to row to the rocks on the shore. For all our knowledge of the River, we were fooled into doing that. The lake looked smooth and calm, and the rocks ahead were so vast that we did not see how fast we were moving until the sail was down. Then we saw we were not stopping. The crates and barrels and driftwood went with us at the same speed as before, and the mountain strode toward us.

"Oh good!" said Gull, lying in the bottom of the boat. "We're really getting on."

"I shall hit him!" said Hern, with his mouth pulled like a grin. "I shall really hit him!" He lugged the oars aboard again, because they did nothing but turn us this way and that, and fell on the sail, trying to hoist it again.

"Don't do that!" Robin and I shrieked. The wind had gone, because we were right under the mountain, and the boat tipped horribly. Hern looked up to argue, but by then we were speeding straight at a huge cliff, and he put his arm over his head instead.

It looked as if we were going to crash into that cliff. You think a great many things very quickly when you see death coming. I thought: It's a bad thing, the way Gull wants to get on! Bad, bad! and at the same time I wondered why there were no great waves dashing on the rock ahead. The water was all smooth, stretched smooth and rapid, with only a few yellow bubbles at the edge.

And then *jerk*. I thought my head had come off my neck. The boat turned in a wrench as the current turned, and we were thrown past the cliff into a narrow gap of roaring water.

Here the rushing was as loud as the night the floods came, with echo upon echo shouting within that. The big walls of rock were so high on either side that there seemed almost no light, and the sky a ribbon high above. The look I snatched at it showed great trees growing in the sides of the rock, looking small as bushes. But I could not keep my eyes off the River. I could not have done as Hern did and taken the keel up. I hung on to the sides of the boat and stared at the foaming water. It was crushed and tormented into a small space with great rocks in it, which tattered it into riding waves, threw it in spouts, and spun it in glassy circles. Our boat spun and tossed and raced with it. One moment we were in the center, white under the light, and the next we were in black water at the sides of the gorge. Far down below in the black water, I could see ferns and grass growing, deep down on the sides of the cliff. I tried to shut my eyes—it was so deep—and went on staring in spite of myself.

I thought I heard screaming voices. I paid no attention until something came battering into the water just by the bows of the boat. The boat slewed round. I saw the spout of a splash just falling back into the water and looked up. There were tiny people up there, on top of the cliffs, black against the sky, and a thin bridge stretched across the gap. It had been broken. Two thicker halves stuck out on either side, and the center had been mended with planks. I saw the light between the planks. The bridge was lined with round heads, and beside each head was a ragged round lump of rock, ready to drop on us.

"They think we're Heathens!" Robin screamed. She dragged a blanket over her head and Duck's, and half over Gull, too. Hern and I were left outside. There was nothing we could do. Our boat swirled toward the bridge. The rocks moved, hung, and then got larger and larger, and we found our heads jerking up to watch and then down at the furious River, not knowing what to look at. All round us were spouts of water as the rocks came down. They jerked us this way and that, and I think it was the jerking that saved us. We were splashed all over, but nothing hit us. Then, before we had time to feel glad, there was more light and Hern was screaming there were rapids ahead.

We were through the falls the same moment. There was a lurch and a swoop, and the boat's nose went down, heaving more water over Hern and me. After that we were out and sliding a boiling, racing width of water most of the way across a second smaller lake. I think the falls were not steep, but I did not dare look back. Sometimes I wake up at night thinking I hear the chunking splash of rocks coming down in the River, and I still tremble all over.

# 5

THIS IS TO BE a very big rugcoat. We have been here in the old mill for days and days now, and though I am weaving close and fine, I have still not half finished my story. Even so, I think I shall finish it long before Robin is well. She is more fretful every day, and her face is the color of candles. I find it so hard to be patient with her. That is why I am weaving. When Uncle Kestrel first brought me my loom and my wheel and my wool, I was sick with impatience, and it all went so slowly. I had to spin my wool and set up the threads on the loom, and even when I began to weave, it took half the morning on the first sentence. But now I have found how to go fast. I set the first part of the pattern and cast the threads, there and back, and then the row to hold it, and while I do that, I am thinking of my next line. By the time I have finished that band of words, I often have the next three or four ready in my head. I go faster and faster, click and clack, change the threads with my feet, click and clack with the shuttles, and so on. And the story grows in the loom.

We swept out of that second lake into the wide, muddy River again. I found I was holding the One in both hands. I never remember picking him up, but my hands were cold and numb with holding him. Robin, with her face very white, was just laying down the Young One. Duck, of course, had the Lady.

"You might have let Gull have her!" I said.

"He doesn't need her," Duck said sulkily. Gull did look peaceful. His eyes were closed, as if nothing had happened. "And I did need her," Duck said. "She went all warm and I knew we'd be safe."

"Of course she's warm, the way you hug her all the time!" I said. "It's a wonder she's not worn down to a log."

"Shut up, Tanaqui," Robin said wearily. "Let's find somewhere to have lunch."

We did not find anywhere to land. The River had spread between hills that must have been nearly a mile apart. There were the roofs of barns and houses sticking up out of the swirling water on both sides of us. We had some thoughts of tying up to the first roofs we came to, but when we reached them, two old people stood up by the chimneys and yelled insults at us. They thought we were Heathens. We put the sail up and went on, eating cold food as we sailed, feeling very dejected. Gull would not eat again. "I'm glad we're getting on," he kept saying.

We did not get on very well. The River turned, and the wind blew from the north, in gusts, straight in our faces. We had to tack from side to side against it. Often we found we were sailing right round a submerged roof, and nearly every one was burned or broken. We smelled burning the whole way. Up on the hills to either side were the burned ruins of more houses, burned haystacks, and burned woods. Where the trees were alive, they were not budding. It was like sailing back into winter. Just a few of the fields had been plowed in spite of the wars, and the earth was a curious red, as if the ground was wounded.

"The Heathens have been here," Hern said. "Everyone's run away."

None of us answered him. I think we were all becoming more and more uneasy at the way Gull insisted on our going toward where the Heathens must be. I know I was. It seemed to me we were in danger from both sides, and I began to wonder at how thoughtlessly we had set off into this danger. True, Zwitt had left us no choice, but there was no reason to have gone down the River more than a mile or two. I wondered why we were going on, and I wished my father were there to tell us what to do.

Toward evening the River rushed again between steep hills of reddish earth that were covered in bare trees. Someone among the trees shot arrows at us. They all fell short as we raced with the flood, but after that we kept a blanket over us, and whichever of us was steering wrapped their head in a rugcoat. We did not dare think of landing until the River widened again and rushed past on either side of islands, long and boat-shaped and half submerged. The first islands were crowded with people who must have fled there from the Heathens. They were dark-haired, like Shelling people. As soon as they saw the boat, they crowded to the edge of the floods, shouting, "You can't land here! No room!" Zwitt could hardly have been friendlier.

Duck was steering. He stood up and put his tongue out at them, the fool, and the rugcoat slipped off his head. Then they all screamed, "Heathen!" and threw sticks and stones after us. We kept clear of all the other islands until night came on.

As it grew dark, we could see fires here and there on the steep shores and the islands. But the last island we came to was dark. It was very small, with only one patch of dry ground under the trees. Robin said we must land there. She was tired out. We were all scared of landing. We drew in as quietly as we dared and went ashore whispering, even though there was no one there. We lit our fire in a hole among the roots of a tree and prayed to our Undying that nobody would see it.

Gull would not eat again. He would not speak, and he was cold. But we were all cold that night. We pressed against one another in the boat, and every time I woke, the rest of them were shivering, too. I was woken by a dream I kept having. As far as I remember, it was just my mother's voice, saying, "The watersmeet!" and with it a slight scent of tanaqui. But I find it hard to separate it in my head from the dream I have been having ever since I started weaving. In that dream I see my mother bending over me, just the shape of her, with fair hair as curly as Robin's, but bushy like mine. "Wake up, Tanaqui," she is saying. "Wake up and think!" There is a scent of tanaqui with that dream, too. And I do think I have been thinking, but nothing comes of it, except that I blame myself.

In the morning the boat, our blankets, the ground, and the bare trees were all covered with frost. It looked odd, the white frost on the blood-red earth. The River here ran pink among the yellow, because of the earth.

Gull would not eat again, and I thought of my dream. I found I was wringing my hands like Robin as I looked down at Gull lying in the frosty boat. I expect it was the cold. Now what is a watersmeet? I said to myself. It is where one river joins another. Hern may say what he likes, but if we do come to another river, I shall fall overboard, or pretend to die, or something, and make sure we stay there.

Then it turned out that Robin had come to a decision, too. "You know," she said, "I don't think we should go any farther. I think we should stay on this island and get Gull warm and well again. I think this is the safest place we're going to find."

Gull, for a wonder, said nothing. He seemed too weak to speak. But Duck said, "Oh, honestly, Robin! We'd starve here!"

Hern said, "We'd be much better off finding a deserted house somewhere. Gull needs shelter, Robin."

"Or there must be *some* people who'll believe we're not Heathens," I said, "and who'll help us look after him. Let's go on, please."

"I think you're wrong," Robin said. "It seems to me we may be killing Gull, taking him on a journey like this."

"He wanted to go," Hern said.

"He doesn't know what's right for him," Robin said. "Do let's stay."

We took no notice. Hern and Duck climbed over Gull in the boat and put the sail up. I poured water on the fire and put the firepot away.

Robin sighed and shook her head and looked about eighty. "Oh, I don't know what to do for the best!" she said. "Promise me you'll stop as soon as you see a good place."

We all promised, easily and dishonestly. I meant only to stop at another river. I do not know what Hern and Duck meant to do, but I can tell when they are being dishonest.

As we sailed on, the sun came up over the hill at the right of the River, leaving it all dark and blue with frost and turning the left bank to gold. The slopes became higher and steeper as we swirled along, one blue, one gold, until the sun melted the red earth into sight again. There were low red cliffs to the left suddenly, which stopped like the wall of a red house. Beyond that the River was twice as wide or more than that. We could see a row of trees to either side, standing in water, and sheets of water beyond that, flaring in the sun. I think the trees marked the real low banks of the wide River.

I turned my head as we sailed past the end of the red cliff. And I saw more water there, winding back behind the cliffs, with red cliffs on the other side of it.

"The watersmeet!" I shouted. I jumped to the tiller and wrestled to get it out of Hern's hand. Duck jumped with me.

"Don't be idiots!" Hern shouted.

We went to and fro and the sail swung. The boat began going in circles. "What are you doing?" Robin shouted.

"We're going to land. We want to land!" Duck yelled.

With three of us shouting and fighting round the tiller and the boat going in circles, we should have been a perfect mark for bowmen, Heathen or our own. But we were lucky. Hern gave in, though he kept shouting. We came surging round into a great bed of rushes under the first red cliff.

They were the tallest rushes I have ever seen. They must have been deep in the floods beneath, but they were high above our heads even so. They parted in front of the boat and closed behind, and the speed we had drove us on between them, still arguing, into a sort of green grove, until we grounded on a beach of dry shingle, hidden from both rivers.

"I suppose this seems safe enough," Robin was saying when a Heathen man came swiftly down a small red path above us and stopped among the rushes when he saw us.

"Who was it called?" he said.

He seemed—how shall I say?—wet with haste or damp with the open air. His skin was ruddier than ours. Otherwise he was not so different, except that he was grown up and four of us were not. His hair was long and golden and even more wildly curly than Robin's or Duck's. I must say I liked his face. He had a gentle, laughing look, and his nose turned up a little. His rugcoat was an old faded red one, not unlike the one my father went to war in, very plain and wet with dew. I could see there was red mud splashed on his legs and that he wore shoes like ours, wet, too. But to our relief, he had no kind of weapon. His hands were empty, spread to part the rushes.

I thought: Well, if this is a Heathen, they can't be so very bad.

"Er—nobody called, really," Hern said, cautiously. "We were arguing about whether to land or not."

"It's lucky you did land," he said. "There's a large party of Heathens in a boat coming down the Red River." Since they were Heathens to him, we knew he meant our people. Not that this made any difference in the danger to us.

We looked at one another. "We'd better wait until they're past," Robin said doubtfully.

"If you like, you can come up to my shelter to wait," the Heathen man said politely.

We did not like this idea, but we did not want him to know we were his enemies. Robin and Hern and I looked at one another again. Duck looked at the Heathen man and smiled. "Yes, please," he said. I kicked at his ankle, but he just moved out of the way. The next second he was scampering away up the path. Robin gave a small ladylike wail and climbed out of the boat, too.

Hern and I did not know what to do. We thought we ought to stay together, but that meant leaving Gull. We bent down and tried to pull Gull up.

"Come along, Gull," I said. "We're going on a visit." Hern said encouraging things, too, but Gull would not move, and we could not budge him.

Damp hair brushed my face, and I jumped. The Heathen man was kneeling beside the boat and leaning between us to look at Gull. "How long has he been like this?" he said.

Hern looked at me. "Months, I think."

Robin leaned eagerly over us. "Do you know what's wrong with him, sir? Can you help us?"

"There's something I can do," the Heathen man said. "I wish you could have brought him here before this, though." He stood up, looking very serious. "We must wait till the Heathen have gone by," he said.

Duck came scooting back down the path. "I saw the Heathen—" he said.

"Quiet!" said the man.

We heard loud voices and the splashy sound of many people rowing. I never saw the people, and they were all talking at once, but I heard one say, "All clear ahead. None of the devils about." It sounded like a big, heavy boat, moving fast with oars and current, and I thought they must be patrolling for Heathen. The sounds moved quickly into the wide stretch of the double River and faded away.

When they had gone, our Heathen said, "My name is Tanamil, which means 'Younger Brother.' "

I was not sure we should tell him our names, for fear he might guess we were not Heathens, not having outlandish names like his. But Robin went all polite and ladylike and introduced us all. "This is Hern," she said, "and Tanaqui, and my brother lying there is Gull. That is Duck—"

Tanamil looked up at Duck, in the path above. "Duck?" he said. "Not Mallard?"

Duck's face went almost as red as the earth. "Mallard," he said. "Duck's a baby name."

Tanamil nodded and looked back at Robin. "I can guess your name," he said. "You have to be a bird, too, a bright one, a bird of omen. Robin?"

Robin went red, too, and nodded. She was so confused she forgot to be ladylike. "How did you guess?"

Tanamil laughed. He had a very pleasant laugh, that I admit, very joyful. It made us want to laugh, too. "I've wandered about collecting knowledge," he said. Then he went serious as he looked down at Gull. "And lucky I did," he said. "He's very far gone."

We all looked at Gull then, thinking Tanamil was exaggerating—until we saw how Gull had changed, even in that short time. He was thinner and paler than ever. He lay with his eyes closed, breathing so slightly that we could hardly see it. We could see the other bones in his head, joining those sharp cheekbones of his. He looked like a skull.

Robin seized Tanamil's arm. She would never have done such a thing in the ordinary way. It shows how upset she was. "What *is* the matter with him? Do you know?"

Tanamil continued to look down at Gull. "Yes," he said. "I know.

They are trying to take his soul. He has fought them long and hard for it, but they are winning."

Hern gave a sort of shiver. He was angry. He is always angry when people talk this way, but I had never seen him as angry as he was then. "Oh, are they?" he said. "And who are *they* in that case, and where are you imagining they are?" He was so angry he could hardly speak.

Tanamil was not offended. He seemed to understand Hern. "The one who is reeling your brother in now," he said, "is a powerful man who sits beyond the edge of my knowledge. I think he is down by the sea."

Hern seemed not to know what to say next. He did not seem angry anymore. "Gull kept saying he must go to the sea," I said.

"Then the man who wants him is there," Tanamil said. "Now I must get to work. We must save your brother without this powerful man suspecting. You understand?" He looked at us all very solemnly. "If what I do seems strange to you, it is done for the best. Will you remember that?"

"Yes," we all said, nodding, even Hern, though I had expected him to object. For all Tanamil was a Heathen, we felt we trusted him. He seemed to know so much.

He told us to get out of the boat and stand beside him in the rushes. We all did so willingly, leaving Gull lying in the bottom of the boat. Tanamil squatted down by the water's edge, where he dug and prized in the ground with his fingers until he had a double handful of wet red earth. We watched, mystified, as he dumped his pile of earth on the dry part of the path and set to work, squeezing, pinching, molding, smoothing at it. Occasionally he glanced in the boat to see how Gull was doing, and continued molding the earth. Shortly Hern began to look sarcastic. The earth was becoming a man-shaped figure, a young man-shaped figure, a figure we could recognize.

"It's Gull!" Duck whispered. "Isn't it *like* him!"

It is very like him. I have it in front of me as I weave. It is Gull to the life, but not so thin as he was when he lay in the boat. The wonder of it is that Tanamil caught the Gull he could not have known—the Gull who once laughed and boasted about going to war, and poled about the River whistling because he found life good. I can remember Gull like that—and an awful tease—but how could Tanamil have known?

When the figure was finished, Tanamil sat comfortably down in the rushes and said, "You can sit down if you want." Only Hern did so. The rest of us stood watching anxiously. Tanamil brought out from his rugcoat a slender reddish pipe, which seemed to be made of a bundle of thin reeds, and began to play it. After the first few notes Hern, who had been scornfully plaiting rushes, looked up, fascinated. It was a sad, sobbing tune that seemed to have a thread of laughter running through it. The notes ran, caught themselves, blended, and ran on, singing. I saw Duck's mouth open and Robin's face entranced. That pipe chimed like bells and ran like water. In it I felt all Spring budding and bursting as it does along the Riverside, and yet it was Spring in the future, overlaid by a sad winter. I hoped it would never stop. I wanted it to run forever as the River does.

I looked down at the red figure of Gull standing in the path. It was drying. I could see it turning pinker, shrinking a little, flaking slightly, and plainly becoming harder every second. I could have sworn the notes of the pipe were sucking water from it and then baking it under my eyes. It became harder, pinker, and smaller yet, until it seemed impossible that any moisture was left in it. Tanamil still played, watching the image as he played, until the pink was whitish. Then he drew to a close so gently that I did not at first realize he had stopped. There was no silence. There was the sound of the two rivers running on either side of us, and the wind stirring the reeds, and birds on the cliffs. All these noises seemed to have caught and held the music.

*"OH!"* said Robin, like a scream. "Gull—!"

I looked into the boat and Gull was transparent. I could see the boards and a corner of the blanket beneath him. I could see how the hair at the back of his head was pressed flat as he lay. As I looked, he was fainter. He was like a pool of liquid with his own reflection in it, and the liquid seemed to be drying up. It shrank, still with the whole of Gull in it, and dwindled till it lay only in the space in front of the tiller.

Hern jumped up. His foot went out to kick the dry image.

"Don't touch it!" Tanamil said, quick as a bark.

Hern's foot went back to the ground. At the same instant the liquid Gull dried away entirely. There was nothing but an empty boat.

We stood staring, with pale faces, too shocked to speak. Tanamil put his pipe away, stood up, and gently moved the image of Gull from the red earth. "There," he said, with Gull in his hands. "He's safe now."

"Safe how?" said Robin.

"Where is he?" said Duck.

"What have you done?" I said. As for Hern, he was speechless.

Tanamil held the dry pink Gull out to Robin, and she took it, utterly dismayed. "What—what do I do with *this?*" she said.

"Keep him safe until you come to your grandfather," Tanamil said.

"We haven't got a grandfather," said Duck.

Tanamil looked round at us all as if he did not know what to say.

"I didn't know how little you understood," he said at last. He considered a moment; then he said, "Gull's soul is not usual. If an enemy took it, he could use it as a spout to drain off the souls of his soul, as it were, and draw through it the souls of his forebears, right down to his first ancestor. I do not know if the man who was trying to take it knows this, but I know he should not have a chance to find out. What I have done makes Gull's soul safe without this man being any the wiser. If I swear by your Undying that Gull is safe, will you believe me?"

"He's safe from us, too, by the look of it," Robin said, and Tanamil laughed.

"Come up to my shelter and warm yourselves," he said, "before you go on."

I do not know how we came to agree to this. Tanamil was a Heathen. He had just taken Gull from us, and the way he had done it proved him to be a powerful magician. Yet we thought of none of these things. We went up the red path between the rushes with him, Robin carrying Gull.

The path came up on a grassy shoulder beneath the red cliff. From there we could see into both rivers. Our own River wound back in a high gorge, mighty, swift, and yellow. The other River ran red and was smaller, though no less swift, and it had a merriment about it that I had not seen in a River before. It sang between red walls. The trees, ferns, and reeds seemed greener there. It was full of birds. We heard the noise of birds at all times while we were with Tanamil.

When I remember Tanamil's shelter, I am confused. I thought it was built against the face of the red cliff, of red mud and driftwood, and that we pushed reeds aside to go in. But I could swear that we went inside the cliff itself. Indeed, we must have been inside the cliff, for I remember a second entrance low down beside the second River, where the red water slapped robustly among the fringed tops of tanaqui. The sunlight came in green through it and danced on the ceiling in curls and ripples.

Inside was a comfortable enough room, with chairs, a table and piles of rugs, some of fur, some woven plain, and a good fire blazing. Tanamil had no Undying at his hearth, Heathen that he was. Robin carefully put the dry little image of Gull there instead. Seeing her do that broke the spell that was on me for an instant—I am now sure that it was a spell. I jumped up, saying, "Oh! We left our Undying in the boat!"

Tanamil smiled his pleasant smile at me. "Don't worry. They'll guard the boat for you."

I sat down again, and for a long time I did not remember we were on a journey or consider our danger or even think of Gull. I had the time of my life instead. We all did, although Robin did not seem to enjoy herself so much at the end. But I cannot remember much that happened. Up till now it was all confused in my head. But by thinking and thinking and discussing it with Duck, I have remembered it better—though I am not sure we have it in the right order.

"That's the trouble with you, Tanaqui," Duck said to me. "You always have to have things in *order*. You're as bad as Hern."

I think Duck is right, though I did not realize it before. If I cannot get a thing straight in my head, it offends me, like a piece of weaving that has gone wrong—like Robin's awful blue skirt. This is why Hern and I are so much more horrified than Duck by our strange time with Tanamil.

# 6

I REMEMBER WE HAD an excellent meal by that good fire. It was food such as I had only heard of before, lobster and fine white cakes and venison, with dried grapes afterward. Uncle Kestrel told us of grapes. They grow among the trees of the Black Mountains, on trailing creepers. When I first heard of the King, my father said he ate lobster and venison every day. I never thought to have them myself. We had wine, too, like our King. Wine is fine pink stuff with a sparkle to it. Tanamil said it was from the Black Mountains. Robin poured a little of hers in front of the dry statue of Gull. Tanamil laughed at her for doing it, and Robin went very pink. But Duck says she did it again at supper.

Now the odd thing is that I remember only that one meal. We must have had another, because we stayed the night. Indeed, I remember sitting out beneath the cliff in the hot sun, looking at both rivers and eating, not once but several times. Yet when I think, I only remember that one meal in front of the fire.

Hern and Duck got very merry. They romped and rolled and fought in the heaps of rugs. I think I did, too, but not all the time. I watched Robin dancing. Robin often used to dance in Shelling when she had time, but she never danced as she did then, when Tanamil played his pipe for her. I remember her dancing in the room, with whorls and wrinkles of sunlight sliding on the ceiling above her, and outside on the grass. I even seem to remember her up on the cliff opposite, across the second River, but that must be nonsense. What I do remember is that she took hold of Tanamil's arm on several occasions, demanding that he pipe for her. That is quite unlike Robin. She is so shy and formal. But I know she did. And when she asked him, Tanamil smiled and piped for her again, clear and lovely music, like a dream of music. And Robin danced and danced.

Duck wanted to learn to pipe, too. Hern and I made an outcry at that. If you ever heard Duck sing! But Tanamil obligingly went out and cut hollow reeds for him. I remember his fingers flying as he cut holes in the reeds and bound them together. He made the mouthpieces from joints in the reeds, where the pith is solid. Then he put Duck's fingers to the holes and told him to blow. Duck blew. Nothing happened.

"Silence! Thank goodness!" said Hern.

"Try saying *Ptehwh!* to it," said Tanamil.

"*Ptehwh!*" said Duck, scarlet in the face. And all the pipes sounded a terrible squealing and braying, as if pigs had got among donkeys. We shrieked with laughter. Duck glowered at us and went outside through the second door, down beside the red River. Shortly we heard halting little tunes from among the rushes.

Hern raised his eyebrows at me. "Ye gods! I didn't think he knew any tunes."

Tanamil taught Hern things, too. I remember them squatting together in the dust, and Tanamil drawing things there with a pointed stick, and Hern nodding. At other times they were leaping on one another and wrestling. I liked the look of that. I pulled Tanamil's arm, like Robin, and said, "Show me, too!"

He showed me. There were things I could not do, not being as strong as Hern, but he showed me the way to use a person's own strength against him. I think that if a grown enemy—say, Zwitt—walked into this mill at the moment, I could throw him to the ground and maybe kill him. But I am not sure that I should use this knowledge. I think of who it was taught me.

Two things Tanamil taught me I *have* used. I forget how it came about, but I know I told him that there were many words I did not know how to weave. He said there was no harm in making your own patterns, provided you taught others what you meant. But he said, "You must use the right pattern for River. That is important," and he showed me, weaving with rushes. He also showed me a more expressive way of twisting yarn. He had me twist rushes until I could do it. He said, "When you use yarn twisted this way, use it for the strongest parts of your story. Your meaning will leap from the cloth." I have done this in several places. I do not mind that it was Tanamil who taught me. It works.

I asked Hern what Tanamil was showing him in the dust with the pointed stick, but he would not tell me.

Later on I remember Tanamil coming to us when the firelight was leaping on the ceiling and mixing with the ripples of sun there. "There's a question you must all ask me," he said. "Each of you ask."

None of us could think what to say. I was reminded of the way Aunt Zara *will* say, "Tanaqui, there is a little word you should say to me. What is it?" And of course I can never think what she means, so I do not say it, and she calls me rude. If only she would say, "Tanaqui, you haven't said please," then I should know what she meant and say it. It was like that with Tanamil. He wanted us to say something particular, which was obvious to him, but not at all to us.

Hern said first, "Would you call yourself a magician?"

"In some ways, yes," said Tanamil, "but that is not what I call myself." And he turned to Duck.

"Do you believe in the Undying?" Duck asked. He had been thinking earnestly, and I could see he thought he was very clever asking this.

Tanamil was amused. He turned his face to the flickering roof and laughed. "Not as you do," he said. "But they exist." Then he turned to me, still laughing.

For a moment I thought I knew what he wanted me to ask, and then it was gone.

"No, no," he said. "You must ask what you *want* to ask."

This was like Aunt Zara saying I must say please because I wanted to—and who does? "Please," I said, but that was not it, of course. "Where do you come from?" I said.

It was not the right question. He laughed again. "I suppose you would say I come from the Black Mountains."

I puzzle over this more and more, because I know the Heathens come from the sea. While I puzzled then, Tanamil turned to Robin. And I do not know what Robin asked. I know she asked, and I think she asked right, and that Tanamil answered, but I have no memory of what was said. Duck says I do not remember because Robin was not there at the time. He says Tanamil came and asked each of us separately, and he says I do wrong to put it in here because it happened right at the beginning of our stay. But I remember it almost at the end, and I am weaving this story.

The next things happened in the night, and I know that was right at the end. We were all asleep among the rugs by the fire. It was more comfortable and warm than we had been since we left home, so I do not know why I woke up, unless it was that Robin and Tanamil were making such a noise with their argument. I only heard a few things they said. I kept falling asleep and waking again to hear them still heatedly at it. I will put what I heard.

Tanamil was saying, "But they're bound to go. They all bound themselves, and I can't keep them forever."

"In that case," Robin said, "I shall have to go, too."

"But you never bound yourself," Tanamil said. "Why should you go?"

Robin said, "I did. I promised my mother, years ago—"

"If your mother knew what I was asking," Tanamil said quickly, "she would tell you to do as I say." That struck me as unfair. Tanamil did not know what my mother would say. But Robin is always saying and thinking that our mother would want this and not like that, and I am sure Tanamil knew it. Robin began to cry. "All I'm asking is that you stay here with me," he said.

All he was asking! I did not care to have Robin bullied like this. I meant to sit up and tell Tanamil a thing or two, but I went to sleep instead.

I woke up to hear Robin shouting, "I tell you *no*!"

And Tanamil shouted back, "*Why*? Why, why, *why*?"

"Because of what you are," Robin said. She was crying again—or still. "It wouldn't be right." I could have shaken her. She had as good as told him we were not Heathens.

"How do you mean, not right?" Tanamil demanded. "Where's the difference between us?"

"Age, for a start," said Robin.

"What a feeble thing to say!" said Tanamil. He sounded as disgusted as Hern would have been. But I was glad because I could see Robin was trying to cover up her mistake. "Have you any other silly excuses?" he said.

"They're not excuses; they're reasons," Robin said coldly.

"That was unfair. I apologize," said Tanamil.

I thought that in spite of her mistakes, Robin was dealing with him better than I could have done. I must have gone to sleep thinking it. When I woke up next, Robin was getting the worst of it.

"I can't see how you can know that!" she was bleating, in her feeblest way.

"I do," said Tanamil. "Next to Gull, you're the one most at risk. I'm not just saying it to persuade you—"

"Then why are you saying it?" said Robin.

"A hit," Tanamil said. "Robin, I can't see much of the future, but I don't like what I see. Stay here and let the others go. They've inherited his toughness. You haven't."

This gave Robin the moral advantage. She is good at taking that.

"And what would you think of me if I drew back just because I was born feeble?" she asked.

That must have been the winning answer. When I woke up again, Tanamil was not in the room and Robin was asleep just beside me. This time it was Duck who had woken me. He was crouched beside me, half rosy in the fire, and the other half of him caught in whorls and ripples of moonlight from the River beyond the door.

"Tanaqui," he whispered, "I've just remembered something. You know that boatload of people Tanamil said were Heathens?"

"Yes," I said. I was suddenly full of distrust for Tanamil. He had taken Gull, and now he was trying to take Robin. I wondered how we had been mad enough to stay with him. I knew he must have cast a spell to make us, and I was scared silly. "What about them?" I said. "They weren't Heathens, they were our people, weren't they?"

"No," whispered Duck. "That was the funny thing. They were real Heathens. They had hair a bit like ours and brown faces—like his—and peculiar clothes with iron hats. Why did *he* call them Heathens?"

Hern was sitting up on the other side of the fire. "Are you sure?" he whispered.

"Positive. I *saw* them," said Duck.

We all looked at the small pale figure of Gull sitting on the hearth. I felt sick. Hern said, "Then he knew who we were from the start. We—"

There was a rilling, splashing noise outside. The rushes at the entrance bobbed, and the moonlight was drowned in the shadow of Tanamil, wading in the water. We dived into our rugs and lay there, so that he would not know we were awake. And we all went to sleep. Duck and Hern remember nothing beyond diving into the blankets either.

Next morning Tanamil was gone. The shelter was as I remembered it when I first started to think about it, built of old wood and red earth, leaning against the cliff. The one door was open to the sun on the grassy shoulder between the two rivers. It was cold. The fire was out, and I think there were no longer any blankets. There were certainly none when I looked back into the shelter before we left. We got up and hurried into the sun, shivering.

Robin was there first, holding the little figure of Gull. "I take it he means us to go," she said dourly. "I think he might have said goodbye."

"He might have given us breakfast," said Duck.

"We've got food in the boat," said Hern. "Come on."

The boat was there, bobbing in a green cave among the reeds, with our food and the Undying still in her.

"I'm relieved to see that," said Hern. "Get in. Let's eat as we go."

"Why the hurry?" I said.

"Who's bossy?" said Duck.

*"I'm head of the family!"* Hern shrieked, turning on him. "Do as I say!"

Duck and I both turned to Robin. She looked at the clay image between her hands and shrugged. "I suppose that's the truth of it," she said.

"Then he'd better be polite about it," Duck said. We glowered at Hern, Duck and I.

"I can't be polite until I've had some breakfast," said Hern. "I'm frantic for it. We've eaten nothing but illusions since we landed. Isn't that so, Robin?"

"I don't think so. How should *I* know?" Robin said as she climbed into the boat.

We poled out from among the reeds into the current of the two rivers and went drifting down a reddish, lazy flood between two lines of trees that ought to have marked the banks. The bread was horribly stale. The cabbages smelled. We chewed carrots, tough cheese, and dried fruit. Duck was so hungry he ate an onion. His eyes streamed. We all felt soggy, irritable, and frightened in a gloomy sort of way. We knew we were back in real life, and we wished we knew the reasons for it: why Tanamil had kept us and why he had turned us out.

"You said we ate illusions," I said to Hern as we finished eating. "But you don't believe in enchantments."

"I believe in what I can see," said Hern. "I saw what happened to Gull. I damn near broke the spell, too. I wish I had. And that food was too good to be real. I can't accept it wasn't real, but I suppose I've got to. It's—it's offensive."

"Bad luck," Duck said politely.

Hern was too gloomy to hit him. He said, "It's the way it's all mixed up in my head that annoys me. I can't remember properly." I saw Hern was having the same trouble as me. "It's maddening!" he said. "Robin, what happened to us?"

"How should I know?" said Robin. She was gloomiest of the lot.

We put the sail up. There were worms, earwigs, and beetles in the folds of the sail, and wood lice and things with many legs making their home under the mast. Hern scowled at them. He scowled at the trees as we beat slowly from line to line of them, tacking against the wind. We did not sail beyond the trees, although there were acres of white water, glittering into the distance beyond, because we did not know how deep it was. There were no people, only trees sticking up from sheets of water.

Hern said, "Does anything strike you about these trees?"

Nothing did. Duck said, as we sailed under spreading branches, "Oaks, elms, willows."

"Go back to sleep!" said Hern. "Tanaqui, you're supposed to notice things. What about these trees?"

I looked up. The oak we were under was large, but quite ordinary. It was just beginning to get leaves, like bundles of yellow rags. The elm and the willows beyond it were just as ordinary, because they were already bright new green. "Everyone knows oaks are late," I said. "Trees always look like this in Spring."

"That's it!" Hern shouted. "Exactly! When we came to the waters-meet, all the trees were bare!" We stared up at the new leaves, astonished. Hern was right. I remembered I had said it was like sailing back to winter, this far down the River. "Now think back to last night," Hern said. "There was a moon. But there was no moon when we set out, was there?"

That was true again. "What do you think has happened?" I said, shivering.

Hern scowled. "A lot of days have passed. I wish I knew how many. I wish I knew why. What was Tanamil up to?"

"Do you think he's made us . . . too late for—for the One's fire?" I said.

If any read my weaving and do not know the One, I must tell you that once a year, as soon as the floods go down in Spring, the One requires to be put in a fire, from which he emerges renewed. It is a peculiar habit, but he is the One and not like the other Undying. I do not know what would happen if the One went into his fire at the wrong time. No one has dared try it.

Hern hunched up and brooded. There was the chalky bleakness in his eyes that always frightens me. My brother Hern is going to be a frightening man if he grows up as angry as he is now. The stoop of his shoulders and the jut of his nose put me in mind of the shadow Uncle Kestrel cast on our wall. Hern stared out chalk-eyed over the white water and said, "We have been taught that the One is our ancestor. We have also been told that Gull's soul could be used to pour out the virtue of our ancestor. We hear that Heathens have skill in this. We meet a Heathen, and strange things happen. It has always seemed to me that the One's habits are insane, until now. But if I believe what I saw happen to Gull, why should I not believe that the One himself is under attack now? The question is—"

"Do stop going on about it, Hern," Robin said. "You must have noticed the days were going by."

"—are the floods going down?" said Hern.

"We didn't notice," I said. "Do you know how long we were there?"

"I didn't count," Robin said. "It felt about ten days."

"Ten days!" I exclaimed. "No wonder the cabbages were bad!"

"Are the floods going down or not?" said Hern.

We looked anxiously at the spreading waters. The River, in its double strength, was bringing down sticks, straw, boughs, leaves, and weed, between the two lines of trees. "Look, look!" Duck cried out, pointing to the nearest floating bough. We looked and found that it was moving not down the River but gently *backward.* We were aghast.

"The River's flowing the wrong way!" said Robin.

For over an hour the sticks, straw, and leaves continued to move gently upstream. Our boat still went forward, tacking against the wind, but we were all in the greatest panic. Duck and I hung over the side watching the debris. We had no idea if this meant the end of the floods or more malign magic.

"That magician by the sea must be turning the whole River now," I said.

"If there *is* a magician there," said Hern. "Think who told us there was." He stared at a place where the water was gently troubled, as if the true current of the River were forcing its way against the unnatural flow. "Gull's soul is one thing," he said. "It can't be very heavy. But it would take magic stronger than I can believe in to turn all this weight of water. There must be some other explanation."

To our surprise and relief, the sticks and weeds turned at midmorning and began going the proper way.

We stayed in the boat all that day. There was nowhere to land in the sheets of water on either side of the trees. But at nightfall we were all sick of raw food. In the dusk we saw what we took for a low island or small mountain out in the flood. We drew up the keel and poled cautiously across to it. It proved to be the roofs of a mighty house, not high, but covering the space of several cornfields. Some roofs were old thatch, some new and steep, of slippery tiles, with painted carvings at the ridge and bundles of tall chimneys.

"I bet the King lived here," said Duck.

We thought Duck was right. But everyone there had gone to the wars and not come back. We tied the boat to the bars of a window and landed on a flat space of tiles, bringing our Undying with us. Hern thought we might have to put the One in his fire anytime. I could not bear to touch Gull for many days after that, so I brought the Young One. As I set him down, I was struck by the resemblance between them.

Gull seems to be made of the same flaky pink stone. Yet I know the Young One was carved many lifetimes ago.

There was only a glimmer of fire in both firepots. We tore off gilded carvings and red and blue rails from the roofs and used handfuls of thatch for kindling. Our fire smoked and smelled bad on the tiles, and smoke spread over the flat water.

After supper we left Robin sitting by the fire with her hands wrapped round the knees of her awful blue skirt and scrambled over the roofs in the near dark. I kept wishing I could see into the drowned rooms underneath. But I had to imagine the grandeur. Hern and I collided coming round the tall chimneys above our boat. While we were laughing, we heard the slop and creak of our boat swinging round to face upstream.

"It's happened again!" said Hern.

We slithered down the steep roof, and sure enough, we could see the boat turned and the rubbish from our supper drifting the wrong way. We knelt with our heads hanging off the roof, trying to see how fast the current went. Hern took a stick and held it with his fingers just out of the water.

"It can't be the end of the floods," he said. "My thumb's wet now."

Somebody laughed on the roof behind us. I thought it was Duck and turned to tell him about the current. But it was a Heathen girl. I could see just enough to know that she was fair-haired and not Robin. I nudged Hern and he looked, too.

"Er—good evening," we said. I don't know how Hern felt, but I was hoping very hard she would think we were Heathens too.

"Hallo," she said. "Why are you two making such a fuss about the tide?"

"Tide?" we said, stupid as owls in a strong light.

"You must know about it," she said. "The sea rises twice a day and comes up the River."

"Oh, we know all about that," Hern said. "We—er—we were just seeing how high it came up."

"Of course," she said.

"We know it's different by the sea," I lied.

"Of course," she said. I know she was laughing at us as she slipped away behind the chimneys.

We felt very foolish and very scared. When Robin and Duck learned we were sharing the roofs with Heathens, they wanted to row away in the dark, but we gave up that idea because we could not see where the two lines of trees were by then. Instead we threw our fire into the water and got into the boat. There we did not sleep for a long time, but we never heard a sound from the Heathens.

# 7

WE DID NOT HEAR the Heathens go, but we were the only people on the roofs in the morning. Hern and I climbed a tower in the middle and made sure of it.

"Now, please," said Robin as we were all getting into the boat, "let's decide where to stop. What kind of place do we want to live in?"

"We're going down to the sea first," said Duck.

"Surely not," Robin said. She gestured to the pink clay brother in the bows of the boat. "Think of Gull."

At once it was certain that Duck, Hern, and I were all settled on going to the sea. "I do think of Gull," said Hern. "I want to see that magician—if there *is* a magician. I'm going to flood him out with real things. I shan't believe a word he says. That's the only way to deal with magic."

"I'd have thought more magic would be better," said Duck. "But I've got to go there, too."

My thought was that we would find a magician by the sea and he would prove to be Tanamil. I growled like a dog, I was so angry—angry with Tanamil and angry with myself for believing anything he said. "I'm going to see that magician," I said, "and I'm going to rescue Gull." I knew I had not the power to do that. I took up the One and shook him, I was so angry. "He'll help," I said. "He'd better!"

"Tanaqui!" said Robin. "You mustn't threaten the Undying! I think you're all mad or—or something."

"Don't you start on about being the eldest and knowing best!" said Hern. "We've all decided."

"I wasn't," Robin protested. "I don't know best. I don't know anything anymore. All I know is that it's dangerous. If I didn't know it was quite as dangerous in Shelling, I'd ask to go home." She bent her head, and tears dripped. Hern sighed.

"We'll find a really nice home when we've been to the sea, Robin," I said.

It took us four days to come near the sea. It might have taken longer if the wind had not backed to southwest and come hurling over the plains of water, bringing ruffles like gooseflesh. With that we made speed even when the tide turned and flowed up the River. Each day it flowed more strongly, until we came to expect it, as we expected the sun to rise. We found it useful, for it showed us where the River truly ran. There were no more trees to mark the River after the first day. Instead there was a very confusing landscape.

I think more people had lived in that part of the land than I knew existed before. It rose into humps and lumps everywhere. The flooded River flowed round them in lakes, in strings of shallow pools, and in a multitude of smaller rivers. Often the first sign we had that we had missed the main River was that we found ourselves sailing beside the posts of a fence. There were houses on nearly every hump of land and more houses half underwater. Not all these houses were burned, but there were no people anywhere. We risked staying in an empty house one night, but none of us felt comfortable there. Even when we put our Undying in the empty niches by the hearth, it still felt like someone else's house.

Many of the humps had animals on them. We have three cats now, Rusty, and Ratchet, and Sweetheart, who came from the island where the gulls were. I love cats. Robin named them. There was one island full of dogs, but they were wild and hungry and barked at us so fiercely that we did not go near them. Most of the humps were full of sheep. They had lambs, because it was Spring. We wondered whether to catch some to eat, but we were not that hungry yet. We had plenty of dried fruit and pickled fish, and there were cows stranded on every hillside. Once we had got used to the way things were, we did not hesitate to milk those cows.

By the fourth evening in that confusing landscape, the mountains we kept seeing in the distance drew in around us, in the form of low, empty-looking hills. They were dark, stony, and infertile. But the island we landed on was grassy and covered with bushes. There little black Sweetheart came running to meet us, purring and mewing. Never have I seen a cat more glad to have human company.

That morning I was woken by melancholy crying. I got up and found the waters covered with white floating birds, and more flying, catching the sun in a way that had me blinking.

"What are these large mournful birds?" I said.

Hern laughed. "Haven't you seen seagulls before?"

"She may not have done," Robin said. "They stopped coming to Shelling years ago. They used to come and cover the field when it was plowed, Tanaqui, and Father said they came inland to get away from the Spring storms."

"But I remember them," Hern protested. "She's only a year younger than me."

"Please, Hern," said Robin. "I'm much too tired to quarrel about seagulls."

"They used to come after the floods," Hern said. "Does that mean the River's going down, then?" He scrambled to test the height of the water. He tried a different way nearly every day to see if the floods were over, but the tides grew stronger and steeper the nearer we came to the sea and defeated all his methods. That day Hern hung a piece of twine with knots in it from a bush. But the end of it floated instead of sinking, and Sweetheart came along and played with it. Hern roared at her. It was very odd: Hern, of all of us, was the one who was determined that the One should go in his fire at the proper time.

Duck picked Sweetheart up. "Don't make such a fuss, Hern," he said. "When the floods go down, it'll be quite obvious."

"But we don't have a bank to measure by!" Hern snarled.

"Then we'll find out some other way," said Duck.

"Stop maddening me," said Hern. "Take that cat away."

Robin was very quiet as we sailed that morning. I should have noticed she was not well, I know, but I was thinking of other things. The gulls followed us. They made a noise like sharp misery, and I was afraid of them. They watched us with hungry eyes like beads. When they floated on the River, they seemed lighter than was natural. I was not sure they were really birds. There was a new light in the air, bleached and chalky, like bones, or Hern's eyes when he is angry, and the gulls wheeled about in it. The hills on either side of us were low and rocky, with no trees to speak of, and they seemed to come together in front of us into a bank of mist. The wind hissed over them. The River filled the wide space in between, gray now, and covered with angry shivers in all directions. Where the water met the land, it rose into high waves with white tops. These waves went riding landward, growing taller as they rode, until they were too tall for themselves, whereupon the white top fell over and smashed on the land. Everywhere was *crash, crash* of falling waves, and the seagulls crying out. I kept looking at Gull to make sure he was safe. I was frightened.

Hern and Duck became frightened, too, when we found we were

not masters of the boat any longer. None of us understands the mass of contradictory currents in which the water flowed to the sea. Sometimes we were racing forward, sometimes we seemed hardly to move, and then, around midday, we were taken by the tide and borne back toward Sweetheart's island. We kept the sail up and tried to beat on, but we found we were taken more and more toward the left. After a whole morning we had gone barely two miles.

"I think we'd better keep leftward," Hern said at last, "and try to land somewhere over there."

"Oh, yes, do let's land!" Robin said. She said it so desperately that we all looked at her and saw that she was ill. She was shivering, and her face was an odd color—almost like the lilac flowers in Aunt Zara's garden. I think we did wrong to bring Robin to the sea.

Hern said, "I'll land in the first possible place."

Duck picked up a blanket and wrapped it round Robin. "Would you like the Lady, Robin?" he said. I confess now that I felt jealous at how kind they both were to Robin. I found it hard to be kind to her, and I still do. She looked so ugly, and she kept shivering for no reason. I hope I did not show my feelings. I put the Lady in Robin's hands, but Robin seemed to forget her, and she dropped to the boards.

"Have the Young One," said Duck.

"No," Robin said, with great firmness.

After endless sailing in heaving gray water, we came near land. It would be midafternoon by then. Everything was bleached, brownish, and sandy-looking and smelling a new smell, like a fresh-caught fish. That is the smell of the sea. And the land was not in a solid line as we had thought, but in islands of heaped-up sand, with the true land just as sandy, some way beyond. In between the land and the islands the sand-colored water raced and sucked, while on the outer side of them it was all waves, crashing continually. How Hern got us ashore on the last island, I shall never know. He must be a better boatman than me.

Here was our final island. It was made of crusty sand. Sharp-edged grass grew on it and bent prickly bushes, all twisted in the wind. The wind had dug out holes and hollows in the sand. We found the largest hollow, facing back to the land we had come from—from there it looked like blue mountains—and we made a camp, dragging the boat up to give Robin some shelter. Down below was a place where all the things in that part of the flood were hurled on the island and pinned there by the racing water.

"Ugh!" said Duck when he saw it.

There were dead hens, drowned rats, cabbage stalks—many horrid remains—but there was wood and waterweed, too. We made a good fire from it. We wrapped Robin in rugcoats and blankets, and she still shivered. We offered her food.

"I couldn't!" she said. "Just water."

"Water!" I said. Hern and I looked at one another. There was a drop in the jar, but there was no water on the island. I went down to the gray flood and tasted it. The River here mingles with the sea, and the sea is salt. I do not know where the salt comes from, but the sea is not fit to drink.

"What do we do now?" I whispered.

"We can't take the boat," Hern whispered back. "She'd be cold without it, and the current's terrible. I can't see any sign of a stream either."

We gazed at the low sandy land helplessly. Naturally Duck chose that moment to say in a loud voice, "I'm dreadfully thirsty!"

"Shut up!" we both said.

But there was Robin heaving herself up on one arm, with rugs dropping from her and her teeth chattering in her blue-gray mouth. "Is the water gone? I'll go and get—"

"You lie down," I said, glaring at Duck. "I'm just going to get some." I took the water jar and stumped off up the sandy hill, with no idea what I was going to do. I was really depressed. When I come to think of it, I find wide-open spaces always make me unhappy. It was the same with the lake. I have been brought up where the land is hilly and close. Here it was as if the land had not been properly made. Everything was flat and sand gray or River gray and hung with peculiar purple-gray mist. You could not see very far, even if there was anything to see. The only thing my eye could cling to was the wide channel of rushing gray water between me and the shore, and I did not see myself getting across that.

All the same, I stumped down toward the channel. I had some notion that the water would not be salty there. And as I went, I thought I heard Duck screaming from the rushing channel. It was the way he screams when he is really frightened. "Help!" he screamed.

I remember I dropped the jar and came down to the water like a plow in a furrow of dry sand. It was not Duck. It was a much smaller child. He was in the channel, thrashing about in the racing muddy water and traveling past in it as fast as I could walk, screaming all the while. There was a horrid while when I seemed to stand there staring. But I think I took my shoes off and got out of my rugcoat while I stared.

"Keep swimming!" I screamed at the child. "Swim for your life!" He heard me. A fountain of water went up from his arms and legs, but I could see he had no idea how to swim. I plowed down into the water.

I remember squawking. It was far colder than the River is by Shelling, and the bottom was no bottom at all. It was just sinking stuff. You had to swim or sink in the mud. I swam madly. I had never swum in a flood before. My father forbade it. But I think, even that first night of the flood, the current was not as strong as the one in that race. My legs were towed sideways before I was afloat. No wonder the child screamed so. I swam with my whole strength, and yet I could not seem to cross that narrow channel.

I think I caught up with that drowning child simply from being heavier. Since I was trying to go forward, I was carried to him on a slant. That is, I was carried to where I had last seen him. He had gone down a second time by then. I thought he was drowned, and I was thinking of saving myself when a heavy sand-colored head bobbed up just by my fingers. I wound my hand in the hair and pulled.

Then it was all panic. The child's terror got into me, too. We both thrashed and screamed and sank. I roared at him to be quiet, and he shrilled at me to let go, and to get him out, and called me names. I called him a crab-faced idiot and fought him until the water was in spouts round us. While we struggled, the current dragged us along against the land, and I saw we were traveling out toward the sea. I put my hand against the bank to stop us. And my hand stuck in the land, up to my elbow. I dream of that still. The bank was as soft as curd cheese. Somehow, I got us out onto it, out of the sucking waters, and the cheeselike land sucked us down instead. I floundered through it, dragging that poor child by his hair. I came to hard sand under my elbows, coarse as sugar, and I cried with relief.

The child cried, too, on hands and knees, with water pouring out of his mouth and hair. His face was red and blue in patches, and his bare feet and legs were raw purple. He was wearing a silly kind of tunic and drawers which must have been cold even when he was dry. He shivered, and I shook.

"Shut up," I said. "You're all right now." He looked at me as if it was all my fault. "You're saved," I said. "By me. You're looking at the person who pulled you out. How did you fall in, anyway?" He seemed vague about that. He muttered something. "I see," I said. "You were fooling about and you slipped. Where do you live?"

He gave me a shifty look. I think he said, "I didn't say that," but he still didn't speak properly.

"Then what did you say?" I said.

"I said some natives pushed me in." He said it very loudly and clearly, so there was no mistake, and he gave me the defiant look people do when they are lying.

"Liar," I said, but I said it without thinking. The wretched child was a Heathen. My wet hair was the same sand color as his, and I knew his would dry fair, too. I thought that if I had let him drown, it would have been revenge for my father at least, but what had my father to do with him? I could not have stood on the island and let him drown. "You'd better go home and get into dry clothes," I said. "Where can I find some water?"

He gave me another sideways look and pointed to the racing channel behind us.

"Very funny!" I said. "Do you think I'm a fool?" He shook his head swiftly. "Water to drink," I said. "I was looking for some when I heard you yelling."

He looked at me from the corners of his eyes, very carefully. Maybe he knew I was not a Heathen. Something made him afraid and respectful of me. "There's water up here," he said, and jerked his shivering chin to the sandy hill above us.

"Show me," I said.

Both shivering hugely, we marched up and inland, over one sandy hump and round another. The wind was cruel. And there, running between two more sand-humps, was a peculiar little stream, very flat and shallow. It came out of the sand about a foot above my head and, instead of flowing down into the River, simply buried itself in the sand and vanished, just beside my mauve feet. I tasted it, and it was good. "Thanks," I said. "Now you've shown me, you can go home, but mind you tell them the truth about what happened. If you spin them that story about the natives pushing you in, I shall know at once, and I shall come and get you." I did not see why he should blame our people for his own silliness.

"All right," he muttered, pushing at the sand with his poor sore toes. I could see I had impressed him. He was a lot younger than Duck.

"Good," I said. "Off you go, then."

He was gone, in a shower of sand, before I finished saying it. He never said thank you. He was a very ungrateful, very Heathen brat.

I knelt beside the stream for a while, playing with its peculiarities. I have since learned that such streams are common at the Rivermouth, but I had never seen anything like it. Dig as I might, I could not find where it came from. Then I noticed that I was freezing cold and that I had no way of carrying the water. I got up and went lumbering on my frozen legs until I could see our island.

It was some way up the shore from me. I could see Duck and Hern bending anxiously over the plowed place where I had gone into the channel.

"Hey!" I shouted. "Where's the water jar?"

Both their heads jerked up. I laughed. They looked out to sea first, expecting me to be there. That was really stupid of them because while I had been digging at the stream, the tide had turned and the water in the channel was rushing inland again. The whole channel was smaller, shallower, and more gentle.

Duck ran away to fetch the jar. Hern tried to yell at me about how I had crossed the channel, and I tried to shriek back about the Heathen brat, but neither of us heard much for the wind. Then Duck came galloping back down the island with the water jar and galloped straight to the water. I suddenly saw he was going to try to cross it.

"Stop!" I screamed at him, remembering the sinking bottom. "I'm wet already." If I had told him about the mud and the current, that would not have stopped him. I ran into the channel myself instead. My feet sank, but nothing like as badly as they had done before. The water came up to my knees—I was so cold by then that it felt warm—and then up to my waist, but that was all. The current was not fierce at all. I could hardly believe it.

"What was the fuss about? I could have come over easily," Duck pointed out when I got to the other side.

"I told you—I'm wet already," I said. I took the jar and waded back. This time the water hardly reached the top of my legs. I shall never understand tides, I said to myself.

When I came back with the full jar, the channel had narrowed again. It was a brisk stream of salt water, which came just to my knees in the middle. On either side of it were wide places of brown sand, but I did not sink in them above my ankles. I could hear it, *trickle-trickle, smicker-smicker*, as the water drained from it, and worms were wriggling up under my toes.

Hern took the jar from me. "Lucky the tide's running out."

"It isn't," I said. "It's running up-River."

"Then why is it so low?" said Duck.

At that we all said at once, "The floods are going down!" It was a great relief to find Tanamil had not made us miss the One's fire after all.

"What a shame Robin's ill for it," said Duck.

"There are Heathen near," I said. "Should we make a fire? I pulled a Heathen brat out of the water."

"It can't be helped," said Hern. His head went pecking forward, as it does when he is determined. "I'm not going to let any Heathen, magicians or otherwise, interfere with what the One thinks is due to him. Let's get some firewood."

It has to be a special fire for the One, newly kindled from our hearth. Usually we do it on the bank of the River near our house. As I went shivering to the camp with the water, I hoped the One would not find it too strange when he came out of his fire on this miserable island. Usually, too, we celebrate with a feast, but I knew there was no question of feasting this time, even before I saw Robin.

Robin was worse. She was shivering as badly as I was, but she had thrown off the blankets and taken off most of her clothes. She said she was too hot. "I'm so thirsty!" she said.

I gave her a long drink and made her get under the blankets again. She would not put on her clothes. She had thrown them up the hill and the cats were lying on them. "Well, if you won't wear them," I said, "I will. I'm soaked." I was so frozen by then that I could not bear to unpack all the lockers in the boat to find my own clothes. I put on Robin's underclothes and her awful blue skirt. My rugcoat was dry, of course, so I put that on, and my shoes. The cats came and sat on the skirt again, with me in it, which helped me to get warm. But Robin still shivered. She looked uglier than ever.

"I'm sore all over," she said.

"You've got the River fever again," I said. "It won't last long."

"Where are the boys?" she said.

"Gull's in the boat," I said. "Hern and Duck are getting wood for the One. The floods are going down."

Robin sprang up again. "Oh, I must see to it! They'll never get it right!"

"Lie down," I said. "They can do it here where you can see them, and you can tell them what to do. But I'll tell them not to do it at all if you get up." I am like that with Robin all the time—not kind. I try to be patient, but she is far more annoying ill than well.

Hern and Duck came back with loads of wood. They had pulled up the thick-branched prickle bushes from all over the island. They were determined to make it a good fire, in spite of the situation. They dug a flat shelf out of the sand above the camp and built the wood up there as Robin told them. We took a long time and did it really well.

When it was ready, Hern, as head of the family, took the One from the boat and put him in the niche we had made in the center of the wood. The One looked just as usual, dark and rigid, and covered with small glisters. It was hard to believe that he knew what was happening. Robin sat up between Duck and me while Hern lit the wood with a coal from our firepot.

We all said, "May the clay purge from you. Come forth again in your true strength."

This is what we always say. Then we watched the flames roar up in the wind. Our campfire was dwarfed. In that light, wide space the flames looked pale and saw-edged. The One was soon lost in them. They raced up from the edge of the hill, whirling round and round, and dropped flaming pieces on the water.

We were staring at the blaze, thinking that it was the best fire we had ever made, when we heard shouts.

"What was that?" said Robin.

"*Hey there! You on the island!*"

"I'll go," said Hern. Naturally Duck and I went over the hill with him.

On the shore opposite, beyond the small stream that was all that was left of the racing channel, a row of Heathen men were standing.

"Hey you!" they shouted. "Come over here!"

# 8

AT FIRST I THOUGHT the Heathen were monstrously tall, with strange-shaped heads. Then I saw that they had on iron hats which came high in the crown. The strange shapes were decorations made of feathers and tufts of fur and colored tassels. They had tunics like the Heathen brat's, but they wore long boots and gauntlets and flapping heavy cloaks, which made the outfit look a little warmer. They were all strong, strapping men. Three of them leaned on spears. The other two carried what looked like short planks with a little bow on one end. We knew those were the bows Uncle Kestrel told us of, which could send a bolt through two men at once.

"The fire gave us away," said Hern. "Pretend we're Heathens, too."

"How can we?" I said. "With the One in his fire."

"Shut up!" said Hern. The Heathen were shouting to us again to come over to them. "Why should we?" Hern shouted back. "What do you want?"

Several of them shouted back and beckoned. We could not hear what they said. "Are they talking about a King?" Duck said. The confused shouting and the beckoning continued, but none of the Heathen tried to cross the channel. They thought, as I had done, that it was still sinking mud there. As we still stood there, the two with bows pointed them at us.

"I think," said Hern, "we'd better do what they want. Tanaqui, go and tell Robin to lie low and look after the One. Don't upset her."

They hoped to cross over to the Heathen while I talked to Robin. I would never have forgiven them for that. But when I went back over the hill, Robin was asleep with the cats curled up round her, and the One's fire was blazing majestically. I threw some wood on the campfire and raced back. I was in time to catch Hern and Duck as they walked into the water. I bunched up Robin's skirt and splashed after them.

The Heathens were taller than I thought. They wore iron waistcoats, which looked even odder than the hats. All of them had brown skins and long noses like Hern's, and from below the metal hats tumbled hair that was either fair as ours or the brown color of the sand. They stared at us with as much interest as we stared at them.

"Just as Ked said!" one of them remarked. "Who would have thought it! Tell me, your honors, which of you pulled a lad from the waters awhile back?" The Heathen accent is hard to understand. Their voices lift in all the wrong places. That was why I had not been able to understand the Heathen brat very well. You have to listen hard, as if you were deaf.

"Er—that was me," I said.

The Heathen raised frosty eyebrows at me. He had a very grizzled and important look. "The lad said it was a youth."

"I was wearing my brother's clothes," I explained.

"She was soaking, and she had to change," said Duck.

"If you think it's important," said Hern.

The Heathens heard us attentively, with strained frowns. I think they found us hard to follow, too. "It is important, your honors," said the grizzled one, "if I am to take the right one to the King." Then he gave an apologizing kind of cough. "Will it trouble you all three to come with us?"

It was strange that he was so polite. It ought to have made me much less frightened. But the men with the bows remained tense and alert, holding an arrow ready to fire and glancing from us to the land around all the time. Looking back, I think maybe that it was not us they intended to shoot.

Hern was very good all through. He did not understand what the man asked straightaway, but he made it seem as if he was considering. "We shall be pleased to see your King," he said, and pecked with his head, graciously.

"This way," said the Heathen. He turned and walked off. Another spear-carrier stepped in front of him, releasing his spear from his cloak. The spear proved to hold a flag full of all sorts of colored devices. We walked behind him over the sandy hills, feeling like part of the Shelling River Procession. I had only seen a flag used for religion before, but this one, as it clapped to and fro over our heads, held no religious picture that I could see.

It was not very far, onto higher land and crustier sand, where grew a stand of trees all bent as if to hold their backs to the sea. There, by another sandy river, was a collection of dwellings no larger than Shelling. As Duck said later, it would have frightened us to death if we had known our camp was so near the King of the Heathens—always supposing we had noticed the King's camp when we saw it. It was of tattered tents and driftwood huts, with rubbish thrown about. It was poor beside the poorest village I have seen since. Yet more flags flew from the rickety roofs as proudly and religiously as you please.

"What kind of King have we come to?" Hern said out of the corner of his mouth.

Duck and I did not feel so scornful. The bowmen could shoot us here as easily as in a palace.

The grizzled Heathen stepped into one of the tattered tents. We waited outside with the flag and the crossbows. Since it was a tent, we could hear what was said inside amid the rattling of the canvas. But we had difficulty understanding it.

I heard, "I have brought no less than three young mages, lord, not knowing quite what else to do." There followed talk I could not hear for the tent flapping. Then, "I think Ked told the truth for once, lord. I find them very hard to understand, and by their dress, they seem to have gone native." After this they spoke so rapidly that I was lost, until the messenger said, "I agree, lord. It may be just what you were wanting."

Meanwhile, we stood feeling slighted and uneasy. We did not know why the King should want us. We thought of Gull and of Tanamil. And we found it ominous that though there were numbers of Heathens about in the camp, they did not come crowding to see us, as people would have done in Shelling. I saw that women and girls kept quietly slipping across behind us to the sandy river, where they fetched water in iron pots. They could not all have wanted water at once. It was an excuse to see us. They were none of them as pretty as Robin, but I liked their clinging dresses. Men and boys were finding excuses to be about, too. Someone tidied a heap of rubbish. Someone came past with a tall horse. A boy staggered with a sack from one hut to another, and so on. We were being seen secretly all the time we waited, and it made us most uncomfortable.

At last the messenger came out and held the flap of the tent for us. "Please go in. My lord is waiting for you."

By this time we were used to the speech. We went in, all of us thinking of Gull and very suspicious. The King stood up to meet us. That was a politeness. But Duck had his mind so firmly on Gull that he said, "No one here's going to take *my* soul."

"I think you know more about that than I do," the King said politely. "Let me assure you that there is no question of that."

He was no older than Gull and not as tall as Hern. We stared at him awkwardly, and he at us. He was really very like Hern, except that he had a slender, unhealthy look, and I think he walked with a limp, though I am not too sure of this, because he was sitting down most of the time. Hern looked surprisingly tall and sturdy beside him. Hern, I am sure, has grown inches since we left Shelling. But they both had the same forward set of the head and the same sharp nose, and they both knew it, too. They looked at one another with strong interest—that interest which can be friendship or hatred at the drop of a pin.

"I am Kars Adon," this thin young King said, "son of Kiniren. The clans owe allegiance to me now my father is dead." He was not boasting when he said this. He spoke as facts, to let us know who he was. I marveled that he named himself Adon. It is one of the secret names of our One, and we do not say it openly. He added, "Perhaps you would like to sit down," and smiled awkwardly at us, before sitting down himself in a folding chair of studded leather and wood.

That chair was not fine, but it was the only good thing in the tent. In front of it, someone had arranged a tree stump, a milking stool, and a wicker basket. Hern sat on the milking stool, which I knew was a politeness because it put him lower than Kars Adon. Duck took the basket, and I sat gingerly on the stump. It rocked rather.

"Tell me," I said, "does your name have a meaning?" Kars Adon followed our speech well. "No," he said, with only a small pause. "It is just a name. Why?"

"Our names mean things," Duck explained. "I am Mallard, he is Hern, and she is Tanaqui. Our father was Closti the Clam."

I could see Kars Adon found this quite outlandish, but he was too polite to say so. "I am of Rath Clan, like Ked," he said, and seemed to look at us expectantly. "I must thank you for rescuing Ked from the River," he said. "I am deeply in your debt."

He meant it. From what he said, I thought the brat must be his brother. "It was nothing," I said, and I did not say what an ungrateful little beast he was. "Is he a near relation of yours?"

"I don't think so," Kars Adon said uncertainly. "He belongs to my clan, of course. But even if he didn't, I'd be grateful. There are so few of us now—" He sighed, but it seemed as if he felt it wrong to be sad. He sat up straight and smiled at us. "What Ked said when he came back made me decide to send for you," he said. "Forgive me. I know you mages are not subject to orders. But Ked swore that the person who rescued him had power to walk on the greediest waters and not only snatched him from the River's mouth but bound him to tell the truth about it. And when Arin fetched you, he saw with his own eyes all three of you walk where he would have been sucked down, and he knew that Ked had told the truth. And we all know," Kars Adon said seriously, "that anyone with power over that monstrous River is a mage indeed. Though I am inclined to think," he added, with a little twitch of a smile, "that forcing Ked to tell the truth shows greater power still."

I was getting truly uncomfortable. I could see Hern and Duck trying not to look at me and laugh. "I don't think we are mages," I said.

"Speak for yourself," Duck said, creaking on his basket. "Personally I have some quite uncanny powers." Sometimes Duck is as bad as Ked.

Kars Adon again looked at us expectantly, as if we were supposed to say something else. When we did not, he said, in an awkward way, as if he were having to remind us of a duty, "Before we go any further, you should tell me your clan and allegiances."

That was a bad moment. Duck and I did not know what to say. I half expected Hern to make up something since I could see he was in that kind of mood, but Hern still said nothing. The stump wobbled under me with my fear and shame. I was ashamed that Kars Adon should so confidently think we were Heathen like himself, and I was terrified he would find out we were not and kill us for it.

"Ked and Arin both said that your speech was strange and you dressed as natives do," Kars Adon said. "I can see that for myself. There are two things you could be." His face grew red under its Heathen brown as he said this. I think, by his standards, he was being very impolite. "You could be of a small Western clan, one of those who came here before we did. Forgive me. Or instead you are some of Kankredin's people." He thought he was being so rude that he could scarcely bear to look at us.

"Who is Kankredin?" said Duck.

Kars Adon was in quite a taking at this. He knew he had been rude, and he wanted to look away, but he was also so astonished that Duck had not heard of this Kankredin that he wanted to stare at Duck to see if Duck was pretending. Between looking and not looking, twisting his hands together, and fumbling at the clasp of his cloak, he made us feel quite as bad. "Kankredin," he said. "Kankredin is mage of mages. It is Kankredin in the ship beyond the sandbars. You must have seen the ship at least!"

Hern's head pecked forward at this. Duck said blandly—I never knew Duck was such a liar—"We suspected there was a ship there, but it was hidden in an enchanted mist."

"Yes, that is Kankredin," Kars Adon said eagerly. "We've been warned to keep clear of his mist. It was Kankredin I wanted to talk to you about. You see—"

"Just a moment," said Hern. "Before you go any further." Now Hern had not said a word up to then. He says he was absorbed in finding out what manner of person this Kars Adon was. "Before you say another word," he snapped out suddenly. And he jumped up from the stool and pounced to the opening of the tent. Kars Adon stared at Hern. This was real rudeness.

"Hern!" I said.

"Stand back there!" Hern said at the door of the tent, speaking very loud and slow. "I want to say something private to the King."

A great many voices made objection to this. I think everyone in the camp was standing there listening in.

"I know that," said Hern. "But you can guard him from where you can't hear. Get over near that hut, all of you."

There were more objections outside.

"What do you take us for?" said Hern. "We could have had the King to the top of the Black Mountains by now if we wanted. I swear to you we are not going to harm a hair of his head or a hair of his soul's head. But I must speak to the King alone. Now move away, all of you."

Feet shuffled off, from all round the tent. It must have been every Heathen in the place. Hern peeked a look round to make sure they had all gone, and then he came back inside. Kars Adon lifted his chin and gave him a haughty stare. I admired that. Kars Adon must have been afraid Hern was going to work all sorts of terrible enchantments on him, but he let Hern know who was King here. As for Hern, I could see him shaking at his own audacity. When he saw the King look, he went bright red.

"I apologize for that," he said, and sat on the stool again—I think his knees gave way. "I had to get them out of the way because I'm going to be frank with you, and I didn't want to be murdered on the spot. Before you tell us about Kankredin, I want to tell you that we are not of your people or of any clan of your people. We are natives, as you would say."

"Is it possible?" said Kars Adon. "You look as we do." He was really frightened now. So was I. When Hern launches himself on one of his rash ideas, you never know what will happen.

"My father's fathers," said Hern, "were born here by the River, as far back as I know. I wanted to tell you that, by way of friendship, and to prevent mistakes. Otherwise—well, you've already let us know there are not many of you, that your father is dead, that you're camped in a bad place without too much food, and in some trouble with Kankredin besides." This astonished me. But Hern was quite right. What Kars

Adon had not told us, we could see by looking at his camp. "So before you give away all your plans and secrets," Hern said, "I shall have to tell you we are your enemies. If I didn't, we'd have given ourselves away somehow, and you'd have killed us, and we'd have lost our chance to help one another. Aren't I right?"

"I . . . suppose so," Kars Adon said. He looked at Hern dubiously. He wanted to trust Hern, for whatever trouble he was in, but he was not sure at all. I did not blame him. I was not sure I trusted Hern either.

"So why did you send for us?" Hern asked.

"He probably doesn't want us anymore," said Duck. He thought Hern was mad.

"I think I do," said Kars Adon. "Only mages can understand a mage. I am sure you have the power to reach Kankredin in his ship. But I do not want to send enemies to him or tell you—" He did not seem to know what to say.

"Tell us as little as you can," I suggested.

"If this will help you," said Hern, "we were going to see Kankredin anyway. We just didn't know his name. And though we are your enemies by birth, our people do not love us. They think we are Heathens, too." It is hard to explain the bitterness with which Hern spoke. He must have been remembering Zwitt and Aunt Zara and Gull in anger for a long time. Kars Adon looked at him and wondered.

"What makes you a Heathen?" Duck asked Kars Adon.

"I don't know what you mean," Kars Adon said.

"Do you believe in the Undying?" I said.

Kars Adon smiled. "We've no use for dolls beside our fireplaces, if that's what you mean. The Undying are not clay figures. But when I die, I hope to be gathered to them."

This made me very indignant, but I could see, all the same, that Kars Adon did in some manner believe in the Undying.

"I will tell you," Kars Adon said suddenly, "since you know so much already. Kankredin has been all the while out on his ship, wrestling with the might of your River. But when my father was killed, he knew, and sent one of his mages to bring us here, where he told us to stay. He promised us that he would conquer the land for us, through the River. But while we wait here, those of us who have not been killed by the natives are being sucked in by the River. The River is a greedy and devouring monster. It has carried off all our ships, except one. Kankredin has angered it with his enchantments, and it rises in ever-increasing might. And we suffer for it, not Kankredin."

It really might have been Zwitt or Aunt Zara talking. But Kars Adon evidently believed it.

"I have known for some time that we must leave," he said.

"Will you go away home?" I asked hopefully.

"That seems the only thing to do," Kars Adon said. "We must build another ship and go. Now that my father is dead, my uncle will let us come back; they had quarreled, you see. It means that I must give up all claim to the throne and perhaps have both hands cut off, but I owe it to my clans." He seemed very calm about this. "But," he added sadly, "Kankredin will not let us out through the Rivermouth for any reason. I want to ask you to make him let us go."

"Fair enough," said Hern. "But what do you really want to do?"

"What do I want?" Kars Adon said. He lifted his head and stared at the gray flapping wall of the tent. "I want to go inland and found my kingdom there, of course. It is a wide country. There is plenty of room for us and the natives. I think there are certainly scattered bands from the clans between here and the mountains. I shall call them in and make a city. I don't pretend it will be easy, but someday we shall be a great people again." The way he said this made me think of flags flying over stone roofs and golden towers, and I really believed he could do it.

"That's a bit hard on us natives," said Duck.

"I shall make treaties with you. If you choose to fight, I shall win," said Kars Adon, lost in high dreams.

"Right. When do you start?" said Hern.

That brought Kars Adon back to earth. He put his chin down and looked bleakly at Hern. Hern looked bleak and chalky back. The windy air in the tent seemed full of flags and half-heard trumpets out of Kars Adon's thoughts.

"You want me to go to Kankredin and get his permission for you to conquer the country?" Hern asked, in his most jeering way.

Kars Adon was so angry that he stood up and took a limping step toward Hern. "I am not the servant of any mage!"

Hern stood up too, showing himself again much larger—not that this daunted Kars Adon. "That's more like it," Hern said. "Then what's keeping you here?"

Kars Adon glared at Hern. "The River. The River drowns anyone who tries to go inland. Tell Kankredin from me that he must leave the River alone."

"I shall do that with pleasure," said Hern. "We've already spoken to the River. You'll find the waters are going down." He could not stop himself from smiling as he said this.

Kars Adon smiled, too. He was so pleased that he put out a damp knuckly hand and wrung each of our hands in turn. "Thank you," he said. "I wish I could offer you a reward or something to eat or drink, but—" He paused a little blankly. I think the Heathen notion of gratitude was to shower food and drink on people, and possibly gold and silver, too, and it seemed to hurt Kars Adon that he could not do it. "I give my protection and friendship freely to all three of you," he said, rather lamely. "I suppose you'll go to Kankredin when the tide starts running out?"

It was lucky he said that. We still had no notion about the tides. I turned to Hern and said knowingly, "Now, the tide turns when?"

"Um," said Hern, pulling his chin wisely.

"It'll be around sunrise tomorrow," Kars Adon said obligingly, "won't it?" He knew all about tides. His people came from the sea. It was odd that he knew so little of the River.

"We'll set off at sunrise," Duck said, as wise as Hern.

"And so will we," Kars Adon said eagerly. "I shall have them strike camp tonight." His flags and trumpets were back. "We should be many miles inland by tomorrow night," he said.

After that we said good-bye with great politeness and went back to our island. Arin and his flag bearer did not come beyond the edge of the camp with us. They were too anxious to get back and find out what had been said. That was fortunate, because when we reached the channel, no one would have believed Ked and I had nearly drowned in it. It was nothing but a ditch of wet brown sand. They would have known we were not mages.

We could see the One's fire flaring beyond the hill of our island. "I hope Robin's all right," said Hern.

"And the One," I said. "Hern, what got into you?"

"I could see he liked straight dealing," said Hern. "And I took a risk. I wanted to find out about this Kankredin. And we did. I'm going to give him a piece of my mind tomorrow."

"But," I said, "you've sent him off—Kars Adon and his Heathens—to get slaughtered inland. Just those few of them can never last."

"We've done our people a service," Duck said complacently.

But Hern said, as we trod across the brown ditch, leaving pale footprints, "It was better than sitting on a sandhill dreaming dreams. If I was him, I'd never have gone there in the first place."

# 9

SUNRISE NEXT DAY came with a fine itching mist of rain. I was woken by miserable wet cats trying to get under my blankets. My clothes, which I had hung on the boat to dry, were wet as ever, and Robin, while she was no worse, was not better. And in spite of the rain, the One's fire was by no means out. It had fallen inward to a flat heap of charcoal, in which blackness and redness came and went as the rain met it, but it was as hot as it was the night before.

This was a serious difficulty. When the One is newly out of his fire, he is at his strongest, and I knew we should take him with us to meet Kankredin. The One signifies that he is ready to come out by putting the fire out and appearing among the ashes. He was not ready. We argued about what we should do. The argument was made more urgent by the sound of the tide racing seaward on three sides of us.

Hern said, "There's no need for anyone to go but me. You two aren't reasonable enough, anyway."

Duck and I refused to stay behind. Duck said he had bound himself to go, too. I wanted to confront Tanamil. "And suppose you're not back when the One is ready to come out?" I said. It had to be Hern, as head of the family, who took the One from the fire.

Then Hern suggested pouring water on the fire and taking the One out at once. That is Hern all over. I would not hear of it. Neither would Robin. By this time Robin had realized what we were intending to do. She started croaking—her voice had become like a raven's, as ugly as her face—on and on at us that we were not to go out to sea, that Mother would not like it, that we were not to go without her, and a dozen other objections beside.

She annoyed me. I am sure the reason we are stuck in this old mill, having failed at everything, is that I got so annoyed with Robin that morning. We should have waited until the One was ready to go with us. The Lady and the Young One were not strong enough alone. But I still think we were right not to take Robin. I do not think her soul would have been safe.

I jumped up. "Let's go," I said to Hern. "If the One doesn't want to come, it's his bad luck. He can stay with Robin." Robin sat up, with blankets sliding off her shoulders. "Lie down," I said to her. "You can't come. I'm wearing your skirt."

Robin was too ill to stand up to me. Normally she has a long, weak persistence, so that I end up losing. But she just lay down and cried.

"Now she's crying!" I said. "She cries like a weapon. Lie down, Robin." I was really horrible. Duck and Hern looked on, subdued. They wanted to see Kankredin too much to interfere. "Let's build her a shelter to keep the rain off," I said to them, "and then go."

The cats got into the shelter gladly. We put food and water in it, and Gull. Nobody argued about Gull. We knew he must stay. Robin was still tearful, but I am almost sure she was glad to be staying, too. We tucked her up where she could see the One's fire before we ran the boat down to the brown racing tide.

Though we put the sail up, it was the tide which took us and snatched us toward the sandbanks at the Rivermouth. It snatched so fiercely that I took up the Young One. I was afraid already. Duck had the Lady in his hands the moment the boat was in the water. Hern smiled scornfully, but he was shaking whenever I looked at him.

It was impossible to see far in the whiteness and grayness of the rain, but I think the River goes into the sea through many channels, among banks of sand and marsh. The place is miles wide, and low and wet. It was lucky Kars Adon had mentioned the tide because the place where our boat went through was shallow enough as it was. Without the race of the water, we would have run aground. We could not see any distance. Our boat drew on swiftly, drawing with it, as it were, the circle of what we could see. At first we saw water; then, on both sides, there was sticky, shiny marsh, sometimes like wet sand, sometimes covered with brown plants. Even in our small circle, there were more birds than I could count. I saw herons wading, River birds swimming and diving, geese, ducks, grebes, coots, and more gulls than I thought possible, glimmering white through the white rain. Everywhere came cries and squawks, splashings, and the beating of wings. And with every yard, our fear grew.

"I bet the fishing's good here," Duck said. His teeth chattered. Yet it felt hot and airless among the beating wings. The rain dewed our rugcoats and filled our hair, and we did not feel cold.

Then we saw something dark through the rain ahead. It was not a ship. We could see the darkness crossed our channel and ran off on either side. Black fear grew in us. We leaned forward, trying to see through the veils of rain. We saw what seemed to be a small boat being poled across in front of the obstruction, just at the limit of what we could see. It went slowly, but we could barely see it all the same. We saw the fair heads of Heathens in it. One was poling, the other stooping and flinging things from the water into the boat. They had gone, slowly to the right, before we could see more.

We knew—though I do not know how—that we had seen something terrible.

"Mother!" whispered Duck. "What were they doing?"

"Fishing, I should think," said Hern. But from the way he shivered in the heat and wet, he did not believe it.

"Let's go back!" I said. But the tide was taking us on all the time, and we could not. "Oh," I said, "why is the One in his fire just when we need him most?" We were slipping forward between the banks of croaking, splashing birds, and I still could not see what the black thing was across our way. I hugged the Young One to my chest and prayed to him to help us.

"Mother!" whimpered Duck again.

"Shut up! She's dead," said Hern.

We slid on. The white rain veiled us. Everywhere was white. We slid in a white circle on gray water, and even the marsh was hidden. I heard a duck croak and a gull cry overhead. My fear of gulls made me look up, but I could not see the bird. The rain seemed to have stopped. Not so fearsome, you think? Next moment our boat drifted upon two ducks, which flew off from almost beneath it, with a great outcry. And we could not see the ducks. You know how ducks run through the water, flapping, until at last they have speed enough to fly. We saw the splash and scuffle in two lines on the water, the spray and drips as the wings beat the surface on either side, and we saw the last splash as they rose on the wing. We heard their quacking. We felt the whir of the wings on our faces. But there were no ducks.

"What's happened?" whispered Duck.

"We've not gone blind," said Hern. His voice cracked. "We can see the water," he said. He was not steering anymore. He was crouched with one arm on the tiller, gazing as if he could force his eyes to see again.

The boat turned sideways and drifted on. I saw the deep V of a swimming grebe, and many scutterings upon the water. I heard birds overhead. But not a single one did I see until, without break or warning, we were out at sea and I could see the birds again.

The obstruction stood behind us. It was a great net, as high as a house, black as midnight and made in large squares. It was hung on posts as far as we could see in both directions, across the marshes and across the many trickling mouths of the River, from one shore to the other. The birds were in the mud behind the net, feeding and flapping as before. We could see them perfectly. In the distance, also behind the net, we saw the boat with the two Heathens in it, still at their strange business.

On the other side of us was wide blueness. The sea is a great field of water. Where it meets the sky, it is a darker blue. It is immense, too big for me. I was glad to fix my eyes on the long black ship moored to lines not far away. It swung on its ropes as I looked. There were two big eyes painted one on either side of its sharp black prow, with which it seemed to stare at us.

"Look, look! In the net!" said Duck.

There were things struggling against the net, on the River side of it. They were not clearly to be seen. They were large, for the most part, the size of geese or swans, and I think they were winged and of a pinkish color. Each one, as it came against the black net, struggled furiously to get through. We could see the struggle more easily than the thing which fought. Some were able to force themselves through the wide mesh. These flew off to the sea over our heads and were lost in the blue. Many, many more gave up the struggle and slithered down the net inside. The water there was full of their strugglings and floppings. It was these that the Heathens in the boat were collecting.

"People's souls," said Duck.

"I don't believe it!" said Hern, staring. "I don't *believe* it!"

Just then the Heathens in the small boat saw us. They shouted angrily and came poling back along the net. Hern quickly swung the tiller and let the wind to our sail. It was a fine breezy day out there. I think the rain and the mist were made by the net. In the breeze and the tide we raced toward the black ship and came in under one of its great eyes. I wanted to hide. It stared so.

"It's only paint," said Duck as he moored our boat to the great chain that held the black ship to the bottom of the sea. Hern hoisted himself up it, onto the deck. Duck looked at me and put the Lady into his shirt, under his rugcoat. I did the same with the Young One before we followed Hern.

The floor of the ship was black and smelled of tar. Overhead it was like a winter forest—ropes upon ropes hanging from masts that were trees braced with iron hoops. There was no one to be seen. But a number of large wicker baskets stood along the sides. Duck opened one. He sprang back, and so did Hern and I, when a host of the almost unseen winged things whirled up out of it, with a noise like roaring flames. They did not hurt us. They flew in a stream over the side of the ship and vanished seaward.

Before we had recovered from the shock of that, a door in the high black stern flew open. Heathens dashed out of it, shouting, "Who are you? What do you think you're doing?"

These were mages. I knew it. When Uncle Kestrel first told us of the Heathen enchanters and their battle spells, I had imagined ugly yellow-haired men with large mauve noses, creased cheeks, and crooked mouths. It surprised me that Tanamil and, later, Kars Adon were not like that. But these men were just like my imaginings. It makes me think a man does not become a Heathen mage unless he is too unpleasant to find friends any other way. They wore gowns that trailed, which they had to hold up as they ran shouting toward us. I was very frightened and clutched the Young One under my rugcoat.

I think Hern had learned from Kars Adon. He stood there calmly and bowed to them a little as they rushed toward us. This made them pause. They did not lay hold of us—as they had meant to when they first saw us—but they crowded threateningly round. With all those ugly faces so close, I do not think Hern was as calm as he looked.

"What do you brats want?" they demanded.

"We are mages with a message from Kars Adon," Hern said. "May we speak to Kankredin if you please?"

The ugly faces circled round us, arguing. "These aren't mages." "Yes, they are. They came through the net." "He won't want to be bothered with brats!" "Put a weight spell on them and tip them overboard." I was very confused. While they milled around us, I kept seeing words and scraps of sentences. Each of them had sayings woven in his gown. It seems they had this art, too. They were large words, and boastful. *I tortured the beast in*—I read. *I took the eyes off Sandar*. Then again:—*made jewels where none were in*—and—*three dead in one spell* and *I sent the hidden death*. It was enough to make one ill.

"Silence!" someone boomed at the other end of the ship. "What is this?"

"Three brats saying they're mages, sir," someone called.

"Did they pass through the net?" the voice boomed.

"Yes, sir. Ladri's shouting about it from the soulboat, sir."

"Then I suppose I'd better see them," roared the voice. "Bring them in."

We were hustled along the deck and through the door at the end. There was a room there with hammocks slung from big beams, but we went straight through that into another room right in the stern. This room had a big window looking on the sea, and one empty chair—a good chair, much better than Kars Adon's. They pushed us in front of it and stood milling behind.

"Some of you get out!" boomed Kankredin. He was sitting in the chair. It was empty till then.

I had thought, after seeing that net of souls, that nothing could frighten me anymore, but I was wrong. Kankredin was not Tanamil. He was not young. He was old—old in the way a stone is old, hard and lasting and as if he had never been otherwise. And like a stone when you turn it over in the earth, a coldness breathed off him. He froze my skin and lifted the hairs on my arms even before I looked at him properly.

It was not easy to look at him. The coldness of him numbed my eyes. I think he had a wriggly gray sheet of hair on either side of his face, and that the top of his head was bald and gray with dirt, with one or two big pink lumps on it. That is what you notice first when a person is sitting down. Then he lifted his face, numbingly, and it seemed to be a plump face, with the eyes thick-lidded, in folds. But as soon as I met his eyes, the face grew and removed itself, to seem large and faint and far away. Hern says he can still see it like that when he closes his eyes, but he cannot tell what he sees. It is the same for me. I remember his voice better, telling the mages to get out. It sounded out of his great chest and belly like the clapper in a bell. But it was a bell in the distance. The voice did not seem to come from Kankredin's mouth. It came clanging from a way off, sounding of fear and horror, defeat and death. As soon as I heard it, I knew we were standing in front of a great evil, and I saw we were mad to have come without the One.

The thing I saw most clearly was the gown Kankredin was swathed in. It was long and voluminous. Unlike the gowns of the other mages, his was woven all over with words, from collar to hem, and the words were much larger and looser than I would weave them. At first I could not look at those words. They leaped from the cloth, close and violent, as if they would do damage to anyone who read them. I had to turn my eyes aside. It was too hard to see Kankredin and too easy to see his gown.

I know Kankredin was not Tanamil. Yet I had, all through, a strong feeling that Tanamil was close by. I looked round for him among the other mages, but these had all left the room by then, except for *I tortured the beast* and *hidden death*.

"Well?" Kankredin clanged out, looking up at us. "You passed through the net without losing your souls, and I daresay you think yourselves mighty clever. What way did you do it?"

It came to me then that we had, most oddly, arrived on the far side of the net, but I could not say how this was. Duck said airily, "I think it may be a spell you don't know."

"There are no spells that I don't know," Kankredin thundered out of the distance. "Have you any means of stopping me taking your soul now you're here? Eh?"

"I don't know until you try," Duck said.

"Then we shall see," said Kankredin. "I see you fancy yourself as a mage, boy. Not much of a one, by the looks of it. What's that spell on the edge of that extraordinary native garment you're wearing?"

Duck lifted the sleeve of his rugcoat. Hern's and mine are plain, but Duck, because he was the youngest, has bands at the wrist, very faded now, which say *Duck* many times, in all the duck colors. Duck was annoyed to have such a babyish thing noticed. "Just my name," he said crossly.

"Pretty poor stuff, eh?" said Kankredin. "And a silly name. And you, girl—turn round and let me see it—what on earth is *that* on your skirt? Eh?"

I was very much ashamed, and angry, too. That skirt of Robin's is my worst piece of weaving ever. It says *A man came over the hill* muddle muddle *lady in the mill* muddle muddle. Then it takes a step down and goes, muddle *from the river* muddle *lived forever*. Terrible. In two broad bands round the bottom. The ugly mages both sniggered as they read it, and Kankredin chuckled. His laughter was as bad as his voice. It had such echoes of cruelty that it made me think someone was being tortured behind his chair.

"What kind of spell do you call that?" he boomed.

"It's a nursery rhyme!" I said angrily.

"In baby talk," said Kankredin. He turned, laughing and torturing, to Hern. "At least you have the sense to go plain," he said.

"I have a message for you," said Hern. It was an odd thing. Duck and I were never as troubled by Kankredin as Hern was. He was pale from the beginning, and before long, he was sweating and breathing heavily. Duck and I each had our Undying, of course, but I think Hern's trouble was more than that. Hern still thought he could fight Kankredin with reason. Reason was overthrown when we saw the souls struggle in the net, but Hern would not admit it. "I've come from Kars Adon—" he began.

"What does that stupid boy want now? Eh?" said Kankredin. He had a terrible way of saying "Eh?" It dragged at you for an answer and bullied you even if you meant to answer. If you resolved to say nothing, you still found you were replying to that "Eh?"

"I am to tell you," Hern said, as if he were struggling, "that Kars Adon is going inland today. He says—"

"He can go, and be eaten by the natives, then," said Kankredin. "I can't be bothered with him. If he had stayed, I'd have let him share my victory, but as it is, I'll make do with the natives. Was that all? Eh?"

"No," said Hern, struggling still. "I want to know what you think you're doing to the River."

"What impertinence is this?" Kankredin boomed, rising to his feet. "Eh?" The cold that came off him made us step back.

Now I must explain that I do not remember well what was said after this point because it was then that I started to read Kankredin's gown. I have to rely on Duck's memory, which is good, but not as good as mine. Hern confesses that from then on his mind felt as if he had his head underwater. His ears were roaring. He remembers little except a struggle with Kankredin to keep his soul.

My reading started first, idly, as Kankredin stood up. As I stepped back, I saw at his left shoulder *I, Kankredin, mage of mages, have set these spells to conquer and confound this land.* It was just level with my eyes. After that, I had to read on. *First I studied deeply*, I read, *to find where the soul and substance of the land lay, for there only may a land be truly conquered. And soon I came to conclude that the soul of the land lies in the one mighty river, which, with his tributary, waters all the country. This river*—this is correct, for he used all through the common weaving for *river*, not the one Tanamil taught me—*this river lies at his source, coiled, I conceive, like a snake or a dragon. Him I catch with this net of words, between sleeping and waking, and bind him fast. But his strength is not yet—*

Here Kankredin sat down, and the next lines were lost in the fold between his belly and his legs. I had to move on to his left thigh.

Meanwhile, Duck tells me, Kankredin was abusing Hern for daring to ask what he was doing to the River. "I am working night and day with the River, bringing his waters down to drown the natives, cleansing the land for us, and you have the gall to stand there asking what I *think* I'm doing!"

Duck answered, seeing Hern struggling and panting, that it was generally thought the River was angry.

"Angry? Of course he's angry!" Kankredin thundered. "He's fighting me tooth and nail. But I'm winning. I have him in a stranglehold, and he won't escape." Duck says Kankredin roared on in this way for some time. Duck listened scornfully because he was sure Kankredin had no idea of the truth about the River. This was just how I felt, reading Kankredin's gown, though Kankredin was saying one thing to Duck and another on his gown.

*—come to my terms*, was the next thing I read. *Thus I keep him tame and pull from him the vital strength of the land. But he has been cunning and fixed his strength in certain of the souls of his people. When I knew this, I sent forth my mages to battle to seek these souls.*

The weaving was large and loose. The next part was on Kankredin's right shoulder. *Then I put my first command on this river that he yield up to me these souls, which he was not willing to do. We strive, and he turns rotten with the effort, bringing sickness, for which I curse him—* Kankredin had pulled the gown up into folds here, at the top of his right leg. I stared and stared, but I could only pick out disjointed fragments at the surfaces of the folds—*refuses the land his waters . . . hides his souls from me . . . send forth greater strength . . . by this I invoke total power—*

"Why do you think I put up the soulnet?" Kankredin roared, as Duck tells me.

"To catch the natives' souls, I suppose," Duck said. "Did you know that quite a lot of the souls were getting through?"

This made Kankredin very annoyed, though he tried not to show it. "So you have mage sight," he said scornfully. "Quite a lot of people can see souls without being mages. Are you telling me to use a smaller mesh? Eh?"

"You'd catch more if you did," said Duck. "What do you do with them?"

"Never you mind," said Kankredin. "That net is a charm on the River, not a soul trap in any strict sense."

"I see," said Duck. Not that he did, he says. But he was enjoying himself, I could tell. I remember thinking, as I stared at Kankredin's gown, that I had seldom seen Duck more confident.

Then, pulled up on to Kankredin's thigh, I read: *and thus we took one with such a soul, outwitting the river by accident, I confess, since his captors had thought he was a clansman like themselves*. I knew he was talking about Gull. I read furiously. *The river would not yield me the soul of the lad, though we strove for three days. But I am cunning. I examined the lad and turned his soul about in my mind. I find his soul is more than the river. It is part of the ancient life behind the river.*

Here came the hem, drawn up above Kankredin's fat vague foot in a dirty sandal. The rest was on the back of the gown. I could have screamed.

I had to get Kankredin to stand up and turn round. I have never been so determined about anything. I looked at Duck and turned my hand round inside my sleeve, hoping that Kankredin would not notice. Duck understood. He had been trying to read Kankredin's gown, too, but he is slower than me, and he could see I was devouring it. So he gave me his daft look, which is his private way of saying, Yes, but it's not easy, and turned to Kankredin's two mages.

"Do you do illusions? Can you make yourselves look like somebody else?" I knew he was trying to find out if any of them had been disguised as Tanamil, and I wondered if I dared to shake my head at him. I was sure the back of Kankredin's robe would tell me.

Kankredin and his two mages gave out sounds of disgust. But this is exactly what they would do if they did not want us to know. Duck did not see it that way.

"Yes, but can you?" he said. "Can you stand up and show me?"

Kankredin saw there was some trick in this. He was terrifying clever. For a moment the fat shape of his face became near and clear to see. His thick lids folded down over his eyes, and he stared at Duck. Duck, for the first time, was troubled by his power. The front of his coat heaved as he grasped the Lady, and he gasped. "That'll teach you to bother me with silly questions," said Kankredin. "Won't it? Eh?"

At this, I thought suddenly: Why is he bothering to talk to us at all? He thinks we're just silly children. I looked at Hern, and Hern was beginning to look the way Gull had looked.

"Stop it!" I said. "Leave my brother's soul alone!"

"Not I," said Kankredin. "There's some strangeness in this soul." He looked full at Hern. Hern put his hands to his face as if he felt giddy.

Duck and I were both terrified. Duck took Hern's arm and pulled him away across the room. And Kankredin sprang out of his chair in a wave of cold air, roaring that Duck was not to meddle.

The next part was very horrible. I had a perfect opportunity to read Kankredin's back, but it was at Hern's expense. And it came to me then that if Kankredin's gown told the truth—and I think it did, as far as Kankredin knew the truth—Hern's soul, and mine, and Duck's were all like Gull's and could be used the same way. Kankredin stared under his fat lids at Hern, and Hern leaned against Duck, shaking. Duck put both arms round Hern and pressed the Lady against him so that they both had a bruise for days. At the same time, he says, he was willing Hern's soul with all his might to look normal—like Korib the miller's son's, like Aunt Zara's, even like Zwitt's. And I read Kankredin's broad back for dear life.

*Thus I, Kankredin, mage of mages, know how to rule the very soul of this land's soul. The river tries to keep the lad's soul from me, but I have bound the lad to come to me. I feel him approaching. He is near. By the power of these words and the hands of my mages, I now erect a soulnet across the mouths of the river wherein shall lodge the souls of all those dead in the land. These my mages collect daily. They shall be captive to me and learn to do my bidding, and I shall not suffer them to go out over the sea to their last home. But the lad who is coming to me will lodge in the net in his own body. Then through him I shall draw forth the soul behind the river's soul. When I have it, I shall come up the river, rolling it before me like a wave of the sea, and the land will lie captive at my feet. I, Kankredin, have spoken.*

I did not read his sleeves. They seemed to be spells from much longer ago. "Duck! Let's go!" I shrieked.

Kankredin turned and looked under his fat lids at me. I did not think we would be able to go.

"There's no mystery about us," I said. "We—we have to catch up with Kars Adon."

"That's right," Duck said quickly. "Take a look at our souls. Can't you see we're quite open and honest?"

"I've looked at your souls," said Kankredin. "Empty things they are. Suspiciously empty. His is not." He pointed to Hern.

"He's older than us," I said. "And I admit you're doing quite right to wrestle with the River. I think you're very clever. I think—" I would have said anything, anything.

Kankredin laughed at me, with his cruel chuckle, and looked at his two mages. "What shall we do?"

"They're absolute idiots," *hidden death* said, but he said it with a sour kind of slyness, meaning something else.

"Exactly," said Kankredin, agreeing to this something else. "All right," he said to us. "If you can get back through the net again, you're free to go. Go and try. I shall enjoy watching you."

I do not remember going out through the room with the hammocks. I think Kankredin hurled us out on deck, where Hern staggered about.

"You get the boat cast off," I said to Duck. "I'll bring Hern." I thought it would be like Gull all over again.

But Hern is tougher than Gull. As Duck raced down the black decking, Hern pushed me away and dived at the baskets ranged against the side. "You do the other side!" he shouted. He went staggering up the whole row, throwing up the lids. I am still amazed at Hern thinking of the trapped souls. But he must have known what they felt like. I threw back wicker lids on the other side of the ship. The roaring wings of the escaping souls mixed with the angry yells of the mages.

Kankredin's voice boomed through it all. "Let them be. We shall take vengeance for that."

The mages left us alone and stood watching as we went down into our boat. I took the tiller. We moved away from the staring eyes of the ship, before all the staring faces of the mages lining the side of it, and two more sitting staring in the soulboat nearby. We felt the jeers in the staring, but there seemed nothing we could do except sail for the net.

I was too shaken to manage the boat well, and the tide was against us. Duck took out an oar to help, but we still drifted crankily sideways. We could see mouth after mouth of the River passing behind the great black net, until the black ship looked small behind us. Then at last we drifted up against the net. A soul or two struggled in it above our heads, and we were just the same, going the opposite way.

Kankredin's voice boomed across the water. "Go on! Go through the net!" We knew he was playing cat and mouse with us.

"He'll fetch us back in a minute," said Hern. "We can't get through."

"We can try this," said Duck. He put the oar away and carefully took out of his shirt the pipes Tanamil had made for him. He saw the way I looked at him. He said, "I'm almost sure Tanamil isn't one of them. And it's worth a try even if it's using their own enchantment against them. Keep us going for the net."

Duck put the pipes to his mouth and played. His music was nothing like Tanamil's. It was bold and jerky and full of breath. But he had scarcely played half a tune when I looked up at the net and found its blackness misted over, with mist beyond.

Kankredin's voice boomed out. "Duck! Stop that silly piping. Stop it!"

Duck faltered and lost the tune. The net swung before me, black and clear. "Go on," I said. "It works!"

"I can't," said Duck. "Not with him shouting at me."

"Duck! Come here to me!" Kankredin boomed.

Hern looked up. "He's not shouting at you. Your name's Mallard. Keep playing, and don't be a fool. He's worried stiff we're getting away." Hern was right. The two mages in the soulboat were poling toward us as fast as they could go.

Duck played again, fierce and squeaky with haste. His face was red with it. The net turned from black to gray, and then it was not there.

We were moving forward in whiteness. In a moment, as before, there were birds all round us that we could not see. This time we were heartily glad of it. Duck played and played us forward into whiteness, until at last he had to leave off and lean over, panting. By then the net was behind us some way and the wide sands of the Rivermouth in front.

"You did it!" I said. "How did you know?"

Duck wiped the pipes and put them carefully away. "Everything goes away like that quite often when I play," he said. "I thought I was out of breath the first time. You know, I think I shall be a magician when I grow up. I shall be a better one than Kankredin."

"Hey! Tanaqui! Look where you're sailing!" said Hern.

He was a little late saying it. I was looking at Duck. We ran deep aground in a reed flat with our keel down, and we stuck. This was how we came to be captured by our own people. Maybe it was Kankredin's malice. I am sure it was my fault for leaving the One in his fire.

I am now at the back hem of my rugcoat. All I have space to say is that we are at a stand. Gull is still a clay figure. Robin is ill. I am afraid she will die. I sit with her in the old mill across from Shelling, with no help from my gloomy brothers. Even if Robin were well enough for us to run away, Zwitt would have us killed if he found us on our own. It is a bad thing to wish to run away from our own King, but I wish I could. Instead all I can do is weave and hope for understanding. The meaning of our journey is now in this rugcoat. I am Tanaqui, and I end my weaving.

# PART TWO

# *The Second Coat*

# 1

I AM TANAQUI. I must begin on a second rugcoat because understanding has come to me at last, and maybe I no longer need to blame myself.

My dream of my mother came to me again the night I finished the first coat. It troubled me. Why should my mother tell me to think? What should I think about except that I have wronged the One twice now? I started the first coat because of this dream, but when the dream came again, I began to suspect that my weaving was not enough. I am glad Uncle Kestrel brought me all my yarn, even that which was under the broken part of the roof. I still feel bitter about that. Zwitt need not have broken our house. But the wool has dried out now, and I think there is enough of every color to make another coat.

I will tell first how I wronged the One again. We were caught while we stuck on the mudbank because we had still not grasped the nature of the mud there. Hern jumped overboard to push us off and sank in it beyond his knees. He was so weak after our meeting with Kankredin that he could hardly struggle back into the boat, and he was very angry with me. I told him that it was because I had made them leave the One in his fire.

"Don't talk such nonsense!" Hern said. "It doesn't mean you have to steer straight into a mudbank."

We tried rocking the boat to loose it. The water trickled from the mud continually and held the keel fast. We should have seen from that that the mud was getting firmer, but we did not. We were too taken up with looking anxiously at the mist where the soulnet stood, thinking Kankredin was bound to follow us. No mages came. I think Kankredin had decided we were not worth the trouble. But we were taken completely by surprise when men of our own people came running over the mud from behind us and dragged us out of the boat, thinking we were Heathens.

We screamed that we were not Heathens, but they did not believe us and dragged us away a full mile over the mud and sand. All the while, they were saying things like "I look forward to hearing these squeal" and "I'm going to take it out on these for Litha. I'll make it long and sweet." I think we were all crying by the time they pushed us over the sand dune and into a camp of some size. We were desperate by then that they should know we were not Heathens.

Someone who saw us being brought in said, "You had a bit of luck, didn't you? I'll put you all down for a reward. Bring them along, and let's see what we can make of them."

They pushed us into a clear space where a great tree lay, dead and silver. The man who had spoken sat on this tree, and many others—the way our people do—came crowding from the tents to look. I heard someone call, "Come on, Jay! Heathens for lunch!"

The man who had hold of me—his name is Sard and I still do not like him—shook me and said, "Now you behave. This is the King. King, understand? He eats you Heathen for breakfast, he does."

I could hardly credit it, but it was indeed our King. I was nearly too awed to look at him. This was not, like Kars Adon, a boy and a Heathen. This was a true King. I took a quick look from under my hair. I saw a small plump man of about middle age. At one time, I think, he has been quite stout, but he lost flesh in the wars, they say. His face is still chubby, however, with a pout to the lips and a humorous twist to it. There were bags under his eyes, and his eyes looked bright and dark, twinkling upon the bags.

"Where were they?" our King said to Sard.

"Run aground on Carne Bank, Majesty," Sard replied, grinning. "I thought even Heathens had more sense."

Our King looked at us. "Where are you from? Where is your clan and how many are you?"

Hern stood with his head down, glowering at our King. "We're not Heathens," he said. Then Duck and I began to clamor at our King, trying to convince him we were not Heathens in every way we knew.

Our King leaned back and folded his arms, sighing. As we talked, I heard him say humorously to the man who stood behind him, "Why do they all make this fuss, Jay?" It was so clear he was not listening that I stopped talking in despair. Hern and Duck had stopped already. "Finished?" asked our King, twinkling his eyes at us. "Right. Now I don't like using unpleasant methods with youngsters, but I assure you I shall if you won't talk. I want to know where your camp is. Who's your chief, or earl, or whatever you call it? How many Heathen are you? Not that it will help much, as you seem to swarm like vermin, but still—we do what we can. Now tell me, and I may spare your lives."

"Majesty, we were truly born in Shelling, up the River," I said. Our King smiled. I cast about for a face that might believe me. All smiled. The man called Jay, who stood behind the King, smiled broadest of all. I knew him. He had only one arm now and his red rugcoat was gray and ragged, but he had smiled like that at Robin, when she stood with her arms all floury. "You came to Shelling," I said. "You took my father and my brother Gull to the wars. Don't you remember?"

"You saw me there," said Hern. "You said I was too young."

"I went to a lot of places," the man Jay said, smiling still.

"And you smiled at my sister," said Duck.

Jay looked at me and choked. "She's a bit young for me."

"Not that one, stupid! The other one," said Hern.

"I do smile at girls," Jay said, grinning widely. "I've even been known to wink at Heathens. They picked this up, Majesty," he said to our King, "from some poor soul they tormented."

"They must have done," our King agreed.

At that I became so frantic that I could think of only one way to convince the King I was no Heathen. "Look," I said, "I'll prove we're not Heathens. Here is one of our Undying." I dragged the Young One from the front of my shirt and held him toward the King.

Our King twinkled at me. "So you're a thief, too?"

"No, no!" I said. "Heathens don't have Undying. We have the Lady as well as the Young One." Duck scowled at me and shook his head, but I went on. "The greatest of our Undying is the One. I can't show him to you because he's in his fire at the moment—he always has to go in his fire when the floods go down—but please believe me!"

"A nice story," said the man Jay.

But our King leaned forward, with a twinkle of interest in his eyes and only the barest smile on his face. I have never known him quite without a smile. "This One of yours," he said. "What color is he?"

Hern and Duck both glared at me, but I said, as if I could not stop, "Dark, with glistering specks, but—"

"Shut up, Tanaqui!" said Duck.

"—but he changes each time he goes in his fire," I said.

Our King gestured to Duck that he was to hold his tongue. Then he leaned to me further, and said, "Name me his secret names."

"They're secret," I said. By this time I was horrified, but it was like the rapids at the end of the lake. I had gone too far to stop.

"Come here and name them in my ear," said our King.

I am ashamed when I weave this, but I did so. I went up to our King—he smelled of sweat and horse and, just a little, of cloves—and I whispered, "He is called Adon and Amil and Oreth." That is how I wronged the One. But I went on and wronged him further because when the King asked me, I told him the One's fire was on our island and that Robin was there, unwell, too. And I described which our island was, in spite of the way Hern and Duck looked at me.

Our King sat back and puckered his face toward Jay and the others nearest him. "Well, what do you think?"

"There's quite a nest of Heathen over there," one of them said. "It looks like the perfect trap to me."

"I know," our King agreed. "But let's say curiosity killed the King. Or that somebody slipped up in Shelling last autumn. Jay— Oh, I forgot. Can you manage one-handed?"

"Provided the remaining hand's tied behind my back" was Jay's reply.

"Good," said the King. "Tie your hand up, take ten men and the best boat—and the elder boy, I think—and let him show you the place. Bring back anything you find there."

"I'm glad you said me," Hern said. He spoke very rudely because he was angry with me. "I'd have had to ask you to send me if you hadn't. I'm head of the family, and it has to be me who takes the One out of the fire."

"Oddly enough, I thought of that," our King said to him. "And I thought the other two could stay as hostages for your good faith. Move, Jay!"

My punishment was that I never saw the One taken out of the fire. The King's camp was right on the other side of the Rivermouth from our island. Duck and I had to wait two hours for Jay to cross and come back. We sat on a sandbank watching the King's men bustling in the camp. Their tents are good, in many colors, but the people are few—not more than fifty, all men. It ought to have seemed more warlike than the poor huts of Kars Adon, because there were no women, no rubbish heaps, and no children but Duck and me, but it did not, and never does. It is more as if our King were traveling for a holiday.

While we waited, Duck was so angry with me that he only spoke once. "Did Kankredin's coat say how we can get Gull back?" he said.

"No," I said. "It said Gull was coming to him. The net is to catch Gull, and he's waiting for him before he conquers the country. And it can't be wrong to tell our own King about the One."

"If he thinks Gull's still on his way," Duck said, "then I was right, and Tanamil isn't one of his mages. And you know we're not supposed to talk about the One to anybody." And he said nothing else.

At last there was a great shout that the boat was coming. Everyone, our King included, went running through the hills of sand to the shore. We ran with them. We were part of the crowd jostling on the shingle, and we helped to pull the boat out of the falling waves. It was large and high. Jay appeared head and shoulders above the gunwale.

"Well?" said the King.

"Everything as described," said Jay. "This is the list—start unloading. Three cats." Sweetheart, Rusty, and Ratchet were dropped down beside our King. They were ruffled and not pleased. Our King looked at them in amusement. "Ten blankets," said Jay, and these were dropped on the shore, too. "Two sacks, containing cheese, dried fish, and onions mostly." The sacks followed our blankets. "And," said Jay, "one sick young lady."

I thought they were going to drop Robin on the shore, too. In fact, they lowered her very carefully, and Hern climbed down to make sure she was safe. They had wrapped her in Jay's rugcoat. She was worse again. She says it was the shock of Jay's coming, on top of worry about us. I put a blanket round her as she shivered on the pebbles, and she cried because Duck and I were still alive.

"And?" said our King, holding out his hand to Jay. "Nothing else?"

"With her," Jay said, nodding down at Robin.

It seemed that Hern had no sooner taken the One from his fire than he gave him into Robin's hands. Robin would let nobody near him. I could not think why Hern had done this, until Hern said, "Come and see," and beckoned Duck over, too.

Robin unwrapped her hand from the great folds of Jay's rugcoat and showed us the One clasped in it. He was gold. He shone all over with a mild orange luster and seemed to be made of metal. Hern and Robin could understand it no more than we could. Hern said he had found the One shining even more brightly in the ashes of the fire. He had dulled a little in the air since. And, Hern says, there was such naked greed on the faces of Jay and the others that he gave the One to Robin, instinctively as it were, to keep him safe. How he thinks poor Robin would be able to keep the One if somebody twisted her wrist, I do not know. She has Gull to keep, too, wrapped in her own rugcoat, and no one knows of him but us four.

Up to this moment Robin has most valiantly fulfilled Hern's trust. She wrapped the One away when the King came up and refused to let him be seen. A faint pink came into her pale face at having to treat our King so, but she was firm.

"He is not to be bandied about and looked at by everyone," she said.

"If you all came into my tent and looked at him over supper?" our King suggested. "I could set up a hearth to make him feel more at home."

Our King was being very polite now, but Robin looked at him severely. She is not used to people making jests all the time, the way our King does. But she agreed.

Our King insisted on a polite and lavish supper. It was a trial to Duck and me, though not to Hern. Hern likes eating and does not care about manners. It was a trial to Robin, too, because she was not really well enough, but I was glad she was there. People believe Robin. When she said we were not Heathens, our King assured her it had been an unfortunate mistake.

"May I see the One now?" he asked when we had eaten fish and meat. There was a pause then, before they brought in chickens, eggs, and sweetmeats. No wonder our King is chubby.

Robin reluctantly brought out the One and stood him on the table among the King's fine dishes. He was the finest thing there. Our King put out a hand to him, looked quizzically at Robin, and at last picked him up. We could see the One was heavy. Robin says he weighs twice what he did.

"Solid gold!" said our King. "I swear to it! This is his latest change, is it?" We nodded. Our King carefully turned the One around to have his face beneath the lamp. Now that he is gold, the One's features are much easier to see. He has a strong nose, a little like Hern's or Gull's. The King saw this. I saw him look at Hern's profile. "How long has this fellow been in your family?" he asked Robin.

"For as long as anyone knows, my father told me, Majesty," Robin replied.

"Hmm," said our King. "Your family must once have been a very important one, young lady, did you know that? And you truly put him in a fire every year after the floods?"

"Every year," said Robin. "My father said we have never once missed."

"That was the sign by which I knew him," our King said, turning the One over. "You have been faithful to the bargain your ancestors made with him. Do you know who he is, this golden gentleman?" He waved the One toward us, from side to side, not wholly respectfully.

"Yes," I said. "He's the One."

"That's a silly sort of name," said our King. "You told me his real names earlier. My fluffy-haired maiden, he is the River—the great River himself! What do you think of that?"

"I think it isn't true," I said.

"Oh, yes, it is true," said he, still waving the One about. "We Kings have a hard time of it and have to put up with a great deal from our subjects—flat contradictions from little girls, among other things—but our reward is that we are told more than most people. I know about your One. As a matter of fact, I had him searched for when the Heathen came. If only Jay had found him when he came to Shelling, I wouldn't be in this pickle now. He could have got us out of it. Only fancy him turning up like this! You'd almost think he did it on purpose. What do you think you're playing at, you stupid golden beggar?" he said to the One. "It wasn't nice to hide away!" This was not quite a joke—or only a joke in the way that everything our King says is a sort of joke. I could see Robin was shocked.

"How do you know he's the River?" Hern asked bluntly. I could say that Hern was tired out after our day's troubles, and it would be true. On the other hand, I have never once heard him speak respectfully to our King.

"Knowledge is handed down from King to King," said our King. "When our people first came to this land, there was a Queen called Cenblith, who may have been a many-greats-grandmother of yours as well as mine, I think. She found a way to bind the River to the service of man. They say she was a witch. I think it just as possible she was simply very pretty, and the River fell for her like a waterfall. Anyway, he submitted to be bound. He agreed among other things to support our people in battle with his not inconsiderable strength, which strength he obligingly let Cenblith put into this small image of himself. But he made one condition: that he be put into a fire once a year. When his dross was purged and he turned to gold, then he would be at his utmost power. And here he is, golden and too late!" The King's eyes twinkled almost as if they were wet, as he looked at the One between his hands.

I remember looking at the One and wondering about the great floods and Kankredin's struggle with the River. I still do not believe the One and the River are the same—or not quite the same.

"He was daft to let himself be bound," Duck said.

"I agree, but I am very glad he did," said our King. He held the One up toward the colored roof of the tent. "Now we can prosper and succeed together," he said. "Now I've got you, you slippery golden beggar!"

"Majesty," said Robin, "the One is ours."

"So he is, young lady," said our King. "You shall stay with me and keep him for me." He passed the One to Robin. "There. Back to his rightful guardians. Keep him safe. We have a lot of traveling before us, now the floods are down."

And travel we did that next morning. This is what has made Robin so ill. She has been hurried here and bumped there and made to sit in the rain until the King is ready. After the first day's travel our King had his physician see her. He said it was the River fever and, as she had had it once, she would soon be well and was quite fit to travel. It is this same physician who took off Jay's arm. Jay says if it were not for that physician, he would still have two arms. I share Jay's opinion. Robin does *not* get well, even resting.

The King has taken a fancy to Hern. He gave him a pony to ride, while the rest of us bumped and creaked in the baggage carts. Every evening, I had to attend to Hern's saddle sores, before I could see to Robin. Now I know why Robin so often exclaimed "Why does nobody help me!" Everything falls on me. For the rest of the day the King has Hern beside him. "Fetching and carrying," Hern calls it. He is not in the least grateful. The trouble is, our King loves people who are rude and familiar with him. This is why he is so fond of Jay. So the crosser Hern is, the more the King admires him.

Hern is in a black mood. He does not show half of it to our King. He says he went down the River to rescue Gull or avenge him. He did not believe in enchantments. Yet first Tanamil and then Kankredin defeated him with spells. He could do less than Duck or I could. He was forced to admit that enchantments exist. This has damaged his respect for his own mind.

"But enchantments are of the mind, too," I said.

"Not of *my* mind," said Hern. "That's why I'm a failure. I wasn't even sure people had souls. Then I saw the souls in the net and knew I was looking failure in the face. It's an awful feeling." Yet that was not the whole story, as I found out later.

Duck is gloomy, too, because he is bored.

All this while our King hastened with us across the country. He does not stay near houses or in any one place for long, for fear of the Heathens. Whenever we come to a farm or a village, the King's men knock at doors and run into houses shouting that the King has come. If the place is empty because of the floods or the Heathens, they take what they can find. When there are people, the King orders what he needs. The people often protest; I know how we should feel if they came banging at our door and carried off all we had saved from winter before the supplies had grown again. The King promises payment and takes so much that we sit high up in the carts on piles of corn and dead sheep.

Collet is our King's memory man, and he memorizes the debt. He tells me that he holds many thousand payments in his head, for food or promised rewards. He does not think they will ever be paid.

It was very rough traveling after the floods. Robin suffered more and more because after a while she became too weak to get out and walk in the worst places. "I can't *stand* this anymore!" she said one evening when the sun was down, but we still went jolting on.

Hern had looked in on us, and he saw how ill Robin was. He went and asked the King if we could stop.

"Oh, the light's good for miles more yet," said our King. "Besides, there seem to be Heathens coming up behind." Our King gets news of Heathens from everyone we encounter. And we went on.

I was so angry that I jumped down from the cart and ran among the horses to the King. "Majesty," I shouted. "The One wants us to stop here!"

I did not think the King would listen, but he did. We stopped at once. After that I chose our camping place every day, speaking for the One. We spared Robin a good deal of jolting like that. It amazes me that our King believes I know the One's wishes, but I think it is the one thing he takes seriously. I have become spokesman for the One. Every day the King asks me jestingly, "And what has the golden gentleman to say to me today, fluffyhead?" I could tell him anything.

"If he believes you, he'd believe anything!" Hern said scornfully.

Our King, of course, talks to everyone, freely and cheerfully, but he talked to me much more after that. I cannot be familiar with him. The weight of kingship and all our Kings before him makes him a heavy matter to me. Our position oppresses me, too. We cannot be called prisoners, yet what else are we? So when he makes his jokes, I do not laugh.

"Fluffyhead, you do come of a serious-minded family," he said to me one day, in a brown field, where the grass lay plastered down with mud in long ripples. "Can't you laugh? I know you've had your troubles, but look at me. I've lost my two sons, my wife, and my kingdom, and I can still laugh."

"I expect you're looking forward to conquering the Heathen and getting your kingdom back, Majesty," I said, "and I'm not."

"Great One!" he said, twinkling his eyes at me. "Do you think so, solemn face? I gave up that idea months ago. The most I hope for is to save my skin until I can get a new heir. It will be my son who benefits from the One's help, not me."

I thought this was just his joke at the time, but it has now become clear to me that our King has indeed no intention of fighting the Heathen again. He inquires daily about the Heathen, but this is in order to avoid them.

Many times it has been on the tip of my tongue to tell him that the Heathen he is running from is only Kars Adon—though I think there are other little bands, too, as Kars Adon said—and that the real menace is Kankredin. But I have not said. Kars Adon is a Heathen and an enemy, but his way is better than our King's. I do not blame our King. Jay has told me how terrible the wars were. But I will not tell him about Kars Adon. Duck will not tell him either. He says our King bores him, and nobody can do anything about Kankredin. As for Hern—well, I found out when we had news of Kars Adon at last.

Summer drew on us as we traveled. We approached the River again, which seemed to revive Robin, and came into the hills at the end of the great lake. The lake was beautiful. It was blue as solid sky. The many trees around it were reflected upside down in the blue. But it was spoiled for me by the people there. They said we were Heathens and stoned us. Duck has a scar from it which will last all his life.

Jay stopped the stoning by saying we were Heathen princes under the protection of the mages. Robin was very angry with Jay.

"What should I have said, lady?" Jay asked. "You try telling them the truth."

While we were there, some men came over the broken bridge, very pleased with themselves. They had fought Kars Adon. They knew it was him by the flags. Kars Adon's people had been surrounded in a valley across the River. Numbers of them were killed before they could fight free.

"Why didn't you kill them all?" our King asked pleasantly.

Hern told me this with a pale face. "The *fool*!" he said. "The stupid fool! Fancy getting himself penned in on low ground!"

Now I know the other part of Hern's misery. As Hern has failed in what he set himself to do, he has taken comfort in the dreams of Kars Adon. He knows it is wrong—that is why he is so moody—but he cannot help himself. I had often wondered why Hern listened so eagerly to the King's daily messages about the Heathen.

He was hoping for news of Kars Adon. Now we have it, it is bad news. Poor Hern. It is lucky our King does not intend to fight the Heathen. Hern would be on both sides at once.

# 2

WE JOURNEYED THROUGH forest beyond the lake. Robin was bounced over tree roots and thrown out of the cart once. It seemed to me that much more of it would kill her.

"Go and tell the King the One wants us to stop until Robin's well," said Duck.

It was an excellent idea. "Suppose I tell him the One wants us to be left behind in an empty cottage, on our own?" I said.

"He won't do that," said Duck. "He wants the One." He was right.

Our King readily agreed to camp until Robin was well. "Still looking very peaky, isn't she?" he said. He pointed through the budding green. "Suppose she rests up in that old mill over there. We'll camp outside, and the village over the River can send us food. We'll give her a week or so. There don't seem to be any Heathen in these parts."

I had no idea we were near the River. It was all forest to me. Imagine my surprise when I found it was the mill across the River from Shelling—the one that is haunted by a woman, that they say the River forbade them to use. I told the King it would do perfectly. I hoped I would see Zwitt's face when he knew.

Jay went over to Shelling in the punt Uncle Kestrel keeps on the millpond and gave them the King's orders. Shortly Zwitt and some other people came over in boats, bringing a few things and protesting about the rest. I think food was short. The floods had been in all the gardens. But Zwitt would protest if he was sitting on a heap of vegetables a mile high and someone asked him for a carrot.

Zwitt saw Hern with the King and knew him at once. He asked to speak to the King alone. I looked out from the mill and saw them walking together among the forget-me-nots by the millrace. Zwitt, by his face, was uttering dire warnings. Our King was laughing and patting Zwitt on the back. I see why our King was so pleased. Now he knows that we told the truth and the One is indeed the One. I think he came to Shelling on purpose. It is what I would have done in his place, I suppose, but my heart is heavy. He will never let us go now. Hern says Zwitt made the King promise him twice as much as usual, as a fee for leaving us alone. But promises are easy.

"Your friends across the water tell me you put bad spells on them," Jay said to me. "Are you a witch?"

"I wish I was. I'd—I'd turn their feet back to front!" I said.

"Temper, temper, now!" said Jay.

I am still very bitter. From upstairs in the mill, where I sleep, I can see the ruins of our house. Zwitt did that. It was to soothe my bitterness and my worry about Robin that I began to long to weave. Then came my dream. Then Uncle Kestrel.

We made Robin a bed in the dry room on the ground floor. It has a door, for loading flour, which opens onto the River, and I have this open in the daytime so that Robin can see the River. All the time I have been weaving it was at its most beautiful. The water is a deep, shining green, like an eye in the light. It flows lazily, slowly. The sun slants down in beams and turns the water green-gold. Midges circle in. Every so often a fish leaps, or a willow bud falls heavily and swims to the doorstep. But Robin does not enjoy it. And I find it so hard to be patient with her.

That first day I was near shaking her. As we were settled, I wanted Gull with us, where I could see him. If we exchanged him for the Young One, no one but us would know the difference. Robin unwrapped Gull and let me have him. But she would not have the Young One in exchange.

"I won't have him near me," she whined. "Take him away."

I have had to hide the Young One in my bed upstairs. If I even speak of him, Robin begins to cry. And yet she clings to the One so that even I hardly get a glimpse of him. The King came in that evening—as he comes every evening—to inquire after his "golden gentleman." Robin would not let our King look at the One at all.

"I wish the King would leave us alone," she said.

Then Sweetheart put a mouse on her bed, and you would have thought it was a poisonous snake. Then Jay came in. Jay made a lot of noise and merriment. He says laughter cures. But the reason he came, I saw of a sudden, is that he is courting Robin. I was shocked. It does not seem right when Robin is ill. Jay is quite old and has loved many women. He boasts of it. That shocked me, too. But I like Jay all the same. My head was in a muddle about it.

"Do you like Jay enough to marry him?" I asked Robin when Jay had gone.

Robin shuddered. "No! I can't bear the way the stump of his arm wags about!"

It is true. Jay's stump of arm seems to have a life of its own. I do not like to look at it either. "Don't you like him at all?" I said. "He likes you."

"Don't talk about it! I don't want him! I shan't ever marry!" Robin said frantically. I could have kicked myself. It was gone midnight before she was calm enough to go to sleep.

When she did, I opened the door to the River and sat thinking. It seemed to be all my fault, this, because I had twice wronged the One. As I sat, I thought I saw a light in the River. I knelt in the doorway and stared, terrified, down into the green-gold depths of the water. There was a huge shadow there, like a man with a long nose and a bent head. If it had not been that I had only just got Robin to sleep, I would have screamed. I was sure it was Kankredin.

"That one-armed jokeman says my Robin is poorly," Uncle Kestrel said. He was rowing toward the door with a tiny light in his boat. Where my shadow came from, I do not know.

It did me good to see him. "It's no good going for mussels," I said. "The King's camp is by the millpond."

"I know that, my love," he said. "I came to see how you all did."

I knelt on the doorstep, crying a little, and told him about our travels, our King and the One. But I did not tell him about Gull. He thinks Gull died on the way.

"Kings and Undying are like that," said Uncle Kestrel. "They take no account of the trouble they cause. You make sure to keep Robin here until she's well. That's what matters. Is there any little thing I can get you from your house?"

"You're the only person in Shelling I love!" I said. "Did they break my loom as well as the roof?"

"Now don't get so fierce," he said. "They did not. They only took their feelings out on the walls and roof." Then he said something that has made me angry ever since. "I'm not excusing them," he said, "but you gave them provocation, you know, even Robin. You all knew you were different, and you acted as if you were better. It made for hard feelings." I was too angry to speak. "You want your loom brought?" he said, and I had to forgive him.

"And my bobbins and my shuttles and my needles and my spinning wheel," I said. "And don't forget my yarn."

"You're trying to sink my boat!" he said. "Sometimes you sound just like your aunt." But he brought them, every one, and my spindles, which I had forgotten to ask for. I have never seen a boat so packed with wool. The loom was perched on top. I had to wake Duck to help me drag it indoors. He could not think what I was so excited about, but I think Uncle Kestrel understood.

Since then I have been weaving, unless Robin finds the noise too disturbing. The King is amazed at my industry. Indeed, I am often very tired, though it gets easier and easier. But I am afraid Robin will die, and I weave to take my mind off it. I pretended to myself that when the coat was finished, Robin would be well, but she is not. Then as soon as it was finished, I dreamed once more that my mother was telling me to think. And I found I had it all to do again.

The morning I started this second coat, Duck lost patience with me. Lately, because he is so bored, he has been spinning for me, and he was at work outside by the millwheel, which has clumps of forget-me-nots growing all over it. "Of all the boring, stupid, gloomy people!" Duck said. He flung the spindle down and waved his arm at the sun-scattered brightness over all the green growing things.

"Look at it! Look at you! You're even worse than Hern!"

I burst into tears and said I hated the King.

"Who cares?" said Duck. "He's keeping Gull safe, and us safe from Zwitt. What more do you want?"

"It's all my fault," I sobbed. "I betrayed the One to him. And I made you leave the One in his fire when we should have taken him to Kankredin. If we'd had the One then, everything would have been different."

"You're just letting yourself be taken in by what the King thinks," Duck said. He took up the spindle and poked moodily in the ground with it.

"I know I didn't obey the One," I said.

"Yes, you did! Don't be a fool," Duck said, stabbing with the spindle. "The One *arranged* it that way! He wasn't strong enough to meet Kankredin. If we'd waited for him, he probably wouldn't have come out of the fire at all. The One alone knows what would have happened if Hern had poured water on it!"

"Stop ruining my spindle," I said. "Are you calling the One a coward?"

Duck looked sideways at me through his hair. He ties it back with a band, but it always falls round his face in white tendrils. "No," he said, and he squatted there, using my spindle to draw patterns round a clump of grass. He reminded me of someone. "The One is deep," he said, "like the River. Tanamil knows. He's the one we should have asked."

"So you understand it all?" I said scornfully. "Tell me."

Duck looked sideways again. "You wouldn't believe me unless you'd worked it all out yourself, anyway."

I knew who Duck reminded me of—Ked, the ungrateful Heathen brat, when he was lying. I wanted to throw him in the mud in the empty millrace for making fun of me. I shoved him over sideways instead, for spoiling my spindle, and went raging into the mill.

I was so angry that I took my rugcoat off the loom and carried it to the River door to read for myself, by my own account, that Duck was talking nonsense. First, I held it up and looked at it. It is a very handsome coat in gloomy colors, touched here and there with bright yellow and burning red. It is also very large. In the front the gloomy colors gather up the center into a shape, and that shape is the same shadow with a long nose and a bent head that I saw when Uncle Kestrel came. I turned it round hastily, when I saw it. There is a lightness on the back that begins from the time we met Tanamil. I did not see that the same shape was there at once. But it is. It is made of grays and sallow greens, which are harder to see. Across the neck of the long-nosed shadow, near the hem, runs a band woven in that expressive twist which Tanamil showed me. It expresses my terror of Kankredin and his soulnet. Nothing else goes right across the coat, except the place where I unpicked my long lament for my father. I do not think even Robin would see this unless I told her it was there.

I was so frightened when I saw that double shadow that I dropped the coat. My skin crawled, and I wanted to wake Robin. But I said to myself, I made this weaving. I wove in it that it held the meaning of our journey. No one is frightened of a thing they made themselves. Read it, Tanaqui, and find out what you meant.

I knelt on the floor, in the doorway, and read what I had woven. It took nearly all morning, even though there were places I moved over very rapidly, remembering what I had woven. It was comforting at first. Here were we all, Robin, Hern, Duck, and I, and poor Gull, being ourselves, and there was my own beloved River in his grandest time, being as usual a part of our lives. And I noticed many things. I have thought about them all these three days I have been weaving my second coat.

I had read down to the place where we found the cat Sweetheart when I could have sworn I heard a seagull cry. I looked up at the red, sandy Gull, beside my loom, first. Then I looked out over the leaf-speckled green River. There were no seagulls near Shelling. I thought I had imagined the sound, from reading about the gulls on Sweetheart's island.

Then Sweetheart herself jumped down the ladder to the upper floor. Cats often appear when you think of them. It is one of their strange ways. Sweetheart was carrying a mouse. She jumped on Robin's bed to give it to Robin.

I knew what Robin would think of that when she woke. I got up to take the mouse away. And moving upright gave me a sight of the other bank of the River, just below the last house in Shelling. I saw Zwitt under the clump of hawthorns there—the may is over now—and another man moving to meet him, as if secretly. This other had darkened his light hair and further tried to disguise himself with a garish rugcoat—and a shoddier piece of weaving I seldom saw—but I knew him by his mauve pointed face and crooked mouth. He was Kankredin's mage, the one with *hidden death* in his gown. I could see the gown looped up under the dreadful rugcoat.

I dared not move while he talked to Zwitt. I was halfway across the dark room by then. And there was my coat, laid out in the doorway, in the full light above the River. Zwitt was nodding, talking eagerly, and pointing directly at the mill. He was telling *hidden death* where we were.

"Tanaqui!" Robin called out fretfully. "Sweetheart's put another mouse on my bed!"

"Ssh!" I said. "She does it because she likes you."

"Take it away," Robin said. "Take it *away*!"

"Oh, please shut up," I whispered. "Something awful's happened!"

The mage turned his crooked face toward the mill and saw my rugcoat. I saw his face change with fear. He leaned out across the River, staring, as if he were trying to read it. As he was a mage, perhaps he *was* reading, with his eyes on two invisible horns, like a snail. I wanted to snatch the coat away, but I dared not let him see me. I stood helpless. Robin, who is no fool, even ill, lay quietly and stared at me as anxiously as I stared across the River. And at last the mage turned away downstream, and Zwitt went back toward Shelling. I took my rugcoat and hid it under Robin's bed, until I could finish reading it elsewhere.

I told Robin. I would like to weave a curse on Zwitt because of the panic and terror Robin has been in. She said we must get away at once. She got up and fell on the floor. I yelled for Duck, and luckily Hern came, too, and we got her back to bed. We are all very frightened. We know we should tell the King that the One says we must leave, but we are afraid Robin will die if we do. And as Duck pointed out, Robin's soul will be caught by Kankredin's net, which is just as bad as if he had caught Gull. We do not know what to do. Duck and Hern have kept watch these last three days, but the mage has not come back. We think he has gone to Kankredin. Hern says this gives us seven days or so. In that time I *must* cure Robin. I have inklings already.

As soon as Robin was settled, I set up new warps in my loom. This was because of the understanding that came to me when the mage was afraid of my weaving. When mages weave, what they weave is so. That is why his gown shows *hidden death*. That death, to whomsoever it was sent, *is* the very words that boast of it. It is the same with Kankredin's gown. The River is bound, Gull's soul endangered, and the soulnet set up by Kankredin weaving those words.

My weaving is a performing, too. I am sure of it. When I compare my close and intricate weaving with that of the mages, so loose, large, and crude, I know I am a greater weaver than they. Setting up my threads, I felt very vengeful and vainglorious. I meant to curse Zwitt, to weave that our King became serious and courageous, and then to say that Kankredin and his net crumbled into the sea. That is why I put in my wish that I could turn the Shelling people's feet the wrong way. I am quite relieved to look across the River and see that their toes still point to the front. I know why. I am like Hern. I need understanding. When I have woven my understanding, then Kankredin will have cause to fear.

This is what I must understand. Why is Gull's soul of such special value? Why is Robin so ill? And what is the One? These questions are all bound to lesser ones, such as what have Hern, Duck, and I sworn to the Undying that we will do? The answers all lie in my first rugcoat, and they are coming to me as I weave.

Robin seems calmer this evening. Before I read my rugcoat, I would have put her panic over the mage down to illness. She has not seen Kankredin. We have not told her much. But now I am sure Robin knows many things the rest of us do not. It is her birthright, as mine is weaving.

I can weave this, yet I get angry when Uncle Kestrel tells me that we gave offense in Shelling! It is not very logical. I read my rugcoat, and I remember, and I know that we all, even Gull, who is the most modest of us, felt and behaved as if we were special people. I think we are now. But the fact is I had no grounds to think it then. I had no business to set myself up. I am ashamed. I could almost apologize—no, not to Zwitt or Aunt Zara.

Here I stopped to light the lamp. Robin seemed asleep, with her yellow candle face turned to the wall. I shut the door to the River and read my first coat again. I do not blame myself about the One now. I see him roosting cunningly in his fire and contriving that I should appear before Kankredin in Robin's skirt, so that Kankredin thought I was of no account as a weaver. I think he arranged I should betray him to our King, too, and that we should be summoned to Kars Adon, though what his purpose was, I still have no idea. If I go back, I can even think that the One used Kankredin's power over Gull for his own end, to bring us to the Rivermouth. And I am certain that Tanamil delayed us until we would arrive as the floods went down.

Just beyond that place, when we first saw the tides, I looked carefully at my account of the Heathen girl on the roof. I noticed that Robin had not been herself even then. I tell hardly a tenth of what we all said—if I put in all Duck and I say, my rugcoat would be too large for a giant—but Robin says barely a tenth of that. But about that Heathen girl—I had left out what she was wearing. I jumped up to ask Hern.

The latch clicked and Jay came in. "My!" he said. "That's a beauty of a coat, lass. Who's the lucky man?"

I said I had made it to take my mind off Robin. True.

Jay glanced at the bed and saw Robin was asleep. He put his face down by the lamp and whispered, "When do you think she'll be well?" He had a significant twist to his face, but I had no idea why. I tried to keep my eyes off the jumping stump of his arm and did not answer. Then Jay leaned closer still and said, "When will she be well enough to listen to advances from an honest man with one arm? I think she likes me enough, and I want to be sure of her before it's too late. Understand?"

I could not think how to tell him what Robin thought of him. "Not really," I said, and looked at the floor because my face was so hot.

"The King," Jay whispered. "The King, little lass! The thought is shaping in his head that he has no wife, and he needs the power of the One. Has he never talked to you? Hasn't he mentioned that he needs an heir?"

"Did he mean he wanted to marry Robin?" I said. "It never entered my head!"

"Lucky for me you didn't understand him," Jay said. He was all merry with relief. "Speak to your sister for me—quickly, soon. Tell her I can't knowingly go against the King, so it's up to her to marry me before the King declares himself. You say that. Tell her she's the sweetest girl I know."

Then he went. I sat and stared at Robin's yellow face. She bounced up out of her pillow as soon as the door had shut.

"What shall we do about *this*?" I said.

"Jay wants the One," Robin said, "just like the King. Oh, I wish I was dead!" It was the first time she had said that, but I know she meant it. She plunged down on her bed, crying, and rolled about wretchedly, tipping the cats off.

"No, stop," I said to her. "I'm thinking of something. I almost have already." I dashed off to find Hern, as I had meant to before Jay came.

Robin called tearfully after me, "Tanaqui, I'm sorry. All I seem to do is complain at you. You're so patient."

Patient! If Robin only knew. "I've nearly hit you a thousand times," I called back, and went flying out into the blue evening.

Hern was sitting moodily against a tree. Beyond him the King's campfires sent merry streaks down into the water of the millpond. I could hear people singing. "Hern," I said, "when Gull and Father went to war, what did you swear to the Undying?"

"I said I'd free the land from Heathens," Hern said sourly. "Ha-ha! Go away."

"Oh," I said. I could not see what the One could make of this oath. Mine was easier. I had asked to be sent to war as a boy, and Ked had indeed taken me for a boy because I was wearing Hern's clothes. "Another thing," I said to Hern. "That Heathen girl on the roof who told us about the tides—what was she wearing?"

Hern scowled. "A sort of blue rugcoat—No. She couldn't have been. Heathens don't wear rugcoats. I don't know."

That was it. "Tanamil wore one," I said.

"Kars Adon would probably say he'd gone native," Hern said gloomily, showing where his thoughts were. There has been no news of Kars Adon since the broken bridge. "Go away."

I went away and looked at my rugcoat under the lamp. When Robin asked what I was doing, I said I was sewing it up and I would go to bed soon.

"I looked at it," said Robin. "It's beautiful. But why do you use that strange word for river? I keep thinking you're talking about the One."

It was like a great light cast. "Robin," I said, "I knew you'd help me!" She meant Tanamil's sign for the River. It is not unlike the sign for *brother*. I had often noticed that. Now I plunged outside for a handful of rushes from the millrace and wove them together furiously under the lamp. I wove the two signs of my own name: *Tan—aqui*. I weave it here to show. See: together, *rushes*; apart, *younger—sister*. Then I took more rushes and wove again: *Adon, Amil, Oreth*, the One's secret names. *Adon* is as much as to say *Lord*, the difference of a thread. *Oreth* I do not see so well. It is a sign for weaving, or knotting, but not the usual one. But *Amil* is *River*, all but a thread. I took all the rushes undone except that name and the front of my name and held them together in front of me.

So now I know. I have been weaving it until late at night because Robin is still too upset to sleep. And I still cannot believe that we are wrong and everyone else is right and the One is indeed the River. But I know what I must do. I must find Duck. He has the Lady inside his shirt.

# 3

DUCK WAS NOWHERE. I took the lamp and went upstairs to bed in the end. And the first thing I saw was the Young One, thrown out of my bed on the floor. I rushed to pick him up. He is so worn and old that I was afraid Duck had damaged him. Duck had thrown him out. He was in my bed asleep. He says he prefers it to sleeping in a tent. I held the Young One under the lamp and made sure he was not broken. The light made the smile move on his worn clay face. Then I shook Duck.

"I'm not asleep," said Duck. He was in his maddening mood. "The King told me about needing an heir, too."

"Then why didn't you come down when I shouted for you?" I said. "I want to know what you swore to the Undying."

"Do you?" he said. I told you he was maddening.

"And I want Mother," I said.

Duck had thought he was the only one who understood. He was annoyed. "You can't have her," he said, and sat up against the wall with his arms wrapped round himself.

"She's my mother, too," I said. "I wouldn't ask if I didn't need her."

"You're not having her," he said. "I found out before you did, and she's mine."

I was too angry to argue anymore. "You selfish little beast!" I shouted, and jumped on top of him. We wrestled and struggled. "I need to talk to Mother!" I shouted. Duck at the same time screamed that the Lady was his and I was stealing her. Half the boards came off the trestles of the bed. We crashed to the floor. I heard Robin call out weakly from downstairs, and the door latch rattle as Hern came in to find out what the noise was. I had my hand on the Lady by then. Duck had my hair in both hands and was shaking my head about.

Then, through the noise we were making, we both heard the River door open below. Robin screamed. Duck and I stared at one another without moving, and Hern said, "I don't believe it! I just don't *believe* it!" just as he did at the net of souls. We heard light footsteps walking from the River door.

Neither Duck nor I remember how we got to the ladder. We were halfway down it before my mother reached the middle of the room. Hern was backed against the other door. Robin was upright in bed, with her hands to her mouth. And the River door was open where I had left it shut.

"What a disgraceful noise!" Mother said to Duck and me. "There's no need to behave like babies!"

I think the way she spoke did more to reassure us even than the cats. The cats had all jumped off Robin's bed and were rubbing purring round Mother's ankles. She bent down and stroked them. My mother is beautiful. She looks no older than Robin, but her face has more angles to it than Robin's and looks more delicate. Her hair is bushy, like mine, just as it was in my dream. But my dream did not show her huge eyes, deep and green as the River, and the long, long lashes round them.

"Lie down, Robin, love," she said. "It's all right."

"You came so suddenly," Robin said tearfully.

My mother smiled at her and at Hern. "I know it's hard to believe," she said to Hern. "Some things you can't see or touch are true, you know. Now what was all that shouting about?"

"Can I speak to you privately, Mother?" I said.

"I hoped that was it," said my mother.

"I want to talk to you as well," complained Duck.

"No, Duck," said Mother. "You go and make Robin's bed. It's all sliding to the floor. It's high time you did a bit to help, instead of leaving Tanaqui to do all the work. You've talked to me for hours already."

"Not properly, not with you really there," Duck said. "That doesn't count."

"Yes, it does," said my mother. She is a very firm mother. She would have been good for Duck. Hern grinned, because he thought so, too. "Don't go away, Hern," she said. "I want to talk to you afterward." Then she went back toward the River door, holding out her hand to me. She stopped on the way, beside my loom and the pink clay Gull. She put her hand to its cheek, smiling. Now, I had left the lamp upstairs. There was only the candle flickering by Robin's bed, so I cannot swear to it, but I think the small statue smiled. "Come along," she said to me.

I hung back on the threshold of the River. "Where?"

"Silly," said Mother. "I'll keep hold of your hand."

We stepped out across the River—I think. But things get so strange when you are with the Undying. There was a moon, and green light rippled through the trees, above and below us. I do not know if I walked on the water, or beneath it, or in some other place entirely. Certainly nobody saw us, but I remember seeing the square of dim light from the mill door to one side as we talked, and the lights of Shelling on the other.

"You've been thinking at last, Tanaqui," said my mother. "I don't suppose you can understand how it felt, watching you weave and willing you to stop blaming yourself and start thinking. I'd almost given up hope. I was telling myself that you'd put so much of the River in your coats, maybe that would do instead."

"Is it important," I said, "to put the River in?"

"Yes," said my mother. "But that is connected with the things I was forbidden to talk about when I married your father. You have to be very careful what you ask me, Tanaqui."

I had supposed some things were forbidden. My father was never talkative, but even he would have told us some of it had he been allowed to. I was prepared to be cunning. "Do you know about Kankredin?" I asked.

"I do," said Mother. "I was there with you. The mage *hidden death* reached him this evening. You have to move fast, all of you."

"We know," I said. "Are you allowed to tell me if Tanamil's a relation of ours? His name is Younger River, isn't it?"

"No. He is of himself," Mother said, to my great relief. "You have charge of him simply because he was bound when my father was bound. He has his name because he made the younger River—even more unwillingly than your grandfather made this one."

"Oh good," I said. "I was afraid he was going to turn out to be our uncle. I think Robin's in love with him."

"So do I," my mother said dryly. "That kind of thing seems to run in our family."

"Can you tell me how to call him?" I asked next. "Do I have to go to the watersmeet?"

"Any lesser stream will do," she told me. "But there's no need to scream like you did before."

That made me a little ashamed, but not much. I was too pleased, and too happy to have a mother again. I leaned against her. She was warm and solid and smelled, just faintly, of tanaqui. "I can't ask about the Undying," I said, as if I was talking to myself, "which means I can't ask if the One is my grandfather. But I know he is. Mother is his daughter. Are we—?"

Mother chuckled. It was like water in pebbles. "Don't get too cunning, Sweetrush."

"Can I ask your name, then, and how you came to marry my father?" I said. "You *are* the lady who haunts the mill, aren't you?"

"While Closti was a young man, I certainly haunted it," said Mother. "He used to come here to fish from the time he was Gull's age. And one day I met him by the millpond. 'My name is Anoreth,' I said, 'and will you marry me?' Anoreth means 'unbound,' Tanaqui—I can tell you that, since you are nearly there already. I suppose asking like that is more the kind of thing you would do than Robin, isn't it? Closti said he had seen me reflected in the water, often and often, and he was only too glad to marry me. But he was betrothed to Zwitt's sister. He had to give the coat back, and they were furious. So was Zara. And I was cast off by my father. That was when the mill was forbidden, through his anger. So when Duck was born, I should have died, but my soul was forbidden to go, you see. I had to ask your father to do for me what Tanamil did for Gull. That way at least I could watch over you all."

It seemed a sad story to me. Now I know why Zwitt dislikes us so much. "Gull," I said. "Can I get Gull back?"

"Ask Tanamil," said Mother.

"I'll go and get him now," I said.

Mother kept hold of my hand. "Wait," she said. "Have a little tact, Tanaqui. Tanamil does not like to remember he's bound, for one thing. Then there's Robin."

"Yes, I know Robin knows things. She knew who Tanamil was," I said. "What shall I do, then?"

"Sleep on it," said Mother. "Kestrel could lend you a boat to get Robin away in."

We went back together through the River door after that. Mother kissed Robin and Duck. Then she took Hern out into the wood and talked to him. I think she knew Hern's mind would not take walking into the River. Hern will not say what she said to him, but he is much happier now.

But I disobeyed Mother this very morning, the day after Mother came. Robin woke around dawn. She was pale and damp-haired and iller-looking than ever.

"I wish I could die quicker than this!" she said.

I had not seen before that Robin *meant* to die. I was appalled. "Kankredin—" I said. I was too sleepy to say more.

"I know all about his net," Robin said. "I shall be expecting it. Duck says quite a lot of souls get through."

"How do you know how fat your soul is?" I said, but I did not stay to argue. The fact is, I do not know what I should do without Robin. I raced upstairs and came back past Robin with the Young One in the sleeve of my rugcoat. "I'm letting the cats out," I said. They were mewing about because they thought it was morning. I went out with them into a white fog. Everything was dripping softly. I looked anxiously into the millrace. The sluices from the pond have been closed longer than Robin has lived, but there was a trickle of water down there among the rushes and forget-me-nots.

I climbed down there and put the Young One on one of the slats of the millwheel. "Tanamil," I said, "Younger River, will you please come here? We need you very badly."

I felt very silly. The flaky stone image did not change or move. When I heard someone coming along the millrace behind me, rustling the wet plants, I felt so foolish that I jumped round to stand in front of the Young One.

It was Tanamil who came along the race, out of the wet whiteness, with fog drops clinging to him all over. My mother did right to warn me. He gave me a doubtful, distant look, as if he had never seen me before. "Did you call me?"

At first I could not think what to say. Then I remembered how we should have asked him the right question, and only Robin did. "Last time," I said, "I should have asked if you were the Young One, shouldn't I?" And I moved so that he could see the Young One on the millwheel.

That was a mistake. He looked aside from the figure, almost shuddering. "That's true," he said, polite and distant. "I am the Young One."

He was so unhelpful that I burst into tears. I am getting as bad as Robin. "Boohoo!" I said, just as if I were a baby. "It's not *my* fault you quarreled with Robin! And now you're like this, and the King wants the One, and so does Jay, and we can't get away from Kankredin even, because Robin's trying to die! Boohoo!" And I went on boohooing until Tanamil shook me.

"What did you say about Robin?" he said. I think he had to say it several times. When I cry, I can hear nothing but me.

"She's trying to die," I said.

"What nonsense!" he said, looking very angry. He came out of the millrace, pulling me almost as fiercely as I pulled the brat Ked, and crashed in through the mill door. Robin sat up with a shriek. "You look like an old woman!" Tanamil said to her. I think he could have been more polite. Just then I found Duck beside me, staring at Tanamil. He looked at me, and we shut the mill door and went to sit outside in the fog.

"I've been wondering whether I dared get him," Duck said. "But I was afraid she hated him for being of the Undying."

"We're of the Undying, too," I said. "We descend from the One on both sides."

"I don't know—we feel suspiciously human to me," Duck said. "Maybe it's just our souls that are different."

"I must ask him how to get Gull back," I said.

"He told us," said Duck. "He said take him up the River to the One, only we didn't understand." He was in a much more obliging mood than the night before. He said, "I'll take him, if you like. I have to go. I swore to the Undying—it was after Zwitt said the River was angry and we weren't to pasture our cow with theirs, remember?—and I swore to see every inch of the River so that I knew more about it than old Zwitt."

"I see," I said. "That means the One wants us to go. We must get hold of a boat again."

Soon after that we were so cold and so curious about what was going on in the mill that when the cats came and mewed at the door to be let in, we opened it and went in with them.

Robin was sitting up cross-legged on her blankets, eating—stuffing, in fact—and her face was pink again. Tanamil was passing her things from the table, which was loaded with finer food than even the King has. He smiled at us and invited us to eat, too. Then he looked at the cats, and there was a fish on the floor for each of them. The mill seemed filled with peace and pleasure. I think Tanamil always brings this feeling. But on that occasion it was more than that; it was Robin, too. I was right. They are in love, and they mean to marry. Robin is almost well again already.

Tanamil assured Duck that the food was *not* an illusion, as Hern said. He has the power to bring anything which is on the banks of streams and lesser rivers, even from the far south, where very few people live. As he was saying this, Hern came in. He was carrying the Young One, accusingly. "Who left him—" he said, and he saw Tanamil.

I was afraid Hern was going to be angry. He was not, but he was awkward. I think Mother talked to Hern of Tanamil. All the same, it has taken Hern most of the day to get used to him. And Tanamil would not look at Hern because Hern was carrying the Young One and Hern did not understand. I had not realized how much Tanamil hates being bound. He hates it so much that he will not speak of it. His face loses all expression when you ask him, and he looks like the image of himself.

"Amil Oreth is bound deeper than I am," was all he would say when I asked. Robin told me angrily to leave Tanamil alone. At that Tanamil seemed to relent a little. He did not speak of himself, but he said to me, "Adon has a double bond to bear now. In the first place, he was cheated by a woman, and it was his own fault. In the second place, he was already bound, so that he could not use his full strength against Kankredin."

We have had such a good day. Hern has neglected the King entirely, and we have sat about in the mill laughing and trying to make plans for getting away up the River without the King or Zwitt knowing. Tanamil sits with his arm around Robin, as happy as we are, and Robin must have eaten more today than she has in the last month. Anything she fancies is instantly on the table. My only regret is that we are not allowed to have Mother here, too. Because of the One's anger when she married my father, Tanamil is not allowed to speak with her. Tanamil is not going to risk the same thing happening over Robin. They are going together to ask the One's permission to marry.

Now the fat is in the fire! Now I see why Tanamil so hates to be bound. I should not have disobeyed Mother. But at least the main fault this time is Duck's, not mine. I will tell it in order.

We were very happy, sitting in the evening sun from the open River door. I had a feeling Mother could be with us like that. I brought my weaving up-to-date and then turned to sewing up my first rugcoat and clipping the ends. Tanamil came over to look at it.

"What made me think I could teach you anything?" he said.

I was very pleased, but I said, "You told me two very useful things," and I showed him the band of expressive weaving at the back, where we went to Kankredin.

"I was there with you," he said. "I knew you would need me; he was almost too strong for me, too. It was lucky he sat down and that you repeat his spellgown broken here. Did you realize it would have made another bond on us?" I had not realized. It is a frightening thought. He told me that he had left when Kankredin said we could go, knowing Duck could take us through the net; it was Tanamil who brought us through it the first time, of course. Robin had told him never to come near us again. The quarrel had been far worse than I had known. I think it was good of him to help us at all, though he says he was thinking so hard of us all, and Robin particularly, that it is a wonder there is anything growing on the banks of streams anywhere.

Then he said, "I was as bad as Amil over Cenblith, but I hope I shan't need to expiate my folly the same way."

"By being bound, you mean?" I said.

"No," he said. "By fire. When it was almost too late, he found how to cheat the woman who cheated him and made her promise to put him in a fire every year. Every fire reduces his bonds by a fraction until they can be broken."

He looked so sad, saying this, that it came to me that it must hurt the One to be in the fire. I had not seen that before. And we put him in the fire so happily. "Did you know the One is golden now?" I asked Tanamil.

"Yes," he said. He picked up my rugcoat and looked at it. "That means his bonds can be broken," he said.

"What are you telling me?" I said. You have to ask the Undying clear questions. They do not tell you things properly.

Tanamil put the thick folds of my weaving back on my knee. "We call this a spellcoat," he said. "I think you should take it to the rising of the River. But I am not certain. You are making a thing here which is beyond anything I know. I dare not risk spoiling it by—"

Here came the disaster. The King came in with Jay, to pay his evening visit to the One. His pouched eyes twinkled merrily at Robin. "My dear young lady! Looking better at last! Restored to health and considerable beauty, isn't she? And how is my golden gentleman?"

Tanamil was standing against my loom, but the King did not see him, nor did Jay. Hern, Duck, and I made faces of astonishment at one another. Robin was too busy with the King to look at anything. She said the One was safe and she was feeling better today.

"Good! We shall be able to move on again," said our King. He circled the room, passing in front of Tanamil without knowing it, and seemed arrested at the sight of my rugcoat. "My dear fluffyhead, this is beautiful! Now I see the purpose of all your industry. I call it truly delicate, my dear!" He took the rugcoat off my knee. My hands went out to stop him, but he whisked it out of my reach. I thought Tanamil might have stopped him. But Tanamil stood as if his hands were strapped to his sides. The King held the rugcoat against himself. It was far too big for him. As I said, he is a small, plump man. But his eyes twinkled delightedly at Robin. "Your sister has made a royal coat for our betrothal, my dear. When shall our wedding be?"

When I think of all our faces, I could almost laugh—though it is no laughing matter. We were all horrified, but Duck was worse even than Tanamil. He stared at the King as if he was a monster and backed away into a corner. As for Jay, he was worse even than Duck. He staggered, as though the King had hit him, and glared at me. I see now that he thought the coat was for him.

"But, Majesty," I said, "the coat's too big!"

"We can turn up a hem or so," the King said, "at the bottom and round the sleeves. I must admit, fluffyhead, that either you miscalculated or you were thinking of another man." The sideways twinkle he gave Jay made no doubt about who he thought the man was. He bowed to me. "Thank you for my coat. I shall salute my bride-to-be." He took Robin's hand and kissed it. He can be very courtly when he pleases.

Robin dragged her hand away. She looked ill again. "I haven't agreed yet, Majesty."

"Nonsense," he said. "This coat is agreement. Shall we marry tomorrow? The headman in Shelling can do the business."

Robin looked desperately at Hern. Hern said, in a cracking voice, "Majesty, we object to Zwitt. You'll have to find another headman to marry you." Hern says this is the law. He says he was lucky to remember it because his mind was spinning.

"Well, frankly, I don't care for Zwitt either," the King said, readily enough. "We note your objection, brother-to-be. We'll use the next headman we find. I'll go and give orders to pack up and leave. Sleep well, my young lady." He bundled my coat under his arm and took it away. Jay went with him, looking as if someone had hit him in the face.

He left us in uproar. Robin was in tears, with Tanamil embracing her. I found I was making the noise old women use at funerals. All my work misused and gone. Just as I had understood its nature and how to use it. Hern was demanding why Tanamil had not stopped the King.

"I'm bound!" Tanamil cried out. "I'm bound, I tell you! I have to do what the King wants."

"Do you mean you can't marry Robin now?" Duck asked. He was very shaken.

"Not unless the King changes his mind," said Tanamil. I think he was near to tears, too. Robin put her face in her hands and wept that he was not to leave her, ever.

Duck stared at them guiltily. "I'm sorry," he said. "I told the King about Jay last night. He cheated. He promised me he wouldn't let Jay marry Robin."

"And he hasn't," said Hern. "Don't you know better than to trust the King, you stupid little—"

"Don't *fight*!" said Robin. "We've all we need without that!"

# 4

THE KING IS LUCKILY not very passionate over Robin. His main wish is to move on. I am weaving this amid the bustle of clearing up to go. The King visits Robin frequently, to remind her she is to be Queen, I think. You would think it would make her ill again, but Tanamil is with her, and she gets better every day. The King is unable to see Tanamil, but he has no illusions about Robin's feelings. He has detailed ten men to watch us night and day.

"Not Jay, I'm afraid," he said to me. "He's not a man I trust in affairs of the heart. But my bride must have a proper bodyguard, fluffyhead."

The bodyguards watch by five and five. Robin has no chance of getting away. Hern says we must stay with her. All I have been able to do is to insist that the One wants us to travel by River. It was not easy. The King has shown a desire to overrule the One. "A King is awfully exposed by water," he says. "We shall be a big slow target for every Heathen crossbow. Are you quite sure our golden friend really wants us to?"

"Yes," I said.

So the King has taken all the boats from Shelling. Zwitt stands scowling at us across the River, but I think it serves him right.

Tanamil has recovered his spirits again. In spite of our worries, we are flooded with his joy and pleasantness, which makes me feel very strange sometimes. I could not think why Tanamil was so cheerful until he came to me and said, "This second coat you're weaving—does it describe the first coat?" I said it did. He smiled and said, "Then I think it may be used instead." I can see he has set his hopes on this. If this coat has power to unbind the One—and it might, since it holds my understanding—then Tanamil will be unbound as well, and he can marry Robin whatever the King says. The difficulty is that the King will marry Robin as soon as he finds another headman.

Sometimes I think Tanamil lacks hardness. I would move against the King if I could, bound or not. But then I think of the way his arms seemed pinned to his sides when the King took my rugcoat away. I think Cenblith did her work well.

Robin has given me the One. She has Gull and the Young One, and Duck has Mother. We have moved a day's journey up the River, beyond the great marshes.

We went in thirty small boats, watched by all Shelling standing on the bank. We were in the marsh most of today. The King's men shot ducks there, which they are cooking for supper. Everyone is scratching because of the mosquitoes. We nearly lost the King in the marsh—a thing I would have been glad to do at any other time, but not when Hern was in the King's boat. Our boat is large and slow, because it carries the bodyguards, and we lost sight of all the rest. It is not surprising. The pools and channels of the marsh change every year with the floods, and the whole is hung with slight blue mist. There are warm springs underneath, which make the mist and cause flowers of all kinds to riot and tangle at this time of year. Every so often the mist and flowers part to show a smoky blue mere. Each time we searched the bleary water for signs of the other boats, but there was nothing but the jump and scuttle of wild creatures.

One such mere was covered with silver birds. When our boat broke through the rushes, they rose into the haze on bent wings. I cried out in fear. "Seagulls! Mages in disguise! Shoot them!" The bodyguards looked at me in consternation.

Tanamil smiled and stood up. He was sitting unseen with Robin. It is as if their troubles have increased their love. They cling together. When he stood up, the seagulls flocked to him and flew calling round his head, while the eyes of the bodyguards rolled sideways, and they muttered of spirits.

"They're only gulls," said Tanamil, and he sat down. The birds flew away. "There are storms at sea. They talk of great waves."

I felt foolish. After all, this could be a sign from the One that Gull will be restored to us. But now that I am sitting weaving on the bank, removed from the peace Tanamil brings, I think the gulls were telling of Kankredin's anger. I am very glad that we are moving at last.

* * *

I have had no chance to weave for three days. At least Robin is not Queen yet, for which it seems we must thank the Heathens.

That morning after the marshes we were woken by numbers of people hurrying along the bank among our tents. The cats hid in my blankets because the people had dogs with them. I sat up and stared through the tent flap at the confusion among the willow trees. There were children and donkeys, men and dogs, and everyone waving lights and shouting. The King had come out with his face creased and crumpled with sleep. But even with the King asking them, the people would not stop or answer clearly. We gathered that Heathens were coming up behind. They shouted that the whole countryside was in flight and fled on.

"That's no reason to give up common politeness!" said the King. "Move!"

We took to the boats and packed and folded our things as we rowed. My loom was nearly left on the bank. I asked Jay to make them load it, but he walked away. Tanamil carried it to the boat. Nobody noticed in the confusion.

Since then we have traveled as fast as oars and sails and men dragging on the bank could take us. We traveled till light was gone. As summer is here, that is many long hours. And when we landed, they were tired and cross and would not unload my loom.

The River is shallower after the marshes, and more winding. It is crowded with willows for a day's journey. In one place a willow had fallen in the floods and lay, still living, across the River.

"Oh, curse this River!" the King said. "He seems to be doing his best to thwart me!"

Our boat was alongside his. Unkingly though it is, I think our King is frightened. I told him the One would not like to hear him speak like that.

"Then tell him to behave more like a benefactor," the King said. "Are you sure he really wants us to go this way?" He looked at me almost pleadingly. Hern looked at me, too. Hern does not understand why Duck and I are so set on going by water.

I told the King I was sure. "Why am I so sure?" I asked Tanamil, while the bodyguard was busy shoving at the willow to squeeze us underneath.

"Your father's people bound us," Tanamil answered out of a mass of pointed willow leaves. "Your father's people know how to unbind us." Why do the Undying never tell you straight? I long to ask Mother a few more cunning questions, but I am not allowed to talk to her when Tanamil is there, and he never leaves us.

The willows stopped after a day. The River, no longer eye green but clear gray, hurried toward us down a valley of green banks. We saw white birch trunks above us and green bracken. Beyond that there were mountains. Some have a dazzle on their peaks which hurts your eyes. One of the bodyguards told me it is snow. It is no good asking Tanamil anything anymore. He is too taken up with Robin. Duck has gone to join Hern in the King's boat. He says all this love suffocates him.

In places where the valley was wider there were humped bridges over the water and houses nearby, built of stone. We found most of them empty. But yesterday the King said, "Ah, people! We shall have our wedding now." Robin looked piteous.

But the people all ran away up the hillside among the bracken. Jay stood up and shouted to the headman that the King needed him.

"Heathen!" the headman shouted as he scrambled upward. He pointed down the River. "Heathen! Run!"

There were no Heathens. We could see some miles down the valley there, and there was no one. Tanamil smiled. I think it was his doing. I see I have wronged him, saying he was soft. He is not powerless to work indirectly against the King, and he does. But he is mad if he thinks he can delay the King's wedding until I have this coat finished. It is barely half done.

However, the King was in a great panic. He said we must put off the wedding and hurry on. So we have come, at a furious speed, to this place. We have only halted here because of a great downpour of rain. The green hills around us were shaded white with it, and large hailstones fell. It was too fierce even for the King's hurry. We went blindly into a wider valley, where the River runs as a small tossing lake, and there we dimly saw a group of trees. The King angrily ordered us to take shelter there. Under the trees there is an old barn or boathouse, built of big gray stones. Here we all wait, while the King paces impatiently up and down and the rain pelts dimples into the water.

They would not at first bring my loom in. Jay, who used to help me in such things, is not my friend anymore. I had to make Hern ask the King. I am sad about Jay. I have wronged him, too. It was not the One he wanted. It was Robin. I do not know why I am so unready to believe that people can love Robin. I have seen Jay look at her just as Tanamil does. And now Jay will not forgive me.

The King could not understand why I should want my loom. "Why, in the name of the golden gentleman, fluffyhead, do you need to keep on weaving coats?" he said.

"I have to make one for Robin, too," I lied. "We always do that in Shelling."

So my loom was carried in, wet as it was, and set up in the doorway. I am sprinkled with rain as I send the shuttles back and forth, but I do not mind that.

"It's all wet, wool and all," the King pointed out.

"The way we prepare and spin our yarn," I said, "that does not matter."

He looked at Robin, who had taken some of the wet yarn to spin for me. Then he frowned at me, in his quizzical way. "Fluffyhead," he said, "it usually matters. Wool shrinks. Sometimes I suspect you of— Do the Heathen have lady mages? I think you may be one."

"No, Majesty," I said. "That I am not."

"Then can you swear to me that you're not making all this pother of weaving on behalf of some other man?" he said.

My heart grew large and bumped a little, but I said, "This is for no mortal man, Majesty."

Then he was satisfied in a dissatisfied way and went to the doorway to look at the rain. Hern sat with his back against the stones of the doorway and scowled out, too, beside my loom. We look out across a rocky, shivering sort of lake. Almost at my feet, rain popples among rushes. I keep looking up and out between rows because this is as near as I have ever been to real mountains. They ring us round, high green shoulders, higher brown shoulders, and headlike peaks which are blue and black and veiled in swimming clouds. Now that the rain is slackening, I can hear water rushing and shouting down all round. It is the sound of streams that run in every groove, some so distant that you see them as a white smear, like a snail's path; others I can see leap and spray.

"I don't see us going much farther by boat," the King said, and turned away, more satisfied.

I think he is right. We shall have to leave the River. The River comes to the lake in a sort of cleft, between two high shoulders of brown hill, and I think it is a rushing torrent there. Up above the cleft, in the highest and blackest mountain, I can see a smear of white that must be our great River at its rising.

Hern has just noticed.

So much has happened since then, and so little time to weave it in.

As I was saying, Hern looked down at the rushes by our feet. "The tide's turned. Look at it running the other way."

I leaned around my loom. The small blobs of foam and twigs that had gathered against the rushes were moving slowly past the bank, toward the rushing water where the River comes down the cleft. It seemed to me that Hern was right for a moment. "But the tide doesn't run up in Shelling," I said.

We looked for Tanamil to ask him. He was leaning over Robin as she spun, over on the other side of the doorway. He did not notice us. Lovers!

"Jay!" Hern called. "Does the River have tides up here?"

Jay came and looked at the water. He ignored me. "No. Tides stop at the Red River. That must be an eddy. The waters run pretty swift out in the middle and force the edges backward. See?" The stump of his arm leaped as if to point.

In the middle of the lake we could see angry waters standing in peaks with the force of their running. I could not quite believe Jay. It was churning there, like the tides do.

And a churning came among the rushes at the doorway. It was all spouting whiteness there. Hern and I were soaked. In the midst of the whiteness Mother stood, with her head and shoulders out of the water, quite dry. She was angry.

"Tanamil!" she said.

Tanamil jumped and put out his hand as if he could push her away. "I can't speak to you," he said guiltily.

"I *must* speak to you," Mother said. "You were trusted to watch, Tanamil! Take your mind off Robin and attend. Kankredin is coming. He and his mages are halfway up the River already, rolling my waters up before them as they come."

"But—" said Tanamil. "Without Gull?"

"Zwitt told them Gull is my son," my mother said. "After that Kankredin guessed how he had been tricked. He'll take Hern or Robin instead. He knows where they've gone. Take that spellcoat back from the King, you fool, and show Tanaqui what to do with it at once!" My mother turned, in a surge of whiteness. A great white swan went beating off across the lake, making the air ring with its wide wings.

I think the King and his men had seen Mother as a swan all along, rearing and hissing at the water's edge. They called to one another to put an arrow in it, saying swans were good to eat, while Mother talked. As I recovered from the shock of what she said, I heard Jay saying, "If I had my other arm, that would never have got away!" I do not like Jay anymore.

Duck came to crouch between Hern and my loom. "Where is the coat?" he whispered.

"In the coffer in the King's boat," Hern whispered back. "I'll create a distraction of some kind. Then you and Tanaqui go and get it."

I looked over at Tanamil. He nodded urgently, but he held out his hands with the wrists together, to show he could do nothing himself.

"Be ready to go as soon as no one's watching you," Hern whispered.

While we waited, I could hardly even pretend to weave.

Duck, however, jerked a handful of rushes from the water and wove them idly into a small mat. He looked bored to tears.

We did not wait long. The King noticed how pale Robin had gone. She had dropped the spindle when she saw Mother and sat staring straight ahead, twisting her hands together. I could see her mouth saying, "Oh no! Oh Mother!" I think she thought it was her fault that Tanamil had neglected his duty. She would not speak to Tanamil when he bent and whispered to her.

"Cheer up, pretty one!" the King said. He came and pinched Robin's cheek. "It was only a swan," he said. "You sweet, timid creature! I really am quite fond of you, you know."

"In that case," Hern said, jumping to his feet, "why don't you get on and marry her?" He marched round my loom, denouncing the King. "You talk about it enough, but you don't do it! What are people going to think? I can't have my sister gossiped about!"

He said a great deal more. Hern can be very eloquent when he chooses. I wish I could have stayed to hear it and to watch the King's face. It was the first time I have seen our King entirely without a smile. But by the time I had slipped round my loom and among the rushes outside, the King had recovered enough to wrench the smile back onto his face. "My dear boy," he said. "My dear boy!" Each time he said it, Hern thundered louder and harsher.

"Robin's name has been sullied!" he was shouting as Duck and I hurried among the trees. Tanamil was in front of us, beckoning. "My family's name is mud!" Hern roared, and we could not help giggling.

"I hope the King won't take Hern too seriously," Duck said as Tanamil slipped down into the King's boat. It did not so much as dip as Tanamil went aboard it, but it plunged for Duck and me.

"The box is locked," said Tanamil. He stood by the King's beautiful carved chest, looking helpless.

Duck laughed and cracked his thumbs. He has double-jointed thumbs. He holds them upright and they hop about, looking as beastly as Jay's stump. He did it now, and the carved lid of the King's coffer hopped in sympathy. I took hold of the lid, and it lifted, pouring rain-water over my feet. "How did you learn to do that?" I said.

"Tanamil taught me," said Duck. Tanamil was out on the bank again. He laughed.

My coat was folded on top of golden things. As I snatched it up and bundled it into my arms, I saw enough plates and goblets encrusted with red and blue stones to have bought our whole country. I turned to follow Tanamil.

Jay landed heavily in the end of the boat as I turned. I saw from his face that he disliked me even more than I knew. He looked at me as Zwitt did. "You thieving fiend's child!" he said. "Your brothers are just as bad. What are you all playing at now?"

"Nothing," I said. "The King has to be married in this coat. I'm getting it for him."

"Liar!" said Jay. "Heathen liar! You may fool the King, but you're not fooling me anymore. Give us that coat. And you can hand over your golden statue while you're at it!" I do not know how Jay knew I was carrying the One in the front of my shirt. He must have been watching me for days.

"Into the River," Tanamil said to me from the bank. I glanced at him and saw he had his pipes to his mouth. I tried to plunge sideways over the side of the boat. Jay's one hand fastened itself into the spellcoat and jerked me back.

"No, you don't!" he said. "You're coming to the King."

I did not care that Jay has only one arm. I bit the hand that held the coat, and I thrust at him in the way Tanamil taught me. We both went over into the water in a spout of splashes. It was bitterly cold. Jay howled and struggled. I had not known he could not swim.

"Duck!" I yelled. "Rescue Jay!"

At that moment Tanamil's pipes sounded. It was a breathy scream, like seagulls, and a crying, like an old woman at a funeral. I felt as if I had been taken out of my head and put somewhere strange and terrible. There was a long streak of light and, in that streak, smooth sliding. Then Tanamil and I were standing by the lake, surrounded by mountains as before, but everything was calm and empty, with a whiteness to it. There were no boats tied to the trees, and the trees stood as if in fog. Yet I could clearly hear a great splashing and large tricklings. Out of nowhere Duck said, "You're all right, you fool! Put a leg over the side. It's your own fault for making Tanaqui bite you."

"Ough! Oughgurrouch!" went Jay's voice.

"What do I do now?" I said to Tanamil in the whiteness.

"If you're ready, you go farther down," Tanamil said. "You must make your way against the River's current to its source."

"Aren't you coming?" I said.

Tanamil shook his head. He had that expression which was no expression. "I can't come any deeper because of being bound," he said. "Besides, I couldn't help you when you come to the source. It has to be one of your father's people who unbinds us. I must go and find Kankredin. Your mother was quite right."

"Oh," I said. I was very disappointed. I suspected he wanted to be with Robin again.

# 5

TANAMIL PLAYED HIS pipes again. It began as a shriek, but it passed to a hurrying, sobbing sound and died away. There was the streak of light and the sliding. This time I knew it: It was the same as when I had looked into the floods at night, not knowing the River was so high. It does not last long.

When I saw things as they really were, I was in the bed of the River, between high shadowing banks, among a flood of another sort. This was all people. People hurried past me in a shadowy crowd, more and more, coming always from the left and hurrying away to the right. My ears were assailed and irritated by the clatter of their feet. The clattering never stopped, yet it was oddly hard to hear. The people never stopped, and they were hard to see. Only when I looked at a person, and turned my head to keep my eyes on him or her as they hurried by, could I see them clearly. In this way I saw four men of our own people, a Heathen woman, two Heathen boys, and a girl about Robin's age who was neither Heathen nor of our people. All were strangers to me. And always they hurried by between the shadowing banks, on and on.

"Gull's rushing people!" I heard myself saying. "These are the souls of dead people. Now I know. The River is everyone who dies."

Speaking like that took too much of my attention. Next thing I knew, I was hurrying with the crowd, panting with haste, on and on. The only difference between me and the rest was that I was still clutching my rugcoat and feeling the One bumping heavily in my shirt.

Nothing seemed to stop me as I hurried. I did not think of stopping, until I saw light shadowy movements in the far distance. The hurrying of the people became broken and hesitant. There was an uneasiness, and we ran waveringly. Then I could see that people were turning about ahead, and some came past, going the other way. They were unwilling and kept trying to turn round. The clatter of our feet was in confusion.

Up till then I had run as one does in dreams, not asking why a thing happens. But now I stared ahead and tried to make out what the light shadows were. I saw huge glassy shapes striding toward me. They were transparent, but green and wavering, as if they were made of water. Though they were still far away, they were enormous and striding fast. I could not see what happened to the uneasy crowd as they met the glassy giants. But I had a sense of nothing beyond them, and I thought I heard among the faltering clatter of feet a voice crying out in despair. It sounded like my mother's.

I was terrified. I tried to turn back and struggle away from the glassy beings. It was most difficult to do. The hurrying was still all the other way, and it swept me with it. I cried out for help.

Then somebody was calling me, above on the bank. "Tanaqui, Tanaqui! Where have you got to, Tanaqui?"

I looked up, expecting my father. I think that, all along, I had been expecting to see my father among the rushing souls. I saw, running along the bank and peering down at the crowd, a fair-haired young man in a faded red rugcoat. He was fiercer and sturdier than Tanamil, but he had a joyful look which was like Tanamil's. I clung with an elbow to the rocky bank and gaped up at him.

"There you are at last!" he said to me. "Mother told me you'd be here. You mustn't go that way. The mages are down there. Come up here on the bank." He held his hand down to me.

"Gull!" I said.

"Who did you think I was?" he said, and pulled me up on the bank.

"But . . . you're grown up," I said. "Are people's souls always grown up, then?"

He was annoyed. "I'm not my soul. I'm all of me. Come along. We've got quite a way to go."

He hurried off along the high bank, the other way to the way the people ran, and I did my best to keep up with him. It was very stony and uneven, quite unlike the smooth trodden ground of the Riverbed. "Why are you grown up?" I panted as I stumbled after him.

"Because I was born five years before you were," he said, striding along. By this time I was falling steadily behind. Gull realized and turned back. "Sorry," he said. "You're loaded to the thwarts, aren't you? Whatever have you got?"

"My rugcoat," I panted. "But it's the One that's really heavy. He went gold, you know."

"I'll carry the coat for you," he said, and took it out of my arms, which was a great relief. "It's a beauty," he said when he had it. "It must be the best you ever did. What have you got it for?" Then he smiled at me. "I'm terribly glad to see you, Tanaqui."

Gull says things like that only when he means them. I was truly pleased. I explained to him about the rugcoat as we walked up the bank above the hurrying multitude of souls, to the perpetual soft patter of their feet. Kankredin's glassy mages were out of sight behind. Everything was shadowy. Gull was the only bright thing I could see. I suppose that should have told me he was not just a soul. But in spite of being with us all the time, Gull did not know anything of our adventures. He told me that he could barely remember the part where he was with us in his body. As I explained, I found it hard not to say, "But surely you remember Robin was ill!" and "You must know what our King is like!"

When I came to the end, I said, "Now what do you think I have to do to unbind the One?" and Gull did not know that either. "I hoped you'd know that," he said. I was thoroughly dismayed.

"But you must know!" I wailed. "I can't ask anyone else here, because it's got to be one of our family that does it!"

"Yes, I know. We bound him; we unbind him," Gull said. "Don't get worked up. Let's think." It did me good to have someone calm like Gull. That is one of the things I have missed. "You've got the One," he said, "and you've got the spellcoat that shows you finding out how Kankredin caught the One and then me. And Tanamil says it was lucky you didn't see all Kankredin's gown—That's it, Tanaqui! The spell is broken in your rugcoat! You try putting the coat on the One in the presence of Oreth!"

In that place, when Gull spoke that name, its echoes rolled in the Riverbed. The hurrying people halted, and their white faces looked up.

"I'll show you where his source is," Gull said quietly. The echoes died, and the people hurried on.

"I can't get used to the way things are the same and not the same," I said. "The One is not the River. Is he this golden statue?"

"He was before the River, and he made it," Gull said. He paced seriously and frowned as he tried to explain. Gull is not a thinker like Hern or Duck. "Making the River, he was bound as the One. He is the River, in a way, or its source at least."

"But the River is people's souls," I said. "And it's water, too."

"It's all those things," said Gull. "But . . . well, if anyone's really the River, I think Mother is."

"Mother!" I exclaimed.

"I can't explain," said Gull. "But I've talked to Mother a lot. I don't think the One likes it, but he doesn't stop me. Mother's not bound, you know, but she's in disgrace for marrying Father. She's told me all sorts of things. You wouldn't believe all the strange places and strange sorts of Undying there are in the land. When we're unbound, I want to go and see some of them. That's what I want to do. I shall have much more fun doing that than what Hern's going to do, I can tell you!"

I remember looking down at the Riverbed while Gull said this. It was narrower by then—a sort of rocky split—and there were far fewer people hurrying along it.

"What *is* Hern going to do?" I said.

Gull laughed. "I'm not telling. You won't believe me."

"Do you know what we're all going to do?" I asked eagerly. "What about me?"

"That I *can't* tell you," said Gull. "It would be terrible bad luck on you. But our Mallard's going to be a mighty mage—I'll tell you that. We go down here. Take careful hold. The rocks are slippery."

The sides of the split were wet. It was the first moisture I had seen in that place. I would have expected moss or mold or green things growing, but there was nothing but wetness. I went down, clenching my hands on rock and feeling my feet slide. Gull came after me more easily, but I saw he was taking care, too.

When we were down, the rocks of the sides were high above our heads, and between them was dimness. Though the place was dark, there was a yellow-greenness everywhere, by which we could see. I looked back down the narrow channel. It was empty where we stood, but there were people behind us, two or three or more, always hurrying away from us. I never saw where they came from. In front of us were rock and an oddly shaped dark hole.

"We go in there," said Gull.

He stooped and went into the hole. I edged in after him. How I felt is hard to explain. I was not frightened. I still went as you do in dreams. Yet there was a terror that was like part of the dream which, had I been really dreaming, would have woken me screaming. Gull moved to one side, and I followed him. It was soft and silent inside the hole. As soon as I moved from the entry, I could see. It was a cave, where the light fell greenish on the rocky back, and it fell in the shape of a figure with a bent head and a nose that was neither straight nor hooked, but both at once. I looked at the hole we had come in by. That was the same shape. Both were the shape of the shadow in my rugcoat. The cave was wet. Drops of moisture stood like dew underfoot and overhead, but the dew neither dripped nor trickled. It was a deep empty silence we stood in.

"Where—where is the One?" I whispered.

"Here," Gull said. "Can't you feel? This is all there ever is."

It was perplexing. I could not put a coat on nothing. If I had been alone, I would have got as bad as Robin and started weeping and wringing my hands. But Gull was there, and he was not worried. In the end I took the golden image of the One out of my shirt. He was so small that it was ridiculous, but there seemed nothing else I could do. I placed him carefully on the dewy rock, so that he stood in the center of the green manshaped light. "Give me the rugcoat," I said to Gull. Gull did so, and I placed the coat over the golden figure so that the head showed but the rest was heaped round with my weaving. I spread the cloth out and stood back to watch.

Nothing happened.

"We haven't got it right!" I said. "What shall we do? We've got to do something before Kankredin gets here!"

"Wait," said Gull. "Feel."

There was warmth growing in the cave. Almost as Gull spoke, it grew from dead chill to the heat of a body. Gull and I both sweated, in big drops, as if we were part of the walls of the cave. Steam gathered about us.

But that was all. We stood and waited in the heat, but nothing else happened. The small golden figure still stood swamped by my rugcoat. The green-yellow light was unchanged, except by the haze of steam.

"What shall we do?" I said.

"You've done something," Gull said thoughtfully. "It's never been warm here before. But I don't think that's enough. There's something else we have to do, I think—and I simply don't know what."

We stood again, and still there was nothing. At last, I could bear it no longer and cried out. "Grandfather!" I cried. "Grandfather, show me what to do!"

There was a green sliding in the cave. I could not see the rocks or the One in my rugcoat, but I could see Gull. He was bent and pallid and out of shape, like a person swimming underwater. Then I could not see him. I was in a still white place, with water roaring and rushing nearby. The sliding came again. This time a chilly wind came with it. I shivered, but I was glad of it after the heat of the cave. After that I was out on a cold hillside in the light of a golden evening. The first things I saw were heavy rain clouds, swimming away to the west in a green sky and limned with a dazzle of gold. Green turf sloped sharply from my feet. Somewhere to my right, water poured shouting downward, tolling an echo like a bell. And beside me more water ran and spread on the turf from steep rocks behind, which were smoking like a fire.

I felt heavy tears dragging in my nose and eyes, but I stopped them. "My grandfather," I said, "has turned me out. I call that ungrateful." Then I looked at my hands, thinking I was carrying my rugcoat again. I was not. My hands were gripped on a bobbin wound with a dark yarn that glistered faintly. And I could feel that the heavy weight of the One was missing from my shirt.

I felt desolate. I knew how Robin felt that morning we woke and found Tanamil had left us. I knew how Hern has felt, knowing he had failed. But neither of them had just lost Gull for a second time. I walked with my strange bobbin across the soaked and steaming grass, not caring or noticing that my clothes were dry where they should have been wet, and barely grateful for the cold wind on my face. I told myself I was going to look down at the thundering water I could hear.

I believed I could throw myself down it, but I had to stop before I came to the brink of the turf. It was too high and too steep. The green country and the purple hills spread like the whole world below and seemed to wheel sickeningly. Almost at my feet was the beginning of our River. It poured in a white cataract from my turfy shelf to somewhere far, far below. It roared as it fell, and everything beneath it was lost in floating smokes and small drifting rainbows. Beyond, and away below, I thought I could see the lake where we had sheltered from the rain, as a bright lozenge laid in the wheeling steepness. I had to take my eyes away and fix them on my tall black shadow, lying nearby across the turf.

"What did I do wrong?" I said. I have been so proud and so sure of myself, ever since understanding came to me in the old mill, and now I saw I had prevented myself understanding truly by being so proud of my own cleverness. "But what about Kankredin?" I said. I tried to look out into the country below, to see if Kankredin was to be seen, but my eyes blurred. It was all green and blue and dizzying.

I looked at my shadow on the turf. There was another shadow stretched out beside mine, longer and large-nosed. I could not move.

"Grandfather?" I said.

His voice is like the sound behind the sound of the waterfall. "Thank you, Granddaughter," he said. "You have been a great help to me. You took Kankredin's hands from my throat."

"Then what didn't I do?" I said.

His answer came after a pause. He sounded sad. "Nobody asked you to do anything—beyond what your family has always done. And I was not very kind to your mother, after all."

"I know," I said. "But Closti—my father—wasn't in the least like Cenblith, you know. You might have forgiven her."

He paused again before answering sadly and hesitantly, "I am very devious, Granddaughter. You—you would not be here now if I had."

It came to me that my grandfather was not only bound and sad, and weighted with shame and loneliness, but even uncertain how to talk to an ordinary person like me. I had not thought it was possible to love him until then. I wanted to turn round and look at him, but I did not dare. I looked at his shadow and said, "Grandfather, tell me what I have to do to unbind you. I want to. It's got nothing to do with Kankredin or Mother or even Gull. It's for *you.*"

Again the pause. "That makes me . . . grateful," he said. "If you mean that, Tanaqui, perhaps you could think of the end of your first coat, where you speak of Kankredin. In what manner did you weave that?"

"In the expressive way Tanamil taught me," I said.

"Then," he said, "think on to the second coat now in your loom. You tell of meeting with your King and what he told you of me. Do you use the same weave there?"

"Yes," I said. I had been in such awe of our King then. And I saw the coat clearly in my mind as I stood there, and my expressive weaving of the King going right across from selvage to selvage. "Of course!" I said. "You were bound twice! By Kankredin and by Cenblith." Then I did nearly turn round to look at him, but again I did not dare.

"It was my own fault," said my grandfather. He spoke musingly, as if he spoke to himself. This is how he must have spoken alone, for many centuries. "I can't ask anyone to unbind us because it was my fault. The first time I was a fool. The second time I was a fool, thinking that I was about to be rid of the first bond in time to welcome my people back. I let Kankredin take me unawares. I knew Kankredin. He has inherited my gifts, but it was too late when I saw that he has put them to the worst possible use."

"Kankredin? Is Kankredin of the Undying?" I said. I could not help interrupting.

"He descends from me," said my grandfather. "All the people you call Heathen descend from me. They went from here, and now they have come back. Kankredin is like you—two lines meet in him—but he has misused his inheritance, and now he wants to take my place."

"Can you stop him?" I said. By this time I was shaken with the urge to look round and see my grandfather, but I could not do it.

"I can stop him if I am unbound," said my grandfather. "That I promise you."

I could not resist turning round. I was so frightened of looking that

I slithered down onto my knees with the bobbin clutched to my chest. I think I gave a whimper of panic. But I turned round.

Kars Adon was standing there, casting a long shadow on the turf beside the blob of mine. He smiled awkwardly at me. There was nobody else there. "You mustn't be frightened," Kars Adon said. "I made them keep out of sight. I was afraid you might go over the edge if we all came."

# 6

I DO NOT KNOW if it had been the shadow of Kars Adon all along, but I think not. I do know this, however: At the bottom of my mind I must have been thinking of Kars Adon as much as Hern had. I was so glad to see him standing there alive that I burst into tears and took hold of his hand; it was cold, and all knuckles, as I remembered from before.

Kars Adon, being such a stiff, polite person, was naturally hugely embarrassed. He twisted his hand out of mine and stepped back. "Please don't cry," he said. Then he thought he had been too chilling, and he said, "I am very pleased to see you up here. We wondered what you were doing."

"Didn't you see the One?" I said. "I was talking to my grandfather."

Kars Adon looked at me with an oddness he was almost too polite to show. "There was no one here," he said. "Who did you think it was?"

"He's called Adon, like you," I said, "and Amil and—"

"Hush!" said Kars Adon. He was very awed. "You mean our Grand Father was here?"

I nodded. I was crying again, to think the One had gone away without my seeing him.

"Then is that why the water coming out of the hill is suddenly smoking like this?" Kars Adon asked.

"Doesn't it usually smoke?" I said, sniffing busily.

"Not while we've been here," he said.

I was cheered by this. "Then it shows I've done something," I said, and my crying stopped.

"If you feel better," Kars Adon said, "I think you should come with us. We are having to move from here. Kankredin is coming up the River, they say, in a great wall of water. As he hasn't sent word to me, I'm assuming he's my enemy, too, now."

"He is," I said. "He wants to be King himself."

Kars Adon twisted his mouth at that. "Thank you. I should have seen that. I could have seen that even when my father was alive, now that I think." He fidgeted a moment with the hem of his cloak, and then he said, "I owe your family a great debt. If it had not been for your brother, I would still be crouching like a mouse in the hem of Kankredin's gown, dreaming of—of glories . . . and risking getting trodden on. Hern made me see how ridiculous that was."

Hern would be glad of that, I thought.

"You'd better come to our camp," said Kars Adon. "I can show you some gratitude now, at least."

"Oh, but I can't!" I said. "My weaving's down in our King's camp, and I have to get it and finish it before Kankredin gets here. You wouldn't believe how important that is!" I took a look over the edge of the turf, down to the tiny slip of the lake below, but I had to snatch my eyes away.

"Is your King down there?" Kars Adon asked, suddenly very eager. I thought he had not noticed my talk of weaving at all, but I found later that I was wrong.

"Yes," I said. "We got to the lake down there this afternoon."

Kars Adon was delighted. "Then that alters everything," he said. "We stay here. I shall send someone down to talk to your King, and they can ask for your weaving then. I think Hern would say that was the right thing to do. You come with me."

He wrapped his cloak around him against the wind and walked away up the turf. He walked with a strong limp; I had been right about that. When I did not come with him at once, he called to me, "Are your brothers with the King?"

"Yes," I said.

"Then everything will be all right," he said, and walked on.

I caught him up easily because of his limp. As we walked round the mountainside together, I asked him if he had been wounded.

His face was pink, and he shook his head. "I was born this way," he said.

In the trees beyond the shelving turf, we were met by six lordly-looking Heathens. They had that grave, anxious look Heathens always seem to have, but I think they were truly anxious. One asked, "Shall you give orders to strike camp now, lord?"

"I've found a better way to settle our troubles," Kars Adon said. "The native King is at hand, and we shall face Kankredin together." He motioned me to walk with him and limped swiftly down the hillside, with the lordly ones following. From the conversation they had as we went, I gathered that the lordly ones had been trying to persuade Kars Adon to leave the place for days, because of Kankredin. They were frightened white by Kankredin, even more than Robin is. It began to give me a sense of how strong Kankredin is, their fear. But it was also quite plain that it stuck in Kars Adon's gorge to flee from Kankredin. He had been looking for an excuse to stay, and he had found it in what I had said.

The lordly ones kept saying that prudence was safety, and who could face the mage of mages? Kars Adon limped on without answering until we came to a trodden path leading out from among the pine trees when he flung over his shoulder, "I was prudent once before and nearly lost the clans. Now I shall trust to our Grand Father." That silenced them.

The Heathen camp spread beneath us. It was very large. Numbers of flags flew over many tents in one of the most favored valleys I have ever seen. It was warm, facing south, and flowers grew there in such profusion that they scented the evening.

"As I promised your brother, I have mustered all the clans that remain," Kars Adon told me, and his chin lifted. I could hear imaginary trumpets. "I want to make my kingdom in this dale." I did not blame him. It is a beautiful place, and no one else lives there.

When we came down among the tents, the first thing I saw was a group of dark boys in rugcoats making up to three Heathen girls in clinging dresses. They were being very polite about it—offering to carry the girls' waterpots and so on—but I was a little shocked. We went round a tent, and there was the same thing in reverse. Some very forward girls in rugcoats were coaxing away at two Heathen boys to give them a ride on their horses.

Kars Adon saw me look. "Your people have been coming here for days now," he said, "fleeing from Kankredin. I made treaties, as I told you I would. You think Hern would approve?"

I did not know what Hern would think. Treaties sound very grand, but the practical result is an awful lot of giggling and a very strange camp. Polite, quiet Heathens looked at us without seeming to look. People of my race crowded and stared. Some of my people were not at all clear they had made a treaty. Kars Adon was hissed by some, and some sat about staring and made no attempt to look after themselves. Most of these, Kars Adon explained, had been too near Kankredin. "I think he has hurt their souls," he said. "They think they are our prisoners. We have to feed them." He sighed. "I often wish that your brother was here to persuade them."

We went to Kars Adon's tent—he had found a great white one big enough to act a play in, from which his garish flag flew proudly—and there we had supper. It was plain food, nothing like the food our King insists on, and confusing. Heathens have the whole meal out upon the table at once, but you do not help yourself. Everything is carried to you by boys. I saw Ked among the serving boys, but he kept to the other end of the table. He is still terrified of me.

I sat eating with a most peculiar mixture of feelings. I was shy, but I felt at home in a way I never did with our King. When I realized this, I began to think I was a traitor, and yet, I told myself, the camp was full of my people, and my grandfather had placed me where I would meet Kars Adon, as if he had intended it. Kars Adon spent the whole time telling me of his plans, and this was oddest of all. "You do agree?" he kept saying. "Do you think Hern would like that?" It was all Hern. It is strange to think that Hern has made as big an impression on Kars Adon as Kars Adon has on Hern. They did not talk together long. But each has gone away thinking deeply of the other and, as it were, trying to live up to what he imagines the other to be. Kars Adon seemed to me to credit Hern with ideals that Hern never had. But how can I tell? Hern has certainly credited Kars Adon with the same, and here was Kars Adon doing his best to achieve them.

After supper Kars Adon sent his lordly ones to the end of the tent and said he must talk privately with me. "Would your King agree to a parley?" he said. "If I offered him a treaty, would he agree to face Kankredin with us?"

The way our King was placed, with fifty men and Kankredin coming up the River, I could not see he had much choice. "I think if you sent someone he could trust and listen to," I said. I did not think he would listen to one of the lordly ones.

"I know the very person," Kars Adon said, and he sent lordly ones in all directions to find this man. "Then you spoke of weaving," he said to me. He was very respectful. Of course weaving to his mind is the mages' art. "Should I ask our messenger to bring you this weaving?" he asked.

"Oh yes!" I said. And then I told him why it was so important. It was something I had never dreamed of myself doing. But he had been open with me, and we were both children of the One. He was equally in danger from Kankredin. I told him of the first coat and how it had loosed Kankredin's bond. "But I don't know what I have to do to unbind him from Cenblith's," I said. "Have you any idea?"

Kars Adon was at his most awkward at this. He wound his fingers in his cloak and twisted about. I think the reason was that he had hoped for just this from my weaving and was ashamed of making me tell him. "I know nothing at all of magery," he protested.

"But nobody knows about this," I said. "And you can look at it fresh."

I think he was flattered. He considered. "What did you give our Grand Father in the first coat?" he said.

"Kankredin's spell broken and our journey down the River," I said. "The second one starts with the King telling us how the One was bound and what happened when we came up the River."

Kars Adon thought deeply. "Would it be," he said at last, "that you are to give him back his bonds and the entire River with it? And perhaps the story of how you discovered this?"

You know, he is right! I knew it as soon as he said it. This is why I am weaving this now. But it is still not quite the whole story, and I know I must go on.

I had not finished thanking Kars Adon for his cleverness when someone came up to us saying, "They say you want something from me, young lord."

We looked up, and there was Uncle Kestrel bending his shaking head to Kars Adon in the most respectful way. "Uncle Kestrel!" I shrieked. I jumped up and hugged him.

"Ah, now, I thought it might be you in our midst," he said. I put a kiss on his beak of a nose. It came to me that my grandfather looks a little like Uncle Kestrel, which is a good thought. It seems that Uncle Kestrel and all the rest of Shelling were forced to run away from Kankredin the day after we left. The River flooded backward and drowned most of the houses. Zwitt was so frightened that he made them go by land to the mountains, while we, because of the winding of the River, took much longer to reach this place.

Kars Adon told Uncle Kestrel to go to our King's camp and arrange a meeting as soon as possible, and he gave him strict instructions to bring my loom and yarn back with him. Uncle Kestrel was a little surprised to be chosen, but it was a good idea. Robin would believe him, and the King would believe Robin. "That weaving," said Uncle Kestrel. "I do nothing but fetch her that weaving." He agreed to go. He keeps his independent manner, but he thought the world of Kars Adon.

I had a lumpy bed that night in a tent with some Heathen girls. They chatter just like our girls when they are on their own. They told me that Kars Adon had asked every one of our people who came to his dale whether they knew the family of Closti. And when Uncle Kestrel came, he had exclaimed, because Kars Adon reminded him so of Hern. Kars Adon spent several hours asking Uncle Kestrel all about Shelling and about Hern. The girls were a little shocked that their Adon, as they call him, should be so interested in natives. I was pleased. I thought all was going well.

In the morning, however, I heard that Uncle Kestrel had not brought my weaving. Our King had made conditions. He agreed to talk and named a place, but he said he would exchange my weaving for the One. He knew I had the One.

"But I haven't got him anymore!" I said to Kars Adon. "I gave him back to himself."

"That won't matter," Kars Adon said. "We can explain. The important thing is that he has agreed to talk." He was overjoyed at that. He set out soon after dawn with me, and Uncle Kestrel and seven of his anxious lordly ones, to go down to the place the King had named, near the lake.

So it was that I have seen every inch of the River, and my coats between them contain it all. As we climbed down past the waterfall, I made myself look at it, although the height and the noise made my head turn round. It streams down hundreds of feet, not wide, but with enormous force, into a great rocky basin beneath the mountain. We climbed down to it over moss and hanging ferns, perpetually wet with the clouds of spray. That day Kankredin was so close that the basin had become a place of white waters, where the fall wound back on itself, up and round, as if it were trying to climb the mountain again. The din was enormous, and there were rainbows at the edge of the winding water as big as rainbows in the sky. Everyone stared at it, shaken. No one liked to say the name of Kankredin, but he was in all our minds.

Beyond that the water boils down to the lake through a curving ravine, in a chain of basins as blue as the eye of a Heathen, and white bubbles fight up through it. The ravine opens into a grassy space just before it reaches the lake. There, between slants of rock, the King was waiting. They were before us, not having had far to come. We came there feeling deafened. Even there the noise was loud. I could not think why our King should choose a place where we could hardly hear ourselves speak.

He was sitting on a stone, smiling at us. He even smiled at me. My loom was behind him, between Hern and Jay. Hern seemed to try to smile at me, too. In spite of what Duck said, he was sure I was drowned until Uncle Kestrel came. But I could see there was something else on Hern's mind. As for Jay, he half closed his eyes and gave me a look of detestation which I find it hard to forget.

Our King did not get up. That was to show Kars Adon he was usurper and invader, which was true enough. Kars Adon bowed to him politely. Our King bent his head, twinkled, and began to shout the names of the important ones with him. The first was a stranger to me, an agreeable-looking man in the rugcoat of a headman.

"This is Wren," bawled our King. "And this"—he pulled Hern forward—"is Hern, my young brother-in-law."

*Brother-in-law!* I thought. I stared at Hern. Hern heaved up his shoulders, spread his hands, and looked "Tell you later." But I did not need to be told. Wren was a headman. Robin was a Queen. Poor Robin. Poor Tanamil. Then I thought: But they hadn't got my rugcoat. I think it's unlawful! I missed the first part of what was said because of this. When I listened again, Kars Adon was leaning forward, shouting earnestly into our King's face.

"We can't afford to be enemies," I heard above the thundering water. "We must make a treaty and unite against Kankredin."

"Treaty?" shouted our King. "You come to my land, kill, lay it waste, dispossess me, and then you bleat of treaties!"

"Things are different now," yelled Kars Adon. I lost his voice in the noise. It came to me in fragments: ". . . make amends . . . proud future . . . kingdom together . . . one tongue . . . same Undying."

Our King's voice carried better. "Who cares about all that? That child Tanaqui stole Oreth from me. I want the One back. She can have her weaving in exchange for the One."

Kars Adon was pleased the King should talk of the One. "Our Grand Father," he yelled, pointing a finger at my loom, "is the most urgent thing we must talk about."

"How dare you shout at me!" thundered our King. "Have you got Amil?" He looked at me and knew I had not got the One. It must have shown in my face. He stood up. I see now that it must have been a signal, though at the time I simply thought he was angry.

Next I knew, the King and everyone except Hern had snatched swords from beneath their rugcoats. I had never seen fighting before. It is swifter and more beastly than you would believe. The worst of it was, Kars Adon, Hern, and I stood stupidly aghast, not believing our King's treachery. Before we moved, three of Kars Adon's lords had lost their lives, and most of the rest of the King's men were jumping down from the rocks where they had been hiding. Uncle Kestrel was hobbling frantically round us, with Jay slashing at him as he ran. Jay impeded our King, or Kars Adon would have died that first second. The King had to make a second stroke at him, and his sword moved to do it as swift and deadly as a snake.

Hern screamed, "You promised me not to!" and tried to get in front of Kars Adon. The King's sword sheared Hern's rugcoat half away. Kars Adon tried to step back. Hern fell into me and, as we went down, I heard the King's sword meet Kars Adon's chest. It was the most awful noise I have ever heard, dull and sticky. The same noise came again. I had glimpses of more Heathens with crossbows. Kars Adon may not have suspected treachery, but someone had. I think it was Arin, who fetched us from the island. The King fell just beyond me, choking, his face mauve and smiling a grin of pain. There was a crossbow bolt in his neck. And Arin stood above us, crashing swords with Wren, the headman, glancing down at our King in satisfaction, until they were both knocked aside by Uncle Kestrel, who toppled over with Jay on top of him. One of them was breathing even more dreadfully than the King.

"Grandfather!" I screamed. "Help!"

The answer was like a skirl of sheer anger, shrieking above the thunder of the falls and the rasp of the fighting. I looked up and saw Tanamil on the rocks above us.

Tanamil had been very unhappy. His hair was a wild yellow cloud, and his rugcoat smeared with mud. I could see misery in his face, even through his anger. He was very angry. His pipes screamed with rage and struck across our ears like terror. All round me, people fell apart from their enemies, staring and shocked. And the pipes screamed on, modulating to a wail and down to sobbing. The heat and the shock died out of us. We began to stir sheepishly, and Hern and I climbed to our feet. I noticed that Tanamil seemed to be looking to the rocks behind me as if someone directed him. I turned. But it was not the One. It was Duck. Duck was crouched there, playing as Tanamil played, with that intent and irritable look you have when you are doing something which is almost too difficult for you. And Tanamil was directing Duck.

To the piping of both, even the noise of the falls grew quiet. Tanamil stopped playing and stepped to a high rock where everyone could see him.

"Stop behaving like beasts!" he said. We all winced. Tanamil angry is a great one of the Undying, without question. Like Gull when I first saw him on the bank of the Riverbed, he was more alive than the rest of us below. Unseeable strength came from him like hammerblows. "Attend to your wounded," he said, "and then attend to your real enemy. The mage Kankredin is nearly here."

Everyone knew Tanamil for what he was. The Heathen hailed him as Tan Adon. A number of the King's people murmured names: Tanoreth, Red One, and the Piper, to name a few. I had not known he had so many names. But Tanamil ignored their murmurs and came down to where Wren, the headman, was bending over the King. The King was not breathing.

"Who did this?" Tanamil demanded.

A shadow fell across the King, of a hawk-nosed man. I whirled round. It was not the One. It was Uncle Kestrel, heaving aside Jay's body as he got up. I was sad about Jay because I would never be able to make him like me again. But I was glad Uncle Kestrel was alive.

"Tanamil!" Hern said. He was desperate.

We all turned to where Kars Adon was dying, with his hands pushed hard to his chest, and blood running from one side of his mouth. Hern and Arin were kneeling beside him. Tanamil pushed between them and raised Kars Adon, very gently, so that he could see us all. "What is your will, lord?" he asked, as gently as he had lifted him.

Kars Adon looked at no one but Hern. "Hern," he said. I wondered how he could speak at all. The effort heaved his chest, bringing blood between his fingers. "Hern, was it the King's sword did that to you?"

Hern looked down under his own arm at the slashed ruin of his rugcoat. He was bleeding along his ribs. He was surprised to discover it. "Yes, it was," he said.

"Then," said Kars Adon, "we are blood brothers." He laughed, and pink froth came from his mouth. "I meant to tell you so much," he managed to say. Then he pushed himself up with his elbows, so that he could see Tanamil, Arin, Wren, and all the rest of us standing round. "This is my will," he said, "all of you: that Hern is King and Adon after me, and that all the clans obey him."

Kars Adon passed into death so smoothly then that we could not tell when he did so. He spoke, and there was no difference to him, but he was not alive. After a moment his hands slipped from his chest, and we knew he was dead. I have asked the One many times to help him get past Kankredin in the River of Souls.

Tanamil laid Kars Adon down, and Hern looked angrily at Arin. The anger was because there were tears in his eyes. "I can't do that—rule the clans—can I?" he said.

"Someone must," Arin said. "It was his will, and you are very like him."

Tanamil said, with some bitterness, "You're the King's heir, too, since this morning. Accept it, Hern. There is a great deal to do."

# 7

AFTER THAT THE day was all hurrying, coming, going, meeting, and mourning. Tanamil seized a word with me in the confusion. "What happened?" he said. "Something came about, but not all. I find I can reveal myself to mortals, yet I had no power to stop the King's wedding. Was something more needed?"

"Yes," I said, and I told him what Kars Adon had said.

"I thought you might need to weave again," he said.

"But I think it's more than that," I said. "The One left me with this bobbin of yarn. What do I use it for?"

Arin came just then, to take Tanamil to the camp of the Heathens. "Your mother can tell you that," Tanamil said, and he left.

I snatched a word with Hern. "The King married Robin?" I said.

"Oh One!" said Hern, and covered his face with his hands. "It was my fault! I made him so ashamed, and all I wanted to do was to cover up for you. The trouble was, I said it in front of everyone, and he felt he had to marry her. Then Jay came in soaking wet, saying you'd run off with the One and were lying drowned for your sins, and the King was so furious that he swore nothing would stop him marrying Robin. He had them dragging the lake for the One. And Robin was too upset about you to bother what the King did. Then Uncle Kestrel appeared. The King went wonderfully calm after that, and I suppose I should have suspected he was up to something. But Tanamil had disappeared, and Duck and I had our hands full with Robin. Wren arrived around dawn. He had his whole village with him, and they were too scared to stop at first. The King made Sard shoot one of them. So they stopped. They were terrified. They say there's a wall of water half a mile high coming up the River. The King said we'd all move when he was married to

Robin, but then he made them wait to look after Robin while he went to meet Kars Adon. He took Wren and me to make sure the rest all stayed. It's not been fun, I can tell you. Then Tanamil! Tanamil turned up during the wedding. He went dashing out across the lake, tearing his hair and yelling, and Robin began crying again. It was terrible. It's all terrible, Tanaqui. I can't be a King, can I, Tanaqui?"

He had wanted to say that most of all. "Gull knew you were going to be," I said. "He wouldn't tell me because he thought I'd laugh. But I wouldn't have laughed. Gull doesn't know how much you've changed."

"Being with the King has taught me what *not* to do, if that's what you mean," Hern said, but it made him happier. He wanted me to tell him what had happened to me, but I was not sure he heard it all. They kept asking things, and he had to hurry away before I had finished.

I found Duck brooding up on the rocks. "Isn't fighting beastly?" he said to me. We talked of that for a while. Then Duck said, "Old Smiler married Robin after all, just this morning. Did you know?"

"Yes," I said. "But I'd taken the rugcoat. What wedding clothes did he wear?"

Duck laughed. "Nobody knew you had. Remember that mat of rushes that I made?"

"Duck!" I said.

"I told you I was going to be a magician," Duck said. "I've got quite good at little things like that. Peacepiping's much more difficult. I thought I was going to let Tanamil down when we started. Anyway, I put that mat in the chest, and everyone thought it was your spellcoat. The King wore it. Nobody knew. At least Hern knew, but he was too upset to say and Robin did, of course, but she kept looking away because she hates people to look silly."

"But, Duck, I don't think the wedding was legal!" I said. I was thoroughly shocked.

"It was all right if the headman did it," Duck said grumpily. "And don't you dare tell anyone. Without that wedding Hern hasn't the slightest right to be King. So keep your mouth shut."

Duck is quite right, of course. I have not told a soul except to weave it in my second rugcoat.

By then a certain order began to appear in the coming and going. The bodies of the two Kings and the others who were killed were laid on the broad grass beside the lake. Wren, the headman, went round the lake to the barn among the trees. When he got there, Kankredin was so near that waves were standing high in the middle of the lake and its water was forced over the lowland. Wren found the barn flooded. Our cats were up in the beams, spitting at the water. Wren's villagers and Robin were up on the hillside above, and Wren brought them back round the lake to the falls, where I was still standing by my loom, wondering what I ought to do.

Robin is no different, in spite of being a Queen and a widow, though she was wearing her best skirt. She burst into tears when she saw me. She says she had known I was not drowned, but she had not been able to believe it. We went down to look at the King. You would not have thought Robin could cry over our King. But she did.

"You didn't *like* him!" I said.

"I know. I didn't treat him well," Robin sobbed. "Nothing treated him well. He wasn't the right man for what he was made to do."

I think Robin is right. But I was glad Tanamil was not near. He would have been hurt.

Tanamil was all this time up at Kars Adon's camp. I am glad he was there. If Arin had gone alone to the camp with news of our King's treachery, there would have been bloodshed, and Hern would have died in it before he could do anything. As it was, Tan Adon, as they call him, came in majesty to the Heathens and bore witness that Kars Adon had named Hern as his heir. Even so, the Heathens from the camp came down beside the falls with black looks and weapons ready. My people whom Kars Adon had sheltered came, too. But it was noticeable that they kept apart, with those too weak to fight sheltered in the midst of them.

Jay is not dead, by the way. While Robin and I were watching the people coming down the falls, Hern and Uncle Kestrel were laying Jay with the other bodies. And Jay sat up, rubbing his head. "I might have known you'd get the best of it, old-timer," he said to Uncle Kestrel. Then he looked at me. It was almost his old, joking look. "I've been sent back from a hurrying host of dead people," he said, "with orders to keep you safe, my lass. There are some glass giants at work down the River. It looks as if they'll be here by nightfall."

Uncle Kestrel thought Jay's mind was wandering. I knew it was not. "He means Kankredin," I said to Hern.

"I was afraid he did," said Hern. He lifted his heel and hacked at the grass with it. "Now I have a chance to do all the things I swore to do," he said. "And I don't think I *can*."

The people from the camp arrived and gathered by the lake. Our people went to stand with Wren and his villagers, near the lake. But the Heathens stood up among the rocks and planted their flags there.

"How shall we do the Adon's will?" a lordly Heathen called out mockingly to Hern.

Hern was very pale. I could see him shaking. He stood out between the two crowds, among the bodies, all on his own. I had expected him to look small there, and I am still surprised that he did not. Hern is thin still, but he has grown as tall as Gull. When Tanamil came to stand near him, the two were the same height.

"First look at this," Hern said, pointing to the corpses. Everyone was quiet. The noise from the falls meant we had to listen very carefully. "These," Hern said, "are the bodies of two kings. They were killed in senseless hatred, when both had lost nearly all they had. Someone is coming up the River who knows of this, and it pleases him very much. This will make it easy for him to suck out our souls, and the soul of this land, and rule us as his slaves. He is coming in a wall of water. And he is nearly here." He pointed down the River, across the lake.

Our people by the lakeside swayed all one way, like grass in the wind, away from the water. The Heathens stood firm, but their crowd was white with faces staring across the lake. The current set it in banks of water, churning toward us, and the space by the lake was flooding as Hern talked.

"This morning," said Hern, "one King married my sister Robin, and the other named me as his heir. This gives me a title to lead all of you against Kankredin. I did not ask for it, and you may choose again later, if you want. But for the next three days I must ask you to fight as one people against our real enemy. The same flags shall fly over us. The same Undying shall guide us. We shall none of us run away. We are going to hold these falls behind us to the death."

Heads swung uneasily to look at the rearing white falls. Everyone shifted with infirm resolution.

"We shall do it," said Hern. "For one thing, we shall lose our souls, anyway, if we do nothing. The main thing is that we have a way to win. My sister Tanaqui can weave against Kankredin, spell for spell. She can unbind Oreth, our Grand Father, so that he can rise and crush Kankredin. She can save us. But she must have time. We must hold Kankredin while she weaves. If we can hold him for three days, we have won."

So Hern did understand about my weaving. I admire him for grasping it so quickly. I did not think he would because it is not reasonable. But I never foresaw that it would all depend on me. I am very frightened. I know how Hern feels.

"If this is any comfort to you," Hern said, looking at the stricken faces by the lake and the grim ones up on the rocks, "the chief power of the mages is that they can take our souls. Everyone is right to be afraid. But Tan Adon, Lord of the Red River, will make you each a talisman which will keep the soul within your body. You can wear that and go into battle with confidence."

Tanamil, for an instant, looked as if he could not believe his ears. But as eyes turned to him, he smiled and nodded.

"So," said Hern, "will you all follow me—just for three days?"

There was the most nerve-racking pause. Hern sat down on a piece of rock. I think his knees gave.

Then Wren stepped out from among our people and went on one knee in front of Hern. I like Wren. "We'll follow you, me and my people," he said. That brought other headmen struggling through the crowd, one by one, and they knelt, too. Zwitt was one of them. Only believe that! He looked very grudging, but he was scared stiff. I think Hern's talk of talismans tempted him.

As the number of headmen increased, the Heathen lords realized they were being outdone. There was some hasty whispering among them. I am not sure that all of them believed Kankredin to be their enemy. But the will of Kars Adon was a powerful thing. All the Heathen flags dipped together, stood, and dipped again. A great shout went up. "Hail Hern Adon! Hail Hern King!" Arin tells me this is the custom among the clans. So, when the last headman went on one knee, both sides were pledged to Hern. I think Hern was near tears, because he scowled so.

After that our King was buried by the lakeside and mourned properly, although the grass was being covered in water while the mourning was done. I saw Aunt Zara among the wailers, but she would not come near us. But Kars Adon was carried up to the head of the falls and buried where the smoking waters of the One's source run across the green turf. Tanamil said it should be so. I can see the grave beside me as I weave. I look at it often and hope that we will be able to complete his dreams for him.

Before we came up here, I overheard Tanamil whisper to Hern, "Why did you promise them talismans? There is *no* way to keep a man's soul in his body."

"Yes, there is," said Hern. "If the man himself believes it's going to stay there. That's how I kept my soul when Kankredin tried to get it. I'm sorry, Tanamil. I had to say it. Give them all mud pies or buttons—I don't care—but make them something, please!"

Duck, who was standing by, burst out laughing. "Come on," he said. "Let's make mud pies."

"Later," said Tanamil. He was very worried. "Hern," he said, "I went down the River last night and saw Kankredin. There was no way I could stand against him. Don't underestimate his strength. I went away. I knew he could take me, and the One, too, through me. The same goes for you, for Duck and Tanaqui, and for Robin most of all. You must take care."

"It's no *good* taking care anymore!" Hern said, and stormed away to talk to men about weapons.

"Well," said Tanamil, looking up the length of the falls, "we must make what defense we can. Mallard, can you make nets?"

"I made the best nets in Shelling," Duck said. Nothing will ever make Duck modest, but he does make good nets.

"These will be spellnets," said Tanamil, "as strong as we can make them."

"Let me help," I said. "I can make nets, too."

"I think you can," said Tanamil. "But only you can weave, Tanaqui. Please go and weave again, as fast as you can. And for the One's sake, leave as little out of your tale as you can. We do not know what small thing may be needed to complete the web."

So I climbed up here to the smoking spring again. Robin came with me. She and Jay arranged for my loom to be dragged up, too, and all my wools. I hope I shall have enough. And here was a strange thing. Robin had Gull with her, and the Young One. When they had placed my loom on the turf, she took out Gull to give him to me. And he crumbled to a mound of red earth in her hands.

I cried out with horror. "Robin! Has Kankredin got him?"

It is true Robin knows things. She was smiling at the handful of earth. "Of course not," she said. "It means he's back, just as Tanamil promised. I think the same will happen to the Young One when Tanamil's unbound."

"Then why isn't Gull here?" I said.

"Hush," said Robin. She poured the earth carefully into the spreading pool of warm water and whispered so that Jay could not hear, "Don't be silly, Tanaqui. What do you think would happen to Hern's plans if Gull came along? Gull's older."

I see Robin is right. My grandfather has sent Gull somewhere else. He has done it to show me that he keeps his promises. But I long to see Gull. Duck and I have decided we shall go and find him if we win against Kankredin.

What Tanamil said so frightens me that I wonder all the time what I have left out. Should I say that I have a corn on my thumb and three blistered fingers? That my eyes ache, and my neck? Should I say how cold I have been in the mountain wind, these last two days? I have been weaving with such haste that I make mistakes. I had to unpick how I saw Kankredin and his glassy mages and weave it again because Duck and Tanamil distracted me when they came over the edge of the falls.

Robin has arranged for a tent to be pitched here and for people to bring me food. I think she left the cats here, too, hoping they would amuse me. But they *will* play with what is left of my yarn and with the shuttles and bobbins. I have had to ask Jay to take them to the camp.

Except when he did that, Jay has stood guard here the whole time. He is not courting Robin anymore. He has seen her with Tanamil, and he looks at her regretfully. But he talks cheerfully enough. "A man with one arm is not much good for fighting," he said, not, I think, altogether truthfully. "I shall stay here and make your last defense, my young witch."

"I don't think I am a witch," I said.

Jay said, "What do witches do if they don't weave spells?"

He is standing on the edge of the green turf at the moment, looking intently down at the fighting. It is mostly from Jay that I get my news. Everyone else is too busy. But I must have news. It must all go in my weaving.

# 8

BEFORE I STARTED to weave again, I called my mother to ask her how I should use the bobbin of glistering yarn. Duck had the Lady. I had to call without. I called, and Mother came. She dragged herself over the edge of the falls into the warm pool beside Kars Adon's grave. When I saw how ill she was, I knew Gull was right when he said she is the River. Kankredin is killing her. She looked as ill as Robin did before Tanamil came. And she was not clear to see either. She sank down in the pool, and I could see the grass through her.

"Mother!" I said. I forgot about the bobbin.

"You mustn't worry, Tanaqui," she said. I could barely hear her. "I've wanted to go down to the sea and join your father for a long time now. Open the way for me, so that I can go."

She was fading all the time she spoke, and when she had said that, she melted from my sight entirely. Oh Mother. I do not know if she is dead or not. If it was not so urgent to weave, I would sit and cry. I feel as I did when I was small and fell in the River in the Spring flood. Before my father could pull me out, I had been rolled against the Shelling jetty nine or ten times. It is blow after blow.

Jay looked at me curiously as I called to my mother, but he said nothing.

I have not had the heart to tell Duck that the Lady in his shirt may be nothing more than a wooden carving now. Nor have I told Hern or anyone. If Kankredin has Mother, we have no hope, but I think he has not, or we could not fight.

All this time Duck and Tanamil had everyone below pulling rushes from the lake. While they worked, he and Duck took a heap of pebbles and splashed a sign on each, so: #. This is to stand for a net to hold a man's soul in, Duck says. They made the back of the pebbles sticky and shared them out. We all wear one, stuck to the front of our clothes. They are in colors according to clans. Our people, having no clans, have adopted whichever clan they feel like. Jay has taken red and blue for the Sons of Rath, the clan of Kars Adon. I wanted the same, but Duck says we must have gold, he and I and Robin and Hern, because we are royalty now. This annoys me, but everyone else says Duck is quite right. You cannot believe how much happier Tanamil's pebbles have made them.

When I think, I believe Hern regards my weaving as a consolation, like these pebbles. He is welcome to his opinion. Sometimes I think I would be happier if he were right.

When the pebbles were done, Duck and Tanamil were weaving the rushes into nets until midafternoon. I did not know, until I came to be weaving of the Riverbed. Then Tanamil, like my mother, dragged himself over the edge of the falls in strong spray and fell in the warm pool. My loom was showered. Duck followed, gray with weariness. He might have rolled back to his death if Jay had not pounced on him and caught his coat. That was when I wove wrong. Duck and Tanamil were both soaked; I have never seen Tanamil wet before. Jay dragged them out onto the turf, where Duck lay whimpering and Tanamil rolled on his back with his chest heaving and seemed barely alive.

"What's wrong with them?" I said.

"It's those nets they've been making," Jay said. "They've put all their virtue into them, by the looks of it."

I have conquered my fear of heights and looked at the nets. They are frail and narrow as ladders, except for the great net spread at the bottom, which is hidden in spray from here. I hear there is another, larger one, farther along the gorge of blue pools, too. The nets I have seen stretch across the falls from side to side, wherever there is a ledge or foothold. Hern has posted his fighters on the ledges at both sides, two groups for every net. Those who go down as reinforcements wait on the broad grass below the turf where I weave. We have made quite a path between there and Kars Adon's camp in the valley.

There is always someone coming or going over this turf, though I have little leisure to look. Someone saw Tanamil lying and fetched Robin. Robin came running.

"What have you done?" she said, on her knees in the warm water.

"Used up my strength for the moment," Tanamil panted. "Made something to put Kankredin in a form we can fight him in. Can't fight water."

"You'd no right to use Duck's strength, too," I said. I was angry about Duck, and about having to unpick my weaving, and sick at heart over Mother.

"Had to," gasped Tanamil. "Not enough of mine."

"Oh," I said. "And you call yourself a god!"

Tanamil fetched himself up onto one elbow and said, very earnestly, a very strange thing. "I never called myself that," he said. "Neither I nor any of the Undying ever made that claim. It is a claim men made for us, and that is how we came to be bound."

I told Tanamil I was sorry. I think this he said is one of the strongest threads of my weaving.

Robin made them both rest in my tent. When she came out, I thought of asking her about my bobbin of thread. I should have asked her before. Robin unrolled a length of the thread, rubbed it between her fingers, and then smelled it. "This seems to be the same stuff that the One used to be made of," she said. "Before he went into the fire that turned him gold. How it comes to be spun, I can't think—but then you can spin gold. Tanaqui, I think the One will tell you how to weave it in. Don't use it till you're sure." So I have waited. So far I am not sure.

Kankredin came that evening. When Jay told me, I left my loom and went with him to a ledge a long way below, so that I could see it and weave it in.

It is the most terrifying sight, though I am in a way used to it by now. He came in a mountain of water, standing a hundred feet tall or more. This mountain burst roaring from the valley and spread across the lake from shore to shore. I saw the trees and the stone barn go flat, like things of paper, as the skirts of the great wave took them. The wave is not transparent, or yet quite solid. It is green-black, stinking of River rottenness, with trees and beams and the greater part of a bridge, and many other things, carried along in it and glimpsed from time to time. But inside it, gleaming out through the dark water, we could see terrible shapes, staring eyes, and glances of bared teeth. I screamed as the monstrous thing came grinding through the lake. It sucked the substance of the lake into itself as it came, and left bare trickling mud behind. Many people on the ledges screamed besides me.

Hern sent messages up and down that it was only water.

Water. Oh Hern! It is the whole River, turned to evil. And only see what the River did when it flooded. But people have come to trust Hern. "Only water," we all said, trembling.

The huge water came on. At the top it curved, and the trees and stones carried in there danced, as if it was about to bend over and break, as I saw the waves do in the sea. But it never broke. I could feel the power that held it upright. No wonder Tanamil ran away from it. The power was confident; I could feel that, too. They were almost at their journey's end, and the One would be theirs before nightfall. They raced toward the chasm of blue pools.

This was where Tanamil and Duck had spread their first net. The great wave ran in, piling behind itself to come into that narrow space, and came on the net unawares. Never have I heard a sound like that great wave breaking. It left our ears numb and our bodies weak. For the top curled before the mages could stop it, and the mass of water crashed down on the chasm. I was drenched by it, far up as I was. Logs, timbers, stones, and trees crashed down there with it. Some people were injured on the lower ledges, but none seriously.

The remaining pile of water faltered, hung, and finally withdrew into the lake with a grating and grinding of rock, where it paused, and its surface seethed with fury. It left the chasm broken wide, into a bay, and Tanamil's net broken with it. Tanamil had known that net would be broken.

"More of a trip wire, really," Jay called it.

But word came that two of the lower nets, including the great net at the bottom, had been broken, too. Tanamil, tired as he was, dragged himself out of the tent and climbed down to mend them. As he passed me coming back with Jay, he told me he had forbidden Duck to go down, for which I was thankful.

The great wave stood seething in the lake, drawing itself higher as water ran into it from the falls. Behind it was all mud and little puddles. But before night fell, people on the lower ledges sent up word that the bodies of two mages were lying behind there among the puddles.

"They are only mortal men as we are," Hern sent word, up and down. Then he made a great pother, from ledge to ledge, to find out if there were, as he remembered, no more than forty or fifty mages. By this time even the most doubting of Heathens had realized that Kankredin cared as little for them as he did for our people. Their lords sent very humbly to say that the college of mages was always fifty. I think Hern knew this. He did it to cheer people.

It did not cheer me. I looked at that hill of water and wondered who could live in it. And then it came to me. People who dealt in men's souls were as dangerous dead as alive. I remembered how Kankredin had suddenly appeared to us, sitting in that chair, and I began to fear that Kankredin was not alive. I whispered to Tanamil about it, when he climbed wearily up from his nets.

"Yes, he is dead," said Tanamil. "No one can work with souls who is alive. All the mages pass through death. Then they clothe themselves in their spellgowns, which are their acts of magery and their new bodies both together."

I had wondered why *hidden death* had worn his gown trailing beneath his horrible rugcoat. I sat at my loom, shaking, in the cold half dark. Two good thoughts came out of my terror. The first is that I, too, have passed through death, and I am more their equal accordingly. The other thought caused me to catch one of Robin's girls and send her down to Hern, to tell him that the way to disable a mage was to cut him out of his gown. Hern sent back to thank me. He sounded almost respectful.

If Kankredin had sent the wave on again at once, he would have destroyed us. Tanamil was climbing down to mend the nets, and I had then woven only as far as my talk with Kars Adon in his camp. I had to stop for the night then. But I could feel that Kankredin was—not uncertain; he still thinks he will win—made cautious. Something had opposed him when he least expected it. I think the nets stopped him from seeing who it was. Duck says they are meant to. So he decided to wait until we puny living creatures were exposed in our folly by day. He can work by dark, but he knows, by the same token, that we also appear mysterious and large in the night. See the way I am beginning to think like a witch! So the wave stood in the lake until dawn, and our army slept by relays on the ledges.

Robin hardly sleeps at all. She has the girls, women, and small children all organized. Some run messages. Some carry away the wounded, and others nurse them. Others again are made into an army for a last defense.

"No," Jay wants me to say. "Not the last defense. The last but one. I'm your last defense."

It rather pleases me that the Heathen girls do not make the best soldiers. You would expect them to. The Heathen men show a toughness and courage that Jay often admires. But none of the Heathen girls is strong, and they are scared of being mannish. It is our own tough village ladies who are the army. Robin has sent Aunt Zara down to the next ledge today, armed with a spindle and a gutting knife. Aunt Zara is a match for any mage. She was always half a witch. That is why she hates me so.

And now I come at last to the battle, which has raged below me as I weave for two days now—as I weave and weave and weave. I dream of weaving when I sleep. But no one has slept much since the dawn when Kankredin moved the wave in against us.

Jay tells me that it came on slowly, observing. Kankredin may not have seen the great net hung in the boiling spray at the foot of the falls.

Or perhaps he despised it, not knowing it was the work of the Undying. I could hear from here the repeated *boom, boom, boom*, as the wave reared and smashed and reared again. Duck came panting over the turf to tell me Kankredin had realized the net's purpose too late. The net broke under the wave, and the wave shattered with it. I could hear the cheering as the mages were swept floundering back into the lake. From there a good half of their captured water escaped, they say, and the River is running again as a trickle. They cannot now come against us as water. But they have amassed the rest of the wave and they use it now as a ladder to rear their onslaught up the falls.

Since midday yesterday they have been coming—as fire, as wolves, as scaly creatures with snapping mouths, and all manner of horrible things. Each mage can make himself seem several of these shapes at once, so men often strike at the false shape and leave the mage unharmed. The worst of their power is that they can come straight up the middle of the falls, where it is hard to reach them. Hern has hung ropes across to help his fighters come at them. And as each fresh batch of nightmare creatures scrambles up, men shout, "Only mortal men!" and they hack at them without fear for their souls. We have lost many men drowned.

When the mages come to the nets, they are forced to appear in their own shapes. They fear this and slash at the nets to break them. Duck and Tanamil sit, with their minds dwelling on every knot in the rushes, holding them together as long as they can. And while the mages attack the nets, Hern's army attacks them, yelling, "Cut his coat off!"

The first day we lost, besides the great net, four small ones. Hern and his people were driven to the fifth ledge. Today is worse. They are up on the ledge but one below me now. The women have gone into battle. The yelling is deadly. Uncle Kestrel is hovering on the edge of the turf, trying to watch. He is fond of Aunt Zara, the old fool. Poor Uncle Kestrel was brought up here, shaking all over, yesterday evening.

"Those mages are too many for me," he said. "I had enough of them last winter. I'll stay here and be your last guard, Sweetrush, with Jay here." I have made him stay in front of me, with the sun at his back. I do not want to confuse his shadow with my grandfather's again.

Robin has just gone down into the fight, taking her nurses with her. Tanamil is waiting by the smoking spring to pipe me to the One. We have agreed I must sew the coat by the Riverbed. Tanamil says there will be time. Time is slow there. I have put needles and thread in my rugcoat and gone on weaving. I have not finished. I have not used my bobbin of strange thread yet. I look out, and all I can see is giddy blue landscape far below. But the sound of the fighting is terrible, and so near.

Aunt Zara has been led back up here, laughing like a madwoman. She has cut the coat off a mage. I knew she would be a match for them. She is so excited and horrified and pleased that she has spoken to me for the first time for six months.

"Right in the midst of him with the gutting knife!" she shouts. "I waited and I aimed, and I got him, right in his midst! Cut the coat off him like apple peel! And, do you know, he was rotten inside. Black and rotten! Think of that, Tanaqui!"

"Aunt Zara, I think you're marvelous," I said. I do. I could kiss her, though I know I shall hate her again tomorrow.

The shadow of the One fell across my loom as I wove this. It is not so much a shadow as a shape of greenish light, with that bent head and nose I know so well. Out of the corner of my eye I saw Tanamil kneel and bend his head to the ground. That would have shown me who it was, even if Duck had not climbed just then over the edge of the turf. What Duck can see I have no idea, but he is shading his eyes as if against a strong light, and he looks as if he might have passed through death, like a mage.

While Duck stares, my grandfather has put a vision in my head. "Weave this, Granddaughter," he seems to say, "and use the thread I gave you. It was Cenblith's."

I saw the shadow of the One, Adon Amil, Orethan the Unbound, rise up in his steamy cave, and rise through the earth, through rock and through clouds, until he stood like a mountain, towering above us. Like this, he took the edge of the turf beside me and pulled it, as I would pull a rugcoat up round my shoulders, and he clothed himself in this and in the land that lay below. And as crumbs fall from a coat as you move it, the falls, the lake, and the green valleys beyond were spilled downward and tipped away toward the sea. With the land rolling and ruined, Kankredin and his mages were tipped, too, helplessly, until the grinding of the pulled earth grated them to powder, scattered them, and buried them. The River was tipped and spilled even after this, until it ran as a thread, which thread became a thousand streams, as many as the threads of my weaving. And the land was a new shape. Only then was my grandfather satisfied.

This vision I have woven with Cenblith's thread, knowing it will come to be. I thought the space of the vision was months, but when it was over, Duck still stared and people were in the middle of movements they had started when my grandfather's shadow fell. They are coming back onto my ledge in confusion, Robin, Hern, and all the army. Jay has his sword drawn. The mages are just below. It is time to finish my weaving and take my second coat through the River of Souls to put it upon the One. Then I will come back to see if my vision has come to pass. And if I have failed, I shall go back to the River of Souls for the third and last time.

# FINAL NOTE

*Spellcoats, as they are called, are mentioned frequently in folklore and legend, but these are the only two examples ever discovered. They were found in the marsh above Hannart, when the new fort was under construction on the mountain known locally as The Old Man. They are both preserved by the marsh to a wonderful degree. The colors are bright and clear, and the threads undamaged. The gold band at the hem of the second coat was slightly spoiled when a dishonest workman tried to pull the threads out, but this has now been restored.*

*The coats were known to be of immense antiquity, but they were not recognized for what they are straight away. We are indebted to Earl Keril for first pointing out that the designs bear strong affinity to letters of the old script. Since then both coats have been carefully studied and the foregoing translation made.*

*The story is largely self-explanatory, but certain obscurities in the text have been amended to avoid confusing the reader. The following remarks may be of use to students.*

*Hern Clostisson seems unquestionably to be the same as the legendary Kern Adon, until now thought to be first King of Dalemark. The nameless King is not known, nor is Kars Adon.*

*Duck/Mallard is dubiously identified with Tanamoril (the name means "youngest brother"), the piper and magician of many folktales. It is not known how far the tales confuse him with Tanamil.*

*Concerning Robin, we may point to the belief that a robin can answer the questions of those in trouble.*

*Gull seems to be the same as the Southern hero Gann, whom the witch Cennoreth went in search of.*

*The Weaver herself has been identified with the Lake Lady, the Fates, and with the southern cult figure of Libby Beer, but not satisfactorily. The witch Cennoreth is the most likely possibility. She is frequently called the Weaver of Spells. A drawback is that, like Gann, she figures only in stories told in the South. However, the name Cennoreth—which is a Southern form; the (unrecorded) Northern form would be Kanarthi—can be interpreted as River Daughter (Cenn-oreth), although another interpretation would make it Woman of the North (Cen-Noreth).*

*The places mentioned are harder to determine. Of several rivers which flow northward, the most probable river is perhaps the Aden, which has a tidal wave, or bore, on occasions, known as the Credin. It flows from its rising in Long Tarn toward the Rath Estuary in Aberath, but it is hard to make the Aden fit the Weaver's description unless we postulate some major upheaval in the landscape since the days of the story. It has been calculated that her account should give the river a source somewhere above Hannart, near where the coats were found, but no river flows north from there today.*

*Elthorar Ansdaughter,*
*KEEPER OF ANTIQUITIES*
*AT HANNART IN NORTH DALEMARK*

# The Crown of Dalemark

*For Rachel*

# CONTENTS

# PART ONE

# *Mitt*

# 1

THE EARL OF HANNART arrived in Aberath two days before Midsummer. He was bringing the Countess of Aberath a portrait of the Adon to put in her collection. As this was a state visit, he brought his son as well and a string of his hearthmen, and his arrival caused a rare bustle.

A tall man dressed like a shepherd watched it all from high in the hills where the green roads ran. He had an excellent view from there, not only into the seething courts of the mansion but of the whole town, the cliffs, the bay, and the boat sheds. The Earl was easy to pick out among the hurrying figures, because he was with a servant carrying the picture. The man watched them go straight to the library, where he knew the Countess was waiting to receive the Earl. Almost immediately the servant was sent away to fetch someone else. The watcher could see him pushing his way, first to the stables, then to the dining hall, and finally to the hearthmen's quarters, where he fetched out a large gangly person and pointed to the library. The gangly one set off there at a run, on long, gawky legs.

The watcher turned away. "So they did send for this Mitt," he said as if this had confirmed his worst suspicions. Then he looked up and round and over his shoulder, clearly thinking that someone else was standing nearby, watching, too. But the green road was empty. The man shrugged and set off walking swiftly inland.

About the same time as this man left, Mitt arrived at the top of the library steps, trying not to pant, and pushed open the creaky door.

"Oh, there you are," said the Countess. "We want you to kill someone."

She was never one to beat about the bush. It was almost the only thing Mitt liked about her. All the same, he wondered if he had heard her right. He stared at her long, bony face, which was set slightly crooked on her high shoulders, and then looked at Earl Keril of Hannart to make sure. Mitt had been ten months now in Aberath, but the North Dalemark accent there still sometimes made him hear things wrong. Earl Keril was dark, with a long nose. Everyone said what a likable man he was, but he was looking at Mitt as grimly as the Countess.

"Didn't you hear?" Earl Keril asked. "We want someone dead."

"Yes. Is this a joke of some kind?" Mitt said. But he could tell from their faces that it was not. He felt cold and disgusted, and his knees shook. "I gave up killing—I told you!" he said to the Countess.

"Nonsense," she said. "Why else do you think I had you trained as my hearthman?"

"*You* would have it that way, not me!" Mitt said. "And I never kidded myself you made me learn all that out of love for me!"

Earl Keril looked questioningly at the Countess.

"I warned you he was rude," she said. She leaned toward him, and they murmured together.

Mitt was too disgusted to try to overhear. He looked beyond their two implacable faces at the painting of the Adon propped on an easel behind them. The light was across the canvas from where Mitt stood, in a bluish haze, but the painted eyes caught his, like dark holes in the haze. They looked ill and haunted. The famous Adon had been far from handsome, sickly-looking, with lank hair and crooked shoulders. Near on a cripple, like the Countess, Mitt thought. She and Earl Keril both descended from the Adon. She had the shoulders; Keril had the Adon's long nose. Earlier that day Mitt would have been thoroughly disappointed to find that the Adon looked like this. Since he came to Aberath, he had heard story after story of the Adon, the great hero who had talked with the Undying and lived as an outlaw before he became the last King of Dalemark several hundred years ago. Now he looked from the painting to the two living faces leaning together in the twilight of the library, and he thought, Fairy stories! Bet he was just as bad as they are! Well, I ran off from Holand, so I reckon I can run off from Aberath, too.

Just then he caught a murmur from Keril. "Oh, yes, I'm sure that he is!" Sure I am what? Mitt wondered as they both looked at him again. "We've gone into your history," Keril said to him. "Attempted murder in Holand. Successful murder in the Holy Islands—"

"That's a lie!" Mitt said angrily. "Whatever you think, I never murdered a single soul! And I gave up trying long before I came here."

"Then you'll have to force yourself to try again," said the Countess. "Won't you?"

"And you came on here by boat," Keril went on, before Mitt could speak, "with Navis Haddsson and his children Hildrida and Ynen. In Aberath the Countess took you in and had you educated—"

"For my sins," the Countess said unlovingly.

"So you see the North has treated you well," Earl Keril said. "Better than most refugees from the South, in fact, both you and your friends. We found Navis a post as hearthman to Stair of Adenmouth, and we sent Hildrida to study at the Lawschool in Gardale. Have you ever wondered why this was?" As Mitt wondered about it, Keril added pleasantly, "Why the four of you were separated in this way, I mean."

It was a pleasantness that made Mitt feel like a sack with a hole in it. Everything trickled away through the hole, and his knees almost let him down. "Where's Ynen then?" he said. "Isn't he with Navis?"

"No," said the Countess. "And we are not telling you where he is."

Mitt watched her long jaw shut like a trap. "I used to think," he said, "that the earls in the North were good. But you're as bad as the ones in the South. Go to any lengths, all of you! You're telling me to kill someone for you or my friends suffer. Right?"

"Let's just say—if you want to see your friends again," Keril suggested.

"Well you're wrong," Mitt said. "You can't make me do anything. I don't care two hoots for any of them."

The two implacable faces just looked at him.

Mitt managed a careless shrug. "We happened to ride on the same boat, that's all," he said. "I swear it."

"You swear it? By which of the Undying?" Keril asked. "By the One? The Piper? The Wanderer? She Who Raised the Islands? The Weaver? The Earth Shaker? Come on. Choose which and swear."

"We don't swear like that in the South," said Mitt.

"I know," said Keril. "So it won't hurt you to swear to me by the Earth Shaker that Navis and his children mean nothing to you. Just swear, and we'll forget the whole matter."

Their faces tilted toward Mitt. Mitt looked away, at the dark painted eyes of the Adon, and tried to make himself swear. If Keril had chosen any other of the Undying, he thought he could have done it easily. But not the Earth Shaker. And that showed how frighteningly much Keril knew. Even so, perhaps he could swear about Navis and Hildy and let on he meant Ynen, too? Navis, cold fish on a slab that the man was, still didn't seem to like Mitt particularly, and as for Hildy, after her last letter, Mitt could almost swear he hated her. But he had shown he was worried about Ynen, like a fool, and there was no way he could even pretend to dislike Ynen or let these two earls hurt him.

"Is Ynen all right?" he said.

"Perfectly, at the moment," said the Countess. She never told lies. Mitt was relieved, until he realized that she and Keril both had the same look, satisfied and unsurprised. They knew he had given in. They had expected it.

"I warn you," Mitt said, "if there's murdering needing doing, I can see two ripe cases for it here in this room. So who do you want killed? What's so special that you need to go to all this trouble with me to have it done?" Keril's eyebrows went up. The Countess seemed surprised. Good, Mitt thought. Find out how important it is from how rude they let me be. "Do you take me for a fool?" he said. "If it was lawful, you both have lawyers to burn, and if it was ordinary, you've hearthmen to do it by hundreds. And I'd lay good money you have spies and murderers better than me any day. So it stands to reason it must be politics—you wanting to lay this on Southern scum like me."

"You said it, not me," Keril replied. "Politics, it is. We want a young lady out of the way. She's very charming and much too popular. The whole of the west coast, including Dropwater, will follow her as soon as she gives the word."

"Flaming Ammet!" protested Mitt.

"Be quiet!" said the Countess. "Listen!" She said it like the snap of a steel trap. End of rudeness, thought Mitt, and swallowed what he had been going to say. It hurt, as if he had swallowed an apple whole.

"Noreth of Kredindale, known as Onesdaughter," Keril said. "I expect you've heard of her." Mitt shook his head, but it was from amazement, because he had indeed heard of Noreth Onesdaughter. The story of the One's only human child was one of the many, many stories he had heard round the small coal fires in Aberath this last winter. He had thought that like other stories, it was from times long ago. But Keril, in the most matter-of-fact way, went on to speak of Noreth as alive here and now. "Unfortunately," he said, "she's extremely well connected. The Kredindale family go back to the Adon's daughter Tanabrid, whose mother was of the Undying. Noreth is cousin to Gardale and Dropwater—though Stair's wife at Adenmouth is the aunt who brought her up—and she's a distant cousin of mine, too—"

"And mine," said the Countess. "Pity the girl's mad."

"Mad or not," said Keril, "Noreth claims that her father is the One himself. As her mother died when Noreth was born, there's no one to contradict her, and this claim gives her a huge following among the ordinary people. She makes no secret that she thinks she's born to become Queen of all Dalemark—North and South."

"And that fool in Dropwater backs her," said the Countess.

So that's it! Mitt thought. They're scared for their earldoms. So they get me to stop her and then blame it on the poor South! "Just a minute," he said. "If she's who she says she is, no one can do a thing about it. And someone who's from the Undying on both sides isn't going to be easy to kill either."

"Quite possibly," Keril said. "That's why we were so interested in what we heard about you from the Holy Islands. Reports from there suggested that you could well ask the Undying to help you." Mitt stared at him, shocked at how much Keril knew and how coldly he was prepared to use that knowledge. Keril leaned forward. "We don't want yet another false king and yet another ruinous uprising," he said. Mitt saw he really meant it. "We don't want another war with the South. We want Noreth quietly stopped before she can lay her hands on the crown."

"The crown?" said Mitt. "But nobody knows where that is. They tell stories here about how Manaliabrid hid it."

"She did," said Keril.

"Noreth," said the Countess, "says that the One will show her where it is." Mitt looked from one face to the other and suspected both of them had a fair idea where the crown was hidden. "The girl claims the One talks to her," the Countess added disgustedly. "I told you she was mad. She says the One has promised her a sign to prove her claim and that this year at Midsummer she will become Queen. Silly nonsense."

"She's in Dropwater at the moment," Keril said, "acting as lawwoman for her cousin, but our information is that she'll be going to her aunt in Adenmouth for Midsummer to drum up support there. We're sending you to Adenmouth, too."

"And," said the Countess, "you're to go there and stop her. But don't do it there. We want this quiet."

"We advise you to join her as a follower—you shouldn't be noticed among all the others—and then look for a suitable opportunity," Keril said. As Mitt opened his mouth, he added, "If you want to see Hildrida and Ynen again, you will."

"But Midsummer's the day after tomorrow!" Mitt protested. A stupid thing to say, but he had been looking forward to the feasting in Aberath.

"It's an easy day's ride," said the Countess, who rarely went anywhere except by carriage. "I shall give out that you have my leave to go and visit Navis Haddsson in Adenmouth. You will go first thing tomorrow. You may go away and pack now."

Mitt had been taught that you bowed on leaving the presence of an earl, but he was too disgusted to remember. He turned and blundered his way across the dimness of the library, past the books and the glass cases that held the Countess's collection: the necklace that was supposed to have been worn by Enblith the Fair, the ring that once belonged to the Adon, a flute of Osfameron's, and the withered piece of parchment that went back to the days of King Hern. Behind him he sensed the two earls drawing themselves up in indignation.

"Mitt Alhamittsson," said Keril. Mitt stopped and turned round. "I remind you," Keril said, "that a man can be hanged when he is fifteen. They tell me your birthday is the Autumn Festival. Noreth had better be dead before then, hadn't she?"

"Or we may not be able to avert the course of justice," added the Countess. "You have nearly three months, but don't cut it too fine."

So there was no possibility of putting things off. "Yes," said Mitt. "I get you." He looked past them to the harrowed, ill-looking face of the Adon. He could see the portrait better from here. He pointed his thumb to it. "Miserable-looking blighter, isn't he?" he said. "It must be giving him a right bellyache having you two as descendants!" Then he turned round and walked to the door, rather hoping he had been rude enough to be thrown into prison on the spot. But there was no sound behind him while he opened the door, and no sound but the groan of the hinges as the door shut on his heels. The man on guard outside straightened up guiltily and then relaxed when he saw it was only Mitt. Mitt marched away down the steps without speaking to him. They really meant him to kill this girl. Even the Countess had not told him off for his rudeness.

His knees were trembling as he came out into the courtyard. He almost wanted to cry with shame. It was the way Keril had muttered "Oh, yes, I'm sure he is!" that seemed to have got to him most—sure Mitt was a guttersnipe, a Southerner with no feelings, the first person earls turned to when they wanted dirty work done. Mitt had known such a person and vowed never to be like that, but fat lot those two cared!

Someone shouted to him across the courtyard.

A knot of people stood there, all about his own age. Earl Keril's son, Kialan, was one of them, and the others were waving to Mitt to come over. Mitt had been rather anxious to meet Kialan. Now he found he could not bear to. He ducked sideways and turned along the wall.

"Mitt!" shouted Alla, the Countess's bronze-haired daughter. "Kialan wants to meet you!"

"He's heard all about you!" shouted Doreth, the copper-haired daughter.

"Can't stop! Message! Sorry!" Mitt shouted back. He did not want to meet the daughters either. Alla had jeered at him for being so miserable when Hildy was sent away, until Mitt got mad and pulled her bronze hair. Then Doreth had told the Countess on him. Mitt had been quite surprised not to be sent away then, too. But that must have given them proof that Mitt did care what became of Hildy. Flaming Ammet! The Countess and Keril must have had this planned for months!

Kialan was now shouting himself. "See you later, then!" Mitt had a glimpse of him waving, tawny and thickset and quite unlike his father—but quite certainly not *really* unlike, not deep down where it counted. Mitt put his head down and sped along by the wall, wondering if Kialan saw him as a dirty Southern guttersnipe, too. Kialan would certainly see a lot of lank hair and two spindly legs and shoulders that were too wide for the rest. Mitt kept his face turned to the wall because that was the real giveaway, a guttersnipe face that still looked starved even after ten months of good food in Aberath. He told himself Kialan wasn't missing much.

He plunged through the nearest door and kept running, through rooms and along corridors, and out again on the other side of the mansion, to the long shed on the cliffs above the harbor. That was the best place to be alone. The people who were usually there would all be rushing about after Keril's followers or getting the Midsummer feast ready. And he was having to miss that feast. Hildy had once said that misery was like this: Silly little things always got mixed up with the important ones. How right she was.

Mitt rolled the shed door open a crack and slipped inside. Sure enough, the place was empty. Mitt breathed deep of the fishy smell of coal and of fish oil and wet metal. It was not unlike the smell on the waterfront of Holand, where he had been brought up. And I might just as well have stayed there for all the good it did me! he thought, staring along a vista of iron rails in the floor, where tarry puddles reflected red sun or rainbows of oil. He felt caught and trapped and surrounded in a plot he had not even noticed till they thrust it at him this afternoon. Everyone had told him that the Countess was treating him almost like a son. Mitt had been pretty sarcastic about that, but all the same he had thought this was the way people in the North did treat refugees from the South.

"Fool I was!" he muttered.

He walked along the rails to the huge machines that stood at quiet intervals along them. Alk's Irons, everyone called them. To Mitt, and to most people in town, they were the most fascinating things in Aberath. Mitt trailed his fingers across the cargo hoist and then across the steam plow and the thing that Alk hoped might one day drive a ship. None of them worked very well, but Alk kept trying. Alk was married to the Countess. It was the only other thing Mitt liked about the Countess, that instead of marrying the son of a lord or another earl who might add to her importance, she had chosen to marry her lawman, Alk. Alk had given up law years ago in order to invent machines. Mitt dragged his fingertips across the wet and greasy bolts of the newest machine and shuddered as he imagined himself pushing a knife into a young woman. Even if she laughed at him or looked like Doreth or Alla, even if her eyes showed she was mad—No! But what about Ynen if he didn't? The worst of this trap was that it pushed him back into a part of himself he thought he had got out of. He could have screamed.

He went round the machine and found himself face-to-face with Alk. Both of them jumped. Alk recovered first. He sighed, put his oil can down on a ledge in the machine, and asked rather guiltily, "Message for me?"

"I—No. I thought nobody was here," Mitt said.

Alk relaxed. To look at him, you would have thought he was a big blacksmith run to fat, with his mind in the clouds. "Thought you were calling me to come and run about after Keril," he said. "Now you're here, have a think about this thing. It's supposed to be an iron horse, but I think it needs changing somewhere."

"It's the biggest horse I ever saw," Mitt said frankly. "What good is it if it has to run on rails? Why do your things always run on rails?"

"To move," said Alk. "Too heavy otherwise. You have to work the way things will let you."

"Then how are you going to get it to go uphill?" said Mitt.

Alk rubbed an oily hand through the remains of copper hair like Doreth's and looked sideways at Mitt. "Boy's disillusionment with the North now complete," he said. "Taken against my machines now. Anything wrong, Mitt?"

In spite of his trouble, Mitt grinned. Alk and he had this joke. Alk himself came from the North Dales, which Alk claimed were almost in the South. Alk said he saw three things wrong with the North for every one that Mitt saw. "No—I'm fine," Mitt said, because the Countess had probably told Alk all about her plans anyway. He was trying to think of something polite to say about the iron horse when the door at the end of the shed rolled right open. Kialan's strong voice came echoing through.

"This is the most marvelous place in all Aberath!"

"Excuse me," Mitt muttered, and dived for the small side door behind Alk.

Alk grabbed his elbow as he went. He was as strong as the blacksmith he looked like. "Wait for me!" he said. They went out of the side door together, into the heap of coal and cinders beyond. "Taken against the Adon of Hannart, too, have you?" Alk asked. Mitt did not know how to answer. "Come up to my rooms," Alk said, still holding Mitt's elbow. "I have to dress grandly for supper, I suppose. You can help. Or is that beneath you?"

Mitt gasped rather and shook his head. It was supposed to be an honor to help the lord dress. He wondered if Alk knew.

"Come on, then," said Alk. He let go of Mitt and lumbered ahead of him through the archway that led to his apartments. Alk's valet was waiting there, with candles lit and water steaming and good clothes hung carefully over chairs. "You can have a rest tonight, Gregin," Alk said cheerfully. "Mitt's going to clean me up today. Part of his education."

Even if Alk did not know he was doing Mitt an honor, the valet certainly did. His face was a mixture of jealousy, respect, and anxiety. "Sir," he said. "The coal. The oil." He started to back out of the room as Alk waved him away, and then came back to whisper fiercely to Mitt. "Mind you don't let him stop you scrubbing him when he's still gray. He'll try. He always does."

"Go away, Gregin," said Alk. "My word by the Undying that we won't let you down." Gregin sighed and went away. Mitt got down to the hard work of scrubbing Alk clean. "Do I take it you've had another of your disagreements with my Countess?" Alk asked while Mitt labored.

"Not . . . the way you mean this time," Mitt said, rubbing away at one huge hairy arm.

"Her bark is worse than her bite," Alk observed.

Alk had to think that, Mitt supposed. He must have had a lot of illusions about the Countess to have married her at all. "Keril's worse," he said. "He's all bite and no bark, as far as I can see."

"So Keril's in it, too?" Alk said musingly. He took his arm away from Mitt, looked at it, and gave it back, sighing. It was still gray. "Now I see you're in no mood to agree with me, but Earl Keril's a good man, shrewd as he can hold together. Knows all about steam power, too. They have a steam organ at Hannart, did you know? Huge thing. But he's not the man to get on the wrong side of if you can help it."

"Well, I have," Mitt said bitterly. "I was on his wrong side before he even set eyes on me."

"Now why was that?" wondered Alk.

He was obviously waiting for Mitt to tell him, but Mitt found he could not bear to, any more than he could bear to go near Kialan. He finished scrubbing Alk's left arm and began on the right, even blacker and larger than the left.

"Something's up," Alk said at length, "that I don't know about, I think. And it can't be quite legal, or she would have told me. Did they tell you not to tell me?"

Mitt looked up to find Alk staring shrewdly at him across his lathery arm. "No," he said. "But I'm not saying. They knew I wouldn't, too, for fear you'd be disgusted and kick me out. How do you like being washed by the scum of the earth?"

Alk frowned. "You scrub even brisker than Gregin, if that's what we're talking about." He said nothing else for a while, until Mitt had scrubbed him to clean pink blotches and was starting to help him into good clothes. As his head came out through the neck of the white silk shirt, he said, "See here. I was only a poor farmer's boy before I came to be a lawman. Keril's Countess Halida was nobody much either, and she was from the South like you." Mitt had not the heart to answer this. It was kindly meant, but so wrong. "Hmm," said Alk. "Wrong track there." As Mitt helped him force his arms down the sleeves, he added, "And it's maybe the wrong track, too, if I was to mention that you're much better placed than you were when you came? You can read and write and use weapons now. They tell me you learn good and quick, and you've brains to use what you learn—well, I know you've got brains. My Countess has not treated you so badly—"

"And that's a lie!" Mitt burst out. "She did it all for a reason!"

"As to that," Alk said as Mitt threaded golden studs into his cuffs, "*you've* not gone out of your way to make her love you, Mitt. And everyone always has a reason for what they do. It's only natural."

"Then what's *your* reason for trying to cheer me up like this?" Mitt retorted.

"Easy," said Alk. "I can't abide misery, and I hate mysteries. Anyone taking half a glance at your face could see something was wrong. And cheering up often brings things to light. I found *that* out when I was a lawman, the first time we had a man accused of murder." Mitt winced at that and nearly dropped a stud. He knew Alk noticed, but Alk only said, "Want me to talk to my Countess about this?"

"No point. Wouldn't do any good," Mitt said. Everyone knew that Alk never went against the Countess. He turned away and got Alk's vast brocade trousers. "Look, I don't want to talk about this no more," he said, helping Alk step into them.

"I see that. And I think you ought to," Alk said.

Mitt obstinately said nothing while he buttoned the trousers round Alk's bulging waist and then fetched the huge embroidered jacket. Alk backed into it with his arms out, like a bear. "Nothing you want to say, then?" he asked.

"Nothing, only a question," Mitt said, meaning to change the subject. "Is the One real?" Alk turned round with the jacket half on and stared at him. "I mean," said Mitt, "I never heard of the One, nor half the other Undying either, until I came here. We don't take much note of Undying in the South. Do *you* believe in any of them?" He went round Alk and heaved the jacket onto him. Then he bent down to help Alk with his boots.

"Believe in the One!" Alk said, and trod into the right boot. "It would be hard not to, here in Aberath, at this time of year, but—" He trod into the left boot and stamped down in it, thinking. "Put it like this. I believed in my machines when they were just a notion in my head and nothing I could touch or see. Who's to say that the One isn't as real as they were in my head—or as real as they are now?" He flipped the fastening at the neck of his shirt to see if Mitt had tied it securely and tramped to the door. "Coming?"

Supper would be ready in the great hall. It came to Mitt that it would be his job to wait on Kialan at table. He could not face it. "I got to polish my gear and pack now," he said. "I'm off to Adenmouth tomorrow."

"Are you now?" Alk turned round in the doorway and looked hard at Mitt again. "Then I'll make sure someone remembers to feed you," he said. "I think I'm on the right track now. And I don't like it, Mitt. I don't like it any more than you do. Don't do anything stupid until I talk to you again."

# 2

MITT HAD TO SET OUT for Adenmouth without seeing Alk again. The Countess had obviously given strict orders. He was roused before dawn, and fed, and pushed to the stables as the sun rose, where he found the armsmaster waiting for him in a very bad temper. Mitt sighed and watched every buckle, pouch, and button being checked, and then every scrap of tack on the horse. He had had some idea of hanging his belt, with the sword on one side and the dagger on the other, up on a nail and then forgetting it accidentally on purpose. But there was no question of that with an angry armsmaster standing over him.

"I'm not going to have you let me down in front of potty little Adenmouth," the armsmaster said as Mitt mounted.

Mitt rather hoped the horse would try to take a bite out of the armsmaster, the way it always did with anyone else, but of course, it did not dare, any more than Mitt did. "I wish you'd let me take a gun," Mitt said. "I can use a gun. I'd let you down with a sword for sure."

His idea was that it would be much easier to shoot this Noreth from a distance than to get close up the way you had to with a sword. But that idea died at the look on the armsmaster's face. "Nonsense, boy! Guns here have to be smuggled in from the South. Think I'd trust you with something that expensive? And sit up straight! You look like a sack of flour!"

Mitt straightened his back and clopped angrily through the gate. He *could* use a gun, and care for it, too. Mitt's stepfather, Hobin, made the best guns in Dalemark. But nothing ever seemed to convince the armsmaster of this. "Yes, sir, good-bye, sir. Good riddance, sir," he said, raising one smartly gloved hand when he was too far away to be caught.

He clopped through the streets of the town, all hung with decorations for the feast he was having to miss, and up along the top of the cliffs, where the sun was a gold eye opening between heavy gray eyelids of sea and sky, and looked down on the boat sheds at the cliff foot as he went. One of those sheds hid the battered blue pleasure boat they had arrived in: Mitt, Hildy, Ynen, and Navis. Ynen's boat. And the Countess had started plotting from that moment on. Today Mitt found he was angry about it, very angry. And the odd thing about being angry was that it seemed to break through the walls that had seemed to hem him in yesterday and give him space to hope. He was going to see Navis. Navis was Ynen's father and a cool customer, and he would think of something. Navis was used to dealing with earls' plots, being the son of an earl himself.

Thinking of Navis, then of Ynen, Mitt rode between the sea and the steep fields on the hills above, where people were scrambling to scrape in a crop of hay despite its being a feast day. Ynen was younger than Mitt, but Mitt had nevertheless come to admire him more than he admired anyone else. Ynen was—steadfast—that was the word. His sister, Hildy, on the other hand . . .

After first Navis, then Ynen had left Aberath, Hildy and Mitt had been together there another short month, while Hildy was coached by the Countess's law-woman in law, geometry, history, and the Old Writing, so that she could pass into the great Lawschool in Gardale. That way, as she told Mitt, she could always earn her living. Nobody was more respected than a lawyer. Hildy was inclined to patronize Mitt, just a little, as Mitt struggled simply to read and write along with all the other duties of a hearthman-in-training. "I'll send you letters," Hildy had promised, when she went away, "to help with your reading." The trouble was, she kept her promise.

Her first letters were carefully printed and quite full of news. The next few were dashed off, with an air of duty about them. Around then Mitt had learned enough to be able to write back. Hildy had answered several of his letters with one of her own, carefully, point by point, but she had been quite unable to resist correcting his spelling. Mitt had kept writing—there had been a lot to tell—but Hildy's letters had become ever briefer and farther apart, and each one was harder to understand than the last. Mitt had waited well over a month for Hildy's latest letter. And what came was:

Dear Mitt,

This grittling the boys on fayside were at trase with peelers, would you believe! They had sein right, too, so it was all kappin and no barlay. We only had mucks. But Biffa

was our surnam and you should have seen the hurrel. Now
highside is doggers and we have herison from scap to
lengday, and everyone looks up to us although we are to be
stapled for it. In haste to trethers.
Hildrida

It was like a message from the moon. It hurt Mitt badly. Hildy and he had had little enough in common anyway, and now Hildy was making it clear that this little was gone. After that letter Mitt had told himself he did not care what became of Hildy, and then Earl Keril came along and forced him to behave as if he did care. As he rode on, he tried to tell himself that he was being noble about Hildy. This was not true. He did not want Hildy hurt, not when she was evidently having fun for the first time in her life.

The sun came up higher. People began passing Mitt on their way to the feasting at Aberath, calling out in the free way of the North that Mitt was going the wrong way, wasn't he? Mitt called jokes in reply and urged his horse on. The horse, as usual, had other ideas. It kept trying to go back to Aberath. Mitt cursed it. He had a very bad relationship with this horse. His private name for it was the Countess. It held its head sideways like she did, and walked in the same jerky way, and it seemed to dislike Mitt as much as the real Countess did. They came to the place where the road forked, a rutty track going along the coast to Adenmouth and a wider and even ruttier one winding back right into the mountains at the heart of the earldom. People were streaming down this wider road and turning along the way Mitt had come, and the horse tried to turn back with them. Mitt wrestled its head round onto the Adenmouth road and kicked its sides to make it go.

"Going my way, hearthman?" somebody called after him.

Hot and annoyed, Mitt looked round to find a boy on an unkempt horse turning out of the main road after him. Another hearthman, by the look of the faded livery. Mitt did not feel like company, but people in the North never seemed to feel you might want to be alone, and it was a fact that the Countess-horse went better for a lead. So, as the two horses slid and stamped in the ruts, Mitt said a little grudgingly, "Going to Adenmouth, hearthman."

"Good! Me, too," said the lad. He had a long, freckled face with a sort of eager look to it. "Rith," he introduced himself. "Out of Dropwater."

"Mitt," said Mitt. "Out of Aberath."

Rith laughed as they set off side by side up the narrower road.

"Great One! You've come even farther than I have!" he said. "What's a Southerner doing this far North?"

"Came by boat—we went where the wind took us," Mitt explained. "I think we missed Kinghaven in the night somehow. How come you knew I was a Southerner? My accent that bad still?"

Rith laughed again and pushed at the fair, frizzy hair that stuck out all round his steel cap. "That and your looks. The straight hair. But it's the name that's the clincher. Dropwater's full of Southern fugitives, and they all answer to Mitt, or Al, or Hammitt. I'm surprised the South's not empty by now, the way you all come to the North. Been here long?"

"Ten months," said Mitt.

"Then you've had one of our winters. I bet you froze!"

"Froze! I nearly died!" said Mitt. "I never saw icicles before, let alone snow. And when they first brought the coal in to make a fire, I thought they were going to build something. I didn't know stones could burn."

"Don't they have coal in the South?" Rith asked wonderingly.

"Charcoal—for those that could afford it," Mitt said. "At least that's what they used in Holand, where I come from."

Rith whistled. "You *did* come a long way, didn't you?"

By this time Mitt had forgotten he had wanted to be alone. They rode with the sea sparkling on one side and the hills climbing on the other, under the douce Northern sun, talking and laughing, while the Countess-horse followed Rith's travel-stained little mount as smoothly as its jerky gait would allow. Rith was good company. He seemed genuinely interested to know what Mitt thought of the North now he was here. Mitt was a bit wary at first. He had found that most Northerners did not like criticism. "It's this porridge they all eat I can't stand," he said jokingly. "And the superstition."

"What superstition?" Rith said innocently. "You mean, like the Holanders throw their Undying in the sea every year?"

"And you lot put bowls of milk out for yours," said Mitt. "Believe anything, these Northerners! Think the One's a pussycat!"

Rith bowed onto his horse's neck with laughter. "What else do we do wrong?" he said when he could speak. "I bet you think we're inefficient, don't you?"

"Well you are," said Mitt. "All runabout and talk and do nothing when a crisis happens."

"Not when it matters, though," said Rith. "And?"

And he went on coaxing Mitt until Mitt at last came out with the real cause of his disappointment with the North. "They told me it was free here," he said. "They told me it was good. I was badly enough off in the South, but beside some here I was rich—and idle. People are no more free here than—than—" He was trying to find a proper description when they came round a bend to find the road blocked house-high with earth and boulders. A stream sprayed from the top in a raw new waterfall and ran round their horses' hooves. "This just about sums it up!" Mitt said disgustedly. "And your roads are all terrible!"

"The Southern roads are, of course, all perfect," Rith said.

"I never said—" said Mitt.

Rith laughed and dismounted. "Come on. This is hopeless. We'll have to lead the horses uphill and come back to the road where it's clear."

Mitt slid down from the Countess-horse and discovered he was more than a little saddlesore. Ow! he thought. I wonder my pants aren't smoking! But he did not like to confess this to Rith, who had ridden all the way from Dropwater and was obviously a seasoned hearthman. A small, tough boy, Rith. When they were both on their feet, Rith only came up to Mitt's shoulders. Makes me look a big booby if I moan, Mitt thought, and he set off dragging the Countess-horse up the hill after Rith. Both horses were huge, heavy, and reluctant. Their hooves slid in the slippery grass. Mitt's horse put its ears back and tried to bite him.

"Stop that!" Mitt slapped its nose aside. "You Countess, you!"

Rith broke into a panting laugh. "What a name! It's a gelding. O-oh! Piper's *pants*!"

Mitt dragged his horse up beside Rith's. The hill, in the mysterious manner of hills, was twice as high as he had thought. Beyond and above them, it was a huge triangle of earthy boulders and trickling water, which had slid down across the road, blocking it for as far as they could see. At the lower edge of it, the sea twinkled, flat and impassable.

"We'd better go up over the hill," Rith said. "I know the way. It'll mean fording the Aden after we cross the green road, but it won't be deep this high."

So they struggled on upward, about twice as high as they had already come, until they left the landslip behind and reached a squishy yellow-green shoulder, where Rith said they could ride again. Mitt nearly yelled as he kicked his way into the saddle. He was raw. But he did not like to mention it. He simply bore it, all the way through a long, marshy valley and then up an endless firm green slope, where they came to one of the things the Northerners called waystones. It was round, like a roughly shaped millstone set up on one edge, with a hole in the middle. Rith leaned over and slapped the thing.

"For luck," he said, grinning. "I'm a superstitious Northerner. I may ask the Wanderer's blessing, too, just to annoy you. There's the Aden down there. What do you say we stop for some lunch?"

Mitt was only too glad to get down. He helped himself off by hanging on to the waystone, which was a way of touching it without seeming to. He knew he could do with some luck. And once he was down, he was so sore that he had to concentrate on small things, like stripping off his gloves and tucking them into the proper place on his belt, and hitching his horse to the waystone, where someone had tied a piece of red twine through the middle for the purpose. Then, moving in a careful, stiff-legged way, he unbuckled his baggage roll and got out the food they had given him. By then the agony had gone off enough for him to sit down beside Rith, bat the Countess-horse's nose aside as it tried to eat his bread, and look at the view.

There were hills all round, yellow and green, with sunlight scudding over them in patches. The green way stretched from the waystone, very level and firm and dry, leading south into the mountainous heart of Dalemark, and the Aden rolled parallel with it about a hundred yards downhill from where they sat. It was a fine big river, wider than any Mitt had seen, and the way it rolled quietly along among all those reeds and willow trees suggested that it might be pretty deep. Mitt hoped Rith knew what he was talking about when he said they could ford it. He leaned back and sniffed the smell of the river and willows mingling with the damp wild smell of heather and rock, the smell of the North, which Mitt still thought of as the smell of freedom in spite of his disillusionment with the North. Perhaps, he thought, not very hopefully, he would be stuck this side of the river and never get to Adenmouth at all. But that would be the worse for Hildy and Ynen.

"You look pretty gloomy!" Rith said, laughing.

"Just thinking," Mitt said hurriedly. "What *are* these green roads? Who made them—really?"

"Kern Adon," said Rith. "King Hern. They're the roads of his old kingdom. That's why they don't go to places where people live anymore. They say that Kern Adon set up the waystones and told the Wanderer to guard the roads, and if you follow them right, they say you arrive at King Hern's city of gold."

"I heard them called the paths of the Undying," said Mitt.

"Oh yes. They're called that, too," said Rith. "My old nurse used to tell me that the Undying sit in the hole in the waystones. What do you think of that?"

"They couldn't!" Mitt said unguardedly. "Not unless they shrunk."

Rith got very interested in this idea. "Then how big do you think the Undying are?" he kept saying, in the same coaxing way he had tried to get at Mitt's opinion of the North. "I've never been able to decide. Do you think they're made of something that isn't as solid as we are, so that they can be of any size? Or what?"

These Northerners! Mitt thought. Rith was laughing, but he was serious, too. They finished eating, and Mitt got up, rather reluctantly, to untie the Countess-horse.

"What size do you think?" Rith said, leading his horse downhill to the river.

"If you must know," Mitt called over his shoulder, "they're people-sized. It stands to reason." He dragged the Countess-horse round to follow Rith. "How could—" He stopped and blinked.

There was no wide rolling river anymore. Rith was on his way down to a sunken crease in the hillside that was choked with small oak trees. Mitt could hear water rushing among the trees.

"You're probably right," Rith called back, "though some of the things they do make them seem smaller. Come on. It really is quite shallow here."

Mitt slowly followed him down among the oaks, wondering just what river it was that he had seen. There was no question in his mind that the real Aden was the yelling, stony stream in front of him now, glinting bright coins of sunlight under the trees. Rivers in the North always seemed to crouch like this one along dips in the hills. And he had not seen a single willow tree since he left the South. Shivers ran down his back, and he approached the brawling little Aden very cautiously indeed.

So did the Countess-horse. At the edge of the water it put its ears back, braced its hooves, and refused to move. Mitt called it names.

"I'll give you a lead," said Rith. He stepped into the shrilling water, which proved to be only a few inches deep, and waded carefully, watching the stones in the bottom, until he and his horse had become dark shadows, patterned with sun between the oak leaves.

At this point the Countess-horse found it preferred not to be left behind and took off suddenly after Rith, dragging Mitt in sheets of bright water. Mitt kept hold of the reins and managed to stay on his feet until he was halfway across, where his foot turned heavily on something that flashed in the sun.

Rith called out, "*Look there!*" in a surprisingly deep, strong voice, and dived toward Mitt.

It was all sun-patterned wet confusion. Both horses got away, and Mitt sat down with a splash. Rith plunged his hands down where Mitt's feet had been and stood up triumphantly holding something that shone. Water poured off his elbows as he held it out for Mitt to see.

"Look at this!"

Mitt floundered to his knees. The thing had evidently once been a little statue—a figurine, Mitt thought the word was. As Rith turned it round, Mitt could see traces of a face and the folds of a robe on the side that was green with river slime. The other side was grated and scratched all over, and that side shone a pure buttery yellow. Mitt in his time had worked enough inlay into gun handles to know what that meant. "It's solid gold!" he said.

"I think it is," Rith said. He sounded awestruck. "Who found it? You or me?"

"You picked it up," Mitt said. "I only stepped on it."

Rith turned the dripping statuette round again. "I wish I could be sure—Look, may I keep it for now and give you your share when I've got it?"

If Mitt had not been so saddlesore, he might have argued. But the cold water was smarting him like acid, and he could think of almost nothing else. "Fine," he gasped, and splashed his way across to the far bank, where the horses were standing head to tail, looking pleased with themselves. Rith followed, stowing the wet figurine in the front of his jacket.

"You're being very generous," he said several times, as they mounted and rode on. "You really mean I can keep it for now?" He was evidently feeling a strange mixture of doubt and elation, but then anyone would, Mitt thought, who had just picked up a pound of solid gold. He thought Rith was nice to be so bothered about it. All through the next hour or so Rith was either exclaiming at the amazing chance that had led them to that spot or asking Mitt if he really minded waiting for his share. "If it hadn't been for that landslide," he said, "we'd never have come this way. Look, are you really sure?"

Mitt got increasingly gruff with him. Mitt's leathers were wet through and rubbing his soreness until he was convinced he was being flayed. Besides, he thought angrily, the way he was caught in the earls' plotting, he couldn't see himself having much use for gold or anything else shortly. He wished Rith would shut up. By the late afternoon, when the sea came into view again blue and crisp to northward, Mitt was wanting to scream at Rith, and he might have done had they not come out on a headland overlooking Adenmouth to find themselves looking down on an accident.

A Singer's cart had overturned on the bridge below. The bridge had no sides, and the horse that had pulled the cart was dangling struggling in the Aden. Mitt saw someone pulling uselessly at the horse. A girl lay on the bank as if she might be dead.

"Come on!" shouted Rith, and his shaggy horse was off down the hill as if it was aiming to end in the river, too.

Mitt followed as fast as the Countess-horse would let him, which was not very fast. The hill was extremely steep. Even Rith slowed down halfway, but this was probably because he could see that help was on its way. They could see into a long green valley to one side, where a party of people were running from one of the farms. More people were running across a second bridge, from Adenmouth itself, and a horseman was galloping ahead of them.

Everyone converged on the bridge, but the horseman got there first. He was a hearthman in Adenmouth livery. As the Countess-horse slithered cautiously down the last slope, Mitt saw the horseman leap to the ground, thrust his reins into the hands of the redheaded Singer's boy, and run toward the struggling horse. There he took one look, cocked his pistol, and shot the horse through the head.

Mitt and Rith came down to the bridge while the horse was still jerking. The bang rang in Mitt's ears like the memory of his worst dreams. The white staring face of the Singer-boy looked just like he felt.

"Anything we can do?" called Rith.

The hearthman turned from slashing at the traces that held the dead horse. Mitt almost laughed. It was Navis. It would be. "Hello," he said.

Navis nodded at him in his cool way. "You see to that girl," he said to Rith. "I think she's alive. Mitt, you help me cut this horse loose."

As the two of them dismounted, Mitt noticed the Singer himself wandering about on the bank, carefully laying out musical instruments from the overturned cart. A dreamy-looking fellow with a gray beard. Mitt ignored the Singer as useless and hobbled over to Navis, while Rith sprinted to where the Singer-girl was sitting up, holding her head.

"Get your knife out and cut here, then here," Navis said. He did not seem in the least surprised at seeing Mitt there. His attention was mostly on the accusing yellow-white face of the Singer-boy. "Your horse had broken two legs—look," he said to the boy. "There was nothing else to be done."

"He was blind in one eye," the boy said. "He walked off the bridge."

"I just wish mine would do that, too!" Mitt said, to make him feel better. "Mine's a right brute."

The boy simply stared at him. "Southerner," he said. "You both are." He turned his back and led Navis's mare to the other side of the road.

Navis glanced at Mitt. "There's a lot of prejudice," he said. "Now cut here." Mitt slashed away angrily. Cool, cool Navis. He had forgotten just how cool.

By the time they had cut the horse loose, the people from the farm and the town had arrived. There was a lot of typically Northern milling about and talking. The chief talker was a lad from the farm, who wanted everyone to know how quickly he had gone for help to the mansion and what the lady Eltruda had said to him. But amid all this there was unnoticed efficiency. In less than a minute many hands had heaved the neat green cart upright and Mitt was able to read the gold lettering on its side.

"Hestefan the Singer."

"You want me?" Hestefan asked.

He was standing beside Mitt with a cwidder in one hand and a fife in the other. Mitt was embarrassed. He had only said it aloud because he still found it easier to read that way. Now he felt he had to say something. "How did you get past the landslip on the road?" he asked.

"Landslip?" said Hestefan. "What landslip?"

Mitt gave him up again and turned to Rith, who said in a worried whisper, "I think that girl, Fenna, has really hurt her head. Can you help me get her on a horse?"

The Countess-horse was at that moment demonstrating that it was not carriage-trained. They had tried to back it into the shafts of the cart, where it divided its attention between trying to take bites out of anyone near and attempts to kick the splashboard in. Mitt ran and hauled it clear. "You good-for-nothing Countess, you!" He dragged it over to the injured girl, where the Singer-boy held it while Mitt and Rith heaved Fenna into its saddle. The chattering crowd seized Rith's horse and backed that into the cart instead. Nobody thought of using the beautiful mare that belonged to Navis. Typical of Navis, that, Mitt thought, taking the reins from the boy. The lad looked as ill as Fenna. "Want me to boost you up behind her, Moril?" Mitt asked. He had gathered the boy's name was Moril.

Moril simply turned away and walked to the cart.

"All right. *Be* like that then!" Mitt said to his back. All this running about made his backside feel as if it was on fire. It got worse when he set off leading the horse into Adenmouth. Fenna had to nudge him with her foot before Mitt noticed she was trying to speak to him.

"Er—young hearthman. Sir."

Mitt looked up. She was pale, but she was dark and pretty, and she spoke with just a trace of a Southern accent, which made him try to smile at her. "Sorry. What?"

"Don't think too hard of Moril, sir," Fenna said. "He loved our old horse. And I heard tell he had another horse killed by Southerners last year."

Well, he's no call to take it out on me! Mitt thought. But he said politely, "Heard tell? I thought he was your brother."

"Oh no, sir," Fenna said. "Moril is Clennen the Singer's son. He'll be a great Singer himself before long."

Rith grinned at Mitt round the nose of the Countess-horse. "These artists! You can tell what they're like from the red hair. Sit straight, Fenna, or you'll fall off."

It was not far to Adenmouth, just across another bend in the Aden, which then poured noisily past low gray houses crowded at the edge of a cove. Mitt was glad. By the time they had gone up the main street to the mansion, he was not sure he could have walked another step. Their arrival caused much confusion, for a good hundred more people came out of the houses to see what was wrong and then followed them into the courtyard of the mansion, where rows of trestle tables that had been set up for the Midsummer Feast all had to be moved to make way for the cart.

Lady Eltruda was out on the hall steps, bellowing instructions in a voice like the armsmaster's. "Navis!" she yelled. "Get that thing through to the stables! Spannet, fetch the lawman! You!" she screamed at Mitt. "You in the Aberath livery! Bring that poor girl to me!"

Before Mitt could move, Rith was dragging Fenna and the Countess-horse toward the steps, zigzagging between tables and shouting back. "Aunt! Aunt! I'm here! I got here, and I got my sign!"

At this Lady Eltruda dashed down the steps, yelling, "Noreth, my dove! Noreth!" and flung her arms round Rith.

Mitt stared. He felt terrible.

# 3

THE CONFUSION CLEARED UP surprisingly quickly. Mitt was almost alone in the yard, wondering what on earth to do now, when Navis put a hand on his shoulder.

"Come to my room," he said. "Tell me your news there."

Funny, Mitt thought, staring slightly downward into Navis's cool, clear-cut face. I don't remember him being that small. Maybe I grew. "I would if I could walk," he said.

Navis smiled a little. "It's not far. But I can't carry you."

He turned and led the way. Mitt hobbled after him, protesting, "I do know how to ride! It's just that I never did it for a whole day before!" They went through the hall, big enough, but a dark little place compared with the one at Aberath, and up a shallow flight of steps. Navis had a comfortable paneled room beyond, as good as one of Alk's. Typical, Mitt thought, looking round. He must be well in with Lord Stair. "How did you know I got news?"

"Hush a moment," Navis said. Two servingmen came into the room. They were grinning rather and carrying a large bowl of something sour and strong. They dumped it where Navis pointed and then hung about, lingeringly, as if there was some joke. "Thank you," Navis said, "but we'd like to be private now."

"What is this?" Mitt said suspiciously as the men left, still grinning.

"Vinegar," said Navis. "Take your leathers off and sit in it. Go on. It works."

Slowly, with misgivings, Mitt did as Navis said. He sat. Yelled. Tried to get out again and found himself held down by Navis's unexpectedly strong hand. Vinegar spilled on the rugs, and Mitt went on yelling, even though he was sure the two men were standing outside the door loving every shriek. "Flaming Ammet!" he roared. "Are you trying to kill me?"

"No," said Navis, and he went on holding Mitt down until Mitt's yells had given way to gasps and then to miserable panting. Then he let go and went to the half-open door. "That will be all," he said, and closed the door.

Mitt heard footsteps retreating. "Can I get out now?"

"The longer you stay in, the sooner you'll be able to ride again," Navis said. "Tell me your news to take your mind off it." It was on the tip of Mitt's tongue to tell Navis he was as bad as Earl Keril, but he did not say it because he suddenly realized it was true. Navis, in his way, could be quite as ruthless as Keril. Earls' blood will out! Mitt thought. He was wondering if he was going to be able to tell Navis anything after all when Navis added, "They wouldn't have let you leave Aberath without very good reason, I'm sure." Very strong bitterness came through his coolness.

He feels just as caught as I do! Mitt thought. "Well, before I start, do you know where Hildy is?"

"In Gardale," said Navis. "Though, from the one letter she deigned to send, I wondered if she wasn't in the moon."

"I got one of those," Mitt said. "Total gibberish. And Ynen? You have any idea where Ynen is?"

"No," said Navis. There was a cold little silence before Navis said, "No. No one has bothered to tell me that. Is that why they let you see me? To bring me a threat?"

"That may be part of it," Mitt said. "They must have reckoned I'd tell you. Navis, they want me to kill that girl Noreth. And I tell you I rode most of the way here with her and she's no madder than what I am!"

"Sit still," said Navis. "You'll get vinegar everywhere." He drew up a chair and sat facing Mitt in his bowl. "Tell me this carefully. *Who* wants you to?"

"The Countess and Earl Keril," said Mitt. "Talk about your past catching up with you! They found out all about me."

"Keril," said Navis. "Keril. Then, Mitt, you are not the only one whose past has caught up with him. I once risked a good deal to send a message to Keril to warn him that his sons were prisoners in Holand. He must have taken it as a threat. What did he say?"

Mitt sat in his bowl and told Navis everything, including his ride with Noreth. The only thing he left out was the way he had thought the Aden was a mighty river. He was not sure he believed that himself now. He found he felt a little tearful as he talked, not for obvious reasons but because Navis was listening and not treating him as the scum of the earth.

"That statue," Navis said. "You were a little over-generous there. Can you persuade her to give you your half?"

"Chop it in two? Why?" said Mitt.

"Because if it *is* solid gold," said Navis, "neither of us need depend on the charity of earls. We could leave tonight. Mitt, I don't like this at all. You hear a great deal about Noreth here in Adenmouth. She is much loved. If anything happened to her, there would be an outcry all down the coast dales as far as Kinghaven. You are an obvious Southerner. Yet they send you after her in full Aberath livery. What are they playing at? Everyone will know Aberath had a hand in it, however villainous they say you are."

"I'm not doing it," said Mitt. "I can't. That's final. But what do we do?"

"We leave," said Navis, "as soon as I think of an excuse, with your share of the gold if possible. We look for Ynen and we cut short Hildrida's education and we hope we can get to them before Keril finds out." He sighed. "Then we all go into hiding again. Meanwhile, keep sitting. You have to be able to ride."

Mitt sat for another hour. During that time the big paneled room darkened, and drops of rain patterned on the tall window. Lady Eltruda's voice was heard bawling for Navis to see about awnings over the yard. Navis hurried away. He came back only to be called away to see about candles. By the time he was back from that, the clouds had passed and red-gold sunlight was slanting into the room. Lady Eltruda bawled that it was going to be fine after all, and Navis hurried off to have the awnings rolled away. Mitt saw why Navis seemed so well in with Lord Stair. People welcomed a little Southern efficiency round here. He grinned as he watched Navis come back and dress for the feast, with the same efficiency, in a ruffled shirt and blue-green Adenmouth livery. You wouldn't think, to look at him, that Navis must have been dressed by a valet all his life until these last months.

"You can get out now and wash," Navis said.

Mitt did so. He was not sore anymore, not even tender. In fact, he was as smooth and leathery as his own buff and gold Aberath livery. "You pickled me!" he said.

"That was the idea," said Navis.

They went out into the hall, which was full of cooking scents and people standing about waiting for Lord Stair to arrive and start the feast. The big doors were open, blowing in a chilly wind. A lot of noise came from the yard, where everyone else in Adenmouth was gathered at the tables drinking beer until the food arrived. Mitt stood, a little lost among all these strangers.

"Oh, *there* you are, Mitt!" said Rith's voice.

Mitt turned and found himself facing an elegant lady. He was utterly dismayed. The only thing that was the same about her was the longish, freckled face with its eager, cheerful look. But that was surrounded by clouds of fair, frizzy hair, done in a most fashionable style, and she had on a slender dress of gray-blue that hung in sheeny folds round a thoroughly female figure. Mitt could see now she was a lot older than he was—eighteen or twenty at least—and that was enough to make him feel a fool. But the thing that dismayed him most was the fact that Noreth was alive, utterly alive, and warm, and a person.

"Come on!" said Noreth. "Where's your tongue?"

"Er," said Mitt. "Your ladyship—"

"I told you," she said, "to call me Rith."

"Yes," said Mitt, "but . . . what were you doing, letting on you were a boy?"

"I always travel like that," Noreth said. "It's far quicker and safer than a carriage, and I don't need to bother to take a guard. My cousin lends me the livery. And I can use the weapons, too. You learn to, during grittling. But listen—" To Mitt's consternation, Noreth reached out and took hold of both his hands. Her hands were strong and warm, but so small they made Mitt's feel like great cold paws. "I'm very nervous," she said. She was. Mitt could feel her hands trembling. "There's something I have to do. Do you know how it feels to do something that means your life will never be the same again?"

"Don't I just!" Mitt said. He sensed that Navis had come up behind him and was watching Noreth coolly. That reminded him that he had to ask for his share in the statue, but he was too confused to know how to put it.

"I had a feeling you did," said Noreth. "Listen, could you—" There was a bustle up on the dais. Someone was calling for lamps to be lighted. Noreth looked round. "Oh, here comes my uncle," she said. "Drunk as usual. I must go. If you could just bear witness about that statue when the time comes?"

"Sure," said Mitt, "but—"

Noreth let go of him and hurried away. Everyone was surging toward the long tables to sit down. Navis beckoned Mitt to a place beside him, just below the important table on the dais. Mitt found there were advantages to being sent to Adenmouth after all. At Aberath he would have been waiting at the tables with the other boys. Here he was a guest, and he could sit and let boys wait on him. He settled down to enjoy himself. The food was good, though Mitt found he did not much care for the traditional Midsummer sausage. Like so much of the food in the North, it seemed to be mostly oatmeal. But there was venison and pork and chicken and beef as well, oyster patties and plum-and-mutton pies, strawberries, raspberries with syllabub, and sweet soda bread. Ale and spirits were passed round the whole time. The sound of voices became a cheerful roar that almost drowned the even greater din from the yard outside. Mitt ate hugely and became very friendly with the hearthmen at his table. There were a great many jokes about vinegar.

Lord Stair was indeed drunk. It was impossible not to notice. He was a large, sallow man, and he sat sprawling in his chair, eating very little and shouting for more drink. Every so often he complained loudly about the food. Nobody took much notice. If people needed to have orders about anything, they asked Lady Eltruda. It looked as if Lady Eltruda, short and fat and loud as she was, had the same power here that the Countess had in Aberath.

"Indeed she does," Navis told Mitt. "I owe my position here to Eltruda. I imagine Noreth does, too."

Lady Eltruda was obviously very fond of Noreth. She kept smiling at her proudly.

The feast drew to a close in sweet cream cheeses and sugared fruit, which Mitt was too full to touch. Lord Stair began to get impatient. His voice roared something about "those idle flaming Singers!" and there were terrific clatterings and scrapings from the yard, where the tables were being moved aside. Hestefan got up from a table near the end of the hall and went to stand in the great doorway. With him, to Mitt's surprise, came Fenna and Moril.

Navis frowned. "I don't think that girl should be here. Nor the boy. They both look ill to me. But I suppose they have to earn their keep."

His voice was nearly drowned in cheering and clapping. Nobody else cared two hoots how the Singers felt, for there was going to be dancing. Tables were pushed aside in the hall, too. Hestefan slung a narrow drum round his neck, looked to see if Fenna was ready on the portable organ and that Moril had tuned his cwidder, and struck up a strenuous jig. Outside and inside, everyone grabbed a partner and danced.

The dancing went on and on. Mitt at first leaned against a table, feeling a little out of things and watching Navis being whirled about by Lady Eltruda. But at the next tune he was grabbed by a young lady in scarlet ribbons, and from then on he danced with the rest. The hall whirled around him, hot and riotous. He kept catching glimpses of Navis dancing with Lady Eltruda, which bothered him slightly, since Lord

Stair simply sprawled in a chair and went on drinking. But once or twice he saw Navis dancing with Noreth, in a very courtly way. Mitt would not have dared dance with Noreth himself. He knew absolutely none of the dances. The young ladies squealed with laughter and pushed him into the right places, and he kept going wrong. Every time his desperate, ignorant caperings got him into a real mess, he seemed to catch the eye of Moril, tirelessly playing his cwidder in the doorway, and there was malicious amusement in Moril's look. It began to annoy Mitt.

It took Mitt unawares when the Singers suddenly changed to a slow, haunting tune and everyone stopped dancing. For a moment Mitt was the only one capering. Moril grinned. "What's this tune, then?" Mitt gasped.

" 'Undying at Midsummer,' of course," said the girl in scarlet ribbons. "It's nearly midnight."

Around him dancing partners were breaking apart and the servers were going round with bottles of rare white wine, Southern wine, to welcome midnight with. Someone put three mugs of it down on the steps for the Singers.

Navis bent over his mug, sniffing deeply. "Now this I *have* missed," he said to Mitt. "Grapes don't ripen this far North."

They exchanged a little smile of pride in the South, even though it had turned them both out. Mitt said wonderingly, "That can't be the only thing you miss!"

"I think it is," said Navis. "Life's never dull up here." Saying this, he thrust his mug into Mitt's free hand and dived toward the doorway. He was just in time to catch Fenna as she dropped the heavy organ and passed out. Everybody stared in shock as Navis turned to Hestefan with Fenna draped over his arms. "What were you thinking of, letting this girl play tonight? Couldn't you *see* she was ill?"

Hestefan gave him a slow, worried look. "She swore she was well, sir, and we needed her part on the organ. I thank you for catching her so quickly."

Navis looked at Moril. "And you? Are you quite well?"

Moril's face did not have much expression, but Mitt could tell that he would not have admitted it to Navis even if he had been playing with all ten fingers broken. "Perfectly, thank you," Moril said.

Here Lady Eltruda raised her voice. Two women came and took Fenna quickly away. Someone shoved the heavy little organ to the side of the doorway. It was almost midnight. A running crowd of men and women were carrying every lamp and candle in the place and putting them down on the ground in two long lines leading from the gates of the yard, through the yard, up the steps, and into a circle in the middle of the hall. It was good luck to place a candle, so everyone fought for the honor except for Lord Stair—and Mitt and Navis, who did not know the custom.

"Let in the Undying!" everyone shouted as the last candle was put in place.

Silence fell, expectantly. From the yard came a strong grating sound as the two big gates were pushed open. At Hestefan's nod, Moril again played the slow, haunting chords of "Undying at Midsummer." To Mitt's ears he seemed to be playing now in an odd, different way. At any rate, there was a queer humming building under the notes. A damp breeze blew in from the yard, where it was probably raining again, bending all the candle flames. A great wavering shadow advanced across the floor and grew up the wall beyond.

Flaming Ammet! Mitt thought, with shivers spreading up his back. I think something really *is* coming in!

But the shadow shortened and fell, and Mitt saw it had been caused by Hestefan advancing up the lane of lights, carrying a small treble cwidder. When Hestefan reached the circle of lights, he turned round and called out, "Welcome the Undying to this house, for this night and the coming year!" Then he played the same slow tune on his cwidder. Mitt wondered why it sounded so much more ordinary now.

A growl of voices welcomed the Undying, too. The custom seemed to be to tip your mug and let a few drops of wine splash on the floor. Navis looked at Mitt. Mitt shrugged. And they both spilled some wine as well, with a private murmur to Libby Beer. After that the feast broke up into groups loudly wishing one another luck for the year. It looked for a minute or so as if things were nearly over.

But suddenly everyone was shouting, "Noreth! Noreth! Noreth, has your sign come?" as Noreth came to stand in the circle of candles beside Hestefan. She was carrying the golden statue, and she held it up for everyone to see.

"Here is my sign," she called out.

Navis murmured to Mitt, "You can say good-bye to your half of it, I think." A number of people were cheering, although Lord Stair was saying loudly in the distance, "Is that girl up to her nonsense again?"

*"Hush!"* someone said.

Noreth called out again. "Will my uncle's lawman please come and stand by me? I wish to make a statement in the proper form of law."

There was a lot of grumbling from the back. One of the men who had been at the high table, rather unsteady on his feet and very embarrassed, came and joined Noreth. She left the circle of light and walked down the lane of candles with him to the door. "I want everyone to hear," she explained to the lawman as they came past Mitt. "Tell me if I say anything wrong." Mitt could feel her shaking with the importance of what she was going to do. It made his stomach give a cold jerk.

"You know ash mush law ash me," the lawman complained, but he went and stood by Noreth as she took up a position in the doorway where she could speak to the people outside as well as those in the hall. The two of them pushed Moril right back to the side of the door. Mitt could see him there, looking awed.

Noreth said, loudly and slowly, "I, Noreth of Kredindale, do this night state and affirm that I am the rightful Queen and heir to the crown of Dalemark, over both North and South and the peoples of both."

It really is true, Mitt thought sadly. The lawman leaned across and murmured to Noreth.

"Oh yes. Thanks," said Noreth. "And over all earldoms and marks therein, not excluding the earls of those marks and the lords under them. This claim I make through my mother, Eleth of Kredindale, descendant in direct line from Manaliabrid of the Undying, and also by right of my father, the One, whose true names are not to be spoken, and from whom all Kings descend. In proof of this my right, my father promised me a token at Midsummer this year, and this promise he kept. This is the token." She held the golden statue up over the nearest lamps so that it could be seen. "Who witnesses," she called out, "that the river Aden today gave me this golden image of my father, the One?"

Mitt jumped and looked round for somewhere to hide. But Noreth turned and looked at him as she spoke. He sighed and pushed his way to the doorway. "If I'd known what you meant when you asked," he said, "I'd have gone straight back to Aberath."

The lawman said, "Do you witnesh thish?" and swayed a little.

"Sure," Mitt said bitterly. If Keril and the Countess had arranged personally for the landslip, they could hardly have pushed him into this any deeper. "I trod on the statue halfway across the brook. She picked it up. That do?"

Noreth replied with an eager, flustered smile. Her hands were still shaking as she held up the statue. She was truly nervous. She was not doing this because she was mad but because she saw it as her duty, as perhaps it was. Mitt felt himself bound to give her a smile in return before he edged away. Beyond Noreth he could see the Singer-lad staring at him resentfully. *Now* what does he think I've done? Mitt thought irritably.

"I call on you all," Noreth said, "to support me in my right. Today at dawn, its being Midsummer Day, I go to ride the green roads until I come to where the crown is hidden, and there I shall be crowned Queen. Let whoever wishes to ride with me and support my claim meet me at the waystone above the quarry at sunrise today."

There was another silence, which was followed by a surge of murmurs, half doubtful, half enthusiastic. Navis whispered to Mitt, "Well, there seems only one thing we can do now." Mitt nodded, but his attention was on Moril in the doorway. He could almost feel the boy making some kind of decision. Sure enough, Moril put his hands to his cwidder and struck up the tune called "The King's Way." Hestefan looked surprised but took the tune up on his cwidder, too, and walked between the two lines of guttering candles to join Moril. Moril, leaning over, plucked once again in the odd and different way. The humming gathered and gathered behind the tune, until it had become more than simply a rousing song. Mitt could quite clearly feel a serious purpose booming behind the notes. Everyone sang:

> "Who will ride the King's Way, the King's Way?
> Who will ride the royal road and follow with the King?"

There was a certain amount of muddle as about half the people tried to sing "Queen" instead of "King," but the singing was truly lusty. It seemed to affect Mitt's head, either the singing or the queer boom of Moril's cwidder, and his memory went a bit faulty after that. He remembered Noreth, glowing in the doorway, holding the glinting statue for everyone to see as they sang. He remembered glancing uneasily at Navis because this song was banned in the South, and finding, to his confusion, that Navis was singing with the rest. Mitt knew the song because he had been a freedom fighter, but Navis was an earl's son, for Ammet's sake!

Next thing he knew, he was back in Navis's room, where Navis seemed to be persuading him to get into bed. Mitt interrupted what he was saying—he seemed to be repeating with great earnestness, "This is serious, Navis, she was serious!"—in order to protest that he didn't need to sleep.

"Please yourself," Navis said. "It's only a few hours to sunrise anyway." Mitt had a confused notion that Navis went away then, saying he had a lot of things to do, and he knew Navis did not come back until the next thing he knew, which was Navis shaking him awake in gray dawn.

"What is it *now*?" Mitt said.

"Time to get up," Navis said. "You and I are going to ride the green roads with Noreth."

"Whatever for?" protested Mitt. "I told you I—"

"Can you think of a better way to keep Hildy and Ynen safe until we get to them?" Navis asked. "You were told to join Noreth. Keril will assume you are doing what you are told. Now get up."

Mitt got up—luckily he still seemed to be dressed—and shortly stumbled out into old food and beer smells in the hall. His bedroll was on the nearest table alongside one for Navis. Navis was just beyond, with his arms round someone, evidently kissing that person good-bye. For a moment Mitt thought it was Noreth and was outraged. Then the girl—no, woman, no, *lady*—stood back with her hands on Navis's shoulders, and Mitt saw it was Lady Eltruda. He stood there in even greater outrage. How *could* Navis! An elderly woman. A married woman. Taking advantage of Lord Stair's being a drunk!

"Take care of my girl for me, love," Lady Eltruda said to Navis. "I trust her to you. She's the only child I ever had."

"I'll look after her, I promise," Navis said, and smiled in what Mitt thought was altogether too loving a way.

At that moment Noreth herself rushed into the hall, once more dressed as a hearthman. "Aunt, where's my bedroll? Aunt! Oh!" she said as she saw how her aunt was occupied. She made a face at Mitt that showed that she felt much the same as he did about it. "I'd better go and look in the stable," she said. "I don't think I ever unpacked. Are you riding with me?"

Mitt nodded.

"Oh good!" Noreth said, and raced away outside.

# PART TWO

# *Maewen*

# 4

MAEWEN CAME BACK to the present with a jump. For a moment there it had seemed as if the noise of the train was not the beat of wheels on tracks, but the sound of water rilling over stones. She had almost seemed to see young leaves rustling overhead, casting a mix of sunspots and shadow on the racing water. In the confusion of glints she could have sworn there was a brighter glint, hands diving for the brightness, voices, and then the brightness taking the form of a dripping golden statuette.

Nonsense, of course. She must have dropped off to sleep while the train was rushing into this deep green cutting—such a deep one that there was no sign of the mountains beyond—and the glint had to be the gold buttons of the guard, just passing on his regular walk down the corridors. The guard smiled gravely at Maewen with his head cocked to one side. Was she all right?

Maewen managed a sort of smile, and the guard passed on. She prickled all over with embarrassment again. It was too bad of Aunt Liss. Mum would just have given Maewen a vague kiss and waved good-bye, but Aunt Liss, being the practical sister, had had to collar the guard and explain loudly and at length. "This is my niece's first-ever train journey. She's going all the way to Kernsburgh to visit her father and I don't like to think of her going all that way without *someone* to keep an eye on her. *Could* you make sure she's all right? *Can* I leave her in your tender care?"

And so on for five minutes, while Maewen wished she were any-where else and hoped the other four passengers in the carriage were all deaf. As if she were ten years old instead of nearly fourteen! The worst of it was that the guard was quite young and rather good-looking. He probably did think Maewen was only ten. She was unfortunately small for her age. He listened seriously to Aunt Liss and eventually took his cap off, baring his beautiful white-fair curls, and bowed slightly.

"Thank you, madam. You can safely leave your niece to me."

Looking back on it, Maewen wondered if the guard hadn't been making fun of Aunt Liss, but it hadn't seemed like that at the time, and Maewen had spent the entire space between Adenmouth and Kredindale trying to hide her hot face and squirming all over.

The silly part was that Maewen usually got on with Aunt Liss, better than with Mum. Aunt Liss was the one who cared. While Mum wandered in her studio covering her strange gawky statues with metal rags and splashes of bright color, deaf and blind to the world, Aunt Liss made sure Maewen had meals and clothes and—most important of all to Maewen—a horse to ride. Aunt Liss earned day-to-day money by running a livery stable. When Mum sold a statue, she earned big money, but that only happened—

"Are you traveling far, young lady?" asked the passenger opposite, making her jump again. He must have got on the train at Orilsway or somewhere. She looked at him, trying to remember, and decided she must have been asleep when he got on because she had certainly not noticed him before. He was one of those wide kind of old men who are almost bell-shaped sitting down. He had a sheet of wriggly gray hair on either side of his wide, plump face. Maewen was not sure she liked the way his eyes were half hooded in fat eyelids—it made him look cunning and rather cruel—but his question had been perfectly polite, and she supposed she had better answer.

"Just to Kernsburgh."

"Indeed?" he said. "And where did you get on?"

"Adenmouth," said Maewen.

"From the farthest north," said the old man, "halfway down the country to King Hern's city of gold. That is a momentous journey, child. At one time it was the royal road to the crown of Dalemark." He chuckled in a windy, breathy way. "And what brings you on the paths of the Undying?"

What a silly way to talk! Maewen thought. There are people who travel between Adenmouth and Kernsburgh every day of the week. "I'm going to visit my father," she said. Up to this moment she had secretly thought this was the greatest adventure of her life, but thanks to this old man, it was suddenly ordinary and boring. "For the holidays," she added drearily.

"Your father," said the old man, in a breathy sort of pounce, "works away from home? In Kernsburgh? Eh?"

"Yes," said Maewen.

"You travel to see him often?"

"No," she said. "This is the first time I've been." And she wished she could end this conversation. She did not like the old man's voice. There was something odd about it.

"Ah, I see. He's only just gone to work in Kernsburgh, is that it? Eh?"

"No. He's worked there for the last seven years." What *was* so odd about his voice? It almost seemed as if the sound was not coming from the old man at all but from somewhere else quite a long way away. Perhaps he was one of those people who had had surgery on his larynx and had to use a false voice box, in which case he was unfortunate and she ought to be polite to him. Maewen tried to explain without giving away her entire family history. "I haven't seen him since I was—was a lot younger." She really did not want to tell him her age, which he would know if she told him her parents had been divorced when she was seven.

"Now why is that?" the old man asked. "Do your parents perhaps not get on? They seem to have lived a long way apart for most of your life."

Cheek! Maewen thought. It's none of his business. "My mother," she explained haughtily, "is a sculptor who prefers to work near the stone she uses. And my father is a very busy man. He's head curator of the Tannoreth Palace."

"Ah," said the old man. She really did not like his half-hooded eyes. She looked away. "So you are truly on your way to the royal palace?" he said. He seemed very pleased. "And traveling all on your own until we met, eh? Now you can travel with me." He leaned forward. The carriage seemed full of his wheezing breath, as if it were coming from outside into him, instead of the right way.

For one horrid moment Maewen thought he was going to pat her knee. She surged herself right to the back of her seat, but that did not seem nearly far enough away.

"I will be with you from now on," he said, leaning at her. "Think of me as a friend."

No! Help! Maewen thought. She looked at the other passengers. Three were asleep, and the other was deep in a book. She thought of putting her feet up and kneeling sideways out of reach of the old man's fat hand hovering to pat her. And the guard only just went past, she thought, so it'll be hours before he comes back again.

"Look at me in the eyes," said the old man, "and tell me you think of me as a friend."

His face seemed to be right in front of hers, filling all she could see. Maewen shut her eyes. Let the guard come! she prayed. Let somebody help!

And here, like a miracle, the carriage door was sliding back and the guard's solemn good-looking face was leaning round it. "Are you all right in here?"

"I . . . oh . . . yes . . . no . . . he—" Stop stammering and say he tried to pat your knee, you fool! "He—" Maewen turned to point at the seat opposite and found herself stammering again, this time with astonished embarrassment. The seat was empty. A quick look round the carriage showed her that there were only four passengers, three asleep, one reading. "But he . . . there was . . . I thought an old man . . . I mean—"

The guard shifted his head to look gravely at the empty seat. "I don't think he'll bother you again," he said, perfectly straight-faced and polite, and he shut the door and went away.

Maewen sat back hot and squirming, worse than before. If one more thing happens with that guard, I think I shall *die*! She must have fallen asleep and dreamed the old man. What had possessed her to have a sinister little dream like that? Probably, deep down, she was terrified of seeing Dad again. Determined to stay awake from now on, she sat looking out at the mountains, dun-colored shoulders, green steeps, black crags, and blue jagged distances, spinning past as the train thundered through the center of North Dalemark. She thought firmly of Dad, to conquer her nerves. He had written over and over again to ask Maewen to visit him. He must really want to see her. But Mum just said irritably that she was not letting Maewen go until she was old enough to take care of herself. "Because he's quite likely to forget you exist after half a day," she said. "You'd starve or worse." She went on to a tirade about how wrapped up Dad was in his work.

Maewen grinned. That, coming from Mum, was rich. But it seemed to have been the main reason for the divorce. Dad just kept forgetting he had a wife and daughter. She felt that if Dad turned out to be a male version of Mum, she could cope. She was used to it. It was worth it for the chance of living in the royal palace of Amil the Great in the middle of the capital city. But what if Dad turned out *unpleasant*? Maewen had always found it hard to believe that you could divorce someone just for being vague. After all, she had never felt the slightest desire herself to divorce Mum. That made her grin again.

By the time the train slowed and rolled creaking into Kernsburgh Central Station, Maewen was feeling quite cheerful and poised. But that was in her mind. Her body persisted in thinking it was very nervous, and her arms felt like string as she tried to heave her suitcase off the train. It was blocking the door, and she could sense the crowd of passengers behind getting more and more irritated. But just as she was getting truly flustered, here was the polite, attentive guard again, giving her a serious smile and picking up her case for her.

"Let me carry that."

He set off into the station, and she pattered after him, grateful even though he was looking after her like a baby. The station was much larger than she had expected, high and ringing with announcements and people's voices and feet, and full of big red pillars that made all the parts of it look the same.

"My father is meeting me," she began defensively.

She saw Dad as she said it, coming through hordes of people going the other way. He was reading from a bundle of notes in his hand, and it was clear that the other people pushing past just did not exist for him. The sight took Maewen instantly back seven years. It was a pure delight the way Dad stood out from everyone else by being so trim and clear-cut—but not for being tall, she realized as Dad came close. He only came up to the guard's shoulder. So that's where I get my smallness from! she thought, and for one mad moment she wondered if Mum had divorced Dad because Mum herself was so tall and willowy.

Dad looked up from his notes and recognized her as if he had only seen her yesterday. "Oh, hello," he said. "You don't look a bit like this photo." He turned the bundle of notes round to show her the snapshot clipped to the front. It was one Maewen had never liked, herself all long-faced and freckled with her arm over a horse, not unlike the horse, and the horse the better-looking of the two. "I suppose that's how your aunt Liss likes to see you," Dad remarked. "She sent the photo, of course."

There was a slight awkwardness then as Dad bent a bit and kissed her cheek and did not quite give Maewen time to kiss him back. He smelled just the same as she remembered, with pipe smoke somewhere. He wheeled away almost at once to stare at the guard. "You needn't have bothered, Wend," he said. "I can be trusted to remember to meet my own daughter, I hope." He had put back his head and gone all haughty. Maewen remembered that haughtiness well. Was it the haughtiness that had caused the divorce, really?

"I was supposed to take care of her, sir," said the guard. "Or so I thought."

Maewen turned to stare at him. She had thought the uniform he was wearing was a railway one, but now she saw it was a paler blue and that the cap was wrong. How puzzling.

"I take it you two have met," Dad said. He was still haughty. He went on with the utmost sarcasm, "Maewen, my chief assistant, Wend

Orilson. Wend, my daughter, Mayelbridwen Singer." Then he swung round and strode rapidly toward the way out, leaving Maewen to dither, not knowing whether to run after him or stay with the puzzling Wend and her suitcase.

She arrived at the exit doing neither, partly chasing Dad and then stopping and turning to look at Wend, wondering if she had the nerve to ask him if Dad had really sent him all the way to Adenmouth to collect her, and then forgotten—and then not daring and running after Dad again. They arrived outside in single file, into a roar of traffic and much hotter sun than Maewen was used to. There was a vast stone, round, with a hole in the middle, upended in the traffic island in front of the station. Its huge shadow fell across the front half of the queue for taxis.

"We won't need a taxi; it's no distance," Dad said. He pointed to the huge stone. "The old waystone," he said, and set off striding into the town, "marking the start of the ancient road system of North Dalemark. King Hern, or most probably his descendants, made the roads, but simple people often thought the gods made them and tended to call them the paths of the Undying."

Maewen pattered after him up a broad thoroughfare, listening to as much as she could hear of a series of little lectures. After the waystone, it was the traffic, then the circular road system invented by Amil the Great, then the goods sold in the expensive shops she could see on either side. Somewhere along the street, Wend caught up, carrying her suitcase, and she thought he said, "I'll explain later," but she was too confused to be sure.

She forgot everything, anyway, when they came between giant gilded gates in a high wall and she had her first sight of the palace. It was across a cobbled court, and it was majestic. Like a very graceful cliff, she thought, almost too big to take in, and all upright lines that made it look taller still. In front of it, right in the middle of the court, there was a very much smaller building. It caught Maewen's attention for being so different from the palace that it looked quite out of place. It was like a house-sized model of a fairytale palace, with three small onion domes and such numbers of spiral towers that it looked almost absurd.

"Whatever is that?" she said.

"That? Oh, that's the tomb of Amil the Great," her father told her, and followed this up with one of the little lectures Maewen was coming to expect. "He completed the old part of the palace two hundred years ago, quite early in his reign. That's Amil's old facade we're looking at now; those recessed arcades along the lower stories were one of his own ideas. He was always full of ideas, but toward the end of his reign the ideas got rather out of hand, I'm afraid. Amil seemed to become obsessed with death and evil. He divided his time between having this tomb built and journeying all over the kingdom to eradicate what he called pockets of Kankredin. He simply meant places where there was injustice or lawlessness, but he had become very eccentric by then, and he preferred to call them that."

"He was very old when he died, wasn't he?" Maewen asked.

"Nearly ninety," said Dad. "Come on inside. Give me that case, Wend. We'll go up in the lift for once." He set off across the big space, over a pattern of cobbles and flagstones, still lecturing. "Amil had seen this country through from two primitive groups of earldoms to a full industrial society, so I think he earned the right to be a little eccentric. That tomb is by way of being his folly."

# 5

DAD HAD AN ENORMOUS, spacious apartment right at the top of the Old Palace, filled with books and old furniture. The main room looked over the leads of the roof, where pigeons waddled to the windows, expecting crusts of bread for breakfast. Maewen's bedroom looked out over the forecourt and the top of Amil's mad little tomb to what seemed miles below, with a huge view of Kernsburgh beyond that, all dark trees and towers and square office blocks. The room was enormous, with almost nothing in it but a bed, a cupboard, and a great threadbare carpet that had been old when Amil's son imported it. Next door was a large clanking bathroom with plumbing so elderly that Maewen was more awed by it than anything else in the palace.

"I'm afraid I can only spare time to be with you in the evenings and early mornings," Dad said over supper. Supper was supplied by one of a bewildering set of young ladies, who all seemed to wait on Dad hand and foot and then turn into secretaries in between. Seeing them, Maewen instantly knew that Dad regretted the divorce no more than Mum did. He was entirely comfortable. After supper he lit a pipe and explained, "We're just moving into the height of the tourist season now. As soon as the palace opens to the public, I have to be everywhere at once. But I've told everyone that you can explore anywhere you want. Tomorrow I'll make sure they all know you, so there won't be any trouble."

That evening they just talked, with Dad puffing clouds of pipe smoke through sunset light slanting in across the leading. Maewen found they got on. Dad seemed to think the same kind of thoughts that she did. Next morning he woke her quite surprisingly early and they had breakfast—supplied by another young lady—with rosy light slanting the other way across crusty rolls and rich black coffee. Just as Maewen was thinking how grown-up and leisurely this was, Dad sprang up and took her on a tour of the palace.

The Tannoreth Palace was vast. Buildings of various ages rayed out around courtyards with fountains, or gardens with statues and summer-houses in them, and hedges and roses, and a small menagerie. At every huge room they came to—and on some of the stairways—at every picture or work of art or curious object, Dad gave her another of his little lectures. In between he was introducing her to bewildering numbers of people who worked in the palace: ladies in overalls polishing the long museum galleries or dusting gilded tables, security men, guides, secretaries, and Major Alksen, who was head of security. Maewen's mind began to seize up. When Dad took her outside to be introduced to the gardeners, she was thinking, I shall *never* remember all this! Our minds are not the same after all. It was too early. Even though she was used to being up with the lark in the holidays to help Aunt Liss in the stables, she could see to a horse on autopilot, half asleep. This was different. No one *introduced* you to horses or expected you to know the history of the barn.

Afterward she found the only thing she could remember from the entire tour was Major Alksen because he was so much her idea of a retired soldier. And Wend, of course. She was glad Dad had not reintroduced her to Wend. Maewen felt too much pure embarrassment to go near him.

But she felt she was letting Dad down, or wasting opportunities, or something. So when Dad had given her another of his swift, awkward kisses and rushed off, Maewen felt herself bound to go all over the palace again.

It took days. Some of the time she joined in the guided tours, having made sure first that the guide was not Wend, and the guides would give her a special smile among all the crowds of foreign schoolchildren, and ordinary families, and silk-suited men and women from Nepstan, and then go on with their spiels. She visited Amil's tomb with one such crowd, but it was a cold, boring arched room inside, with a lot of gold lettering on the tombstone, and she only went there that once. She preferred indoors.

Here she usually started her sightseeing in the Old Palace, where most of the pictures were. That was easy to find because of the art students. They lay on the floor in what had been the great hall but was now a ballroom, copying the perspective in the ceiling picture. On the walls of this room Amil the Great, with his mane of fair hair and a roll of plans trailing from one hand, supervised the building of the palace.

Amil was wearing purple breeches, which Maewen thought were decidedly unfortunate. They looked worse in the copies the students made of them. On the ceiling there was the whole of Dalemark spread out, from the plains and slow rivers of the South to the mountains of the North, and full of battling figures, as Amil (in the same purple breeches) led his armies against the rebellious earls at the start of his reign.

Next door to the ballroom was a smaller room where oil paintings hung in frames. This was where Maewen's favorite pictures were. She got into the habit of stepping over the students lying on the floor and then pushing between the easels and the busy students in the smaller room in order to look at the portraits they were copying. The biggest was of the Duke of Kernsburgh, posed haughtily looking over the shoulder of a trailing crimson cape, in front of a new castle on a hill.

"Amil the Great's chief minister," Dad told her when she asked that first evening, "and one of the most ruthless men in history."

Maewen could see the Duke was ruthless—it was in every fierce, clear line of him—but there was something familiar and almost friendly about him, too. She almost felt as if she knew him. She kept trying to decide why. He looks as if he was very nice to his friends, she decided. But if you weren't one of his friends, you had to watch it. He'd put you to death without turning a hair.

The Duke was flanked by two dismal portraits of the Adon, both much, much older, and beyond that was an even older portrait of Enblith the Fair, who was supposed to have been the most beautiful woman ever, daughter of the Undying and a famous queen. The portrait was cracked, but even so Maewen could only suppose that ideas of beauty had changed. Enblith reminded her very strongly of Aunt Liss—and no one had ever called Aunt Liss a beauty, even when she was young. I bet she *managed* people into thinking she was lovely, Maewen thought. That was all women were supposed to *be* in those days. And she pushed between easels to the portrait that truly fascinated her.

It was called *Unknown Minstrel Boy*, and she kept wishing she knew more about him. He was probably about her own age, and he had red hair—which Maewen had always secretly wished for herself—with the paleness that always goes with such hair. He was rather richly dressed in dark maroon satin, so either he was a very good minstrel or a young aristocrat posing as one. Good minstrel, Maewen decided. It was in the way his pained eyes met yours and yet looked way, way beyond, full of thoughts and knowledge and strong sadness. Someone's let him down badly, Maewen thought when she first met those eyes. She wished she knew who had and why. And kept going back to look.

She wanted so badly to know about that boy that in the end she joined the afternoon guided tour that went round the pictures. The advantage was that the students had gone home by then. The disadvantage was that this tour was always taken by Wend. It took Maewen several days to muster courage to go with it. When she did, the mere sight of Wend started her fizzing with embarrassment again. Wend saw her and gave her a polite little bow and a restrained smile. Maewen felt her face flooding with red. It was the awful way Wend never seemed to show any emotion but politeness. But she clenched her teeth and followed the other tourists.

The picture of the minstrel boy was famous for several reasons, she discovered. Nobody had ever been able to find out who the boy was, although he was important enough to have been painted by the best artist of the time. And he must have been important to Amil the Great, too, because Amil made a special bequest of the picture to his grandson, Amil II. Books had been written about the picture. Some theorists suspected the boy was Amil himself, before he won the throne. Amil the Great had also carefully preserved the cwidder that had been painted with the boy. It was obviously old, even then. The minstrel boy had his hand dreamily wrapped across the cwidder, half hiding the strange old lettering inlaid on the front. And the actual selfsame cwidder was in a glass case just beside the portrait, very fragile and cracked-looking, despite careful restoration.

"Well, fancy that!" said everyone, raising cameras and jostling for the best shot of it.

After that Wend took the party into the ballroom, where he told them that the paintings on the wall and the ceiling had been done in the time of Amil II. Nobody knew what Amil the Great really looked like, and the purple trousers were a pure invention. This so amused Maewen that she left Wend's embarrassing presence in order to go down to the hallway and buy a postcard of Amil in his breeches and write a "Wish you were here" message on it to Mum and Aunt Liss. Then she made a foray into Kernsburgh itself to post it.

The city was even more crowded than the palace, and the traffic was terrible. A very few glances into the shops as she passed showed Maewen that she had barely enough money even for ordinary presents for Mum and Aunt Liss. Kernsburgh sold things from all over the world, and it was expensive. But the distressing thing to someone who had been brought up in the country like Maewen was that the place seemed to have almost no trees once you were down on street level.

"Where do all the trees go?" she asked Dad that evening.

It was a perfect example of the way she and Dad got on. Dad knew just what she was talking about although he was busy laying out sheets of stiff paper and notebooks on the other end of the table. "In people's gardens, I think," he said. "I believe Amil the Great planned it that way, because there were no trees on the site when he started to rebuild Kernsburgh."

"Then he made a mistake," Maewen said. "It's all buildings and cars, and it makes me cough."

"You'd have coughed worse when the place was new," Dad said. "Two hundred years ago it would have been smog from coal fires. Though I'm never sure it was such a good thing when they discovered oil under the Marshes. It makes the Queen a rich woman, I suppose, but it has its drawbacks."

"Where *is* the Queen?" Maewen asked. "I've been almost all over the palace now, and—"

"Oh, she very rarely comes here these days," Dad said. "She's pretty old, you know, and she prefers the warmth in the South. She almost only ever comes to the Tannoreth for state occasions."

"And the Crown Prince?" Maewen asked, feeling rather let down.

"He lives in Hannart," Dad answered absently, busy with a notebook. "Doesn't get on with his mother or with public events."

"What are you doing?" Maewen asked him.

"Trying to establish our family tree," said her father. "It's a hobby of mine—and damned exasperating, too. You can come and look if you like."

Maewen came and leaned on his square, warm shoulder, and he spread scrawled books and careful diagrams out for her to see. "Here," he said. "My family. As far as I can tell we go back to one of the traveling Singers. I *think* his name may have been Clennen, but Singers wandered about so and were so little documented that it's a fiendish job to find out for sure. Compared with that period, the last hundred years were a doddle, and I thought those were bad enough. And when we get to your mother's family, things get even worse. Here." Dad pushed sheets of paper in front of Maewen, hectically scrawled all over in pale pencil. "See? There's some connection with Amil II's brother Edril, but that's as far as—"

"You mean Mum descends from Amil the Great!" Maewen exclaimed.

"So do a lot of people. If you mean that accounts for your mother's standoffish vagueness," Dad said dryly, "I hardly think so. If you remember that everyone has four grandparents and eight great-grandparents, you can see that almost everyone has to be related if you go back far enough. We're talking here about doubling the number of ancestors each person has every generation, and halving—or even quartering—the number of people those ancestors could have come from. The population of Dalemark was quite small until a hundred years ago."

He was lecturing again. Maewen tried to listen. She was quite interested in the difficulties Dad had sorting out the two generations around the time of Amil the Great. School history didn't tell you half the confusions and revolutions there had been then. But there was so much of it. It had been dark for hours and she was yawning before Dad said, "Well, that will have to do for now. I've another long day tomorrow."

Once she was in bed, Maewen tried to sort out how she felt about Dad and the divorce. She was very fond of Dad—achingly, fiercely fond—but not so much when he lectured. And try as she might, she could not be upset that he was quite happy to be divorced from Mum. She had expected to feel sad—she felt she *ought* to feel sad—but whenever she passed the big busy office on the floor below and saw Dad conferring with secretaries, snapping instructions at Wend, or consulting with Major Alksen—and sometimes all three at once—she was glad she did not have to live with him and Mum at once. These were two strong-minded people who were both utterly buried in their work. And one of those, Maewen felt, was enough at one time.

Next morning, as she chucked pieces of bread onto the leads for the fat waddling pigeons, Maewen discovered that sorting that out about Dad had somehow let her off having to remember everything about the palace. As it was another baking hot day, Maewen decided to go for a swim. Major Alksen had said she could use the staff bathing pool. But he had not said where it was. She set out to find him and ask him.

Downstairs she went to the office. It was so busy that though she could hear Dad's voice, she could not see him among all the other hurrying people. And the secretary nearest the door said that Major Alksen had already gone down to his security post. Maewen went down again to the great upper galleries of the palace, which were cool and quiet and empty yet, until the palace opened to the public. These long rooms were a sort of museum, where curios and clothes belonging to past kings and queens sat in cases among statues and pieces of carving that had once been on the outside of the palace. As a lot of the things were very valuable, Major Alksen was often there, patrolling with a radio phone, checking security. As she came into the first room, Maewen could hear his footsteps ringing in the distance somewhere and his voice talking into his radio. "Coming through Gallery Two now. All secure. Over." She made toward the sound.

The person she saw when she went round the corner was Wend. Maewen stopped. How had he sounded so exactly like Major Alksen?

Luckily Wend's handsome face was set intently on distance as he listened to the voice on his radio. He had not seen her. Full of embarrassment again, Maewen started to tiptoe softly round the corner.

"Don't go, Maewen," said Wend. "I'll be with you in a moment. Right. Everything in place here. Over and out."

What excuse could she possibly give for rushing away? Maewen wondered. So sorry, I need to swim this second. Forgive me, but I have to go and depress myself at once by seeing Amil's tomb. Excuse me, I must go and look at the Duke of Kernsburgh—urgently. Or she could just run away. But Wend was already turning toward her, and the only thing she could think of was to let him explain why he had been sent to meet her as if she were ten years old and get it over with.

"You must have wondered," Wend said to her.

"No, no!" Maewen said. It seemed as if she did not want to get it over after all. "No, no, I never wonder—"

"Who that old man on the train was," said Wend. "The one I sent away."

This was so entirely unexpected that Maewen said, "Oh!" Then because she could feel her face was as red as it could be, she said, "He wasn't there. I dreamed him."

"No," said Wend. "He was—well—*there*, even if he wasn't what you'd call quite real. I'm afraid he's about to become a very big threat to you unless you let me help you. *Will* you let me help—or at least let me explain?"

"I—er—" Maewen was even more flustered. She was suddenly sure that Wend was mad. This was the only explanation for his grave, polite, *sane* look and the way it made her squirm every time she was near him. "Who *was* the old man?"

"A piece of Kankredin," said Wend. "A pocket of evil. And"—he smiled—"I promise you I am not mad."

This was worse than ever. "Yes, you are! You must be!" Maewen cried out, and she knew she would squirm even harder about this when she had time to think about it. "Kankredin's just a legend from the days of King Hern—and Hern killed him, anyway, when he conquered the Heathens."

Wend looked his most serious, and there was a sympathy about him as if he understood precisely how she was feeling—which, if possible, made Maewen feel worse. "Yes, I know how the story goes," he said. "People tell it like that because it's more comforting, but it wasn't the way of it, I assure you. Hern helped defeat Kankredin, that is true, but Kankredin couldn't die because he was dead already. The only way he could be conquered was for someone to unbind the One himself. You've heard of the witch Cennoreth. She unbound the One, and Kankredin was broken and scattered into a million pieces. But he wasn't dead. He came together over the centuries—concentrated, if you like, into larger and larger pockets—and eventually he was strong enough to take over the South and divide it from the North. Amil the Great found a way to destroy quite a bit of Kankredin, but even that didn't really defeat him. He was just scattered, and some parts of him came forward in time to these days. Other parts simply stayed around and arrived here and now by keeping secret and outlasting anyone who believed he was there. I'm not sure which kind of pocket you met, but I think from the way it behaved, it was one of the parts sent forward in time."

"I don't believe you," Maewen said. "How do you know?"

Wend shrugged. "I was there for nearly all of it. Hern was my brother."

Maewen stared at him. "But that's"—she was going to say "nonsense!" but she stopped herself, because you had to be careful with mad people—"not possible, Mr. Orilson. You see, that would make you so old you'd almost be one of the Undying." And no one believes in the Undying anymore, anyway, she thought, but I'd better not tell him that.

Wend nodded. There was a sad, priggish sort of sanity to him that Maewen found deeply suspect. "I found it hard to believe, too, when two of my brothers died and I didn't even age. It is hard to admit that you are anything but mortal. But the Undying exist whether people believe in them or not. I am one. You have probably heard of me. I was known as Tanamoril for a while. Then I was called Osfameron."

Osfameron! The Adon's friend who raised the Adon from the dead! He's further round the twist than I thought a person *could* be! Maewen stared at Wend, all alone in the long empty museum room. Do all lunatics look this sane? I wish I knew. He'd look quite normal if he wasn't so good-looking. Keep humoring him until he gets called away to his duties. "What do you think this piece of Kankredin wanted with me?" Maewen asked gently.

"I think," said Wend, "that he was trying to get control of you."

Maewen's spine felt as if cold fingers were being trailed down it. She backed into the nearest glass case in order to feel safer. "Why—why would he want to do that?"

"Because you are the image of a young woman who lived just over two hundred years ago," Wend told her.

"That makes no sense!" said Maewen.

But Wend continued talking as if he had not heard her. "A very important young lady," he said. Looking at his constrained and serious face, Maewen thought that this was the heart of his mental disorder, whatever it was. She leaned on the glass cupboard and let him go on talking. "Noreth," Wend said. "Born to rule all Dalemark. My grandfather the One was her father, and she knew from her childhood up that she was to take the crown and rule both North and South. When she had it, people would have risen to her all over the country, whatever the earls had to say."

"What happened? Wouldn't she do it?" Maewen asked.

"I don't know what happened. She was willing enough." Just for an instant Wend seemed to feel wretched about this. Then his face smoothed over. "I was guarding Noreth on the royal road," he said. "The midsummer after her eighteenth birthday, as was right, she set off from Adenmouth to ride to Kernsburgh for the crown. Nothing should have gone wrong. I was as watchful as I could be. But somewhere along the way Kankredin got to her as he was trying to get to you, and she . . . simply disappeared." Wend swallowed a little. Then, with his face all cold and smooth, he said, "That was how Amil, so called the Great, was able to claim the crown."

Maewen stayed pressed against the glass. "And," she said, gently and humoringly, "you're telling me this because I look like this lady."

"No," said Wend. "I'm telling you because I'm fated to send you back in time to take Noreth's place."

"Fated?" said Maewen. "That's a strong word. You need me to agree first, and I haven't."

Wend came nearer to laughing than she had ever seen him. "You forget," he said. "I was there. So were you. So I know I did send you." He had a funny lighthearted air to him, now that he had arrived at this point. "As I see it now," he said, "I must have asked the One to send you to the moment on the royal road when Noreth disappeared, so that you could find out what happened and tell me when you came back here."

"Oh." Maewen looked down at her two somewhat scruffy sandals planted on the glossy floor. Then I must have been—I will be—as mad as he is! Though of course, if he really *was* there, he is over two hundred years old, and that means he can't be mad. It all hung together. And she knew mad people's fantasies did often hang together. That was why they found it so difficult to get out of them. Perhaps the best way to deal with Wend was to show him it was nonsense by daring him to send her into the past. No. He could turn violent then. Best just to go. She slid carefully away along the glass cupboard and braced her sandals to run.

Wend smiled his polite smile. "Thanks. I was needing to get at this showcase. Your father wants some of the things moved."

He fetched up his bunch of keys and advanced on the lock of the sliding door. He was far too near. Maewen could feel her stomach squirming and those queer pins and needles in her back that she always got when she was about to do something wrong. Strange the way Wend always made her feel like this. She slid farther away, warily watching him as he undid the electronic lock and then the ordinary one. Any second now she would be far enough away to risk running for help.

Wend reached inside the glass cupboard and gently, almost reverently, picked up a small gold statue that was standing there among vases, salt cellars, rings and other golden objects. While Wend turned to her holding the statue in both hands—she could see it was heavy—Maewen craned to see the label it had been standing on.

FIGURE OF KING OR NOBLE (GOLD).
PREHISTORIC. ORIGIN UNKNOWN.

"This is the image of the One that my family once guarded," Wend said. The radio on his belt beeped as he spoke. He frowned. "Would you take this to your father for me? Someone wants me."

He held the small golden image out. It was the ideal excuse for going away. Maewen reached out gladly and took hold of the image in both hands. The thing was so worn and old that all you could say of it was that it had once had a face and wore a long sort of poncho robe, but the instant she touched it she had the queer doing-wrong feeling worse than before. Her teeth ached with it, and her hair tried to lift. She snatched her hands away. But by then the pins and needles were worse down her hands and legs and through her face. It seemed to affect her eyes, so that the long empty room grew foggy, and her ears, so that she could only dimly hear Wend's beeping radio.

# 6

THE FOGGINESS WAS COLD as well as thick. Maewen lost all sense of direction. She staggered and found her sandals were getting wet in short grass beaded with fog drops. It felt icy. "Oh—ouch!" she cried out.

Her voice had the unechoing clarity of somewhere outside—and high up, too, she thought, having been brought up among mountains. Anyway it was nothing like the woody, stony echoes inside the museum gallery. She looked up and around in a panic. Everything was mist, thick white mist, except for—thank goodness!—one pink streak of dawn over to the right. And there was something dark ahead through the mist. Maewen took a couple of excruciating cold, wet strides toward the dark thing, enough to numb her feet, and found the thing was a round stone a little higher than her waist with a hole in the middle. A waystone? It was only about a tenth the size of the one outside the station in Kernsburgh, but she supposed that was what it might be.

She stood shivering in her scanty summer shorts and shirt, staring at the stone resentfully. It's real! she thought. Wend tricked me! I'm in shock! I'm going to die of exposure, and I haven't the *faintest* idea where I am! Or *when*!

Here she noticed that the pins and needles feeling was no longer with her. It had been replaced—some seconds ago, now she thought about it—by a much better feeling, a feeling that everything was going to be all right. Well, I hope so! she thought. I *could* scream, only there doesn't seem to be anyone around to hear.

She began to feel definitely warmer.

She looked down in time to see her sandals closing over and growing up her legs into stout-looking boots. Her shorts were growing downward into felty, rather baggy trousers that tucked into the boots. A faint jingling alerted her to the fact that her shirt was also growing, and multiplying, into linked mail with one thinnish shirt under it and another, thicker one on top. A heaviness on her head caused her hand to leap up there. She touched metal. She now had a light domed helmet on.

She felt a mad, hilarious pleasure. I'm a warrior maid! I'm changing into a fighting girl under my own eyes—what I can see of myself! Her feet were still frozen inside the boots, and her hands were no warmer, but she nevertheless had a warm, cared-for feeling. Something—the golden statue?—was looking after her.

There was another jingling over to the right. Maewen whirled like a wild animal. The jingling mixed with a *pruff* of breath, a sound that she knew very well. She moved warily over that way, jingling herself. Sure enough, looming out of the mist, dark against the pink stripe of dawn, was a horse, standing patiently waiting for someone. Not a bad horse, though rather shaggy, as far as she could see, and it was saddled and bridled, with a roll of baggage behind the saddle. It turned and blew steamy breath at Maewen as if it knew her.

Maewen had not realized how much she had been missing horses. Almost by reflex, she gathered in the reins, put her foot in the stirrup, and swung up into the saddle. Ouch! Effort! The mail and the boots were *heavy*. It was only when she was up that it occurred to her that the horse almost certainly belonged to someone else. What did they do to you for horse stealing? Oh well. Say I'm awfully sorry, there was this thick fog and I thought it was mine. Would that work? It felt so much better to be mounted that she hardly cared. Deal with the owner when we meet her. She reined around toward the little waystone and tried to make out where she was.

The mist was clearing gradually, downward, dropping into a valley below the stone, but that was still all she could see. "Hello?" she said uncertainly.

"Oh—your pardon, lady. I never heard you come."

Maewen bunched herself, again with wild-animal wariness, as a tall man unfolded himself from where he had been sitting against the other side of the waystone and bowed to her, hastily and politely. When he straightened up, she saw he was Wend. She went warier than ever. His hair was a good deal longer, grown into wavy whitish ringlets that were not very well combed, which altered the shape of his face somewhat, and instead of the neat uniform she had seen him in a few minutes ago, he was wearing patched and baggy woolens with an old sheepskin jacket on top. The sort of clothes, Maewen thought, that a poor shepherd might have worn two hundred years ago. She stared at Wend, wondering if she really was in the past. And does he know me? Does he think I'm Whatshername?

Wend stared back with the usual grave politeness. "I am Wend, lady," he said. "If you remember, we met before." So he *does* know me, Maewen thought. "And I am here to follow you from waystone to waystone along the royal road, until you come to Hern's city of gold and claim your rightful crown."

He's briefing me, Maewen thought, and so he should—tricking me into pretending to be this Northeen, or whatever she's called! The trouble was Wend still made her fizz with embarrassment. He spoke in a very strong Northern accent, of the kind that Mum and Aunt Liss always objected to when Maewen spoke that way. It seemed quite natural to Wend, but she had heard him speak quite normally only a minute ago, and she could not get over the feeling he was putting on an act. It irritated her. "I think I need to know a bit more than that," she said angrily.

Wend bowed humbly, which irritated Maewen even more. "True, lady. Then I will tell you what no one else knows. I am the one they call the Wanderer, and I keep the green roads—"

He stopped talking and looked over his shoulder. There was a brisk jingling of tack below and nearby. Maewen once more bunched up like a wary wild animal and watched two more riders scramble uphill out of the fog. They seemed to bring the fog with them, fog of their own breath, fog of their horses' breath, and fill the air with their presence.

"Good morning, Noreth," said the smaller of the two. "You got ahead of us very quickly. We were hoping to ride up with you." He was riding a truly magnificent mare. His clothes were like the ones Maewen had so recently acquired, mail coat and cap and all, except that on this man they had a neater, wealthier look. Maewen was shocked to find that she knew his face. She had last seen those clear-cut ruthless features staring over a painted shoulder out of the portrait of the Duke of Kernsburgh.

It gave her a vivid, physical shock, like touching a live wire. Up to then Maewen had not really believed she had been sent two hundred years into the past. But here was a live man, breathing out warm, live, foggy breath, whom she *knew* to have been dead for well over a century. It made it real. It made it much more frightening. She looked rather frantically across at the taller rider, wondering if she would know him, too. He was young and gawky and obviously in the middle of growing even taller. His clothes, which were quite neat, too, sat on him as if they were his best clothes and he was used to wearing something much scruffier. And his horse looked villainous.

He was a total stranger, but Maewen's feelings about that changed from relief to dismay when this young one smiled at her. He smiled in a cheerful, friendly way, with just a touch of shyness, as if he knew her quite well. And she had simply no idea who he was. O great *One*! she thought. Why hasn't Wend *warned* me about these people?

She looked at Wend, waiting humbly by the waystone, but had to look back when the man with clear-cut features spoke again. "As you see," he said, "Mitt and I have come to be your followers on the royal road."

Maewen was thrown into confusion again. He sounded so sarcastic. It was just the way a man like this one *would* speak—and it made her feel about five years old. But it was a double confusion. She suddenly found she had no idea *when* this was. She had been assuming, in a muddled and buried way, that she had been bounced into this Noreth woman's place somewhere halfway to Kernsburgh. But from what this man said, she could be right at the start of Noreth's journey from the North. It gave her a low, grinding sort of worry to add to all the other things. Among the other things was the thought, If Kankredin got to Noreth *that* early, how soon will he get to *me*? And a slightly more trivial thought, but just as worrying, was that this man on the fine mare was not going to be made Duke of Kernsburgh until some years on in Amil the Great's reign. If she was Noreth and at the start of Noreth's journey, then Amil the Great was somewhere else in Dalemark and nowhere near being King yet. So this man was not Duke of Kernsburgh yet. And she had no idea what to call him. At least she now knew the younger one was called Mitt.

She gave Mitt a flustered smile and tried a stately bow on his companion. He bowed back, ironically, and raised an eyebrow at Wend. He was, naturally, one of those who could slide one eyebrow up without the other one moving at all.

"I am Wend, sir," Wend said humbly, "and I follow the lady, too."

"Well, well. That makes three of us," the man said. "How many more are we expecting?"

Maewen could not answer since she probably had less idea than he did. In fact, she had no idea what they expected her to do. She simply sat on her purloined horse and hoped that Wend would have the decency to give her a hint.

Wend said nothing. They all sat, or stood, while the horses fidgeted and the pink of the sky spread and faded toward a gray morning. Below, the mist seemed to be thinning, but not enough to show any landscape that might give Maewen some idea whereabouts they were. She began to feel stupid. This had the feeling of a party when none of the guests turn up.

The man who would be Duke of Kernsburgh obviously felt the same. "Not much sign of a mighty band of followers," he remarked.

Mitt was horribly embarrassed. "*Navis!*" he protested.

Navis! Maewen thought in the greatest relief. Or should I call him Your Grace? No. Stupid. Not yet.

"I suggest we give it till full daylight and then be on our way," Navis said.

It was more of a decision than a suggestion, as if Navis was in charge, but Maewen was simply grateful for someone deciding *something*. "Yes," she said. "That's fine."

It was the first time she had spoken in front of Navis and Mitt. She saw Mitt give her a puzzled glance, as if her voice, or her accent, or something, was not quite right. She glowered at Wend. She was angry enough to smash his smooth, grave, handsome face. He had tricked her into this, and now he was not giving her any help at all. If one of these two noticed she was not Noreth, it would be his fault, and it would serve him right.

Luckily—probably it was lucky—Mitt was distracted by someone else arriving at last. There were clatterings and a light rumbling from the thinning mist below. It could be quite a number of people. Everyone turned that way. The first thing to appear was a lop-eared glum-looking mule. Then a darkness behind it resolved into the rounded canvas cover over a cart, the whole thing painted a sober dark green. The bearded man driving the cart looked as sober as the rest of his turnout. As the cart tipped forward onto the level land beside the waystone, he looked up and reined in the mule as if he were surprised to see anyone there at all. Maewen read the name in sober gold lettering: Hestefan the Singer. Now this was interesting. Her mind shot to Dad's family tree. He could be one of her own ancestors. And she had had no idea that Singers still roamed the land as late as two hundred years ago.

"This is a surprise, Hestefan," Navis said. "Did Noreth inspire you to follow her, too?"

He was even more ironic than he had been before, but Hestefan answered quite simply, "I thought I'd come along. Yes." His voice rolled out foggy breath, full and trained-sounding, but not very deep.

"But," Mitt chipped in, "Fenna's not fit to travel, is she?"

A boy stuck his head out of the back of the cart. "We're not fools," he said. "We left her in Adenmouth." The gathering sunlight struck red on his head. Maewen could not take her eyes off him. She knew him, too. He was the unknown Singer-boy from the portrait in the palace.

"And Lady Eltruda was good enough to lend us a mule," Hestefan said.

"Lady Eltruda is always generous," Navis said. He seemed to mean this. At least he did not sound nearly as ironic as usual, saying it. "And what of others following? Did you pass any large numbers of folk hurrying to join Noreth?"

Hestefan slowly shook his head. "We were the only ones on the road." Maewen caught the Singer-boy, and Mitt, too, looking at her as if they were afraid she would be very disappointed at this news.

Then everyone was looking at her expectantly.

"Er—" Maewen said. "Well, I suppose we'd better be getting on, then." Thinking that she had better lead the way, she turned her horse toward the green path stretching from the waystone. Then she paused. Wend was on foot. "Will you be able to keep up?" And serve you right if you can't!

Wend put a horrible old baggy cap on his head and smiled his restrained smile up at her. Maewen was growing to hate that smile. "I walk the green ways every day, lady. Unless you gallop, I shall be beside you."

I wish he wouldn't *talk* like that! Maewen thought as the small party set off.

Nobody talked much at first. Maewen was glad of the silence. She had so much to sort out. For one thing, she was still full of quivering animal wariness, first from thinking Wend was mad and then from finding he seemed to have told her the truth. On top of that was the sheer shock of being, really and truly, two hundred years in the past. And one thing sorted itself out of that: This expedition, with herself in place of Noreth, had to be very important. The mere fact that two of the people who had been important enough for their portraits to hang in the palace were on it made this certain. It was frightening—too much responsibility for an ordinary girl who just happened to look like this Noreth. Perhaps, she thought hopefully, Noreth escapes and comes back to take over later. But if that were going to happen—

Here Maewen came hard up against a question which had been nagging at the back of her head from before she laid hands on the golden statue, from the moment Wend first mentioned Noreth. If Noreth was that important, why haven't I seen her name in a history book somewhere? And I haven't, not even once. Dad never mentioned her. None of the guides said a word about her, and they were forever on about Amil the Great. The really frightening thing was that, as Maewen now seemed to be Noreth, *she* was the one who was going to vanish utterly from the face of history. She shivered and tried not to think about Kankredin.

Well, Amil the Great comes along soon. I just have to hand over to him, she thought. That was a much better thought than the idea that she was all alone here having to make history—or fade out of history permanently. I'll simply go on until he turns up. She raised her head and began trying to see where they were.

The green road curved gently ahead, sloping upward a very little, carving its way into the mountains by what seemed the easiest route. At first it ran between high hillsides of brown rock and Maewen could not see very far. The shapes of mountains do not change, she reminded herself. When I see them, I'll know. Even though two hundred years ago there was no big refinery at Kredindale, and Weaversholm was probably hardly a town, there would be something to give her bearings.

But there was nothing to see for some miles, except every so often a rowan tree, leaning like a guardian over the path, or a stream carefully channeled under it. Corners had been built up to keep the road level. Maewen wondered about this road. There was nothing like this that she knew of in her day. Did Wend *mean* it when he said he kept the green roads? She looked at him, striding beside Hestefan's mule. Two hundred years old. He had to be. He had to be of the Undying, then.

She looked round again to find the path coming out on an upland and, like a relief, blue peaks and khaki shoulders of mountains in all directions. They swung slightly right. Maewen stared at the high horseshoe top of Aberath Tor and knew at once where she was. In the far North, right up near Adenmouth somewhere. She and Mum and Aunt Liss lived—*would* live—just twenty miles west of here. But it was no good rushing off home at a gallop. She might find the house—it was old—but there would be strangers living in it. A miserable, lonely thought. And she had been right. Wend had pitched her in right at the start of Noreth's royal ride, and Noreth had been kidnapped, so she was in for *days* of this. Oh—damn!

Maewen turned another glowering look on Wend. And this made her notice that the rest of the party was not entirely happy either. Mitt and Navis rode side by side, but this was so that they could argue in low voices. As she looked, Navis snapped, "I never believed you could be such a prig!"

Mitt answered, "Call *me* names! It was you took advantage!"

"It was *not* taking advantage," Navis retorted. "Surely, with your background, you must have *some* idea of what it means to be married to a hopeless drunkard!" He turned haughtily away, found himself looking at Hestefan, and turned haughtily from Hestefan, too, as if Hestefan displeased him as much as Mitt did.

Hestefan took no notice. He just stared dreamily at the mule's ears. Probably he was a dreamy type, but just then he looked as if he was having rather bitter dreams. The boy—Moril, she had gathered his name was—sat equally dreamily beside Hestefan, plucking at his big old cwidder, but he was no happier. He did not have quite the tragic look that Maewen remembered from the portrait, but she could see he was brooding on something miserable. Whatever this was might have had something to do with Mitt. In between arguing with Navis, Mitt made various friendly remarks to Moril, and Moril either pretended not to hear or else gave a short, snide answer that stopped any conversation dead.

Nobody but Maewen seemed to have met Wend before. After their latest argument Navis tried to talk to him and ignore Mitt. Wend's replies were so polite and humble that Navis raised both eyebrows and gave up. Serve Wend right! thought Maewen. Then she thought, This won't do! What a dreadful way to start an important journey!

Angrily she turned her horse sideways to the rest of them. "What's the *matter* with you all?"

They stared at her out of a confusion of horses and mule half pulled up. Mitt's horse refused to stop and went bucking backward into the stones of the verge. He hit it. "Behave, you Countess, you!"

"Matter?" Navis said with his head haughtily up.

He reminded Maewen of someone like that, but she had not the patience to think who just then. "Yes," she said. "There are only five of you, and every one of you is deliberately annoying all the others. You're to *stop* it, do you hear! Why can't you all be cheerful?"

Mitt, who had on the whole been trying, Maewen had to admit, gave his horse another bang and said resentfully, "That's great, coming from you! Who's been off ahead the whole time, looking like a wet week?"

Moril grinned at this, as if he could not help it.

Maewen glared from one to the other. Boys! "All right. I'll try as well. But I order the rest of you to be cheerful, too!"

Navis asked smoothly, "And how do you suggest we fulfill your orders?"

"*You* can do it by stopping being so damn sarcastic!" Maewen shot back. "And you"—she pointed to Hestefan—"can come out of your dream."

This seemed to alarm Hestefan. He stared at her in a stunned, terrified way which seemed entirely wrong for the kind of person he was.

Maewen did not understand, and it cooled her down rather suddenly. She had been about to go on to Mitt and suggest he made peace with Navis and then to Moril and tell him to stop the dumb insolence, but Hestefan's stare made her see that she really knew nothing about what had happened among these people before she met them. Maybe they were right and she was wrong. So she swung round on Wend, as the only one she knew. "And you're to stop being so polite all the time!"

Wend snatched off his cap and seemed about to give one of his humble bows.

"No," said Maewen. "Don't even think of it!"

Navis threw back his head and bellowed with laughter. Mitt snorted. Moril actually giggled. Even Hestefan gave a shaky smile. Maewen thought there might even have been a bit of a grin on Wend's face, too. Thank the One! Maewen heaved a deep startled breath and rode on again, staring at a large bird—eagle?—circling among the nearest mountains, to help herself cool down. How had she *dared* snap at Navis? No matter. It had worked. She could hear people talking behind her in an ordinary, cheerful way now. But she thought she had better go round each of the party and talk privately to them if she could. That way she might piece together what had made them so gloomy.

Mitt came up to ride beside her as she was thinking this. "You've got that golden statue safe, have you?" he said. "Don't forget that it's half mine."

Maewen went hunched and wary again. She had no doubt which statue he meant. The trouble was, it was two centuries away, locked in a glass case in a palace which was not built yet. "Oh yes. Safer than houses," she said, which, she thought, was certainly true.

# 7

HOLDING THAT FIRST conversation with Mitt was one of the hardest things Maewen had ever done. Long before they stopped for what Navis called "a nuncheon," she could feel sweat starting in beads on her face. The air grew milder anyway, warm enough for Maewen to remember that this was, after all, Midsummer Day, but it was not that. It was the sheer difficulty of keeping her end up. She kept looking at Wend, hoping he would give her a hint or so, but Wend simply strode along, easily keeping up with Navis's mare, and said nothing to anyone. Maewen took this to mean that Wend was only going to come to her rescue if she made a really bad mistake.

In a way this was comforting because it meant she had not done anything really wrong yet, but it was frightening, too. She knew her face was a mass of dots, dots of freckle and dots of sweat. She hated herself like that. She kept sneaking looks at Mitt's long, bony profile, hoping he was not too disgusted.

Mitt usually turned and grinned at her. After a while Maewen realized that he was as flustered as she was. At first she thought it was because she was supposed to be Queen. Then Mitt said, "I'll tell you straight, Noreth. It came as a shock last night, finding out you were so old."

Old! Maewen thought. Oh, *bother* these freckles! He must be at least fifteen! How old does he think I am? Eighteen, said her memory. Noreth went on her ride the Midsummer after she was eighteen. That would seem old to Mitt. "Don't hold it against me," she said. "Please!"

Mitt laughed. "I'll try not to."

This did not make the conversation any easier. Maewen was trying to find out who Mitt was—he had a dreadful Southern accent for someone so far north—and how he knew Noreth, and how he was connected with Navis, and why Moril disliked him so, and why Mitt talked as if he lived in Aberath, not Adenmouth, and what had made him come on this expedition, and Mitt would keep talking about that golden statue. His beastly horse did not help. It kept trying to bite her leg.

Each time Mitt hauled its head round and cursed it. "Stop that! I told you, you Countess, you!"

After about the sixth time, Maewen had to laugh. "It's a gelding. Why do you call it Countess?"

"I told you yesterday," Mitt said, obviously surprised.

Help! "Oh, so you did," Maewen said hurriedly.

It was like that all the time. But Maewen kept on, because she did need to know, feeling ridiculously flustered for someone riding in the clear open air with mountains slowly wheeling around them on all sides. And at last she seemed to have the story of the statue sorted out. Mitt and Noreth had found it together in the river Aden. Maewen frowned a little at this. There was that odd dream she had had in the train. . . .

"And I need my share of the money," Mitt told her. "I need it bad. It's to help Navis out, too, or I wouldn't keep nagging about it."

Mitt believed in plain speaking, Maewen could see. She liked that, but it made her feel dishonest. "The statue is quite safe . . . honestly," she repeated. She began to hope devoutly that the horse she was riding might have belonged to Noreth. It had been wandering by the waystone. Noreth had meant to meet everyone there, and then she had been kidnapped, so it could have been her horse, if you supposed the kidnappers had hauled her into a carriage and turned the horse loose. If that was so, then the golden statue just *could* be in the roll of baggage behind the saddle.

They stopped to eat in a grassy bay surrounded by high rocks. Maewen made haste to lead her horse to one side across the moist green tender grass, where she hunted through that baggage roll, pretending to look for food. Food she found—bread, cheese, apples, and a fine small pie—though not very much of it, not nearly enough to last all the way to Kernsburgh. She found a clean undershirt and drawers and some socks. They were all her size, so it did begin to look as if this was indeed Noreth's horse, but there was no statue. What about this roll of blanket, then? It felt unpromisingly soft and light, but Maewen unrolled it all the same. As she did so, someone spoke, close beside her.

"You won't find the statue there. It has been stolen."

It was a man's voice, deep and rather echoing. "What do you mean, stolen?" Maewen said, wondering how whoever it was knew. She looked round, expecting to find herself talking to Navis or Hestefan.

She was confounded to see Hestefan many yards away, still dreamily sitting on the driver's seat of the cart, and Navis unsaddling his mare right on the other side of the green bay. It had not sounded like Wend. Wend was anyway sitting against the wheel of the cart, fetching a loaf out of his knapsack. Mitt was over beside Navis. Moril came crawling out of the cart beside Hestefan as she looked. Everyone was too far away to have spoken—unless of course one of them was a ventriloquist. Maewen looked up at the rocks, and all round, and then bent to look under the horse's belly. There was no one else. But the blanket came unrolled as she stooped, showing that it was nothing but blanket. There was no golden statue anywhere in this baggage.

"Who are you?" she said, keeping her eyes warily on all of the other five people. "Where are you? How do you know?"

She had spoken too softly for anyone to have heard her, and none of the others moved. But the voice answered her, seemingly out of the air beside her. "I am the one who has always advised you. And I can feel the statue near. One of those five has it."

"Thanks very much!" Maewen rolled the blanket up. "I can't tell you how that sets my mind at rest!" She thought she was in a state of shock again. Her mind was whirring with it. Whoever had taken the statue could only have taken it from Noreth. Therefore, one of her companions must have helped kidnap Noreth, and that person knew Maewen was a fraud. Why had that person not said? Or was this voice lying?

"I am glad to find you so calm," the voice said. "You speak like the Queen you will be."

Calm! thought Maewen. She rammed the blanket and clothes back in the container and turned back across the grass, juggling pie and cheese and apple with hands that seemed too shaky to hold them.

Moril met her as she came. He was eating a large hunk of bread—one-handed, because his other hand was supporting that cwidder of his. Maewen had yet to see Moril put it down. It was as if it were part of him. She noticed now, without any surprise, that it was the same cwidder that had been in that portrait of Moril, the one that was in the glass case beside it. She was noticing everything just then. She felt like a hunted hare, wild big eyes staring. She noticed that Moril did have a scatter of freckles on his pale skin, rather like hers, only not so many. She noticed he was looking at her wonderingly.

"What's the matter?" he said with his mouth full. "Have you seen a ghost?"

"Yes—or I heard one at least," Maewen said. "Out of the air. A man spoke."

"I thought something happened," Moril said. "I think I need to break my rule again. Just a second." He bit off another mouthful of bread, tossed the rest down on the grass, and put both hands to the cwidder. For a moment he chewed and thought, and then he played a short run of mellow rippling chords.

Peace swept through Maewen, running like strength up her back and down her arms, and relaxing muscles in her face that she had not known were there. She found herself smiling dreamily, thinking that, whatever that voice had been, it had no way to harm her. "Thanks," she said.

Moril left the cwidder humming and looked at her critically. "It was easy," he said. "You're really quite a relaxed person." And he added, very seriously, "Things do happen on the green roads. There are lots of stories."

He bent to pick up his bread. Mitt and Navis sauntered over. Moril must have seen them out of the corner of his eye, because his face went blank and unfriendly, and he went away at once, back to Hestefan.

Maewen sat against the cartwheel to eat, looking out across broken rocks to blue-black mountains, in front of dun-colored mountains, with more jagged mountains beyond that, all under a heavy gray sky. She must get to know Moril, she thought. He had seemed to be one of those dreamy types, entirely wrapped up in himself, but he noticed things, dreamy or not, and that—whatever—he had played on his cwidder had been . . . Well, go on. Say it, Maewen. Magic. That boy is some kind of magician, and I want to know how he does it.

Far off among the mountains an indigo peak caught the sun and was for a moment yellow and green and purple.

Wend pointed a fist holding a piece of cheese. "City of gold!" He and Moril and Hestefan spoke almost in chorus. "Hern's golden city."

"Go on," said Maewen. "It *can't* be! Kernsburgh's miles south of here."

"It's what we say, lady," Wend explained, "when a peak catches the sun—to show we remember the city even though it's long ruined and gone."

"Ruined and *gone*!" Maewen said. "But—"

"It is, though," Hestefan said reprovingly from the cart above her. "Did you not know?"

"I—" Maewen craned round at what she could see of the gray beard. What did Hestefan remind her of? She should have known about Kernsburgh. All the guides in the palace had never seemed tired of pointing out that Amil the Great had rebuilt the city. But none of them had thought to say that he had rebuilt it from nothing. "Ruins and rubble?" she asked.

"More like grass and humps in the ground by what I heard," Mitt told her.

"Oh—*bother*!" Maewen said. "How am I supposed to find a crown in a place like that?"

"How indeed?" Navis murmured.

"A way will be found, lady," Wend said.

Maewen supposed Wend knew. But as they mounted again and moved off, she could not help thinking that this mission was becoming more impossible with every mile they went. She wondered if Noreth had realized and simply run away. Maewen would not have blamed her. Six people set out wandering the old roads—one of those six accused of theft by a voice in the air, too!—in search of a crown buried in a city that did not exist anymore, with no provisions and almost no baggage, and this was supposed to prove that the wrong girl was Queen. As if the earls in their earldoms would let even Noreth get away with it! Maewen uneasily remembered that earls were like little kings in those days, bad kings in the South and better ones in the North, but all of them kings. And kings always made a point of keeping their thrones.

But Amil the Great did it somehow, she told herself. Don't be too long turning up, Amil. I'll hand over to you with the greatest pleasure.

The green road all this while was taking them through another gorge, overhung by more rowan trees. Maewen found she was nervously looking at the skyline, high above, in case an earl had sent a party of hearthmen to make sure they got no farther. It must be an earl who had kidnapped Noreth. One of her five companions was in the pay of an earl.

She felt a great deal better when the road took them out onto a green plain, high, high up. Chilly reviving wind swept over her. Far below, and yet seeming to stand up into the sky, was the gray sea, chopped by white galloping waves.

"This is better," Mitt said, coming up beside her. "Maybe it's being brought up a fisherman; I always like seeing the sea. Or maybe it comes of being a Holander. Eh, Navis?"

Navis had come up on the other side. He was looking out at the sea just as Mitt was—as if it was home, really. He said, "I miss the blue of the sea farther south, but I wasn't displeased the Countess sent me to Adenmouth. Plenty of sea there. And I've never for one moment regretted leaving Holand."

It was odd to hear Navis talk without sarcasm at all. Maewen wondered how to find out what they were both doing so far from Holand, but before she could think how, Navis said to her, "You, of course, will have a special interest in this stretch of sea."

"Why? Do you know something I don't know?" Maewen shot back. A silly thing to say, but Navis had that effect on her.

"I was meaning that we must be quite near Kredindale," Navis said, "where I gather you were born, Noreth. Isn't it your cousin Kintor who's lord here?"

Maewen said quickly, "Yes, but we don't get on." That, she hoped, would stop Navis expecting her to go and visit her cousin. But he can't be right! she thought. It was miles round the coast from Adenmouth to Kredindale. It took ages, even by car. But as they moved on, she saw the long spit of green, scribbled with the ditches of a sea marsh, stretching out into the sea below, where, in her day, the big refinery stood. She had seen it from the train only days ago. It seemed that the old road had cut straight through the mountains.

"Whatever you feel about your cousin," Navis said, "I imagine you could hope to gather quite a number of followers here."

Followers! I hope *not*! Maewen thought. Whatever would I *do* with them?

"Yes, I reckon you're going to have to have an army," Mitt agreed. "Show those earls you mean business."

They were probably both right, but Maewen just could not see herself leading an army. She would feel such a fool. She rode on wondering how to get out of having one.

The coastline made a grand curve, and the road followed it, but so high that Maewen could not see the big Kredindale Valley she knew must be down there somewhere. There, as they came round the curve, was the waystone marking the way down to the valley and—horrors!—really quite a big crowd of people gathered on the clifftops beside it. As Maewen's group came into sight, there was a lot of shouting. She heard the name Noreth! over and over again, and—she couldn't help it—she pulled her horse to a standstill, terrified. Her eyes blurred, and her knees shook.

She said stupidly, "What do you think they want?"

"To talk to you, evidently," Navis replied.

He seemed to be right. A group of people, men and women, was running toward her eagerly, with one man out in front, and the crowd itself was pressing forward behind them, more slowly, in a jog-trot filled with windy wavings of scarves, hair, arms, ribbons, and some kind of long, snapping banners. Midsummer flags, Maewen thought. They must be holding their Midsummer Fair up here. She wanted to shake her horse into a gallop and leave. Fast. But the crowd was blocking the road. And they all looked so glad to see her.

Oh Noreth! she thought. Why did you have to let me in for this?

Wend strode up beside her. "May I hold your horse, lady, while you get down and speak with them?"

Mitt had seen how she was feeling. "I'll go with her. D'you mind holding the Countess, too?" he asked Wend.

"And mine," Navis said, hurling his reins over his mare's head.

Maewen was too grateful almost to be ashamed at how obvious her terror must be. It felt much better walking toward the eager man with Mitt towering slightly behind her on one side and Navis pacing sedately and briskly on the other.

"Noreth Onesdaughter," the eager man greeted her. "We heard tell you'd ride the roads this Midsummer, and you must forgive us that we lay in wait for you, in a manner of speaking, but—" Here the small group of men and women caught up and stood panting, nodding, smiling and staring. "We are all the gang heads at the mines," the eager man explained. "I am Tankol Kolsson, and I speak for the heads. Lady, will you talk to Lord Kintor, your cousin, for us? We are at our wit's end truly and truly do not mean to be lawless the way his new law-woman says we are."

At this all the others in the group burst out talking, too. "Willing workers all," Maewen heard. "The land being that poor" and "No sale in summer so he'll only pay half!" overlaid by "The mines now the main way to make a living" and "Next to nothing if you've a family to feed!" This was half drowned by someone saying over and over, "Then Lord Kintor would have to sell his horses and that we do not want," and someone else saying just as often, "Pay half for what we fetch out and put only a quarter back in winter—that's starvation, lady!" During this the entire crowd arrived, so that Maewen was surrounded and buried in people all shouting, "It's that new law-woman of his! Make him send her away!" or, "We're only miners, lady, and we don't know what to do!"

Mines, she thought distractedly. Miners. She remembered the Kredindale of her day, and the big spoil heaps that had been landscaped with grass and trees down by the coast, with the ruins of chimneys and old mine shafts farther up the hills. There was a colliery museum somewhere. Maewen remembered Aunt Liss's saying that when she was a girl, Kredindale had been nothing but coal mines wherever you looked. It looked as if it had started being like that very early on. But she had no idea what all these shouting people expected her to do about it.

"Hold hard!" Mitt shouted. "Do you mind not all talking at once!"

Into the slight hush that this made, Navis called, "Let's get this straight. You're in some kind of quarrel with Lord Kintor, and you want this lady to put it right."

Amid the shouts of agreement Mitt said to the eager man, "You. Tankol. If you're spokesman, you tell her."

Tankol was only too ready to tell. The trouble was, he was not one of those people who could tell a thing simply and quickly. Maewen listened for a good quarter of an hour, almost glad of being surrounded by people because the sea wind was cold, even though she found the pressure of all their attention nearly unbearable. At the end of that time she had gathered that her supposed cousin had hired a new law-woman who had told him he would have to sell his horses because there was no demand for coal. There were lots of figures, too, halves, quarters, thirds, which had something to do with the wages miners earned. The main thing Maewen really gathered was that neither Tankol nor anyone else had the least desire to leave Kredindale and follow Noreth as an army.

She ought to have been relieved. She was, in a way. But she was also exasperated. If even the people in Noreth's birthplace did not consider following her, this really did make her mission impossible. But there had to be more to it than this. Mitt and Navis seemed to be following what Tankol said. Maewen turned to them. "Can you explain?"

"A rather familiar story," Navis said dourly, "one I thought I'd left behind with the South."

"Isn't it just!" Mitt agreed. "He's saying this Kintor of yours has hired the law to help him diddle the miners. Kintor's hard up, mind you, because folk can burn peat for nothing. And she's told him—this law lady—that he can halve their wages in the summer and then put a bit back in the winter, without them being able to do a thing about it. If they complain to him, it's unlawful. If they hold meetings about it, that's not lawful either. So what are they to do?"

"They seem to have been smart enough to get around the law by having their meetings as the Midsummer Fair up here, while they waited for you," Navis said. "But one does wonder how many miners' wages your cousin is paying his new law-woman."

Maewen was beginning to feel glad that she could disown this Kintor as her cousin. All the worried faces staring at her had the hollow eyes of people who never quite got enough to eat. Everyone was in holiday best, to judge from the ribbons and embroidery, but they were poor clothes, old and darned and carefully looked after. "Why don't they want him to sell his horses?" she asked.

"Famous bloodstock," Navis said. "Everyone is proud of them."

"Yeah. This is the free North," Mitt said bitterly.

"Free to some," Tankol retorted, quite as bitterly. "You're an Aberath hearthman, lad. You don't know you're born."

Because Mitt looked about to become extremely angry, Maewen said almost without thinking. "Then why don't you go on strike?"

Every face, Mitt's and Navis's, too, turned to her, perplexed. Oh help! she thought. They've never heard of strikes yet. Strikes were unheard of until industry started. And when did industry get going? Maewen wondered frantically. Not quite yet, she was sure. But wasn't it quite early on in Amil the Great's reign? Yes, because she remembered learning that Amil had encouraged industry, particularly in the North. But, oh dear, all the same. Everyone was waiting for her to explain, and she was going to have to send history in a circle, because she only knew about strikes because there had *been* strikes, probably because she had told everyone about them one windy afternoon in Kredindale, because . . .

"It means," she said, "that you all stop work until my cousin agrees to pay you a fair wage."

"But we can't. We'd be turned off work," Tankol protested.

"Oh come *on*!" Maewen said. "My cousin needs you to work the mines. If you all stop, he can't sack you all because he'd starve, too."

"But," said one of the women, "it's like Young Kol said. It's not lawful."

They were so slow and sad and doubtful that Maewen wanted to shake them. "Look. It's not unlawful if one of you is sick and can't get to work, is it?"

"No." Everyone agreed to that.

"Then you all get ill at once," Maewen explained.

This caused a startled, interested silence. Mitt broke it by pointing out what Maewen had always thought was the weak part of strikes. "They'd never get away with that in the South," he said. "The Earl would just send his hearthmen to hang the ringleaders, sick or not. Maybe your Kintor won't do that in the North here. But he'd have to do something. If he didn't, they'd *all* be ruined, him and them together. It goes," Mitt added, just as if he had read Maewen's mind, "in a circle, like."

It did. Maewen wanted to shake Mitt, too. "But there's going to be a huge demand for coal," she said. "Any day—well, any year now—in five years, anyway. I know. There'll be machines—"

Mitt frowned disbelievingly. "You mean, like Alk's Irons?"

Maewen did not know what he meant, so she turned back to persuading the rest of them. "It's true. I really do know. Tell Kintor that if he'll just pay you properly and wait, people will be yelling for all the coal you can mine, and more!"

She heard murmurs, back in the crowd, dubious and awed. "The

One speaks to her. She might know, at that." But Tankol, who was clearly a more practical type, said, "You wouldn't be willing to walk down the dale and tell Kintor that yourself, would you, lady?"

"We don't get on. He wouldn't listen," Maewen said. Besides knowing I'm not Noreth, I'll bet. Great One, this is difficult! "Now what I think you should do is wait to go on strike until people start wanting coal again in the autumn, and Kintor really needs you. Then you all say you're sick and—and those that want to can come and join me at Kernsburgh and be my army."

"After Harvest," someone said. "We could, if the harvest's in."

Maewen could feel them all slowly beginning to agree. She felt warm with victory. How was that for brilliance? How was that for a way to recruit an army without having one? How was that for killing several birds with—

Navis canceled all that by asking coolly, "After Harvest? But what, may I ask, will you be doing, Noreth, for the three months in between?"

Doesn't it take that long to get to Kernsburgh then? Oh *hell*! "I shall be very busy," Maewen said.

Navis's eyebrow slid up. But quite unexpectedly Tankol came to her rescue. "Of course she will, hearthman. We all know she'll want to be searching out the Adon's gifts to take to Kernsburgh."

Both of Navis's eyebrows soared. "I beg your pardon? Adon's gifts?"

Tankol, and several other people, gave Maewen knowing smiles. "Southerner, isn't he?" Tankol said. "Knows nothing. But we all know they answer to the true Queen, and even the strongest claim *can* be stronger. Very well, lady. You've mapped us our way. We work all summer and then fall sick of starvation, and those of us still with our strength bargain with Kintor and then vanish away to Kernsburgh. What say, all? Is this what we do?"

To Maewen's considerable amazement, there were shouts of agreement. Navis was possibly even more dumbfounded, but he kept his head even though they were suddenly being jostled every which way in a cheering crowd. He seized Maewen's arm strongly, and quite painfully, just as it seemed that she might be swept away from himself and Mitt, and he shouted, in a ringing voice that came out over all the other voices, "The army is to gather at Kernsburgh. Bring weapons and food if you can. For now, will you please supply the lady Noreth with provisions for her ride."

Maewen thought that last demand was a bit much. These people were so poor. All the same, when Navis and Mitt dragged her clear of the crowd, more than half the people in it were already running the other way to see what the pens and stalls under the banners could supply.

They found Moril angrily hanging on to Mitt's horse. Hestefan was off the cart, hauling at the mule. Wend, who had enough to do with Navis's mare and Maewen's horse, said, very irritably for him, "That vile gelding with the teeth bit the mule. Tell the boy to take care of it."

Wend doesn't like Mitt, Maewen thought. Doesn't anyone like *anyone* on this expedition?

# PART THREE

# *Ring and Cup*

# 8

"CONGRATULATIONS, NORETH," Navis said as they rode away from Kredindale. Behind them Hestefan's cart was laboring and creaking with its load of provisions. "Tell me, do you intend to call for an army in every dale we pass?"

Maewen had been afraid he was going to ask her that. While Mitt and Navis had been riding about choosing cheeses and bags of oats, and rejecting numbers of skinny upside-down hens, Maewen had put in quite a bit of thought. "I don't think so," she said judiciously. "Kredindale was special. Now they know I'm calling for an army, word will get round."

"I admire your faith," said Navis. "So we—"

"And I admire the way you got all the food organized," Maewen said quickly, to stop him saying what she knew he was going to say next.

"Think nothing of it. I was an officer in Holand before you were born," said Navis. "Although," he added thoughtfully, "it was last year in Adenmouth that really taught me to do ten things at once." Then, just as Maewen was sure she had distracted him, Navis went on, "But as I was about to say, your plan is that we spend the intervening months searching for certain objects with which to bolster your claim? Just what are these Adon's gifts?"

Maewen tried not to sigh. But then people did not get made Duke of Kernsburgh by being easy to distract. The trouble was, she had no more idea than Navis did. "I think," she said, "that the best person to ask is Hestefan. Singers always know more about these things."

"I shall," said Navis. "But you are aware, are you, that none of the earls are going to take kindly to our wandering the green roads like this? Three months will give them ample time to deal with your claim."

Maewen knew he was right. She had been wondering whether to answer this one by saying piously that the One would provide, but she had a feeling that Navis would simply laugh at that. So she did the only other thing she could think of and smiled a secretive, knowing smile—or she hoped it was—and then asked Navis how he came to be in the North.

He had had an adventurous escape from some kind of danger in Holand, she gathered, though as he would only talk about it lightly, in scraps, as if it were a joke rather than a flight for his life, Maewen never quite understood what the danger had been. He had met Mitt for the first time in the Holy Islands. "Mitt appeared to be having dealings with the Undying. Quite beyond my depth," Navis said lightly.

He was so easy to distract that Maewen felt rather sad. She knew he was letting her change the subject, and that had to mean that Navis did not really care what they did in the next three months. Someone like Navis was not going to join this expedition without some other, personal reason. Maewen suspected that he and Mitt were going to leave and go off on their own as soon as that personal reason led them in a different direction.

"Don't worry, Noreth," Navis said. "I promised your aunt I would take care of you. I intend to see you right."

Maewen was still surprised by this when they stopped for the night. The road had plunged them back into the heart of the mountains again, through narrow places full of pine trees, then out again into a sort of crossroads in the green ways. It was a large, lumpy meadow among the crags with quite a number of waystones round the edge. They camped in a flat space among the lumps. People obviously used it regularly. There was a fireplace, a surprisingly clean latrine pit, and sort of caves scraped in some of the humps for sleeping in.

"Where is this?" Mitt asked while Moril was lighting a fire with the bag of coal the miners had given them.

Wend answered, but he spoke to Maewen as if Mitt was just a servitor. "This is Orilsway, lady." Orilsway! Maewen thought. But I went through this in the train. It was a *town*! "It is the northern crossway," Wend explained, pointing to the various waystones. "That leads to Aberath, and that to central parts, with Hannart at the end. South-easterly, you may go by Ansdale and Loviath, to Gardale and beyond, but I take it, lady, we'll be wanting the way down the end there that goes south to Dropwater."

Maewen looked up at Wend's serious face. Always serious. Why can't he unbend a little? she thought irritably. "I'm considering," she said. "I'll tell you which way in the morning."

Supper was fresh bread, curd cheese, and pickled cherries. Mitt loved pickled cherries. It was not a thing he had met in the South. But Navis spit his first and only one into the fire. "I take it the cherry crop was large in Kredindale," he said. "They should have left it for the birds. Hestefan, tell us about the Adon's gifts."

Hestefan looked up from the other side of the fire. "These are well known to everyone in the North," he said.

"But not to me," said Navis. "Or Mitt."

Mitt threw a handful of cherry stones on the fire. "Speak for yourself, Navis. They're supposed to be the things Manaliabrid gave the Adon in her dowry. There's a sword and a cup and a ring, and the Countess has got the ring in that old collection of hers, back in Aberath."

"And the cup's in the One's chapel at the Lawschool in Gardale," Moril said. "I saw it when I went to see my sister."

"The sword is in Dropthwaite," said Wend. "It is well hidden, but I have seen it."

"And would they answer to the true Queen?" Navis asked Hestefan. "Tankol seemed to think they would, and he's the sort of practical man I'm inclined to believe."

Hestefan had been looking from one to the other, for all the world, Maewen thought, like a schoolmaster who had come prepared to teach and found his class knew all the answers. He had reminded her of a schoolmaster ever since she first saw him—Dr. Loviath, who taught her physics last year, that's who he was like! He said, in exactly Dr. Loviath's repressive way, "There are various kinds of hearsay about the gifts—nothing I have seen myself and nothing anyone is known to have proved."

Mitt, who thought Hestefan was a right stick, took up another handful of cherries and said, "Alk told me the ring always fits the right one's finger. He says it fits the Countess, and not him, because she's descended from the Adon. Mind you, it's a small ring. And you should see the size of Alk's fingers!"

"So that is not proven," Hestefan said, frowning. "Singers are bound only to tell the truth. I can say nothing more."

Moril seemed puzzled. "Yes, but we can tell what people *say*," he said. "And I know they *say* that only the Adon's true heir can draw the sword."

"I can say nothing more," Hestefan repeated.

Maewen tried to smooth things over by asking, "Can you tell me something I've always wondered? Was the Adon of the Undying?"

It did not work. Hestefan stared at her rather as he had stared before, when she told him to come out of his dream. Then he said grudgingly, "I think not, though he was of their blood. He died twice, you know."

Chalk up two more of us who don't get on, Maewen thought. Hestefan and me. Thoroughly disgruntled, she got up and went to sit on top of a hump some distance away, where she watched the last of the light fading from the highest peaks. The sky was still silvery, but the mountains were bluer and bluer. Over the other way the campfire made it seem quite dark. What was the matter with her? Why should it bother her that nobody in the group got on? She was only a fraud and a substitute, who was in danger of making history go in circles after this afternoon.

That seemed to be it. This afternoon she had done something which really would affect history, and because of that, whether it was impossible or not, she wanted this mad venture of Noreth's to *succeed.* She wanted to take it and make it work. Maybe, when the time came, she would not tamely hand over to Amil the Great. That would be changing history indeed—if only she could think how to do it.

"You dealt very shrewdly with those miners," the deep echoing voice remarked in her ear. "My advice has not been wasted on you."

Maewen jumped and looked round carefully. For as far as she could see in the gloaming, she was alone on her damp green hillock. She could see Navis, Hestefan, and Wend over in the orange light of the fire. Besides, she knew their voices now, and it was none of those three who had spoken. Moril's voice was still a husky treble, and Mitt's tended to crack and rumble. It was that ghost again. Ghosts cannot hurt one, but Maewen did not like the bluish wafts of mist that were gathering in the spaces between the hummocks. She got up casually and started to go back to the fire.

"Now you must acquire the Adon's gifts," the voice said, still at her ear. She walked faster, but it was still at her ear, sending deep, deep vibrations through her. "Find the Adon's gifts. They will prove your claim. They will also give your followers a purpose, and your search will confuse the earls."

This was exactly the idea that Maewen had been fumbling for in her own mind. Perhaps this voice *was* part of her mind. That made it worse. "I'll consider it," she said, and fled.

By the fire everyone seemed to be getting up and settling for the night. But there was no sign of Moril. Moril was the one Maewen wanted. She needed some more magic from that cwidder. She thought she heard it, twanging gently, beyond one of the hummocks to the right. She swerved and ran that way, over a hump and down the other side, where she very nearly trod on Mitt, sitting rather as she had been sitting herself.

Mitt sprang up with a hoarse squawk. Maewen yelled.

"Thank you very much!" Mitt said. "That's all I need for a perfect day!"

"Is anything the matter?" Navis called from the fireside.

"Nothing," Mitt called back. "Just saddlesore. Vinegar!" he said disgustedly to Maewen. "He made me sit in vinegar. Maybe I'd be worse without it, but it doesn't do your temper any good, I can tell you! And then you come charging over this mound. What's up? You seem a bit off from yesterday."

"I was wanting Moril," Maewen said.

"He's off over here somewhere," Mitt said. They wandered that way together, between two lines of vague dark mounds. "Looks a bit like a street," Mitt remarked. "I shouldn't wonder if this wasn't a town once. What do you want Moril for?"

It was soothing wandering between hummocks with Mitt. Maewen found it much easier than she had expected to say, "I'm being haunted. A ghost keeps speaking to me, and Moril helped last time."

Mitt was truly puzzled. "What do you mean, a ghost? Last night you were saying it was the One, your father, who spoke to you. Or is this another voice?"

Help! thought Maewen. Why didn't Wend *tell* me?

"It's—it's always very alarming when he does," she said.

"That's the Undying for you," said Mitt. "What did he say?"

How can he be so matter-of-fact? Maewen wondered. Even for two hundred years ago. But she remembered what Navis had told her. Mitt knew what he was talking about. "He said I ought to have the Adon's gifts," she said. She wanted to ask Mitt if he thought the voice was really the One's, but Noreth seemed to have told him already that it was, so she could hardly do that. Instead she said, "If this is Orilsway, Aberath is only a little way to the north. I can go and get the ring from there tomorrow."

Mitt laughed. It was a hacking, unhappy noise. "You'll be lucky! They'd cut your throat on the spot, girl. I know. I *know* that Countess."

Maewen began, "But—" Then she saw that Mitt, once again, probably knew what he was talking about. Two hundred years before she was born, people really did cut throats. Earls could get away with it then. She changed her objection to "But I need that ring. What should I do?"

"I'll get it for you," said Mitt. It seemed obvious to him that this was what Noreth was angling for. And it ought to be child's play. "I was looking at that ring only two days ago," he explained. "I know just where it is. If I go off now, I can sneak in while it's dark and pick it up with no one any the wiser."

"But you're saddlesore," Maewen protested. "And your horse isn't fresh."

"Teach that horse a lesson," Mitt said blithely. "And I'm not that bad. I was just having a moan."

He was lying a bit about the soreness. Ouch! Flaming Ammet! he thought as he mounted the surprised and reluctant Countess-horse. But he kept his mouth shut. Noreth's face, which he could see as a pale, anxious oval, was lifted toward him from beside the hummock he had used to mount. She was worrying, anyway. As he set off beside the half-seen waystone that marked the road to Aberath, he thought that she would have to give over this habit she seemed to have of worrying about everyone. She'd go off her head with it if she got to be Queen.

The green road, as they all seemed to be, was level and smooth and surprisingly easy to follow in the dark. The Undying did a good job, Mitt thought, if it was them who made the roads. And he was pleased to find that after years of indoors work, he had not lost the knack he had learned as a fisher lad of finding his way in the night. You did it the way they said bats did, mostly. Sort of by feel. Whenever the road turned, he could feel the air pressing off the bigger bulks of rock, and he knew to veer left or right, even when he could not see the pale grayishness of the track. The Countesshorse, to be fair to it, had the same knack, when it consented to go.

It made quite a fuss at first. After a mile of head tossing, loitering, and pretending to go lame, and hearty cursing from Mitt, it chose to surprise him by consenting to go. They thudded on at a fair pace. Mitt, in order not to think of the trouble he might be in if he got caught at the mansion, tried to work out why he was going off to get this ring for Noreth.

It might have belonged to the Adon, but whatever Alk said, Mitt was fairly sure it was just a ring. The Northerners could believe in these things if it made them happy, but Mitt had been brought up by the practical Hobin, making guns for a living in Holand, and he knew that the only virtue that ever got into a piece of metal was fine, careful workmanship.

Right. That was the ring. Did he believe the One wanted Noreth to have it?

Mitt had a little more difficulty here. He had never met this One the Northerners made so much of. Or had he? Mitt narrowed his eyes into the mild wind of the night as he remembered finding the golden statue and that great deep voice crying, "*There!*" That had surely not been Noreth shouting. Well, keep an open mind there. But would the greatest of the Undying be that bothered about a ring?

You could say it was Mitt himself bothering. If he took this ring, it would prove to the Countess that Mitt was not her hired murderer. That could be true. But it was fairly clear to Mitt that he was riding through the night like this simply because Noreth thought she needed the ring. That nervous, freckly look of hers made you want to do things for her. So you did them. And then trusted to Navis to get them all out of the consequences, Mitt added to himself as he came out beside the waystone above Aberath.

The Countess-horse knew where they were. It slithered gladly down the raked track to the town. Mitt was almost sorry for its disappointment when he dragged it over to the woods beyond the first fields and—to its incredulity—left it tied to a tree. It made its feelings plain, quite loudly, and several other horses answered it from stables in the town.

"Shut *up*!" Mitt told it. "Be quiet or *I'll* bite *you* for a change!"

He ran away round the fields toward the cliff. Reproachful horse noises followed him for a minute and then stopped with a sigh Mitt could hear even at that distance. He grinned and ran with long strides. His legs ached from being wrapped round a horse so long, and it was good to stretch them in spite of his soreness. He supposed he had vinegar to thank that he could run at all. He only stopped running when he was looking down at the pale heaving sea. There he paused to speak to the Undying he did know.

"Alhammitt," he said. "Old Ammet. Do you hear me? I'd be much obliged if you and Libby Beer could keep an eye on me in the mansion. If I get caught there, quite a few people are going to be in trouble."

There was no sign from the glimmering sea, but Mitt felt better as he hurried along the clifftop to the place where all the children regularly scrambled round the wall. He nipped round, quietly and carefully, and there he was out in the space by Alk's shed. It was so easy Mitt could hardly believe it.

It went on being easy. Mitt slithered in among the buildings of the mansion, from well-known spot to well-known spot, and not a person moved or a sound disturbed the place except for the faint crunch of his own feet when he crossed the gravel court in front of the library. There were one or two dim lights in some of the upper windows. Otherwise he would have thought the place was empty. It reminded him of times in Holand when he sneaked into strange places with a forbidden message. In fact, it was too much like that. The mansion did not feel like anywhere he had ever lived anymore. Nor was it now, he thought ruefully, as his feet carefully inched through the dark archway and met the flight of stairs up to the library.

At the top his hand met the door and found the handle. Gently, gently, he turned the great latch ring and pushed the door open on the woody, booky mustiness inside. It was so dark in there that he realized he was going to have to find the glass case where the ring was by memory and feel. But since he was going to have to break the glass and someone might hear, he shut the door behind him as gently as he had opened it. He took a step into the room.

*Cree-eak.*

"Flaming Ammet!" Mitt muttered. "Wish I'd remembered how *noisy* this dratted floor was!"

Light came on, blindingly, with a metal clapping sound.

# 9

MITT DID NOT EVEN feel despair. He felt dead. He was caught, as he had always known he would be one of these days. He simply stood, blinking to see through the light, wondering if it was only the Countess lying in wait for him or Earl Keril as well.

The light was a dark lantern standing on the selfsame case he had intended to rob. When Mitt tore his eyes sideways from it, he could see the bilious visage of the Adon's portrait, still on its easel. Beside that, in a big dark wood chair, Alk was sitting, bulky and blinking. Either the light had blinded him, too, or he had been asleep—asleep was most likely, because Alk yawned before he spoke.

"I told you," he said, "not to do anything stupid until you'd talked to me. Did you shut the door?"

Mitt nodded.

"Then come over here," said Alk.

Mitt went, still without any word to say, over several miles of violently creaking floor, until he was beside the table and the glass case, and in front of Alk's chair. Alk put out a beefy hand and carefully closed down the iron shutter of the lantern until the library was nothing but shadows all round them.

"Now stand over there," Alk said, pointing the other beefy hand.

Mitt moved, regretfully, away from the table and the glass case, and stood at the edge of the pool of light, beside the easel. Alk was alone, but this was no comfort. Mitt knew very well how quick and strong Alk was. Alk had put him where it was impossible for Mitt to get to the door before Alk did.

"Doing a bit of studying tonight," Alk remarked, yawning again. "Or so I told my Countess. I had a bit of a conversation with her, like

I told you I would, and I wasn't pleased with what she had to say at all. To put it bluntly, as soon as Keril was out of the way, we had words—which is not a thing we've ever had before." He blinked at Mitt, as sleepy and glum and grim as Mitt had ever seen him. "What do you think about that? You being the cause of those words."

Mitt cleared his throat, which had somehow closed solid. "I'm sorry."

"Glad to hear it," said Alk. "So then I had a think. And it seemed to me that in your shoes I'd be trying ways to wriggle out of the bind they'd got you in. Am I right?"

Mitt cleared his throat again. His voice still came out hoarse and desperate. "I'm not doing any killing!"

"So I should hope!" said Alk. "But I'm glad to hear you say it. What's she like, this Noreth?"

"Freckly," said Mitt. "Full of life. I took her for a boy at first. She's all right. She's got her head screwed on more than you'd expect, considering."

"Has she, now?" said Alk. "Then what's she up to, riding the King's Road with you for a follower? That doesn't sound too clever to me. There's more earls around than Keril and my Countess who'll want to put a stop to that."

"I know. Put like that, it sounds right daft." But daft though it was, Mitt found himself defending Noreth. "She cares about people, and she's got some good ideas. People will come to her. And she *has* got a claim."

"As to that," Alk said, "so have a lot of people got a claim. She's saying she descends from the Adon over beside you and his second wife, Manaliabrid—right? Now I've been reading up again on all that."

His big hand made a gesture, down by the lantern and the glass case it stood on. There was a spread of books there, several of them open, others with markers in. One of the markers was a shoehorn; another was a six-inch nail. Typical of Alk. Mitt would have grinned at any other time.

"My law stuff is a bit rusty after all these years," Alk explained. Mitt was not sure he believed that. "But I've been finding out that even the Adon didn't have that good a claim to be King. But he took the crown, so we'll take it from there. Now if this Manaliabrid was who she said she was, she certainly made his claim better. She claimed to be of the Undying, daughter of Cennoreth and great-granddaughter of the One. Well, no one seemed to doubt she was, so we'll give her that. Now she and the Adon had two children, a son and a daughter. And either these two were a great disappointment to their parents, or *they* weren't any too sure of their claim either, because neither of them made the least push to rule after. The son, Almet, took the kingstone, but all he did with it was go off to the South and govern a little lordship that's dead and gone now, somewhere near Waywold. And the daughter, Tanabrid, was quite satisfied to marry and settle down in Kredindale. After that there were marryings and intermarryings, the way there are, and Kredindale gets related to half the earls of the North. What I'm saying, Mitt, is that the claim's rubbish. Her cousin Kintor has a better claim, and so has my Countess or that soft-faced boy in Dropwater."

Mitt felt a bit light-headed. The last thing he had expected was for Alk to sit there talking family trees at him. He could only suppose that Alk was trying to make him feel foolish and give up the whole idea. So probably the Countess had not told him about Hildy and Ynen. "Yes, but—"

"You're going to say she says her father was the One," Alk interrupted. Mitt had not been, but he held his tongue. "Now there we're into the difficult part." Alk leaned back in his chair. It creaked horribly. "Even King Hern only claimed the One as his grandfather—which is probably just what we say when we call the One our Grand Father." Alk tipped his face round to look at Mitt, across what had been a beautifully ruffled lawn collar but was now dirty laundry. "I've seen the One," he said, to Mitt's surprise. "Several times. Not a thing I talk about to everyone. You'd know why, if it ever happened to you. And . . . well . . . it's like coming into a shadow all of a sudden, or the shadow coming into you. A bit like this." Alk's hand went out and downward across the narrow slit he had left in the shutter of the dark lantern. A huge hand-shaped darkness swept across the floor and Mitt and the wall of books beyond. Mitt shivered. "See?" said Alk. "He's there, but not solid—but I could be wrong. And Noreth's mother's not alive to tell me I'm wrong, is she?"

When Earl Keril had said something like this, Mitt had not felt it mattered. Coming from Alk, it did. "But the One talks to her," he protested. "I think I heard him. And it scares her."

"I don't doubt you," said Alk. "That's the most difficult part of the difficult part. If the One has an interest in all this, us mortal folk had best tread very wary. You don't cross the One. I wish my Countess would see that. But that Keril's one of your new, reasonable folk, and the Undying are just out-of-date beliefs to him. And she listens to him." He leaned his massive arms on top of the books and pondered glumly.

After a moment Mitt said, "Were you expecting me . . . to come back here?" His voice was still annoyingly hoarse.

"After a fashion. It was one of the options," Alk replied. "I was here on the off chance you'd take the option of going along with this

Noreth and helping her claim. I knew I was right when that nag of yours started sounding off in the meadows. Woke me up. Probably woke the dead, too. She's after the Adon's gifts, isn't she?"

Mitt's heart sank. He felt himself sag slightly.

Alk noticed. He never missed much. "I thought so. She knows, and you know, she's got no real claim. You were going to pinch this ring here, weren't you?"

Mitt managed a small, throaty "yup."

"And I thought you never believed it answers to the right blood!" Alk smiled slightly, his face all slabs of shadow and curves of light. He shook his head. "I wish I knew how the man who made it *did* it. I've tried all ways to catch it changing size, but I never can pin it down. And my Countess can put it on any finger and both her thumbs, and it'll fit her. I made Gregin try it, and it fell off him. So I've no doubt it would fit your Noreth whatever size her hands are."

"Small." Mitt's eyes went longingly to the glass case, where the ring picked up gleams of light underneath the lighted pane of glass, as if it were underwater. It looked as always very big, nearly big enough to fit one of Alk's massive fingers. If it did not fall straight off Noreth, it would be a miracle indeed.

"But it's a stupid way to get out of a mess," Alk said. "And I know you're in a mess, Mitt. Take this ring, or put a foot wrong any other way, and my Countess will have you—or Keril will. My sense is, they don't mean you to live too long. Or maybe they mean you to spend the rest of your days as their hired murderer. My Countess wouldn't admit to one or the other, but it has to be that."

Mitt nodded. He had worked this out, too. He tried to imagine Alk twisting the information out of the Countess, and he just could not see it. It was like imagining one of Alk's engines running straight up a house.

"And the only way you can keep out of that," Alk continued, "is to stay completely lawful and not give them a handhold. If you do that, I'm on your side. Will you promise me you won't murder or steal or anything like that?"

Alk didn't understand. It was clearer than ever to Mitt that the Countess had not told Alk about Hildy and Ynen. "What else *can* I do?" Mitt said, trying to talk round it.

"Uh-uh," said Alk. "Promise, I said."

"I'd rather not," Mitt said. "Something might come up."

"Fish feathers," said Alk. "I put it to you, you've done nothing outside the law yet. You went off to visit Navis Haddsson. You came back to have a chat with me."

"I came to pinch that ring," Mitt said, looking at it gleaming below the glass.

"But only I know that, and you're not going to," Alk said. "Whatever threats they made to you, I'll stand by you if you give me that promise."

Whatever threats? Perhaps Alk did know about Hildy and Ynen then. Mitt looked searchingly at Alk's big shadowy face. It gave nothing away. "What can *you* do against Keril?" he said.

"Hold him to the law," said Alk. "I don't know! Everyone round here seems to have forgotten I used to be a lawman once upon a time! And the law's the same whether you're an earl or a fisherman. Are you going to give me that promise?"

"I—" Mitt was not sure he dared.

"I'll make it easier for you," said Alk. "You didn't come here to steal that ring. You came here to ask me to *give* it you."

*"What?"* It was odd how the library seemed to be a brighter, warmer, freer place all of a sudden. "You couldn't do that," Mitt said, trying not to laugh. "She'd notice."

"I made a copy," Alk said, "trying to get it to change size the same way. And I couldn't do it. It's just a ring. But it looks just the same. Now what d'you say?"

"I promise," Mitt said. "You won't know me, I'll be so lawful."

"That'll be the day!" said Alk. Smiling a little, he fetched out a small key that was marking a place in another of his books and stood up to move the lantern and unlock the glass case. The dim light swept around the room, and his vast shadow blotted half the library into darkness. "Remember," Alk said as he turned the key, "that the One has an interest in this, and don't go forgetting you promised."

Mitt looked at that vast shadow and shivered. "I'll bear it in mind."

Alk lifted the glass lid, fetched out the ring, and held it where the light from the lantern was strongest. It was a plain heavy ring, made of gold, and its only ornament was the big seal carved out of some kind of red stone into the haggard-looking profile of the Adon. Alk's huge, deft fingers twiddled it. "Safest way to carry it is to wear it," he said. "Put your hand out."

Mitt spread his long, bony hands into the light. Alk tried to slip the ring on the ring finger of Mitt's right hand. It stuck at the knuckle. "I got big lumps there on all my fingers," Mitt said.

"You put it on then," said Alk.

Mitt took the heavy ring and, still barely able to believe Alk was letting him have it, tried it on finger after finger. Each time it slid only as far as Mitt's first knuckle. The only finger it would fit, and only with a struggle, was the little finger of his left hand.

"Well, at least it won't fall off," Alk said. "Off you go then, and give it to your Noreth. And if she wants you to do anything else unlawful, you say no. Understand? And I'll back you up."

"Thanks," Mitt said. It was truly heartfelt.

He was not any too clear about much of the journey back. He scrambled back round the mansion wall. That took concentration because it meant balancing on the edge of the cliff above the sea. After that some kind of reaction hit him. Things came and went. He remembered getting onto the Countess-horse, because it tried to bite him as usual, and—dimly—going up the rake to the green road, because that took all the concentration he had left. But as soon as the horse was on the road to Orilsway and there was nowhere else it could go, Mitt was probably asleep in the saddle. He thought he dreamed that Alk had given him the Adon's ring. It had to be a dream, he decided, waking up about a hundred yards from the camp, because it was just not probable that Alk would do a thing like that. Why had he woken up? He thought it was the Countess-horse, which had gone from a stumbling plod to a much more eager pace. No, it seemed to be because something was wrong with his left hand.

*Wrong!* That was an understatement. He felt as if his little finger had been clamped in one of Alk's vises. And someone was still twisting the vise. Throb, throb, throb. Mitt could *feel* his finger swelling. He dropped the reins and wrenched at the ring. It would not budge. Flaming Ammet! He could have pulled his finger off sooner than moved that ring! He had to have light—help—something! He shot down from the horse and rushed toward where he thought the camp was.

Maewen sprang up. She had been half listening, not really asleep, hoping she had not got Mitt into trouble with this Countess of his. She heard mad, blundering footsteps, followed by a cracking voice swearing and then demanding, "Where *is* this flaming camp then? They *can't* have all gone off and *left* me!" Maewen ran in that direction. And there was Mitt, a demented leggy figure in the near dark, racing toward the southernmost waystone, apparently wringing his hands.

"What's the matter?"

Mitt rushed up to Maewen and towered over her, still pulling at his finger. "I got you the ring. The flaming thing's stuck on my finger! I think I'm in it for life!"

Maewen seized the hand he flapped in her face. She could feel the ring, a tiny metal waist in a finger that seemed as large and hot as a fresh-cooked sausage. "Oh my lord!" She tugged. Mitt yelped. It was most well and truly stuck. "Don't you know any better than to put on a ring that's too small for you?"

"How should *I* know? I never wore a ring in my life!"

"Well, you should have *thought*! People were small in the old days!" But this *is* the old days. *He's* not small. Never mind.

They bent over Mitt's hand, both of them in the same panic. "I'm stuck in this thing for*ever*!" Mitt squalled.

"Lick it. See what lots of spit does," said Maewen. "Or soap." There had been no soap in her baggage roll. But surely soap *was* invented by this time? No one struck her as *that* dirty. "Or—water—water might cool your finger down."

"I've got some soap," Moril said from beside them. "Shall I fetch it?"

"Yes, and a light, too," said Maewen.

Moril dashed away. Mitt put his hand to his mouth and slobbered on it mightily. Maewen helped him spread the spit up and down the swollen finger. Then she pulled. Mitt pulled. Neither of them had budged the ring one fraction by the time Moril dashed up again with a piece of soap and a lighted lantern from the cart. By the light Moril looked both awed and scornful.

"That's the Adon's ring?" he said.

"Yup," said Mitt, soaping for his life.

"It only fits people with royal blood," Moril pointed out.

"I know *that*!" Mitt snarled. "I only wore it not to lose it, you stupid little—"

"Cool it, cool it," Navis said, arriving with a slopping leather bucket.

"Oh no!" said Mitt. "Keep him away from me! He'll try to boil it off or something!"

"It's only cold water," Navis said. "Put your hand in it."

"Yes, that should take the swelling down." Wend agreed, coming, yawning, up beside Navis.

Mitt plunged his hand in the bucket. Took it out, soaped it, hauled on the ring, sighed, and put his hand in the water again. He did this four more times. "I'll bring this water to the boil, at this rate," he grumbled. As he plunged his hand in for the sixth time, Hestefan arrived, yawning, rubbing his beard and wanting to know what the fuss was about. By this time it was plain to Maewen that she could not have kept the theft of the ring secret, as she had meant to, any more than if she had shouted it from the top of the nearest mountain.

As Mitt took his hand out of the bucket for the seventh time, Wend said wearily, "Here. Let me." He seized Mitt's bony wrist in one hand and the ring with the other. And dragged.

*"Yow!"* said Mitt. "Leave me my hand!"

But the ring was off. Everyone was silent while Wend held it under the lantern light, where they could all see the red stone flash, and then passed it to Maewen.

She felt sweat popping out among her freckles. "This is the Adon's ring," she said, making a clean breast of it, "that Mitt very kindly—er—obtained for me. I intend to collect all the Adon's gifts. Tomorrow we're going to Gardale."

"How convenient," Navis murmured to Mitt. But Mitt was watching Maewen across the finger he was sucking. They were all watching.

Maewen realized there was no way she could distract them. She was going to have to put this ring on, now, under the light, and it was not going to fit. It was huge. Mitt's fingers might look long and bony, but each of them would have made two of hers. If Dad was right, she told herself, Mum does go back to Amil the Great somewhere. But she was afraid that drop of royal blood had got very watered down by the time it came to her. She took a deep breath—and an even deeper risk—and slipped the wide gold band round her right thumb, this being the only place it had even a chance of fitting. And it fitted. Everyone sighed.

"I'll see to your loathsome horse," Navis said to Mitt. "You get some sleep."

# 10

IT TOOK SOME DAYS to get to Gardale, even straight through the heart of the mountains. Long before they got there, everyone except Mitt was heartily sick of pickled cherries. Mitt was simply sick with himself. The Countess-horse was tired and subdued, and he rode slackly at the rear, watching clouds come down and stream like gray scarves below spiky black mountain peaks, and then seeing those mountains wheel aside to show more and yet more ranged behind, and clouds stream against those mountains, too. It seemed as if the green road was gradually rising to take them through the central heights of the North.

Mitt supposed it was all very beautiful and grand, though it was not what he was used to. It was harsher than the sea and even more obviously cruel. And empty. One of the times they stopped, Navis remarked that they had not met another soul on the way. "Everyone is at home celebrating Midsummer, I imagine," he said. "It makes this the best time to travel and not be found."

Mitt simply grunted, "Good." His mind would not seem to let go of that promise he had made to Alk. In a way it was a weight off his mind. That worried him. It seemed so feeble to shelter behind a promise. Smug. Now I can do no wrong, you said, and ended up doing nothing, like a total failure. At the same time he had a gloomy feeling that the promise clamped him round as tight as that ring had, and that meant doing nothing, too, and total failure *that* way. It was worse than Keril and the Countess.

Maewen kept rubbing the red stone of the ring on her thumb. It became quite a habit. The voice had told her to get this ring, and she had got it. Somehow that made her uneasy. She had the same fizzing, doing-wrong feeling about it that Wend had given her in the train and in the palace. Without exactly admitting it to herself, she was careful never to be alone somewhere where one of the others could not hear. She suspected, again without admitting it, that the voice would only speak to her when she was on her own. And that was all mixed up with a nasty suspicion that the voice was part of her own mind, perhaps something to do with being sent back in time. It was bound to make your mind play tricks on you.

She would have liked to talk to Mitt or Moril about it. But Mitt either rode glumly on his own or else made the kinds of jokes that meant he did not feel like talking, and Moril was usually inside the cart, playing scales and pieces of tunes on different instruments. When Moril did emerge, it was to drive the cart while Hestefan sat with his legs hanging over the tailgate, practicing different instruments, too. Their small procession went to shards and trills of music most of the time, higher and higher into the central peaks. The clouds came damply about them. It was never easy to sleep at night.

Maewen stayed with Navis. She liked Navis. He was so efficient and imperturbable. It fascinated her the way he never let an evening go by without polishing his mare's tack and his own boots. In the mornings he brushed his hair and his clothes, and then, unfailingly, he shaved in whatever water was going, usually icy cold from a mountain stream. And he was so sharp, too. One morning Navis cut himself shaving. He exclaimed with annoyance and tried to keep the blood from running into the collar of his shirt. Wend, without a word, produced a clump of cobwebs from somewhere.

Navis said, "I thank you," gratefully. But as he pressed the cobwebs to his chin, Maewen saw his eyes go narrow and turn for just an instant to Wend's smooth chin. After that Navis's countenance was as bland and composed as ever, but Maewen knew he was wondering why Wend, a grown man, never seemed to shave or grow a beard either.

It interested Maewen, too. Maybe this was a sign of the Undying. But she did not like Wend enough to ask him.

From that day on, the green road was up in the clouds. Everything was moist and white. As Mitt rode in the rear, everyone ahead had turned into quiet gray shadows. A dewdrop gathered on his nose.

"I hate this!" he told the Countess-horse. It was the sort of remark he knew it would agree with.

Moril hopped out of the cart and walked beside Maewen's horse. She did not blame him. It was warmer walking, and no one was going fast in this fog. After a while she dismounted herself, and they walked side by side, talking, leading her horse. Maewen was surprised and glad at how ready Moril was to talk. He told her how it felt to lead a Singer's life, and the new way he wanted to treat the old songs, and about his plans for the future. She encouraged him. Ever since she had seen that portrait, she had had an ache somewhere about Moril. And without putting it to herself that she was once again trying to change history, she wanted badly to comfort him. It would be wonderful if she got back to the Tannoreth Palace to find that the portrait smiled instead of looking wretched.

Coming behind, Mitt honestly tried not to hear what was obviously a private conversation. He wondered about pushing past and riding on ahead where he could see the sketchy gray bulk of the cart, but the road was in a narrow ravine here, with wet black rocks close on either side, and it would have meant forcing his way through beside Moril or the horse, which would remind both of them that he was there, overhearing. He could see Moril's pale face turned eagerly to Noreth, as he told her about the dangers in the South, where Singers were often called upon to carry illegal messages. Noreth certainly had a way with her, Mitt thought ruefully. She drew me out the same way. Now Moril was telling her how he had come North last year after his father had been killed.

Moril's voice cracked a little. Mitt reined back the Countess-horse and tried to keep well behind. He knew that if he were to tell Noreth about *his* father, he would want no one listening in. But the horse had a long, rangy stride, and he kept catching up. He was up close behind again in time to hear Moril explaining that Hestefan was no relation. "He came to Hannart while I was there," Moril said. "And I asked him to take me with him. We went off secretly because I knew Earl Keril wanted me to stay."

Keril's name was enough to send Mitt backward again. This time he dismounted and walked, too. It was warmer that way, as well as slower. He tried to keep the three shapes ahead looking like pale gray shadows, out of hearing and almost out of sight. But Mitt's stride was as long and rangy as the Countess-horse's, and somehow, before long, he was able to overhear again.

"I told Hestefan I'd follow you on my own if he didn't want to come," Moril was saying. "But he said he'd better come because great events afoot need a Singer to record them. I'm sorry he's so neutral. I'm not. I think it's like the time Osfameron followed the Adon. Did you know Osfameron was my ancestor? My big cwidder used to be his."

Something about this seemed to make Noreth modest and uncomfortable. Mitt could hear her trying to change the subject. He waited for them to get ahead again. The mist seemed to be thicker here, perhaps because the ravine had widened. They were going past a chain of dimly seen lakes, each one like faintly rippled milk under the fog. Mitt thought he kept well behind while they passed three of these lakes, but he must have caught up again gradually, because he was able to hear Moril's voice then, evidently in the middle of something upsetting.

Noreth's answer floated back clearly. "But Navis couldn't possibly have known about Olob when he shot Dapple. Be *reasonable*, Moril."

"I know," Moril answered. "I didn't say it was reasonable. Anyway, he's Earl Hadd's son, and I hate him for that."

"He couldn't help being born," Maewen said patiently. "And Mitt's definitely not a noble, and he *didn't* shoot your horse. You can't just lump him in with Navis like that."

"Can't I just!" Moril said. "I hate all Southerners." For a while neither of them said anything else. Mitt, walking on the soft grass beside the milky lake, thought they had gone out of hearing again. Then Moril said, "I'll tell you why I really dislike Mitt. He makes jokes all the time—about serious things."

I do not so! Mitt thought indignantly. It occurred to him that though Noreth might have forgotten he was there, Moril probably knew perfectly well.

"A lot of Southerners do that," Maewen said. "It doesn't mean they aren't serious."

"Mitt's *never* serious," Moril said contemptuously. "Look at the way he joked when he was bearing witness about the One's statue. That made me so angry I broke my rule. I told you how I swore not to use the power of my cwidder. Well, I knew it was *serious* that you'd been given a sign to set out on the King's Road. So when you told everyone to follow you, I started to play the song with the power, to show people that it was important and they shouldn't follow you unless they really meant it."

Noreth, Mitt noticed, did not point out that the song seemed to have misfired a little. She said, "That was nice of you." And Mitt wondered if perhaps Moril did not know he was just behind them after all.

"You should watch Mitt," Moril said. "He's trying to suck up to you, the way all Southerners do. But he's shifty, too. He may even have been sent North as a spy."

Right! Mitt thought. That does it! Moril knew he was there. He had no doubt of it now.

Maewen said, "Now you're being ridiculous, Moril. I shan't listen to you if you're going to talk like that."

Mitt thought it was nice of her, but he was not in the least mollified. As the mist began to thin to a moist yellow, and Navis shouted back that there was a good place to stop for a nuncheon, Mitt thought, If that little sneak says *one more thing!* He towed the Countess-horse out of the mist to find everyone else sitting on wet rocks unpacking bread, cheese, and pickled cherries. Here, the ravine with the lakes had opened into what was almost a meadow. The horses moved about in it, trying to crop the grass, half hidden in golden shifting mist that might have been the top of a cloud.

The bread was stale. Everyone ate quickly and packed up again. "We're at the highest point the green roads go, lady," Wend told Maewen. "From now on it is down toward Gardale."

"Oh good," she said. "Real food. If I eat one more pickled cherry, I might scream. Or does anyone know a way to cook them to make a change?"

"I might have a notion," Mitt said. "On a skewer, like, with cheese and a bit of that bacon."

They were all moving about, getting ready to go on. Moril gave Maewen a meaning look as he went toward the cart. "See what I mean? Sucking up to you."

Mitt went after Moril with giant strides, roaring, "You take that back, you little slime-bag!"

Moril turned round against the tail of the cart. He was prepared. He was holding his cwidder in front of him like a shield. "What should I take back?" he said coolly. "*Didn't* someone order you to suck up to her?"

There was enough shrewd truth in this to make Mitt even angrier. The cwidder made a poor, fragile shield, but a year in Aberath had taught Mitt the value of a beautiful old instrument like that. He knew it was less of a sin to break Moril instead. "You little coward!" he said, grabbing for Moril's arm.

Moril swung aside and tried to pluck a chord on the cwidder. Mitt's hand, lashing out in what was now the wrong direction, hit the strings as Moril's fingers plucked them. The cwidder boomed. It was a mighty chord, and it seemed to boom on and on. Mitt felt the hairs on his outstretched arm stand upright. What Moril felt he had no idea, but he felt something strongly. There was shock all over his white face. To Mitt it was as if he had just punched a cwidder made of solid granite.

Then they were both in rushing cold water up to the shoulders.

The other four travelers scrambled for the panicking animals. Wend seized the mule's bridle on the other side from Hestefan, and together they hauled mule and cart through the rushing shallows and out onto the strip of turf beside the rocks. The three horses were all farther in. Maewen was soaked all over as Mitt's horse floundered past her and galloped away down the bank, but she managed to catch her own before it followed Mitt's. Navis was just beyond her, soothing his mare while he dragged her through rolling stones and racing current. Maewen and he made it to the cliffside almost together, where they turned, both dripping, and stared at a sudden mighty river where there had only been grass before.

The river was a good half mile wide and one of those tricky, spiteful stretches of water, full of upreared rocks and vicious back eddies, flowing with a force that made it hard to stand up in. Mitt and Moril were a long way out in it, much farther away than Maewen had expected, staggering this way and that and, as far as she could see, still screaming insults at one another in spite of it. At the moment when she looked, they were submerged to Moril's shoulders and Mitt's chest. Moril had his cwidder held high in both hands. He was raising a bubbling wave of water under his chin as he pushed and surged, and almost fell sideways into a hidden pothole, trying to make his way to the nearest big rock. She could hear Mitt's voice faintly through the incredible noise of the water, roaring at Moril.

"Stop them, somebody!" she said.

Mitt surged after Moril, grabbing angrily. The result was that Mitt went sideways into the same hidden pothole and vanished underwater. He emerged almost at once, flailing sheets of spray and yelling with rage.

"A bit hard to do anything from here," Navis observed.

Moril made it to the rock. He put the cwidder carefully down on a dry space and, scrabbling and hauling, managed to drag himself onto the rock, too, brown and skinny with wet as a drowned weasel. Mitt was still in the water with a white wave frilling round his neck. Moril knelt on the rock and called down at him derisively.

"If you want to stop this," Hestefan said, coming up beside Navis, "someone must go and take that cwidder away. It's a thing of great power. Moril ought not to be trusted with the thing."

Navis shrugged. "Really? I should never have guessed. And how do you suggest we remove the cwidder? But while you consider that problem, please do not underestimate Mitt. I have reason to believe he can call on power of his own."

Maewen thought both of them were being utterly unfeeling. She looked at Wend for help. Wend was pale, subdued, and awe-stricken. "It's not for any of us to interfere, lady," he said. "They have put themselves in the hands of the One himself."

"O-oh!" Maewen said. *"Fiddlestick!"*

She looked helplessly out at that distant rock.

Out there, up to the neck in racing river, Mitt said, "What do you mean, look what I made you do? Of all the feeble, wingeing things to say! It's *your* flaming cwidder that did this!"

To his surprise Moril seemed quite ashamed. But his white face remained mulishly set. "I meant the rest of it," he said. "You try to get on this rock, and I'll kick you off!"

"And a fat lot of good it's going to do us, each squatting on a different rock!" Mitt bawled up at him. "We got into this river together. It stands to reason it's going to take both of us to get out."

Moril looked from bank to bank of the improbable river. Mitt had already looked. He knew water. He had been brought up with it, both fresh and salt, and it was kind of instinctive with him. He hoped what Moril saw would bring him to his senses. Wisps of fog hung over the shrilling water, making it hard to see far, but it was possible to pick out a sheer, dark cliff on either side. Trees clung to niches in the cliffs here and there, so high that at first glance they looked like bushes. And those were the only other living things in sight. There was no sign of Navis, Hestefan, and Wend, or of the horses and the mule. As he discovered this, Moril's face unbunched into wide-eyed alarm.

Good, Mitt thought. His teeth were beginning to chatter, and this river scared him badly. He knew it. He had seen it before while he sat with Noreth by the waystone above Adenmouth. This one had the same smell, the same feel to it, and the thing which scared him most was that it did not seem to exist. "Listen," Mitt called up to Moril, "I'll give you my life history if it makes you feel better. I know you hate us Southerners—I heard what you said to Noreth—but I swear to Ammet you got no reason to hate me!"

Moril went on hands and knees and leaned down to look at him. Mitt actually had hopes that Moril was going to help him scramble up, until Moril said, "Yes, I knew you'd listen in. I was trying to annoy you."

Mitt roared with frustration. "Flaming Ammet! What's wrong with you? I think your *mind's* mixed up! You behave like the whole world's out to get you!"

That got home to Moril. He was pinched and staring and hurt for the time it took to draw breath, but then he went calm again. "And you're jealous," he said. "I meant you to be."

Jealous? The word seemed to take all the heat out of Mitt's body. He felt as cold as the water rushing round him. An instant later the heat came back, tenfold. He could feel his face burning above the frill of water round his chin. He was surprised the frill didn't start to steam. He tried to tell himself that he hadn't a clue why one word should affect him like this, but if one of his own words could affect Moril as badly, why not? Moril's mind *was* mixed up. And Mitt had a thousand clues about his own condition: Rith's cheerful freckly face and man-to-man way of talking and then Noreth, the young lady in the fashionable dress who was so nervous about what she had to do, and then the girl trying to hold them all together on the road. As soon as he picked up these clues, Mitt could look up into Moril's pinched and greenish face and see that some part of the mix-up in Moril's mind was the same thing. The same clues were there. They had both been unhappy. They had both fallen at the same young lady's feet. Both of us! Mitt thought bitterly. How flaming *stupid*!

"All right!" he shouted up at Moril. "So I am jealous! So are you! Calf love, they call it. And it's not going to get either of us *anywhere*!"

A surge of pink swept across Moril's face. He blinked. "I . . . wasn't only angry about that," he said.

"Neither was I!" Mitt shouted back. "Let me come up, and let's have it out, shall we?"

To Mitt's extreme relief, Moril at last held out a thin wet hand to help him up. Gripping it, Mitt hauled himself upward, skidding and slipping and clawing at the rock with his other hand. His boots weighed like lead, and the sodden leather of his clothes seemed to have the whole river in them. As Mitt floundered onto the top of the boulder, dripping and panting, Moril hurriedly crouched in front of his cwidder.

"Don't get it wet!"

That made sense. If the cwidder was spoiled, they would be in this for good. Mitt stood at the edge of the rock and let the water course and sluice and trickle off him where it did no harm. He was freezing, but to his surprise the air was warm. He could see himself beginning to steam as he said, "Well then. What's biting you?"

Moril bent his head and fiddled with some pebbles lodged in a crack of the boulder. "I— It's not that I *think* the whole world's out to get me. I *know* the whole South is. I . . . killed an awful lot of them last year."

"What? With that cwidder?" said Mitt.

Moril nodded. "When they tried to invade the North. It can move mountains. I closed Flennpass."

"You did Noreth a favor then," Mitt said. "In advance like. They can't get at her till she's ready, and from what I heard she can come down at them on the sheep tracks whenever she wants."

He looked down at Moril's head, wet and brown, feeling almost sympathetic until Moril said, "You don't understand. I don't dare go near Dropwater—it's so full of Southerners—and I've no proof that you and Navis haven't been sent to kill me. Almost the only person I can *trust* is Hestefan."

"Get away!" said Mitt. "I heard you tell Noreth what friends you are with Earl Keril. That's what got me mad."

"Yes, but he treats me like—like a child," Moril said. "And I'd done something so . . . awful I needed to go away and work it out for myself."

"Just as long as you don't have your workout on me," Mitt said. "You don't look much of a child to me if that's any comfort to you. How old *are* you?"

"I shan't be thirteen for another month," Moril said regretfully. "How old are you?"

"Fifteen come Harvest," said Mitt.

"I thought you were more than that," Moril said, marveling. "You come from a slum somewhere, don't you? You've got that old-and-young look they all have in Holand and places. But I thought you were at least as old as my brother."

"Comes of earning a living as soon as you can walk," Mitt answered. "But then I reckon that applies to both of us."

From there it was the most natural step for Mitt to sit down on the edge of the boulder and swing his soggy boots above the streaming water while he told Moril about his life in Holand and his journey North and then about the Countess and Keril. Moril frowned at this. "I like Keril," he said, dubious and thoughtful. "Could he be up to something deep?"

"No," said Mitt. "No deeper than he wants Noreth out of the way before she can get to be Queen."

Moril's face came alight, the way it had when he talked to Noreth in the fog. "She *must* be Queen! It's like the old stories, like Enblith and Tanamoril. I want to help her. I know the old things are still true."

"Well, well," said Mitt. "You make me feel old. Here was I going to say that the country needs bringing together because the North is poor as an empty barrel full of mice—let's face it—and the South is rich—or it would be if those earls didn't take it all. Noreth wants to do that, so I'm for her. Very dull and political."

Moril laughed. "So you ride off in the night, like an old story, to steal her the Adon's ring."

"As to that," Mitt said, knowing his face had gone hot, "it proved I wasn't going to stick a knife in her, didn't it?"

"That made me jealous," Moril said frankly. "You must let me steal her the cup. Anyway, I'm dull and political, too. She said she thought the Singers ought to be paid by the Queen to stay in one place and make better music than they can going round in a cart. A royal academy, she said. I like that idea."

"She's got good ideas," Mitt agreed. "I really loved the way she settled those miners. All right. So we're both on the same side. Are you feeling happy enough about it to think how we get out of this river?"

# 11

MORIL PICKED UP HIS CWIDDER, carefully so as not to wet it on his clothes. "Can you read what it says on the front of it?"

There were swirls and dots there, made of mother-of-pearl, inlaid on either side of the strings. Mitt recognized it as the Old Writing, but that was all. "Not me," he said. "It takes me all my time to read the usual stuff."

"I can't read it either," Moril confessed. "But I was told that one bit says, 'I sing for Osfameron'—and that's *my* name, along with Tanamoril—and this other bit says, 'I move in more than one world.' "

"What's this?" said Mitt. "You mean we're in another *world*!"

"I . . . don't know," Moril admitted. "You always have to tell the truth with the cwidder. It works on how you think when you play it."

"Then let's get at what we were both thinking," Mitt suggested. He looked at the water boiling round the front of the boulder. "You were thinking I want this Southerner drowned deep. That right?"

Moril ducked his wet head uncomfortably. "Not quite. At least, I was probably meaning the sea. I was thinking, Let this Southerner go back where he came from, and I knew you came by sea—"

"How?" Mitt demanded.

"I heard about you in Lavreth last spring," said Moril. "It's all round the North that a Southerner came north by the wind's road with the Undying before and behind to guard him. Singers call the sea the wind's road in a lot of the old songs."

"I never knew *that*!" Mitt said. "And it's true, too, in a way!"

"They told me in Adenmouth that you were the one," Moril told him, "and I didn't like you because I could see you had something bad on your mind."

Mitt shivered. He was beginning to feel awed by Moril's perceptiveness, not to speak of that cwidder of his. A dangerous enemy, Moril, if they hadn't both chanced to get themselves into this mess together. "Stuck out like a sore thumb, did it?" he said ruefully. "You'd think I'd do better than that after a lifetime of guilty secrets. All right. So you wanted me back at sea."

"And you hit the strings, too, and we were both in this river. What were you thinking?" Moril asked.

Mitt stood up and scowled at ribbons of foam tearing backward from the nearest jagged rock. He was fairly sure that he would not have been so blindly furious with Moril if he had not been feeling so trapped himself. Then Moril had brought it all to a head by asking, "Didn't someone order you to suck up to her?" That had brought two pictures into Mitt's mind. One was of the Countess, sitting upright in her chair, making it clear that Mitt had to do what Keril wanted. The other was of Alk, bulging out of that selfsame chair, turning the whole thing round with that promise, making Mitt feel just as trapped, because the One was supposed to have an interest.

"In a funny way," he said, "I may have been thinking about the One. That's where I was at when my hand hit, anyway."

Moril tipped his face up. His eyes were squinted with dismay. "You were? Then we've gone back into the One's river, before he destroyed Kankredin. I hope he's not too angry."

"You mean we're back in history?" Mitt demanded. "Or dead, really?"

"More like . . . the place in the stories where the One really is, I *think*," Moril said doubtfully. "It's hard to explain, but the other world the cwidder moves in is the place where the stories are."

Mitt looked again at the torrent tearing past their boulder and thought that he had seldom seen anything more real. Equally real were his steaming, clammy clothes. He had a notion that the One was taking the opportunity to point out that *he* was real, too. No wonder Alk had been so cautious. "Then we get back by apologizing and asking the One to let us go?" he said.

Moril nodded, looking as sober as Mitt felt. "I'll ask, if you like, because I know the way. You get ready to hit the strings in the same place as you did when I nod."

"I don't know where I did hit!" said Mitt. "And it won't do to get it wrong, will it?"

"You hit the lowest string," said Moril. "This one—it's always the dangerous one—and I wasn't touching it, because I didn't want to kill you or anything, but I heard it sound. Just pluck it, with one finger when I say."

Mitt put forth one doubtful finger and knelt ready. Moril seemed to settle himself—no, it was not simply that. Mitt could feel the power building in the cwidder. It hummed along his shaking finger. He felt even more awed by the thing.

Moril drew a big breath and spoke in the strange formal way that Hestefan had used to invoke the Undying at Midsummer. "Great Grand Father of the golden bonds, Unbound and Undying, understand my asking. Hear and help. History's flood took us and tore us from our traveling. Restore us to our own realm out of the river you made. Mitt and Moril ask this by Manaliabrid most humbly, and by Cennoreth, Clennen's son begs you cast aside your anger." He nodded at Mitt: *now.*

Mitt's finger twanged the thickest string heartily. He thought he saw the way of this speech, and he could not resist doing it, too. "By the Adon and Alhammitt and his *all*-fruitful lady," he said as he twanged.

Moril's fingers made the rest of the sound. It was a many-toned roaring.

It seemed as if the sound of the river had increased, almost unbearably, to a sound that fogged their eyes as well as their ears. They felt the river was now thundering over a cliff in a waterfall, whose thunder gradually faded to a long, deep chord, and then a growling vibration. As the sound faded, it seemed to carry the river away with it. The water became foggy and quiet. The golden whiteness of the fog spread to the very riverbed, and for a second or so it was the great transparent ghost of a river, silently rushing over green ground. At the instant that Mitt realized that the green was really grass, the river was gone, except for the faintest vestige of that chord, still sounding and dragging on him like a current. During the next instant it took him to realize that the dragging was taking *all* the river with it, including the water that filled his boots and soaked his clothing. He was dry. So was Moril. Moril's hair went from draggled brown to true red again. And though they were dry, though there was a little feeble sunlight on them, the air was so much colder that they were both still shivering.

From Maewen's point of view, the river vanished as suddenly as it had come, leaving Mitt and Moril crouched on an outcrop of rock just across the green road. She was not sure whether to cheer or to run and shake them. It had been maddening watching them. All they seemed to do was sit on that rock in the river and talk for an hour. Maewen kept shouting to them. Navis had shouted, too, after he had rounded up Mitt's horse, but the boys had taken no notice. Hestefan and Wend maddened her almost as much. Both shook their heads and said, "They'll not hear from where *they* are."

Moril and Mitt climbed off the rock and crossed the road, both looking self-conscious.

"So soon?" said Navis. "We were expecting to wait all night."

Mitt tried to give him an explanation. It sounded lame and stupid to him, and he was glad when everyone was distracted from it by Hestefan. Hestefan seized Moril by one shoulder and ranted at him. He began in a low, penetrating voice. "This is neither the time nor the place for such tricks. We have a journey to go on, fellow travelers to consider, and a performance to give in Gardale." His voice gradually increased as he went on to, "You could have spoiled your cwidder, or—worse!—lost it. You nearly stampeded the horses. You could have drowned us all!"

Everyone listened uncomfortably. Moril was staring at Hestefan as if he had never heard anything like this in his life, and that made it clear that this was not just a master giving his apprentice a dressing-down, but something more. Maewen could see that Hestefan had been terrified by the sudden river, and she supposed he was working it off on Moril. Then Hestefan's voice increased again.

"Now give me your cwidder at once, and I shall lock it in the chest until you are old enough to be trusted with it."

Moril clutched the cwidder and stepped backward. "No. You've no right—"

"I have every right!" Hestefan enlarged his voice as only a Singer could. It rang in the rocks. "My apprentice has been fooling with something too powerful for his years. You have no notion what that cwidder is!"

"Yes, I have," Moril said, dogged and white. "And it belonged to my father, not to you. You've no right to take it away."

Mitt felt he had better intervene. "Now look. He didn't do any harm with it."

Hestefan ignored Mitt. "Give me the cwidder here," he said, and held his hand out sternly for it.

"There's no need—" Mitt tried to say.

But at this point Navis intervened, too. He came up beside Moril and said, in his most sarcastic way, "Is it possible the master envies his apprentice? Surely not?"

Hestefan turned and glared at Navis.

Wend looked urgently at Maewen. "Lady!"

Maewen had been feeling like she did in school, watching one of the teachers tell off someone else in her class. Hestefan was so very much like Dr. Loviath that she could not help it. And of course, if a teacher decides to tell someone off, no one else in the class dreams of interfering. Wend's look made her realize that it was not like this at all. She tried to gather her wits.

"Stop it," she said to Navis. "Er—Hestefan, I'm not sure this is right. Moril told me this morning that it was your daughter, Fenna, who was indentured to you, not him. He said he came with you from his own choice. Doesn't that make him your—er—colleague instead of your apprentice?"

"Well yes," Hestefan said, very displeased. "But considering his years and his actions, common law would hardly make that distinction."

That displeased look made him so like Dr. Loviath that Maewen had to fight herself not to agree humbly. As so often happens, she found herself going too far the other way. "But I'm the leader," she said, "and I say he isn't *really* your apprentice. So I say you can't take his cwidder away even if he did something—er—rather mad with it."

"That was my fault, too," Mitt put in, but in a very gruff and unfriendly way. He was having trouble even looking at Noreth after what Moril had said.

Hestefan lifted his chin and jutted his beard at Maewen.

A black mark and detention! Maewen thought. And Mitt glowering, too. If you're a leader, everyone hates you. So will Moril after this. "And, Moril, you were trying to hurt Mitt with that cwidder, weren't you?"

Any other boy would have protested that Mitt was bigger than he was. Moril impressed Maewen by just saying, "Yes."

She felt like a beast, but she was launched on her way now and found she had to go on. "Then, until we get to Gardale, someone else is going to take charge of it. Moril, will you give your cwidder to Wend, please?"

It was hard to tell if Moril, Wend, or Hestefan was more surprised. Hestefan turned away and climbed into the cart, still jutting his beard. Moril at first clutched the cwidder closer. Then, with a glance at Mitt that certainly meant something, he passed the beautiful gleaming instrument over to Wend. Wend took it so reverently that it seemed to slide into his hands. He hung the worn leather strap across his shoulder and looked down at the cwidder as if it was a lamb he had just rescued from the snow. His left hand formed a chord on the strings as if it could not help itself. "May I?" he asked Moril.

"If you *can*," Moril said. "I'll fetch you the case."

Wend's right hand played on the strings as if it were stroking the lamb's head. He only played a sequence of chords and arpeggios, but he became a new person doing it. His face came alive, into a slight, rapt smile, full of thoughts and energies that had not been there before. The way he stood altered, to accommodate the cwidder, into the stance of someone much stronger. For the first time since Maewen had met him, he looked happy. Oddly enough, that made him look ten times more dangerous, too.

Why couldn't he be like that all the time? Maewen wondered as she turned away to mount her horse again at last. Instead of trying to pretend he was not an Undying among all us dying-people? She tried to catch Mitt's eye to see what he thought, but Mitt was raw with shame about that word *jealous*, and he turned away quickly. Hestefan gave her an unloving look from the seat of the cart.

*Two* black marks and a whole week in detention! Maewen thought. She thought Navis was right. Hestefan had wanted Moril's cwidder. As they rode on, she found herself wondering why Hestefan had chosen to follow Noreth if he disliked her so much.

The handing over of the cwidder had a surprising effect on Moril. While Wend strode along, looking strong and different, Moril behaved like a boy let out of school. He went scampering along beside Mitt's horse, shouting cheeky remarks up at Mitt. Mitt answered the same way, and both of them laughed themselves silly. After a while they began taking turns to ride, with a lot more silly laughter when the Countess-horse tried to throw Moril off.

Maewen rode out ahead, feeling lonely and unloved, listening to the pair of them laughing in the foggy distance behind. I suppose owning a thing like that cwidder *is* a big responsibility, she thought, but she had a stupid, hypersensitive feeling that Moril and Mitt were fooling about because of *her*. I was *told* to come here and be the leader, she thought. No need to be paranoid.

As if that word had triggered it off, the deep voice spoke to her, at her ear in the gathering fog. "You did well not to let the Singer get his hands on the cwidder," it said.

Maewen's hands shook on the reins. She had known that the voice would catch her alone sooner or later. *Was* it the One? Somehow, because it was telling her what she wanted to hear, she doubted it. After seeing that sudden mighty river, she had a feeling that the One was more likely to tell her something unexpected that she did not want to know about at all. No. It was some kind of ghostly effect of her own mind on the green road.

"You will need that cwidder, and the Singer-boy to play it," the voice continued, "when you come to find the crown."

Maewen had not meant to answer, but she found herself saying, "And what about the cup and the sword?"

"The Southerner can steal both of those for you," said the voice.

"Oh? Can he? Just like that?" Maewen said.

"I tell you so," said the voice. "You must accept my advice or you will never find the crown. And I tell you not to alienate the Singer-boy."

"All right." Maewen was working on her horse, slowing down so that Navis and Wend could catch up with her. "All *right*. Just go away now, will you?"

She could hear Navis behind now, asking Wend how much farther it was to Gardale, and Wend answering that it would take another day. Maewen fell in on the other side of Navis, and as she had hoped, the voice did not speak to her again.

The fog thickened. By nightfall, when it was blue-dim, they stopped in another of those lumpy places that might once have been a town. There was a well-made fire pit where Moril built a cheerful coal fire. Maewen reminded Mitt of his idea for cooking pickled cherries. Mitt could not bring himself to be natural. Gruffly he borrowed skewers from the cart and kept his back turned while he stuck them with cherries, cheese, and dried meat to roast. It was terrible. Mitt tried to be polite and found himself agreeing fawningly with Noreth that a lentil stew would help. He tried to correct that and went gruff again. He could not seem to get it right. Plainly by the firelight, he could see the hurt, puzzled look among Noreth's freckles. He could feel her wondering what she had done to offend him, and of course there was no way he could tell her.

Never mind. I'll be seeing Hildy again in Gardale, he thought. For some reason he knew that would make things better.

While the lentils plopped and bubbled and turned too thick, Maewen tried to put Mitt out of her mind by thinking what she should do in Gardale. Should she make a speech? She had told Navis that her army would arrive by itself, but that was over on the coast. They were now a long way inland, where people would not know about Noreth. The trouble was that she had no idea what to expect. She had been to Gardale in her own time. She and Aunt Liss had driven there on a sight-seeing trip. But she had a feeling that this was only going to confuse her.

Around then Wend politely asked Moril's permission and played the cwidder again. Lilting tunes from the old days rang in the crags. Everyone seemed to feel better. They ate caked lentils and Mitt's sooty skewered things quite cheerfully, and when they had finished, Hestefan surprised them all by telling tales. Most of them were stories that were around in Maewen's day, too, but she had only read them in books. It was another thing again to hear Hestefan tell them, gravely and plainly, as if every strange occurrence were the exact truth. The stories were suddenly unknown and new. Maewen had known what was going to happen nearly every time, but it still surprised her.

*This* is what it means to be a good Singer, she thought, and he really is good!

"I thank you," Navis said when Hestefan finished. "I have never heard those tales better told."

Hestefan bowed as he sat. "And I thank you. Never have I told them so well for so little in return."

Navis laughed and tossed Hestefan a silver piece. Hestefan took it with a bit of a twinkle. It looked as if they were actually beginning to like one another. Maewen caught a little smile on Wend's face as he carefully put the waterproof case round the cwidder, and she wondered.

The fog was worse in the morning. Probably they were down into the clouds again. Certainly the green road sloped gently downhill as if it were leading them back to the valleys. Before long it was branching past waystone after waystone, and Maewen was glad to have Wend striding out in front to show the right way. And this day, for the first time, there were other people using the road. It made sense, as Navis remarked. Up to now they had been ahead of or behind all the folk who had gone somewhere else to celebrate Midsummer. Now they came up with all those people returning home and also the usual traffic of people going into Gardale.

They passed riders, groups of walkers, and families with carts all coming toward them. Hestefan called out cheerfully to each. But when they passed the first person going the other way, who was someone driving a flock of geese, he said ringingly, "Hestefan the Singer here! Watch for me in Gardale."

Maewen tensed. Hestefan had to advertise, of course, but so did she. She wondered whether to call out in the same way, Noreth Onesdaughter here! and ask the gooseman—no, it was a woman all bundled up against the fog—ask the goosewoman, then, to join her at Kernsburgh. She dithered. She hated the idea, and besides, the woman might tell the Earl of Gardale. On the other hand, perhaps she *ought*. For once she would have welcomed that deep voice speaking to her out of the air to tell her what to do. But of course, there were too many people near.

Meanwhile, more and more white triangular geese kept appearing out of the fog. As Maewen, still dithering, opened her mouth to imitate Hestefan, Mitt's horse demonstrated that it considered geese a lower life-form. It began moving at them in pounces, with Mitt hauling on the reins and cursing it. After ten feet of rocking-horse-like progress, the Countess-horse won and plunged in among the geese. Mitt fell off into an outrage of honking, flapping, and running. Geese ran in all directions, except for two, which ran for Mitt with spread wings and outstretched necks. The lady driving them shouted mightily—most of it very rude things about Mitt and the horse.

Navis was into the fray almost instantly, using his riding crop on everything. The lady shouted at Navis, too. But the two geese fled, Moril caught the Countess-horse, and Navis hauled Mitt up. Everyone else chased geese for a while. By the time the flock was assembled again, Maewen's nerve was gone. Even if the goose-lady had not been so very angry, she thought, watching Navis and Hestefan being wonderfully polite to the woman, the proper time to declare Noreth as Queen was when she had reached Kernsburgh with the Adon's gifts and had something to show those earls. The decision made her feel utterly relieved and completely feeble in about the same proportions.

"I think this is yours, madam," Navis said, bowing and handing the goose-lady the stick she had dropped.

"Just keep that big looby off his back and out of my geese," she answered.

"Certainly," Navis agreed. "But I'm afraid that would mean buying him a real horse, and we neither of us have the funds just now."

At this the woman hooted with laughter. Mitt struggled back into his saddle again feeling like an utter idiot.

After that he kept tight hold of the beast whenever another traveler loomed through the fog.

# 12

WHEN THEY CAMPED that night, Wend said that Gardale was only a mile or so away, below in a valley they could not see.

It was odd, Maewen thought, that it had taken all this time to get that near, even coming straight through the center of the mountains. When she had driven here with Aunt Liss, it had only taken four hours, and that was with a detour on the way to look at Hannart. Her sense of distance was all confused.

Her sense of *everything* was all confused. She was dreading Gardale. Mitt was still being so distant and gruff that she knew she was not going to ask him to steal the Adon's cup for her. And Moril was younger than she was, and she was not going to ask him either. She would have to do it herself. But she still felt hurt at the way Mitt was behaving. She wanted to apologize, although she had no idea what she had done to annoy him. Perhaps they should all just go away and not bother about the cup.

No. Out of this muddle of thoughts came one thing that was clear—probably. Maewen and Aunt Liss had done the usual tourist thing and seen round the college at Gardale, where the old Lawschool was. Part of the Lawschool was the Chapel of the One. There had been—would be—a cup on the altar there, with a notice saying that this was only a replica of the cup that had been stolen two hundred years before. So it looked as if she had stolen—would be going to have stolen—the darned thing. In a mad, circular way, that meant she had to go down into Gardale and steal it because she already *had*.

It came on to rain. Oh, I give up! she thought.

Moril and Hestefan had the best of it. They vanished into the cart. The others draped the oilskin covers off their baggage over three large rocks and crawled underneath, where they spent a hot and sticky night, steamily full of the plopping and thrumming of rain. It was so uncomfortable that everyone woke and crawled out again at dawn. The rain stopped and became thinning mist, almost mockingly.

Maewen was clammy all over, and itchy, and—well—plain dirty. She could smell herself. She wanted to clean her teeth. But nobody seemed to bother about tooth cleaning any more than they appeared to worry about baths. At that moment Maewen felt she would have given her left ear and probably several toes as well for a nice hot bath full of rose-scented bath oil. And there was not even a hairbrush in her baggage roll! While Navis was shaving and Hestefan was clawing the kinks out of his beard, Maewen did what she could by taking her hair down from the little helmet, shaking it out and scratching hard at her scalp. Her hair smelled awful, of horse mostly, but dirty human hair was part of the smell, too.

"What wouldn't I give for a *bath*!" she said as she crammed the helmet back on her head.

"Me, too," Mitt said, surprisingly, looking up from tightening the buckles on the Countess-horse. This was always a wary business, of circling and darting, in order not to get kicked or bitten, and he was glad to be distracted. "I never thought I'd live to hear myself say that," he said. "But I got spoiled this last year in Aberath. Alk's got the whole place mined through with lead pipes and a furnace down in the dungeons. Water comes out boiling."

A chuckle rose up in Maewen's throat. Things were all right again. Mitt was back in form. Now she could almost look forward to Gardale.

Mitt kept talking about Alk as they wound their slow way down into the valley. It matched a tender place in his mind where that promise to Alk was. So he was not sure why he was suddenly so cheerful. Maybe it was that the fog had gone. You could see mountains navy blue against pink dawn, peak after peak, right away to far-off Mount Tanil, which had a quiet feather of smoke coming out of its pointed head. Near to, there was still no sign of a valley—only a chasm of dark blue emptiness with mist boiling up out of it as if there were a giant version of one of Alk's Irons down there.

"I hear there's this great huge steam organ they have in Hannart," he remarked, as the roiling, rising mist put him in mind of it.

Maewen nodded. She had seen the carefully preserved remains of that organ on that trip with Aunt Liss.

Maybe, Mitt considered, it was the sight just now of Noreth with her hair down from her helmet in long, frizzy clouds. Like that, she was the young lady he had felt so respectful to in her aunt's hall, so different and so far away from Mitt that it was silly to be awkward with her. Or maybe he was simply looking forward to seeing Hildy again.

The track that led down from the waystone was nothing like as grassy and well made as the green roads. Mostly it was rubble and raw earth and quite dangerously frayed at the edge of the great drop-off, where the mist heaved and rose. It led down in zigzags beside a furious stream of white water splayed over wet rocks, and at every hairpin bend, the cart threatened to come off and pitch into the depths. Hestefan led the mule. Everyone else took turns leaning on the outer side of the cart, boots braced in sliding gravel, either above white water or horrifying mist-filled steepness, helping to ease the cart round. When Maewen took her first turn, a nattering and honking above made her look up. There were white triangular splotches some bends overhead. The goosewoman seemed to have caught up.

The splotches and the noise came nearer every bend. "The geese get down here more easily," Navis remarked to Mitt as they leaned side by side against the gold letters. Mitt laughed, and hoped they would not have to meet the goose-lady again.

As they slowly descended the track, the white stream enlarged into a mountain river roaring on a bed of green rocks, under a cliff hung with holly trees and small perilous rowans. The mist continued boiling its way upward as they went down. Somehow it had miraculously changed from mist to a proper cloud hovering against the upper crags. The sun caught it there and turned it to a cloud of gold film, with the green-black bones of the rock showing through. Everyone began to feel dry again at last.

About then Maewen caught sight of a woman standing on the other side of the loud green river. At least she thought she saw someone, between two of the rowan trees. But when she turned her head, there were only the two trees. She saw Mitt's head jerk, as if he had seen someone there, too. Then, as if he was struck by a sudden thought, Mitt turned his head back and up to look at the zigzags of the track above. Maewen looked, too. There was nothing up there. No gaggle of geese, no woman driving them. She could not even hear the geese chatting anymore.

They're out of sight on a bend, she thought.

Mitt thought, Libby Beer! Now what's she playing at?

Wend came hurrying down to the cart in a slide of small stones, unslinging the cwidder from his neck as he came. "Is it all right to give this back now?" he called to Maewen. "I'll have to leave you for a while. I'll wait for you by the waystone south of Gardale Valley."

"Yes, I suppose so," Maewen said, rather taken aback. "What if we take all day, though?"

"I'll wait," Wend promised, handing the cwidder to Moril. Moril settled it on his knees, and quite a weight of responsibility with it, from the look of him. They went on down. The last Maewen saw of Wend, before a shoulder of the hill hid him, he was leaping in great, splashing strides across the river.

Going to see that lady, Maewen thought. She *was* there, then.

At the next bend of the path Wend vanished from her mind. The path came out above the great green wedge shape of the Gardale Valley, with Gardale Town nestled into the pointed end just below them, seemingly at their toes, a mass of smoking chimney stacks. Maewen was astonished. She had known the place was bound to be smaller, but not *this* small! It was more like a large village than a town.

Two more turns of the road brought them into green meadows outside the town, and Maewen still marveled. She knew it was absurd, but she had been expecting the high blocks of buildings and the tall shops she had seen on her visit with Aunt Liss. This Gardale was all low. The houses were all built of greenish stone, and none was more than three stories high. The amount of smoke from all those chimneys astonished her. The track suddenly turned into a proper road paved with the same greenish stone and took them across a bridge over the same river, now flowing quietly and more brown than green, between stone walls where small boys sat fishing.

After that they were in the main street, and Maewen could hardly breathe. It's like a foreign country! she thought. There were crowds of people. She had thought she had become used to being in the past. Now she knew she had only become used to the people traveling with her and the way those five people dressed and talked. Everyone who crowded the street here seemed to have more lines on their faces—or fewer—as if they all worried about different things from those that concerned people in Maewen's own time. This set their faces into quite another shape, like people who spoke a foreign language. As to their clothes, the hearthman's livery she had grown used to was the rarest kind here. The men wore bright wools and sober velvets in any number of styles, from tight-fitting suits with a colored blanket thing folded over one shoulder, through the looser sorts of clothes that Moril or Hestefan wore, to the elderly fellow pushing past in a long dark blue velvet robe with a jeweled chain round his neck. The women were in so many styles and colors—nipped waists, loose pleats, long flounces, calf-length gathers—that even when Maewen saw the outfit was homemade and probably redyed from another color, they still made her feel dowdy and wrongly dressed. The place smelled of people and, almost chokingly, of smoke with, underneath that, most definitely cesspits.

"It seems very busy," Navis remarked. "Market day?"

"That and more, I rather think," Hestefan said. People had seen his cart by then and were pressing up to it all round, wanting to know when the Singer would perform. Hestefan enlarged his voice, in the Singer's way, so that though he seemed to be speaking normally, his voice rang round the street. "In the market square in an hour's time."

"Oh but—" Moril started to say. Then he saw faces turning and nodding eagerly. He gave up.

"What are our plans?" Navis asked Maewen. They were down to a slow walk, boot to boot, as they pressed through the crowd.

"Go to the college—Lawschool," Maewen said.

"That suits me," Navis said, and he bent to the nearest person to ask the way.

It was out on the other side of the town. They had to go through the market square, where there was a frenzy of buying and selling going on, and such shouting mixed with smells of new bread, fruit, leather, and cattle dung to add to the cesspit smell that Maewen's stomach began to feel unhappy. Hestefan cast a professional eye over the chaos and agreed with Moril that they would have time to visit the Lawschool before people were ready to listen. So the whole party continued, out through the farther end of the market square and down another street, to where the crowds and then the houses quite abruptly stopped and the street became a white dirt road leading across more green fields. There were animals—cows, goats, and a donkey or so—tethered out in the fields, but the only other people in sight were a small party of horsemen some distance ahead on the road.

"Hannart livery," Navis said. He and Mitt exchanged a significant, worried look. "I think we'll let them get well ahead."

That suited Maewen. In these times Hannart was a name to conjure with. As everyone reined in and hung back at the mule's slowest pace, she looked anxiously at the horsemen until they vanished behind a clump of trees. "Do you think someone told the Earl of Hannart that the Adon's ring was stolen?" she asked Mitt.

"I don't *reckon* so," Mitt said, almost equally worried.

"I'll give a false name," Maewen said, "if anyone asks."

"A wise precaution," Navis agreed. "At times like this I could wish Mitt and I were not so obviously Southerners."

The Hannart horsemen had vanished by the time they came round the clump of trees and saw the Lawschool. Maewen had another moment of sheer surprise. She had known the school would have to be the oldest part of the college she and Aunt Liss had visited, but she had expected that this would be the part with all the towers and tall, pointed windows. She had not expected it would be these low, graceful greenish buildings topped with clusters of long, stylish chimneys. The windows were wide, one and all, and they had diamond panes. In the middle, an elegant archway filled by a wrought-iron gate joined two blocks of the buildings together. The rest were joined by a high stone wall.

"Looks a good place for studying," Mitt said. He tried to smile, but he knew his face had gone pinched and worried. Those Hannart riders were inside. He could glimpse horses between the bars of the gate.

By the time they reached the gate, there was nothing to be seen through it but a garden and a cobbled path leading away between lavender bushes. An official walked to the middle of the gate. Maewen bit the inside of her mouth, or she would have laughed. He was wearing exactly the same uniform that the porters at the college wore in her day: baggy knee-length breeches and tunic in dark blue, with a wide white collar. It was obviously old-fashioned even two hundred years before that. He had bad teeth. She saw them as he spoke.

"Visitors for Sending Day? Which of the scholars are you for?"

Navis hesitated a fraction because of those riders from Hannart. "Hildrida Navissdaughter," he said, with a shrug you could only have seen if you knew him.

"And I'm for Brid Clennensdaughter," Moril called from the cart.

The porter smiled at them. Maewen had to look away from his teeth. "I'm sorry for it, but you're all too early. Sending Day doesn't start till midday. Come back then, and I'll let you in with pleasure. You're not the only ones I've had to turn away. You'll find the town's full of you. But," he said to Hestefan, "you can come half an hour ahead if you want to set up to sing. The other Singer will be coming back then."

Hestefan frowned to hear of another Singer to compete with and began to turn the cart round. "Thank you. I shall only perform in the town then. But my apprentice will be back to see his sister."

Nobody pointed out that the riders from Hannart had been let in at once. Nobody even remarked that since they had been let in, this meant they were not just a chance band of hearthmen but members of the Earl's household on important business. Yet they all knew it, even Maewen. They rode back the way they had come very soberly.

The other Singer was now camped just outside the town. They saw him as soon as they came round the trees, a neat black, white, and gold cart at the edge of the wide green, surrounded by sacks and bundles of provisions. Someone—presumably the Singer—was sorting through the bundles in a rather hopeless way.

Moril, at the sight, tugged excitedly at Hestefan's arm. Hestefan whipped up the mule. The green cart, in a most uncharacteristic way, went rollicking and bumping across the turf toward the black and white one. Moril stood up on the seat, waving and shrieking, "Dagner! *Dagner!*"

The Singer, a slightly built young man with reddish hair, who looked very little older than Mitt, had just picked up one of the sacks. He turned round at the noise and let out a bellow of his own. "*Hestefan!* MORIL!" He dropped the sack and came racing over to hang on to the step of the green cart, laughing as if this was the most wonderful meeting in the world. The three of them fell into instant eager talk.

As Maewen came up with Navis and Mitt, she thought she had never seen Hestefan look so animated. They hung about a short distance away, none of them sure how private the Singers wanted to be, and admired the new Singer's turnout. The horse, which was enjoying a nosebag, was as black and glossy as the black paint on the cart, and its harness was white. The austere colors served to show up the fact that instead of a name painted on the cart, there was a large and complicated coat of arms.

Moril turned and shouted to them, "It's my brother! Isn't it wonderful! Dastgandlen Handagner!"

"Oh, I've heard of him," Mitt said, decidedly impressed. "Aberath folk said he was the best."

"Let us be introduced," Navis said.

But before they had come within talking distance, Moril had said something to Dagner which seemed to alarm him acutely. Dagner backed away from the green cart, asking anxious questions. Next moment he was running for his cart and hurling the sacks and bundles in anyhow, latching the tailgate, and running again to take the nose bag off the horse. The horse's head came up. It looked as surprised as everyone else. "Sorry, Stiles," Dagner called out. "Later." With that he was in the driving seat and untying the reins, and the cart was in motion. All in seconds.

"But what about *Brid*?" Moril yelled.

"You're here now. You can give her my love!" Dagner shouted back. "Get *up*, Stiles. I want your best pace." The horse broke into a trot. The black and white cart went in a swift near circle past Navis, Mitt, and Maewen. Dagner leaned out to call as he passed, "I'd have followed you, too, lady, if this hadn't happened!"

Maewen realized he was talking to her and managed to shoot a smile in reply. Then the horse was going faster still. The black and white cart went careering away into the distance, raising a cloud of moisture and grass seeds behind its flying wheels.

"What got into him?" Mitt asked.

"I told him Fenna was hurt," Moril said. "He's in love with her. He's going straight to Adenmouth by the green road above Hannart." It was clear Moril was very pleased by his brother's devotion.

"And why does he carry a coat of arms?" asked Navis. "It looked like the arms of the South Dales to me."

Moril grimaced. This was something which did not seem to please him so much. "It is," he said. "Dagner's Earl of the South Dales. Since last year, when our cousin got killed. He told me Earl Keril made him put the arms on his cart, but I know Dagner only agreed because it takes up less space than his names do." He looked fondly after the galloping cart. "Dagner's only proud of being a Singer," he said.

Navis had one eyebrow right, right up. "Is Tholian dead then?"

"Yes," said Moril.

"Well, well," said Navis. "One hesitates to say good riddance, since he was obviously a near relation of yours, but—"

"We have to sing in the market square," Hestefan interrupted. He was back to his schoolmaster manner.

"Well, well," Navis said again as they followed the green cart back into the town. "Tholian dead! If I had to choose between Tholian and Keril, I might, even at this moment, choose Tholian."

"Never met him," said Mitt.

"You have no idea how lucky you are," said Navis. He did not say anything else until they were in the confusion of the market again. Then he said, "Mitt, how about a decent breakfast at the inn?"

"That," said Mitt, "is the best thing I heard today."

The two of them threaded their horses between the stalls toward the large inn at one side of the square. Maewen had no money. She was watching them rather wistfully when Navis turned round and called, "You, too, lady. This is my treat."

Maewen followed gratefully. They clopped under a huge archway into a stable yard, where a boy with a raw face and yellow hair spit out the straw he was chewing and came to listen to Navis's instructions. He wanted the horses to have a good breakfast, too. Maewen patted her horse and let the boy take it away with the other two. A nice horse, she thought, as she followed Navis into the inn, but one without any character at all. If it *was* Noreth's horse, the girl must have used it like a bicycle. What *had* become of her?

The front rooms of the inn were wide open to the square, where tables were set out under a sort of covered way supported by old gnarled pillars with creepers trained up them. A nice arrangement in summer, Maewen thought. It reminded her of the pillared balconies at the front of the Tannoreth Palace. But what did they do in winter? Kernsburgh was many degrees warmer than Gardale even now. People in these times seemed to be so hardy. They lived out of doors much more than Maewen was used to.

The only free table they could find was a long way from the end of the square where Hestefan had stopped his cart. Maewen could hear his voice faintly, behind all the rest of the din, calling to people to come and listen, but any view was blocked off by a gnarled pillar and a big stall selling iron pans. It was a slight disappointment. Maewen had never yet heard the Singers perform. Still, as she agreed with Mitt, it was good to be sitting in a proper chair listening to Navis ordering food from a cheerful, hurried man in a dirty apron.

"And beer for three," Navis finished.

Help! thought Maewen. Coffee came from abroad, of course, and it was not much drunk until a hundred years later than this. She would have preferred water—except from the way this town *smelled* she was sure the water was not fit to drink. Oh well. Beer couldn't be that bad, or people wouldn't drink it. Hestefan and Moril were singing now. Maewen leaned back, trying to pick out the sound from behind the shouts, the talk, the yelling of animals, and the bonging of the pans in the ironware stall. It was not a tune she knew.

The food came promptly on enormous wooden platters, sizzling hot: bacon, kidneys, eggs, mushrooms, and hot bread to go with it, with butter and honey for the bread. With this arrived three pewter tankards of sour-smelling yellow stuff. Maewen tried it. Yuk. But she was very hungry, and all that food needed something to wash it down. She kept drinking, in valiant sips.

Mitt could no longer contain his anxiety. "They let Hannart in early," he said to Navis. "I don't like that. What do we do?"

"Play it as we see it," Navis answered. "At least we're here."

"And what's this Sending Day?" Mitt asked, wolfing down food he hardly noticed.

"As I gather, it's the day most pupils go home for the summer," Navis said. "Not that anyone thought to inform me. I asked Noreth's aunt."

"Then you can take her away," Mitt said.

"So can Hannart," Navis pointed out. He was, as usual, trying not to show his feelings, but Mitt could tell Navis was as strained and gloomy as he was himself.

There was applause from the distance. Hestefan began a new song.

Maewen thought it was perfectly lovely, but it was low and sweet, and she kept losing it in the noise.

"Suppose," said Mitt, "that Hannart has been and gone by the time they let us in?"

"There's a closing ceremony," Navis replied. "Surely even Hannart can't remove a pupil before that. And of course neither can we."

"First moment we can then," Mitt said urgently.

"Whatever's possible," Navis agreed.

They ate in worried silence after that. Hestefan seemed to be telling a story. There were bursts of laughter and clapping, but Hestefan's voice was almost inaudible. Maewen was straining to hear when Navis pulled himself together and turned to her politely.

"I fear we have been leaving you out of our private concerns, lady," he said. "As you may have gathered, we became your followers not entirely out of personal conviction."

"Speak for yourself," said Mitt. "I'm convinced." He turned to Maewen, waving a hunk of bread and honey in one bony hand. Here was something to take his mind off Hildy. "Tell us your beliefs, Noreth. Convince him."

*Help!* thought Maewen. She stared at the pots and pans swinging on the stall, hoping for inspiration. Mitt was leaning toward her eagerly as if he thought she really did have beliefs. Probably Noreth did have beliefs, but Maewen had no way of knowing what those were. She had simply been getting by on a messy muddle of beliefs from her own day, mixed up with what she knew had happened in the last two hundred years. Dalemark had changed, almost out of recognition, in that time, and not wholly for the better at that.

"It is possible she just follows the will of the One," Navis remarked in his usual sarcastic way.

This bounced Maewen into speaking. She did not want to let Mitt down. "I believe there has to be change," she said. A disgustingly safe thing to say. Something seemed to be wrong with her, adding to her difficulty. Her face buzzed, and the sounds from the market had gone quiet and distant. Moril was singing. She could just pick out his voice among the deep belling chords of his cwidder. She would have liked to think it was the cwidder doing this to her, but she was fairly sure it was the beer. And the way Gardale smelled like a filthy farmyard. Maewen swallowed. "There's a lot in Dalemark that hasn't come out yet," she said. "Wonderful people, and talents and richness. Some of the reason it hasn't come out is that all the ordinary people are too poor for different reasons"—am I going to be sick?—"but the *main* reason is that everybody is too busy thinking of themselves as North and South. They need to be one country and—and be *proud* of it before—before they can show what's . . . really in them." There. I believe that. Maewen pushed back her chair. She knew what was wrong with her now. A truly vicious stomachache. Nerves? Those mushrooms? She could not help it that Mitt's eager face was going puzzled and disappointed. "I'm sorry . . . I have to— Do you know where is the—"

Navis understood instantly. "It'll be round in the stable yard. First door. Women to the right."

Maewen bolted that way. She raced under the arch. And—bless Navis!—there was the door. It was dark inside, with a sticky mud floor, but she was led to the right door by the smell. Yuk! She nearly *was* sick. Inside, it was clean enough in its primitive way, with whitewashed walls and a bundle of rags instead of paper, but the *smell*! Why hadn't things smelled anything like this bad up on the green roads? Did Wend really look after that kind of thing as well as the roads?

It was not a place to stay long in. Maewen finished as quickly as she could and unlatched the door to the dark muddy passage with relief. That's better. Now I can go back and talk sense to Mitt.

A hard arm grabbed her round the throat. A hand, with the faint glint of a knife accompanying it, rose and came down, stabbing.

*"Help!"* Maewen screamed. The hard arm cut her scream off to a squawk. She struggled furiously. What an *awful* place to be killed in! I *will* not die here! She twisted sideways against the grip on her throat and kicked where she could feel legs behind her. The rest of her twisted and bucked mindlessly. It was horrible the way she could *feel* the man. Intimate. Beastly. It never occurred to her to use the knife and short sword she had just hitched aside to fasten her breeches. She kicked madly, trying to fall out of the man's grip into a sort of squat. That unbalanced him. The hand with the knife swept away sideways and banged on a wooden wall as he tried to stay upright. His arm loosed her throat enough for her to give a high, whistling scream.

"With you!" someone said. Doors banged. Wood resounded. The knife gleamed in half daylight. It had grown. No, it was a sword, being held by someone else. Maewen only glimpsed it before her attacker dropped her as if she was on fire and fled, kicking her as he barged across her, shoving the swordsman aside, and banging out through the door. Maewen could feel the pounding of his running feet as she lay on the sticky mud floor.

"Are you all right? *Noreth!* Where are you hurt?"

It was Navis. His hand was pulling at her arm. Maewen tried to sit up and found she had suddenly no strength at all. Navis hauled her upright and dragged her out into the comparatively pure-smelling yard.

"Where are you hurt?"

"I—I'm not . . . I . . . How did you— Who *was* he?"

"I wish I knew," said Navis. "It was far too dark. As I didn't see him when I came along behind you, I conclude he was hiding in there."

"What a horrible place to hide!" Maewen managed to say. "Why did you—"

"I told you," said Navis. "Your aunt told me to look after you. Let's get the horses and go out on the common. You should be safe out of the crowds. We should have stayed there as soon as we saw Hannart was in town."

# 13

MAEWEN SPENT WHAT was left of the morning sitting on the grass outside the town, more or less where Dagner's black and white cart had been, hedged in by Mitt, Navis, and the three horses. Even this did not make her feel safe. If someone came to untether a cow, or a goat bleated, or a lark went up from the grass, she jumped and stared round, expecting her throat to be grabbed and a knife to appear. She was, slowly, beginning to feel more rational when crowds of people came streaming out of town to follow the road to the Lawschool. Maewen started shaking again.

"Nearly midday." Navis stood up and brought her horse over.

Maewen mounted, hoping she would feel better high up on a horse. It seemed to help a little. They rode sedately over to join the stream of carts, carriages, riders, and walkers on the road, and she found herself hanging back nervously.

"Get the Southerner to steal the Adon's cup for you," the deep voice said suddenly in her ear.

Maewen felt like a water bed, trembling all over from being trodden on. "Is that all you can say? Where *were* you? Why didn't you warn me?"

"You are not hurt. The Southerners were there to help," said the voice.

"Oh thank you!" said Maewen. "You're such a comfort!" She was trembling with indignation now. What use was a ghostly adviser who did not care that you might have been killed? Angrily she caught up with Mitt and Navis as they joined the busy road. They had almost reached the clump of trees before she realized that she felt much better. It made her smile. Perhaps the voice knew what it was doing after all.

Outside the gracious buildings of the Lawschool there was now a picket line set up for horses, and boys in that old-fashioned uniform to guard it. The man with bad teeth was now letting people through the gate in slow twos and threes. Mitt jigged with impatience as they joined the line of people waiting to go in, and even Navis looked anxious.

Moril got down from a waiting carriage which had evidently given him a lift and came jogging over to them with his cwidder bumping on his back. He was folding up a pie and corn cakes in an expensive-looking linen napkin and chewing as he arrived. "They gave me lunch, too," he explained. "I wondered where you'd got to."

"And where is Hestefan?" asked Navis.

Moril looked a little anxious. "He said he'd have a rest and meet us at the waystone with Wend. I don't think his health's very good. He's looked ill ever since the cart overturned."

"You think he got hurt then?" Mitt asked.

"Yes, but he won't say," said Moril.

They came to the gate and the man with bad teeth. Moril gave him a beaming smile. "Do you think you could take care of my cwidder until I come out?" That was how he got the ride in the coach, Maewen thought, watching the porter try to pretend that no one had ever asked him such a thing and then give in and take the cwidder carefully in his arms. Singers learned to get round people.

"Through the garden and turn right to the small quadrangle," the man said, as he said to everyone.

Nobody looked at the garden. Moril and Maewen passed through on the cobbled path, trying to keep up with Navis and Mitt. They swept through an archway on the right and came to a square court surrounded by buildings. Here stood a long row of young people in gray, with broad white collars. Some were much younger than Moril; some were nearly grown-up. Most seemed around Maewen's real age. Many of them were already greeting parents and other relatives, and most of the rest were staring sideways at the archway, looking for their own families. There were no hugs or shouts and almost no jigging about. Evidently the way of this school was to pretend you were very grown-up. It made things very awkward. Mitt, Navis, Moril, and Maewen went crabwise along the line, and the ones waiting stared coolly past them, until Navis stopped in front of a thin dark girl, whose pale face seemed to be set in a permanent little frown.

"Hildy!" he said. There was delight and relief all over him. Mitt was the same.

The dark girl turned from whispering to the enormous girl bulking beside her and stared at Navis. "Father! Fancy you being here!" Her face lit up. For a moment it looked as if she were going to break out of school custom and hug Navis. Then she remembered the grown-up behavior and took hold of both his hands instead, smiling all over her face. It made her look much younger. "Father, this *is* good! Now I'll have someone to show round and shout for me at last grittling after all!"

"Are you all right? Is all well here?" Navis asked her.

"Absolutely *mountaintop*!" said Hildy. "I love it here. But this is Biffa." She turned and pulled forward the huge girl beside her. "Biffa's my besting. Do you mind if she comes round with us? She's a win-through like me, and her parents can't afford to come today. Please. She won't have anyone if I go off."

"I shall be honored," Navis said. Huge Biffa turned pink right down to her white collar and stood bulking helplessly, smiling. She had a very sweet smile. It transformed her slab of a face and made everyone see why Hildy liked her.

"Good," said Hildy, and began to tow Navis away, ignoring the rest of them completely.

Navis hung back. Mitt said, "Hello, Hildy."

Hildy glanced over her shoulder. "Oh. Hello, Mitt." It was barely friendly. Maewen found she could not bear to look at Mitt's face. The hurt in it and the disillusionment were so huge and so plain that it hurt her, too, just from the one glimpse she had of it.

Navis firmly pulled Hildy back again. "My dear daughter," he said. "Not so hasty. Let me introduce my friends. This young lady is, ah, Ilona Kernsdaughter."

Maewen bowed, impressed that Navis remembered to invent her a false name. Hildy's eyes swept over Maewen's travel-stained hearth-man's livery and back to her face, which she seemed to study freckle by freckle. Hildy's eyes were very dark, very observant, and not very warm. Maewen felt thoroughly uncomfortable. She was wondering whether to bow again, ironically this time, when Hildy seemed to decide that Maewen met some standard she approved of. The little frown cleared from between her eyebrows, and she smiled and bent her head to Maewen.

"Who is placed in my care by her aunt," Navis continued. "This lad with me is Moril, from a line of famous Singers."

Singers were obviously something Hildy respected. She bowed and smiled at Moril, who stared gravely and did not bow back.

"And," Navis finished dryly, "Mitt, of course, you know."

Mitt had his face under control by then. It still stared pale and blank, but he grafted a joking smile onto it. "Turned up again like the bad penny," he said.

Somehow this hurt Maewen more than the way Mitt had looked at first. When Hildy nodded coolly and turned away, Maewen could have slapped her. He's looked forward to meeting you and worried about you—which is more than you deserve!—and you do *this* to him! she thought. You little—little *cow*!

They all moved off, with Mitt drifting in the rear like a sleepwalker. Moril spoke to huge Biffa. "Do you happen to know where I'll find my sister?" He said it shyly but somehow made it plain that he had no use for Hildy. "She's called Brid Clennensdaughter."

Maewen caught a look of sheer awe above her on Biffa's face. "Brid!" said Biffa. "Is Brid your *sister*? She's Great Girl this sessioning. She won all the prizes on tally. She's somewhere about with the Adon."

Eh? thought Maewen. But the Adon's dead, centuries before this.

Hildy turned half round from in front. "She means she's with the Earl of Hannart's heir," she said. "He came to see her because she's the Earl of the South Dales' sister."

There was a reverent note to her voice that told Maewen that Hildy was a snob. This probably accounted for the way she treated Mitt. Mitt had caught the reverent note, too, and his face was worse than ever.

"They say," Biffa added shyly to Moril, "that the Adon's in love with your sister."

"*Is* he?" said Moril, as if he thought he might have something to say about that. "Where's the best place to find them?"

"Skreths—no, maybe Climbers," said Biffa. "I'll come and show you if you like."

She led Moril off, while Hildy called instructions about where to meet again and Biffa called back about when. Both of them seemed to be talking gibberish. And when Biffa had vanished round the nearest corner, Maewen realized that there were only three of them left. Mitt seemed to have slipped off with Biffa, too. She could hardly blame him. She would not have stayed to be ignored by Hildy either. No, it was worse than ignoring. It was more unkind than that. From what Moril had told her, Hildy was an earl's granddaughter, but Navis was only a hearthman now. He was not going to be Duke of Kernsburgh for some years yet. There was no reason, no *excuse* for Hildy to think so well of herself.

She gloomily followed the girl on a grand tour of the school. It soon became a great blur to Maewen, confused in her mind with tours of the Tannoreth Palace—except that this tour was strewn with other pupils in white collars leading brightly clothed relatives who all looked as bewildered as Maewen. When she thought of the visit she had made here with Aunt Liss, she became even more confused. None of it was the same. When she remembered some of the buildings, they seemed smaller or in the wrong place. And parts of it were like any old school.

Maewen's head ached, and her stomachache came back. She trailed behind Hildy and Navis, wanting to sit down, while Hildy dragged Navis along by one hand, saying things like, "and this is where hardimers set trethers. Even if you're sailing in grybo, they can make you a comedown for squarks." She never once bothered to explain. Navis looked increasingly ironic. Maewen thought, Hildy doesn't want us to know what it really means. She's one of those that like to be on the inside knowing things, with everyone else on the outside, not knowing.

Perhaps this was unkind. Maewen knew she was still feeling odd because someone had tried to kill her. She made an effort. She came politely up beside Hildy while they were crossing an enormous courtyard that did not exist in Maewen's day and tried to join in the talk. But after a very short time of politeness, she found herself saying, not altogether kindly, "Why did you treat Mitt like that? He's been looking forward to seeing you."

"Really?" said Hildy. "How stupid of him. I suppose it comes of being uneducated."

"*Is* he uneducated?" Maewen said, even less kindly.

"He's practically *illiterate*," said Hildy. "He can hardly read." She made it sound like an infectious disease. She added, "He used to *fish* for a living." Her manner of saying it told Maewen that Hildy was quite aware of Maewen's unkindness, that she had met it often before, and that she expected it and did not care two hoots.

Hmm, thought Maewen, dropping back again. I suppose that says volumes about her early life. She has problems. Well, I suppose unpleasant people *do* have problems, or they wouldn't be unpleasant, but that doesn't mean I have to like her—*or* forgive her! And she went on trailing behind. She ached all through. Some of it seemed to be an ache of the heart about the way Mitt must be feeling.

Been here before, Mitt was thinking. It's only what I'm used to. Only to be expected, really. Hildy's back in the life she was bred for and that's that. But though this stopped his hurting—a little—he was still hurting in other ways he was not used to at all.

He had thought Hildy was his friend. He had not known friendship could be such a fragile thing. Probably Ynen, if they found him, would not want to know Mitt either. And who cares? he said to himself, sauntering behind the mountainous Biffa and the much smaller Moril. The size of Biffa made him grin, hurt as he felt. She was a good few inches taller than he was, and Mitt knew he was around six feet these days.

"My parents keep the mill over in Ansdale," Biffa was saying to Moril, "and they're both taller than me. If you think I'm big, you should see my brother. Size runs in our family."

"It's not far to Ansdale," said Moril.

"Two days," and Biffa. "That would be four, if one of them came to fetch me. They can't afford the time. But they sent me the horse hire to come home. I don't have to stay all through the recess like Hildy does."

Mitt wondered what kind of mountainous horse Biffa would have to hire to ride home on, but the sick, choked, hurt feeling kept him from joining in the conversation.

They crossed an echoing cloister and came out into a bright, hot courtyard with steps at both ends. "Climbers," said Biffa. "There she is."

A number of hearthmen in Hannart livery were sitting on the steps opposite, indulgently watching Kialan Kerilsson walk about the court talking with a dark-haired girl in Lawschool uniform. Mitt checked a bit at the sight. He had not properly attended to where Moril was going. But of course! he thought bitterly. Kialan comes here to see his fancy, and they let him in early because he's an earl's son, and he probably doesn't even notice he's getting special treatment. There's earls for you. Mitt thought he might go away. Then his misery said, What the hell—I'll give him a rude message to his father. And he walked down the steps with Biffa and Moril.

"Brid," Moril said sternly.

The girl spun round. She was very pretty, even prettier than Fenna, and not as old as Mitt had expected, probably only his own age. "*Moril!*" she screamed, and unlike the pupils in the sober line, she rushed at Moril and flung her arms around him. The two of them hurtled round and round, both talking at once and laughing, with Kialan throwing remarks at Moril and laughing, too. Mitt stood back, hurting.

"I only came to fetch her back to Hannart," he heard Kialan say.

Brid's voice rose in a Singer's soprano, with a good strong edge to it. "Of *course* I'm not throwing away Singer heritage, Moril, *or* law learning! But it's *my* life, and I decide it!"

"So she'll be here for three more years," Kialan said ruefully. "Satisfied, Moril?" He probably was in love with Brid, Mitt thought. See the way he looked at her. His chest gave a wrench at the thought.

Out of a further babble of talk, Moril asked, "Is your father here?"

Kialan shook his frizzy head. "No, I came over alone. Why?"

Alone except for twenty hearthmen, Mitt thought, and was taken by surprise when Moril said, "Good. Then you can meet my friend Mitt."

Mitt's chest gave another wrench, that Moril called him a friend, and then a sort of hop at the eager way Kialan instantly swung round and stared, with his head up so that his nose made him look like a questing eagle. "Mitt?" Kialan said. "From Aberath? Really?" Mitt nodded warily. "What are you doing here?" Kialan asked, no less eagerly.

Mitt intended a laugh. It came out as a hacking sort of caw. "Visiting on Hildy Navissdaughter."

Kialan's mouth bunched like a prune. "That white-faced little sow. She'll be worse than Earl Hadd before she's through; she's the image of him already! Her brother Ynen's worth ten of her."

Mitt's chest did odd things again. He was not sure what he felt, but he somehow made no protest when Kialan signaled to Brid to keep talking to Moril and seized Mitt's arm and walked him out of their hearing. It was a lordly thing to do. Mitt found he hardly cared. The way he was feeling showed him that Kialan was a lordly type who would have acted like this if he'd been born a fisherman's heir. It was a strange discovery. He faced Kialan, pricking with odd new sensitivity.

"Am I glad to meet you at last!" Kialan said. Mitt knew he meant it. "I was looking for you all over when I was in Aberath. Did you really sail north with the Undying?"

"In a manner of speaking," Mitt said as they walked up the steps together. "It was Ynen's boat, but I helped bring Old Ammet aboard."

"I want to hear you tell it," Kialan said, "but that'll have to wait." He stopped halfway up the steps and again pulled Mitt round to face him. They were near enough of a height to look into one another's faces, but Kialan was chunkier. Kialan said, slowly and carefully, "It was lucky I didn't run into you in Aberath. I'd have blurted out all sorts of jolly messages from Ynen—or I would have until that evening. My father spoke to me before supper then and told me you weren't supposed to know where Ynen is. And of course I couldn't go against my father."

Mitt looked into Kialan's light-colored eyes, a good many shades bluer than his own, and realized that Kialan was telling him all the same. His chest did strange things again. "When did you last speak to Ynen?" he asked, testing the situation.

"This lady—Noreth—is she riding the green roads?" Kialan asked, testing Mitt in return.

"Alive and kicking," Mitt said. "She's around the school somewhere if you want to meet her."

For a second Kialan looked as if he would dearly have loved to meet Noreth. Then he shook his curly head regretfully. "My father would be furious. In answer to your question, I spoke to Ynen this morning before I set off to come here. He wasn't allowed to send his love to his sister—" He looked questioningly at Mitt.

"All right," Mitt said. "I'll tell her."

"Thanks," said Kialan. "I'd promised Ynen. And you're riding with this Noreth Onesdaughter?"

"Down to Kernsburgh," said Mitt. "I suppose."

"I'll join you there," said Kialan. "With Ynen. Wait for us if we're not there first. It's going to take a bit of planning." He swung Mitt round again, and they strolled back down the steps. "So where did you make landfall?" he asked loudly, for the benefit of the hearthmen across the courtyard.

"Holy Isles," said Mitt. "And right weird they were."

"I've heard they are," Kialan agreed. "Where then?"

"Blown north again to Aberath," Mitt said. "We never saw the coast till then. We'd no idea we'd come that far."

"Amazing," said Kialan. "Well, thanks for telling me." He let go of Mitt's arm.

"You're welcome," Mitt said, backing away. "Tell Moril I'll be with Navis when he wants us."

"Right," said Kialan, strolling back toward the others. Brid waved and called out something happy to both of them.

Mitt could not face happy scenes. He went the other way, back up the steps with long, busy strides, pretending he had something important to do. His mind was all over the place. He needed to be alone to think. But there were people everywhere, in happy, chatting groups. Back and forth went Mitt, looking as busy as he knew how, through gardens, under arches, across a wide paved court, into buildings again. And always there were people. Until at last he came out into a gravel court where there was a small separate building, a funny domed place that looked older than all the rest. Nobody seemed to be about here. Mitt went cautiously in through its arched doorway. Inside, it seemed to be a stone summerhouse with a stone table up some steps at one end. Mitt sat on one of the stone benches that curved round the walls, between bundles of twisted greenstone pillars, and gave himself thankfully up to thought.

So Ynen was in Hannart, then, right under Keril's eye. It made sense. Even Navis would hardly try to get Ynen out of there. But Kialan could. Who would have thought it? Mistrustfully Mitt tried to tell himself that Kialan had not meant a word of what he seemed to mean. He was just acting for his father, getting Mitt to betray himself. "And I did—didn't I just!" Mitt said aloud. But as the words echoed round the domed room, he knew that Kialan had been entirely straight with him. Kialan was all right. The bitter, disillusioned feeling that made Mitt not want to trust anyone was about Hildy, not Kialan. He knew very well how Kialan came to think so differently from his father. Mitt had only to recall that glimpse he had had, of Kialan shuffling through Holand, a prisoner of Navis's father, to know it. Over a year ago it had been now, but Mitt remembered it as fresh as if it were yesterday. No doubt Kialan remembered even better. Kialan knew all about how it felt to be in the power of an earl.

All the same, Kialan had no call to say Hildy was like Earl Hadd. Mitt decided he hated Kialan for that—all the more because he suspected Kialan might be right.

"Damned *earls* and their families!" Mitt said out loud, clenching both hands on the edge of the stone seat. His eyes glared ahead at the stone table and the lopsided metal cup on it. Hildy and Kialan between them had mixed his mind up properly.

His eyes suddenly told him what they were seeing. That stone table was an altar. There was an image in a niche above it of an old man lifting up a mountain. The One. That meant that the lopsided cup had to be the one Noreth wanted—the Adon's cup.

Mitt clutched the stone bench even harder. It was the perfect opportunity. All he had to do was walk over, pick the thing up, and stuff it down the front of his jacket. Noreth would rejoice. And with the school swarming with people, if somebody did notice the cup was gone and raise a shout, how were they to know which of the crowd had taken it? If Mitt took it and went *now*, through the valley and up to the green road, he could be gone before anyone could do anything. So why was he sitting here like an idiot, clinging to a stone seat until his fingers hurt?

Because it was stealing. Because he had made that promise to Alk. Because he had spoken words to Old Ammet and to Libby Beer—who had been around yesterday and today, perhaps to remind Mitt of those words. Mitt grinned, a bent, unfunny smile. Funny the way it was never enough to swear and promise just the *once*. You seemed to have to rethink and repromise every time the subject came up. Mitt's smile narrowed away. This time he would be stealing from the One, and even sane, level Alk was cautious with the One. On the other hand, Noreth was the One's own daughter, and the One wanted her to have the cup. And now, after Hildy and Kialan had mixed Mitt's mind up, he felt like doing something bad. It would be a waste not to, really.

Mitt unclenched his fists from the bench and stood up. He listened. All the voices and footsteps he could hear were off in the distance.

What he could see of the gravel court through the doorway was empty. So. Get it over with.

Mitt took three long strides to the altar. There he flinched and froze. He could have sworn a shadow, like an old man with a long nose, had swung through the room as he took the third step. As if someone had flitted across the doorway. But he stood and he waited and he listened and no feet crunched on the gravel outside. The new view he had of the court from here was empty. He stretched out a cautious hand and grasped the cup round its wide, uneven stem.

The domed room filled with crackling blue light.

Mitt leaped back. One arm was over his face and watering eyes. The other hand was fizzing, prickling, and stinging, and he shook it frantically. The light was gone by then. Mitt blinked away tears and dazzle, panting. No wonder no one bothered to guard this cup. The thing looked after itself. He looked round nervously, hoping that no one had been near enough to see the One's chapel suddenly fill with light.

Somebody must have been. There were shouts outside, loud and desperate, from somebody young.

# 14

MAEWEN HAD HAD ENOUGH of Hildy by then. Navis was being far too patient with her. "Now look, my dear," he was saying, as they wandered through the garden by the gate, "it really is vital that you come away with us today. If you remain here, you're playing into Earl Keril's hands. He's using you as a hostage for my behavior—not to speak of Mitt's."

"Let's *not* speak of Mitt," said Hildy.

"All right, we'll speak of you, then," Navis agreed. "Everyone else goes away from here today, isn't that right? Surely you would prefer not to be left all alone in this place all summer."

The fierce little frown grew between Hildy's brows. "Why are you bothering now? I was alone here for nearly two weeks at spring recess—at least, Biffa was here, too, but it was *nearly* alone—and I didn't mind."

"Things have changed since then," Navis said patiently.

"What things?" said Hildy.

"Politics. I know now that you were sent to this place as part of a plan," Navis explained. "The plans I've made to counter the earls' move could make it very dangerous for you. Keril knows you are here. He has only to take you away. Anyway, the only safe thing for you to do is to be with me for the next three months. I—"

"Three *months*!" Hildy interrupted. "But then I'd miss Harvest grittling and modes *and* the start of middle vokes— *No*!"

"Well, yes, I'm afraid you would," Navis admitted. "But you'd be alive. You'd not be in prison. You can always come back next year, if things go our way."

"*If!* Next *year*! Miss a whole *year*!" It was clear Hildy could not believe her ears. "Just for politics! No *way*!" She meant this so much that she actually made an effort to explain. "Father, you're asking me to go back to junior vocation studies, just for *politics*."

Navis looked exasperated and, for him, surprisingly helpless. His eyes flicked to Maewen. Maewen realized she must be some of his difficulty. She supposed it was because Navis had told Hildy she was someone called Ilona Something and Navis was not sure he dared explain who she really was—or who Navis *thought* she was. Oh, what a muddle! Maewen was sick of this. It was with enormous relief that she saw Biffa coming towering through the garden toward them. Maewen rushed to meet her.

"There you are!" Biffa said. "I hunted everywhere. Then I thought she'd decided to show you the One's chapel and I came this way. Have you been there?"

"Not yet," Maewen said. "Which way is it?"

But Biffa was gazing over Maewen's head. "What's wrong with Hildy? She looks near on in one of her rages."

Maewen looked back at Navis and Hildy, bent toward one another arguing, against a great bush of lavender full of bees. She saw the anger in Hildy's white face and the worry in Biffa's healthy pink one, and she wondered how Hildy had managed to be friends with such a nice girl. "Navis wants to take her away with him," she explained, "and she won't go."

"Why ever *not*?" said Biffa. "She's been right gloomy all this week, saying she'll be alone all summer here—you wouldn't believe!"

Maewen could believe. "Then go and persuade her. Navis is worried to death," she said. "Which way is the One's chapel?"

"Over there," Biffa said, pointing. "You'll just have time before grittling." She strode over to the lavender bush to loom anxiously over Hildy.

Maewen sighed as she trudged off the way Biffa pointed. She knew Biffa would persuade Hildy. She supposed it was a good thing, if Hildy *was* in danger. But the idea depressed her too much for her to bother to work out what the danger might be. There would be Hildy all the way to Kernsburgh, frowning angrily and pretending Mitt did not exist. And Mitt would have that look all the time, with that horrible jokey smile grafted on top of it. It hardly bore thinking of.

Chalk up another black mark to this Keril, she thought, as she came through the bushes and saw the One's chapel across a gravel court. It was just as she had remembered it. But she had not remembered it *here*. The buildings must all have been in different places after two hundred years. I wonder why she didn't show us it, Maewen thought. No, I know why. It's not something she can call a silly name and mystify us with. Or maybe she'd call it Wunners.

The thought amused Maewen enough to give her the courage to advance slowly and quietly toward the small, domed building. She was not happy with the idea of stealing this cup. But she did think she ought to do something for herself. And of course she was in the fortunate position of knowing that she had done it. Just rush in, snatch it, and out, she told herself as she advanced cautiously, slantwise to the door.

A funny blue flash made her jump round. The gravel crunched under quick footsteps. Maewen swung round further, almost in time. Someone muffled in a gray robe grabbed at her with one hand and raised a knife in the other.

"No, not again! *Help!*" Maewen screamed.

She went on screaming because this time he had not grabbed her throat. It was so much like last time that she was sure it was the same man. He had her arm instead of her throat, and he was trying to twist it so that she would hold still for him to bring down the knife into her neck. In spite of the way it hurt, Maewen seized the wrist of his knife hand with her free hand and frantically held it away. She could see his face over her head. It seemed to be made of gray cloth, except for his glaring eyes. The sight turned her weak. She could only push at his wrist and keep screaming, "*Help!* I'm being *killed*!"

Gravel scrunched and spurted, stinging her face. Someone said, "Flaming *Ammet*!" and then, "Drop that, you hooded horror, you!" Mitt's unmistakable large bony hand closed over the fist that was trying to stab Maewen. Everyone swayed, and grunted, and slid, in a shrill jangling of gravel. Then the attacker wrenched his hand, and his knife, free and ran, with Mitt after him like a greyhound. Maewen was left standing in a patter of small stones, still shouting.

"Oh save me, Mitt!"

She heard herself say it, as the madly running gray man plunged into the bushes and trees of the garden and Mitt hurtled after him. She stood staring, feeling a total fool. Tears were running down her face, though she had no memory of when she had started crying. How—how totally . . . *girly*! "Oh save me, Mitt!" she mimicked herself. Honestly!

She tried to walk to the chapel then, but her legs wobbled and refused to go, even though at the time they were carrying her round and round on the spot, like someone in a mad, giddy dance. She seemed to be trying to see all sides of the yard at once in case there were any more gray attackers. She made herself stop that. She managed to stand still and wipe her eyes, but that was all she could manage before Mitt came hurtling back with Navis running beside him. Both of them looked so anxious that tears came leaking down Maewen's face again.

"Bastard got away in the bushes!" Mitt said disgustedly.

"What are you doing on your own here?" Navis demanded.

Maewen swallowed. "Cup," she managed, but that was all.

"That's easily solved," said Navis. "Stay with her, Mitt."

Before Mitt could say anything, Navis had crossed the gravel and briskly vanished into the chapel.

"Are you all right?" Mitt asked Maewen. He put both hands out uncertainly, with half a mind to take hold of her shoulders. But then he did not quite like to touch her. Maewen instantly found she was hurling herself against him. She pressed her face against his chest. Through the hard mail she could feel Mitt panting and his heart thumping. She was sure she was embarrassing him horribly, but this did not prevent her from wrapping her arms round him, tightly. One of Mitt's arms came gingerly round her shoulders and he patted her back. "There, there. It's all right."

"Oh Mitt, I'm so sorry!" Maewen blurted. "About me and about Hildy—about *everything*!"

"There, there," Mitt repeated.

That was all they had time for before Navis trod briskly out of the chapel again, carrying something bundled in a large handkerchief. "Quite simple, you see," he said.

Mitt stood back a bit, with a damp spreading patch on his jacket where Maewen's face had been. "Simple?" he said. "It's got a hex on it sizzles off like a thunderbolt when you touch it!"

"This being the North, I considered that," said Navis, "and I didn't touch it. Look." He opened the silk handkerchief a fraction to show the cup nestled in it. Then he calmly stowed the bundle in one of his wide pockets. "We'd best take ourselves off to the great court," he said as he made sure this pocket was arranged not to bulge more than the one on the other side of his coat. "We must attend a closing ceremony, it seems."

They went there slowly. Maewen was still shaking, and her legs were not steady. Navis courteously put his hand under her elbow to help her along. Mitt avoided touching her. Maewen kept seeing him rubbing at the wet patch her face had made on his chest. She could hardly look at him for embarrassment.

"You persuaded Hildy to come along?" Mitt asked, rather too casually, giving his chest a further rub.

"Not yet," said Navis.

Mitt's face went tight and bony, like a skull. "She's *got* to."

"I know," said Navis. "I'm hoping that extremely large friend of hers can make her see reason. In that hope I explained the whole situation to both of them."

"Biffa?" said Mitt. "Is that safe?"

"I trusted her," said Navis. "And this you won't believe! The girl's real name is Enblith!"

"After Enblith the Fair!" In spite of his skull face of worry, Mitt began to giggle.

"Unkind, isn't it?" Navis said. "Her parents made a serious miscalculation there. Not that she's *un*beautiful, poor girl. Just too big for one to see it."

Maewen wondered how anyone could be so cool with the stolen cup in his pocket. Mitt tried to match Navis in coolness. He said, "I found out where Ynen is. It seems like bad news, but it could just be good—very good."

"Later. Hush," said Navis.

They came round a corner in a covered walk and found themselves at the top of wide steps overlooking the biggest courtyard. People were crowded on the steps below them, serious, parently people, all looking across to the main school building, where a line of gray-coated teachers stood. One stood out in front in a blue and gray gown. In front of them the courtyard was filled with rows and rows of uniformed pupils in bright white collars.

They had missed quite a bit of the ceremony. The gowned teacher was saying, in a voice that carried almost as well as Hestefan's, "For those who now go out into the world, this is a solemn leave-taking. For those who will return here next Harvest, it is a temporary parting, accompanied, I hope, by new resolves and higher endeavors. I would like you all seriously to consider . . ."

Maewen let the strong voice fade to a drone in her ears. I don't believe it! she thought. Headmasters must have made this speech ever since schools were invented!

Something scuffled behind. She and Mitt both jumped round. But it was only Moril, tiptoeing toward them. He looked white and worried. Mitt, at the sight of him, self-consciously rubbed at his chest again. "What's up?"

"The cup!" Moril whispered back. "I went to get it and it wasn't there!"

"Never fear," Navis murmured. "The sacrilege has been committed already."

"Is that why you all look so worried? Why don't we just go, then?" Moril said.

People on the steps turned round and said, "Hush!" Navis put a finger to his lips. Maewen pulled herself together enough to take hold of Moril's arm and tow him back round the corner.

"We have to leave with everyone else or they'll know exactly who's got it," she whispered.

Moril was no fool. She saw him realize this as she was telling him. "Sorry," he said. "But I told Mitt *I'd* get it. He—"

"It wasn't Mitt. It was Navis."

This obviously astonished Moril. Well, it astonished Maewen, too, now she came to think of it. Navis was an adult and a sensible person. If he thought it was necessary to take the cup, this somehow made the whole matter more serious.

When they came back round the corner, the headmaster was saying, "We will now sing our customary prayer to the One, who is the special guardian of our school. What comes after that is something my staff and I know nothing about."

For some reason almost everyone laughed. Then the gray rows of pupils broke into song. It was a solemn and simple invocation to the One and like nothing Maewen had heard before. Mitt was as startled as she was. The song was beautiful. The strange old tune swelled and mounted, warm and chilling at the same time, and full of reverence. While it lasted, something seemed to fill the vast courtyard that was not of this world. Maewen's back prickled. Navis has done an awful thing! she thought. But Navis never turned a hair.

Moril listened critically. "I never care for those old tunes," he said. "What's going— Oh, I remember."

The headmaster and the other teachers had vanished from the front of the building as if the ground had swallowed them up, and the ranks of gray-uniformed pupils were suddenly seething. Nearly every one of them was pulling over his or her head a colored hood of some kind, and most were putting on clumsy gloves, too. Quite a number of the hoods were gray, or gray with a blue or orange tuft on top. As soon as Maewen saw them, she understood how her attacker had managed to be so thoroughly disguised. He must have raided a cloakroom. The hoods covered faces except for the eyes. Sober pupils had now become blob-faced monsters, with formless gray, green, or red heads. The sight upset her.

There was confused shouting, muffled and strange, from under the hoods. It sounded like "Bad on" and "Herry's gone."

After a second Kialan came sauntering down the steps at one side, trying, from the look of him, not to look as silly and sheepish as he felt, and stopped slightly to one side of the milling monsters.

"They always ask the most important visitor to start it," Moril explained.

"Eye, eye, eye," came the muffled shouts. "Owe it eye."

Kialan nodded. Someone on the steps tossed him a great brown ragged ball. Kialan took it in one hand, bent over sideways with it, and heaved it high into the sky. He probably intended it to come down somewhere in the middle of the crowd, but either the thing was weighted oddly or Kialan miscalculated his throw. The ball came down again almost where he was standing. Kialan saw it come and simply ran for his life.

"Nor don't I blame him!" Mitt said.

The whole crowd of monsters closed on the spot, fighting like maniacs. Many fought with fists and feet. But weapons appeared, too, which must have been hidden under the sober uniforms. There were clubs, whips, and sticks, and at least one person was wielding a short plank. It looked as if someone would be maimed or trampled to death any second.

After a stunned minute Navis said, "This, I take it, is grittling?"

"That's right," said Moril.

"How comforting to know," Navis said, "that the South is, after all, a comparatively peaceful place. And here was I thinking that all the bloodshed happened south of the passes."

"Yes, but what are the *rules*?" Mitt wanted to know.

The rest of the spectators were shouting, "Up the reds!" and "Yellow, yellow, yellow!" as if they knew what was going on. Moril was not very sure, but he thought each of the colors was a team, and the aim was for one team to get the ball into its own special place round the edge of the big court. There were lots of places. There seemed to be at least seven teams. The fight rushed this way and that.

"I hope they don't make a mistake and score with someone's severed head instead of the ball," Navis murmured. "How long does it usually take, and how many deaths result?"

"I don't know," Moril confessed. "Brid doesn't do it."

It seemed to take hours. Hours of yelling, battling, and thwacking, of giant surges and furious counterattacks. Long before it was over, Maewen was hiding her eyes. The sight of all this fighting, after someone had twice tried to kill her, was just too much. She wanted to leave. But as she had sensibly told Moril, they dared not leave.

Moril was not happy either. "It reminds me of Flennpass," he said.

Mitt, on the other hand, had discovered that it was easy to pick Biffa out in the fray, and he was yelling with the rest. "Come *on*, Biffa! Hit him! Ammet, that girl's strong. Go to it, Biffa! Go it!"

And eventually the ball went into someone's goal area in a tumble of gray bodies and a great deal of shouting.

Shortly after that Hildy and Biffa joined them on the steps. They were both dangling blue hoods and were very flushed. The hoods were padded all over, particularly across the nose, and they must have been boiling hot in them.

"Well?" said Navis. "Did you win?"

Hildy's chin lifted haughtily. "*Of* course. You must have seen."

"I saw murder, mayhem, and confusion," Navis retorted. "Are either of you seriously maimed?"

"Of course not—not with Biffa as our surnam," Hildy said.

"It was great!" said Mitt. "Don't mind him. Hildy, Ynen sends you his love."

Hildy glanced at Mitt as if it were very tiresome to have to answer. "Thanks," she said, and turned back to her father. The look settled on Mitt's face again. It was not so much hurt as mortally wounded, Maewen thought. She wished someone *had* maimed Hildy.

"Father," Hildy said, "I've come to a decision. I intend to be a really good law-woman and—"

"An excellent intention," said Navis. "Is this recent? Did it come upon you during the grittling?"

Hildy stamped her foot. Maewen hardly blamed her. Navis could be maddening. "Oh, I wish you wouldn't be so—so *unserious* all the time! You always try to stop me doing things by making me look silly!"

"Let us get this clear, Hildy," Navis said, almost angrily. "I have never, ever wanted to prevent you being a lawyer. I am not trying to stop you now."

"Yes, you *are*!" Hildy cried out. "If what you told me goes wrong, then we'd be on the run and I'd *never* get back here. I'd have to sacrifice what *I* want to politics, just like I have done all my life! I'm not going to. I refuse to come with you. I'm staying *here*!" She spun round and marched away down the steps, angrily swinging her blue hood.

Navis watched until she was lost in the surging, mingling crowd. His eyes were narrowed. He looked vicious and wretched.

"Excuse me, sir," Biffa said, looming shyly over him.

Navis jumped and looked up at her. "Didn't anything I said get through to her?" he asked Biffa.

"Not really," Biffa admitted. "But it got through to me. That's what I wanted to talk to you about. I know she ought to be away from here, somewhere where no earls will think to look, and I thought— Anyway, if I asked her to come home to our mill with me for the summer, I *know* she'd come, and no one would expect that, because we're poor. But—but the trouble is I only have the hire for one horse."

Navis's face relaxed. "May the One bless you, my child!" he said. "That would solve the summer. But I was talking about an autumn campaign, if you remember. Can you think of a way to stop her coming back here?"

Biffa shyly twisted her hood. "That's the other thing I wanted to tell you, sir. We get the autumn storms real terribly in from the Marshes, over in Ansdale. Sometimes you can't get down to the valleys until weeks after Harvest. I was over a month late getting here last autumn. That's how I came to know Hildy. We were both latecomers, as well as on scholarships. But Hildy came a month after me, and she won't know."

"Aha!" said Navis. "This is deep cunning, my dear!" Biffa went very pink and shot a flustered smile at Mitt, then at Maewen and Moril. "Well, if you think you can keep my thankless daughter safe," Navis went on, briskly undoing his money belt, "here is the hire of a horse for her and money for her keep. Is this enough?"

Biffa looked at the pile of gold coins he pushed into her hand, and her eyes went large. "It would do me a year, sir—or two, if I went steady. I'll give it Hildy now, not to be tempted. That's the third thing I wanted to tell you: We ought to go *now*, in among everyone else, so that when those Hannart people look round for Hildy, she's gone. Wouldn't you say so, sir?"

"Absolutely right," said Navis. "Biffa, you are an extremely intelligent young woman."

Biffa went an even brighter pink. "Yes, I know," she said. "But me being so big, people never think of me as clever. I trade on it quite a lot." Everyone laughed. It was too much for Biffa. She turned and ran.

"Quite a character," Navis said.

"Do you *trust* her?" Mitt said.

"I think it's all right," Moril said. "She sort of worships Hildy—you know the way girls do."

"But all that money!" Mitt muttered as they joined the shuffling mass of people trying to get through the garden and out of the school gate. "I wouldn't trust *myself* with that lot. And she said she traded on her size."

It was a nerve-racking time. They shuffled and stopped and shuffled again, and the garden lawn got trampled under many feet. They were too far from the gate to tell if the cup had been missed, or if the many holdups were because Hannart hearthmen were waiting at the gate for Hildy or Maewen. And that gate was the only way out.

"I think it's merely the confusion of so many departures," Navis said. He was completely cool. He seemed to be one of those people who just got cooler the more danger there was.

As they shuffled nearer the gate, it began to look as if Navis was right. The opening was crammed with parents and pupils and younger brothers and sisters, all with luggage and lunch baskets. Pupils kept forgetting things and shoving back into the school to find them. Many families had hired porters to carry the pupils' trunks, so the way was constantly being blocked by men with handcarts, shouting, "Porter for Serieth Gunsson!" as they came in and, "Por-ter! Mind your backs!" as they shoved their way out again.

After a while Moril said quietly, "Biffa and Hildy are in the crowd behind us."

Maewen wished she was taller. It took her five minutes of twisting and standing on tiptoe to see the two girls. Both carried bulging bags. Very sensibly they had mixed themselves up with a family of tall men who were fetching home a boy pupil even taller than Biffa and were talking busily with them as if they belonged.

"A relief," Navis said, after he had turned casually and seen them, too. "So young Biffa *is* honest then."

They reached the gate at long last. People were just shoving their way through without being stopped but without any order either. The man with bad teeth was standing to one side. He stopped Navis.

"Excuse me, sir." Everyone waited for the worst. "Excuse me, one of your party left a cwidder with me."

Moril shoved his way through, while the rest of them tried hard not to look as relieved as they felt. The man turned and fetched the cwidder out of his cubbyhole beside the gate.

"Here you are. One cwidder, safe and sound. Is it you the Adon's waiting for?" He pointed sideways through the opening.

There, beyond a confusion of carriages and carts, the Hannart horsemen stood in a huddle. Kialan was in the midst of them, looking bored and impatient.

Moril took it in without a blink. "No. It's my sister. She's always late."

"No, lad, she's out there," the man said.

They could all see Brid as he spoke, on a horse beside Kialan.

"Well, it's not me. I don't live in Hannart," Moril said. "I expect they're waiting for Hildrida Navissdaughter. Isn't that so?" he asked Navis.

"My daughter," Navis said, looking quite at ease, "is even more inclined to be late than your sister."

The man laughed a mouthful of bad teeth. "Women!" he said, handing Moril the cwidder.

They went out through the gate. Mitt and Maewen felt weak at the risk of it all, but Navis and Moril wandered nonchalantly along the line of horses and Navis gave Moril a leg up to ride double with him until they came to the cart. As he arrived on top of the mare, Moril gave Kialan a friendly wave. Kialan waved back. They saw him scan the three horses and try not to look puzzled.

Moril giggled. "Expecting Hildrida to be with us and all set to pretend he didn't see," he said as Mitt and Maewen mounted. "Now he can't think what's going on. Good. It distracted him beautifully."

Mitt batted aside the Countess-horse's biting mouth. "What do you mean?"

Navis set a sedate pace round the walls toward the main part of Gardale Valley. It was sensible, although Maewen could see the cup flopping heavily in Navis's pocket and the sight made her want to gallop. "Moril means," he said, "that while he was waving to Kialan, Hildy and Biffa came out and almost instantly cadged a lift in a carriage. If that carriage takes them into town and they hire horses at those stables in the first street, they could be away almost as soon as we are."

"And Kialan can't tell Keril," said Moril. "Keril's rather good at getting things out of people."

"I believe you," said Mitt.

As their three horses rounded the corner of the school walls, Maewen had a good view of a man in Hannart livery pushing his way out through the gate and running toward Kialan, shaking his head. Before they were quite out of sight, Kialan was giving a genuine display of someone annoyed and baffled and at the end of his patience. As the walls hid them, the Hannart horsemen were turning to ride off the other way.

Miraculously, nobody at all seemed to have noticed the cup was missing.

# PART FOUR

# *Sword and Crown*

# 15

WEARINESS HIT MAEWEN as soon as they were well away from the school. The Gardale Valley was as beautiful as she remembered from her visit with Aunt Liss, and much the same except there were far fewer houses. They took narrow lanes where wild roses grew in the hedges, miles of them, that blurred in her mind. She was so tired she almost missed seeing Hestefan's cart and would have ridden straight past if the others had not stopped.

The cart was parked on a triangle where three lanes met. The mule was hitched to an oak tree almost the same color as the cart and dozing on its feet. Moril jumped off the mare and went racing anxiously over, with the cwidder bumping on his back. He looked over the tailgate and came back. "It's all right. He's asleep inside." The relief in his face was mixed with worry. "I don't think he's well."

"He's not a young man," Navis said. "And I'm sure he was injured, or shocked at least, when your cart overturned."

"Let him sleep," Mitt suggested. "They say sleep cures."

Moril unhitched the mule, which was not anxious to move, and drove the cart behind the horses. Hestefan did not stir. The miles went by slower still. Moril was white with worry.

"And no wonder," Navis murmured to Mitt. "What becomes of him if Hestefan dies?"

"There's that brother of his," Mitt said stoutly. "He's fond of the old lolly, that's all. Worry about Hildy instead. And I'll tell you about Kialan now."

The two of them talked in low voices. Maewen continued to ride in a daze, long, long lanes through the valley, a long, long haul up a slanting track into the hills beyond. After what seemed an age, her horse humped itself onto level green turf at the head of the track, and there was the waystone casting a huge hollow shadow in the evening light. Wend's shadow was even bigger as he stood up to meet them.

Seeing him, Maewen relaxed from a watch she had not realized she was keeping. Safe at last! she thought. Wend was Undying. He had the power to keep her safe. Most of her weariness dropped away. She realized it had been a smoke screen her mind had put up to disguise how terrified she had been that someone would jump out from behind a hedge and try to kill her again. She was so glad to see Wend that she leaned down from her horse and wrung his hand.

Wend was surprised, but she could tell he was very flattered, too. His face looked like that of a normal human person who was glad to see friends again. "There's a good camp in a mile or so," he said.

It was a very good camp. It was a green lawnlike place set back from the road, spread beside a pool from a cascading stream. There were rocks to sit on and a small wood of rowans and silver birches leaning over the place. "Protection," Wend said, patting a graceful silver trunk.

"Libby Beer?" Mitt asked.

Wend looked at him. "You know her?" he asked sharply.

"You might say so," Mitt said. "We've met once or twice."

Wend stared at him gravely for a moment, as if he were reappraising something. Then he turned away, looking puzzled.

The fresh, safe feeling in the camp revived everyone. They all bustled about, seeing to the horses and making a fire. When Hestefan crawled out of the cart, rubbing his eyes and saying he didn't know what had come over him, he was greeted with jokes and laughter from everyone. There did not seem to be much wrong with Hestefan. He helped Wend fill Wend's hat with wild strawberries as energetically as Mitt and Moril were hunting mushrooms farther upstream. Among them they provided quite a feast.

Maewen kept looking at Mitt, wondering if he was still feeling bad about Hildy. She simply could not tell. The fact was, Mitt had no idea himself. At times, while Navis was giving Wend and Hestefan the story of all they had missed in Gardale, he thought that if only someone would give him definite proof that Hildy and Biffa were safely on the way to Ansdale, he could forget Hildy entirely—almost with relief. Trouble with me, he thought, watching Wend's straight, fair face turning to Noreth in alarm, I'm like a stupid dog that asks to be kicked.

"Twice?" said Wend. "Lady, I must ask you not to go down from the green roads again. The paths can keep you safe."

"But did you get the cup?" Hestefan asked.

"Navis did," Moril said. He was still sore about it.

"Please show us," Hestefan said politely to Navis.

Maewen forgot Mitt. This was going to be alarming. Nervously she watched Navis feel in his pocket and pull out the bundle of silk handkerchief. It was twilight by then and greenish. As the handkerchief fell aside, the firelight made mild dancing gleams on the silver of the cup. Navis bowed to Maewen from his seat on a boulder. "Your cup, Noreth," he said, handing it to Mitt to pass over to her.

Mitt was not expecting Navis to hand him the cup. He came out of his thoughts with a jump and fumbled. The handkerchief unrolled. For an instant the green light and the flicker of the fire just vanished, overwhelmed in blue fizzling light. "*Ouch!*" said Mitt. While everyone blinked and saw yellow dazzle, he hastily rewrapped the cup and passed it to Maewen. "Careful. There's a strong hex on it."

Maewen took the bundle. This was worse than the ring. They were all expecting her to unwrap it and take hold of it and she was probably going to be electrocuted. But, she told herself, swallowing hard, if I *had* been electrocuted, Wend would have mentioned it in the palace. Here goes. Pulling away the handkerchief, she said, "Look, everyone. This is the Adon's cup." She took firm hold of the lopsided silver bowl of it and held it out.

To her huge relief, nothing fizzed. Everyone's dim faces were turned to the cup. After a moment or so Maewen realized they were looking at the way her hands looked dark against it, darker than natural. The cup seemed to have grown brighter. Yes. It had. It was filling with a spreading gentle blue glow, shining like a blue lamp in the near dark, making her hands look bloodred against it. It was so beautiful, and so welcome, that her eyes filled with tears.

Several people let breath out noisily. "It is the cup," Wend said. "It knows you as it knew the Adon."

Well, thank the One! Maewen thought as she wrapped the thing up again.

Under the friendly rustling of the rowans and birches, they all slept well. But toward dawn, around the time when the pouring of the stream began to sound less soothing and more like a noise, and people began to turn and shift because the grass was flat and the bones of the earth came through, Mitt had a strange dream. There was danger in it, and wonder, and the two were mixed up confusingly.

It began with him looking down on the camp from above. He saw the silver cup glowing and another, yellower glow nearby. After a while he knew the yellow glow was from the golden statue. It was very important. Mitt looked at it and thought, Noreth won't need it so much now. I can have my share. But that was not why it was important. Mitt puzzled over this, until his attention was distracted by finding he could see the green roads winding away from the camp. While he was looking at them, he dreamed he was back in the camp, lying under his blanket, dreaming he was looking at the green roads.

He dreamed and looked at the roads with interest. They went in all directions, snaking among the mountains, linking place to place. He could see them all, right down past Dropwater to Kernsburgh and beyond that, into the North Dales and on into the South. Yes, there had been green roads that led through the South, but they were not kept up any longer. Things moved over them, keeping them hidden, dangerous things. But they had been meant to cover all Dalemark.

Mitt dreamed that he would have been happier about seeing it all if the roads had not kept coming back to him, lying under the rowan trees and in danger. Since the idea of danger made him impatient, he turned his attention out again, to the roads, gray under late yellow moonlight, and took a look at the people traveling on them. Quite a few people were up early or traveling through the night. Hildy was one. She and Biffa were riding, a long way over toward that smoking mountain, nearly into Ansdale already. Kialan was riding, too, well on the way to Hannart. This meant danger. That troubled Mitt, so he looked North, where the young Singer who was Moril's brother was up early and hastening toward Adenmouth. Beyond, and coming toward Dagner, there were more riders. These meant danger, too.

There was a black patch of danger centered on the camp under the rowan trees.

Mitt ignored it obstinately and kept watching the roads. He saw the Undying moving on them, too, unnoticed by ordinary people. They looked so much like ordinary people that Mitt wondered how he knew they were Undying. But he knew King Hern, coming down the King's Way to build Kernsburgh, though King Hern looked like a gawky boy only about Mitt's age, and he knew Manaliabrid, hurrying into exile with the Adon and a small boy who was the Adon's son. The Adon turned out to be a short man, much more like Navis than Mitt expected, and Manaliabrid had a strong look of Noreth about her. Wend was with them, to Mitt's surprise, looking much the same.

Now he knew he was dreaming. So it did not surprise him that the green roads were winding away into the past. He lay and marveled at the way they turned back and forth through history, up to the present, into the place where he lay in such danger, and then went winding and snaking on into the far future. The Undying went walking on, taking the roads through time, and history went with them, ignoring them, forgetting the Undying were making history. He watched the roads snake out again into the South, and battles, and other strange things. He would have enjoyed watching more, if the roads had not kept on winding back into the rowan trees and showing him Noreth was a danger.

"No," Mitt said to his dream. "She may be *in* danger, but she's not *a* danger."

And the dream kept telling him, "Not Noreth. You."

"Ah, come on! *She's* all right," Mitt told the dream. "If there's any danger, it's those earls."

Then he woke into white mist with gray trees like shadows in it, feeling very irritable and rather frightened.

Everyone else seemed annoyingly refreshed. When Wend asked Maewen, "Where to next, lady?" she answered cheerfully, "To get the Adon's sword."

"Then we go toward Dropwater," Wend said.

When the road branched at the next waystone, they took the right-hand branch and found themselves almost at once in the stony bottom of a vast valley. It dwarfed everyone. Sweeps of hill rose on either side, barren, and curved tight as a wind-filled sail. Mitt supposed he was put in mind of sails because the wind streamed in this valley, with a sour sort of whistling, as hard as he had ever known it at sea. Like wind at sea, it kept sweeping bands of misty rain across them, which made the barren hills look even more harsh and empty. They look stretched, Mitt thought, staring up at the bare yellowness, through little itching raindrops. A vision came to him of the One, immeasurably huge, taking the hard rocky edge of this land and pulling until it was so tight it would stretch no more. Rivers, rocks, and creatures went tumbling and rolling as the One pulled—

Mitt shivered and hunched into his jacket. He had a dim memory that he might have seen something like this in his dream. He put it, and the idea of danger, resolutely out of his mind. It did no good to get nervous fancies.

It was a drear day's ride and a cheerless camp that night, which could not have been more of a contrast to the camp under the rowan trees. The wind came from all directions. The flames of the fire blew out raggedly, making more smoke than warmth, and the smoke seemed to follow you about wherever you sat. Everyone, even Moril and Hestefan in the cart, rolled themselves in all the coats, cloaks, and blankets they could muster, but nobody slept very well. The wind seemed to get in everywhere. Mitt was so cold that he got up almost before it was light. It had rained again, and everything he had was damp. Since it did not seem to matter how much colder or wetter he got, he went off to wash in the stream beyond the pile of boulders where the horses were. It was a cheerless little stream, clattering down through gray stones with a sound like teeth chattering.

The sound of his going woke Maewen. She rolled up into the gray day, moaning. She had never been so cold or so damp in her life. The one good thing was that her stomach had stopped aching. As if the green roads cured you, she thought as she stumbled off to the latrine beyond the horses. She came back to find everyone else huddled in dead heaps. This was depressing. She went back to the boulders and started to attend to the horses.

She was alone. The deep voice spoke to her at once. "I have considered," it said. "Your way is now clear before you."

"Is it indeed?" said Maewen. "Welcome back. Where were you when I needed you to warn me about the *other* man with a knife?"

At the stream Mitt discovered that it *was* possible to be colder. The water was icy. It must have been snowmelt from some high mountain out of sight from here. The bits of him he could bear to dip in turned blue. He washed in a hurry, with great splashings and snortings, and put his clothes back on quickly. The sun was up by then. It was no wonder he was cold, Mitt saw. The stream was in deep blue shadow. But there was misty yellow sunlight on the boulders. Shivering all over, Mitt went over there to get warm.

He could hear Noreth talking on the other side of the rocks, and a deep voice answering her. So Hestefan or Wend was up. Mitt went cheerfully round the boulders.

"You were in no danger. Help was at hand whether I warned you or not," the deep voice said.

Mitt stood, confounded. Noreth was brushing Navis's mare and entirely on her own. He could see Wend, still asleep by the dead fire in the distance. Navis was the other hump. And Hestefan was just crawling out of the cart.

She said the One spoke to her, Mitt thought. But I never really believed it till now. He backed quietly away behind the boulders so that Noreth would not think he was prying and stood in the sun there. But he could still hear both voices.

Maewen said, "I'm not going down into the dales anymore. I'm staying up on the green roads. Wend says I'm safe here."

"You are not safe here," said the deep voice.

There was a pause. "Why not?" came Noreth's voice. She sounded quite calm. Mitt was not to know Maewen was shaking all over. He was thinking he had better back away some more, out of hearing, when the deep voice answered.

"The Southern youth you call Mitt," it said, "is the worst danger you have encountered yet. You must kill him before he destroys you."

After this Mitt could no more have moved than he could have flown.

"But Mitt *rescued* me from the second murderer," Maewen protested.

"For his own ends," said the voice. "And this Mitt will not be easy to kill while the man Navis is alive. Navis will defend Mitt for *his* own ends. For this reason I advise you to kill them both at the same time."

"You can't mean this!" Maewen said.

"After you have found the Adon's sword, both of them are expendable," said the voice. "Stab them as they sleep, the night before you reach Kernsburgh."

"Really?" said Maewen. "And what about Wend and Moril and Hestefan? Are they expendable, too?"

"I told you," the voice replied imperturbably, "you will need the Singer-boy to find you the crown. After that, he will be as much of a liability as the Southerners, and you may stab him as soon as you have an opportunity."

"You're asking me"—said Maewen; she was trying not to giggle, even though it was not funny at all—"you're asking me to arrive at Kernsburgh with nothing but a pile of corpses."

"You will be joined there by a sizable army. Display the bodies as the bodies of traitors and explain that all traitors to the crown must suffer the same fate."

"Thanks a bunch!" said Maewen. "That's quite a program!"

"Do as I say," said the voice, and the deep notes of it made both Mitt and Maewen shudder, "or fail, and die yourself."

There was silence then. Mitt stood where he was until he heard vigorous horse-grooming noises from the other side of the boulders. Then he did his best to walk casually over to the camp. Nobody there seemed to notice that he was shaking all over. But they were all cold and all shivering.

Breakfast was nasty. There was no decent bread. The outsides of all the cheeses had gone moldy. Almost the only thing eatable was the pickled cherries, and Mitt discovered that he hated them by now.

They moved on up the stretched and windy valley, and neither Mitt nor Maewen spoke to anyone much that morning.

Maewen's thoughts were chaos. *Was* it the One who spoke to her? Or was it just a time-confused part of her own mind, reacting with violence to the violence she had met in Gardale? There was no doubt she had been in danger from *someone*. Or if it was the One, he was angry. Those he had singled out—Mitt and Moril had tried to steal the cup, and Navis had taken it. She had known during the song that Navis had done something awful. It might be because of the cup. But it did not really matter *what* spoke or why. It hurt. Maewen's head was now full of nasty suspicions of Navis, Mitt, and Moril. Right back at the beginning of this ride, she had seen that each of them had come to follow her for their own secret reasons, and Mitt and Navis had shown her some of those reasons in Gardale. It was Hildy who was important to them. That hurt.

Oh, I want to go *home*! Maewen thought this so strongly that she almost said it aloud. In fact, she did utter a sort of noise, which caused Hestefan and his mule, who happened to be alongside her just then, both to turn and look at her. But no sooner had she almost said it than she saw she did not quite mean it. She wanted to find out what had happened to Noreth and to try to change history, even though she knew now that one of those three was going to do her some terrible harm. Correction. *Mitt* was going to do her some terrible harm. Navis was a cool customer, Moril was a deep one, and he had that cwidder, but Mitt was the one who did things. The knowledge made her throat ache, as if Mitt had tried to strangle her—and maybe he *had*, at the inn in Gardale.

Mitt kept thinking, This is a *laugh*! The One was playing games with him. Or he had it in for Mitt, which was much more likely. Mitt wanted to ride away from the whole mess. It would be lovely to settle down on a farm, somewhere near enough the South to be like what he was used to, and leave the One to stew. But he needed his half of the golden statue for that, and Noreth was not likely to part with it now. Not now she knew Mitt had been told to kill her. Anyway, he had to stay with her until Kernsburgh. If Hildy was safe, Ynen was not, and Kialan might not manage to bring Ynen there after all. He would have laughed at the mess if he'd felt like laughing. Meanwhile, he had to warn Navis and Moril somehow. And talking of warnings, that dream had been a warning, hadn't it just!

Mitt came out of his thoughts to find he was warm—more than warm, almost too hot, for a wonder. He undid his jacket. There was light, white rain steaming over them, but he was too warm to care. This makes a change! he thought. It must be almost record heat for the North.

They had come out of the stretched valley and were now following the green path across a high gorse-grown heath. The mountains had melted to white-purple distance, and the one behind, Mitt saw, peering through the misty bands of rain, did indeed have snow on the top of it.

"Where is this? Why is it so hot?" he said. It was the first thing he had said since breakfast.

Moril grinned at him. "Welcome back. It's the Shield of Oreth."

"It is a large upland that opens toward the South," Hestefan explained from beside Moril on the driving seat. Schoolmaster again, Maewen thought. The warmth was making her feel better. "We'll be having the warm air from now until Kernsburgh. This used to be fine land. Even in the Adon's day it was full of people."

Hang on! Maewen thought, coming properly out of her misery. If this was the Shield, she had looked out the train at it. There had been farmlands and factories, trees and towns. But Hestefan could be right. Up among the gorse and heather on either side there were piles of stone in faint, broken squares, which could have been ruined houses.

"Where did all the people go?" she asked.

"Fled in the wars after the Adon died," said Moril.

"Who owns it now?" Navis asked, looking out over bracken and heather beyond the gorse bushes as if he would not mind owning some of it himself.

As Hestefan went into a complicated account that suggested that Hannart or Dropwater might have a claim, but nobody wanted this land, anyway, Maewen frowned. She rather thought Navis would be owning some of it before long. The Duke of Kernsburgh owned the big brewery here in her day. Would she dare change history to the extent of cutting Navis out of it? *Could* she? No, of course not. That was a relief. But that did not apply to Mitt or Moril, who were not really in history at all.

She looked sideways at Mitt. He was turning his head to watch a slightly bigger pile of stones with an old apple tree drooped over them. I could farm here, he thought. It would take a deal of hard work, but I reckon it would be peaceful.

The rain blew away into the mountains, leaving a tearful sort of blue sky overhead. Everyone steamed in the heat. And the cart went along in its own cloud made of wreathing spirals of steam. Flies came out of the heather and circled the horses. They made the Countess-horse restive, but Mitt rode along with his chin down, hardly noticing. That dream was nagging at him. Farming had not been in it anywhere. Something was wrong.

By this time they were seeing occasional small farms built of gray stone, with square fields around them scratched out of the heather. The Shield was not quite as derelict as Maewen had thought. The farms grew bigger and more frequent as they went on. By midday, when they stopped to eat, there was farmland all round, and walled lanes leading to distant farmhouses on both sides of the green road. There were even a few trees. They stopped to eat under a mighty old ash on a corner by a lane.

Navis reveled in the heat. While the horses crowded into the shade with Maewen and Hestefan, Navis sat against the drystone wall in the sun and stretched both arms out. "This is more like it!" he said to Mitt.

"It is and all," Mitt agreed. "First time I've been warm since I came North. I'll be back in a moment." He picked up a couple of pickled onions—better than those cherries—and a handful of the manky cheese and set off up the lane. That dream was now mixing in his mind with what he had heard this morning, and he wanted to be alone to think. Something was badly wrong.

He almost wondered whether he might not simply walk away. He came to another lane and turned into it because it was narrow and had no walls and he felt freer there. He climbed higher with it, until he was walking in the warm wind between low hedges with a field of grain on either side. Gray-green both fields were, like the sea over sand in dangerous shallows. The barley on the right surged in the wind, in green waves over silky white, as if it were the sea indeed. The wheat on the other side stood stiffer, and the wind rasped in it like sea over shingle. But the land smell was wrong for the sea, dusty and juicy.

Great homesickness overtook Mitt. "Flaming Ammet!" he said. "Why did I ever leave the coast?"

"You know you had no choice," someone told him.

# 16

MITT'S HEAD SNAPPED UP. A tall golden man came walking along the lane toward him and bent his head in a solemn nod of greeting as Mitt looked. At this season Old Ammet had a face that was neither young nor old. He could have been the same age as Navis, except that the long golden hair blowing about his head and shoulders made him seem young.

"Now it's you," Mitt said. "Why do you Undying keep pushing me about?"

"It's not our fault, Alhammitt," Old Ammet answered. "The times are pushing *us*. And I should remind you that when you chose the wind's road, you chose the green road, too."

"I know, I know," Mitt said. "Once I got on, there's never been a moment I could have got off. But I keep having to choose all the same! And every time I choose and try to get right, things turn round on me and try to make me go the other way. The One told Noreth to kill me this morning—and Navis and Moril. You tell me what I'm supposed to do about that!"

Old Ammet looked at him gravely, in a way that reminded Mitt of Wend all of a sudden, except that Old Ammet was blowing and rustling in the wind. "I am not here to tell you what to do."

"No," Mitt said bitterly. "You Undying never do give a straight answer. You just push."

"It is not my place," said Ammet, "to question our Grand Father, whom they call the One. His law is that we do not tell his mortal family what to do. That is to make people into puppets."

"Then the One just broke his own law," Mitt said.

"I am here to tell you to think about that," said Ammet.

There was a silence full of the warm wind and the rustling and streaming of Ammet's white-blond hair, while Mitt digested this. "I don't get it," he said at last. He found Old Ammet looking so kind that it made him feel terrible.

"I should remind you that we gave you our names to say at need," Old Ammet said.

Mitt nodded. He felt his face screw up. There were indeed four names, the greater and lesser names of Old Ammet and Libby Beer, tucked away in the corner of Mitt's mind. That part of his head always felt like a sore tooth, where you kept putting your tongue even though you knew it would hurt. "You mean, I could say your biggest name at her?"

Ammet laughed. It felt as if the wind had turned to a warm gale. "That name is not to be used that lightly. It will be many a long year before you will need to say my Great Name. But you have three other names. I am here to tell you that if you use those names properly, the Shield of Oreth can be covered again with fields like these."

His hand spread to show Mitt the surging barley and the stiff rustling wheat. Mitt looked wistfully, thinking of that farm he might have. "You'd like that, wouldn't you?" he said.

"We would, Alhammitt," Old Ammet agreed. He smiled at Mitt, rather sadly, over his shoulder among his flying hair, as he walked away round a turn in the lane.

Mitt stood looking a moment. The lane ran straight as a ruler through the two fields. Then he sighed and turned to go back.

Moril was standing a few yards down the hill. The two of them simply stared at one another for a moment. Then Moril licked his lips and cleared his throat. Still, his voice came out scratchy with awe. "Wh-who was that?"

"Old Ammet," said Mitt. "The Earth Shaker." His voice was not in much better shape. "What are you doing here?"

"You forgot to take any bread," Moril said.

"It was like a flaming gray rock this morning," Mitt said. "There'll be critters in it by now."

"Well, anyway, I brought—" Moril started to hold out the bundle in his hands. And stopped and stared at it. Then he unwrapped the cloth and held out a crusty new loaf. Mitt could smell the newness of it on the wind. He looked ruefully down at the cheese and onions he had not yet bothered to eat. The onions were the same but the cheese was now a fresh pale wedge. It smelled as wonderful as the bread.

He held it out to Moril. "Want some?"

Moril nodded. He arranged the cwidder on his back and sat down by the hedge. As Mitt sat down beside him, it occurred to him that this cwidder was as much of a sore place to Moril as those names were to him—and more of a nuisance, too. Moril had barely let go of the thing since Hestefan had threatened to take it away.

They tore the crusty fresh loaf in two, broke the cheese in half, and ate like wolves. "All the same," Mitt said, going back to what Moril had first said, "it's not like you to run after me with bread."

"I wasn't spying," Moril said, with as much dignity as someone who is crunching a pickled onion can. "I only *saw* him. I didn't hear a word he was saying. And he must have known I was there, because of the bread."

"So?" said Mitt.

"Something's wrong," said Moril. "This morning I was on top of the rocks, trying to get warm. I heard that voice telling her to kill us."

Mitt felt his appetite go. "And?"

Moril swallowed the pickled onion as if it was a lump in his throat. "I heard it before. I heard it tell her to find the Adon's gifts. It seemed all right then."

Mitt went on eating although his appetite had gone. If you had once been poor in Holand, you never wasted a chance to eat. "So what do you think?"

Moril was eating in the same dutiful way. Singers met hard times, too. "I think," he said, "that it isn't the One that speaks to her."

Mitt knew this was why Old Ammet had looked kind. It was something he did not want to think about. "Who is it then?"

"Kankredin," said Moril.

So it was out. Mitt nodded. "I think you're right. You know what this means, then?"

"He started talking to her when she was young and worked her up to this gradually," Moril said, thinking about it. "He's disembodied, so he could pretend to be the One."

"Probably, but I don't mean that," Mitt said. "Just stop and think what it means if she got to be Queen. *She* may be all right, but she'd go everywhere with this voice telling her to do what Kankredin wants. And she'd do it, too. She does."

"But," said Moril, "this morning she was sounding sarcastic, rather the way your Navis does."

"Maybe, but she'll do it in the end," Mitt said. "Don't you see? He works her along, like you said. He tells her she's got to be Queen and she's the One's daughter, and she sets out to ride for the crown. For all we know, she's got no claim at all. Alk thought not. It means this whole ride is a load of old crab apples."

"So what should we do?" Moril asked.

Mitt smiled his most unfunny smile. "It looks as if I better do what the Countess and your Keril wanted in the first place. Kill her somehow. It's a laugh!"

It was a horrible thing to say. Mitt almost choked on it, thinking of Noreth's nervous, freckly look—which seemed to get to him more now he knew her so much better—and how plain frightened she had been when that man attacked her in the Lawschool. He was still surprised at how *very* frightened she had been. She would be the same, or worse, when she found Mitt after her.

He was fervently relieved when Moril said, firmly and quietly, "No."

"But she's got to be stopped," Mitt protested hopefully.

"Yes, but if she's dead," Moril said, "won't Kankredin just move on to somebody else? Somebody who's more—you know—ruthless?"

Like Navis, Mitt thought. That would be worse. The idea snapped his brain clean out of the bind Keril and the Countess seemed to have put on it. "Then it's Kankredin we ought to go after." This was the way Old Ammet had been trying to make him think, he realized. "Can this cwidder of yours do anything there?"

Moril put his chin on his knees and twiddled the last crust of his bread while he thought. "It's got to be truth," he said. "I think, if we could catch him talking to her again, I could make him appear in his true shape. Would that be enough?"

"Could be just right!" Mitt said. "I've a name or two up my sleeve I could use as long as I know where he is."

Moril put the crust of bread in his mouth. "I hoped you might have," he said, munching it. "There are stories about you."

They got up and dusted off crumbs. "Don't give Kankredin any kind of hint," Mitt said.

"What do you take me for?" said Moril. They smiled at one another, conspirators, but not at all happy about it.

Mitt thought, as they walked back between the rustling corn, The worst of it is, if it goes wrong. I might have to kill her, anyway. The hot sun seemed to weigh on him. He felt as if he was in mourning already.

The others were waiting impatiently under the ash tree. They said, almost in chorus, "Where *were* you?" The rest of the bad gray bread had been tipped into the ditch. Mitt and Moril looked at it guiltily.

"We got lost," Moril said. "I think we ought to stop at a farm for more bread."

"Teach your grandmother," said Maewen. Mitt could see her, as they mounted and rode on, looking from him to Moril and wondering what they had been plotting. She had her nervous, freckly look. He knew he ought to do something about it, but the Countess-horse was balky in the heat and kept Mitt busy wrestling with it all through the long, blazing afternoon. Despite his warning to Moril, Mitt kept wanting to tell the horse, Cheer up! Come Kernsburgh, you could be carrying my dead body! He could see himself, too, dead hands trailing on one side, limp boots swinging on the other, and the whole thing starting to smell in the heat. He had to keep biting his tongue not to say it.

Maewen and he did not say one word to each other until they were camped that night—in a proper field with cowpats in it, near a farm. While Wend and Navis were away at the farm, buying bread, and Mitt and Maewen were doing the horses, Mitt took a deep breath and said, "Are we not on speaking terms or something?"

She jumped and turned to him gratefully. "Yes. Probably. You didn't have to wait under that tree and listen to Navis and Hestefan being sarky to one another."

Though Mitt knew there was much more to it than that, he said, "If you shoot someone's horse, he's not likely to love you. Mind you," he added, watching Hestefan fussily washing down the wheels of the cart, "if that Hestefan wasn't a Singer, he'd be teaching school and living alone in a house with the door barred."

"Yes! Wouldn't he!" Maewen said, quite delighted.

They chatted lightheartedly after that, until they saw Wend and Navis returning with cans of milk and armfuls of cheese and bread. Maewen said guiltily, "Oh dear. I bet Navis paid for it all. I hate the way we seem to be living off him."

Mitt's attitude to money was much more carefree. "Well, we can't hardly wave a golden statue at them," he said.

It was the wrong thing to say. She gave him a nervous, freckly look and went off to meet Navis. Mitt sighed. All the same, he and Moril took good care never to be far away from Maewen in case the voice spoke to her again. But nothing happened that night.

When they went on next morning, they found the farms thinning out again, giving way to more and more bracken and tumbled rocks. The Shield here descended slightly in a series of waves, downward toward Dropwater and the coast, and the green road went with it, up and over and down, up and over and down. The warm, itchy rain came over in waves, too. You could look back and see each white shower traveling back along the way you had come, up and up and up, like a ghost going upstairs, until it was lost in the high green distance.

In the middle of the afternoon Mitt was looking back after the latest shower, having watched it as it came climbing up and swept over them, when he thought he could see a darkish blot, right up at the top, where the road and the rain went out of sight. Next time he looked, the blot was more definite, wavering forward in the high distance.

"Ay-ay," he said. "Looks like there might be a troop of horses coming down behind."

Heads snapped round. Hestefan and Moril leaned out on either side of the cart. It was what everyone had been dreading.

"Looks to be at least twenty," Wend said.

"In good order," said Navis. "Quite a body of hearthmen, I would say. Can anyone see what livery?"

"Too far off," said Hestefan.

"But coming quite fast," said Moril.

"And they must have seen us," said Navis, "if we can see them." He turned to Wend. "Is there anywhere we can get off this road while we're in a dip and they can't see us?"

Wend's solemn face twisted anxiously. "Not for some miles."

"Then get in the cart," said Navis. "Let's get there as fast as we can."

Wend took three running strides and heaved himself over the tail-gate of the cart. Hestefan whipped up the mule. The cart set off rattling up the next rise, and the rest of them kept pace. It was maddeningly slow to Maewen. The mule was trying, but the cart was heavy, and it slowed down over every long, undulating rise. She grew a crick in her neck from looking back. The horsemen were gaining steadily. Every time she looked, there were fewer hills between them. Before long, they could tell that there were, in fact, only about fifteen of them. But as Mitt said, that was quite enough against six.

"Perhaps they aren't after us at all," Maewen said hopefully.

"Would you bet on that?" Navis asked. "Between us we have stolen a cup and a ring and attempted to start an uprising. I *wish* I could see the livery. That would give us a clue."

*And* stolen a horse, Maewen thought guiltily, looking at the patient ears of the horse she had hoped was Noreth's. Would someone ride all the way from Adenmouth after a stolen horse in these days? She wished she knew.

"And someone may think we sneaked Hildy along," Mitt said, with his head turned back over his shoulder. "Are they Hannart?"

The rain was blinding over in white clouds. It was never possible to see the horsemen except as a wavering dark blur, but they saw them most of the time. When the cart was down in a dip, the blur was cresting a rise, and as the cart labored uphill, the pursuers had already been down in the next dip and were wavering into sight again. They came closer and closer.

Navis was looking off into what could be seen of the countryside. It rose steeper and steeper to the left and not so steep to the right. Most of it was covered in head-high bracken. If they did go off the road, the cart would make tracks in that bracken that a blind man could follow. "How much farther?" Navis snapped at Wend.

"Just down to the river," Wend said anxiously. "Not far."

By the time they came down the last slope to see a small river cutting across the green road, the horsemen were only three hills behind. They were almost invisible in what seemed to be a final cloud of rain. As the cart splashed into the moist edge of the river, weak sunlight traveled after the rain and made everything golden white.

"Stop a moment," Wend called. He leaned out of the back of the cart. "Will you play your cwidder now?" he asked Moril.

Moril leaned out to look at him. "Does it matter what?"

"Yes." Wend jumped down into squashy turf. "Play anything you can think of about the witch Cennoreth," he said, going to the mule's head.

Moril wrenched the cover away from the cwidder and hurriedly plucked out the chorus to "The Weaver's Song":

*Thread the shuttle, throw the*
*shuttle,*
*Weave the close-bound yarn.*

As he moved on to the tune of the verses, Wend led mule and cart in a half circle, with much splashing and swaying, until it was facing up to the left, along the riverbank.

"Follow me upriver," he said to the others, under the music.

They rode after him along the wet grassy verge, none of them very hopeful. The light was brighter and more golden than before. Mitt looked at the tracks of the cart and the prints the horses were leaving and thought that even in another shower of rain the riders behind could hardly miss them. Maewen wondered if Moril had got the music wrong in his hurry. She knew "The Weaver's Song," and she had never known it had anything to do with the witch Cennoreth. Navis rode trying to look back up the green road, but the rise of the land cut off the view almost at once.

"This is going to take a miracle," he murmured.

The lawnlike riverbank turned into a proper track, leading easily upward among bracken and rocks. As the cart clattered onto the higher, rockier part, they all distinctly heard the drumming of several dozen hooves, mixed with the rattle of tack and mail, and a few voices. Navis stopped his mare and, in a resigned way, fetched out his pistol and cocked it. Above, the cart went on, and Moril continued to play.

To everyone's amazement, the drumming of hooves barely paused. It slowed and broke into separate noises, but that was mixed with the splashing of water and the *clack* of rolled stones as the party crossed the river. Then the regular drumming took up again and faded off into the distance.

"Missed us!" Mitt said. He could hardly believe it.

"Let's hope they don't come back before we're out of sight," Navis said, turning his mare back to the path.

Above the rocky section, the river was a mere stream, flowing out of a fair-sized lake, cupped inside steep black crags. The banks were squashy with marsh, but the path avoided it by mounting higher, among clumps of tall rushes. Maewen could not resist leaning sideways to trail her hand in the feathery heads. They were the scented kind of rushes. Clouds of strong pollen filled the air with a lovely smell, like nothing else she knew. Mitt sneezed. Navis pushed through the rushes in clouds of more pollen and caught up with the cart. Moril had stopped playing by then.

"Are you sure this is safe?" Navis asked Wend.

"Of course, sir," Wend said. "This is Dropthwaite where my sister's croft is. No one can find us here." He smiled in his pent-up way and pointed out into the lake where a number of fat white ducks were swimming beside a patch of white-flowering weed. "Those are my sister's ducks." The way he smiled, Maewen thought he and his sister must have some private joke about them.

# 17

THEY CAME THROUGH the rushes to find a small ragged field with a stone trough in the middle. Hens wandered there. Two goats were tethered farther off, and there was a vegetable garden beyond that. The croft was a low stone house built against the crags, among fruit trees and lilacs. Everything was warm and fragrant because the rocks went round the holding in a high horseshoe and cut off all but the west wind.

Wend walked through the orchard with long strides and knocked at the house door. It was opened almost at once by an old woman leaning on a stick.

"His sister?" Navis said, watching the two talking eagerly together.

"More like his granny," said Mitt. "Still, we might get a bed for the night out of it." And a bedroom had a door you could bar, in case Kankredin persuaded Noreth to do her killing now.

Oh yes! Maewen thought. And a *bath*!

Navis looked nervously back down the path. "They won't find us here," Moril said to him. "Promise." Navis looked at Moril's cwidder, but not as if he was convinced.

Wend came striding back. He seemed almost as carefree as when he had taken charge of the cwidder. "She says you're welcome to camp in this field here," he said cheerfully. "And if the young ones like to go to the door when the horses are seen to, she'll have milk and eggs and cheese ready for you." Whistling a little tune, he untethered the goats and led them away round the side of the house.

Bother! Mitt and Maewen thought, though both for different reasons.

"The old lady likes her privacy, I see," Hestefan said glumly. Evidently he had been hoping for a bed, too.

"It's not a very big house," Moril said as he unhitched the mule. Apart from Wend, he was the only one who was happy with the arrangement. Navis continued to watch the path, and he insisted on setting up the camp where it could not be seen by anyone coming up from the lake. This meant a long trudge across the grass to the trough, which Mitt felt was unnecessary. He was the one who fetched the water. The trough fascinated him. Clear water bubbled up in it the whole time, but it never, for some reason, overflowed.

When the horses were rubbed down and feeding, Moril jerked his head toward the house. Mitt winked and left Navis to see about the rest. They were both a little put out to find Maewen coming with them through the orchard trees. They did not consider Noreth as one of the young ones. Maewen saw it. But she had come along almost without thinking, and it seemed a little late to go back now. Besides, she was curious about this sister of Wend's.

Wend opened the door to them. "Come you in," he said. "This way."

He led them quickly through a kitchen-room and opened a door to the back of the house. Maewen looked around curiously, but all she had time to see was a scrubbed wooden table and a banked-up fire of smoky peat, with a copper kettle singing on it. The room at the back of the house was even harder to see at first. It had only one window, which was half blocked by a big loom with woolen cloth being woven on it. It smelled of warm wood and, even more, of slightly oily wool. The ceiling was low and beamed. The walls were dark from being paneled in old wood—very beautifully carved, in a mass of half-seen designs—and the rest of the dim space was nearly full of stack upon stack of tall, chubby wooden things. These things were where the wool smell was coming from. Large bobbins, they seemed to be, wound with woolen yarn of every conceivable color.

Wend's sister got up from her seat at the loom and edged through the bobbins toward them. She was tall, and she moved very spryly. When she was near enough to be seen clearly, all of them had a moment when they thought the old woman who answered the door must have been Wend's old mother. Then they realized she was the same lady. But she looked much younger, though older than Wend. Her face was thin and only a little lined, and her hair was white, mass upon mass of it, wriggly and curly and pinned back with combs that glittered black among the white. Mitt thought there was just a look of the Countess about her, but a kinder look than the Countess's. Maewen, too, found this lady reminded her of someone, but she could not place it. She thought she must have been stunning when she was younger, when all that hair was surely flaxen fair. The lady's eyes were still stunning, huge and blue-green.

"I'm pleased to meet all of you," she said. Her voice was much more educated than Wend's, and that reminded Mitt of the Countess, too. "I hear you're looking for the Adon's sword."

"Oh, did Wend tell you?" said Maewen. "Yes. We've got his cup and"—she held up her hand with the ring on its thumb—"this."

"Then one of you is truly riding the royal road," the lady said, looking from Maewen, to Moril, to Mitt, with very strong interest. "At last! I thought no one would ever get round to it again! Very well. The sword is here. You'd better see if you can get it down."

"The sword is *here*!" Moril was so astonished that his voice went up into a squeak.

The lady swung round on him. "What makes you so surprised?"

"Well," Moril said awkwardly, "I heard . . . the Singers say . . . that the Adon's wife—Manaliabrid—hid his sword when she went back to the Undy—er, her own people."

"And so she did," said Wend's sister. "My poor daughter. She'd thought her Adon was of the Undying, too—and as I told her, so he might have been for all we knew, but when a man sets himself up as King, he puts himself in the way of assassins, and sooner or later one of them will strike lucky. There are many ways to kill the Undying, though we don't die easily."

"Manaliabrid," said Moril, "is your daughter?"

"That's right," said the lady. She folded her arms and looked amused at the awe in Moril's face. "And the name you'll have heard for me is Cennoreth. Am I right?"

"Then you're a witch," said Mitt.

"You're the Weaver," said Moril.

Both of them turned to look at Wend. "My sister is both," he said.

"So I should hope!" Cennoreth snapped.

"But you—" Moril said to Wend.

"Tanamoril," said Cennoreth, energetically making her way between the piles of bobbins, "Osfameron, Oril, Wend, Mage Mallard—when a person lives a long time, names tend to pile up. Now, do you want this sword or not? Here it is."

There was a fireplace at the end of the room opposite the window, made of stone as beautifully carved as the wooden walls. Hung on the wooden panels above the stone was a long dark thing. Maewen and Mitt both took it at first for a stuffed fish. But when they had edged over there along the narrow path between the bobbins, they saw it was actually a sword, probably quite a plain one, in a blackish leather sheath.

The reason it was so hard to see in that dim room was that it was tied to the wall by innumerable long strips of leather. The leather thongs had been knotted to about a hundred rusty nails hammered into the paneling above and below the sword, and then knotted and overlapped and knotted again, until the sword was in a kind of basket of leather strips.

"Hey, Moril!" said Mitt.

Moril was still over by the door, looking across his shoulder at Wend, full of awe and amazement. Mitt could hardly blame him. This was the man Moril had been named after, twice over, the hero of half the stories the Singers learned to tell, and Moril's own ancestor into the bargain. Wend was shifting about self-consciously, as if—just like a normal person—he had no idea what to say. He was obviously relieved when Moril switched his attention to Mitt.

While Moril was making his way through the bobbins, grinning and going like a sleepwalker, Wend said awkwardly, "These things happen—if you live long enough. You should think nothing of it—or not too much."

"Think nothing of it!" Moril said, looking up at the sword and its thongs. "That's asking a bit much! Those pieces of leather are knots and crosses. There has to be a catch."

"Quite right." Cennoreth stood by the hearth with her arms folded. "You're an observant boy. You must understand that none of it is my doing. My daughter nailed it up there. Remember she was mad with grief—though I suppose you're all too young to know how that feels—and try to forgive her. She was disappointed in her children, too. She expected too much of them, but there you go, I'm only her mother, and it didn't matter what I said. So she set this sword up, knots and crosses, like redhead said, for the children of her blood and the Adon's. That's rather a lot of people these days, but that's another thing she wouldn't listen to, when I told her how it would be if enough time passed."

"So what's the catch?" Mitt asked.

Cennoreth shrugged. "The knots must be undone without touching sword or scabbard, and the sword must be drawn before it touches wood, stone, or earth. My daughter," she said, "expected too much of her children's children, too, if you ask me, but I wasn't consulted."

They all stared up at the sword in its cat's cradle of leather. The thongs were black with age, and there was dust all over them. Maewen could see that each knot, beside being pulled fiercely tight to start with, had shrunk and hardened over the years—how many? two hundred?—and must by now be nearly impossible to undo. Just to think of the lasting fierceness of the misery that did this was appalling. Could one wet the leather and loosen the knots that way? "What happens if you break the rules?" she asked.

"She didn't say," said Cennoreth.

"Though you may take it that you won't get the sword, lady," Wend added from the other side of the room.

They stared up at the sword again. It was high above Maewen's reach. I suppose if I knelt on the mantelpiece—the leather could just be old enough to crumble away when I touch it. Anyway, I don't really *need* this sword—though it seems a shame, when I've got the ring and the cup.

Moril thought awhile. Then he sat down on the nearest pile of bobbins and started taking the case off his cwidder.

"What are you doing?" Mitt asked him.

"The leather was straight to start with," Moril said. "The cwidder could tell the truth and make it straight again."

It could, too! Mitt realized. Things unfolded with a crisp *snap* inside his head, and he saw that he and Moril had been so taken by surprise that they had not thought this through. Why don't I *think*? he asked himself angrily. If Kankredin was talking to Noreth, and Noreth had listened to him all her life, then even if he and Moril could do for Kankredin—which was a stupid thing to plan when even the One could not do it—then the last thing either of them should do was to help Noreth become Queen. That meant the whole country under Kankredin. So—break the rules, quick.

Mitt was the only one tall enough to reach the sword. "No. That's going at it the slow way," he told Moril.

Moril's fingers went slow and fumbling on the cwidder. As Mitt turned away and pulled out his knife, he knew Moril had seen the danger, too. Mitt pushed between Maewen and Cennoreth, reached up, and, quick as he could, slashed along the length of the sword, between the multitude of knots.

"Get ready to catch it!" he cried out merrily.

He had meant to call out too late. But to his annoyance, not all the age-hard thongs parted. He was forced to slash again, and again after that. Even then only the pointed end of the scabbard came loose. Mitt watched it with satisfaction, descending slowly to the mantelshelf, tearing the other thongs as it came.

Maewen yelled out, "Careful!" and flung herself forward with both arms up at full stretch. She was just in time to catch the tip of it. The cwidder resounded as Moril set it hastily down and jumped forward to pretend to help her. He grabbed hold of the scabbard above Maewen's hands and blundered artfully around her. But Maewen hung on grimly.

All Moril managed to do was dislodge a long iron-handled hearth brush from beside the grate. It fell among their legs with a clatter.

Bother! Mitt thought. Hadd's *pants*! He took hold of the sword's hilt, thongs and all, and pulled. That ought to bring it down *and* make sure it touched the wall or the fireplace on the way.

The hearth brush seemed to set off an avalanche. Fire irons went on falling, with mighty clangs: ladles, toasting forks, a slotted spoon, shovels, two pokers, a mighty black roasting spit, a set of hooks for cauldrons. Cennoreth seemed to have a whole blacksmith's worth of implements in her hearth. Maewen and Moril stumbled on a firedog. Mitt found long tongs between his legs and reeled aside. This burst the last of the thongs. Maewen and Moril crashed backward onto Cennoreth's feet, both trying to save themselves by hanging on to the scabbard. Mitt was left holding aloft a naked sword.

It was indeed a very plain blade, he saw. "I reckon we broke all the rules there," he said in mock regret.

"You touched at least half a dozen knots," Moril gasped hopefully.

There was a strange look on Cennoreth's face. Possibly she was trying not to laugh. "No, he didn't," she said. "I was watching quite carefully. Which of you is supposed to be having the sword?"

"She is," said Moril.

"Then please give it to her and then clear up my hearth," Cennoreth said. "I think I'd better look at my weaving."

Maewen got to her knees and held the scabbard out. Mitt slithered the sword inside it with an angry flourish. It looked ceremonial, done that way. Mitt had not the slightest doubt that Manaliabrid would consider that Noreth had won the sword. He turned away disgustedly to help Moril collect fire irons and prop them in noisy bundles by the grate. *Clatter*. It was not that simple to defeat Kankredin's plans. *Clang. Boing*. Well, it wouldn't be, would it? Kankredin was of the Undying, and that meant strong. After all, Old Ammet was so strong that just saying one of his na— Oh flaming *pants*! Mitt stopped with pokers bundled to his chest and looked up at the dangling, broken thongs and torn-out nails. *This* was why the Earth Shaker had reminded him of those names! And he had never even thought of using one. *Clatter*—flaming—CRASH. There.

Dejectedly Mitt followed Moril and Maewen over to the window. Wend was standing, leaning on the loom, watching Cennoreth smooth and smooth at the most recently woven end of her cloth. You could see the likeness between them now, Maewen thought, although Wend looked so smooth and young. But she also saw another likeness. That dreamy, devoted way Cennoreth was smoothing at her weaving was like

Mum's, when Mum was on a new statue. They were rather the same shape, though Mum's hair was straighter and darker. Cennoreth clicked her tongue and shook her head as she stroked the cloth, again like Mum. A comb fell out of her hair, and she rammed it back impatiently. That was even more like Mum. "This is a pretty snarl!" she said.

It was odd cloth—even odder than Mum's sculptures, which Maewen secretly considered quite mad. At first sight it looked as if the witch had used every color off all the bobbins at random, changing color so often that it all went down to reddish brown muddle. But after you had looked at it awhile, letters seemed to appear in the weave, small and close and almost making words. Then just as you thought you had found a word, you found instead patterns, large patterns and small ones, rambling and winding all over the cloth in various bright colors. The pattern Cennoreth was smoothing at was a rusty orange that suddenly turned into bright red. Indeed, it had turned red so suddenly and recently that the scarlet yarn was still in the shuttle, hanging down from the half-woven edge in a row of other shuttles, ready to be used in the next line.

"There's no need to stare," Cennoreth said. "My grandfather asked me to go on weaving. It's not my fault it comes out as it does. Just look at this! I can't think what you're doing with my son-in-law's sword, young woman. You're not who you should be at all. What's your real name?"

Their four faces stared at Maewen, and the shock on three of those faces was lurid in the low light from the window. Moril's mouth came open. Wend was white. He and Mitt both edged back from Maewen, and Mitt frowned, calculating and enlightened, as this cleared up several mysteries he had not properly considered before.

Maewen backed, too, clutching the sword. She felt she might have dissolved with horror without something to hang on to. "M-Maewen," she said. Cennoreth looked at her. Under those accusing blue-green eyes, Maewen found she had to correct herself. "Er, Mayelbridwen Singer, really."

"Hmm. That sounds like an outlandish version of my daughter's name," Cennoreth said. "Where are you from?"

"The present—I mean, your future," Maewen confessed.

Everyone was startled. "That can't be *possible*!" Wend said.

"Oh yes—or at least, it's quite true," said Cennoreth. "That red snarl is from no bobbin here in this room. I was planning how to get that color dye, but I haven't done it yet—though I suppose I will in time. I *thought* it felt strange when I threaded the shuttle the other day, but there's been a fog, and the light wasn't good. I didn't really see it till now."

Wend seemed completely shattered. His face looked older than his sister's. "Unpick—unpick it!" he burst out. "Before it's too late, Tanaqui—unpick!"

"Don't be silly," said his sister.

"But you've unpicked before!" Wend said.

"Not often and not for centuries," she retorted. "And only when the One has asked it of me."

"But *I* asked you last time!" Wend cried out. He seemed quite desperate. "Don't you remember? I asked you when that slimy traitor killed the Adon. You unpicked then!"

"Duck, that was unpicking a death," she said, very seriously. "You wouldn't want me to unpick a living person."

"Why not?" Wend demanded. "She's an impostor. Unpick! Send her back! I don't want her here!"

Maewen clutched the sword and stared from one to the other. Wend must be mad, after all. "But you *do* want me!" she said. "You sent me here! You told me in the palace you wanted me to take Noreth's place!"

Wend rounded on her, so angry and tall and so full of queer power that she backed away again. "I do not want you! Why should I send you here?"

"Because," Maewen faltered, "because the real Noreth disappeared and you know I look—"

*"Disappeared!"* Wend shouted. His eyes were not mad, Maewen saw, but so full of grief and shock and anger that they glared as if he was not really seeing her.

"I thought you knew," she said. "What you said, you know, by the waystone—at Adenmouth—"

*"What!"* said Wend. "For so long?" He rounded on his sister. "Where is Noreth of Kredindale?"

Cennoreth ran her finger down the rust-colored pattern, and on down the scarlet twist of wool, until she came to the thread hanging off in the shuttle. "It's not here. That part isn't woven yet." Wend made an angry noise. "Don't you understand, Duck? I don't know *either*."

Maewen could have sworn that Wend was crying as he swung round again and glared at the boys. "And do *you* know?" Moril and Mitt shook their heads. "You wouldn't!" Wend said disgustedly. "You only think of yourselves. Don't you understand? All my hopes were on Noreth. There could have been a Queen again!"

"No, there couldn't," Maewen said unwisely. "There was a Ki—"

Wend swung round and shouted at her. "What do you know about this? You're not Noreth! You're no one! *You're* not the one I've kept the green roads for, all these years! You can go hang, and the green roads with you! Not one step more do I go with any of you!"

He turned and stormed through the room, going from space to space between the bobbins in enormous strides. The door to the kitchen-room slammed behind him.

Very shaken, Maewen looked at Mitt and Moril. She was afraid they were going to be as angry with her as Wend. What she saw growing on both their faces was simple, devout relief. Mitt even gave her a shaky grin as he asked Cennoreth, "He do this often, your brother?"

Cennoreth was frowning out of the window, at the rocks and apple trees there, busily and absently attending to her weaving, tying off a thread of dark green yarn beside the hanging scarlet shuttle. Very like Mum when something upset her, Maewen thought. At Mitt's question, Cennoreth gave a start and looked down at what her hands were doing. "Oh dear," she said. "You must forgive my brother. There are times when he feels that every mortal soul just lets him down. He *can* behave like this when his heart is very much in something. I expect he has gone to look for the real girl." She sighed. "I think you'd better go and collect the supplies I promised you; they're on the table in the kitchen. Your friends will be waiting."

She turned back to her loom. Mitt and Moril nodded at one another, and the three of them worked their way through the bobbins to the kitchen door. There was no sign of Wend in there, but on the table stood a crock of milk, butter, a bowl of eggs, and a round of cheese. Maewen looked up from wondering if Wend had put them there, to find Mitt and Moril facing her meaningly across the table. Here it comes! she thought.

"Who *are* you, really? You said Singer," Moril asked her.

"That's a surname," Maewen explained. "My dad said we had Singer blood. Believe it or not, he was showing me some of our family tree the night before I left, but the part from this time was really confused, and I've no idea whether I'm related to you." It felt so good to be able to be herself again that she could have chattered on for minutes. "I may be called Singer, but I can barely sing a—"

"How *long* into the future?" Moril said.

"Oh. Er—two hundred years, I think."

Mitt and Moril looked to one another. "That long!" said Mitt. "Then you'll know what's going to happen here—right?"

"Not really," Maewen confessed. She was rather dashed to find that what they were really interested in was their own future. She had wanted to amaze them about planes and computers and television. "History doesn't tell you about the Undying or the green roads or anything," she explained. "It's mostly kings and politics. Noreth didn't come into any of the history I learned, but I'll tell you who does: Amil the Great. I'm almost sure he's almost now."

*"Who?"* said Mitt.

"Amil," Moril said, rather accusingly. "That's not a king's name. It's one of the names of the One."

"What about him? Tell," said Mitt.

Maewen racked her brains. "Well, there was a big uprising, and Amil the Great took the crown and united all Dalemark. He reigned for ages and rebuilt Kernsburgh and changed the whole country."

"Ah," said Mitt. This sounded good. Let him and Navis only get in on that, and Earl Keril and the Countess could go whistle. "When is this uprising going to start?"

"I can't remember the date," Maewen confessed—which was *stupid*, considering how often she had heard it in the palace—"but it can't be more than a year away now. I've been thinking all along that I've only got to keep going until Amil comes."

"Then *where* does he start?" said Mitt. He needed to know where to make for.

Maewen flogged her brain again, feeling quite resentful at being released from her imposture only to stand up to a history test. She would have told him so, too, if she hadn't thought she owed it to them. The trouble was, what she remembered was a muddle. "I *think* it began in the South, down on the coast— No, because I seem to remember that the North Dales and Dropwater came into it, too. And Kernsburgh, I think. Yes, I'm pretty sure that some of it began near Kernsburgh."

"Kernsburgh." Mitt and Moril looked at one another again. She could see that both their minds were hard at work. "Kialan's bringing Ynen to meet us at Kernsburgh," Mitt told Moril. "If he can."

"Kialan," said Moril, "would make a good king."

"My money's on Ynen," said Mitt. "I grant you that Kialan's kingly, but Ynen's got the character." Both boys looked at Maewen. "I reckon," Mitt said, "that our job is to go along there and hand over that sword and that ring and the cup, to one of them."

"Yes," Moril agreed. "I don't think we can stop. The One's got an interest in it. You can tell from this king's name." He frowned down at the little white goat cheese in front of him on the table. "But I don't understand. What's *happened* to Noreth?"

This was the part Maewen had been dreading. Both of them were eyeing her, picking out the features that did not match their memory of Noreth—or, maybe, wondering if she was a murderess. "I don't know," she said. "Honestly. She was gone when I got here. I found her horse—

at least I suppose it's her horse—wandering about by the waystone. I thought maybe one of the earls might have kidnapped her."

Again Mitt and Moril exchanged looks. "It could be," Moril said. "About the only earl in the North who won't want to stop her is Earl Luthan."

Mitt said, "Then we'll look for her . . . after."

There was a silence, filled with the soft singing of the kettle on the banked peat and clacking from the loom next door. A memory teased at Maewen, now she had space to think. "I remember! Wend told me, back in the palace when he was tricking me into coming here, that Kankredin had got to Noreth somehow."

Both of them pounced on this. "The voice," said Moril.

"Now we'll tell you something," said Mitt. "That voice that talks to you. You think it's the One, don't you?"

"But it's not," said Moril. "It's Kankredin."

"How do you know?" Maewen said guiltily.

"By what it tells you—mostly," Mitt said.

"But I'm the only one who can hear it!" Maewen protested.

"We've both heard it," Moril told her. "And we know it's Kankredin."

He and Mitt looked at one another again. "If he's got rid of Noreth," Mitt said, working it out, "he got you instead because he thinks you'll do what he wants. *Do* you want to?"

"No!" Maewen said fervently. "If you heard— No!"

"Then don't let's talk about it outside this house," Moril said.

Maewen looked up from the bowl of eggs, big pale blue duck eggs and brown hen eggs mixed, which she had mostly been staring at, and gazed round the kitchen. Low beams with strings of onions hanging from them, copper pans, chairs with knitted cushions and a wall of shelves with glass jars on them, holding colored mixtures that may have been dyes—it all belonged to Cennoreth. It made sense that Kankredin could not hear them here, even if he seemed to be everywhere else. She shuddered. That voice. She knew it was Kankredin now. It was the same voice that had so frightened her from the old man in the train—the way it had not seemed to come from a person—but she had not realized, because there had not been a face to connect it to.

"No," she said. "I won't say a word. You know I— Secretly, I was afraid I might be going mad!"

"Not you!" said Mitt. "So we'll keep him thinking we don't know it's him. Right?"

"Right," said Maewen.

They were all suddenly jolly with relief. Maewen felt like a person who has long had a splinter festering under a fingernail, after someone has come along and pulled the splinter out. Mitt laughed as he picked up the bowl of eggs and the cheese. "One thing," he said. "I bet you got that idea about the miners from history books, didn't you? Telling them to go on smash."

"Strike," said Moril, and he laughed as he picked up the crock of milk.

This left Maewen free to snatch up the loaf and rush out of the door, crying out, "Wallop! Smash! Strike!" She raced through the trees, waving the sword in one hand and the loaf in the other. "We got the sword!" she shouted.

Mitt and Moril were forced to follow more slowly for fear of spilling milk and breaking eggs. Moril had gone sober again. "Penny for them," said Mitt.

"She never heard of Noreth," Moril said. "So what happens to *her*? She can't be in history either."

# 18

NAVIS HAD EVIDENTLY decided that the meadow was safe. Maewen caught him in the act of dressing after a bath in the stone trough. As she dashed across the field, Navis was scrambling into clothes, in time to behave as if nothing at all unusual had happened when she reached him. Hestefan left off polishing a row of cwidders and ambled across to look. By the time Mitt and Moril reached them, Navis was saying, "Antique, certainly, and worth devoting half the evening to, no doubt. We had more notable blades in the armory in Holand, but if we *are* to have an uprising, I suppose every weapon counts. And is Wend staying the night with his sister?"

"Didn't he come out here awhile back?" Mitt asked.

"We haven't seen him since he went away with the goats," Hestefan said. "Should we have done?"

"I'm not sure," said Moril. "He may have left."

There was no sign of Wend that night. When he had not appeared by nightfall, Mitt and Moril shared the buttered eggs they had set aside for him. Maewen was chiefly relieved that Wend had not rushed out and denounced her to Navis and Hestefan. She thought Navis might not have taken it too badly, but Hestefan would have been outraged. Navis, however, took Wend's absence as a sign that they were not safe and rigged up a trip wire across the rushes some way down the path.

There was no alarm in the night. They woke to a gray morning to find that the meadow cupped in the crags was smaller and more ragged. There was no garden and no fruit trees. Maewen discovered this first, when she went to have a bath in the stone trough before the rest were awake. The trough had gone. Where it had been, there was a muddy hole in the ground. She looked for the house. Where it had been, there was a thicket of crab apples and wild cherries against the rocks, overgrown with brambles and dog roses. Inside the thicket she could just see the broken walls of a small stone house.

"No hens either," Navis said, coming up beside her. "It was improvident of us to eat all the eggs." By this time the others were coming across the field in a dismayed straggle. Navis slid an eyebrow up at Mitt. "Would you say the Undying have deserted us?"

Mitt shrugged unhappily. "No idea."

Hestefan stood by the muddy hole and looked slowly round, stroking his beard. "I know this place now," he said. "This *is* Dropthwaite, and this"—pointing to the mudhole—"is the source of the river Dropwater. I have camped here before. It is said that the Adon once lived in hiding in those ruins over there."

"Then that serves to authenticate the sword," Navis said, and went briskly off to inspect his trip wire. It took him a long time to find it. The rushes had been replaced by thistles and brambles. When they did find the wire, it was lying loosely a long way up the hill. From there they could all see that the lake of yesterday was now only a large green pond.

Hestefan stared at it gloomily. "This change is the worst of all possible omens."

"Oh come on," Maewen said, forgetting how Hestefan seemed to dislike her. "We got the sword."

Hestefan turned his gloomy look on her. "The City of Gold is always on the most distant hillside," he said. Before Maewen or Mitt could ask him what that was supposed to mean, he said, "I believe we should all now disperse on our separate ways."

Moril gave a short protesting "Oh!" and Mitt said, "Well, Navis and I can't, and that's final."

"But you may disperse by yourself, by all means, Singer," Navis added.

Breakfast made no one feel much better. Hestefan was, if possible, even gloomier, when they set off, to find that the path was mud and marsh, with hardly room to get the cart past the pond. As they came slowly down the bank of the river, Navis murmured, "The Undying make quite a difference."

Everyone was glad when they came to the place where the green road crossed the river and found it just the same. They could even see the place where the pursuing horsemen had trampled through the spongy turf, in and out of the water.

"Go cautiously," Navis said, "since the pursuit is now ahea—" He turned round in surprise as the cart came splashing through the river, too, with water whirling from its wheels. "I thought you were leaving us, Singer."

"There are only two ways to go," Hestefan pointed out. "I chose not to turn back."

This seemed to be Hestefan's way of saying he was not going to leave them after all. They went on together, the same party, apart from Wend striding alongside, and the river Dropwater went with them, too, sometimes winding in the distance, sometimes skirling along beside them, and growing steadily larger. A long way farther on, they came to the place where the band of hearthmen had camped for the night. There was not much to see, merely hoofprints and the cold ashes of their fire, but it sent Navis very cautious again. From then on he was either watching for prints in the green road or scanning the distance on either side.

It was empty distance, all green sheep runs and faraway dark peaks, but there were sheep and, once or twice, a shepherd a long way off. Maewen found herself staring every time they saw a shepherd, expecting him to come striding toward them and turn out to be Wend. But no shepherd did more than turn and look at them. She was quite surprised to be missing Wend so much.

When they camped that night by the river, Navis insisted that they find a place a long way back and hidden from the road. Hestefan drove the cart after him along the riverbank just as if he had never threatened to leave, remarking cheerfully, "We've made good time without a walker to slow us down. We'll be at Dropwater tomorrow."

As they dismounted, Moril hopped off the back of the cart and came over to Mitt. "That's a relief," he said. "I wouldn't have known what to do if he'd decided to leave. I'm sure he's not well."

Maewen led her horse into the river, still thinking about Wend. She had been sure he would get over his anger and come back, but now she began to see that he was not going to. It was Noreth he followed, not her. So what was she going to do? She had, she saw, been relying on Wend to get her back to her own time. Perhaps she never would get back. She thought of Mum and Aunt Liss and Dad and felt a touch of fear—but only a touch. She was surprised not to be much more frightened.

"The Wanderer is no loss," said the deep voice. "You never needed him."

Maewen jumped and shuddered, wondering if it—he—could read her mind. "Didn't I?" she said. "That's a weight off my mind!"

Sarcasm always seemed to pass Kankredin by—if it was Kankredin. The voice went on imperturbably, "From now on, look for an opportunity to stab the Southerners. The danger from them is growing."

"Anything you say!" Maewen told it bitterly.

It was a great relief to her over supper to hear Navis arranging with Mitt for the two of them to keep watch that night in turns. Those pursuing hearthmen had been a blessing in disguise. Kankredin could not expect her to try to kill them tonight. But she was terrified of what might happen when he found she had no intention of trying.

They went on again next day through the same rolling green country, with Mitt yawning and Navis red-eyed. Maewen was inclined to be sorry for them until Mitt said, "I'm used to it, and Navis is one of those who just get sharper for it. Mind you, I've only seen him lose four nights of sleep, but he never turned a hair then."

She realized Mitt was right when Navis spotted the faint marks where the party of hearthmen had turned off the green road to the left, to follow a disused-looking path that led toward the mountains. Navis pounced on it like a cat. "Where does that lead?" he asked Hestefan and Moril.

"You can cut through to the North Dales that way," Moril said.

Navis narrowed his eyes at the path and then raised them to the mountains. They were nearer here. Ahead they curved inward and seemed to stand right over the green road. "And can horses work their way round through the tops to come back to the road?" he asked.

"Possibly," said Hestefan. "But the river goes down to Dropwater there." He pointed to the craggy eminences ahead. "We only have to go down into the valley to be safe."

"If they don't reach us first," Navis said.

From there on he rode with his pistol ready in his hand. When, around midday, they reached the crags, and the road wound in among them, Navis's eyes were continually flicking to the skyline above, watching for an ambush. Mostly he watched to the left. But if there was a heathery dip in the crags above the Dropwater, which now roared beside the road as a wide wild torrent, Navis was sure to check that, too.

Half a mile farther on, the Dropwater suddenly spread wider still, into an immense flat sheet of racing water, and seemed to plunge off the edge of the world into vague blue distance. The road curved so that they could see where it fell and fell and fell, nearly a mile of falling white water, in smoky rainbows and wet thunder. The noise was enormous.

"Quite something, isn't it?" Moril yelled.

Maewen turned to shout back and saw a squad of armed men running toward them from farther up the road. Her hands leaped to the Adon's sword, lying crosswise in front of her saddle, and then fell away.

Navis swung round with his pistol ready. She saw him lower it. There were so many armed men. They were all wearing dark red and blue livery, except for the man in front who seemed to be waving at them, and she was sure she had seen those colors before— Oh. Maewen looked down at herself. She had grown so used to her clothes that she had thought of them as just clothes. But she was wearing the same dark red and blue. The man in front was in expensive scarlet silk and red leather, and he was definitely waving to her.

Maewen slid down from her horse. This was like Kredindale, only possibly worse, she thought, as she went hesitatingly to meet him. To her gratitude, Moril realized she would need help and hopped off the cart to come with her.

"Who *is* he?" she half shouted, under the roar of the falls.

"Luthan!" Moril yelled in her ear. "Earl of Dropwater. Noreth's cousin. He's been her hearthlord these last two years. Don't nod at me! Smile at *him*!"

Maewen stretched her mouth into a grin. At least, she thought, this saved them from any ambush.

The Earl of Dropwater pelted up and stood in front of her panting and smiling. "Cousin!" he bawled.

"Hearthlord!" Maewen shrieked back. He was awfully young. She took him for her own age at first sight. But as he laughed and seized hold of both her hands, she saw he was older than that, maybe at least eighteen. He was one of those people who have pretty pink and white faces, all curves. As he laughed, he tossed back glossy black hair.

"At last!" he shouted, fluttering long dark eyelashes Maewen truly envied him for. "Where have you been? We expected you yesterday at the latest."

He clearly had no idea she was not Noreth. Well, you see what you expect to see, Maewen thought. "How did you know when to expect me?" she bawled back.

Luthan put an arm round her shoulders and led her up the road, past the people who had been running with him, and among masses more. There was what looked like a small army strung out along the way, and horses for them standing in patient rows under the crags. "There's less noise along here. We can hear ourselves speak," Luthan said.

Mitt looked at Moril, who nodded and scampered off beside Maewen. Mitt slid to the ground and hurriedly led Maewen's horse and the Countess-horse along behind them. Navis looked at him questioningly and then rode up behind Luthan.

Luthan turned round, surprised. "Noreth, who are these?"

"My followers, of course," Maewen said. They came to a moist green ground beyond the rocks where Luthan had a fine tent set up. The noise of the waterfall was cut off by crags in the way. Maewen could speak normally as she said, "This is Navis Haddsson, and this is Mitt. This is Moril Clennensson."

Luthan's curvaceous face lit up. "The Southerners who came on the wind's road? I've heard of you. And of course, I've met you, Moril, now I think—though I knew your father better. My cousin certainly knows how to pick her followers." He smiled at Maewen and really seemed to mean it. She felt like a beast deceiving him. She felt worse as numbers of men and women in Dropwater livery came crowding round to smile and say hello. They were probably Noreth's personal friends. And all she could do was smile back and hope they did not think she was behaving oddly.

"Now, to business," said Luthan. "You were awfully secretive when you left, Noreth, but I guessed what you were up to. You're riding the King's Road, aren't you? Well, the whole North knows you are. What made you think I wouldn't follow you?"

Maewen found herself thinking, Flaming Ammet! She seemed to have caught that from Mitt. Here was the army she had been trying to avoid having. "It—it's going to be very dangerous," she said lamely.

Luthan swept that aside. "Danger—nothing! I court it! I intend to follow my true Queen!" He meant it. Maewen squirmed. "But I won't keep you guessing about how I knew. They sent word down by sea from Kredindale. They told the whole coast. All the coastal dales are ready to come to you as soon as you give the word, and of course, I got ready at once. You'll need my help. There's worrying news, too." Luthan's curved brows set in a serious line. "My agent in Hannart sent a carrier pigeon. Earl Keril has set out for Kernsburgh, and it looks as if he wants to stop you. I was going to invite you down to the mansion, but in view of that news, I think we'd better break camp and be on our way."

"You mean you're coming, too?" Maewen said. Oh flaming Ammet, oh *bother*!

Luthan smiled meltingly. "My Queen, what do you think I've been telling you? I am coming, and all my hearthpeople with me."

Navis coughed. "When did the Earl of Hannart set out, and how long will it take him to reach Kernsburgh?"

Luthan blinked his beautiful eyelashes. "Er. Um. Yesterday. He'd be there tomorrow evening if he rode hard."

"Yesterday." Maewen could see Navis thinking that it was not Earl Keril's band that had been after them, then. "And Dropwater is on the other point of a triangle, am I right?" Luthan nodded, in another flutter of eyelashes, and turned back to Maewen. "Then," said Navis, forcefully, "if you would be good enough to strike camp at once, my lord, I think we must ride through the night."

Luthan all but sprang to attention. "Oh. Yes. At once, sir." He ran away, waving his arms and shouting orders. Moril snorted. He butted his head into Mitt, and both of them bent over, howling with laughter.

"It's not funny!" said Maewen.

"Only some of it," said Navis. "But allies are allies." He watched the Dropwater people running about for a while, and he sighed. "These children have no idea they are about to fight a war. And," he added, "no idea how to hurry either. Mitt, stop giggling and come with me. I'll need a serious aide." He shook his mare into motion and rode into the confusion. Mitt popped his eyes at Maewen and legged after him.

It was like magic. The confusion stopped as soon as Navis took over. He seemed to know just which gaggle of people to speak to and which to leave alone. And if two or more inefficiencies happened at once, Navis had only to nod to Mitt, and Mitt was at one of them, sorting it out as quickly as Navis. Maewen was impressed. Barely half an hour later they were ready to go. There was even a spare horse for Moril. Navis came riding up with it himself. "Because I take it you are ready to leave us now," he remarked unlovingly to Hestefan.

Hestefan's beard jutted at him. "If you recall," he said, "sir—Navis Haddsson from Holand—I told you a long way back on the road that where great events are toward, a Singer must needs be there. But by all means remove my apprentice. I'll follow at my own pace."

"As you please," said Navis, and he murmured as he wheeled away, "*Crawl* behind, if you like. I don't know what it is," he remarked to Mitt as soon as they were well away from the green cart, "but I can't abide that fellow. He sets my teeth on edge—rather the way my brother Harchad always used to."

Mitt shuddered. "That's a bit steep, isn't it? Your brother Harchad only killed a few hundred folk each year and terrified the rest. Hestefan's a Singer, Navis. Maybe it's the beard reminds you."

They rode. The cart was soon only a green smudge behind. They rode under Navis's direction as fast as they could without exhausting their horses. They stopped to breathe them and rode again, on over the green undulations of the Shield, rising now, toward the high plateau that held Kernsburgh. Before nightfall the more distant mountains had wheeled into the blue jagged shapes Maewen remembered seeing from Dad's apartment. The peaks of the North Dales, Dad had told her. They set off again into the sunset to ride some more.

The Countess-horse had had enough by then. It stopped with all four feet planted and tried to bite Mitt's leg while Mitt cursed and bounced and shook the reins. Navis looked. He beckoned with a trim, gloved hand. One of the Dropwater hearthwomen instantly rode up with Earl Luthan's spare horse for Mitt. Nobody seemed to object that after that Mitt rode on a mare that was almost as good as Navis's own. When Maewen next saw the Countess-horse, it was in the rear carrying someone's baggage. She was impressed all over again. This was the kind of thing, quite certainly, that was going to get Navis made Duke of Kernsburgh during the next year or so.

Otherwise she did not enjoy the ride. At least the actual riding was a pleasure. It was good not to have to keep to the pace of Wend or the cart. It was Luthan she did not enjoy. He was beside her far too often, and he would keep reminding her, with significant smiles, of all the things he and Noreth had done together. "Do you remember the Harvest when we threw plums?" he said, and Maewen had to pretend to remember. Or, "You know that time with the lawbooks? Ham the Markinder still hasn't got over that." This was bad enough. But Luthan's smiles grew more and more melting. Finally he sighed and said, "Noreth, it seemed an age, an endless age, after you had gone. Dropwater was empty. Empty and void."

This is *dire*! Maewen thought. Moril, jogging on the other side of her, thought so, too. "But," he said, "Dropwater *isn't* empty. It's full of plum trees and people."

Luthan was not at all embarrassed. He smiled meltingly again. "You know what I mean. Lovers are allowed to say these things."

Maewen gave up trying not to hurt Luthan's feelings and lost her temper. "Stop being so silly! I am *not* your lover!" Then she bit her tongue. For all she knew, Noreth was very fond of Luthan—though if she was, Maewen was beginning to wonder why.

Luthan sighed, and laughed a little. "Oh dear. Have I overstepped again? I never know where to have you, Noreth. I think I've won your heart, and then you bite my head off."

So that was all right. But it did not stop Luthan. When Mitt was relieved of the Countess-horse, he rode Luthan's spare mare firmly up between Luthan and Maewen. Whenever Luthan said anything sighing or melting, Mitt grinned, grinned like a death's-head. It was soon too much for Luthan. He gave up and rode on ahead. But then, as far as Maewen was concerned, it was almost worse. Moril and Mitt could not seem to stop teasing her about it.

"Your handsome lordly lover got it bad for you!" Mitt said.

"Every lady's dream!" Moril sighed. "An earl in red silk!"

"With eyelashes," said Mitt. "Don't forget the eyelashes. All bat and flutter, this dream lover!"

Moril giggled. "Now he's gone off to write a poem about you."

"No, he hasn't. Even he's not that much of a wimp," Maewen said.

"He *is* writing a poem, you know," Moril said. "He's dictating it to his scribe. The poor man's got real trouble, trying to write it down on horseback."

Maewen refused to look, so she had no idea whether this was true or just Moril's idea of a joke. Besides, it grew dark then, too dark for poems—or so she hoped. They stopped again, and ate and drank, and then went on. After that Mitt and Moril were too tired to tease her. They just rode.

Eventually, far into the night, Navis consulted Luthan and the Dropwater armsmaster and decided they could afford a longer stop. Everyone saw to horses, ate food they did not feel like, and fell down and slept for three hours. Then Navis had them all up and on their way again.

"Flaming Ammet!" Mitt groaned. "Is this necessary?"

"Yes," said Navis. "We have to be in a good defensive position before the Earl of Hannart arrives."

"Because of Ynen?" Mitt yawned.

"Not entirely," said Navis. "You and I have necks we need to save, too."

Mitt puzzled about this as he yawningly mounted Luthan's mare among all the blue-brown shadows of other people mounting, too. It seemed tremendous cheek for him and Navis to use the Earl of Dropwater's hearthpeople just to save their necks. Noreth was the excuse, of course. But somehow he did not think this quite accounted for Navis's urgency. Navis had something else in mind which Mitt was too sleepy to work out.

Dawn came as their small army set off again, whiteness pouring down the sky and blueness rising from the ground to meet it. Then the blueness was ripped open to the left by a dazzling bar of orange. In seconds, the grass was green again and the riders turned from brown shadows to solid, colored shapes.

There were more solid shapes advancing down the green road to meet them. The orange dawn flashed on gold braid and threw turning glints from steel and leather. It was a smaller group than theirs, but everyone in it was orderly and very well armed.

"It looks as if Earl Keril got here first," Maewen said.

"No," Mitt said, squinting up his eyes to look. "That's not Hannart colors, it's— Flaming Ammet! It's Alk! What's *he* doing here?"

# 19

ALK WAS RIDING an enormous horse. Mitt knew it well. It was about the only one in Aberath which was up to Alk's weight. By the horse and the hugeness Alk was unmistakable, as he gestured to the rest of his party to halt and rode out ahead of them alone. Though Mitt knew Alk would be wearing his own special armor under his pale leather clothes, he still thought this was very brave—or very foolish—of Alk. Luthan's people had guns and crossbows. They might be tired, but after the way Navis had worked them, they were jumpy as cats.

"Nobody fire!" Navis called sharply. Fifty weapons were up.

Luthan came awake with a jump. "That's right, Navis. Hold fire, everyone. We've no quarrel with Aberath."

Speak for yourself! Mitt thought nervously as Alk came to a ponderous halt halfway between the two bands.

"Good morning," Alk called. "I need to speak to some of you. Here's my list: Navis Haddsson, Alhammitt Alhammittsson, Hestefan the Singer, Tanamoril Clennensson, and a lady known as Noreth Onesdaughter, if she's with you. I'd be grateful if they all came out here and the rest of you went back a bit. I need to talk to them in private."

They exchanged mystified looks. Mitt and Moril had been yawning. Maewen's eyes had been nearly shut. But they were all suddenly wide awake. "I suppose we should see what he wants," Navis said. "We *are* four to one."

"That doesn't count with Alk," Mitt said. "I've seen him throw a *horse*."

Navis bowed politely to Luthan. "We'll try not to keep you waiting long," he said. Luthan gave him a polite, bewildered nod. Navis edged his mare out of the throng, and the other three followed him.

Alk looked them over as they approached. Mitt had never seen him look so glum and grim. "Where's Hestefan the Singer?"

"Following behind," said Navis. "His mule couldn't keep up. Are you likely to detain us long, my lord?"

"My lord." Alk rubbed his chin. It rasped. Behind him Mitt could see a cluster of faces he knew well from Aberath. All of them had a weary, fed-up look, and none of them greeted him. "My lord?" Alk repeated. "Now, I reckon you're at least as much of a lord as I am, Navis Haddsson. My reading is that when you call people that, you don't mean any respect at all. So don't call me that. As for how long we'll be, this'll take as long as it takes. You all gave me the slip once, when I'd nearly caught you up at Dropthwaite, and forced me to get ahead of you. I've been hanging around for you, up and down the green roads, for a day and a half now, so now you can just wait for me, Navis Haddsson. That reminds me—" Alk's glum manner vanished. He turned to Mitt. "This is something you'll appreciate, Mitt. I'd been in Aberath such years that I'd forgotten what these green roads were like. Lovely level runs, you get on them—bends beautifully cambered, not a sharp curve among them—and never a steep gradient anywhere! It would only take a little tinkering and filling in, and I could lay tracks and run my steam engines all over the North!"

Maewen had been watching Navis look as put down as she had ever seen him, but this snatched her attention back. So *that* was why there were no green roads in her day! They were all railways! "So that's—" she began, and stopped herself.

But the small noise caught this huge man's attention. "And who are you, young lady?" Alk asked her.

"Noreth Onesdaughter," she said. "You asked to see me."

"With respect, young lady," said Alk, "I don't think you can be."

He was terrifyingly grim about it. Mitt and Moril gave her looks that were plain frightened. As for Navis, he looked at her, narrowed his eyes, and looked again, in a way that made Maewen feel as if she were dropping fast through the earth, leaving sun and grass and friendliness behind. "Wh-what makes you say that?" she managed to ask Alk.

"The reason I came after you all." Alk settled himself stonily upright on his huge horse. "Four days," he said. "Four days after Mitt set out for Adenmouth, Lady Eltruda of Adenmouth arrives in Aberath. Came herself. Asking for justice. On a charge of murder. She brought the murdered corpse with her, because the victim was her niece. Noreth of Kredindale. The girl's throat had been cut."

"I don't believe this!" Navis burst out. His face had drained to a blue-white, except for his eyes, which were rimmed with red. "Does Eltruda—the Lady of Adenmouth—suspect that I—"

"You're on her list," said Alk, "though I can't say she likes the idea."

Navis sagged. There were big, deep lines on his face that had not been there a minute before. He's really fond of her! Mitt thought wonderingly. That little, loud lady. Who'd have thought it?

"It seems," Alk continued, "they didn't find the girl's body right away because whoever did her in killed her in the stables. Then shoved her in an empty stall and piled straw over her. It was only luck they found her. I reckon the killer hoped it would be longer than that before they did."

His eyes wandered over all four of them, bleak as stones. Mitt shivered. He had never seen Alk like this. This was Alk the lawman. Seeing it, Mitt had an inkling at least of why the Countess had married Alk. Like this, he must have frightened even the Countess.

"Lady Eltruda," said Alk, "ought to have been a law-woman. She did a fine job. Everyone in Adenmouth she's accounted for, and had them all prove where they were and what they were doing. She has it narrowed down to everyone who went off on Midsummer morning. You'd better believe this. I do. I suspect you all, plus"—his eyes traveled to Maewen—"you. I've seen the body. You could be her twin sister, but you're not her. She looked older." His eyes traveled to Moril and on to Navis. "*You* told Fenna you'd sworn to follow Noreth, and *you* promised Lady Eltruda you'd look after her. But when you both went off, she was already dead." His eyes went to Mitt and, if possible, were bleaker still. "And you came and made promises to me in Aberath, so you could get that ring for someone who wasn't Noreth. Did you know she was dead then?"

"I didn't—I didn't know. I swear—" Mitt stammered.

"Nor did I," Moril whispered. "I was with Hestefan all—"

"*All* the time?" said Alk. "You went and talked to Fenna, up in her bedroom, and after that you were running around, no one knows where, looking for your cwidder."

Moril wilted. Navis said nothing. Maewen put her hands to her face. The poor girl. And here was I cheerfully thinking she'd just been kidnapped. Maewen knew, too well, what Noreth's last moments had felt like. Grabbed round the throat. The knife coming round. Or maybe Noreth had been glad to see the killer and turned round smiling—oh, are you coming, too?—and then she saw the knife. Tears came rolling down her face. Poor Noreth.

"This gets us nowhere," Alk said. "I came for justice, not playacting. And I made inquiries as I came. When Karet came back up from Gardale with the news that the Adon's cup had gone from the Lawschool, I thought, Can you believe anything that Mitt says? You stole it, didn't you?"

"No," Navis said. "I did."

Alk stared at him in genuine surprise. After blinking a bit, he said, "Then where is it?"

Navis answered by fetching the cup from his pocket, still wrapped in the handkerchief. Alk stared at it for a moment. He considered. Then he nodded at Maewen. "Give it to her. And you," he said to Maewen, "take hold of it without that wrapping and tell me your name is Noreth of Kredindale. Go on."

Maewen wretchedly took the cup and just stopped herself from wiping the tears off her face with the handkerchief. "My name is Noreth of Kredindale," she said, "Why—"

"Quiet," said Alk.

Maewen obediently shut her mouth. The man had a personality as huge as his body, she thought, wiping her face with her sleeve. You did what he said.

"Now say your real name," said Alk.

"I'm Mayelbridwen Singer," Maewen said sadly.

She was still thinking of Noreth. She saw everyone staring at the cup before it occurred to her to look at it herself. It was shining blue all over its lopsided shape. Even in the gold haze of dawn it was bright. And at the end of her long shadow, stretching away on top of her horse's longer shadow, right out across the grass and bracken, there was a blue haze where the shadow of the cup should have been. She saw Alk's followers turning to look at it.

"Marvelous!" said Alk. "Clever work! When I was a boy at the Lawschool, I heard they used it for truth telling in evidence." For a moment, in spite of their anxiety, all four of them had an irresistible vision of Alk at grittling. His side must have won every time. Even Navis nearly smiled. "But I never saw it at work before this," Alk said. "Now tell me another lie, young Mayelbridwen."

Maewen's mind would not come up with a lie at first. Then her horse sidled, no doubt puzzled by the blue light on its back, and she caught a glimpse of scarlet, where Luthan was standing, patting his horse's nose and staring at the cup. She said, "I'm in love with the Earl of Dropwater." The blue light went from the cup as if someone had turned a switch. Moril gave an unhappy chuckle.

"Now another truth," Alk commanded.

Maewen nearly began, "I'm in love with—" but she swallowed it down and said, "Oh—er—we found the Adon's sword. It's behind my saddle."

"Did you indeed?" said Alk as the cup lit blue again, like a small sheeny moon. "I thought no one knew where that sword really was. Well, well. Now pass the cup to the Singer-lad." Maewen reached across and handed the cup over. As Moril's hand closed round it, the blue light went again. Alk nodded. "You say your name," he said to Moril.

"Osfameron Tanamoril Clennensson," said Moril. And the cup was alight and blue again. He stared at it wonderingly.

"Untruth," commanded Alk.

"I—er—I can't play the cwidder," Moril said. And he was holding a simple silver cup.

"Now say— Did you kill Noreth of Kredindale?" Alk said.

*"No!"* said Moril, and again the cup flared blue. Moril screwed his eyes up at it as if he might cry.

"Now pass it to Navis," Alk ordered. When Navis had stretched out and taken the cup and it was once more a mild silver, Alk said, "And did *you* kill Noreth Onesdaughter?"

"I most certainly did *not*," Navis said, and screwed his eyes up like Moril when the cup shone blue in his hand.

Mitt waited anxiously. Alk was leaving him till last because he thought Mitt was the guilty one. He could see that. It was a wretched thought. But the cup itself was beginning to worry him just as much. If it was behaving as it was supposed to with the others—and from Alk's look as he tested it, it was—then it had behaved all wrong with Mitt, spitting blue sparks at him both other times he touched it. Mitt suspected the thing disliked him. He did not trust it not to prove him guilty out of sheer malice. He could see the faces of his onetime friends in Aberath behind Alk, shut away from him, sure he was a murderer.

"Now to him," Alk said to Navis.

Navis held the blue-glowing cup out to Mitt. That, and Mitt's worry, made his new horse turn round restively, giving him a sight of Luthan and all his people staring. Ammet only knew what *they* were thinking.

"Take it!" Navis snapped.

Mitt spared a hand for the thing. *"Ouch!"* It was like nettles, squirting blue rays between his fingers. He had to let go the reins and hang on to the cup with both hands or he would have let it fall. It hurt. It crackled blue streams round his wrists and knuckles. The cup clearly hated him as much as the Countess-horse did. *"Ow!"* And Luthan's spare horse did not help, bucking around in fear, until Navis grabbed it and pulled on the bit.

"Can you bring yourself to tell a lie?" Alk said, watching callously.

"You being . . . sarky is . . . all I need!" Mitt said with his teeth clenched. "Burn you! I—I— You don't make steam engines!" The blue rays faded inward between Mitt's fingers and vanished. The prickling lasted an instant longer, and then that went, too. Mitt shook the plain silver goblet he was now holding, and the other hand as well. The relief! "Burn you, Alk! This thing hates me! I won't dare tell the truth now, I warn you!"

"I dare you," said Alk. "Did you kill Noreth of Kredindale?"

*"No!"* Mitt spat, hunched against another assault from the cup. It spat at him again, with a sharp sizzle, but, to his surprise, it was nothing like so painful. More like a tingling. The blue rays reaching through his fingers were almost glorious. "Ah. Calmed it down," he said.

"Turn it off, turn it on. I thought that might do it," Alk said. He looked smug, like someone who had won a bet. As Mitt thankfully passed the cup back to Navis, he said, "Then I declare you all clear of the charge of murder. Now," he added to Maewen, "let's have a look at that sword, young lady."

"But why?" said Navis.

"It might do to swear some more on," Alk said.

Navis looked harrowed. "Please," he said. "I have to get to Kernsburgh in case my son, Ynen, is there."

Maewen hurriedly scrabbled the sword loose, knowing Navis was right.

Alk grinned. "It's just curiosity, really. I love clever metalwork. Just draw the sword and show it to me, young lady, and then you can all go."

Maewen tried to draw the sword in the same hurry—too hurriedly. She jammed it sideways somehow, and it refused to emerge. "It's stuck!" she said, hauling uselessly at it. Mitt and Navis leaned over to help. They both wanted to get going. Both their horses, and Maewen's with them, got the wrong idea and started to move and were pulled back. All three surged round in a circle, and Moril's horse joined in. Alk calmly moved his own horse back, where he sat watching the confusion. It was only resolved when Navis seized the leather scabbard Maewen was waving about and planted the hilt end on Mitt's saddle. Both pulled. The sword came loose with a slithery clang.

"There," said Mitt. He rode over and pushed the sword under Alk's nose. "Satisfied?"

"I'll say!" Alk looked it over admiringly. "It may look plain and a silly old fashion, but it's better work than any of us could do today. I'd give an eyetooth to meet the man that made it. He'd have taken a year and a day to do it, you know. No one bothers to take that sort of trouble today. All right. Put it away, and let's all get to Kernsburgh."

"All?" said Navis. He was more depressed than Mitt had ever seen him. "I've no more patience for jokes."

"No joke," said Alk. "I said I'd come to Kernsburgh with the rest of you. Keril listens to me."

"I don't think you understand," Navis said wearily. "You have just removed my pretext for dragging the Earl of Dropwater there with me."

Alk's eyes went to Maewen. "Is that so? Who heard me do that, apart from you and two lads who knew, anyway? Didn't you?" he asked Moril.

"Kankredin might have heard," Moril said.

"All the more reason for going there," said Alk. He turned his vast horse round to join his hearthmen.

"Just a moment," Navis said. He seemed to have revived wonderfully. Alk stopped and turned his head questioningly. "If I have no pretext," Navis said, "you must have one."

"Must I?" Alk lifted his helmet and scratched his head. "I suppose it stands to reason," he admitted, "that if I pull the rug out from under you, you'll need somewhere to stand." He grinned. "Let's say I've got the same pretext as you have."

Navis laughed and wheeled round to ride back to Luthan.

"What did he mean?" Maewen asked as their three horses shimmied about, glad to be moving again.

"Not to tell Luthan you're not Noreth, I think," Mitt said, although, knowing Alk and Navis as he did, he was not at all sure.

She made a face. Moril laughed. "Don't look now. Luthan's on his way to ask you all about what Alk wanted."

Maewen naturally looked. Luthan was mounted again, trotting up the road with an eager, tender, questioning look. "What shall I *tell* him?"

Navis reached Luthan first. He spoke quickly and quietly to Luthan, and whatever it was he said, it seemed to satisfy Luthan entirely. He shot Maewen a look of deep understanding and rode gravely beside Navis as their party joined Alk's.

The two groups together made quite an impressive force, Mitt thought, as he rode in the midst of it. This ought to show Earl Keril they meant business—if this *was* what Navis and Alk had in mind. Since he was not sure, Mitt found himself thinking about Noreth instead, dead before she set foot on the King's Road. Kankredin must be angry about that. Wend had fooled him, and everyone else, by sending Maewen in her place. Except that Wend hadn't seemed to know what he was doing. Mitt was anxious about that. Wend had withdrawn his protection from

Maewen, and she could well be in danger if Kankredin turned on her. Mitt decided not to let her out of his sight.

He was surprised, and a little ashamed, to find that when he thought he was thinking of Noreth, it was Maewen he was really worried about.

About an hour later they reached Kernsburgh. At least, it was where Alk and all the Dropwater people said Kernsburgh was.

"It is. Honestly," Moril assured Mitt and Maewen.

They had halted in a half circle three or four riders deep, facing an ordinary small waystone. Beyond it the green turf rose and fell in a hundred humps and hummocks. And that was all.

"City of Gold," Alk said genially. "Always on the hill beyond."

Navis beckoned Mitt and cantered among the grassy mounds to organize his defense. Everyone followed slowly, Maewen among the last. This felt weird. Where they had first stopped could have been the space which Kernsburgh Central Station was going to fill, except that the waystone was all wrong. Those low mounds were where she had last seen shops and office blocks, and the slightly higher hummocks ahead, up which Navis was riding slantwise, were where the Tannoreth Palace would be someday soon. The green crease she was following, full of hoofprints and horse droppings, was probably King Street. And instead of cars and lorries, there was a much quieter confusion of riders in two different liveries. Maewen could so little believe this was really Kernsburgh that she had to look up toward the distant hills to make sure. There she saw the blue jagged shapes she saw from Dad's apartment, the North Dales Peaks. But the oddest part was the way there had obviously been a city here once, under all these lumps. She felt as if time had stood upside down and she really was in the far future, looking at the remains of the Kernsburgh she had known.

A great shout jerked her attention back to here and now. Mitt was down from his horse, leaping across the hummocks, yelling. Maewen shook her own horse to a fast trot and arrived at the top of the palace mounds in time to see Mitt delightedly greeting two newcomers. The tall, curly one was plainly Kialan. Navis had his arm round the shoulders of the small pale boy with Kialan. They were alike enough for Maewen to know that this was Ynen. There were two weary-looking horses in the hollow behind the two. It looked as if they had ridden all night as well.

"I'm sorry we kept out of sight," Kialan was saying. "There was a big troop of horsemen in war gear on the road last night. We had to leave the road to avoid them. We couldn't see who they were in the dark, but we didn't think they should see us."

"It was probably Alk," said Navis, "but we'll take precautions."

Maewen was watching Ynen frisk round Mitt like a terrier puppy round a greyhound. I'm so glad! she thought. He *likes* Mitt! I don't think I could have borne it if he'd been like Hildy. Ynen was so unlike Hildy that she thought maybe he was a bit of a softie. Then Ynen looked up at Maewen, and she knew he was not soft at all. He smiled at her uncertainly, not knowing who she was.

"Are you Noreth?" Kialan asked her. Lordly, Maewen thought. He reminded her of the boys at the sixth form college.

"We all thought so, but apparently not," Navis said. "Mayelbridwen, I believe, is the name."

Just then, there were agitated noises from Luthan a little way off. Mitt went haring over there to see what was wrong. Maewen found she could not face the puzzled looks from Kialan and Ynen, and she followed Mitt.

In another hidden hollow Luthan was standing over an immense heap of mixed bread and grapes. There was another heap beyond that looked like oats. "Where did all *this* come from?" Luthan demanded.

Mitt narrowed his eyes at the stuff. The loaves were the kind plaited into a wheat shape which he had last seen in the Holy Islands. The grapes were the sweet green Southern kind. He grinned. "A present," he said, "from the Earth Shaker and She Who Raised the Islands."

"You're joking," Luthan said uncertainly.

"I am not," Mitt said.

However it arrived, the breakfast was very welcome. By the time Navis had the place organized, everyone was glad to sit down and eat at their posts. Alk's people, and most of Luthan's, were posted hidden behind mounds in a great circle. Kialan and Ynen were sent to help pass a loaf and a bunch of grapes to everyone, while Maewen and Mitt were busy pouring a pile of oats in front of each of the horses picketed in the middle. Luthan's hearthwomen were standing by a third of the horses to mount a cavalry charge if necessary.

"There's still quite a heap of bread and grapes left," Kialan said as he arrived at the horses with an armload for the hearthwomen.

"As if they might be expecting more people," Ynen said, following Kialan with his arms clutched round loaves and grapes dangling from his fingers. "I got these for us."

Mitt wondered about this as they went to eat in the central hollow. What did the Undying think was going to happen? He had a sense that this was a lull before things got frantic. And once things got frantic, he knew they would go on that way for quite some time.

Before Mitt could mention this feeling to the others, Navis arrived with Alk and Luthan. "There," Navis said. "That should stop anyone interfering while we look for the crown. Has anyone any idea where it is?"

Everyone shook their heads. Wend would know, Maewen thought. Oh, bother the man!

Luthan broke apart a loaf. "They say," he said, "that the crown is buried in the ruins of King Hern's palace. You may be sitting on it," he added, with a melting smile at Maewen.

"Then it's going to take digging to find," Alk said, sitting on the slope with a loaf in each hand.

"Long, careful digging," Kialan agreed. "They took six weeks' digging to find the second spellcoat up above Hannart."

"I doubt," said Navis, "that we have six hours."

"Then we think it round another way," said Alk.

Moril arrived then, with his vaguest look, and was introduced to Ynen. Ynen was delighted. It turned out that he had met Moril's brother, Dagner, in Hannart, who had told him a great deal about Moril. The two of them chattered as they ate. They were the only ones talking. Everyone else was wondering how to find the crown, except Luthan, who kept giving Maewen such melting looks that she wanted to tell him to start digging. But he won't, she thought. It would spoil his scarlet suit.

"This won't do," Mitt said at last.

"No," Kialan agreed. He nudged Moril with his boot. "Moril, do the Singers have any sayings that might help us find the crown?"

Moril looked up. His face was full of a kind of nervous awe. "You want to go and get it now?"

Everyone stared at him.

"I've been walking around," he said, "trying to work it out. I *think* the cwidder will do it. We have to go to the waystone."

Everyone sprang up. "Why didn't you *say*?" Ynen cried out.

"I second that," said Navis.

"Leave him be," Kialan said, as they all raced down the hummock. "He's like that. One of us should have asked him before."

They raced past the hobbled horses, where the hearthwomen were fixing bayonets to long guns. Mitt knew how they felt. Every one of the women was trying to pretend this was just a training exercise, and very much hoping that was all it would turn out to be. As they ran on, more hearthmen sprang up alertly from among the green humps and then subsided, seeing they were not being attacked. Further heads reared up from across the green road and disappeared, as the eight of them gathered round the waystone.

"What do we do?" said Kialan.

"Go through," said Moril. "I think." He knelt down and carefully put his face to the impossibly small hole in the middle of the waystone.

"Look any different through there, does it?" Mitt asked hopefully.

"No," Moril said, crawling away backward. He slung the cwidder round to the front of him and stripped off its cover, thinking hard.

"I don't wish to cast a blight, lad," said Alk, "but not even young Ynen is going to get through there."

Moril frowned. "I know. I wish I could think how—"

"Wait a minute," Maewen interrupted.

As she spoke, there was a yell and a splatter of gunfire from the mounds over to the right. Here comes the frantic bit, Mitt thought.

"Uh-oh," said Alk.

Luthan's curvaceous face went a little less pink. "My sector," he said and went dashing away.

"Good," said Maewen. "Moril, in the time I come from, this waystone is as tall as a house—and I think the hole is lower down. Does that help?"

Moril's white face lifted to her. "Yes. That's a truth." He put his fingers to the strings of the cwidder and bent his head. Mitt, now he knew a little about the working of the cwidder, could feel Moril concentrate and the power begin to build. He knelt beside him, as if that could help.

There was another shot and a great deal of yelling, fierce and strident, from over to the left. Alk flinched in that direction and turned back. "I'd better go," he said. "That's my part. Here, Mitt. Here's a keepsake for you. Catch." He tossed Mitt something small and round and heavy.

Mitt was just in time to catch it. "What's this, then?"

"Told you I made a copy of the Adon's ring," Alk called over his shoulder. "Put it on. I may have a hole in me like that waystone when you see me next."

Mitt gave the ring a distracted look and shoved it on his nearest finger. Moril had begun to play, rippling music like waves from a stone dropped in water, expanding and expanding, and rippling again. The waystone looked no different, but Mitt could feel the solid booming beneath the ripples, and strange, shrill stretching sounds buried in it, that told him that something was happening. Counterpoint against the music came more shots and clamor, this time from behind.

Navis looked over his shoulder. "Now I must go. You young ones find that crown, and we'll cover your backs."

"But you'll need me," Mitt said, half getting up.

Navis put a hand on his shoulder and held him down. "Not yet. You go. Luck ship and shore."

A strange thing to say, Maewen thought. She looked back at the waystone and saw the impossible sight of Moril stepping through the hole in the center, carefully holding his cwidder. The waystone looked no larger. Moril looked no smaller. Yet he stepped through, and there was no sign of him on the other side. Ynen hopped eagerly through after him, and he disappeared, too. Then Kialan stooped to follow. He was so much bigger that Maewen held her breath. But Kialan stepped through as calmly and easily as if he did this impossible thing every day. Mitt went next, in a gawky scramble of elbows and long legs. By this time the yelling and the gunshots were coming from all round. As Maewen bent down to follow Mitt, there were white puffs of smoke coming from every mound she could see. She saw the hearthwomen in the center grimly getting on their horses.

A strange voice behind her yelled, *"Charge! Come on, charge them!"*

Maewen had no time to think that the hole was too small. She simply scrambled through it, and was barely surprised to find that it was easy.

# 20

MAEWEN HAD A GLIMPSE of Kialan and Ynen following Moril down a silent golden street, casting blue-black shadows as they went. There was a warm sun and a feeling of humming peace in this place. But Maewen could clearly hear screams and shots and crashing in the distance all round. The battle was only a hairbreadth away. She knew it could come bursting through Moril's paper-thin enchantment any second. When someone came at her sideways in another long indigo shadow, it was just like Gardale again. She put her hands to her face and screamed.

"Hush!" Mitt said, giving her a shake.

It was only Mitt, who had waited for her. Maewen knew this, but still she whimpered and sobbed.

Mitt shook her harder. "Will you hush! Moril made this out of *sounds*, don't you understand! You're going to break it if you carry on. What are you, a baby?"

Maewen pulled herself together. "Of course I'm not a baby. I'm thirteen. It was just the battle out there."

"Thirteen? Really?" Mitt found this wonderful and remarkable. He had been thinking of Maewen as the same age as Noreth, and here she was younger than he was! It seemed to turn everything round. As they set off to follow the others, Mitt slid his hand carefully down Maewen's arm and took hold of her hand. It was the most momentous and the most exciting thing he had ever done in his life.

*Click!*

"Snap!" said Maewen, as Mitt swung their joined hands up to see what the noise was. They both laughed. On Maewen's thumb and Mitt's forefinger were two identical gold bands and two identical gloomy profiles carved out of what seemed exactly the same kind of red stone. "Alk's copy?" Maewen asked.

"Yes. He made it to fit himself by the size of it," Mitt said.

After that it became a more normal thing to hold hands. They walked on, following the square gold-yellow stones of what seemed to be a street. Everywhere was misty, white mist with the sun in it, and the other three were out of sight ahead by then. But there seemed nowhere else for them to have gone except along the street.

At first there appeared to be houses on either side, though these were fuzzed out above the first story by the mist. But after a while they seemed to have come into a garden or a parkland. There was a feeling of openness. Delicate trees spread green-gold branches in the mist, and others were spires and blocks of gold-dark. It seemed moist underfoot. Maewen thought she could hear birds, but when she listened, they were somehow out of hearing. Seabirds? Mitt thought. Land birds? There were smells, too, delicately scrawled on the air. Mitt's head came up at the smell: the peat smell of the North, of a distant farm, the hot tang of the South, water lazily running, and even, amazingly, the far-off salt of the sea. This was a smell he had once thought of as home. Nearby, willows were budding.

It can't be this wet here! Mitt thought. But it was, secretly. The scent was conveying him the secret that under Kernsburgh the rock was porous and riddled with channels of water flowing down to the sea. Then they can sink wells, he thought with some relief. It had worried him slightly that Kernsburgh did not seem to have a water supply. He found himself saying to Maewen, "There's going to be war and fighting for the next two years."

"They can't do much rebuilding till that's over," she agreed.

"They can make a start. That's not what I meant," Mitt said. "I meant it was all building to war when I left the South, and I get the feeling I'm going to have to be part of it, but I don't like to think of you getting hurt in it."

"I don't want to be left out," Maewen said.

"But you don't like war," Mitt pointed out. "What I mean is, you might stay here and start the building."

"Only if you promise to come back and see me after the war," Maewen said. "I'll come after you if you don't."

"All right," said Mitt. "I promise. In two years." In the strange scented gold mist it did not seem ridiculous to talk of these things.

"I'll hold you to that," Maewen said, laughing.

They wandered on. Shortly they came out into a wide golden courtyard where they found the other three, none of whom seemed to notice that Mitt and Maewen must have come by a side way. Ynen was pointing to a statue on a pedestal.

"Ours are the only shadows, here," he said. "Look."

He was right. All their shadows were long and blue-black. The statue ought to have laid a zigzag shadow up a flight of stairs, but it did not. Moril stumbled on the stairs because they were so hard to see. Kialan caught his elbow to stop him falling, all in a crisscross of inky shadows, and accidentally jarred the cwidder. It sang out melodiously. The sound seemed to shake the entire place. Everything blurred. For a moment, even the inky shadows were faint. Nobody dared breathe. They all stood still until the sound died and the faint golden buildings came back.

The tall building at the head of the steps, though it was lost upward into mist, was remarkably like the Tannoreth Palace. Like, but quite unlike, too, Maewen realized, staring up at it while the others tiptoed gently up the steps. It had almost no windows, and its roof was supported on mighty pillars shaped like buds—long whorled buds, like the ones on magnolias—and yet it had the same shape and gave her the same feel as the palace she knew. She climbed the difficult steps on cautious, whispering feet and joined the others in the long gold-stone tunnel.

They trod forward as gently as they could, all horribly aware that this palace of gold was only the most fragile illusion. The stony air from the tunnel made both Ynen and Mitt want to cough. Neither of them dared make that much noise, and they had to keep clearing their throats as gently as they could. Then the tunnel branched.

"Where to?" Moril whispered.

"Follow your cwidder," Kialan breathed.

Moril seemed to consider this meant straight on. They tiptoed after him, deep into the heart of the palace. Now they seemed to be in a corridor whose golden stone roof was only an inch or so above Kialan's head or Mitt's. Both of them ducked when Moril led them under a heavy lintel and down misty steps into a warm oblong room. It was not a big place. It had stone benches along each side and a large stone seat at the far end. The first thing they all noticed was that this seat had a strange gap underneath, as if something that was meant to go there was missing. The second thing they saw was a thick golden circlet on the seat of the chair.

They all knew this was the crown. Everyone waited for everyone else to go forward and pick it up. Before any of them could sort out the courage to do it, a young man jumped up from the right-hand bench.

"At long last!" he said. He was very glad to see them. He strode joyfully over to the stone seat and picked up the crown. "I thought I would never do this again!" he said as he turned round, holding it in both hands.

Everyone stood very still. He was a tall young man, with rounded shoulders wider than Kialan's or Mitt's, and there was a sort of gawkiness to him that reminded them all of Mitt. His face, when he turned sideways to look from Moril, along the line to Maewen, was like Ynen's. He had the same nose, long and pointed. When he turned full face, to look at the whole group of them in a puzzled way, he reminded Maewen of Wend, though everyone else was reminded of Maewen, with a fleeting likeness to Moril and Kialan. And Mitt was reminded of Old Ammet, too, because the young man had the same flying white hair.

"What's the matter?" said the young man. "Why don't you speak?"

"Is it all right? It won't shake the place apart?" Moril whispered.

The young man laughed. "Not here. This part has to be more solid. It used to be my strongroom."

"Er—then, who are you?" Mitt asked. "If you don't mind being asked."

"My name's Hern," said the young man. "I used to be King here a long while ago."

All five of them gasped, and then drew breath, one after another, to ask the King if he was of the Undying—and then let the breath go, not quite sure. He had the same unshadowed golden look as the rest of the palace. If you caught him out of the corner of your eye, bright rays seemed to stand out from him, and across him, that almost canceled him out of sight.

Hern laughed again. "Don't be afraid. I'm only here because I asked the One on my deathbed if I could present the crown to the new King."

"Whatever possessed—" Kialan, Moril, and Ynen all began together.

"—me to do such a stupid thing?" Hern asked. "I know. What you ask the One for, you get."

"Then you *are* of the Undying," Mitt said. "In a manner of speaking."

Hern looked at him. His face was bleak and ribby as Mitt's face had been in Gardale. "In a manner of speaking is right. I was afraid all my life that I was going to turn out to be of the Undying. And because of that, I was always very careful never to let anyone make a picture or an image of me—that's how the Undying are bound into godhead, you know—and then I go and ask for the wrong thing, and my reward is this half-life." Mitt opened his mouth to say something, but Hern shook his head. His face relaxed and went businesslike. "No. Let me first ask who claims this crown. All but one of you have a perfect right to it."

Nobody answered. Each of them shot dubious looks at the others.

"Oh come on!" said Hern. "Isn't this what you came for?"

Maewen cleared her throat. "Yes. But I think we were supposed to get it for Amil the Great."

Hern shrugged. "That's news to me," he said. He came toward them, carrying the golden circlet. All of them made a move to back away and then stood, feeling cowardly. But it was alarming. Hern was misty and shot with beams of light, but his personality was as strong as it must have been when he was a King. As if that was the main thing left of him, Mitt thought. And the crown itself was thick, real, and solid between Hern's misty hands, of such pure gold that it shone orange in the golden light.

Hern halted in front of Moril. "Do you claim this crown?"

Moril gulped. The others could see him thinking that his answer would really be addressed to the One, and he had Hern's example to show him that he had better say exactly the right thing. "No," he said, "I don't want to be King. I want to be a new kind of Singer—a very good one, if I can."

Hern nodded and moved on to Ynen. "You?"

Ynen licked his lips. He was whiter even than Moril. "No, not me. I—I want to be a sailor, and they wouldn't let me if I was King, because I might get drowned."

Hern said nothing. He simply moved on to Kialan. "And you?"

"I—" said Kialan. He had to stop and try again. "I know I have a claim, and it isn't because of the way my father would hate it, it's—Well, I don't feel *big* enough. Inheriting Hannart's quite enough for me, honestly."

Hern frowned at this, which made Kialan flush bright red and then stare unrepentantly. But Hern said nothing again and moved on to Mitt. Mitt had expected Hern to pass him by. He backed away. "You're not including me in this?" Mitt said.

Hern nodded.

"Then include me out," Mitt said. "I'm not fit, I'm common and—and—" He searched for the feeling he had just now in the strangely scented parkland. "Listen, I don't mind helping in the war. The country needs a change. But all I want out of it is a bit of peace and maybe a farm somewhere."

Hern frowned at this, too, and Mitt looked as unrepentant as Kialan. Hern turned to Maewen. "I can't offer the crown to you," he explained, "because you are not really born yet. I'm sorry."

"I understand," Maewen said, but she knew she sounded wistful. "The only thing I really want is to be allowed to stay—" She caught herself up. The One alone knew what Mum and Aunt Liss would feel, but this was what she *wanted* and she knew, like Moril, that she had to phrase it right. "Stay in Mitt's time, I mean."

Mitt turned and gave her a smile that warmed them both. Hern, meanwhile, retreated, still holding the crown. When they looked back at him, he was sitting in the stone seat, looking exasperated.

"Let's get at this another way," he said. "We have eliminated one of you. We know that the one who accepts this crown will be King. Let's call him King—for the sake of argument—Amil, since that is the name you seem to have brought with you. Who will be Amil?"

"If you like," Ynen offered, "we could take the crown and give it to my father."

"Yes, or mine," Kialan agreed.

Hern gave them that bleak, ribby look again. "You didn't attend to what I said at first. I am to hand the crown to the next King. That means to one of you, since no one else is here to claim it." He let them think about this, uneasily, for a moment. Then he said, "When I made my unlucky request to the One, what I had really wanted was to give the new King the benefit of my advice, but since I didn't ask that, that is something I am not allowed to do. Instead I shall ask you what advice you would give to this new King Amil. Think carefully. You may be advising yourself."

There was utter silence. Nobody could think of anything.

Hern laughed. "I shall start you off. How about: People's *idea* of what they can do is even more important than what they *can* do?"

"Oh, I know that!" Moril said. "It's in the King's Sayings. The Singers all know those."

"There, you see?" Hern said. "I couldn't give you that saying if it hadn't been out in the world already. I said it at the battle with Kankredin. This is why I can't give advice to the new King. The One knew, though I didn't, that a dead man's thoughts stop with his life. Listen to the Singer. He'll tell you my thoughts."

"Yes, but I didn't know they were *yours*," Moril said.

"Hang on a minute," said Mitt. "What do you mean, you can't give advice? You just gave us a whole load of it!"

"Did I?" said Hern.

He said it perfectly neutrally. This made Kialan say, almost exasperated, "You did, you know. He's right. You warned us straight off to be careful what we said, or the One would take us at our word."

"Roundaboutly," said Mitt. "Using yourself."

"A King should always set an example," Hern said. "That's in my Sayings, too, isn't it?" he asked Moril.

Moril nodded. "And," said Kialan, "you told us to attend to your exact words."

But Mitt broke in across Kialan. "No, before that! Didn't you listen? There was that about not being bound like the Undying."

The two of them were leaning forward eagerly. Hern's face was intent. Oh I see! Maewen thought, from her standpoint as a nonqualifier. We're in Round Two now. Ynen seemed to have dropped out. He was staring sadly at Hern. Maewen saw Mitt notice Ynen's sadness and wonder about it as he spoke.

"Then you made a song and dance about your sayings being dead and over with," Mitt said, "just so we'd notice they weren't."

"Yes, the exact opposite of what you seemed to be saying," Kialan agreed. "Your thoughts *have* gone on after you."

"That's not new," Moril put in. "It's in a song by Osfameron."

Moril would be disqualifying himself, Maewen thought, if he went on sticking just to what Singers knew. Perhaps Moril did not mind. Maewen had thought she did not mind, but now she knew she felt sad and alone and left out.

"I'm glad it's not new," Hern said. "I have no business having new thoughts. It wouldn't be reasonable."

Mitt could not help grinning.

"What are you smiling at?" Hern asked.

"You," Mitt said, "must have been a regular eel in your day. Not reasonable, my big toe! You keep turning up new ideas."

A slight, enjoying smile bent Hern's mouth. "I was always very hot on reason," he said. "If I had been able to give the new King advice, I would have told him never to rely on things being reasonable. I did, and it caused me no end of trouble."

"There you go again!" said Mitt.

Kialan laughed. Hern's smile grew slightly. "I defy you," he said, "to discover any other new thoughts I've shown you."

"Well," said Kialan. "You *can* have new thoughts. Osfameron may have written that song about thoughts flying on, but you were dead when he wrote it."

Hern shook his head. "Won't do. Osfameron is my brother."

Kialan looked very dashed at this and turned to Mitt for help. "He said *shown*," Mitt said. "And he did tell us to listen to every word. Let's see." He looked at Hern. "You've shown us what comes of asking for the wrong thing, and then shown us yourself getting round that, and giving advice like you meant to. That's how to keep the rules and break them, too. I like that. It takes a cool head. But there's more," Mitt said, thinking aloud, which was the way he always thought best. "Maybe this was what Kialan was driving at. Yes—you're still at it. You're not beat yet. You're showing us that."

"*Is* it a new thought, then, to say, 'Keep on, there's always hope'?" Hern said. "I thought that was a very old saying."

"Yes, but you're the first person *I've* met who's still saying it when he's *dead*," Mitt answered. "That has to be new."

Hern laughed and stood up. "I believe you. Bend your head, Alhammitt, so that I can put this crown on it."

*"What!"* Mitt backed away in horror. "Now, look. I told you. And I was only saying what Kialan said."

Hern looked at Kialan. "Was he?"

"Not really," Kialan admitted.

"Tidying it up, then," Mitt said pleadingly. "Take the thing away. I'm not qualified."

"Yes, you are," said Hern. "*I* told *you*. Your right descends from the Adon's son Almet, who went to live in Waywold."

"Pretty sideways, I'll bet!" Mitt said.

"Only as sideways as direct descent, from father to son," said Hern. "If that was not so, why does the Adon's ring accept you?"

Mitt looked down at the Adon's seal, snugly above his knuckle. "This is just a copy."

"No," said Hern. He nodded toward Maewen. "Hers is the copy."

Mitt shot a disbelieving look from Hern to Maewen and rapidly tried the ring on his little finger, then on his thumb. Each time it slid over his lump of knuckle and fitted as if it had been made for him. "This is plain ridiculous!" he said. He turned round. For a moment it looked as if he was going to storm from the room.

"Wait!" said Hern. It was the voice of command that Navis was so good at using. Mitt almost stopped. But he shook his shoulders and put one foot on the steps. Hern said quickly, "Accept the crown, and you may ask the One one favor."

Mitt turned back. "You mean that?"

"I do," said Hern.

"Now?"

"Crown first," said Hern. "Bend your head."

Mitt sighed and bowed his head down. "Extra bit of advice," he said, looking sideways at Kialan. "Kings drive a hard bargain."

Hern chuckled as he settled the thick gold band carefully over Mitt's lank hair. "A King should have a sharp mind," he said. "That may be in my Sayings somewhere. I am sorry that I cannot give you the kingstone as well as the crown. The stone is in the South. A man in Holand called Hobin knows where to find it."

Mitt stared at him from under his own forehead. "Hobin? Gunsmith? He's my stepfather!" He straightened up slowly and put one hand uneasily to the crown, thinking it might slip, but it seemed steady enough. Like the Adon's ring, it was an exact fit. "Hobin!" he said. "You Undying really got me hemmed in, haven't you?"

Hern nodded as he stepped backward. "It was the same for me. Now you can ask your favor."

"All right," said Mitt. "Then, do you really have to sit here, century after century, waiting for the next new King to come along?"

Hern went very still. "This I know is in the Sayings of the King," he said. "Never be beguiled by pity. Are you talking pity?"

"No," said Mitt. "You've been showing us you're stuck here and you don't like it from the moment you first spoke."

"Mercy, then?" asked Hern. "This sits well on a King."

"No," said Mitt. "Flaming Ammet, I don't know what it's called! I'll have to take a leaf out of your book and *show* you. Take a look at Ynen. He's miserable because all he can think of is that you have to sit here, year in and year out, waiting for a King that may not come. Only he doesn't like to say so because the One made you sit here. Isn't that so?" Mitt asked Ynen. Ynen went pink and nodded hard. "See?" Mitt said to Hern. "I don't know the word for what I'm doing, unless it's having the cheek to say things no one else dares to say. Is that kingly?"

Hern did not answer. He laughed.

"Laugh away," Mitt said. "I'm going to ask the One to take you off duty."

Hern went on laughing, but the sound was confused now and fading. The beams of light, which had half hidden him if you looked at him sideways, came to cover him however you looked, crisscrossing and elongating confusingly. He was like a candle seen through tears. Then the beams separated and slid away. Each silvery streak carried a dim piece of Hern's shape with it, as if he were dissolving underwater. Mitt set his teeth and clenched his hands until the Adon's ring bit into him. This was exactly like his worst nightmare when he was small. He had been fairly sure this would happen, but it had seemed worth asking all the same. He made himself watch until Hern had rippled away into nowhere.

The rippling did not vanish with Hern. It remained as a greengoldness, like air shaking in heat. The stone seat, and that whole end of the room, wavered as if they were under clear, shallow water. Mitt's hands remained clenched. The scent he had recognized outside, of peat and farm, willows budding, and slow, deep river flowing to the far-off sea, was back again, stronger and more potent. And the rippling had formed a shape, a huge gold-green shadow with a profile like Hern's or Ynen's. Mitt had no doubt, nor had any of the others, that there was a presence standing behind them, casting this shadow, but it was beyond any of them to turn round and look.

When the One spoke, the voice came from behind them. "Hern has long ago gone down the River to the sea."

Mitt relaxed. Ynen murmured, "Oh good!" Maewen wondered how anyone could mistake Kankredin's voice for the One's. This voice was like the whole land speaking, the settling of rocks, the grind of water through granite, the slow shift of earth, and the wind blowing, and it burred in your ears in the same way as the low string on Moril's cwidder.

"It is not easy," said the One, "for my mortal children to speak with me face-to-face."

This was true. All of them were aching to turn round and see the One, and all of them knew it was quite impossible.

"Witness this, all of you," said the One. "You have a new King."

No one was sure what to do, until Moril led them in a ragged chorus. "We witness we have a new King."

"I thank you," said the One.

The rippling shadow stooped then. It was as if the One bent to have a private word with each of them, all at the same time. Maewen heard the great voice at her ear, saying, "I cannot promise you what you asked. Too many imponderables lie in between. I am sorry."

To Mitt the One said, "You have been offered the name of Amil, which is my name. Before you choose between that name or your own, you must know that I have sworn to root out Kankredin from my land. If you take my name, that will be your task, too. What name do you choose?"

Mitt knew it was a real choice, even if Maewen had told him which way he chose. He weighed it up. Alhammitt was a good name, except that it was the name of half the men in the South. Amil was a name no one else had, but it carried the One's burden with it. Well, Mitt had carried burdens all his life. Kingship was another one. One more seemed to make no difference on top of that. "I'll take Amil," he said.

Then he turned round, like someone waking up, wondering what the One had said to the others. The rippling shadow was gone, and with it, most of the golden mistiness. He could see they were standing in a place that was no more than an oblong trench, with walls made of big blocks of yellowish stone that were broken off at about waist height.

Beside him Maewen was fiercely blinking back tears. Moril looked much the same. But Ynen and Kialan both looked happy, in a stunned kind of way.

"I think we have to go back through the stone," Moril said.

# 21

WHEN THEY TURNED ROUND, they found three stone steps the color of oatcakes leading into a green-gold landscape of humps and hillocks. Had it not been for the silence, and the mist still clinging to the near distance, they would have thought they were back in the Kernsburgh outside the waystone.

They walked, slightly downhill, through a dip on the gold-green turf. The humps of Hern's palace were small behind them. Ruins were like that, Maewen thought. Buildings, even palaces, seemed to take up far more room than they really did.

At first they were very silent and sober. Everyone kept glancing at Mitt, walking in the midst of them with the crown gleaming orange against his hair. He seemed taller. Nobody knew quite what to say. At last Maewen decided that someone must say something.

"Do you want us to call you Your Majesty?" she asked.

"Flaming Ammet!" said Mitt. "Don't you dare!" He grabbed hold of her hand. "Don't any of you treat me different," he said. "I'm going to need you all around for sanity."

Everyone broke into relieved laughter. After that they were able to talk together quite normally until Moril said, "Hush a moment."

His cwidder was humming, and humming louder for every step they took forward. Something dark was rising out of the mist ahead. The cwidder was almost growling as they reached it. It was the waystone, but it was not small any longer. It towered in a mighty arch above them, even bigger than the one Maewen remembered outside the station.

Moril murmured, "Wider than the world, or small as in a nut." It must have been a quotation. Kialan recognized it and grinned at him as they all stepped through the waystone together, with Ynen, who was last, almost treading on Moril, who was just ahead of Kialan.

They were back on green grass under a gray morning. The waystone was waist-high behind them, and they were in a battle.

The fighting was noisy, it was vicious, and it was all round them. Everywhere they looked, people ran and struggled and hacked at one another. Riders and loose horses galloped and screamed. They had a glimpse of Luthan, still on horseback, furiously hacking at someone in a wavy helmet and shiny armor that gave him a chest like a pigeon. Luthan's face was bright with blood that clashed with the red of his clothes. One of his arms was the wrong red, too, and the mail was dangling from it in strips. They just had time to see this before the horses and fighting swirled and both Luthan and his opponent vanished. The air was full of drifting puffs of white smoke, shouts, clangs, and the slurring whisper of crossbow bolts, which were even crueler than the guns, because you could barely hear them coming.

Kialan threw himself behind the waystone. "Get down, all of you!"

The waystone was a tiny piece of cover, but it was the only one available. The rest crowded up against Kialan, kneeling or crouching, Mitt on one knee with one hand steadying the crown.

"What's going on?" Moril gasped. He was doubled protectively across his cwidder. "Those look like Southerners! That armor!"

Ynen took a look through the hole in the waystone. "They are, too! I *think* they look like Andmark."

"Earl *Henda*!" Mitt exclaimed. Everyone except Maewen bobbed up for a hasty look. "Hundreds of them," said Mitt. "Where have they all come from?"

"It must have been *them* we heard in the night— Ynen and me," Kialan said, doubled over his own knees. "I remember thinking I heard supply wagons."

Mitt bobbed up again to look through the savage smoky confusion. He bobbed down again, almost at once, and a speeding crossbow bolt whizzed above all their heads, but he had had time to see a row of big black wagons drawn up some way beyond the green road. "They're using the wagons for cover," he said. "The ones with guns."

"Who do you think's winning?" Kialan asked.

Mitt shook his head. It felt heavy with the crown. The battle had obviously gone long beyond the stage where you could tell what was going on, but there had looked to be far more Southerners than Northerners. He had a feeling the Northerners were getting beaten.

There was another noise now. It was hard to pick out among the din. Mitt thought he had noticed it only because he seemed to feel it in his bones as much as his ears. For a moment, he wondered if he had accidentally said the name of the Earth Shaker. The earth seemed full of drumming.

There was a tremendous shouting behind.

They all whirled round to find a wall of horsemen galloping down upon them. The world seemed full of thousands of pounding horse legs, flying divots of turf and hollow drumming thunder. Kialan spread his arms out and pulled the four of them into a tight bundle in front of him. *"Down!"* he yelled, and fell forward on top.

Even so, they all ducked and flinched as the horsemen swept up to them. Horses were all round them, all over them. One rider actually hurtled over their heads, leaping the five of them and the waystone, too. The ground shook in earnest.

"O great One!" Kialan groaned, with his head up to follow that particular rider. "That was my father. Now we're in the soup whatever happens!"

The noise of fighting suddenly doubled. They could almost feel the riders from Hannart crash into the battle. Beyond the edge of the waystone Maewen saw a horse rear, screaming and gushing blood. Something else tumbled into view, with a clothy *thwump*, and she saw it was the rider, thrown down like a broken doll in a strange position. He was not moving, but his horse went on screaming, and so did others she could not see. She nearly screamed herself. She wanted to be sick. Her eyes felt twisted and hot. Mitt had been right to say she did not like war. It was horrible. And the worst of it was that she had helped cause it by riding the King's Road instead of Noreth. The only reason she did not scream and kick and beat the grass with her fists was that it would be letting Mitt down. She crouched, swallowing.

A bullet went *whang* on the edge of the waystone. That nearly hit me! she thought. Beside her Kialan yelled out an extremely filthy word. Maewen jumped round to find him clutching his arm. There was a slice of granite standing out from his sleeve and blood was trying to flood out around the slice. His sleeve was soaked red already. Kialan repeated the filthy word and took hold of the piece of granite to pull it out.

"Don't do that!" Mitt shouted at him. "Stop the bleeding first!"

"But it hurts," Kialan said. There were gray-green smudges of shock under his eyes.

Maewen could see how much it hurt. And Kialan had had his arms spread out to keep them from being trampled. He didn't deserve this. She wanted to do something to help. She bobbed up. The fighting was a frantic seething out beyond the green road. The space in between was full of loose horses and quiet, doll-like dead people. One of the horses wandering there was her own—or Noreth's, except that poor Noreth would never have any need of it now. Here was something she could do.

"I've got a roll of bandage in my saddlebag," she said, and jumped up to get it.

Mitt and Moril both screamed at her to come back, but there were scarcely any bullets now. The fighting had rolled back again and was now around that line of black wagons. Maewen covered the space to her horse in perfect safety and told herself she was being brave at last. The horse stood docilely. She heaved and fumbled at the straps on her baggage roll. Quick, quick, before Kialan bleeds to death! It seemed to take a hundred years just to undo two buckles.

Then the voice spoke to her. "There is a loaded pistol someone has dropped on the ground at your feet," it said. "Take it and—"

"Oh shut up!" Maewen told it. "Kialan's hurt."

"Moril!" said Mitt.

"I know. I heard him." Moril bent hurriedly over his cwidder, trying to make the power gather. Mitt could feel it was slow and difficult to gather again so soon, and the screams and roaring of the battle did not help.

"I made sure the Adon was injured," the voice told Maewen smugly. "These are my instructions. Shoot the Southerner with the crown first, and then—"

"I said *shut up*!" Maewen screamed. The buckles were undone. The bandage was—where? *Where*? Oh, here it was. She took the roll and backed away. Pistol? Oh yes. There, almost under the horse's feet.

The voice rose to a blare. *"Pick it up, you stupid girl. Shoot them all and take the crown!"*

"Quickly!" said Mitt.

"No," said Maewen. She aimed her boot at the pistol and deliberately kicked it as far away as she could.

Mitt groaned. Moril put all his fingers under the lowest string and plucked, desperately. The cwidder responded with a deep brassy *twang*, as if Moril had struck a gong instead.

The horse in front of Maewen drifted away sideways. Although it seemed like a solid horse, it behaved just like smoke and shredded into the air, in brown wisps. In its place was the ghost of a man, twelve feet high or more, bell-shaped and robed, bent over to glare at Maewen with human eyes under fat eyelids. He was hollow. She could see the empty space in the middle of him, and somehow this was the most horrifying thing about him. I was riding *that*! she thought.

It did not seem to bother Kankredin that Maewen could see him. He blared, "I am the One! You must do as I command!"

Mitt made a movement to stand up. The ghostly fat-lidded eyes caught the movement. The vague hand in the hollow sleeve made a small gesture, as Maewen said, "No, you are *not* the One. And you never fooled me for a moment." She was shaking, but she was glad to find she could be brave in this way at least.

The towering shape bent toward her. The sheets of wriggly hair on both sides of its face fell forward, and the huge, vague hands reached. Mitt found he could not move his legs. Beside him Moril's hands seemed to be stuck to the cwidder, in crooked shapes. But Mitt did not need to walk. He drew breath and shouted.

"YNYNEN!"

Then he moved, in spite of not being able to, and took off like a sprinter. Somehow he covered the distance between himself and Maewen, just in time to knock her over and fall on top of her before Ammet answered his call.

There was a howling wind, full of chaff. They were peppered with stinging grains of wheat, first from one side and then from everywhere. It made them both cringe. But in spite of that, in spite of grain coming at them like hailstones, and flying straw and blinding chaff dust, Maewen and Mitt both craned round to see the ghost of Kankredin spinning in a spinning trumpet shape of wheat-filled wind.

It was over almost as they looked. The ghost drew tatters of itself together and dissolved away backward. The trumpet shape unraveled and streamed away across the green land, carrying chaff and grain far and wide.

"Did you get him?" Maewen asked.

"Not sure." Mitt dragged himself to his knees. There was no sign of Kankredin. The gong note Moril had evoked from the cwidder was still in the air, sounding on and on. If Kankredin was near, he would be visible. "Had a feeling Ammet only got part of him," Mitt said regretfully, "but I think he's gone."

Maewen scrambled up with the bandage. The crown had fallen beside her. She picked it up, thick and orange and heavy, and it left a bare oval shape in the grain that covered the grass. "I *knew* there was something strange about that horse," she said as they went back to the waystone among drifting chaff and pattering grain.

Moril looked up as they came. Mitt nodded. Moril put one hand on the throbbing string to stop the sound, and then flexed both hands as if Kankredin had cramped them. Behind Moril, Kialan had Ynen's belt buckled round his arm to stop the bleeding. He was holding it tight for

Ynen while Ynen tore pieces off both their shirts to bandage the place where the slice of stone had been.

"Rather a waste of two good shirts," Kialan said. His face was a better color. He looked up at Mitt. "What happened to the crown?"

Maewen realized that she was holding it. "Bend your head down," she said to Mitt.

None of them noticed that the noise of fighting had all but stopped. As Mitt bent his head and Maewen fitted the crown carefully over his hair, Earl Keril came crunching toward them over the scattered grain. He was a little disheveled, but he barely looked as if he had been in a battle. He hooked his thumbs in his sword belt and watched Mitt and Maewen. "Well, now," he said pleasantly. "I had five possible outcomes in mind when I sent you to Adenmouth, but this was one that I confess never occurred to me."

Mitt straightened up. He was slightly taller than Earl Keril. "Get me hanged and make sure there's no uprising," he said. "Right?"

"Hanging you may yet be the solution," Earl Keril said in the same pleasant way. "Let me put to you my point of view. The North had been agog for some years with stories that Noreth Onesdaughter"—he bowed pleasantly to Maewen—"would take the royal road the year she was eighteen. Then, all of a sudden, *you* arrive in Aberath in a manner which fulfills every prophecy ever made, and all the common people are hailing you as the new King come at last—"

"I never knew that," Mitt said. "I had no idea. If you'd let me alone, I wouldn't be here now. But you set me on to murder Noreth."

"Naturally I hoped that the two claimants would cancel one another out," Keril agreed. He looked at Maewen again. "Rather than the one crown the other. But we were prepared for other outcomes, too. To that end the Countess took you in and educated you, and I took steps to make sure you would remain under the sponsorship of Hannart and Aberath—"

"Sponsorship is one word for it," Mitt said. "Nice try."

"I asked you to see my point of view!" Keril snapped. "When I was young and ignorant, I took part in an uprising. I know better now. I would go to greater lengths than this to stop another. People die in uprisings, by thousands, most horribly."

"When *I* was young and ignorant," said Mitt, "I lived in Holand. People died there all the time, only slowly. And the rest were too scared to help. There needs to be an uprising. One that works this time."

The two of them stared at one another unlovingly. "If this is your attitude," Keril said, "I shall see you hanged at Harvest. There are plentiful grounds."

Moril, Kialan, and Ynen surged to their feet, Kialan saying, "Listen, Father—" and Ynen protesting, "Don't undo the belt yet!"

"Be quiet!" said Keril. "I'll deal with you two later. What I want to know—"

Hasty feet crunched over the grain, and Alk and Navis arrived, one on either side of Keril. Alk's leathers were torn all over, showing battered links of mail underneath, and he had a streak of blood on his chin. One side of Navis's face was black with powder. He looked tired to death, but he spoke to Keril with the utmost courtesy. "My lord, we have to thank you for your timely intervention."

Alk grinned. "We were goners without you, Keril."

Keril turned his unloving look on them. Navis said, "Is there some trouble, my lord? May we assist?"

"Yes," Keril said grimly. "I want to know how this Mitt of yours contrived to have a Southern war band to meet him."

"I did no such thing!" said Mitt.

"Those are Henda's men, my lord," Navis said. "As you surely know, Henda can be trusted to respond to anything that might be a threat to his earldom entirely on his own."

"But how did he know?" Keril said. "Did you tell him, Navis Haddsson?"

"Oh come now, Keril," said Alk. "You saved Navis's life yourself. You heard the Southerners calling him traitor."

Keril hitched his shoulders irritably. Navis bowed to him. "As to how Henda knew, my lord, since I had heard of Noreth Onesdaughter at least two years ago, I can only suppose Henda's spies told him at the same time." Mitt stared. This was news to him. "One of those secrets," Navis said to him, "that my brother took good care not to have known on the waterfront in Holand."

"So I am to understand," Keril said to Navis, "that Navis Haddsson commandeered the hearthmen of Dropwater and Aberath to fight Henda, knowing that Henda would oppose Navis Haddsson's candidate for the crown."

Navis's eyes went to the golden band round Mitt's forehead. He smiled slightly. "My lord, I did not expect Henda. I expected you. But you are right to believe that I hoped Mitt would be King."

"Why?" Keril asked icily.

Navis shrugged. "Aside from obvious personal wishes, my lord, one of the pictures in my rooms in Holand was a portrait of the Adon. My impression is that you, too, my lord, were struck by Mitt's resemblance to the Adon. I thought about it much of the time we sailed North. But

I would have waited a few years to do anything about it. You forced our hands."

"I'm glad I did," said Keril. "Your candidate is not of age and has no right to that thing on his head."

Alk had been exchanging looks with Moril. Now he said, "Right, Keril. Why don't we ask?" And he nodded at Moril.

Moril stood forward. "The One called us to witness just now," he said, loudly and formally, "that we have a new King. The One gave Mitt the crown and his own name of Amil."

"I hereby witness this as lawful," Alk said. "Come on, Keril. Accept it."

Keril still seemed entirely unwilling. Moril, carefully and meaningly, arranged his fingers on the cwidder. "I could summon the One," he said.

Keril looked uneasily at the cwidder. "You always were a bit of a mystic, Moril," he said. "But this is a reasonable age—"

He was interrupted by howls and yells and catcalls in the distance behind him. "Traitor!" they heard. "Traitor! There's the traitor!" The shouting was coming from hearthmen in all three liveries. It seemed to have something to do with the row of supply wagons beyond the road. Navis set off that way at a run. Alk and Keril followed. Mitt pointed a thumb at Keril's back. "Never rely on things being reasonable," he said.

"Sayings of the King," Moril said, laughing.

They jogged toward the wagons, with Ynen and Kialan following more slowly. As Mitt reached the crowd milling round the wagons, Navis waved. People fell back respectfully to let Mitt through. Everyone's eyes for a moment fixed wonderingly on the crown. "What is it?" said Mitt.

"We invite you to look at this," Navis said. And, with a smooth stare at Keril, he added, "Your Majesty."

He waved again. Several hearthmen hauled on the dark weatherproof covering of one of the wagons. As they dragged it away, the trim green-painted cart underneath came into view.

Hestefan was on its driving seat. When he saw Mitt, Maewen, and Moril all staring at him, he writhed away backward. "I didn't do it!" he said. His fine Singer voice cracked into hoarseness. "I was made to! They forced me to come along!"

"What do the Southerners say about it?" Mitt asked.

Alk nodded to the nearest person from Aberath. "Go and fetch the Andmark captain to the King."

The Southerners were sitting in a large huddle a little way off with their hands on their heads. Luthan and his hearthwomen were walking round and round them with their bayoneted guns. Luthan's clothes were ruined, and his arm was in a sling. He looked warlike and efficient as he nodded at the message and beckoned someone from the midst of the Southerners.

The man was most unwilling to move. In the end Alk strode over and brought him out of the huddle, almost dangling from his big fist. "Here we are, Majesty," he said. "One captain."

The prisoner looked at Mitt and looked puzzled. "It was supposed to be a woman we had to ambush," he said. "What's going on?"

"Never mind that, Captain Fervold," Navis said. "Just tell us what this Singer had to do with it."

"Never forget a name, do you, Navis Haddsson?" said the captain. "It must be ten years since—"

"Twelve years," said Navis. "Tell."

"Simple enough," said Fervold. Alk let go of him, and he straightened up, looking relieved. "Orders were to land secretly at Cressing Harbor, come up by night to the green road, and rendezvous with the Singer at dawn, and he would show us where Kernsburgh was. Then we were to ambush the, er— Anyway, get to them before they got the crown. And we'd have got you, too, if you hadn't been a day late. But we missed the green road in the dark both nights, and the Singer didn't turn up to put us right until well on in the morning. What did he do? Give us away? Our information was we'd only find five folk here."

"Your bad luck," said Alk. "So Hestefan was working for the South?"

"Has been for years," said Fervold.

At this Hestefan cried out, "They made me! I tell you, they *made* me!"

Alk turned to him with his lawman's look. "And did they also make you murder Noreth of Kredindale?"

Hestefan straightened up and jutted his beard. "What nonsense is this? How could I have done? Look. She's standing there!" He pointed at Maewen.

"I'm not Noreth," Maewen said. It was embarrassing to say it in front of all these people, but a great relief, too.

"And I have seen Noreth's murdered corpse," said Alk. "The others who might have killed her are proved clear. I accuse you in law and before the crown of cutting Noreth's throat."

"Never," said Hestefan. "On my honor as a Singer. Never."

"Better get that cup out," Alk said to Navis.

Maewen had a different idea. She tugged at Mitt's sleeve. "This may not be right, because it was Kankredin who said it, but if he did kill her, he may have stolen a golden statue."

"That statue!" said Mitt. "You know, that clean slipped my mind! Where would Hestefan hide something really valuable?" he asked Moril.

He had to nudge Moril and say it again. Hestefan was saying, "A Singer is honorable. Our word is our bond. We are sworn to speak true and purvey no lies. Nor do we do dirty deeds and dastardly acts. This accusation soils all Singers."

Moril was staring at Hestefan as if he could not believe what he was hearing. "Sliding panel under the cart at the back," he said colorlessly, and went on staring.

Mitt whispered to Alk. Alk passed the cup back to Navis and, leaving Hestefan still ranting, he strode round to the rear of the cart. It heaved. There was the sound of wood splintering. Alk came grimly back with gold shining in one massive fist. "Shut your mouth, Hestefan. Where did you come by this?"

Hestefan gaped at the statue. His face had gone gray and piteous. "I tell you I did not kill her! The woman is of the Undying and cannot be killed! I took that statue—yes, yes, I admit—the first time I tried to cut her throat, but she was alive again half an hour later on the green road. I had no choice but to go with her and kill her again. And as I knew she would not die, I sent word in Kredindale to Henda's agent there to send a boat South for an armed band to cut her in pieces. And sure enough, she did not die, though I killed her twice in Gardale." He rocked about on the seat of the cart. "I had to do it. I had to do it for Fenna!"

"Deranged, I think," Navis said, leaning wearily on the nearest wagon.

"How come—you did it for Fenna?" Mitt said.

Hestefan looked at him and did not seem to see him. "Fenna is in Earl Henda's dungeons. The Earl will kill her painfully if I do not do as he wants."

"Oh nonsense!" said Navis. "You and I both know that Fenna is in Adenmouth recovering from a cracked head."

"That," said Hestefan, "is not my Fenna. That Fenna is the daughter of Henda's court musician. He sent her with me so that no one would know I had lost my daughter."

"You think this is true?" Alk asked Navis. "*Is* it true?" he said to Fervold.

"No idea," said Fervold. "But knowing our Henda, it could well be."

"True or not, the man's confessed to murder," Earl Keril said, stepping in to take command. He nodded to some of his hearthmen. "Take him down to Dropwater—it's nearest—and ask Earl Luthan to see him hanged."

Mitt could see that Keril had stepped in because it was what he was used to. Keril was thinking of himself as the senior Earl here. It made him angry. In spite of all that had been said, Keril was simply discounting the crown on Mitt's head. And it made him even angrier that Keril had done to Mitt himself exactly what Hestefan said Henda had done to him—and Keril had not even seemed to notice.

"*Wait* a minute!" he said. "You can't hang him. We need him. Singers can go where other people can't."

Keril stared at Mitt with his lips pressed together hard. He glanced round and saw that everyone else, including the hearthmen he had nodded to, had turned respectfully to Mitt. He pressed his lips together harder still. But he said nothing.

"Hestefan," said Mitt. Hestefan looked up, still not really seeing Mitt. "Hestefan, I want you to go and tell Henda that you carried out his orders. Tell him Noreth is dead. Can you do that?" Hestefan nodded, blinking, as if he were beginning to be able to see again. "But," said Mitt, "you're to go to Andmark through Holand. You're to go to Hobin the gunsmith in Holand—got that?—and tell Hobin that I've got the crown and he's to bring me the kingstone. Understand?"

"Well . . . yes . . ." Hestefan said slowly. "But if Henda hears I did that—No, no! I can't!"

"Oh yes, you *can*!" Moril said. "My father did that kind of thing all the time! *Do* it!" Hestefan turned to Moril, shivering so that his beard juddered. This made everyone look at Moril. Moril was as white as a person can be, so white that he was lurid, and the look of betrayal on his face made everyone look away again quickly. "Do it," Moril said, "or I'll curse you, Singer's curse, with the power of this cwidder, so that the curse will follow you beyond your grave! You've betrayed all Singers!"

"Ah no." Hestefan held up a shaking hand against him. "I only did what any man—"

"You aren't just *any* man!" Moril shrieked at him. "You're a *Singer*! I thought you were a good one. I trusted you. I know better now. So go to Holand. Go *now*!" He turned his back on Hestefan, looking as if he was going to be sick.

Keril turned to Mitt. "And what about our Southern prisoners?" he said, with a politeness and sarcasm that outdid Navis. "Are you finding a use for them, too?"

This was enough to make Mitt find a use for them on the spot. "*Of* course! This crown is the crown of all Dalemark. I'm going to need an army that comes from the South as well as the North. They can all swear to me on the Adon's cup, and the ones it doesn't shine for can flaming well stay here under guard. I don't want word out round the South until Hestefan's got through to Hobin."

"And what will they do here? Sit with their hands on their heads?" Keril asked.

Mitt laughed. "No. They'll be digging. They can start on the foundations for the palace I'm going to build here. After that they can go on and flaming well rebuild Kernsburgh."

"That's the stuff!" said Alk. "I'll be the guard. Want me to make some drawings for the buildings? That's much more my line than fighting. Let's see—Luthan's scribe had pen and paper." He looked at the statue in his hand and then looked round for somewhere safe to put it. "Seeing you thought to look for it," he said to Maewen, "just hold it for me while I do some sketches."

He passed her the statue. As soon as her hands were on it, she was not there any longer.

# PART FIVE

# *Kankredin*

# 22

SHE WAS NOT THERE any longer. She was back in the museum gallery of the Tannoreth Palace, in exactly the same spot where she had been standing when she left. Wend, who was in the act of locking the golden statue away again, jumped round and stared at her.

Wend was as neat and trim and handsome as ever. Maewen was instantly aware that she was dirty, and moist all through with showers of rain she had given up noticing days ago. Her mail smelled of rust. Her boots were filthy. The livery of Dropwater smelled of wet wool, horse, and person. Under the little helmet her hair felt damp and clotted.

"You're back!" said Wend.

"Yes." The animal wariness she had acquired in those days of journeying told Maewen that Wend had not expected to see her again. It was in every line of Wend, as he carefully placed the statue on its shelf and locked the glass front. She noticed it, even though she was distracted by her hearthwoman's clothes dissolving away from her, leaving her again in grubby shorts and shirt. Her hair tumbled back to her shoulders, and it still felt damp and clotted. She was even more distracted by the shrill beeping of the radio clipped to Wend's uniform, but she still noticed.

"What happened?" Wend casually rattled keys, but that wariness showed Maewen he was, underneath, very eager to know.

"Hestefan the Singer murdered Noreth before she even set out from Adenmouth," she said. She was ashamed of the wariness—it showed her Wend was full of fury and frustration, carefully hidden—but she could not help knowing it. They all had this wariness: Moril, Mitt, Hestefan, Navis, everyone. It was the way you lived in those days.

"I'd thought it was . . . one of the others," Wend said, across the *wheep-wheep-wheep* from the radio on his chest.

Thought it was Mitt, you mean! Maewen thought. The wariness again. The noise from the radio was getting on her nerves, so she said, "I think you ought to answer that."

Wend unclipped the radio and flipped the switch. "Orilson here. Over."

Major Alksen's voice blasted from it like someone talking into a tin. "About bloody time! Wend, get down into the front court soonest. There seems to be something going on in Amil's tomb—animal or something shut inside. Over."

"Coming, sir," said Wend. "Over and out." He clipped back the radio, forced a smile at Maewen, and said, "Tell me about it later."

Maewen watched him hurry away down the gallery. Tanamoril, Osfameron, Mage Mallard—he was all those heroes of all those stories, and he could be one of her own ancestors, too—and he had come down to this, a museum attendant in league with Kankredin. She knew how Moril had felt about Hestefan. It made a bad taste in your very bones. Playing the good guy on the train so that she would trust him. Yuk.

It was like knowing the answer to a crossword clue by instinct and then working out the clue after that. That photograph. Aunt Liss had sent it to Dad. Wend had seen it and known she was like Noreth. It had to be Wend. How would Kankredin know to look?

Maewen looked at the golden statue, a buttery shine from behind the glass. She was fairly sure that if she hunted along the cases, somewhere she would find a lopsided silver cup and a ring with a big red stone that had the Adon's profile on it—maybe two rings—but she had not the energy to look. Her boots had dissolved into sandals again, showing her toes outlined in brown dirt. She needed a bath. She had to wash her hair. She looked at her thumb. There was a clean white band round it where the false ring had been. Yes, there would be two rings. The One had turned everyone's cunning schemes round—Wend's, Kankredin's, Earl Keril's, that Earl of Andmark's, Maewen's own ideas—and used them against themselves. Maewen herself had not been able to change history; she had just helped it happen as it should.

She really had to have a bath.

Instead she set off round the gallery, very slowly, toward the line of huge windows that looked over the front court. She did not mean to look in the cases as she went, but she could not help seeing the sword. It seemed to throw itself at her eyes, in spite of its dark color, in its dingy, somber sheath. Maewen took a step back, having almost walked past it, and read the label:

ONE OF SEVERAL SWORDS REPUTED TO BE THE ADON'S. LEGENDS CLAIM THAT ONLY THE RIGHTFUL MONARCH CAN UNSHEATH THE ADON'S SWORD.

That's true, she thought. I couldn't draw it. Mitt had to do it both times. She dawdled toward the windows, with heaviness on her heart. Ordinary life was so very ordinary. Everything was *over*.

When she came to the first window, she looked cautiously out from one corner of it. There was the wide cobbled yard, with its paved patterns and the absurd onion-domed stone tomb in the middle. A very fine example of Amilian stonework. There was Major Alksen, too, and all his people, Wend included, in a cautious circle all the way round the tomb, slowly moving inward. What did they think was in there?

Whatever was in there squealed, a long, descending *hee-hee-hee*. Maewen could hear it quite clearly even through the glass. Horse. Something began banging in her throat, and she felt her face go pale as she realized *which* horse. It had not whinnied much, but Maewen knew horses, and she knew this one only too well. She wanted to lean out of the window and scream to Major Alksen, *Don't go near it! That's Kankredin in there!* Wend must know. He was letting them all move in on it, not knowing what they were up against. Major Alksen was right beside the tomb now. He was putting his hand on the grille over its door.

There was a disturbance in the air over the little domes of the tomb's roof. Major Alksen did not see it. It was very faint, like the ghost of the trumpet-shaped whirlwind Mitt had summoned, but the new wariness in Maewen had prepared her to expect it. She was looking right at it as it went spiraling up to hover level with the roof of the palace. She saw Wend's head tilt slightly as he saw it, too, but his face was expressionless and he did not say anything to anyone. Meanwhile, Major Alksen threw open the grille and then the door, and his lady helper threw open the ones at the other end at the same moment. They went in. They came out. They walked with blank, puzzled, irritated movements. Nothing there. All the other people in the circle moved uncertainly, let down, but ready for some kind of trick.

Maewen discovered she was watching this in glimpses, mostly with her back to the wall so that the hovering cloud of Kankredin would not see her. Her throat pounded harder and her legs felt weak as she caught up with the way her new wariness was making her behave. He's come for me! she thought. He's not going to forgive me in a hurry! Had Wend summoned him? Or perhaps by the action of coming and going back over two hundred years Maewen herself had opened the way for Kankredin. Or again, with One-like cunning, maybe Kankredin had used the force Mitt had thrown at him to help him take that open way through time. It could not be coincidence that Kankredin had arrived just as she had taken hold of the golden statue. It just could not be.

She was very frightened indeed.

This was worse than any time on the green road. It was more horrifying than being attacked twice in Gardale. Why? At first Maewen thought it was because that had only been Hestefan, and this was Kankredin. But she had not known her attacker was only an elderly Singer in Gardale. No—it was because this was her own time. This was modern life, when things like this were not supposed to happen. And worse still, she was alone. All the friends who might have helped her had been dead for two hundred years.

That was when it hit her. Dead. Two hundred years. It was Mitt's tomb she had been looking at, down there in the court.

Grief thundered down on her, hard and continuous as the waterfall at Dropwater. Maewen fled under it, round the gallery, and up the stairs, and upstairs again to her father's apartment. There she ran a bath. Even with both taps full on, the water did not pour as fiercely as grief poured on Maewen. She sat in the bath and she washed herself and she washed her hair without, for a single instant, thinking what she was doing. Instead her mind was going through, going through that entire journey from Adenmouth to Kernsburgh. She found she remembered things about Mitt she had not even known she had seen until now.

When the water was cold, she noticed it with a dull sort of jump, and got out and dried, and dried her hair. By that time she had been through everything twice and was starting round again. She even laughed in several places—that time when the ring stuck, for instance. By then the grief had stopped pouring and set into a full ache, so that her throat hurt, and her chest, as if she full, full of sorrow as a person could get. Her hair dried wild and floating and fluffy, as it always did. It was a good inch longer. Aunt Liss would have noticed, but she was fairly sure that Dad never would. There was more than a touch of Cenoreth's wriggliness to it—or Kialan's, or Kankredin's. She put on her nicest dress. That was not to let Mitt down when she had to face Kankredin alone. She looked quite good in the mirror.

I might have been the Queen, she thought, in an experimental way, watching herself. And watched herself shake her head. Somehow that was never a possibility. So I might have been feeling like this, anyway, even if I never touched the statue and Alk passed it to someone else, she told herself. She did not believe that either. Whatever she believed, there was no point to might-have-beens. *Now* was enough—and bad enough.

Mitt had left her a legacy, although he did not know it (at the word *legacy* Maewen had a moment when she thought she was going to cry, but she did not seem to be able to cry; she was hard and dry inside). She had heard the word Mitt shouted to bring that whirlwind, and she had no doubt it would work for her, too. She could use it on Kankredin—and Wend—if need arose.

Out on the leads the pigeons were landing, taking off, circling uneasily. They knew. Kankredin was hovering as a nearly invisible cloud somewhere near. But before she went into battle, there were things she wanted to do.

Maewen let herself out of the apartment again and raced downstairs, down, and on down, until she came to the old part of the palace where the pictures were. She had spent too long in the bath. The art students were all there, and she had to edge round their easels and step over them as they lay on the ballroom floor, in order to look at the paintings on the walls and the ceiling.

She shook her head at the fair-haired Amil in his purple trousers. Whoever painted that had not had a clue what Mitt looked like. Or *had* he? she wondered, remembering King Hern. *Was* it deliberate? she thought, looking up at the battles in the ceiling. Navis was up there, and a huge man who was supposed to be Alk, and a fierce-looking woman. Was she the Countess? She did look a bit like a horse. And now Maewen knew whom to look for, she could spot Kialan and Ynen, neither of them much like themselves—and the young man with red hair, carrying a cwidder and half hidden behind a troop of horses, was surely intended to be Moril, and that was nothing like him. She still had no idea who the savage type in fur was, down in the South.

There was no real portrait of Mitt, she knew that now. All the same, she went on into the polished room where the pictures hung. It was full of people, large men from Haligland, who all looked a bit like Kialan, talking foreign talk and wearing silly national-dress kilts and badges—a convention of some kind. Maewen pushed among them with urgent curiosity. Here were the two old, old portraits of the Adon—quite right: One said it was from Holand, the other from Aberath—and both were startlingly like Mitt, or rather, like Mitt painted by someone who had not got it quite right. She could see why Mitt might not want his portrait painted. That bony, ill look. Or was that the reason?

But here was Navis as Duke of Kernsburgh, staring keen and haughty over his shoulder. The artist had got Navis to the life. And round here was Moril. Moril looked more than betrayed. He looked heartbroken. Maewen wondered whether he ever got over what Hestefan had done. She rather thought not. It was funny, though, because it was not that Moril had been so enormously *fond* of Hestefan. No, she thought, as her eye fell on the cwidder in the picture; it was because they were both Singers. If you were a Singer, there were things you just did not do.

Maewen pushed between two broad backs from Haligland to look at the real cwidder in its glass case. Yes. It really was Moril's. And it had looked so much newer and more used when she last saw it. Shame that a thing of such power should lie crumbling in a glass case. But though her name was Singer, Maewen knew she had not the least chance of using it as it could be used. Shame. Waste.

She backed away and worked her way out to the exit. And caught the eye of another portrait, one she had never bothered to do more than glance at before. A woman. A thin white-faced woman with black hair piled up high and an angry little frown between the eyebrows. Hildy. O great *One*! Misery came thundering down on Maewen again, more than she had thought possible—and here she had thought she was as full of it as she could be. Memories came with the misery: Mitt brushing at the damp patch of her tears in the Lawschool; the straight, greasy feel of Mitt's hair when she put the crown back on him; the incredible knuckliness of Mitt's hands. . . .

Maewen caught up with herself to find she was racing upstairs again, pushing past a big party of tourists and then another, and then hammering on upward alone. By the time she flung through the doorway of the palace office, she hardly had breath left to pant. She leaned against the wall to recover, watching the usual frenzy, people rushing all over, papers being passed, typing, telephones ringing. Dad sensed she was there. He put down a telephone to turn to her over his shoulder and raise his chin inquiringly.

That pose! *Now* Maewen knew whom Navis had all along reminded her of. Both of them were short men. And just like Dad, Navis was in his element giving orders and attending to a thousand things at once. No wonder Mitt had made Navis a duke and let him organize the kingdom! Dad saw she needed something and came over to the door. That was like Navis, too.

"What's the matter, Maewen?"

Nothing, she wanted to say. I'm only in love with a King who died over a hundred years ago. Stupid. Keep your mouth shut. "Dad, who did Amil the Great marry?"

He raised an eyebrow, although unlike Navis, he could not do it without raising the other eyebrow slightly, too. "Is this important? All right, I see it is. Well, she was never very prominent. She seems to have been rather a retiring character, because very little is known about her apart from the fact that she was very tall, and I believe she was also very kindhearted—"

"Her *name*, Dad!" Maewen said. "Not a lecture."

"Didn't I say?" He was surprised. "Enblith—though she is *not*, of course, to be confused with Enblith the Fair."

"Thanks."

Fancy that! Maewen thought as she ran away downstairs. Biffa! *Biffa!* Well, Mitt had shown some sense, at least! And it was really a very good choice, she thought, patrolling round the museum gallery while she waited for Kankredin to show himself. Biffa was nice—so nice, in fact, that it was entirely likely that Mitt had lived happily ever after. Maewen tried to feel glad. But in moments she was saying, "I expect he forgot about me entirely after a day or so. I don't suppose he thought about me *once* in the rest of his life."

Her voice rang out, peevish and hurt. Don't be so ridiculous! she told herself. Kings have to marry. Besides, he *had* to remember you in order to get the waystone changed to a huge one, like I told Moril it was. And—well, the waystone was not really a message, since it *had* to be there—but Maewen stood suddenly stock-still, wondering if Mitt might not indeed have left her a message, buried in history. She was on her way upstairs again, before the idea had had time to be fully formed.

"Dad!" she said from the office doorway.

Dad was reading a bundle of papers, but he came over to her. "Yes?"

"Dad, how did the Tannoreth Palace get its name?"

"Amil named it," Dad said. "I'm sure I told you the first day you were here. Nobody knows quite where he got it from. The first part, *tan*, is the old word for 'young' or 'younger,' and we assume Amil was thinking of Hern's old palace, which may have been on the same site."

"And the *noreth* part?" Maewen asked.

"Nobody knows. It seems to be just a name—Maewen, forgive me, but I *must* get this read before the Queen's Office phones me."

Maewen galloped away downstairs again, thinking, Young Noreth—no, the *younger Noreth*! Not Noreth, but the one who was younger. Great One! He named a whole palace after me, and I'll never be able to say thank you! It made her eyes prick, and it warmed the heavy hurt inside her without making it any better. She walked twice round the gallery, hugging Mitt's message to her. Then there were other things that she just had to know. Upstairs she dashed again.

"Dad!"

She forgot how many times she rushed up to the office or quite what order she asked the other questions in. Each time Dad was surprisingly patient—like Navis, if you really needed something. Or was it, in some confusing way, that Navis had had some kind of family feeling for Maewen? One of the first things she asked was, "Dad, who did the Duke of Kernsburgh marry?"

Dad frowned. "I really don't remember the name of his first wife. But his second wife was the widow of the Lord of Adenmouth." He clicked his fingers. "What *was* her name? Eltruda, that was it!"

"Thanks, Dad." Noreth's aunt. It all fits. And downstairs again to patrol round the gallery.

Upon one of her reappearances in the office, one of Dad's young ladies handed her a cheese roll, saying it was lunchtime. Maewen had no appetite. She carried the roll about as she patrolled. She was carrying it when she saw Wend coming and fled from him up to the office again. There she had to stop and eat the roll, chokingly, for fear of offending the young lady.

"Dad, who did Hild—er, the Duke of Kernsburgh's eldest daughter marry?"

"Hildrida. Dear me. That family seems to be an obsession with you," Dad said. "I really can't remember. She certainly *did* marry, because her descendants are still Wardens of the Holy Islands, but— Not that Hildrida ever spent much time in the Islands. Amil was there far oftener, and so was Hildrida's brother, Ynen, building up our navy. That was when Dalemark first became a big sea power, you know. Ynen tried out the first steamships there."

Bless Dad and his lectures! Maewen thought. You always got twice the answers you asked for. Sometimes on her visits to the office she got more than she wanted, like the lecture she got when she asked who Hobin was. That lecture started, "You mean Bloody Hobin of Holand? He was the center of the uprising in the South at the start of Amil's reign. Like so many revolutionaries, he got quite out of hand. . . ." Maewen did not attend to this one much, because it was all about Hobin and nothing about Amil.

But there were times when she got next to nothing, as when she asked, "Moril the Singer, Dad? Does history say anything about him?"

"No," Dad said. "I never heard of him."

"Hestefan the Singer, then?"

"Nope," said Dad. "You must remember that things changed very fast in Amil's reign. Singers were right out of date by the time Amil died."

Poor Moril. Next time Maewen charged upstairs, she asked, "Earl Keril of Hannart, Dad. Was he a great nuisance to Amil the Great?"

Eyebrows up, like the image of Navis, Dad said, "Are you writing a historical novel or something? Far be it from me to discourage such a venture. But let it be accurate, please. Earl Keril supported Amil, like most earls of the North, but he never seems to have been very deep in Amil's confidence. Historians usually put Hannart's decline down to this period."

"Thanks." Oh. So history had Keril as just a politician who backed the wrong move. Right, in a way, but so wrong, too.

Maewen went thoughtfully away. She was tired. Today had literally lasted two hundred years. But even if she could have borne to sit and wait for Kankredin, Maewen's misery would not let her keep still. She patrolled wider and wider, through most of the palace by the afternoon.

Halfway through the afternoon the loudspeaker outlets crackled all over the palace. Here it comes! Maewen thought, and stood stock-still where she was, between two state bedrooms.

"Attention. Your attention, please." It was Major Alksen's voice. "A bomb has been reported concealed on the palace premises. I repeat. A bomb has been reported somewhere in the palace or grounds. I must ask everyone to leave as quickly and quietly as possible. This applies to all visitors and staff alike. Please leave the palace and its grounds as quickly as you can. Doors and gates have been opened front and rear. Please leave by the nearest exit you can find. Please do not return until the bomb is located. Attention, please . . ."

The message went on and on, repeating.

The palace resounded softly as hundreds of people's feet hurried through rooms and down stairs to find the doors. Presumably Dad and his ladies were on their way out, too. Maewen wanted to know. Once more her feet took her on the familiar journey to the office. But the stairs were blocked by the office staff pouring down them.

"Your father, dear?" said someone, barely stopping. "Mr. Singer's gone down to Security. He'll probably stay with them until the bomb squad gets here. You come down with us."

Maewen hung back and let them pass until the stairway was empty. Dad was not safe, but there was nothing she could do. She went softly down again. The palace was weirdly empty, much emptier than she had ever known it. Maewen went on a zigzag course, quite unimpeded, from back windows to front ones, and then back windows again, as she went down. She saw people pouring out through gardens at the back and through the court at the front. Nothing would happen until everyone was gone. She was sure of that. Kankredin was after *her*. Maybe he would also destroy the palace as a belated revenge on Mitt, but he would not blow up all the tourists. Kankredin valued power over people, and you could not have that if all the people were dead.

She went on down, checking windows. By now she had come to the floors that opened onto the cloister balconies at the front. The windows were big glass doors, and Maewen had to go through those, into a roofed space held up by thin pillars, and then lean over the parapet to see into the front court. When she did this at the highest balcony, there was still a scatter of people hurrying away through the court and out under the arched gateway. At the next floor, everyone had gone. Everywhere was empty and still— No, it was *not*!

Maewen leaned on the parapet and did not dare move. Over the multiple domes of Amil's tomb, a big cloud of something nearly invisible rolled and coiled on itself. She could see it mostly by the way it distorted the wall and the city buildings beyond, in ugly, glassy waves. It was not person-shaped—yet. Kankredin was busy assembling himself. Maewen licked her lips. There was so much of it. Kankredin seemed to have brought more of himself from somewhere. The ugly shimmer was easily five times the size of the ghost thing that had been her horse. She supposed she ought to shout that word, but she had a feeling that the thing hovering there was too big to be dealt with like that.

On the other side of the court the gates in the big main gateway were softly closing, switched by remote control from Security, shutting her in with Kankredin. But Dad was inside, too. She had to do *something*.

Before the gates had quite swung closed, a man in an old leather jacket slipped between them and pushed them shut with his back. He must be the bomb disposal expert. Maewen had heard that bomb men were daredevils who dressed all anyhow and enjoyed risking their lives. The trouble was, he was not up against a bomb. She saw him realize. He stood as still as Maewen, staring up at the heaving, invisible cloud. Then his head switched— There was something odd about— There was somebody else in the court, running. Maewen could hear running footsteps. Then see who. It was Wend, racing toward Amil's tomb.

The man by the gate gave a great shout. "GET BACK, YOU FLAMING FOOL!"

*That was Mitt's voice!* Maewen was head down, leaning far out over the parapet, without knowing she had moved. She *knew* she was right. Except it couldn't be true. The man was not gawky enough—was he?

Above the tomb, the coiling movement, which had been bunching and bending over itself ready to move down on the man by the gate, now swayed round and turned to face the movement Maewen had made. She saw—no, *felt*—eyes in its midst. Eyes that knew her. Eyes that hated her. Fat-lidded eyes she knew.

Mitt's voice yelled a word. It was not the word Maewen knew. This was a word that made your brain clench and then prefer to forget you had heard it. It was a word that dragged shivers from deep, deep under the earth. A word that shook the palace. The invisibleness above the tomb coiled hurriedly round to throw itself at the shouter.

In the act of coiling it was caught, and held, and thrown high, high in the air, mixed with and part of a tremendous jet of water, a huge tsunami. Water burst from the tomb in a giant dark horn, throwing pieces of building aside like a card house. Maewen stared, with her neck twisted, at the immense column of water hanging into the sky, darker and darker with dissolving shreds of the coiling cloud, and all spouted to yellow froth at its distant top.

Then it fell.

Maewen threw herself flat beside the parapet. Even so, she was soaked. The open balcony bucked under her. Salt water stung her eyes. Salt? And the roar of falling tons of water was more deafening than any bomb. It went on and on, mixed with the crashing of stone. Maewen scrambled up in the midst of it, unable to care that she was deaf as a post. Three pillars that held up the balcony were missing nearby, and there was a gap in the parapet where she had been leaning. Unable to care about that either, she walked over balcony that swayed and grated until she reached the nearest whole pillar. Clinging to it, she stared at the courtyard awash with angry, gray, leaping waves. The gate was down. The gateway was mostly rubble. Water was roaring out into King Street. The salt that ran on Maewen's face was partly tears. No one could have survived that.

But he had. He must have been swept over to the side wall. She could see him, nearly out of her view, where it was blocked by the ragged edge of the balcony, clawing himself along the wall, first shoulder-deep, then, very quickly, only waist-deep. The water was rushing away all the time, going back underground. Maewen could dimly hear the surge and growl of it running away. But she was staring at the man's soaking, lank hair. It *did* look like Mitt's.

Then he had clawed himself out of sight. Maewen had turned to dash away down into the court when she heard him speaking, right under the balcony. "Come on, get up, you fool. Walk." It was Mitt's voice, no doubt now.

Wend's voice answered. "Let me go. I deserve to drown."

And then Mitt's voice again: "If that was true, the Earth Shaker wouldn't have left you alive. Come on, stand up."

Maewen heard splashing, and coughing. Wend said, "Don't you understand? I was working with Kankredin."

Mitt answered, "Well, you had the sense to phone and tell me when you realized how much of him he'd collected here. He's an expert in blackmailing and tempting and all that. Stop kicking yourself. What I want to know— Watch it! These steps are all broken." There were flounderings, and the sound of wet stones rolling and splashing. Then Mitt's voice came from right underneath, where the palace door was. "What I want to know is how did he persuade you?"

"Noreth," said Wend. Maewen could tell he was crying. "My daughter Noreth! All these years I thought you were the one who'd killed her."

"Of all the idiots!" Mitt answered. "There were several hundred people you could have *asked*!"

Maewen found she could wait no longer. She had not dared believe it was really Mitt until now, but this proved it. She dashed back through the open window-doors and sped through the ballroom to the nearest stairs. Halfway down she found herself pausing—with an impatient skip, because of the vanity of it—to look at her draggled self in the grand mirrors: wet, salty hair, tear-stained face, damp rag of a best dress. Well, he's seen me look just as bad, and he knows I'm only thirteen. But, as she sped down again, she found herself repeating, Only thirteen. He's two hundred years old. I'm only thirteen. Over and over.

Across the slippery grand hall she sped. Rubble rolled under her racing feet, and she splatted in pools of seafoam. And there was the open door at last, open onto heaved-up paving stones and steaming water. A gust of sea scent blew in through it. Maewen hurtled out of it and stopped. There was only Wend, leaning against a pillar, soaking wet. In the distance, across uprooted cobblestones strewn with seaweed, bloodred and olive green, Mitt was just climbing over the rubble that had been the gate.

*"Mitt!"* she screamed.

He heard her. He stopped. She could see him think about it. He turned round and gave her a cheerful wave before he jumped off the pile of rubble and walked away down King Street.

Maewen was left gazing. Between her and the remains of the gate there was a scummy, odd-shaped pool, turgid with tainted waves, draining away into the ground as she looked at it. That was where the tomb had been, of course. That tomb must have been one of Mitt's biggest jokes. By the time he had had it built, he must have known he was of the Undying. No wonder he made it so absurd. Maewen almost smiled, in spite of her misery. He's two hundred years old. I'm thirteen.

She turned to Wend. Wend was staring straight ahead, dripping. "I owe you an apology," he said.

"Yes," Maewen agreed. "Did you take this job at the palace to wait until I turned up?"

"No," said Wend. "I was never sure where you came from. I took the job for something to do. There's so much time, you know."

He said it very drearily. Maewen could see time stretch on and on, before and behind him.

"Why did you tell Noreth she was the One's daughter?" she asked.

"I didn't. That was an idea her mother had," Wend said. He laughed, a nasty hacking sound, like a bad cough. "The One told me she would ride the royal road. He lied."

"Are you sure that wasn't Kankredin?" Maewen asked.

Wend turned and stared at her, as if this had never occurred to him. Beyond him she saw Major Alksen in the distance, followed by Dad, gingerly picking his way toward the empty slot that had been Amil's tomb.

"Come with me," Maewen said to Wend. "I've got an idea about you." When Wend did not move, she took his chilly hand and dragged. "You ought to get into dry clothes, at least."

"No problem," Wend said. His clothes began to steam as if he were out in hot sun. But he made no protest when Maewen dragged him, in a trail of steam, through the rubbly hall and to the stairs. Thank goodness, she thought. For what she had in mind, it would be better that Major Alksen and Dad were busy outside. But why am I doing this? she wondered as she towed Wend upstairs. He thought he was sending me to be killed. He knew he was sending me to Kankredin. Am I trying to be worthy? But she knew why, really. She knew how Wend felt.

She dragged him through the ballroom and round into the smaller room where the pictures hung. She pushed him in front of the glass cabinet where the old cwidder lay.

"Get that out," she said. "Play it. It's yours, anyway."

"Oh no," Wend said. "I gave it to my son. And it's the Queen's property now."

"Is it?" said Maewen. "I think Moril gave it to Mitt, not to Amil, and as Mitt's still alive, it's *his*. I know he won't mind you having it in the least. It's wasted, lying there."

"Maybe," Wend said. He looked down at the old beautiful instrument as if he were very tempted. "But someone will notice if I take it."

"You are beginning to annoy me!" Maewen said. "From all I've heard, you're one of the greatest magicians there ever was. Surely you can make it *look* as if the cwidder's still there? Nobody's going to try to play it, after all."

"True." Wend stared down at his uniform, now dry and trim. In a hopeless, fussy way, he picked a piece of dry seaweed off it. For a moment, he stared at the red-brown spray of weed as if he had never seen such a thing before. Then he smiled. He took his keys out, unlocked the cabinet, and raised the glass lid, tossing the seaweed spray inside as he did so. Then he picked up the cwidder. To Maewen, it looked as if he drew the ghost of the cwidder out of itself. There was a cwidder lying in the cabinet, fat, mellow, and glossy. Wend had an identical cwidder in his hands and was hitching the strap over his shoulder.

"You'd better replace that strap," she said. "It's awfully frayed."

Wend smoothed the strap. "I know. I made the strap, too. It'll hold." His face already looked different. It was newer and happier. It became serious-happy as he turned the pegs and brought the strings into tune. And it changed to a dreamy pleasure as he picked out a little tune. The cwidder hummed, almost purred, with happiness. "Forgive me," Wend said. He looked up at the portrait of Moril, as if Moril was really there.

"He will," Maewen said. "It was always a burden to him."

Wend sighed. "Yes, and that's odd. Or perhaps not. It was my power I put in the cwidder—a good half of it." He strummed another hasty tune. It made him stand in a different, easy way, and he looked stronger. "I should never have passed that power on," he said, and looking as dreamy as Moril often did, he turned and walked out of the room.

"Oughtn't you to tell my father you're leaving?" Maewen said.

"A message is on his desk now," Wend said, conjuring a small waterfall of notes as he walked off. His uniform had gone. He was wearing a shabby leather jacket, rather like Mitt's.

He was really going. Maewen hurriedly called out the selfish part of why she had done this. "Wend! How can I get in touch with Mitt?"

Wend paused. "Through Cennoreth, I suppose." Then he turned and looked at her over his shoulder, like Navis in the portrait behind her. His face had gone beyond happy to become the face of a man of power. Oddly enough, that made him look kinder. "Mitt gave me a message for you. I'm sorry—I'd forgotten until now. I've no idea what he meant.

He said, 'Tell her to make it four years, not two, to allow for inflation.' Does that mean anything to you?"

It certainly did. Maewen almost laughed as she watched Wend walk away. Four years! No way! She was going to get the train to Dropthwaite tomorrow, and somehow, she was going to find Cennoreth there.

# A Guide to Dalemark

**Aberath,** the northernmost earldom of North Dalemark; also the town on the north coast, situated on the Rath estuary at the mouth of the river Ath.

**Aden,** the small river running north to the sea at Adenmouth, thought by some to be all that remains of the great River of the spellcoats.

**Adenmouth,** a small town and lordship in the extreme northwest of North Dalemark, and part of the earldom of Aberath.

**Adon,** a name that seems to mean "High Lord" and has several applications:

1. One of the secret names of the One.
2. The name or title of the heroic King of Dalemark about whom there are many songs and legends. The Adon was an Earl of Hannart who married Manaliabrid of the Undying as his second wife and went into exile with her and the Singer Osfameron, during which time he was murdered by his jealous half brother Lagan and brought back to life by Osfameron. He then became King, but on his death his two children disappeared, leaving Dalemark without a King and riven by civil war.
3. The title of the eldest son and heir of the Earl of Hannart.

**The Adon's gifts,** the legendary gifts Manaliabrid brought to the Adon as her dowry. These are:

1. A ring said only to fit the finger of one with royal blood.
2. A cup which was believed to acknowledge the true King and also to shine in the hands of anyone telling the truth.

3. A sword which, it was said, only the true King could draw from its scabbard.

**"The Adon's Hall,"** one of the old-style songs composed by the singer-mage Osfameron, in which Osfameron seems to be thinking not only of the Adon in exile in a ruinous hall but of his own cwidder and of the Sayings of King Hern.

**Al,** the most common short form of Alhammitt, the commonest name in South Dalemark. The name of a castaway picked up by the yacht *Wind's Road.*

**Alda,** the wife of Siriol; a confirmed alcoholic.

**Alhammitt**

1. The true name of the Earth Shaker.
2. The most common man's name in South Dalemark.
3. Mitt's actual name.

**Alk,** a lawman from the North Dales who took office under the Countess of Aberath and shortly married her. His status then became that of Consort of Aberath, with the courtesy title (which was seldom used) of Lord. Alk devoted his time to inventing steam engines and eventually, almost single-handedly, brought about the industrial revolution of Dalemark.

**Alksen, Major,** the head of security at the Tannoreth Palace.

**Alk's Irons,** the name given by the people of Aberath to the steam machines invented by Alk. The most notable of these were a plow, a hoist, a press, a pump, and a locomotive.

**Alla,** the elder daughter of Alk and the Countess of Aberath.

**Allegiances,** the personal ties of primitive Haligland. A man or woman would be born into one clan, sent as foster child to a second, swear friendship to a third, and marry into a fourth. This formed a network of friendship and obligation which you were bound to tell to a stranger when you told your name. Allegiances defined you as a person. If you did not tell, or had no allegiances, you were either a criminal or a social outcast.

**Almet,** the son of the Adon and Manaliabrid, who declined to be King after his father.

**Amil,** one of the secret names of the One, which appears to mean either "Brother" or "River." It later became the name of the line of kings that began with Amil the Great.

**Ammet,** a straw image thrown into the sea every year at the Sea Festival in Holand in South Dalemark, which was said to bring luck to the city. Small images were also made and sold for luck. Even greater luck was supposed to come to any boat that found Ammet floating beyond the harbor and brought him aboard. The name is a corruption of Alhammitt, one of the names of the Earth Shaker. See also **Poor Old Ammet**.

**Andmark,** the earldom in the center of South Dalemark which was probably the wealthiest in Dalemark. Henda was Earl of Andmark until he was killed in the Great Uprising.

**Anoreth** of the Undying became the wife of Closti the Clam. The name means "unbound."

**Ansdale,** a remote valley east of Gardale. The birthplace of Biffa, whose family kept the mill there.

**Arin,** a senior lord of the (Heathen) invaders from Haligland and chief warrior-minister of Kars Adon.

**Armor** was markedly different in the two halves of Dalemark. Southern soldiers wore helmets and breastplates with exaggerated curves designed to deflect bullets, over tough leather, with knee-length boots and big gauntlets. Many carried guns as well as swords, and foot soldiers carried pikes.
Northern soldiers still used chain mail under sleeved jerkins of leather or tough cloth. The mail was long enough to protect the wearer to the wrists and knees, and the helmets were round, coming low enough in the back to protect the neck. Gloves were leather with mail or studs on the backs. Weapons were usually crossbows, swords, and daggers. Guns were few and could only be spared for picked hearthmen.

**Arms inspectors** were employed by all the earls of South Dalemark to keep strict watch on gunsmiths, armorers, and weapons makers, who were not allowed to work without the inspectors' seal on all their equipment. The earls rightly feared that the craftsmen might otherwise sell weapons to the common people or make weapons for the earls that were deliberately flawed. Despite the inspectors, many armorers seem to have done both these things.

**Arris,** a rough spirituous liquor brewed throughout South Dalemark from discarded grapes and sprouting corn. All that can be said in its favor is that it was much cheaper than wine.

**Ath,** the river that runs north into the sea at Aberath. It is thought to be one of the remnants of the great River of prehistory.

**Autumn Festival,** the usual name in the South of Dalemark for Harvest, the feast that celebrated the gathering of crops.

**Autumn floods** in the prehistoric Riverlands were as regular as spring floods but never so large. They were due to the rains that fell in the autumn storms.

**Autumn storms** were a regular feature in Dalemark. In historic times they reached as far north as Gardale and could be very severe. The worst lasted for days, with the gale swinging from northwest to southwest. With a shorter storm the winds tended to gust even stronger but not veer so much. If the gale was southerly, the storms came repeatedly for several days.

**Bad luck** gave rise to many superstitions all over Dalemark. Those which require explanation are:

1. Giving. It was considered disastrously unlucky to give, or promise to give, something and then not give it. This is why Ganner was forced to give Lenina to Clennen and also why he seems to have been certain she would one day come back; he had not incurred bad luck by refusing to give her away.
2. Festivals, feasts, and ceremonies. Enormous bad luck was incurred if anything happened to interrupt these. Note that the Heathens interrupted the One's fire ceremony; that both Mitt and Al interrupted the Sea Festival; and that Fenna interrupted the Midsummer Feast by fainting.
3. A death brought great bad luck and could only be countered by a marriage on the same day. Lenina and Ganner take advantage of this belief.
4. Speaking a falsehood to the Undying brings more bad luck than any of the foregoing.
5. An unlucky person can bring bad luck to others. Gull was considered to be doing this, and Kialan believed he was such a person.
6. A person or group can carry their own cloud of bad luck around with them and nothing will go right for them until the cloud passes away.

**Barangarolob,** the full name of the horse that pulled Clennen the Singer's cart. Clennen, who loved long names, named him after the

Adon's horse Barangalob, with the inserted superlative particle *ro* meaning "youngest" or "much younger."

**Barlay,** Lawschool slang. "No barlay" means "no quarter given."

**Beat the water,** as part of the Holand Sea Festival in South Dalemark. People pretended to beat the sea with garlands of fruit and flowers. The ancient aim seems to have been to subdue the sea for the following year.

**Beer** was drunk throughout the North of Dalemark instead of water, wine, or coffee until near the end of Amil the Great's reign. One of Navis Haddsson's many profitable enterprises was to set up a large brewery in the Shield of Oreth, but the best beer came from Hannart and still does. The lager brewed in Kinghaven is to be avoided at all costs.

**Bence,** captain in chief of the fleet of the Holy Islands and commander of the *Wheatsheaf.* Bence was not a Holy Islander. He was born in Wayness in the earldom of Waywold.

**Besting,** Lawschool slang for best friend.

**Biffa,** pupil at the Gardale Lawschool, a native of Ansdale and best friend of Hildrida Navissdaughter. The name is a shortened pet-name form of Enblith.

**Big Shool,** one of the larger of the Holy Islands.

**Black Mountains,** the highest range of mountains in prehistoric Dalemark. It is possible, though not certain, that they were thrown higher in the mountain-folding at the start of the reign of King Hern, to become the Black Mountains of historic Dalemark, in which case the name may refer to the large deposits of coal to be found there.

**"Both hands cut off . . ."** refers to the law of primitive Haligland, whereby any member of the High Lord's (King's) family who was suspected of treason could be legally deprived of both hands, not as a punishment but as a precaution against a threat to the throne.

**Bradbrook,** a lordship on the coast of Waywold in South Dalemark.

**Brid,** daughter of Clennen the Singer and sister of Moril and Dagner, who fled North with Moril. Soon after her arrival Brid went to Gardale and trained as a law-woman, and thence to a professional appointment in Loviath. After the Great Uprising she became

Countess of Hannart and eventually the first head of the Royal Dalemark Academy of Music, which she helped her brother Moril to found.

**Bull,** the most usual form in which the Earth Shaker appears. For this reason bulls' heads are carried in the Holand Sea Festival. It is said that the Bull is most frequently seen in the Holy Islands.

**Canden,** the younger of two brothers from Waywold in South Dalemark, devoted to freedom fighting. He moved from Waywold to Holand, where conditions were much worse, deliberately to foment rebellion. In Holand he joined the secret society of the Free Holanders and shortly proposed the firing of one of the Earl's warehouses. The older Free Holanders refused and stayed at home, while Canden led the younger ones to the warehouses. There he found that they had been betrayed and that soldiers were waiting for them.

**Canderack,** the earldom on the west coast of South Dalemark, where the best wine was grown. Until the reign of Amil the Great, Canderack owned a fleet that rivaled Holand's.

**Canderack Head,** south of Canderack Bay, an important landmark for shipping on the South Dalemark coast.

**Carne Bank,** a mudbank at the far east of the prehistoric Rivermouth, notorious for quicksands and shallows.

**Cenblith,** a queen of prehistoric Dalemark who first took the One for her lover and then bound him to the will of mortals, apparently either by forcing him to make the great River or by carving an image of him.

**Cennoreth,** one of the Undying, known in legends as a witch and often called the Weaver. It was said that whatever she wove became truth. She was sister to the legendary King Hern and mother of Manaliabrid, wife of the Adon.

**Chindersay,** one of the outer ring of the Holy Islands, notable for the dark color of its rocks.

**Cindow,** a village northeast of Markind in South Dalemark.

**City of Gold,** King Hern's lost city of Kernsburgh, which gave rise to the saying "The City of Gold is always on the most distant hill," meaning that your ideal is never *here*, under your hands, but always out over *there*.

**Clans,** the tribe families of the Heathens of Haligland. The clans are very large and contain all classes, from aristocrat to lowborn. For instance, Kars Adon and Ked both belonged to Clan Rath, but Kars Adon was King while Ked was lowborn and had no real relation to the royal family.

**Clennen Mendakersson,** one of the most famous and characterful of the old-style Singers, a musician, composer, and teller of tales. He married Lenina, niece of the Earl of the South Dales, and was the father of Dagner, Brid, and Moril. He was murdered near Markind in South Dalemark on suspicion of being a spy, and bequeathed to Moril a cwidder with strange powers, which he claimed had been handed down to him from their ancestor Osfameron.

**Climbers,** Lawschool slang name for the cloistered court with steps.

**Closti the Clam,** father of Tanaqui the weaver and a native of Shelling in the prehistoric Riverlands kingdom of Dalemark. He was called the Clam for his extreme uncommunicativeness, which may have been caused by the early death of his wife, Anoreth, or perhaps by the command of the One. He was killed in the invasion of the Heathen Haliglanders before he could tell his children many very important facts.

**Collen,** one of the two Southern forms of the name Kialan; a name fairly common in Markind.

**Collet,** the steward of the King of the Riverlands, whose duty was to memorize the King's debts for lodging and provision.

**"The Color Song,"** composed and sung by Dagner Clennensson.

**"Come Up the Dale with Me,"** an apparently innocent love song from South Dalemark which was actually urging rebellion. It was banned.

**"Come with Me,"** a song being composed by Dagner Clennenssen, which Clennen objected to on the ground that it could be seen by spies as urging rebellion.

**Coran,** a townsman of Derent in Waywold in South Dalemark, later well known as a freedom fighter.

**Countess**

1. A female who is earl in her own right, like the Countess of Aberath.
2. The wife of an earl.

3. Mitt's name for his bad-tempered horse, which was not even female.

**"Cow-calling,"** a traditional patter song to a lively tune. Each verse is two lines longer than the last, until the singer is addressing the whole herd of cows.

**Crady,** a large town in the south of Andmark in South Dalemark.

**Credin,** the tidal wave which, at certain seasons, runs up the river Aden from the sea. A lesser wave usually runs up the river Ath at the same time. It is thought the name derives from memories of the mage Kankredin.

**Cressing Harbor,** a small fishing port to the northeast of the Point of Hark. It was the nearest landing for ships from South Dalemark and much involved in smuggling goods and people from both sides.

**Cruddle,** one of the traditional instruments played at the Holand Sea Festival, a sort of triangular fiddle with three gut strings. The player held the cruddle under his chin and scraped the strings with a loose horsehair bow. Cruddlers were seldom musicians. Their sole aim was to make as much noise as possible.

**"Cuckoo Song,"** a comic song with rather indecent words composed by Clennen the Singer.

**Cwidder,** a musical instrument rather like a lute but with some of the properties of an acoustic guitar. Cwidders are found in all sizes, from small trebles through medium-sized altos and tenors to large bass and deep bass. Moril's cwidder was a large bass, but it could be used as a tenor. Cwidders were much used by Singers because they were both versatile and easy to carry.

**Dagner,** the elder son of Clennen the Singer and a noted composer. Dagner became Earl of the South Dales very early in his life but was so reluctant to leave his life as a traveling Singer that he only took up his earldom after fifteen years, at the urgent request of Amil the Great.

**Dalemark,** the fifteen earldoms of Aberath, Loviath, Hannart, Gardale, Dropwater, Kannarth, the North Dales, the South Dales, Fenmark, Carrowmark, Andmark, Canderack, Waywold, Holand, and Dermath, with the so-called King's Lands (the Holy Islands, the Marshes, and the Shield of Oreth), that, together with their peoples and history, make up historic Dalemark. For prehistoric Dalemark, see **Riverlands**.

**Dapple,** the mottled gray horse belonging to Hestefan the Singer. It was blind in one eye. There was usually something amiss with Singers' horses because they could only afford to buy them cheap.

**Dark Land,** the place where the souls of the newly dead gather before they make their way to the constellation of the River and on to oblivion.

**Dastgandlen Handagner,** the full name of Dagner Clennensson, who was named for the twin brothers of the Undying encountered by the witch Cennoreth. It was said that Clennen could not resist long names.

**Derent,** a prosperous town in the northeast of the earldom of Waywold in South Dalemark.

**Dermath,** the earldom in the extreme southeast of South Dalemark.

**Diddersay,** one of the Holy Islands.

**Dideo,** a fisherman of Holand in South Dalemark, one of the older members of the Free Holanders, who knew how to make bombs. Dideo put this knowledge to use for Mitt, and again in the Great Uprising, when he had a hand blown off by one of his own bombs, but he survived this and ended his days on the City Council of Holand.

**Dike End,** the birthplace of Mitt, farmed by his parents for the first six years of Mitt's life. The name comes from the situation of the farm and the nearby village at the end of the great Flate Dike, quite near where it runs into the sea about ten miles west of the port of Holand.

**Doen,** one of the Holy Islands.

**Doggers,** Lawschool slang for top of the game league.

**Doreth,** second daughter of Alk and the Countess of Aberath.

**Dropthwaite,** a secluded valley at the source of the river Dropwater where the Adon is said to have hidden as an outlaw. A center of tourism in modern Dalemark.

**Dropwater,** after Hannart, the richest and most influential earldom of North Dalemark, situated facing southwest astride a wide fjord that is ideal for shipping, and sheltered by the mountains from the normal harsh weather of the North. The chief riches of Dropwater come from wool and leather goods, but it was mostly famous for its strong plum brandy and, above all, for the spectacular giant waterfall at the head of its dale.

**Duck,** the pet name of the youngest son of Closti the Clam, who later became famous as Mage Mallard.

**Duke of Kernsburgh,** a new title created by Amil the Great and bestowed upon Navis Haddsson. It was designed to ensure that Navis outranked all the earls.

**Earl**

1. The aristocratic ruler of one large segment of Dalemark. In the old days, prior to the reign of the Adon, earls held their places as officers of the King but, when Dalemark ceased to have kings, each earl became a small king in his own right, with absolute authority over everything in his earldom. Many misused this power, some brutally, and all went to great lengths to keep it.
2. The title of a clan chief among the Heathens of Haligland. This later became the modern title.

**Earldom,** a division of Dalemark ruled by an earl. It was said that earldoms came into being when King Hern divided his kingdom into nine and set nine men in charge, whom he called earls after the name of the clan chiefs, to govern under him. These divisions he called marks. Later six more marks were added in the South when Hern's conquests had reached that far. The system worked well, provided the King was strong. The common people traditionally regarded the earls as only the officers of the King and continued to think this way even after there were no kings.

**Earth Shaker,** the title of Alhammitt, one of the elder Undying, who had become the god of corn and of the sea. The title might describe the sea, but it possibly also refers to what happens if any of the Earth Shaker's secret names are spoken.

**Edril,** the younger grandson of Amil the Great and one of Maewen's ancestors.

**Egil,** a hearthman in the service of Earl Keril of Hannart.

**"The Eighth March,"** the last of a set of marching songs usually called "The Seven Marches," and only sung or played in North Dalemark because the words were offensive to the South.

**Eleth of Kredindale,** the mother of Noreth, who died soon after Noreth was born, declaring to the end that her daughter was the child of the One.

**Elthorar Ansdaughter,** keeper of antiquities at Hannart in North Dalemark in the time of Earl Keril, a law-woman of great learning who gave up the law in order to study the history and prehistory of Dalemark. She was present at the discovery of the spellcoats and translated them, sometimes rather inaccurately.

**Eltruda,** the Lady of Adenmouth, wife of Lord Stair, and younger sister of Eleth of Kredindale. Being childless herself, Eltruda brought Noreth up when Eleth died. On the death of Lord Stair, Eltruda married Navis Haddsson and became a considerable force in Dalemark politics and almost legendary for her quarrels with her stepdaughter, Hildrida.

**Enblith the Fair,** Queen of Dalemark some hundreds of years after the reign of King Hern, daughter of the Undying and said to be the most beautiful woman who ever lived. The musician-mage Tanamoril found Enblith living as a pauper in the woods and tricked the King into marrying her.

**Falls**

1. In prehistoric Dalemark the great River rose as a waterfall said to be half the height of a mountain. This was the site of Hern's battle with the mage Kankredin.
2. In historic times the falls at the head of the dale of Dropwater, where the river Dropwater fell nearly three hundred feet to the floor of the valley, were among the most admired sights of North Dalemark.

**Fander,** a revolutionary in Neathdale in South Dalemark, a grocer by trade, who provided the family of Clennen the Singer with bacon, lentils, and, for some reason, a large bunch of rhubarb.

**Farn,** the southernmost of the Holy Islands.

**Fayside,** one of the dormitory houses in the Lawschool at Gardale.

**Fenna,** the daughter and apprentice of Hestefan the Singer.

**Fenner,** Ganner Sagersson.

**Fervold,** captain of Earl Henda of Andmark's private army.

**Fire,** a ritual bonfire which had to be lit for the One every spring as soon as the River ceased to flood. The fuel had to be specially arranged with the image of the One at its center and kindled with coals from the hearth of the officiators. The lighting of the fire was celebrated with a feast. When the fire died down and the One was revealed in the ashes, only the eldest male of the family was allowed to remove the image.

**Firepot,** a clay pot with a lid and cunningly placed vents in which a fire could be kept alight and carried until needed. Until the invention of the wheel-and-flint tinderbox, firepots were in use all over Dalemark and continued in use by Singers and traveling traders until some time after the reign of the Adon.

**Fishmarket,** a broad thoroughfare in Holand in South Dalemark where fish was sold until the days of Amil IV.

**Flags** were considered potent symbols in Dalemark from prehistoric times onward:

1. In the old Kingdom of Riverlands flags were religious symbols and only carried in the holiest ceremonies to honor the Undying.
2. To the Heathen invaders from Haligland flags were equally holy as expressing the honor and status of a clan. They were carried at all times and defended to the death in battle.
3. In historic Dalemark flags were nearly taboo. They were only flown at Midsummer Fairs and by ships at sea. No earls and few kings dared fly flags until Amil the Great designed the royal standard of the crowned wheatsheaf. To this day only the monarch flies a flag.

**"Flaming Ammet!,"** an oath peculiar to Holanders and a favorite of Mitt's. Since Ammet was an image of the Earth Shaker made of wheat straw, the notion of it on fire amounted to blasphemy.

**Flapper,** Ganner Sagersson.

**Flate,** the general name for the flatlands surrounding Holand in South Dalemark, most of which were at, or below, sea level.

**Flate Dike,** the main drainage ditch for the lowlands around Holand. It was wider than most roads and ran dead straight for nearly fifteen miles, the water in it flowing like a river to an outlet ten miles west of the port of Holand.

**Flate Street,** a street in a poor but respectable district to the west of the city of Holand in South Dalemark, where Earl Hadd provided Hobin the gunsmith with a house and workshop.

**Fledden,** a small town to the north of Andmark in South Dalemark, the birthplace of Earl Henda and one of the few places where Henda could rely on absolute loyalty. The inhabitants held the curious belief that the color yellow was unlucky.

**Flennpass,** the last of the passes open in the mountains between North and South Dalemark. It was said that the musician-mage Osfameron had closed the other three passes at the time of the Adon.

**Flind,** a common name in South Dalemark.

1. A vintner outside Derent in Waywold, who brought Kialan and a supply of wine to Clennen the Singer.
2. A nonexistent person mentioned in a password as part of Siriol's plans for Mitt's escape.

***Flower of Holand,*** the boat belonging to Siriol on which Mitt served as apprentice, part of the fishing fleet that sailed regularly from the port of Holand in South Dalemark.

**"Follow the Lark,"** a song about bird catching whose secret meaning was "overthrow the earls," composed during the last rebellion before the Great Uprising.

**Fort Flenn,** the fort at the northern end of Flennpass, in the hands of the North and designed to hold the pass against incursion from the South.

**Fredlan,** one of the Singers, who traveled in a cart with his family, giving performances all over Dalemark.

**"Free as Air and Secret,"** a song pretending to be about the delights of the countryside which secretly urged rebellion, composed during an early uprising in South Dalemark.

**Free Holanders,** one of many secret societies of freedom fighters in the city of Holand in South Dalemark, the one to which Mitt belonged from the age of eight. Its members were mostly fishermen who believed ardently that they should free South Dalemark from the tyranny of the earls but who could seldom agree how this should be done. However, when the Great Uprising finally came about, all the Free Holanders were active in it, both in the fighting and in the reshaping of the government afterward.

**Gander,** Ganner Sagersson.

**Gann,** a great hero in the legends from South Dalemark who performed many great feats with his sword, Soulmaker, which was forged for him in secret by the Undying smith Agner while both were captives of the mage-king Heriol. Some stories give Gann as the brother of the witch Cennoreth. See also **Gull**.

**Ganner Sagersson,** Lord of Markind in the earldom of the South Dales, who had been betrothed to Lenina Thornsdaughter as a young man. When she left him for Clennen the Singer, Ganner did not, despite pressure from his household, marry anyone else. He seems to have expected Lenina would eventually come back to him (see **Bad Luck**). Ganner was a just and efficient administrator and one of few Southern lords to survive the Great Uprising untouched. He became regent for the South Dales on the death of Tholian.

**Ganter Islands,** a cluster of three islands in the Holy Islands.

**Gardale,** a prosperous valley, town, and earldom in the southeast of North Dalemark, site of the famous Lawschool.

**Garlands** of apples, corn, and grapes were worn by all those taking part in the Holand Sea Festival and afterward thrown into the sea.

**Golden Gentleman,** the name given by the King of the Riverlands to the image of the One when he finally found it in the keeping of Robin Clostisdaughter.

**Gosler,** Ganner Sagersson.

**Gown,** the distinguishing garment of the mage among the Heathens of Haligland. The gown had spells woven in it which appeared as words and, once put on by a mage, was never taken off, even for washing.

**Grand Father,** the most respectful of the titles of the One, possibly derived from the fact that most kings and many earls claimed to be descended from the One.

**Great Girl (or boy),** Lawschool slang for the pupil who comes top in the oral examinations held just before Midsummer.

**Great Ones,** the term for the Undying in the Holy Islands.

**Great Uprising,** the name for the countrywide revolution in Dalemark which brought Amil the Great to the throne. The Uprising began in the North around Kernsburgh and, almost simultaneously, in the South in the city of Holand, where a mob stormed the palace of the

Earl and then had to fight a bloody battle with soldiers hastily sent by Dermath and Waywold. In the North a number of lords and earls who did not at once side with the rebels were killed or forced to go overseas.

**Green roads,** the system of highways said to have been made by King Hern. They remained for many centuries, being remarkably well engineered, never steep, despite running through the peaks of North Dalemark, and deliberately grassed for ease of travel by horseback. Many people believed that the Undying made and maintained the green roads, particularly as they continued to exist long after the main centers of civilization had moved down to the valleys. The roads were used as drove roads and by those who wished to travel quickly from dale to dale, until Alk took them over as railways in the reign of Amil the Great.

**Gregin,** Alk's valet in Aberath in North Dalemark.

**Grittling,** the traditional ball game of the Lawschool at Gardale.

**Guilds,** organized companies of craftsmen and merchants in South Dalemark. Most guilds were formed at the time of the Adon, when the men of many trades realized that the South was becoming increasingly estranged from the North, while the Southern earls grew ever more powerful. Almost every trade, including the Singers, took hasty steps to obtain the protection of the law, usually by petitioning the Adon for a Royal Charter, so that in after years the earls could not easily disband them. The guilds generally kept a low profile, looking after their own members and the widows and orphans of members, training apprentices, educating children, saving money, and paying taxes promptly. They had considerable power and were suspected by the Southern earls to be quietly financing the various uprisings, though nothing was ever proved.

In the North guilds were almost unknown.

**Gull,** eldest son of Closti the Clam and Anoreth of the Undying, the only one of Closti's sons to go to the wars. Gull was captured early in the fighting by the Heathen invaders and interrogated by the mage Kankredin, who returned him to his own side little better than an idiot. Gull is thought to be the same person as the Southern hero Gann, and if this is the case, it seems that Gull did eventually recover from Kankredin's treatment of him.

**Guns** were invented at the time of the Adon but never much used in North Dalemark. The South used guns extensively, although they were forbidden to all but earls, lords, and their hearthmen. The early guns were clumsy and inaccurate and used mostly for sport until Hobin invented the rifled barrel, which had a spiral groove down the inside that caused the gun to shoot far more accurately. There was then a rush to buy guns. Waywold and Canderack drove a thriving trade smuggling guns to the North.

**Gunsmith's Guild,** to which Hobin belonged, together with all other gunsmiths, was a very sober and respectable body of men who, in fact, spent the majority of their meetings laying careful plans for the Great Uprising.

**Hadd,** the angry and tyrannical Earl of Holand in South Dalemark who, after a lifetime of injustice, quarreling with Earl Henda, terrorizing his family, and overtaxing and suppressing his subjects, was murdered at the Sea Festival by an unknown marksman.

**Halain,** a spy for the Earl of the South Dales who had infiltrated the freedom fighters in Neathdale in South Dalemark.

**Halian Tan Haleth,** Lord of Mountain Rivers, is an old name for Tanamil. A legend about him was woven into the rugcoat given by Anoreth to Closti on their marriage but is otherwise unknown.

**Halida,** the wife of Keril, Earl of Hannart, who was born a poor relation of a lord in Canderack in South Dalemark. When Keril was taking part in an uprising in South Dalemark as a young man, Halida helped him escape capture and fled North with him.

**Haligland,** a country on the other continent, peopled by emigrants from prehistoric Dalemark several centuries before the reign of King Hern. Once in Haligland, they developed a clan system, a science of magery, and a religion of the One. Modern Haligland is an oil-rich republic, still with a clan system and a fanatical religion, but one which denies vehemently any connection with the uncanny.

**Ham,** the partner and mate of Siriol aboard the *Flower of Holand*. Ham's full name, like so many in Holand, was Alhammitt. He was a large, good-natured, unintelligent man who was killed in the violence following the storming of the palace in Holand during the Great Uprising.

**Hammit,** a South Dalemark name, one of the many abbreviations of Alhammitt.

**Hand organ,** a musical instrument with pipes, bellows, and keyboard, like a very small church organ. It had a sweet, piping tone, strong enough to be heard above the noise of a crowd. The player carried the organ on his or her right arm and pumped it with the left hand while playing the keyboard with the right.

**Hands to the North,** an unknown group of secret freedom fighters in Holand in South Dalemark. They were quite possibly invented either by Harl Haddsson as cover for his attempt to assassinate Earl Hadd or by Harchad Haddsson as an excuse to pull down buildings to give *his* assassin a clear shot at Earl Hadd.

**"The Hanging of Filli Ray,"** a popular ballad about a young outlaw who was hanged for having the temerity to court a lord's daughter. The version sung in the South concluded with the arrival of the Earl, who reveals, too late, that Filli Ray is his son. In the North it is the King who arrives too late.

**Hannart,** the leading earldom of North Dalemark, famous for its music, its flowers, its buildings, and the frank, outspoken nature of its people, and reputed to be the first civilized area of Dalemark. Certainly some of the buildings in the town of Hannart itself are thought to date back to the days of King Hern. Throughout much of history Hannart stood for freedom, justice, and opposition to the South and its ways. Its heyday was from the reign of the Adon to that of Amil the Great, when it was also a center of learning, but it became steadily less important from the time of the Great Uprising until it passed by marriage into the royal family and was adopted by the Crown Prince as his country retreat. Nowadays Hannart is mostly famous as a beauty spot and for the remains of the giant steam organ at the north end of its dale.

**Harchad,** second son of Earl Hadd of Holand in South Dalemark, head of Hadd's secret police and master of his spies, said to be the cruelest man in Dalemark.

**Hardimers,** the name given to disciplinary officers at the Gardale Lawschool.

**Harilla Harlsdaughter,** eldest girl cousin of Hildrida and Ynen and betrothed at an early age to the Lord of Mark by her grandfather, Earl Hadd.

**Harl Haddsson,** the eldest of the Earl of Holand's three sons, a fat and seemingly indolent man, who became Earl of Holand for a year following the death of Hadd, during which time Holanders took to saying that Earl Hadd was preferable. He was killed when the mob stormed the palace in Holand during the Great Uprising.

**Harvest,** the Northern term for the Autumn Festival.

**Headman,** the leader or chieftain of a village in prehistoric Dalemark. The office combined the functions of major, priest, and judge and was usually handed down from father to son.

**Hearthmen,** a privileged band of soldier companions sworn to a lord or earl and personally responsible to him only, who lived in their hearthlord's mansion with him and formed a private army when need arose. A lord was also said to be the hearthman of the earl who was his overlord if he had sworn to follow the earl to war. In the South of Dalemark hearthpeople were always men, but many lords and earls of the North swore in women, too. The maintaining of hearthpeople was forbidden by royal decree in the reign of Amil II.

**Heathens,** emigrants from Haligland who invaded the prehistoric kingdom of Dalemark and eventually intermarried with the natives. They brought with them their women and children and the mage Kankredin and his college of lesser mages, intending to settle, and introduced to the country both the worship of the One and many magical practices that were previously unknown. Their main, disastrous invasion is described in the spellcoats, but it seems certain that small boatloads of Heathens had been arriving for decades previously, compelled by the harsh conditions in Haligland to find better living and possibly inspired by legends of their former home in the Riverlands.

**Henda,** Earl of Andmark in central South Dalemark, a violent and paranoid man who spent much of his time quarreling with the Earl of Holand and lived in constant dread of plots from the North. He was beheaded by his own hearthmen during the Great Uprising.

**Herison,** Lawschool slang meaning "the right to start grittling until the next full moon."

**Hern,** the second son of Closti the Clam and Anoreth of the Undying, who became the first known King of Dalemark. Most of what is known of him is legend, like the story of his defeat of the mage Kankredin, but numerous laws, customs, and sayings are said to be his, and it is fairly certain that he founded the city of Kernsburgh,

moving the seat of the throne there from his early base in Hannart and constructing the system of roads now known as the green roads or the paths of the Undying.
The name Hern means "heron."

**Hestefan,** one of the traveling Singers, of whom little is known beyond the facts that he befriended both Dagner and Moril Clennensson and became a follower of Noreth of Kredindale during her bid for the crown of Dalemark.

**High Mill,** a village twenty miles northeast of the port of Holand, on the rising ground toward Dermath, well known as a beauty spot.

**Highside,** the dormitory house at the Gardale Lawschool to which Hildrida Navissdaughter belonged.

**High Tross,** one of the islands of the Holy Islands, so called from its high and rocky outline.

**Hildrida Navissdaughter,** one of the company who sailed North to Aberath in the yacht *Wind's Road*, granddaughter of Hadd, Earl of Holand, betrothed to Lithar, Lord of the Holy Islands, at the age of nine. After spending several years at the Lawschool in Gardale, Hildrida was able to annul this betrothal, and practiced as a law-woman in the North Dales until Amil the Great appointed her Warden of the Holy Islands upon her marriage. Hildrida seems to have preferred living in Kernsburgh, however, where she became a leader of fashion and notorious for her quarrels with her stepmother, Eltruda.

**Hildy,** the pet name of Hildrida Navissdaughter.

**Hobin,** known as Bloody Hobin, the elder of two brothers devoted in different ways to freedom fighting. He was born in Waywold in South Dalemark of a family which seems to have been secret hereditary guardians of the kingstone, and he became a brilliant and innovative gunsmith, highly respected by his guild and much in favor with the earls of Holand, Waywold, and Dermath. He then moved to Holand, where he married Milda, Mitt's mother, and bided his time, building up a hidden stock of weapons and an organization of sober revolutionaries like himself, until word came from the North that Amil the Great had seized the crown. Hobin sensed the time was ripe and at once led a massive revolt in Holand, which spread to Dermath and Waywold and rapidly became a bloodbath. Hobin killed so many people, many of them innocent, that Amil himself was forced to intervene. It was said that Hobin shot himself rather than submit to a King. This may be true, but the story that he shot his wife and daughters at the same time is probably a fabrication.

**Hoe,** a village on the rising ground west of Holand in South Dalemark.

**Hoe Point,** the second major landmark for ships sailing northwest out of Holand. Sailors took care to know it well because a strong current flowed northward from there.

**Holand,** the leading earldom of South Dalemark, a sizable city, a flourishing seaport, and the seat of Earl Hadd, situated in the extreme south of Dalemark.

**Hollisay,** one of the Holy Islands, named from the number of holly bushes that grow there.

**Holy Islands,** a scatter of islands in the bay between the Point of Hark and Carrow Head, famous as a haven for shipping. The islands are home to a strange, fey people and full of legends of the Undying. They are part of the King's Lands and owe no allegiance to any earl, but in the long interregnum between the Adon and Amil the Great they were regarded as part of South Dalemark and claimed by whoever was the strongest earl. Amil the Great rectified this by appointing a Warden of the Islands and spent much time there himself helping Ynen Navisson build his new fleet and experiment with steamships.

**Holy Isle,** the centermost island of the Holy Islands and rightly named. Only those who are meant to go to it can find it.

**Honker,** Ganner Sagersson.

**Horsehair drums,** traditional crude drums made of horsehide with the hair still on it, beaten loudly at the Holand Sea Festival, probably because Old Ammet was thought to govern the wild horses of the sea.

**Horses of the sea** were said to belong to Old Ammet and to appear galloping round a ship that was doomed.

**Hurrel,** Lawschool slang for a big push at grittling, a real scrimmage.

**Incantation,** a measured alliterative way of speaking, passed down from Singer to Singer and only used on the most solemn occasions.

**Irana Harchadsdaughter,** one of Earl Hadd's many grandchildren, cousin of Hildrida and Ynen, betrothed at an early age to Agnet, third son of the Earl of Waywold in South Dalemark.

**"I sent the hidden death . . . ,"** one of Kankredin's two chief mages, who seems to have had no name apart from the boastful spell woven into his gown.

**"I sing for Osfameron, I move in more than one world"** are the words inlaid in Moril Clennensson's cwidder in the old writing, by which the cwidder describes itself. Compare Tanaqui's weaving. It is possible these words cause the cwidder to behave as it does.

**Island people,** the inhabitants of the Holy Islands who are something of a race unto themselves, being small and brown, with dark eyes and pale hair. Their sing-song accent is unlike any other in Dalemark. They are said to be remnants of the first people ever to settle the country.

**Isle of Gard,** the ruling island of the Holy Islands where the Lord's mansion and the main fleet are.

**"I tortured the beast . . . ,"** one of Kankredin's two chief mages, known only by the words woven in his gown.

**Jay,** herald and captain to the King of the Riverlands. Jay seems to have started as a minor, though trusted, herald, but he distinguished himself in the wars with the Heathens, when he lost an arm and endeared himself to the King by his cheerfulness, and became the favorite of the King in exile.

**Jenro,** a Holy Islander, coxswain aboard the flagship *Wheatsheaf.*

**"Jolly Holanders,"** a sea shanty that was known and loved all over South Dalemark.

**Justice,** an essential part of the corrupt legal system of South Dalemark before the reforms of Amil the Great. A justice was appointed and paid by an earl and did the earl's bidding, sitting as a magistrate and hearing only such cases as interested his employer or could bring the justice himself a bribe. The South had no access to the Lawschool of the North, and justices seldom had any legal training. They had to rely on their clerks, who were equally corrupt, to tell them what the law was.

***K*** at the beginning of a personal name was only used in North Dalemark. In the slurred and softer dialect of the South a *K* becomes either *C* (pronounced *KH*) or *H*. For instance, the Southern form of the name Keril is Harl; or there are sometimes two forms of a Northern name, as in the name Kialan, which appears in the South both as Collen and as Halain.

**Kanart,** an Earl of Dropwater killed in battle during the Adon's wars.

**Kanarthi,** the conjectured Northern form of the name Cennoreth.

**Kankredin,** an evil magician, sometimes called the mage of mages, who accompanied the Heathen invaders from Haligland, intending to use them to help him usurp the power and position of the One. Kankredin was himself of the Undying and had increased his powers by magically passing through death, which made him virtually impossible to kill. Though legend claims that King Hern overthrew him, Kankredin appears again in stories long before the time of the Adon and was later said by the North to be the cause of all the evils in the South. It is claimed that Amil the Great frustrated an attempt by Kankredin to take over the North, too.

**Kappin,** Lawschool slang for fighting to hold the team's position.

**Karet,** a hearthman of Aberath.

**Kars Adon,** son of Kiniron, who became clan head and High Lord after his father died in the invasion of prehistoric Dalemark. Though Kars Adon was barely fifteen and crippled from birth, he was held in great honor by all his subjects. This was partly due to the custom of the clans, but mostly to the character of Kars Adon himself.

**Kastri,** the Adon's son by his first wife and ancestor of Earl Keril of Hannart, who accompanied his father and Manaliabrid into exile.

**Ked,** a lowborn member of Clan Rath, aged about eight, who had a bad reputation as a liar.

**Keril,** Earl of Hannart, descended from the Adon and generally considered the most influential man in North Dalemark. As a young man he had high ideals and set out to free the South by helping in an uprising. The rebellion failed, and Keril had to be rescued and smuggled North by Halida, whom he married. He arrived back in Hannart to find his father dying and himself with a price on his head in the South. This seems to have given Keril a strong distaste for revolution of the violent kind. As an earl he supported the Southern freedom fighters surreptitiously, with money and advice, apparently hoping for a peaceful political solution, no doubt with himself as chief negotiator, for he possessed a lively and devious political mind. Unfortunately this same deviousness caused him to miscalculate gravely in the case of Navis Haddsson, and he had, as a result, to watch the gradual fading of Hannart as a power in the land.

**Kern,** the Northern form of the name Hern.

**Kernsburgh,** the capital city of Dalemark, situated nearly at the center of the country. Kernsburgh was founded by King Hern and flourished for many centuries until the kingship shifted to Hannart, Canderack, and elsewhere, after which it fell into ruins. At the time of the Great Uprising it was little more than grassy humps in the ground. Amil the Great's first act as King was to rebuild Kernsburgh, and from then on the city grew continually, to become the seat of government, center of commerce, and international metropolis it is two hundred years later.

**Kestrel,** the husband of Closti the Clam's elder sister, Zara, an old man who married late in life when Zwitt refused to marry Zara after Closti had jilted Zwitt's sister. Kestrel, it seems, did not wish to see Zara suffer through no fault of her own.

**Kialan,** younger son of Keril, Earl of Hannart, and later his heir.

**King of the Riverlands** of prehistoric Dalemark. Tanaqui never gives his name, perhaps out of respect, or perhaps because she never knew it. She clearly shows that he was not the correct man for dealing with the Heathen invasion, although he seems to have done his best at first, until his family was killed and his spirit broken.

**Kinghaven,** in the earldom of Loviath, the main port city of North Dalemark and otherwise notorious for brewing bad lager.

**King's Sayings,** a collection of proverbs and wise thoughts memorized by all Singers and supposed to be the words of King Hern himself.

**King Street,** the main thoroughfare in Kernsburgh.

**"The King's Way,"** a traditional song with a rousing tune which celebrates the customary journey of the new King down the green roads of North Dalemark to Kernsburgh to claim his crown. This song was banned in the South, where the earls did not wish to remind people there had once been Kings.

**Kiniron,** the younger brother of the King of Haligland who led the main invasion of the clans to prehistoric Dalemark, where he died of wounds from the fighting.

**Kintor,** Lord of Kredindale and cousin of Noreth Onesdaughter.

**Knots and crosses,** one of the oldest and most potent charms of binding and, of course, the basic pattern of a net. See also **Nets.**

**Konian,** the elder son of Keril, Earl of Hannart, executed in Holand in South Dalemark after a travesty of a trial.

**Korib,** son of the miller in Shelling and an excellent shot with the longbow.

**Kredindale,** a valley, town, and lordship in the extreme northwest of North Dalemark where deposits of coal were found very early in history. From the reign of the Adon, mining became the main occupation of the valley until the mines were closed in the reign of Amil III. Kredindale was the birthplace of Noreth Onesdaughter. Its name is thought to be derived from Kankredin.

**Labbard,** King of Dalemark prior to the Adon, an indolent and incompetent man who openly declared that he would rather sit and drink cider than rule the country.

**Ladri,** one of Kankredin's mages, whose task was to collect the souls caught in the soulnet.

**Lady,** the wooden image of a woman which the family of Closti the Clam kept, according to the customs of prehistoric Dalemark, in one of the niches reserved for the Undying.

**Lagan,** the villainous half brother of the Adon, a student of sorcery and, some legends say, a pupil of Kankredin. Lagan seems to have been consumed with jealousy both of the Adon's status and of the Adon's love for Manaliabrid. Having conspired to have the Adon sent into exile, Lagan then followed him, disguised himself by sorcery, and stabbed him to death. The Adon was recalled from death and later killed Lagan.

**Lake,** a large body of water in the center of prehistoric North Dalemark, which must have been extensive even when the River was not flooding, to judge from the petrified remains of freshwater life to be found all over the central peaks. By historic times this lake had shrunk to a row of small tarns, the largest of which is Long Tarn.

**Lalla,** housekeeper at Lithar's mansion in the Holy Islands and an aspect of Libby Beer.

**"Lament for the Earl of Dropwater,"** an old ballad song composed during the Adon's wars, mourning the death of Kanart, who was one of many earls who opposed the Adon.

**Lathsay,** one of the Holy Islands.

**Lavreth,** a coastal town northwest of Hannart in North Dalemark.

**Lawman,** a position of great power and prestige in North Dalemark. Lawmen served earls, lords, and town governors as advisers, justices, or planners for the future and in many other ways, often for very large fees. Quite a few lawmen married into the families of lords or earls. Since the law was open to everyone, however lowborn, training as a lawman was a favorite way to rise in the world.

**Law of the sea** was very largely unwritten but was held throughout Dalemark waters to be much more binding than the law of the land. It stated, among other things, that all ships must go to the assistance of any boat in trouble.

**Lawschool** at Gardale in North Dalemark, the only such school in the country until the reign of Amil the Great, very famous and much sought after. It took only those pupils who could reach a very high standard in its oral entrance exams, but a pupil could join the school at any age from nine to fifteen and then be assured of the very best education, both in law and other studies, and nobody ever failed to get a job after graduating. The Lawschool was well endowed with funds and gave quite a number of scholarships to poor students every year. Students entering the school found it a world in itself, with many strange customs and words that were not found anywhere else.

When Amil the Great founded lawschools all over the country, the status of the Gardale school diminished. In the reign of Amil III it became simply a part of Gardale University.

**Law-woman,** a female lawyer, had even more prestige in North Dalemark than a lawman and could command an even higher fee.

**Lengday,** Lawschool slang for Midsummer Day.

**Lenina Thornsdaughter,** niece of Earl Tholian of the South Dales, wife of Clennen the Singer, and mother of Dagner, Brid, and

Moril. Lenina was brought up as an aristocrat in the Earl's household in Neathdale in South Dalemark and left there when she became betrothed to Ganner Sagersson. Clennen saw Lenina at the betrothal feast and persuaded her to marry him instead.

**Libby Beer,** the name of the image made of fruit that was yearly thrown into the harbor in Holand in South Dalemark at the Sea Festival. The name is certainly a corruption of one of the little-known names of She Who Raised the Islands, the Undying mother of fruitfulness and wife of the Earth Shaker.

**License,** a legal document with the seal of an earl attached, showing that the holder was allowed to exercise his or her trade anywhere in South Dalemark. Licenses were expensive. Their main value was the unspoken assumption that the holder was allowed to travel between the South and the North. Without a license, a traveler would be arrested at the border.

**Liss,** Maewen's aunt, who ran a livery stable near Adenmouth in the north of Dalemark.

**Litha,** a woman of the prehistoric Riverlands who was killed by the Heathen invaders from Haligland.

**Lithar,** Lord of the Holy Islands, who was of special value to the earls of South Dalemark, both because of his fleet and because, as lord of the onetime King's Lands, he was not the subject of any earl. He was betrothed to Hildrida Navissdaughter when he was twenty and she was nine years old.

**Little Flate,** a village on the slightly rising ground southwest of Holand in South Dalemark, which was the first landmark for ships sailing out of Holand. Sailors gave it a wide berth because of the shallows just offshore.

**Little ones,** the name Holy Islanders give those mortals under the special protection of the Undying.

**Little Shool,** one of the Holy Islands, barely yards from its neighbor, Big Shool.

**Lord,** a lesser ruler under the earls, who owed allegiance to the earl in whose earldom his lordship was, paying taxes and providing fighting men when his earl required him to. A lord was also supposed to obey every other command from his earl, but not all lords did so. Otherwise a lord lived in his mansion, kept hearthmen, and ruled his subjects just as an earl did, but on a smaller scale.

**Lord of Mark,** lord of the northernmost lordship in South Dalemark, a plump and middle-aged widower, betrothed to Harilla Harlsdaughter when he was thirty-eight and she was ten years old.

***Lovely Libby,*** one of the big merchant ships sailing out of Holand in South Dalemark. Like most of the tall ships of Holand, she was named from the Sea Festival for luck.

**Loviath**

1. The earldom on the northwest coast of North Dalemark.
2. The name of Maewen Singer's physics teacher.

**"Luck ship and shore,"** the ritual reply to the traditional greeting "The year's luck to you" at the Sea Festival in Holand in South Dalemark.

**Lucky ship,** any ship sailing out of Holand that could retrieve the image of Poor Old Ammet from the sea. The yacht *Wind's Road* was doubly lucky from having accidentally brought the image of Libby Beer as well. Anyone noticing this fact had to be a Holander.

**Luthan,** Earl of Dropwater and cousin of Noreth of Kredindale. Because of his almost accidental support of the King's side in the Great Uprising, Luthan—and Dropwater with him—became extremely important in the reign of Amil the Great. Luthan was made chancellor and was twice elected prime minister.

**Lydda,** Siriol's daughter, a plump, good-natured girl who married a sailor from the merchant fleet of Holand. Her husband later took over Siriol's boat and business.

**Maewen Singer,** a teenage girl hijacked from modern Dalemark to take the place of Noreth of Kredindale. See also **Mayelbridwen.**

**Mage Mallard,** the Undying musician-mage, youngest son of Closti the Clam and brother to the Weaver and King Hern. See also **Duck.**

**Mages** were fairly common in primitive Haligland and much respected because much feared. No one dared insult a mage of any kind, but the greatest fear and respect were reserved for the so-called college of mages, which was always made up of fifty of the strongest and most experienced enchanters in the land. When

Kankredin came to head this college, he seems to have made it a condition that every mage should have passed ritually through death before he joined, which was not the case before his time. College mages were always male, but female mages also existed, with a coven of fifty of their own.

**"A man came over the hill . . . ,"** a rhyme woven into the skirt of Robin Clostisdaughter by her sister Tanaqui, but hopelessly garbled. As far as can be understood, the rhyme seems to be about the meeting of Closti with Anoreth, or else it refers to a much older but very similar story.

**Manaliabrid**

1. The Undying wife of the Adon, daughter of Cennoreth the Weaver.
2. The full second name of Brid Clennensdaughter (her first name was Cennoreth).

**"Manaliabrid's Lament,"** a song in the old style, said to have been composed by Osfameron after Lagan killed the Adon. It has a tune of strange broken phrasings, so unlike the usual style of Osfameron that many consider that Manaliabrid may have composed the "Lament" herself.

**Mansion,** the large semifortified house of an earl or lord, always the most prominent in the area. Besides housing the lord's family and many servants, the mansion had to be big enough for a band of hearthmen, advisers, lawyers, clerks, and numerous other assistants.

**Markind,** an area in the very south of the South Dales, the lordship of Ganner Sagersson, and notable for its many little hills and valleys, which are, in fact, the worn-down remnants of volcanoes.

**Marks,** an old name for the fifteen divisions of Dalemark that later became the earldoms.

**Mark Wood,** a large forest at the northern edge of the third and highest Upland in the earldom of the South Dales, part of the lordship of Mark. It was full of clearings stockaded against possible invasion by the North, where wood was cut and charcoal was made. The inhabitants hated the North heartily and put up the stoutest resistance met by the army of Amil the Great at the start of the Great Uprising.

**Marriage by proxy,** a custom among earls of holding a wedding without the bride's being present. Her place would be taken by a woman who was married already. The practice probably originated to save the nobly born bride the trouble and expense of a journey, but it was widely used if the bride was unwilling, or a child, or both.

**Marshes,** a huge area of volcanic swamp to the east of Dalemark. Throughout historical times the Marshes were considered worthless, remarkable only for curious plants and birds, and they became King's Lands because nobody else wanted them. When, in recent times, oil was discovered there, they remained the property of the crown but added considerably to the wealth of the country.

**Mattrick,** chief among the freedom fighters in Neathdale in South Dalemark.

**Mayelbridwen,** a form of the name Manaliabrid from Fenmark; Maewen Singer's full name.

**"May the clay purge from you . . . ,"** the start of the ritual spoken when the image of the One was put into its yearly fire. The speakers of this invocation had, for generations, no idea that what they were uttering was a spell for the unbinding of the One.

**Medmere,** the valley where Clennen the Singer was murdered. The round lake in the middle is the center of an old volcano.

**Middle vokes,** Lawschool slang for the second stage of the training course.

**Midsummer flags,** traditional bright banners flown at Midsummer Fairs all over Dalemark. The devices on them—the Eye, the Sheaf, the River, et cetera—are versions of the Old Writing. The flags are thought to be the debased remnants of flags once carried in religious ceremonies.

**Milda,** the mother of Mitt and afterward the wife of Hobin the gunsmith, who was the father of her two daughters. Sadly, neither Milda nor her daughters survived the Great Uprising. Though there are several highly colored stories about their deaths, the most likely theory is that they perished in the terrible violence and confusion after the mob stormed the Earl's palace in Holand, when the earls of Dermath and Waywold sacked the city in reprisal.

**Mitt,** short for Alhammitt. Mitt was born at Dike End in the earldom of Holand in South Dalemark, on the day of the Sea Festival. He moved to the city of Holand as a child, where he became a freedom fighter and was forced to escape to the North to avoid arrest. After just under a year in Aberath, in training as a hearthman, he left to follow Noreth of Kredindale in her bid for the crown.

**Modes,** Lawschool slang for a progress report on the term's work.

**Moril,** younger son of Clennen the Singer. Clennen bequeathed to Moril a cwidder said to have belonged to the minstrel Osfameron. After the death of his father, Moril went to Hannart in North Dalemark, where he briefly joined Hestefan the Singer before leaving to take part in the Great Uprising. He played a considerable part in the Uprising and afterward became court musician and chief architect of the Royal Dalemark Academy of Music, collecting traveling Singers from all over Dalemark and gathering them together in Kernsburgh. This caused such changes and improvements in the making of music that by the end of Amil the Great's reign the old traveling Singers had ceased to exist.

**Mount Tanil,** a very tall volcano on the edge of the Marshes southeast of Gardale, thought by unlearned people to be the home of the One.

**Mucks,** Lawschool slang for gloved hands, the gloves often weighted by being stuffed with metal or stones.

**Natives,** the term given by the Heathen invaders to the prehistoric inhabitants of Dalemark, who were mostly dark and squarely built. After the invasion many of these people went South, where they intermarried with the settlers there to give rise to the average Southerner, pale-skinned and brown-haired. Those who stayed in the North interbred with the invaders to produce the brown-skinned, light-haired Northerner.

**Navis Haddsson,** third son of the Earl of Holand, a brilliant and efficient soldier and a ruthless politician, who was forced to escape North from the palace plots in Holand (he was disliked by both the old Earl and the new for having shown too much sympathy for the plight of the common people of Holand). He spent nearly a year as a hearthman in Adenmouth before leaving to follow Noreth of Kredindale and to take part in the Great Uprising. It was probably thanks to Navis that the bloodshed was not greater. Early in the reign of Amil the Great, Navis was made Duke of Kernsburgh, partly in reward for his services and partly because he then outranked the earls it was now his job to control. A year later he married Eltruda, widow of Lord Stair of Adenmouth.

**Neathdale,** a large market town in the South Dales, the seat of Earl Tholian. Because it was the last major town before the North, Neathdale flourished both on legal trade and by smuggling goods and people in and out of North Dalemark. The earls' spies and security forces were particularly active there, which led to the Siege of Neathdale during the Great Uprising.

**Nepstan,** a country in the far South.

**Nets,** a potent item of magecraft, akin to weaving. The netmaker, working with power, could design his net to perform various tasks. Kandredin's soulnet, besides trapping departing souls, was intended to draw Gull's soul to him *and* to bind the One. Tanamil's nets likewise had several purposes: concealing the army, blocking the mages, and forcing them to assume their true shapes.

**New Flate,** the drained flatlands some miles west of Holand in South Dalemark, where Halain, grandfather of Earl Hadd, was supposed to have had dikes dug and drained the sea marsh. In fact, the New Flate was probably older than that. It was very fertile farmland but was denied prosperity until the reign of Amil the Great by the ridiculously high taxes imposed by the earls of Holand.

**Noreth,** known as Onesdaughter, of whom it was said that the One spoke to her all her life, telling her she was to take the crown when she reached the age of eighteen. She was born in Kredindale to the Lord's unmarried daughter, Eleth, who died soon after Noreth's birth, declaring that the child's father was the One himself. If this was true, it gave Noreth the strongest possible claim to be Queen. She was educated first in Adenmouth, where she was left in the care of her aunt Eltruda, and then at the Gardale Lawschool, from which she graduated early, then spent the next two years at Dropwater as junior law-woman to her cousin Luthan. The Midsummer after her eighteenth birthday Noreth returned to Adenmouth, where she formally declared her intention of riding the royal road to claim the crown.

**North,** the seven earldoms of Hannart, Gardale, Aberath, Loviath, Dropwater, Kannarth, and the North Dales, all these being north of a line drawn east and west from the Point of Hark. This was the earliest part of the kingdom of Dalemark and also the most mountainous, where the people, though generally poor, had a long tradition of independence and freethinking. The earls of the North quickly learned that injustice was not to be tolerated (quite a few earls lost either their lives or most of their subjects to the mountains while this lesson was being learned), and the laws of the North were therefore fair and lenient, applying to earl and commoner alike. From well before the reign of the Adon, the North was known as the place of freedom. It was also, perhaps because it was the oldest-settled part of Dalemark, renowned for strange old beliefs and even stranger happenings.

**North Dales,** the earldom immediately to the north of South Dalemark. Though it was cut off from the South by a range of high mountains, the people there were used to dealing with the South (often as smugglers) and were in some ways more akin to the South than to the North.

**Northern Cross,** the most noticeable constellation in the night sky at all seasons, invaluable to sailors because it revolved around the true north. Other well-known constellations are Enblith's Hair, the Flatiron, the Big Cat, the Kitten, Hern's Crown, and the River. Astronomy was not much studied in Dalemark until the reign of Amil the Great, so that although it was known that the world was round and circled the sun, little account was taken of the planets. Sailors called them the Unreliable Stars, for always moving about, or the Unchancy Ones.

**Old Flate,** the flatlands toward Waywold in South Dalemark, part of the earldom of Holand which had once been drained and farmed but allowed to return to marsh in the course of the two centuries before the Great Uprising because of the ruinous taxes imposed by the earls of Holand. The Old Flate became the haunt of snakes, criminals, and disease.

**Old Man,** the highest mountain in Hannart, at the south end of the dale, thought to be named for the One.

**Old Man of the Sea,** a seeming priest who appeared to certain people in the Holy Islands, an aspect of the One.

**Old Mill,** across the River from Shelling in prehistoric Dalemark, where the first spellcoat was completed and the second begun. It had become a forbidden place for the villagers after the marriage of Closti and Anoreth. Some said it was haunted by the ghost of a woman, others that it was the abode of bad spirits, and still others that the River had cursed the place. As the King's men found mussels being cultivated on a system of ropes in the millpond, it appears that not everyone in Shelling believed these tales.

**Old Smiler,** Mage Mallard's derisive name for the King of the Riverlands.

**Old Writing,** a system of syllabic signs in use before letters were developed, which came to be thought of as magical. It was often used in spells or for inscriptions intended to be potent.

**Olob,** the shortened name of Barangarolob, Clennen the Singer's horse, which Clennen often said he would not part with for an earldom.

**Ommern,** one of the Holy Islands, the greenest.

**Ommersay,** one of the larger of the Holy Islands.

**One,** the greatest of all the Undying, whose face could not be looked upon and whose names could not be spoken. The One was said to have fathered the human race by his union with the witch-queen Cenblith, at which time he made the great River of prehistory and was for centuries bound by magic at its source. He was at length unbound by the Weaver and shook the country into its present mountainous state when he defeated the mage Kankredin.
The One was worshiped as a god by the invaders from Haligland and for a long time remained a god in the North of Dalemark, where many beliefs and customs about him still remain, but he was almost unknown in the South. Nowadays he is regarded simply as an old superstition.

***Or, er, ro,*** a particle inserted into a name to give the meaning "younger" or most often "youngest." Compare Barangalob and Barangarolob, Tanamil and Tanamoril, Osfamon and Osfameron, et cetera.

**Oreth,** one of the secret names of the One, the least known, meaning "he who is bound."

**Orethan the Unbound,** the name by which the One was known after the Weaver released him from the spells of Cenblith and Kankredin. This name is almost never spoken.

**Oril,** one of several names taken by Mage Mallard to disguise the fact that he was of the Undying.

**Orilsway,** a town which grew up at the junction of the green roads in the far north of Dalemark, possibly taking its name from Mage

Mallard in his guise as the Wanderer. When the green roads were abandoned as highways, Orilsway fell into ruin and was only rebuilt and resettled after the coming of the railways.

**Osfameron,** one of the two names taken by Mage Mallard in his guise as a minstrel and meaning "Osfamon the younger." It is not known who Osfamon was. Under this name Mallard became the friend of the Adon, whom he raised from the dead, and also created the cwidder with which he is said to have made mountains walk, later bequeathed to Moril Clennensson.

**Palace** of Earl Hadd in Holand in South Dalemark. Most earls, even in the South, lived in much humbler mansions, but Earl Hadd, perhaps because he insisted on his entire family's living with him, enlarged and renamed his dwelling. The palace was largely destroyed in the Great Uprising.

**Pali,** a prison guard in Neathdale in South Dalemark who was a secret freedom fighter.

**Panhorn,** an intricately curled horn with four mouthpieces and eight valves, very difficult to play.

**Paths of the Undying,** a name for the green roads of North Dalemark used by those who believed that the Undying created and maintained them.

**Peace-piping,** a very difficult form of musical magecraft in which the mage must first use his pipes to echo the anger of combatants and then reduce their feelings to calm and shame. Moril Clennensson unwittingly used a form of peace-piping on Tholian, Earl of the South Dales.

**Peelers,** Lawschool slang for willow wands with the bark peeled off.

**Penner,** Ganner Sagersson.

**Pennet,** a village between Waywold and Holand in South Dalemark.

**Piper,** the name most often used, from the time of the Adon onward, for Tanamil of the Undying, onetime lord of the Red River. It was said that being released from bondage at the same time as the One, Tanamil went to the Holy Islands, where his piping may still sometimes be heard on calm evenings.

**Point of Hark,** the high rocky peninsula that divides North from South Dalemark waters.

**Poor Old Ammet,** the full name of the image made of plaited wheat decorated with fruit and flowers and ribbons which was thrown into the harbor in Holand in South Dalemark each year at the Sea Festival. Opinions vary as to whether this ritual echoes some personal sacrifice by one of the Undying or is simply a charm for improving the harvest, but what is certain is that any boat which picks up Poor Old Ammet beyond the harbor has good luck ever after. This is rare; the tides and currents have to be exactly right. Usually the image sinks in the harbor.

**Portable organ.** See **Hand organ.**

**Porter,** the main spy for North Dalemark, operating under the noses of all the earls of the South, and the most wanted man in the South. He reported to Hannart almost everything the Southern earls wished to keep secret, organized freedom fighters, and ran a rescue service for wanted men and women. The Porter was operating for most of the eleven years prior to the Great Uprising.

**Prest,** one of the Holy Islands, large, with high crags.

**Prestsay,** a small rocky island in the Holy Islands.

***Proud Ammet,*** a big merchant ship based in Holand in South Dalemark, where Earl Hadd's assassin seems to have been when he fired. Like all the big merchant ships, this one was named from the Sea Festival.

**Ratchet,** a cat found by the children of Closti the Clam on their journey up the great River, named from the sound of her purring.

**Rath Clan,** sometimes called the Sons of Rath, the royal clan of primitive Haligland into which Kars Adon and Ked were born. The clan colors, which appeared on banners and in clothing, were red and blue.

**Rattles,** rotating wooden rattles, where the noise is produced by a wooden flange meeting a ratchet, which are traditional at the drowning of Old Ammet in the Holand Sea Festival. The rattle users are always small boys dressed half in red and half in yellow.

***A Reader for the Poor,*** a book designed to teach working people to read. It was written by a clerk in Carrowmark who had little imagination. A typical page begins, "Ham beats the cask. He knocks in five nails. Will that make it hold water?"

**Red One,** one of the names for Tanamil the Piper.

**Riss,** a seaman aboard the flagship *Wheatsheaf* in the Holy Islands.

**Rith,** a boy's name, fairly common in North Dalemark.

**River,** the mighty prehistoric watercourse which flowed north through Dalemark from a source somewhere near Hannart. It was said that the One made the River, and that the River was both the One and the soul of the land, and that it was the path of souls on their way to the sea. The River was destroyed by the One when he shook the land to rid it of the evil mage Kankredin. It only remains nowadays as two small rivers, the Ath and the Aden, and in the belief that the souls of the dead travel down the constellation of the River to oblivion in the sea of the universe.

**Riverbed,** the spirit land behind the great River, otherwise called the River of Souls.

**Riverlands,** the correct name for the prehistoric kingdom of Dalemark.

**Rivermouth,** the place where the great prehistoric River of Dalemark ran out into the sea in the north, through a delta of marsh, quicksand, and changing tides and currents. Its remains can be seen today in the bay between Aberath and Adenmouth, where there are still treacherous currents and constantly changing shoals.

**Robin,** the eldest child of Closti the Clam and Anoreth of the Undying, whose birthright was knowledge. Unlike her brothers and sisters, Robin passes clean out of all history and legend after the narrative of the spellcoats. It is possible that stories about her have been lost or attributed to her more spirited sister, Tanaqui.

**Royal road,** the green roads of North Dalemark between Adenmouth and Kernsburgh. Tradition said that each new monarch should make this journey on the old roads before claiming crown and kingstone at Kernsburgh.

**Rugcoats,** the poncholike garments of woven wool worn by men and women over their other clothing in prehistoric Dalemark.

**Rugcoats for weddings** were presented by a girl's family in prehistoric Dalemark to a husband-to-be as a sign that the two were officially betrothed; the groom then wore the rugcoat at the wedding. These rugcoats were always of specially fine weaving, usually with words all over. It was believed that the coat brought luck to the wedding, and possibly children, too. If the bridegroom did not wear the coat at the wedding, it was a sign that the bride would soon be either deceived or a widow. If the groom gave the coat back before the wedding, the betrothal was broken off.

**Rushing people,** the souls of the dead that hurry along the Riverbed toward the sea.

**Rush mat,** woven by Mage Mallard to deceive the King of the Riverlands. Weaving in any form is a potent spell.

**Rusty,** a ginger tomcat found by the children of Closti the Clam on the journey up the great River.

**Sailing in grybo,** Lawschool slang for being in the clear, without black marks.

**Sard,** a trusted soldier of the King of the Riverlands—trusted because he enjoyed killing.

**Scap,** Lawschool slang for the spring solstice.

**Scarnel,** a pipe made of pea or bean stalks, hollowed and varnished, traditionally played at the Sea Festival in Holand in South Dalemark by any number of amateur players. The sound is indescribably horrible.

**Sea Festival,** celebrated in autumn and called the Autumn Festival or Harvest elsewhere in Dalemark and peculiar to Holand in the South. Two images, one of straw and one of fruit, are carried down to the harbor in a procession of men clothed in red and yellow, draped with garlands and wearing traditional hats, accompanied by music from traditional instruments and by other lesser images; at the harbor with solemn words the two greater images are thrown into the sea. This is followed by feasting.

**"The Second March,"** one of seven tunes used by soldiers to march to all over Dalemark. "The Second March" has a jaunty tune and is generally more in favor in the North.

**Sein right,** Lawschool slang for the right to start grittling. The team with sein right could choose weapons and set up the first move.

**Sending Day,** at the Lawschool, the day on which pupils returned home for the summer. Pupils' families were asked to attend the closing ceremony before they removed the pupils.

**Sessioning,** the Lawschool word for school term.

***Sevenfold,*** a merchant ship based in Holand in South Dalemark which had the good luck to pull Poor Old Ammet out of the sea. Every man aboard was said to have made his fortune subsequently. *Sevenfold* herself was sold when she became old to a merchant in Waywold who renamed her *Fair Enblith* and was not particularly lucky with her.

***Sevenfold II,*** a merchant ship sailing out of Holand in South Dalemark, so called when the first ship of that name was sold. Her cockboat was found by the yacht *Wind's Road*. Like most Holand shipping, both *Sevenfolds* were named from the Sea Festival.

**"The Seven Marches,"** the set of lively tunes to which soldiers marched in both North and South Dalemark. Each march had well-known words.

**Shelling,** a village much like other villages on the west bank of the great River of prehistoric Dalemark, the birthplace of Closti the Clam and his children.

**Shelling River Procession,** held once a year at Midsummer to honor the River as a god. This was one of four yearly ceremonies in which flags were carried, and probably gave rise to the custom of flying flags over the stalls at Midsummer Fairs all over historic Dalemark.

**She Who Raised the Islands,** the most common term for the lady of the Undying who, as wife of the Earth Shaker, has power nearly equal to his but is, on the whole, more benign. As Libby Beer she provides fruit and nourishment, but in her stronger aspects she is the earth itself and the only one of the Undying able to control the Earth Shaker. She is adored particularly in the Holy Islands, where she takes the shape of a beautiful red-haired woman dressed in green.

**Shield of Oreth,** a mountain plateau in the southwest of North Dalemark that faces the milder weather of the sea. The name is from the least known of the secret names of the One, and it should perhaps be noted that at least three of the Undying and the Adon's sword were to be found there. In early historic times the Shield was well farmed and populous, but it fell into wasteland during the Adon's wars. Navis Haddsson was given ducal lands here and was fond of saying that of all his achievements, the one which gave him most pleasure was the restoration of the Shield to farmland and prosperity.

**Singers,** a race of men and women, most of whom claimed descent from Tanamoril or Osfameron, who traveled the country of Dalemark singing, playing music, and telling stories. Because Singers were among the few people able to move freely between North and South, they also carried news, letters, and often fugitives. Some even acted as spies, but this was rare: Singers had their own rigid customs and standards, chief among which was always to tell the truth and never to perform a vile or a violent act. They also passed down by word of mouth innumerable old customs, sayings, beliefs, and incantations, many of which were lost when Moril Clennensson disbanded the Singers in the reign of Amil the Great.

**Siriol,** the owner of the *Flower of Holand*, a fisherman and a prominent member of the Free Holanders, the society of secret freedom fighters to which Mitt also belonged. Mitt was apprenticed to Siriol for a while until his indentures were bought out by Hobin the gunsmith. Siriol greatly distinguished himself during the Great Uprising and afterward became first a councillor and then semipermanent Mayor of Holand.

**Six steps** up to a front door were standard in Holand in South Dalemark, where the land is only inches above sea level and there is constant danger of flooding, particularly during the autumn storms.

**Skreths,** Lawschool slang word for the cloister to the east of the school.

**Small Western clan,** any of several minor clans that sailed from Haligland to prehistoric Dalemark during the years before the main invasion.

**Soulboat,** a small skiff specially enchanted to hold the souls of the dead once they had been retrieved from Kankredin's net.

**Soulnet.** See **Nets.**

**Souls** of mortals were believed until quite recently to be the prey of witches and sorcerers, whether joined to a body or not. The mages of primitive Haligland claimed to be able to steal a man's soul while he slept, and Kankredin is said to have been able to take someone's soul at any time he wished. Souls of the Undying and those descended from them were a different matter because they were believed to be combined not only with a body but with the entire country, too.

**South,** the eight earldoms of Dermath, Holand, Waywold, Canderack, Andmark, Carrowmark, Fenmark, and the South Dales. This part of Dalemark has a warm climate, a rich soil, and few high mountains. In early historic times it was very wealthy, but it became steadily poorer under the oppressive rule of the Southern earls, until, shortly before the reign of Amil the Great, the South was actually often poorer than the North and only ruled by fear. The North regarded this regime with disgust; the South was deeply suspicious of the North; and each considered itself superior to the other. The South, in fact, was noted for a number of virtues not seen in the North: efficiency, coolheadedness, perseverance, and clear-sightedness, combined with a strong sense of humor.

**South Dales,** the earldom closest to North Dalemark and in many ways not unlike the North in climate and geography. But being this close to the freethinking North had a bad effect on the earls of the South Dales: They were the most tyrannical, warlike, and unjust of all the Southern earls.

**Spannet,** a stablehand in Adenmouth in North Dalemark.

**Specials,** guns made secretly by Hobin of Holand in South Dalemark which he sold only to a chosen few. Each gun had some unusual feature, and all were better than any of the weapons he sold in public.

**Spellcoat,** a poncholike garment woven with word pictures that either told a story or stated facts. The garment, in the weaving, became the spell that made the story or fact come true. See also **Weaving; Words.**

**Spirits** were thought to be everywhere and to govern everything in prehistoric Dalemark, and it was necessary to please or soothe them every day. Some of the more powerful spirits almost had the status of gods and were confused by many with the Undying. The unusual thing about Closti's family is that they did not share this belief. Hern, in fact, rejected spirits out of hand as "unreasonable."

**Spring floods,** as a result of the snow melting in central Dalemark, are extensive even in modern times. In the uncontrolled River of prehistoric times there was always much flooding, which not only devastated homes but also brought fertile silt, driftwood, and fish.

This violent mixture of destruction and benevolence caused many people to regard the River as a god.

**Square rigging,** the old type of sail which is simply a sheet of canvas hung between two yards across the mast and swiveled at both ends to catch the wind. South Dalemark very early gave this up in favor of the far more efficient fore-and-aft rigged triangular sail, but the North still clung to the old rig right up to the reign of Amil the Great, when Ynen Navisson reorganized all shipping to form his fleet.

**Square-topped pillar,** a waist-high primitive altar only found in the Holy Islands.

**Squarks,** Lawschool slang meaning "being too bumptious."

**Stair,** Lord of Adenmouth in North Dalemark, a confirmed alcoholic.

**Stapled,** Lawschool slang meaning "to be posted on a notice board as a wrongdoer." Any pupil who was stapled lost certain privileges for a month.

**Steam organ,** at Hannart in North Dalemark, a huge music-making machine built into the side of the mountain, operating like a church organ but powered by steam. It was said to have been the brainchild of the Adon and brought sightseers to Hannart from the moment it was built. It is clear that the people of the Adon's time knew all about steam power two centuries before the industrial revolution but considered it only worthwhile for providing entertainment.

**Stirring,** Holy Islands dialect for rowing a boat.

**Stork,** the totem standard of the King of prehistoric Dalemark, where birds had a significance and potency which it is now hard to define. No one but the King or his accredited agents dared carry the Stork. Thus the people of Shelling knew at once that the messengers were there by royal decree.

**Surnam,** Lawschool slang for the one who spearheads an attack at grittling.

**Sweetheart,** a black cat rescued from an island by the children of Closti the Clam on their journey up the great River.

**Sweetrush,** a pet name for Tanaqui the weaver.

**Talismans,** charms for keeping the soul in the body made for King Hern's army by Tanamil the Piper. Many centuries later Dalemark people still call pebbles found with a chance pattern of cross-hatching piper's pieces.

**Tally,** the Lawschool term for its list of prizes.

**Tan,** a particle added to the front of a personal name to mean "the younger," as in Tanabrid, Tankol, Tanamil, et cetera.

**Tanabrid,** the daughter of the Adon by his second wife, Manaliabrid of the Undying, who married the Lord of Kredindale after the death of the Adon.

**Tan Adon,** Young Lord, one of the names for Tanamil the Piper.

**Tanamil,** one of the elder Undying, whose name means "younger brother" or "younger river." It is said that Tanamil was enslaved by Cenblith at the same time as the One and forced to create the Red River. There are many legends about him, some of which confuse him with Tanamoril, the mage-musician. Tanamil, however, is earlier than Tanamoril, for he is said to have played a major part in King Hern's defeat of Kankredin, after which he is said to have gone to the Holy Islands, where he can sometimes be heard playing his pipes at sunset.

**Tanamoril**

1. Moril's full second name. He was called after his famous ancestor.
2. The name taken by Mage Mallard in his earliest disguise as a minstrel. Under this name he assisted Enblith the Fair to become Queen because, according to some stories, she was his daughter.
3. The name means "youngest brother" and also refers to both Mallard's and Moril's position in their families.

**Tanaqui**

1. The second daughter of Closti the Clam and Anoreth of the Undying. She was a skilled weaver who made the two spellcoats which were dug up from the hillside above Hannart in North Dalemark. Her name is a punning one, meaning both "scented rushes" and "younger sister." There has been speculation as to whether Tanaqui is herself of the Undying and, if so, is to be identified with Cennoreth the Weaver, but this is probably without foundation: Tanaqui was plainly a real person. See also **Weaving**.

2. The scented rushes that are nowadays rare, growing only in certain habitats in North Dalemark.

**Tankol,** otherwise known as Young Kol, head foreman of the mineworkers at Kredindale in North Dalemark.

**Tannoreth Palace,** built by Amil the Great in Kernsburgh at the start of his reign, to Amil's own design, and still the royal palace although the present monarch seldom lives there. Amil appears to have invented the name Tannoreth himself (as he invented so many other things in the course of his long reign). It means, if anything, "the younger Noreth."

**Tanoreth,** the "young bound One," a name for Tanamil the Piper.

**Tears,** a potent magic. When Mitt weeps on an image of Libby Beer, he unknowingly invokes her protection.

**Termath,** the southernmost port in South Dalemark, the seat of the Earl of Dermath.

**"The year's luck to you,"** the ritual greeting between Holanders on the day of the Sea Festival.

**"This is my will,"** a form of words used by a dying King to name the next King. These words had the force of law. King Hern, having named his son Closti as King, is said to have continued, "and it is my will that I name all Kings after you."

**Tholian,** the name of several earls of the South Dales. After the last Tholian perished in an abortive invasion of the North a year or so before the Great Uprising, the name was discarded as unlucky.

**"To tide swimming . . . ,"** the ancient charm of invocation to the Earth Shaker and She Who Raised the Islands, spoken as part of the Holand Sea Festival. Any who doubt that this is indeed a charm should note that the words *go now and return sevenfold* are thrice repeated in it.

**Trase,** Lawschool slang for a team attack at grittling.

**Trethers,** Lawschool slang for roll call, for which all pupils had to be present to answer their names.

**Tross,** one of the largest of the Holy Islands.

**Trossaver,** one of the Holy Islands, held to be the most beautiful.

**Tulfa,** the Southern spelling of Tulfer Island.

**Tulfer Island,** a large island some eight leagues off the coast of Dropwater in North Dalemark, closely allied to Hannart by marriage.

**Undying,** immortals. There are three kinds:

1. The gods and closely related spirits of prehistoric Dalemark, whose images were kept in niches by the hearth and worshiped and placated daily.
2. The Elder Undying, who had the status of gods and whose souls were supposed to be enmeshed in the land. They were worshiped in numerous rituals throughout Dalemark which still remain as fragmentary customs and superstitions, particularly in the North. Though there never was any organized religion and only a few buildings were dedicated to the Undying, it is clear that everyone in early historic times, from the King downward, joined in rituals of worship or invocation to the Undying at certain times of the year. The Elder Undying can be distinguished by their ritualized names—e.g., the One, whose names are not to be spoken; the Weaver of Fates, et cetera.
3. People who live forever. There seems to be a gene of true immortality in the blood of Dalemark. Such people—for instance, Tanamoril or Manaliabrid—are born rarely, possibly one every three or four centuries, but do seem to exist. They nearly always possess unusual powers or abilities and often claim descent from the Elder Undying. It has been said that these immortals are the same as the Elder Undying, except that the Elder Undying unwisely allowed themselves to be bound into godhead by mortals wishing to worship them, but there is no proof of this theory.

**"Undying at Midsummer,"** a very ancient tune of invocation to the One at the time of his greatest power.

**Updale,** a small village in the center of the second Upland, north of Neathdale in South Dalemark.

**Uplands,** the most northerly section of South Dalemark. The land here rises in three steep escarpments to meet the mountains of the North.

**Virtue,** power, life force, or magic.

**Wailers,** mourners, women who traditionally sit over a dead person making sounds of grief. The sounds have strict rules, which have to be learned. Wailers are usually elderly women or those without children who have had time to learn the rules.

**Wanderer,** the one of the Undying who walks the green roads of North Dalemark, keeping them in good repair. He is the patron of all travelers and invoked even in the South at the start of a journey.

**Warden of the Holy Islands,** the title bestowed on Hildrida Navissdaughter by Amil the Great.

**Warm Springs,** mentioned in the spellcoats, halfway along the southern stretch of the great River and certainly of volcanic origin. Dalemark lies across two tectonic plates, and the land has always been prone to earthquakes and volcanic upheavals. Most historians believe that the shaking of the land by the One was in fact caused by the colliding of the two continental plates. There is evidence in Markind of a much earlier upheaval accompanied by massive volcanic activity.

**Wars** in Dalemark were frequent, but three only need concern us:

1. The prehistoric invasion by Heathens from Haligland.
2. The Adon's wars when the Adon claimed the crown, one of the few civil conflicts in which earls from both North and South appeared on either side.
3. The Great Uprising, when Amil the Great took the crown, which ended in the establishment of modern Dalemark as one kingdom.

**Watersmeet,** in the prehistoric Riverlands, the junction where the Red River flowed into the great River.

**Waystone,** a flat, round stone with a hole in the middle, set up on its narrow edge to mark the start of a green road in North Dalemark. It was the custom to touch the waystone for luck at the start of a journey.

**Waywold,** the earldom next door to Holand on the south coast of South Dalemark.

**Weaver,** the lady of the Undying who weaves the fates and fortunes of mortals. She is said by some to be the same as the witch Cennoreth.

**"The Weaver's Song,"** a well-known nursery song that may originally have been an invocation to the Weaver.

**Weaving** was always to some extent a magical skill and not simply to do with making cloth. In early historical times each pattern woven was held to have significance. Note that Tanaqui takes it for granted that whatever she weaves will contain at least some words, usually at the hem or wrists of the garment, but quite often in bands throughout. See also **Words**.

**"Welcome aboard, Old Ammet, sir!,"** the traditional greeting from the crew that found Old Ammet floating in the sea, showing respect proper to one of the Undying.

**Wend Orilson,** assistant curator at the Tannoreth Palace in Kernsburgh, who claims to be one of the Undying.

**West Pool,** the second harbor of Holand in South Dalemark, shallower than the main harbor and protected by walls and gates, where the rich have always kept their pleasure boats. Harbor dues here are very high.

***Wheatsheaf,*** the flagship of the Holy Islands fleet.

**Wheatsheaf crest,** the badge of Holand in South Dalemark, much feared in the time of Earl Hadd, when Harchad Haddsson gave each of his paid spies a small gold button stamped with this crest.

**"Wider than the world, or small as in a nut,"** a quotation from a song by the Adon, sung by Kialan on the road north. The song is called "Truth" and, at one level, describes the working of the cwidder bequeathed to Moril Clennensson.

**Wind's Road**
1. An archaic term for the sea, used in spells and invocations.
2. The name of the yacht in which Mitt and his friends escaped north.

**Wine,** made all over South Dalemark. The best vintages, red and white, are from Canderack, and the worst from Holand, and there are one or two superb reds from Andmark. The Holy Islands make a strange sparkling white and a brandy so good only earls can afford it. Apart from this, everywhere north of Markind tends to make cider instead and distill from it the spirits called gley. The main drink of the North is beer, except in Dropwater, where they make a sort of plum brandy.

**Winthrough,** Lawschool slang for a scholarship student.

**Wittess,** one of the Holy Islands, low and green.

**Words,** a term used by Tanaqui and Kankredin for the clusters of woven signs in the spellcoats which only the learned or the initiated could read in the cloth. These signs not only formed words in the normal sense but were also potent ingredients of a mage-weaver's spell.

**Wren,** the headman of an unknown village in prehistoric Dalemark who led his people northward, fleeing from Kankredin. He was the first man to swear allegiance to King Hern.

**Yeddersay,** one of the outer ring of the Holy Islands.

**Ynen,** son of Navis Haddsson, who became Amil the Great's admiral in chief. Ynen not only experimented with steamships but built the conventional navy up to the extent that Dalemark quickly became an important sea power.

**Ynynen,** the lesser of the Earth Shaker's two Great Names. Readers are strongly advised not to say this name beside the sea or in a boat.

**Young One,** the red clay image of a smiling young man which the family of Closti the Clam kept in one of their fireside niches reserved for the Undying.

**Zara,** the sister of Closti the Clam, who was to have married Zwitt, the headman of Shelling, if Closti had not jilted Zwitt's sister. Zara was then forced to marry Kestrel or remain a spinster. Zara never forgave Closti or his family for this, though she seems to have retained a strong fondness for Zwitt.

**Zwitt,** the headman of Shelling beside the great River of prehistoric Dalemark. When Zwitt was young, he was betrothed to Closti the Clam's sister Zara, while Closti was betrothed to Zwitt's sister. Closti, however, fell in love with Anoreth and married her instead. Zwitt, in revenge, refused to marry Zara. This caused continuing bad blood between Zwitt and Closti's family.